FROM THE PAGES OF
LEAVES OF GRASS

I am the poet of the body,
And I am the poet of the soul.

(FROM "SONG OF MYSELF," 1855, PAGE 48)

Walt Whitman, an American, one of the roughs, a kosmos,
Disorderly fleshy and sensual . . . . eating drinking and breeding,
No sentimentalist . . . . no stander above men and women or apart
    from them . . . . no more modest than immodest.

Unscrew the locks from the doors!
Unscrew the doors themselves from their jambs!

(FROM "SONG OF MYSELF," 1855, PAGE 52)

I have perceived that to be with those I like is enough,
To stop in company with the rest at evening is enough,
To be surrounded by beautiful curious breathing laughing flesh
    is enough,
To pass among them . . . to touch any one . . . . to rest my arm ever
    so lightly round his or her neck for a moment . . . . what is this
    then?
I do not ask any more delight . . . . I swim in it as in a sea.

(FROM "I SING THE BODY ELECTRIC," 1855, PAGE 121)

To the States or any one of them, or any city of the States,
Resist much, obey little.

(FROM "TO THE STATES," PAGE 173)

Shut not your doors to me proud libraries,
For that which was lacking on all your well-fill'd shelves, yet
    needed most, I bring,

Forth from the war emerging, a book I have made,
The words of my book nothing, the drift of it every thing.

(FROM "SHUT NOT YOUR DOORS," PAGE 176)

[These women] are not one jot less than I am,
They are tann'd in the face by shining suns and blowing winds,
Their flesh has the old divine suppleness and strength,
They know how to swim, row, ride, wrestle, shoot, run, strike,
    retreat, advance, resist, defend themselves,
They are ultimate in their own right—they are calm, clear,
    well-possess'd of themselves.

(FROM "A WOMAN WAITS FOR ME," PAGES 263–264)

City of the world! (for all races are here,
All the lands of the earth make contributions here;)
City of the sea! city of hurried and glittering tides!
City whose gleeful tides continually rush or recede, whirling in
    and out with eddies and foam!
City of wharves and stores—city of tall façades of marble and iron!
Proud and passionate city—mettlesome, mad, extravagant city!

(FROM "CITY OF SHIPS," PAGE 444)

O Captain! my Captain! our fearful trip is done,
The ship has weather'd every rack, the prize we sought is won,
The port is near, the bells I hear, the people all exulting,
While follow eyes the steady keel, the vessel grim and daring;
        But O heart! heart! heart!
            O the bleeding drops of red,
                Where on the deck my Captain lies,
                    Fallen cold and dead.

(FROM "O CAPTAIN! MY CAPTAIN!" PAGE 484)

LEAVES OF GRASS

First and "Death-bed" Editions

Additional Poems

❈

Walt Whitman

Edited with an Introduction and Notes
by Karen Karbiener

George Stade
Consulting Editorial Director

BARNES & NOBLE CLASSICS
NEW YORK

ℐℬ
BARNES & NOBLE CLASSICS
NEW YORK

Published by Barnes & Noble Books
122 Fifth Avenue
New York, NY 10011

www.barnesandnoble.com/classics

Leaves of Grass was published anonymously in 1855. Throughout
his life, Whitman revised *Leaves of Grass* and regularly issued new editions. The
final authorized ninth, or "Death-bed," edition was published in 1891–1892.

Published by Barnes & Noble Classics in 2004 with new Introduction,
Notes, Biography, Chronology, Publication Information, Inspired By,
Comments & Questions, For Further Reading, and Index.

Leaves of Grass
ISBN-13: 978-1-59308-083-9
ISBN-10: 1-59308-083-2
LC Control Number 2004102191

Produced and published in conjunction with:
Fine Creative Media, Inc.
322 Eighth Avenue
New York, NY 10001

Michael J. Fine, President and Publisher

Printed in the United States of America

QM

11 13 15 14 12

WALT WHITMAN

Walt Whitman was born on May 31, 1819, on a farm near West Hills, New York, on Long Island. In 1823, Walter Senior moved his growing family to Brooklyn, where he worked as a carpenter and introduced Walt to freethinkers and reformers like the Quaker preacher Elias Hicks and women's rights activist Frances Wright. One of Whitman's most vivid childhood memories was of being hoisted onto the shoulders of General Lafayette during a visit the Revolutionary War hero made to New York.

While many notable American figures of the mid-nineteenth century, such as Henry Wadsworth Longfellow and Nathaniel Hawthorne, were the privileged sons of well-established families, Whitman was, at least on the basis of his humble origins, indeed a man of the people. His mother, Louisa Van Velsor, an unfailing supporter of her literary-minded son, was barely literate; of the seven Whitman offspring who survived infancy, Eddy was mentally disabled, Jesse spent much of his life in an insane asylum, Andrew died young of alcoholism and tuberculosis, and Hannah married an abusive man who repeatedly beat her. Whitman was confronted with these often sordid family matters through much of his adult life.

Walt dropped out of school when he was eleven, though he continued to read widely and soon entered the newspaper business as a printer's apprentice. Before long he was editing and writing for some of the most popular newspapers of the day. He reported on the crimes, fires, civic achievements, and other events that shaped rapidly growing New York in the 1830s and 1840s; he reviewed concerts, attended operas, and socialized with other writers and artists; and, always observing, notebook in hand, he walked the streets of the city that had fueled his imagination since his youth and inspired such poems as "Crossing Brooklyn Ferry."

Whitman came onto the literary scene quietly. The First Edition of *Leaves of Grass* received little notice when it appeared in 1855, though such distinguished American men of letters as Ralph Waldo Emerson recognized the twelve poems included in the slim volume, with Whitman's photo on the frontispiece, as a major literary achievement. Whitman spent the rest of his life revising and editing *Leaves of Grass*, incorporating new collections of poems into subsequent editions of his masterpiece. Though he more or less gave up journalism by the early 1860s, he continued to observe with a reporter's eye, working his experiences into his poetry. The often disturbing wartime poems he included in such collections as *Drum-Taps* and *Sequel to Drum-Taps* took root in the visits he made to soldiers in Washington, D.C., hospitals during the Civil War. His romantic relationships also worked their way into his poetry, especially those in his "Calamus" collection, making Whitman one of the first American poets to openly address homosexuality.

Many of Whitman's contemporaries were shocked by *Leaves of Grass*, and in 1882 a Boston printing was banned when the work was declared immoral. Even so, the poet continued to gain a reputation in America and, even more so, in Britain. After suffering a stroke in 1873, Whitman moved from Washington to Camden, New Jersey, where he spent the greater part of his remaining days writing, overseeing new editions of *Leaves of Grass*, and receiving visitors. Just ten days after writing his last poem, "A Thought of Columbus," Walt Whitman died on March 26, 1892.

TABLE OF CONTENTS

———◆———

THE WORLD OF WALT WHITMAN AND *LEAVES OF GRASS*
ix

INTRODUCTION BY KAREN KARBIENER
xiii

LEAVES OF GRASS: *First Edition, 1855*
1

LEAVES OF GRASS: *"Death-bed" Edition, 1891–1892*
147

ADDITIONAL POEMS
699

ENDNOTES
787

PUBLICATION INFORMATION
819

INSPIRED BY *LEAVES OF GRASS*
877

COMMENTS & QUESTIONS
881

FOR FURTHER READING
891

INDEX OF TITLES AND FIRST LINES
897

LIST OF PHOTOGRAPHS

Original frontispiece to the First Edition of *Leaves of Grass* xlvi

Title page to the First Edition of *Leaves of Grass* 1

"Christ likeness" 2

"Out of the mines" 137

Title page to the "Death-bed" Edition of *Leaves of Grass* 147

"Laughing philosopher" 148

"Walt Whitman & his rebel soldier friend Pete Doyle" 273

Walt Whitman holding a butterfly 634

Walt Whitman as a dandy 698

Walt Whitman with Nigel and
Catherine Jeanette Chomeley-Jones 753

Walt Whitman sitting with cane 786

THE WORLD OF WALT WHITMAN
AND *LEAVES OF GRASS*

———◆———

1819   Walter Whitman is born on May 31 in West Hills, Long Island, the second of nine children of Louisa Van Velsor and Walter Whitman, a carpenter. Herman Melville is also born this year. "Ode to a Nightingale," by John Keats, appears.

1823   The senior Whitman moves his family to Brooklyn, anticipating that a building boom will create a demand for carpenters.

1830   Young Walt leaves school, works as an office boy, and continues his education through reading.

1831   Whitman takes an apprenticeship at the printing office of the *Long Island Patriot*.

1832   Whitman moves to the printing office of the *Long Island Star*, Brooklyn's leading newspaper.

1836   He begins teaching school in East Norwich, Long Island, the first of many such positions he will take over the next several years.

1838   Whitman founds a weekly newspaper, the *Long Islander*.

1840   He campaigns for presidential candidate Martin Van Buren.

1841   The *Democratic Review* publishes some of Whitman's prose and verse.

1842   The *New World*, a Manhattan newspaper, publishes Whitman's sentimental temperance novel, *Franklin Evans; or The Inebriate*.

1846   After several years spent writing for several Manhattan and Brooklyn newspapers, Whitman begins a two-year stint as editor of the *Brooklyn Daily Eagle*. He begins attending opera, a passion that will continue for decades. Whitman sits for the first of what will be more than 130 photographs over the course of his lifetime (he was the most photographed nineteenth-century writer after Mark Twain).

1848   Whitman becomes editor of the *New Orleans Daily Crescent* but soon returns north to found the *Brooklyn Freeman*.

1850–   These are crucial yet mysterious years in the development of
1855   Whitman's poetics. He works intermittently as a freelance journalist, builds and sells houses in Brooklyn, and lives with his family. The details of how he prepares for and writes his great work *Leaves of Grass* remain unknown.

1855   Whitman publishes *Leaves of Grass* on July 4 to little notice. His father dies seven days later. Whitman sends a copy of *Leaves* to Ralph Waldo Emerson, who replies with a congratulatory letter.

1856   In September, Whitman publishes the second edition of *Leaves of Grass*, with added poems and Emerson's letter. Henry David Thoreau visits Whitman at his home.

1857   Whitman returns to journalism as the editor of the *Brooklyn Daily Times*.

1859   Dismissed from the *Times*, Whitman prepares another edition of *Leaves of Grass*. He begins to frequent Pfaff's, a restaurant that is the epicenter of New York bohemian culture. There he meets Fred Vaughan, a stage driver; the relationship with Vaughan probably inspires some of Whitman's homoerotic poetry.

1861   The American Civil War begins.

1862   Whitman travels to Fredericksburg, Virginia, to search for his brother George, who is reported missing in battle and turns up wounded.

1863   Whitman settles in Washington, D.C., where he works as a clerk for the Army Paymaster's Office and makes lifelong friends of John Burroughs and William D. O'Connor, both writers. In his spare time, he visits wounded soldiers in the capital's overflowing hospitals.

1864   Family matters, including the recent death of his brother Andrew and the mental deterioration of his brother Jesse, force Whitman to return to Brooklyn temporarily.

1865   The year the Civil War ends is a significant one for Whitman. Returning to Washington, he becomes a clerk in the Indian Bureau of the Department of the Interior but is dismissed within six months on grounds of alleged obscenity in

Leaves of Grass. He meets Peter Doyle, an eighteen-year-old former Confederate soldier, and the men begin a long-term romantic relationship. Whitman publishes *Drum-Taps*, his book of Civil War poetry, and *Sequel to Drum-Taps*, which contains "When Lilacs Last in the Dooryard Bloom'd," an elegy to Abraham Lincoln, slain in April of this year.

1866   William O'Connor publishes *The Good Gray Poet*, a pamphlet that defends the poet against his firing and charges of obscenity.

1867   Another edition of *Leaves of Grass*, including *Drum-Taps* and other Civil War poems, is published. John Burroughs publishes *Notes on Walt Whitman as Poet and Person*, the first biography of the poet.

1868   The first foreign edition of Whitman's poems is published in England, where Whitman attracts a sizable following.

1871   *Democratic Vistas*, *Passage to India*, and the Fifth Edition of *Leaves of Grass* are published.

1873   On January 23 a paralytic stroke leaves Whitman partially disabled, and his mother dies on May 23. Whitman moves to the home of his brother George in Camden, New Jersey.

1876   Whitman publishes *Two Rivulets* and a "Centennial" Edition of *Leaves of Grass*. He develops a close relationship with Harry Stafford, an eighteen-year-old errand boy.

1879   After traveling as far west as Denver, Whitman falls ill and stops in St. Louis to stay with his brother Jeff.

1880   Whitman returns to Camden, then travels to Ontario to spend the summer with Richard Maurice Bucke, a physician who becomes a lifelong friend and will be Whitman's biographer.

1882   Facing criminal obscenity charges, Boston publisher James Osgood ceases distribution of a new edition of *Leaves of Grass*. The edition is published in Philadelphia, as is the autobiographical *Specimen Days and Collect*. Oscar Wilde pays two visits to Whitman and sends him an enlarged photographic portrait. Henry Wadsworth Longfellow and Ralph Waldo Emerson die.

1883   Richard Maurice Bucke publishes his biography, *Walt Whitman*.

1884   Whitman purchases a house at 328 Mickle Street in Camden, New Jersey, where he receives his many friends. A daily visitor is Horace Traubel, Whitman's so-called "Spirit Child," who will recount his conversations with the poet in his multi-volume *With Walt Whitman in Camden* and who will be one of the executors of the poet's estate.

1887   Whitman draws large crowds to a lecture in New York City and is the subject of a portrait by Thomas Eakins.

1888   In June, Whitman suffers another stroke. *November Boughs*, a collection of new poems and previously published prose pieces, appears.

1889   Whitman is enthralled by the glow of the electric street lamp installed on Mickle Street.

1890   Weary of English poet and essayist John Addington Symonds's incessant inquiries about the homosexual content of the "Calamus" poems, Whitman fabricates the story that he is the father of six illegitimate children.

1891   Whitman publishes *Good-Bye My Fancy*, a collection of prose and verse, and prepares the final, "Death-bed" Edition of *Leaves of Grass*. Herman Melville dies.

1892   Whitman dies on March 26 and is buried in Camden's Harleigh Cemetery. His last, spoken words are to his nurse, Warry Fritzinger: "Warry, shift."

INTRODUCTION

Walt Whitman and the
Promise of America

———◆———

"America," the voice says, decidedly.

> "Centre of equal daughters, equal sons,
> All, all alike endear'd, grown, ungrown, young or old."

There is a pause. Then, with renewed vigor and a deliberate beat:

> "Strong, ample, fair, enduring, capable, rich,
> Perennial with the Earth, with Freedom, Law and Love"
> (from "America," pp. 638–639).

"Listener up there!" the poet calls from the pages of *Leaves of Grass*. Walt Whitman listens—*really listens*—and responds—*actually responds*—to America through his poetry. The page functions as a "necessary film" between the reader and the elusive, contradictory "I" of the text, but Whitman himself often longed to dispose of this medium and confront his audience face to face. He was compelled by the powers of the human voice; Whitman might have realized early dreams of becoming an orator had he possessed a stronger tonal quality or more dramatic flair and talent. But even as a writer, he never stopped measuring the worth of words by their sound and aural appeal. "I like to read them in a palpable voice: I try my poems that way—always have: read them aloud to myself," the aging poet told his friend Horace Traubel (*With Walt Whitman in Camden*, vol. 3, p. 375; see "For Further Reading"). Getting his listeners to listen to him, as he absorbed and translated them; sensing and deriving energy from the presence and participation of an audience, as his own physical self and voice inspired them: These were foremost concerns for the poet now known as America's greatest spokesperson, a man who still speaks to and for the American people.

Thomas Edison's recording of Whitman reading his poem "America" is the closest Walt came, in a literal sense, to addressing his audience (that is, if it is indeed authentic; see Ed Folsom's article "The Whitman Recording"). Edison patented the phonograph in 1878, and the public flocked to see and hear demonstrations of the new device that "spoke" in a faint metallic tone. Whitman himself visited New York's Exhibition Building to see displays of Edison's phonograph and telephone in 1879. A great admirer of technological progress and inventive spirits, Whitman and Edison struck up a friendship and apparently decided to make a recording in 1889. The poet spoke into a small megaphone, attached to the recording apparatus with a flexible tube; the inventor turned the crank. The winding sound of the spinning wax cylinder is clearly heard for the first few seconds of the recording.

And then the voice starts. Students of Whitman are often surprised by how "old" he sounds, forgetting his many paralytic strokes in the 1870s and the ill health that plagued him in his final years. His choice of poem for this apparently onetime opportunity also seems unusual, since "America" is not a popular favorite with Whitman or his readers. But given the strong beat of the poem's many monosyllabic words, Whitman may have chosen the reading for its sound as well as its meaning. The urgency of his voice increases as he moves from the musical cadence of the first two lines to the solemn grandeur of the next. His pronunciation of "ample" as "eample" sounds explosive, and the accent perhaps betrays the Dutch heritage of his family and his beloved city. And the luxurious curl in the word "love" is intimate and inviting. The sensual Whitman can still be heard—even felt—well over a hundred years after his physical death.

The sudden cut after the last word suggests that Whitman and Edison had run out of cylinder space before recording the last two lines: "A grand, sane, towering, seated Mother, / Chair'd in the adamant of Time." The omission does not damage the poetic quality of the first four lines; in fact, fans of Whitman's earlier, energetic descriptions may consider the final image too static, too conservative or classical. But this late poem was written by a poet reacting as much to intimations of his own mortality as to America's growing obsession with capitalism and divisions of labor. By the time Whitman wrote "America" in 1888, he no longer believed he would see the promise of America fulfilled in his day; if true democracy were to be achieved, Americans would have to will it into existence. Whitman forcefully projects this solid, secure image of America—an America where the values of community, equality, and creation are at the center rather than the margins—in defiance of the divisive, material culture he first recognized after the Civil War. In both the recorded four and the original six lines of the poem, Whitman's last word on America is love.

Whitman might be disappointed by how removed America still is from his idealized vision, but he would have been pleasantly surprised by the relevance and impact of his message today—especially to his fellow New Yorkers. Though the printshop where *Leaves of Grass* was first struck off was unceremoniously demolished in the 1960s to make way for a housing project, the city has since confirmed and created symbols of the enduring presence of the poems: "Crossing Brooklyn Ferry," hammered into the Fulton Ferry landing balustrade in Brooklyn, underscores one of the most dramatic Manhattan views; an inspiring section of "City of Ships!" faces the World Financial Center from the marina's iron enclosure; other verse cruises the length of the city below ground, as part of the "Poetry in Motion" series exhibited on the subway.

The events of September 11, 2001, affected every American's sense of security and allegiance but brought New Yorkers together in a particularly powerful way. With a renewed sense of connection among this diverse group of people, and support for its heroes and survivors, came a turn to their first spokesperson. Even a century and a half later, Whitman's images of American courage are strikingly modern. As more firehouse walls and church walls became temporary memorial sites, more of *Leaves of Grass* became part daily life in New York City. This passage, inspired by Whitman's own eyewitness accounts of the great fires of 1845, became a popular posting:

> I am the mashed fireman with breastbone broken . . . .
>   tumbling walls buried me in their debris,
> Heat and smoke I inspired . . . . I heard the yelling
>   shouts of my comrades,
> I heard the distant click of their picks and shovels;
> They have cleared the beams away . . . . they tenderly
>   lift me forth.
>
> I lie in the night air in my red shirt . . . . the pervading
>   hush is for my sake,
> Painless after all I lie, exhausted but not so unhappy,
> White and beautiful are the faces around me . . . . the
>   heads are bared of their fire-caps,
> The kneeling crowd fades with the light of the torches
>   ("[Song of Myself],"* 1855, p. 68).

"The proof of a poet," wrote Whitman in his 1855 preface to *Leaves of Grass*, "is that his country absorbs him as affectionately as he has absorbed it" (p. 27). For decades now, American popular culture has participated in a conversation with Whitman that continues to grow more lively and intimate. The absorption of Whitman by the mainstream is clearly demonstrated in film—an appropriate medium, considering the poet's interest in appealing to the ears and eyes of readers. When Ryan O'Neal quotes the last lines of "Song of the Open Road" as part of his wedding vows in *Love Story* (1970), he pronounces Whitman as the spokesman for love that knows no boundaries of class, creed, or time; "Song of

---

*Titles of First Edition poems are presented in brackets. Whitman did not title the twelve poems in the First Edition but gave them titles as he included them in subsequent editions (see "Publication Information").

Myself" is used similarly in *With Honors* (1994) when read over the deathbed of Simon Wilder, a beloved eccentric (played by Joe Pesci) found living in the basement of Harvard's Huntington Library. Whitman stars with Robin Williams in *Dead Poets Society* (1989), and represents proud individuality and independence of spirit—socially and sexually. "I Sing the Body Electric" inspires dancers to celebrate physicality in *Fame* (1980); as Annie Savoy, Susan Sarandon also uses the poem to celebrate her body in the sexiest scene of *Bull Durham* (1988).

The musicality of Whitman's long lines have inspired American composers from Charles Ives to Madonna, who quotes from "Vocalism" in her song "Sanctuary": "Surely whoever speaks to me in the right voice, / Him or her I shall follow." Well over 500 recordings have been made of Whitman-inspired songs, with such artists as Kurt Weill and Leonard Bernstein lending Whitman's words a classic pop sensibility. Bryan K. Garman's *A Race of Singers: Whitman's Working-class Hero from Guthrie to Springsteen*, introduces Whitman's influence on rock and folk musicians, far too vast for adequate treatment here. As a single example of the continuing presence of Whitman through generations of singers, consider this: The popular alt-country group Wilco (along with British singer-activist Billy Bragg) recorded a 1946 Woody Guthrie song entitled "Walt Whitman's Niece" and included it on the 1998 release *Mermaid Avenue*. Guthrie himself never recorded the song; one wonders how far the joke of the title would go with his own audiences.

Many Americans get the joke now, and can smile about it. Others still don't find it funny. For few writers have provoked such extreme reactions as Walt Whitman—America's poet, but also America's gay, politically radical, socially liberal spokesperson. And few books of poetry have had so controversial a history as Whitman's brash, erotically charged *Leaves of Grass*. When the First Edition appeared in 1855, influential man of letters Rufus Griswold denounced the book as a "gross obscenity," and an anonymous *London Critic* reviewer wrote that "the man who wrote page 79 of the *Leaves of Grass* [the first page of the poem eventually known as "I Sing the Body Electric"] deserves nothing so richly as the public executioner's whip." Finding himself on the defensive early on, Whitman wrote a series of anonymous self-reviews that clarified the goals of *Leaves* and its author, "the begetter of a new offspring out of literature, taking with easy nonchalance the chances of its present reception, and, through all misunderstandings and distrusts, the chances of its future reception" (from Whitman's unsigned *Leaves* review in the *Brooklyn Daily Times*, September 29, 1855).

Five years later, Whitman's own mentor Emerson, who advised against including the highly charged "Children of Adam" poems, tested his "easy nonchalance." Holding his ground yet again, Whitman explained to Emerson that the exclusion was unacceptable since it would be understood as an "apology," "surrender," and "admission that something or other was wrong" (*The Correspondence*, vol. 1, p. 224). In 1882 Boston publisher James R. Osgood was forced to stop printing the Sixth Edition when the city's district attorney, Oliver Stevens, ruled that *Leaves of Grass* violated "the Public Statutes concerning obscene literature." After looking at Osgood's list of necessary deletions from *Leaves of Grass*, Whitman responded: "The list whole and several is rejected by me, & will not be thought of under any circumstances" (Kaplan, *Walt Whitman: A Life*, p. 20). The sixty-three-year-old immediately sat down and wrote the essay "A Memorandum at a Venture," a diatribe condemning America's close-minded and unhealthy attitudes toward sexuality. Whitman's poems continued to provoke harsh criticism and calls for censorship through the nineteenth and twentieth centuries: As recently as 1998, conservatives were given another opportunity to condemn the book's suggestive content when President Clinton gave Monica Lewinsky a copy as a gift. Lewinsky's own critique of Whitman, enclosed in her thank you note, facilitated the controversy: "Whitman is so rich that one must read him like one tastes a fine wine or good cigar—take it, roll it in your mouth, and savor it!"

Whitman would have probably laughed in approval of Lewinsky's reading. Despite the relentless public outcry and his permanent defensive posturing, he also "took in" and "savored" his poems as well as the writing process. From the publication of the First Edition in 1855 until his death in 1892, he continued to revise and expand his body of work. *Leaves of Grass* went through six editions (1855, 1856, 1860, 1867, 1871, 1881) and several reprints—the 1876

"Centennial" Edition that included a companion volume entitled *Two Rivulets*; the 1888 edition; and the "Death-bed" Edition of 1891–1892. He also published a collection of Civil War poems entitled *Drum-Taps* (1865) and added a *Sequel to Drum-Taps* (1865–1866). Though he began writing poetry relatively late, he never stopped once he started: Plagued by bronchial pneumonia for three months before his death, Whitman completed his last composition ("A Thought of Columbus") on March 16, 1892, ten days before he died. So ended a literary life that had not seen the rewards of wealth, love, or the recognition of his fellow Americans; the poet could only hope that future readers and writers would embrace his message and carry it forth. Acknowledging that he had "not gain'd the acceptance of my own time" in 1888, Whitman described the "best comfort of the whole business": "I have had my say entirely my own way, and put it unerringly on record—the value thereof to be decided by time" ("A Backward Glance O'er Travel'd Roads," p. 681).

> I myself but write one or two indicative words for the future,
> I but advance a moment only to wheel and hurry back in the
>   darkness.
> I am a man who, sauntering along without fully stopping,
>   turns a casual look upon you and then averts his face,
> Leaving it to you to prove and define it,
> Expecting the main things from you ("Poets to Come," pp. 176–177).

"I greet you at the beginning of a great career, which yet must have had a long foreground somewhere, for such a start," Ralph Waldo Emerson wrote to Whitman a few weeks after the first publication of *Leaves of Grass*. Whitman was so pleased with the letter that he included it in the 1856 Edition of *Leaves of Grass* as promotional material, going so far as to imprint the first words on the spine of the book. Emerson was correct on two counts. The 1855 Edition marked the start of a poetic legacy that endures 150 years later. And yes, the foreground was a longer one than that of most first-time poets: Whitman was thirty-six when his first book of poetry was published. But Emerson could have never anticipated the "preparations" that led to this great publication, simply because Whitman's literary apprenticeship was radically different from Emerson's own, or any other traditional poet's, for that matter.

Emerson himself had privileged beginnings—intellectual, social, economic. He was born into a line of ministers, was encouraged by his brilliant and eccentric aunt, went to Harvard, and traveled extensively. His friend Henry David Thoreau studied under clergyman William Channing at Harvard and was guided by liberal thinker Orestes Brownson. Henry Wadsworth Longfellow and Nathaniel Hawthorne were both descended from established colonial families; they were classmates at Bowdoin, and both had time and money for European travels. All of these men had supportive networks that extended beyond the family as well: Emerson, Thoreau, Hawthorne, and others formed the core of the Transcendentalist movement; several of them participated in communal experiments such as Brook Farm; and some of them were neighbors in Boston or Concord.

In comparison to the Massachusetts "colony" of writers, their New York contemporaries were disconnected and had seen harder times. Herman Melville, born like Whitman in 1819, never met the poet; after his popularity began to wane with the publication of *Moby Dick* (1851), Melville worked as an outdoor customs inspector for the last two decades of his life. Whitman did meet Edgar Allan Poe, whom he described as "a little jaded," in the offices of the *Broadway Journal*. Poe disliked New York and was too busy wrestling with inner demons to make any friends in his adopted hometown. Whitman never had the same opportunities to travel as Melville did, never profited from wealthy family connections as Poe had, and had less monetary or social success than either of them.

Born on May 31, 1819, in West Hills on Long Island, Whitman spent his first three years on the family farm. "Books were scarce," writes Whitman's longtime friend John Burroughs of the Whitman homestead. Walter Whitman, Sr., a skilled carpenter, struggled to keep his family fed and clothed; he moved his growing family to Brooklyn in 1823 to take advantage of a building boom.

Four of the seven children who survived infancy were plagued with health problems: Jesse (1818–1870) died in an insane asylum; Hannah (1823–1908) became neurotic and possibly psychotic; Andrew (1827–1863) was an alcoholic who died young; and Edward (1835–1892) was mentally retarded at birth and possibly afflicted with Down's syndrome or epilepsy. The second son after Jesse, Walt assumed a position of responsibility in the family. After about five years in public school, he dropped out to help his father make ends meet.

The family certainly needed the help. The senior Whitman's fine craftsmanship can still be seen at the Walt Whitman Birthplace on Long Island (the beautifully laid diagonal wainscoting in the stairwell, for instance, was allegedly his handiwork), but he seems not to have had a head for business. The family moved frequently because of bad deals or lost jobs. There is no direct proof, but there is reason to suspect Walter was an alcoholic. His son was obsessed with the Temperance movement through the early 1840s, and many of Whitman's early prose writings preach of the horrors of alcohol (Whitman's temperance novel, *Franklin Evans; or The Inebriate*, was published in 1842). Critics have also made much of the absent or abusive fathers who often appear in Whitman's poetry, such as those from "[There Was a Child Went Forth]": "The father, strong, selfsufficient, manly, mean, angered, unjust, / The blow, the quick loud word, the tight bargain, the crafty lure" (p. 139). Whatever his faults were, Whitman's father was also responsible for training his sons as radical Democrats, introducing them to such Quaker doctrine as the "inner light," and providing Walt with two lifelong heroes: the freethinker Frances Wright and the Quaker Elias Hicks. In his prose collection *Specimen Days* (1882–1883), Whitman fondly remembers going with his father to hear Wright and Hicks give speeches, events that helped shape and define the poet's love of the spoken word.

Whitman negatively compared the "subterranean tenacity and central bony structure (obstinacy, willfulness), which I get from my paternal English elements" to the qualities inherited from "the maternal nativity-stock brought hither from far-away Netherlands . . . (doubtless the best)" (*Specimen Days and Collect*, p. 21). Though

Louisa Van Velsor Whitman was almost illiterate and confessed to having trouble understanding her son's poems, she was a great support for Walt. Indeed, she kept the family together despite her husband's unreliability. Whitman's feministic opinions were undoubtedly inspired by her strength: "I say it is as great to be a woman as to be a man, / And I say there is nothing greater than the mother of men," he writes in "Song of Myself" (p. 210). Significantly, Whitman's father died within a week of the first publication of *Leaves of Grass*—in a year that represented a high water mark in the poet's life—while Louisa's passing contributed to making 1873 one of Whitman's darkest years. He described her death as "the great dark cloud of my life" (*Correspondence*, vol. 2, p. 243).

Louisa's natural intelligence and Walter's self-schooling inspired their son to think creatively and independently about his education. Whitman never regretted leaving Brooklyn District School Number 1 at the ripe age of eleven. Even when he returned to the classroom to teach between 1836 and 1841, Whitman was unhappy and felt out of place. His attempts to use the progressive pedagogical approaches of Horace Mann were criticized, and he felt trapped by the small-mindedness of the farming communities in which he worked. For Whitman, the path to enlightenment demanded mental as well as physical engagement.

> . . . in libraries I lie as one dumb, a gawk, or unborn,
>   or dead,)
> But just possibly with you on a high hill, first watching
>   lest any person for miles around approach unawares,
> Or possibly with you sailing at sea, or on the beach of
>   the sea or some quiet island,
> Here to put your lips upon mine I permit you ("Whoever
>   You Are Holding Me Now in Hand," p. 277).

Throughout his writings, Whitman returns again and again to the shores of his beloved Paumanok (Algonquian for "Long Island"), his place of birth as both man and artist. The young boy was never far from the water's edge, from his first years on Long Island to his youth in Brooklyn, where he picked up bones of Revolutionary

War soldiers in the sand by the Navy Yard. As the space between the world of the everyday and what he called his "dark mother the sea," or the two extremes of reality and the subconscious, the shore represented a place of emotional equilibrium and communion. "My doings there in early life, are woven all through L. of G," he wrote in *Specimen Days* (p. 13). Whitman describes the Long Island coastline as a sort of outdoor lecture hall, "where I loved, after bathing, to race up and down the hard sand, and declaim Homer or Shakespeare to the surf and sea-gulls by the hour" (p. 14). In the rite-of-passage poem "Out of the Cradle Endlessly Rocking," the speaker explains that his own songs were "awaked from that hour" the sea had sung to him "in the moonlight on Paumanok's gray beach." The murmuring waves deliver the knowledge of death that will transform the boy into the poet of life, the "solitary singer."

Inspiration for the poetry came from nature; love of the words themselves was acquired in a Brooklyn printing office. One of Whitman's first employers was Samuel E. Clements, editor of the *Long Island Patriot*. Here and at several other Brooklyn and Long Island newspapers, Whitman learned about the art of printing from the most basic task of setting type. It was fast, competitive, potentially fun work for boys with quick minds and fingers. In a series of articles entitled "Brooklyniana," Whitman describes his apprenticeship as one might recall a first love or sexual encounter:

> What compositor, running his eye over these lines, but will easily realize the whole modus of that initiation?—the half eager, half bashful beginning—the awkward holding of the stick—the type-box, or perhaps two or three old cases, put under his feet for the novice to stand on, to raise him high enough—the thumb in the stick—the compositor's rule—the upper case almost out of reach—the lower case spread out handier before him—learning the boxes—the pleasing mystery of the different letters, and their divisions—the great 'e' box—the box for spaces right by the boy's breast—the 'a' box, 'i' box, 'o' box, and all the rest—the box for quads away off in the right hand corner—the slow and laborious formation, type by type, of the first line—its unlucky bursting by the too nervous pressure of the

thumb—the first experience in 'pi,' and the distributing thereof—all
this, I say, what journeyman typographer cannot go back in his own
experience and easily realize? (Christman, ed., *Walt Whitman's
New York: From Manhattan to Montauk*, p. 48).

Whitman learned to love language from the letter on up. Words
weren't just inanimate type on a flat page; they were physical, even
three-dimensional objects to hold and to mold. Even the spaces
between words were tangible to him. Here was a connection be-
tween manual labor and enlightenment, action and idea, hand
and heart.

A good part of Whitman's literary apprenticeship, then, was
started and encouraged by his work for New York's burgeoning
newspaper industry. He eventually tried and enjoyed each step in
the process of publishing. In 1838 he temporarily abandoned teach-
ing to start up his own newspaper called the *Long Islander*—serving
as compositor, pressman, editor, and even distributor (he deliv-
ered papers in a thirty-mile circuit every week, on horseback). And
though he sold this enterprise after about ten months and returned
to teaching, he found his way back into the newspaper business
within three years. In the next years he would pursue his interest
in writing even as he helped print and edit a number of Brooklyn
and Long Island papers. In the fifteen years before publishing
Leaves of Grass (1855), Whitman worked for some of the most pop-
ular penny dailies of his day and published a substantial body of
journalism.

Surprisingly, during these same crucial fifteen years, Whitman
saw in print only twenty-one of his poems and twenty-two short sto-
ries. His first poem, "Young Grimes," was published in the *Long
Island Democrat* on January 1, 1840—clearly imitative, since it
followed the model of a popular poem entitled "Old Grimes," by
Albert G. Greene. "Young Grimes" is as conventional as "Old
Grimes" in its rhyme, meter, religious expression, and sentimen-
tality; there seems to be no signs of America's great outlaw poet in
its didactic lines. Even as he progressed through the decade, Whit-
man did not make substantial improvements to the formulaic
poetry he contributed to the penny dailies. For example, "The

Mississippi at Midnight," originally published in the *New Orleans Daily Crescent* on March 6, 1848, bears much more similarity to Whitman's earliest verse than to the twelve poems of the 1855 *Leaves of Grass*: Its forced rhyme, predictable meter, and hyperdramatic tone suggest that Whitman had not yet found his poetic voice.

Whitman himself supplied a visual corollary for different stages of his literary career. His interest in physical representations and images, encouraged by his printing apprenticeships, led to a lifelong fascination with the developing art of photography. No American writer (with the possible exception of Mark Twain) was more photographed than Whitman. More than a hundred images of the poet are now in public domain and available online on the Walt Whitman Archive (www.whitmanarchive.org). An image of Whitman circa 1848 depicts a haughty young dandy; his high collar and necktie lend him a traditional air, and his pose (he is strangely uncomfortable-looking as he leans on a cane) seems affected and self-conscious. His hooded and supercilious expression contrasts with the eye-to-eye contact of the poet of *Leaves of Grass*, who confronts the reader directly from the frontispiece of the 1855 Edition. This image, an engraving made from an 1854 daguerreotype taken by Gabriel Harrison, shows Whitman with loosened collar, exposed undershirt, and wrinkled chinos. Hands in pockets, hat cocked, physically forward, the 1855 Walt resembles one of the masses but looks radically different from other poets; he strikes one as straightforward and up-front, yet at the same time less predictable and conventional. Between 1846 and 1855, then, Whitman's image ironically grew younger and more edgy. He exchanged a Brooks Brothers "stuffed shirt" look for the suggestive appeal of a sexy Gap ad, and his radically altered literary style reflected this new look.

"Whitman, the one pioneer. And only Whitman," wrote D. H. Lawrence in 1923. "No English pioneers, no French. No European pioneer-poets. In Europe the would-be pioneers are mere innovators. The same in America. Ahead of Whitman, nothing" (Woodress, ed., *Critical Essays on Walt Whitman*, p. 211). The sentiments were echoed by the likes of F. O. Matthiessen, William Carlos Williams, and Allen Ginsberg. Langston Hughes named Whitman the "greatest of American poets"; Henry Miller described him as "the bard of the future" (quoted in Perlman et al., eds., *Walt Whitman: The Measure of His Song*, pp. 185, 205). Even his more cynical readers recognized Whitman's position of near-mythical status and supreme influence in American letters. "His crudity is an exceeding great stench but it *is* America," Ezra Pound admitted in a 1909 article; he continued: "To be frank, Whitman is to my fatherland what Dante is to Italy" (Perlman, pp. 112–113). "We continue to live in a Whitmanesque age," said Pablo Neruda in a speech to PEN in 1972. "Walt Whitman was the protagonist of a truly geographical personality: The first man in history to speak with a truly continental American voice, to bear a truly American name" (Perlman, p. 232). Alicia Ostriker, in a 1992 essay, claimed that "if women poets in America have written more boldly and experimentally in the last thirty years than our British equivalents, we have Whitman to thank" (Perlman, p. 463).

How did a former typesetter and penny-daily editor come to write the poems that would define and shape American literature and culture?

Whitman's metamorphosis in the decade before the first publication of *Leaves of Grass* in 1855 remains an intriguing mystery. Biographers concede that details about Whitman's life and literary activities from the late 1840s to the early 1850s are extremely hard to come by. "Little is known of Whitman's activities in these years," writes Joann Krieg in the 1851–1854 section of her *Whitman Chronology* (most other years have month-to-month commentaries). Whitman was fired from his job at the *New Orleans Daily Crescent* in the summer of 1848, then resigned from his editorship of the *Brooklyn Freeman* in 1849. Though he continued to write for several newspapers during the next five years, his work as a freelancer was irregular and his whereabouts difficult to follow. He seems also to have tried his hand at several other jobs, including house building and selling stationery. One wonders if Walt's break from the daily work routine had something to do with his poetic awakening. Keeping to a regulated schedule in the newspaper offices had been a struggle for him, and he had been fired several times for laziness or "sloth." Charting his own days and ways—in particular, working as a self-employed carpenter, as had his idiosyncratic father—may well have enabled him to think "outside the box" and toward the organic, freeform qualities of *Leaves*.

Purposefully dropping out of workaday life and common sight suggests that Whitman may have intended to obscure the details of his pre-*Leaves* years, and there is further evidence to support the idea that Whitman consciously created a "myth of origins." In his biography of Whitman, Justin Kaplan quotes the poet on the mysterious "perturbations" of *Leaves of Grass*: It had been written under "great pressure, pressure from within," and he had "felt that he must do it" (p. 185). To obscure the roots of *Leaves* and build the case for his original thinking, Whitman destroyed significant amounts of manuscripts and letters upon at least two occasions; as Grier notes in his introduction to *Notebooks and Unpublished Prose Manuscripts*, "one is continually struck by [the] omissions and reticences" of the remaining material (vol. 1, p. 8). Indeed, some of the notes surviving his "clean-ups" were reminders to himself to "not name any names"—and thus to remain silent concerning any possible readings or influences. "Make no quotations, and no reference to any other writers.—Lumber the writing with nothing," Whitman wrote to himself in the late 1840s. It was a command he would repeat to himself several times in the years preceding the publication of *Leaves*.

Whitman's friends and critics also did their share to create a legend of the writer and his explosive first book. In the first biographical study of Whitman, John Burroughs claimed that certain individuals throughout history "mark and make new eras, plant the standard again ahead, and in one man personify vast races or sweeping revolutions. I consider Walt Whitman such an individual" (Burroughs, "Preface" to *Notes on Walt Whitman as Poet and Person*). Others insisted that *Leaves of Grass* was the product of the "cosmic consciousness" Whitman had acquired around 1850 (Bucke, *Walt Whitman*, p. 178) or a spiritual "illumination" of the highest order (Binns, *A Life of Walt Whitman*, pp. 69–70).

What sort of experience could inspire such a personal revelation? For a man just awakening to the inhumanity of slavery and the hidden agendas of the Free Soil stance, witnessing a slave auction might do it. This was but one of the life-altering events that occurred during Whitman's three-month sojourn in New Orleans in 1848. Another, substantiated by his poetry rather than Whitman's own word, was an alleged homosexual affair. Several poems in the sexually charged "Calamus" and "Children of Adam" clusters of 1860 are suggestive of an intense and liberating romance in New Orleans. The manuscript for "Once I Passed Through a Populous City" has the lines "man who wandered with me, there, for love of me, / Day by day, and night by night, we were together." "Man" was changed to "woman" in the final draft of the poem; see *Whitman's Manuscripts: Leaves of Grass (1860)*, edited by Fredson Bowers, Chicago: University of Chicago Press, 1955, p. 64. In "I Saw in Louisiana a Live-Oak Growing," the poet describes breaking off a twig of a particularly stately and solitary tree: "Yet it remains to me a curious token, it makes me think of manly love" (p. 287). The emotional release of "coming out" might well explain the spectacular openness and provocative energy of *Leaves of Grass*; additionally, Whitman's identification of his "outsider status" could have helped spark his empathy for women, Native Americans, and other marginalized groups that are celebrated in the 1855 poems.

Whitman's personal transformations, as well as America's political upheaval, characterized the 1840s and early 1850s. His growing political awareness was no doubt inspired by the unprecedented corruption of the day: Vote buying, wire-pulling, and patronage existed on all levels of state and national government. In New York, Fernando Wood was elected mayor in 1854 as a result of vote fraud: In the "Bloody Sixth" ward, there were actually 4,000 more votes than there were voters. And three of the most corrupt presidencies in America's history—Millard Fillmore (1850–1853), Franklin Pierce (1853–1857), and James Buchanan (1857–1861)—were certain to catch the attention of an aspiring young journalist. "Our topmost warning and shame," Whitman wrote of the three incompetent leaders, who exhibited especially poor judgment on the issue of slavery.

The debate over slavery divided the country in the decades before the Civil War; even within regions, the answers were not as clear-cut as they would seem once sides were drawn in 1861. According to one estimate in 1847, two-thirds of Northerners disapproved of slavery, but only 5 percent declared themselves Abolitionists. Immediate emancipation, it was feared, would flood the North with cheap labor and racial disharmonies. The word "compromise," with all its political and moral ambiguities, was a favorite with politicians. Fillmore was responsible for the Compromise of 1850, which admitted California to the Union as a free state but also lifted legal restrictions on slavery in Utah and New Mexico; to satisfy the South, he instituted a stringent Fugitive Slave Law at the same time. In 1854 Pierce signed the Kansas-Nebraska Act, allowing settlers of Kansas and Nebraska to decide for themselves the issue of slavery. The result was "Bleeding Kansas," the 1854 congressional election that was decided by 1,700 Missourians crossing the border and casting illegal votes for the proslavery candidate. Additionally, in this crucial year before the first publication of *Leaves of Grass*, fugitive slave Anthony Burns was arrested in Boston, put on trial, and shipped back to Virginia. At a huge rally in Framingham, Massachusetts, William Lloyd Garrison burned copies of the Declaration of Independence, and Henry David Thoreau delivered the powerful address "Slavery in Massachusetts."

Whitman, too, was incited to protest. Through the 1840s and 1850s, he watched with increasing anger as the Whig Party collapsed, and as the Democratic Party gave itself over to proslavery forces. His editorials throughout this period indicate that his political understanding and stance was becoming more concrete, less forgiving. And in 1850, a series of four political poems appeared, indicating that Whitman had finally stepped away from imitative verse and started investing his poetry with a more personal, immediate voice and message. "Song for Certain Congressmen," first published in the *New York Evening Post* of March 2, 1850, mocks Americans for considering compromise of any sort—particularly compromise of human rights (before the Compromise of 1850 became law in September, the country debated the status of slavery in the new western states for several months):

Beyond all such we know a term
    Charming to ears and eyes,
With it we'll stab young Freedom,
    And do it in disguise;
Speak soft, ye wily dough-faces—
    That term is "compromise" (pp. 736–737).

"Blood-Money," published March 22, is an indictment of Daniel Webster's support of the Fugitive Slave Law; "The House of Friends," a criticism of the Democratic Party's support of the Compromise, was published June 14. "Resurgemus," published two months later, celebrates the spirit of the European revolutions of 1848. The fact that it became the eighth of the twelve original poems in *Leaves of Grass* (1855) demonstrates that Whitman saw this effort as more than an apprentice-poem; indeed, the prophetic, confrontational last lines foretell of the arrival of a Whitmanesque redeemer: "Is the house shut? Is the master away? / Nevertheless, be ready, be not weary of watching, / He will surely return; his messengers come anon" (p. 743).

Along with personal revelations and the awakening of a political conscience, a spiritual conversion contributed to the metamorphosis of a Brooklyn hack writer to democracy's poet: Walt Whitman became a New Yorker.

Of the three types of New Yorkers, "commuters give the city its tidal restlessness; natives give it solidity and continuity; but the settlers give it passion," writes E. B. White in his essay "Here Is New York" (reprinted in Lopate, *Writing New York: A Literary Anthology*, pp. 696–697). Whitman belonged to the third category. Though born on a Long Island farm, he discovered at an early age that the city fed his soul. When his parents moved back to the country in 1833, the fourteen-year-old boy decided to stay on alone in Brooklyn and work in the printing industry. An employer helped him acquire a card for a circulating library; on his own, he started attending the theater and participating in a debating society. Looking for work during difficult times, Whitman left New York during his late teens and early twenties to teach school on Long Island. He disliked the job and eagerly returned to the world of city journalism in 1841. Until 1848 Whitman bounced from one Brooklyn or Manhattan publisher or newspaper to the next; he reported on local news, reviewed concerts and operas, and wrote his own fledgling poems and short stories. When he was fired from his editorship of the *Brooklyn Daily Eagle* in 1848, Whitman made an impetuous decision to try working in New Orleans. Not surprisingly, the now-confirmed New Yorker was back within three months. Later that year, Whitman secured his position in his beloved Brooklyn by buying a Myrtle Avenue lot and building a home on the site (with a printing office and bookstore on the first floor). Though he sold this property in 1852, he continued to call Brooklyn (and occasionally, Manhattan) home until 1862, when he left to search for his brother George, who was wounded at the battle of Fredericksburg, and settled in Washington, D.C.

When the Whitman family first moved to Brooklyn in 1823, it was a village of around 7,000 inhabitants. Paintings such as Francis Guy's *Winter Scene in Brooklyn* (1820) depict its country lanes, free-ranging chickens and pigs, and clapboard barns. By the time *Leaves of Grass* was published in 1855, Brooklyn had become the fourth-largest city in the nation. Manhattan, too, had rapidly expanded; its population rose from 123,706 in 1820 to 813,669 in 1860 (Homberger, *The Historical Atlas of New York City*, p. 70). City life, largely confined to the area below Fourteenth Street in the first decades of the nineteenth century, moved so rapidly northward that plans for a "central park" (starting at Fifty-ninth Street) were proposed in 1851. Travel around the city was facilitated by several new rail lines, five of which were incorporated in the 1850s; and "the number of omnibuses shot up from 255 in 1846 to 683 in 1853 (when they carried over a hundred thousand passengers a day)" (Burrows and Wallace, *Gotham: A History of New York City to 1898*, p. 653). People were flocking to the city from the outside: While 667,000 immigrants arrived in the United States between 1820 and 1839, 4,242,000 came between 1840 and 1859. "By 1855 over half the city's residents hailed from outside the United States," note Burrows and Wallace (pp. 736–737). Most of them were impoverished peasants and workers from Ireland and Germany.

Visitors and residents alike were quick to comment on the negative aspects of the city's social and economic boom. British actor Fanny Kemble marveled at the diversity of the city's population in her 1832 journal, but was outraged by the prejudice and racism she witnessed (Lopate, pp. 25, 27). Touring New York in 1842, Charles Dickens was taken aback by the treatment of the poor, as well as the pigs roaming noisy, filthy streets (Lopate, pp. 57–58). Thoreau spent a few months in the city in 1843 but was appalled by the crowds: "Seeing so many people from day to day one comes to have less respect for flesh and bones," he wrote to a friend. "It must have a very bad influence on children to see so many human beings at once—mere herds of men" (Lopate, p. 73). Poe mocked the dirty dealings of city businessmen in "Doings of Gotham," a series of articles written for out of towners in 1844. And native New Yorker Herman Melville was the first to capture the urban alienation still felt by Manhattanites, in his 1853 tale "Bartleby the Scrivener."

Writing for Brooklyn and New York newspapers for much of the 1840s and part of the 1850s, Whitman was employed to take note of the changes and report on the city's big events. He wrote about the opening of the Croton Aqueduct in 1842, which brought running water to city residents; he commented on the Astor Place Opera House riots, in which more than twenty people were killed in 1849; he attended the opening of the Crystal Palace on Fifth Avenue and Forty-second Street in 1853. But his interest in city life extended beyond his duties as a reporter. After work, he'd leave his office on "Newspaper Row" (just east of City Hall Park) and take long walks, wandering through the "Bloody Sixth" ward and the crime-infested, impoverished streets of Five Points. Another favorite activity was "looking in at the shop-windows in Broadway the whole forenoon . . . . pressing the flesh of my nose to the thick plate-glass" ("[Song of Myself]," p. 65), especially with the opening of so many elegant photography studios in the 1840s. The Museum of Egyptian Antiquities and the Phrenological Cabinet of the Fowler Brothers and Samuel Wells were other frequent destinations. To cover longer distances, he rode the omnibuses up and down the glorious avenues, singing at the top of his lungs. Whitman started carrying a small notebook, jotting down his thoughts during his daily morning and evening commutes on the Brooklyn ferry. And somewhere along the way, he fell in love with the noise and filth, crowds and congestion, problems and promise of New York.

> This is the city . . . . and I am one of the citizens;
> Whatever interests the rest interests me . . . . politics, churches, newspapers, schools,
> Benevolent societies, improvements, banks, tariffs, steamships, factories, markets,
> Stocks and stores and real estate and personal estate
> ("[Song of Myself]," p. 79).

Whitman found cause to celebrate the same elements of city life that others had criticized or overlooked. He was the first American writer to embrace urban street culture, finding energy, beauty, and humanity in the meanest sights and sounds of the city.

> The blab of the pave . . . . the tires of carts and sluff of bootsoles and talk of the promenaders,
> The heavy omnibus, the driver with his interrogating thumb, the clank of the shod horses on the granite floor,
> The carnival of sleighs, the clinking and shouted jokes and pelts of snowballs;
> The hurrahs for popular favorites . . . . the fury of roused mobs
> ("[Song of Myself]," p. 36).

The cultural offerings of New York were another source of inspiration to Whitman. He fully embraced the city's opera rage, which began in April 1847 when an Italian company opened at his beloved Park Theatre. The Astor Place Opera House also opened that year; with 1,500 seats it was America's largest theater until the Academy of Music opened in Manhattan in 1854. From the late 1840s through the 1850s, Whitman saw dozens of operas, on assignment and for his own pleasure. By the time *Leaves of Grass* went to press, he had heard at least sixteen major singers make their New York debuts. Jenny Lind, P. T. Barnum's "Swedish nightingale," had been a smash success at her debut in Castle Garden in 1850; but a personal favorite of Whitman's was Marietta Alboni, who arrived at the Metropolitan Opera in 1852 and is said to have inspired these passionate lines:

> I hear the trained soprano . . . . she convulses me like the climax
>   of my love-grip;
> The orchestra whirls me wider than Uranus flies,
> It wrenches unnamable ardors from my breast,
> It throbs me to gulps of the farthest down horror,
> It sails me . . . . I dab with bare feet . . . . They are licked by the
>   indolent waves,
> I am exposed . . . . cut by bitter and poisoned hail,
> Steeped amid honeyed morphine . . . . my windpipe squeezed in
>   the fakes of death
> Let up again to feel the puzzle of puzzles,
> And that we call Being ("[Song of Myself]," 1855, p. 57).

The wonder of this ecstatic revelation is that it is both a private and a public experience. His feelings are inspired by human connections: Alboni's voice, the orchestra's resonance, the excitement of his fellow concertgoers, the hum of electric city life just outside. If anything has ever defined the idea of a "New York moment," it is this brief and wonderful merge of inner being with common understanding. An accumulation of such moments, plus years of taking in the city and reimagining it on paper, led to the creation of the self-declared "Walt Whitman, an American, one of the roughs, a kosmos" ("[Song of Myself]," p. 52). And since Whitman perceived New York to be at the heart of America, his love for the city enabled and inspired the love of his country. The diversity, energy, and ambitions of New York represented the promise of America: By finding his voice on city streets and ferries, he was able to sing for his country's open roads and great rivers.

> City of the world! (for all races are here,
> All the lands of the earth make contributions here;)
> City of the sea! city of hurried and glittering tides!
> City whose gleeful tides continually rush or recede, whirling in
>   and out with eddies and foam!

City of wharves and stores—city of tall façades of marble and iron!
Proud and passionate city—mettlesome, mad, extravagant city!
("City of Ships," p. 444).

If the poet's heart was based in Manhattan, the title "Leaves of Grass" for not one but several of his books seems an odd choice. And what of the green cover and gold-embossed, organic-looking lettering that made the book resemble a volume of domestic fiction more than a serious effort? The title and appearance were not the only surprises of the 9- by 12-inch, 95-page volume: Most notably, no author's name appeared anywhere on the cover or first pages. Though the image of Whitman as a provocative and confident working man looked up from the frontispiece, his name came up only about halfway through the first poem—which was, confusingly, also entitled "Leaves of Grass," as were the next five poems.

The quirky details were all deliberate. The title echoed the names of literary productions by women (such as *Fern Leaves from Fanny's Portfolio*, Fanny Fern's popular book of 1853), and the outward appearance also was designed to get readers to question the sexist boundaries of the book industry (note, too, that Whitman's preferred trousers through the late 1850s were "bloomers," the loose-fitting pants that were the male equivalent of those worn by women's rights activists, such as Amelia Bloomer). "Leaves of Grass" was also an obvious metaphor for the unregulated, "organically grown" lines of the poems in the "leaves" of the book. But Whitman was also using "grass" as a symbol of American democracy. Simple and universal, grass represents common ground. Each leaf (Whitman thought the proper word "blade" was literally too sharp) has a singular identity yet is a necessary contributor to the whole. Likewise, each reader will find that he or she is part of *Leaves of Grass*—a book about all Americans that could have been written by any American (hence, the absence of the author's name).

When the first publisher Whitman approached refused to print the manuscript on the grounds of its offensive contents, he took it to the Rome printing shop on Cranberry and Fulton Streets in

Brooklyn Heights. The Rome brothers were friends and neighbors, and they agreed to work on the volume if Whitman would lend a hand with the job. "800 copies were struck off on a hand press by Andrew Rome . . . the author himself setting some of the type," noted Whitman (*Correspondence*, vol. 6, p. 30). Legend has it that most of the copies remained in a back room of the shop "until they were finally discarded as liabilities" (Garrett, *The Rome Printing Shop*, p. 4). The price of two dollars was apparently deemed too high by Whitman, because a second issue printed later that year with a plain paper cover cost one dollar. "All in all a thousand copies were printed but practically none sold," writes Florence Rome Garrett, the granddaughter of Tom Rome (Garrett, p. 4).

Leaves of Grass was bound to be a quiet release, since the book was not printed or supported by a large publishing house with wide distribution, and did not even have a recognizable author's name on the cover. A British name, in particular, would have helped, since midcentury America still looked toward England for artistic models and inspiration. Though political freedom had been established for decades, America was still a long way from gaining cultural independence. "Why should not we have a poetry and philosophy of insight and not of tradition, and a religion by revelation to us, and not a history of theirs?" asked Emerson in *Nature*. Whitman replaced Emerson's interrogation with imperatives in his preface. "Of all nations the United States with veins full of poetical stuff most need poets and will doubtless have the greatest and use them the greatest," he insists in the preface to the First Edition (p. 10). This twelve-page, double-columned preface that stood between the reader and Whitman's twelve poems remains his definitive declaration of independence: These new American poets would represent and inspire the people, assuming the roles of priests and politicians; the new American poetry would be as strong and fluid as its rivers, as sweeping and grand as its landscapes, as various as its people.

As a living embodiment of the new poetry, the American reader was responsible for its grace, power, and truth. The urgent tone of the preface exposes Whitman's desperation over the state of 1850s America—a country corrupted by its own leaders, torn apart by its own people, and facing an imminent civil war. His demands on readers were meant to shake awake a slumbering, passive nation and inspire a loving, proud, generous, accepting union of active thinkers and thoughtful doers:

> This is what you shall do: Love the earth and sun and the animals, despise riches, give alms to every one that asks, stand up for the stupid and crazy, devote your income and labor to others, hate tyrants, argue not concerning God, have patience and indulgence toward the people, take off your hat to nothing known or unknown or to any man or number of men, go freely with powerful uneducated persons and with the young and with the mothers of families, read these leaves in the open air every season of every year of your life, re-examine all you have been told at school or church or in any book, dismiss whatever insults your own soul, and your very flesh shall be a great poem and have the richest fluency not only in its words but in the silent lines of its lips and face and between the lashes of your eyes and in every motion and joint of your body (p. 13).

What is requested here is just as astonishing as how it is stated. The unidentified speaker of the preface possessed an extreme, provocative confidence that could be seen in the eyes and stance of the image on the frontispiece. His prophetic message for America was delivered in lines that evoked the passages and rhythms of holy books; the above section, for example, may be compared with Romans 12:1–21 in the New Testament. But while the writer had perhaps elevated himself to the status of a prophet, his run-on sentences, breathless lists, and general disregard for proper punctuation suggested that he was neither scholar nor trained or "proper" writer. Most outrageous of all was his direct confrontation of the reader—the use of "you" that really meant "you." This personal advancement from writer to reader, this attempt to jump off the page into the audience's immediate space and time, was a new and startling literary technique. And if the combination of audacious demands and prophetic, finger-pointing tone in the preface did not deter readers from moving on to the poems, they would find the same revolutionary style and content in the very first lines.

> I celebrate myself,
> And what I assume you shall assume,
> For every atom belonging to me as good belongs to you
> ("[Song of Myself]," 1855, p. 29).

First-time readers of these lines still find the egotism tremendous and off-putting. The irregular length and randomness of the lines, along with the use of ellipses of various sizes, looks strange enough to the eye trained on Henry Wadsworth Longfellow's neat verse or Alfred Tennyson's stately measures. But the idea of engaging in a conversation with this relaxed figure, who sensually melds with the natural landscape around him (to the point where one is uncertain of the definitions of "loveroot, silkthread, crotch and vine"), puts a more cautious reader on the defensive. In 1855 the son of Nathaniel Hawthorne was appalled by the poet's position on the grass, claiming that he "abandons all personal dignity and reserve, and sprawls incontinently before us"; 150 years later, one might still wonder at a man who unabashedly declares that he will "become undisguised and naked"—and what's more, celebrate every "atom" of himself.

"Song of Myself" (as the poem was finally titled in 1881) may begin with "I," but the poem's last word is "you." In between, the poet does inject a great deal of ego; his posture is clearly that of the poet-prophet with instructions and predictions for his listeners. The most important part of his message, however, concerns the reader's intellectual and spiritual independence:

> Stop this day and night with me and you shall possess the origin of
>   all poems,
> You shall possess the good of the earth and sun . . . . there are
>   millions of suns left,
> You shall no longer take things at second or third hand . . . . nor
>   look through the eyes of the dead . . . . nor feed on the spectres
>   in books,
> You shall not look through my eyes either, nor take things from me,
> You shall listen to all sides and filter them from yourself
> ("[Song of Myself]," 1855, p. 30).

In *Leaves of Grass*, Whitman recognizes the role of the poet as of the highest order. But he also notes that the role is open for everyone (hence, the lack of an author's name on the front cover). This seeming irony is the first that Whitman's readers must get past: the idea that the poet is inspired and must be heeded, but must be heeded regarding a lack of adherence. "He most honors my style," explains the poet in "[Song of Myself]," "who learns under it to destroy the teacher" (p. 86). Throughout the poem, Whitman encourages the reader's active participation and independent thinking with unpredictable breaks as well as provocative questions without "right" answers (many of them bear a resemblance to Buddhist *koans*). At the end of the poem one is left with a sense of the poet's spirit not shining over but running under the bootsoles of his protégés.

Equality between writer and reader was not the only difficult balance Whitman attempted to achieve in the poems of *Leaves of Grass*. As part of his plan for a new democratic art, he questioned and disrupted many other long-standing cultural boundaries: between rich and poor, men and women, the races and religions of the world. His most direct way of doing so was by observation and aggressive questioning, as in his discussion of a slave at auction in "I Sing the Body Electric":

> This is not only one man . . . . he is the father of those who
>   shall be fathers in their turns,
> In him the start of populous states and rich republics,
> Of him countless immortal lives with countless
>   embodiments and enjoyments.
>
> How do you know who shall come from the offspring of his
>   offspring through the centuries?
> Who might you find you have come from yourself if you
>   could trace back through the centuries?
> ("[I Sing the Body Electric]," 1855, p. 125).

Such passages were obviously meant to shock and provoke the American conscience, especially considering that slavery was still a legal and accepted activity. Whitman, who was close friends with Paulina Wright Davis, Abby Price, and several other reformers, also attacked the common acceptance that women were the "weaker sex." Eight years after the first women's rights convention took place in Seneca Falls, New York, he set out to liberate a population still falsely confined by their society's written and unwritten rules, their own fears—even their clothing:

> They are not one jot less than I am,
> They are tann'd in the face by shining suns and blowing winds,
> Their flesh has the old divine suppleness and strength,
> They know how to swim, row, ride, wrestle, shoot, run, strike,
>   retreat, advance, resist, defend themselves,
> They are ultimate in their own right—they are calm, clear,
>   well-possess'd of themselves
> ("A Woman Waits for Me," pp. 263–264).

A less confrontational method for "democratizing" his image of America was the "catalogue," a list of people, places, items, events that sometimes went on for pages. Whitman might have been inspired by the new art of photography in creating these lists; reading through them has an effect that's similar to looking through a photograph album, though a closer comparison may be to watching a video montage. By verbally connecting the marginalized and the mainstream, Whitman puts them "on the same page"—in the book, and hopefully in the mind of the reader.

> The affectionate boy, the husband and wife, the voter, the
>   nominee that is chosen and the nominee that has failed,
> The great already known, and the great anytime after to day,
> The stammerer, the sick, the perfectformed, the homely,
> The criminal that stood in the box, the judge that sat and
>   sentenced him, the fluent lawyers, the jury, the audience,
> The laugher and weeper, the dancer, the midnight widow,
>   the red squaw . . .
> I swear they are averaged now . . . . one is no better than the
>   other ("[The Sleepers]," 1855, pp. 116–117).

Whitman's idea of a "passionate democracy" encouraged an awareness and appreciation of others as well as one's own self. The strong sensual and erotic passages in *Leaves* must have been especially shocking in the mid-nineteenth century, when underwear was called "unmentionables" and piano legs were covered with pantaloons because of their suggestive shape; but even in the twenty-first century Whitman's openness about sexuality makes readers question their own body consciousness and personal taboos. "Spontaneous Me" is but one of the poems describing masturbation; "I Sing the Body Electric" includes a lengthy catalogue of all body parts—including sex organs—described with the meticulousness of a physiognomist; "Unfolded Out of the Folds" takes place at the entrance of the birth canal (also described as the "exquisite flexible doors" in "Song of Myself"); "To a Common Prostitute" honors the profession of the most marginalized of women; "[Song of Myself]" contains passages suggestive of oral sex ("Loafe with me . . . ," p. 32), voyeurism ("Twenty-eight young men . . . ," p. 38), and homoeroticism ("The boy I love . . . ," p. 86). Whitman also describes scenes of shame, as in the "wet dream" episode of "[The Sleepers]" ("Darkness you are gentler . . . ," p. 111). Whitman apparently realized that, in order to institute change regarding societal sexual hang-ups, he had to sympathize with his embarrassed readers as well as provide models for a healthy, open-minded attitude.

Once the doors of perception were cleansed, the relationship between body and soul would be seen as it really is: connected, infinite, divine.

> Divine am I inside and out, and I make holy whatever I touch
> 　　or am touched from;
> The scent of these arm-pits is aroma finer than prayer,
> This head is more than churches or bibles or creeds
> ("[Song of Myself]," 1855, p. 53).

It would be a mistake to overlook Whitman's down-home sense of humor, tickling the edges of some of his touchiest passages ("I dote on myself," he purrs later in the same passage. "There is that lot of me, and all so luscious"). But there is serious, deliberate provocation here. He is raising the significance and worth of the physical realm to meet that of the spiritual. Whitman was not denying the existence and importance of God, or attempting to lower the soul's worth: He simply saw God in everyone and divinity in everything, and wanted to encourage his fellow Americans to do so, too.

> Why should I wish to see God better than this day?
> I see something of God each hour of the twenty-four, and each
>   moment then,
> In the faces of men and women I see God, and in my own face
>   in the glass;
> I find letters from God dropped in the street, and every one is
>   signed by God's name,
> And I leave them where they are, for I know that others will
>   punctually come forever and ever
> ("[Song of Myself]," 1855, p. 88).

Simple language, complex ideas: This is Whitman's *Leaves of Grass*. Achieving balance between contrary notions, questioning the accepted or unquestionable, pushing every known limit or boundary— all characterize the work. And Whitman made things more difficult by sometimes modifying some of his basic tenets, such as the idea that all men are created equal: His elegy "When Lilacs Last in the Dooryard Bloom'd" celebrates the "redeemer-president" Abraham Lincoln above all humanity, even himself. Whitman's glorification of the physical, too, changed as his body aged. In later masterpieces, such as "Passage to India," he finds inspiration in the amazing output of the intellect (such as the Suez Canal and the transatlantic cable crossing) rather than in the miracles of the human form. Though unconditional truisms seem to run through his oeuvre, they are often more nuanced than casual readers recognize: His interrogations in such poems as "To the States," for example, have taught generations of radicals that one can be actively critical and still patriotic. Even his ultimate vision of America as an abstract ideal, as expressed in his aptly titled 1888 poem "America," seems far removed from the voluptuous, fluid, fertile image of the nation in the 1855 preface.

All these revisions and reconsiderations are signs of an active and flexible mind, one unwilling to settle or stagnate despite the appeal of worldly success and the acceptance and burdens of heartache, disease, loss, and age. Whitman was himself pleased with his unending evolution and wrote some of his finest poems about his passages as man and artist. In "There Was a Child Went Forth," the poet details the people, places, and events that form the character of he "who now goes and will always go forth every day." The "doubts of night-time" that trouble him are further explored in "The Sleepers," in which he learns to embrace the continuous, ever-changing cycles of life rather than fear the darkness and the unknown.

But Whitman's most inspiring rite-of-passage poem was borne out of actual personal and professional crises he experienced between 1855 and 1856. Despite the critical and commercial failure of the first publication of *Leaves*, Whitman set to work almost immediately on the revisions and new poems of the Second Edition. The artist may have felt the need to write, but the man found life getting in the way. "Every thing I have done seems to me blank and suspicious," Whitman wrote in a notebook entry in late 1855. "I doubt whether my greatest thoughts, as I had supposed them, are not shallow—and people will most likely laugh at me.—My pride is impotent, my love gets no response" (*Notebooks and Unpublished Manuscripts*, p. 167). "Crossing Brooklyn Ferry," in which Whitman uses his twice-daily ferry ride as a metaphor, describes the poet's journey through the "dark patches" to a moment of emotional equilibrium and spiritual poise. His movement through crisis brings him in communion with "others that are to follow me" and secures "the ties between me and them, / The certainty of others, the life, love, sight, hearing of others" (*Notebooks and Unpublished Manuscripts*, p. 199). "Crossing Brooklyn Ferry," perhaps more successfully than any other poem, unites Whitman and his reader across the "impassable" boundary of time.

> Closer yet I approach you,
> What thought you have of me now, I had as much of you—I laid
>   in my stores in advance,
> I consider'd long and seriously of you before you were born.

Who was to know what should come home to me?
Who knows but I am enjoying this?
Who knows, for all the distance, but I am as good as looking at
    you now, for all you cannot see me?
("Crossing Brooklyn Ferry," p. 320).

A few years ago, I took a group of my Cooper Union students on
a literary tour of Brooklyn Heights. As we emerged from the subway
onto Henry Street, I pointed left to our first "site": the general area
of the printshop where Whitman had helped typeset the First Edi-
tion of *Leaves*, now a housing development fittingly named Whit-
man Close. Our efforts to find Whitman's spirit alive and well were
not off to a promising start. In fact, the poet really seemed dead for
the first time, even to me.

A sophomore art major named Alice Wetterlund decided to use
the lull to perform her recitation (each student was required to
memorize and present at least ten lines of Whitman's verse or
prose). As she began to recite, she struggled to make the words
heard over the street bustle. Then she spotted a utility truck being
used by the members of a local carpenter's union who were stag-
ing a strike in front of the old St. George Hotel. One of the car-
penters was using a megaphone from inside the truck to promote
union sentiment and camaraderie among the strikers.

Before I realized what she was up to, Alice ran over to the van
and addressed the speaker. His announcements suddenly ceased.
Alice disappeared for a moment; in the next, her distinct voice car-
ried over the hubbub of Henry Street, proclaiming the entirety of
"A Woman Waits for Me."

Traffic slowed down. Strikers stood still. And when Alice had fin-
ished reciting the poem, a brief silence was swallowed up by honks
of approval, shouts, and cheers from the carpenters, and our own
wild reactions to her stunt.

Whitman repeatedly asks his readers to be progressive in every
sense of the word, and to work constantly toward the fulfillment of
America's promise. He hoped that "greater offspring, orators, days"
than himself and his own would rise, and must have considered the
idea that he himself would eventually fall behind the times. His fol-
lowers have certainly refreshed and expanded his message, but

Whitman's own words have such powerful and continuous relevance that he seems to address us face to face, rather than talk at our backs. Deliberately leaving off the end punctuation at the close of the 1855 edition of "Song of Myself" (p. 91), he remains ever a step ahead:

> Failing to fetch me at first keep encouraged,
> Missing me one place search another,
> I stop some where waiting for you

Karen Karbiener received her Ph.D. in English and Comparative Literature at Columbia University in 2001 and teaches at New York University. A scholar of Romanticism and radical cultural legacies, she is the general editor of the forthcoming *Encyclopedia of American Counterculture* (M.E. Sharpe, 2006). She is currently curating an exhibit for the 150th anniversary of *Leaves of Grass*, entitled "Walt Whitman and the Promise of America, 1855–2005." She lives in and loves her hometown, New York City.

Leaves

of

Grass.

—•—

Brooklyn, New York:
1855.

"Christ likeness"—About 35 years old, c.1854, possibly taken by
Gabriel Harrison, although the photographer and place of sitting are
unknown. Courtesy of the Bayley-Whitman Collection of Ohio Wesleyan
University, Delaware, Ohio, and the Walt Whitman Birthplace Association,
Huntington, New York. Saunders #5.

CONTENTS

First Edition, 1855

[Preface] 7

[Song of Myself] 29

[A Song for Occupations] 91

[To Think of Time] 102

[The Sleepers] 109

[I Sing the Body Electric] 119

[Faces] 126

[Song of the Answerer] 130

[Europe, The 72d and 73d Years of These States] 133

[A Boston Ballad] 135

[There Was a Child Went Forth] 138

[Who Learns My Lesson Complete] 140

[Great Are the Myths] 142

INTRODUCTION TO FIRST EDITION

Walt Whitman was a poet of great first inspiration. That fact might come as a surprise to anyone who knows how many times Whitman revised and expanded *Leaves of Grass* over his lifetime. But the twelve "core poems" of the First Edition are arguably Whitman at his best. This is Whitman in the raw: His stance is defiant and provocative, his vision all-encompassing, his voice uninhibited, his demands radical. The passion and energy of his message and the rushing flow of the unregulated lines still feel revolutionary, 150 years after the book's publication. The appearance of the First Edition even heralded a new way of presenting poetry: Neither cover nor title page gave an indication of an author's name. Instead, across from the title page appeared the image of a man who might have easily been the reader. Everything about this book signaled the author's desire, and ability, to be an American literary pioneer. Indeed, Whitman had overseen this project from his first vision for it, to composition, to typesetting, to production and distribution; he even wrote anonymous reviews of *Leaves of Grass*.

"An American Bard at last!" Whitman proclaimed of himself in a self-review published in 1855. Whitman wrote two such reviews that year to offer explanations of his unusual project and stir up interest in *Leaves of Grass*. According to Florence Rome Garrett, granddaughter of the printers who helped Whitman produce the First Edition, "practically none sold." The public's ambivalence may have been fostered in part by the lack of an author's name — not that placing "Walt Whitman" on the cover would have done much to encourage sales. At best, fellow Brooklynites might have recognized Whitman as a writer and sometime editor of the city's more liberal newspapers; others might have remembered that he and his father had both worked as carpenters, and that while Whitman Senior's weakness may have been alcohol, Walt's was laziness. The name "Walt Whitman" had rarely been associated with poetry before 1855. The "Additional Poems" section of this Barnes and Noble Classics edition contains the only poetic efforts Whitman is known to have published before the arrival of *Leaves of Grass* in 1855. Even the single poem in the 1855 edition that had previously been published—"Resurgemus," published in the *New York Tribune* on June 21, 1850—underwent radical transformation before becoming the eighth of the twelve poems. The interest in reading through the first edition of *Leaves of Grass*, then, derives not only from looking at it as a point of departure for later editions, but also from marveling at this remarkable, as-yet mysterious first effort.

—Karen Karbiener

[PREFACE¹]

AMERICA does not repel the past or what it has produced under its forms or amid other politics or the idea of castes or the old religions . . . accepts the lesson with calmness . . . is not so impatient as has been supposed that the slough still sticks to opinions and manners and literature while the life which served its requirements has passed into the new life of the new forms . . . perceives that the corpse is slowly borne from the eating and sleeping rooms of the house . . . perceives that it waits a little while in the door . . . that it was fittest for its days . . . that its action has descended to the stalwart and wellshaped heir who approaches . . . and that he shall be fittest for his days.

The Americans of all nations at any time upon the earth have probably the fullest poetical nature. The United States themselves are essentially the greatest poem. In the history of the earth hitherto the largest and most stirring appear tame and orderly to their ampler largeness and stir. Here at last is something in the doings of man that corresponds with the broadcast doings of the day and night. Here is not merely a nation but a teeming nation of nations. Here is action untied from strings necessarily blind to particulars and details magnificently moving in vast masses. Here is the hospitality which forever indicates heroes. . . . Here are the roughs and beards and space and ruggedness and nonchalance that the soul loves. Here the performance disdaining the trivial unapproached in the tremendous audacity of its crowds and groupings and the push of its perspective spreads with crampless and flowing breadth and showers its prolific and splendid extravagance. One sees it must indeed own the riches of the summer and winter, and need never be bankrupt while corn grows from the ground or the orchards drop apples or the bays contain fish or men beget children upon women.

Other states indicate themselves in their deputies . . . but the genius of the United States is not best or most in its executives or legislatures, nor in its ambassadors or authors or colleges or churches or parlors, nor even in its newspapers or inventors . . . but always most in the common people. Their manners speech dress friendships—the freshness and candor of their physiognomy—the picturesque looseness of their carriage . . . their deathless attachment to freedom—their aversion to anything indecorous or soft or mean—the practical acknowledgment of the citizens of one state by the citizens of all other states—the fierceness of their roused resentment—their curiosity and welcome of novelty—their self-esteem and wonderful sympathy—their susceptibility to a slight—the air they have of persons who never knew how it felt to stand in the presence of superiors—the fluency of their speech—their delight in music, the sure symptom of manly tenderness and native elegance of soul . . . their good temper and openhandedness—the terrible significance of their elections—the President's taking off his hat to them not they to him—these too are unrhymed poetry. It awaits the gigantic and generous treatment worthy of it.

The largeness of nature of the nation were monstrous without a corresponding largeness and generosity of the spirit of the citizen. Not nature nor swarming states nor streets and steamships nor prosperous business nor farms nor capital nor learning may suffice for the ideal of man . . . nor suffice the poet. No reminiscences may suffice either. A live nation can always cut a deep mark and can have the best authority the cheapest . . . namely from its own soul. This is the sum of the profitable uses of individuals or states and of present action and grandeur and of the subjects of poets.—As if it were necessary to trot back generation after generation to the eastern records! As if the beauty and sacredness of the demonstrable must fall behind that of the mythical! As if men do not make their mark out of any times! As if the opening of the western continent by discovery and what has transpired since in North and South America were less than the small theatre of the antique or the aimless sleepwalking of the middle ages! The pride of the United States leaves the wealth and finesse of the cities and all returns of commerce and agriculture and all the magnitude of geography or shows of exterior victory to enjoy the breed of fullsized men or one fullsized man unconquerable and simple.

The American poets are to enclose old and new for America is the race of races. Of them a bard is to be commensurate with a people. To him the other continents arrive as contributions . . . he gives them reception for their sake and his own sake. His spirit responds to his country's spirit . . . he incarnates its geography and natural life and rivers and lakes.[2] Mississippi with annual freshets and changing chutes, Missouri and Columbia and Ohio and Saint Lawrence with the falls and beautiful masculine Hudson, do not embouchure where they spend themselves more than they embouchure into him. The blue breadth over the inland sea of Virginia and Maryland and the sea off Massachusetts and Maine and over Manhattan bay and over Champlain and Erie and over Ontario and Huron and Michigan and Superior, and over the Texan and Mexican and Floridian and Cuban seas and over the seas off California and Oregon, is not tallied by the blue breadth of the waters below more than the breadth of above and below is tallied by him. When the long Atlantic coast stretches longer and the Pacific coast stretches longer he easily stretches with them north or south. He spans between them also from east to west and reflects what is between them. On him rise solid growths that offset the growths of pine and cedar and hemlock and liveoak and locust and chestnut and cypress and hickory and limetree and cottonwood and tuliptree and cactus and wildvine and tamarind and persimmon . . . and tangles as tangled as any canebrake or swamp . . . and forests coated with transparent ice and icicles hanging from the boughs and crackling in the wind . . . and sides and peaks of mountains . . . and pasturage sweet and free as savannah or upland or prairie . . . with flights and songs and screams that answer those of the wildpigeon and highhold and orchard-oriole and coot and surf-duck and redshouldered-hawk and fish-hawk and white-ibis and indian-hen and cat-owl and water-pheasant and qua-bird and pied-sheldrake and blackbird and mockingbird and buzzard and condor and night-heron and eagle. To him the hereditary countenance descends both mother's and father's. To him enter the essences of the real things and past and present events—of the enormous diversity of temperature and agriculture and mines—the tribes of red aborigines—the weatherbeaten vessels entering new ports or making landings on rocky coasts—the first settlements north or south—the rapid stature and muscle—the haughty defiance of '76, and the war and peace and formation of the constitution . . . the union always surrounded by blatherers and always calm and impregnable—the perpetual coming of immigrants—the wharfhem'd cities and superior marine—the unsurveyed interior—the loghouses and clearings and wild animals and hunters and trappers . . . the free commerce—the fisheries and whaling and gold-digging—the endless gestation of new states—the convening of Congress every December, the members duly coming up from all climates and the uttermost parts . . . the noble character of the young mechanics and of all free American workmen and workwomen . . . the general ardor and friendliness and enterprise—the perfect equality of the female with the male . . . the large amativeness—the fluid movement of the population—the factories and mercantile life and laborsaving machinery—the Yankee swap—the New-York firemen and the target excursion—the southern plantation life—the character of the northeast and of the northwest and southwest—slavery and the tremulous spreading of hands to protect it, and the stern opposition to it which shall never cease till it ceases or the speaking of tongues and the moving of lips cease. For such the expression of the American poet is to be transcendent and new. It is to be indirect and not direct or descriptive or epic. Its quality goes through these to much more. Let the age and wars of other nations be chanted and their eras and characters be illustrated and that finish the verse. Not so the great psalm of the republic. Here the theme is creative and has vista. Here comes one among the well-beloved stonecutters and plans with decision and science and sees the solid and beautiful forms of the future where there are now no solid forms.

Of all nations the United States with veins full of poetical stuff most need poets and will doubtless have the greatest and use them the greatest.[3] Their Presidents shall not be their common referee so much as their poets shall. Of all mankind the great poet is the equable man. Not in him but off from him things are grotesque or eccentric or fail of their sanity. Nothing out of its place is good and nothing in its place is bad. He bestows on every object or quality its fit proportions neither more nor less. He is the arbiter of the diverse and he is the key. He is the equalizer of his age and land . . . he supplies what wants supplying and checks what wants checking. If peace is the routine out of him speaks the spirit of peace, large,

rich, thrifty, building vast and populous cities, encouraging agri-
culture and the arts and commerce—lighting the study of man, the
soul, immortality—federal, state or municipal government, mar-
riage, health, freetrade, intertravel by land and sea . . . nothing too
close, nothing too far off . . . the stars not too far off. In war he is the
most deadly force of the war. Who recruits him recruits horse and
foot . . . he fetches parks of artillery the best that engineer ever
knew. If the time becomes slothful and heavy he knows how to
arouse it . . . he can make every word he speaks draw blood. What-
ever stagnates in the flat of custom or obedience or legislation he
never stagnates. Obedience does not master him, he masters it.
High up out of reach he stands turning a concentrated light . . . he
turns the pivot with his finger . . . he baffles the swiftest runners as
he stands and easily overtakes and envelops them. The time stray-
ing toward infidelity and confections and persiflage he withholds
by his steady faith . . . he spreads out his dishes . . . he offers the
sweet firmfibred meat that grows men and women. His brain is the
ultimate brain. He is no arguer . . . he is judgment. He judges not
as the judge judges but as the sun falling around a helpless thing.
As he sees the farthest he has the most faith. His thoughts are the
hymns of the praise of things. In the talk on the soul and eternity and
God off of his equal plane he is silent. He sees eternity less like a play
with a prologue and denouement . . . he sees eternity in men and
women . . . he does not see men and women as dreams or dots.
Faith is the antiseptic of the soul . . . it pervades the common peo-
ple and preserves them . . . they never give up believing and ex-
pecting and trusting. There is that indescribable freshness and
unconsciousness about an illiterate person that humbles and mocks
the power of the noblest expressive genius. The poet sees for a cer-
tainty how one not a great artist may be just as sacred and perfect
as the greatest artist. . . . The power to destroy or remould is freely
used by him but never the power of attack. What is past is past. If he
does not expose superior models and prove himself by every step
he takes he is not what is wanted. The presence of the greatest poet
conquers . . . not parleying or struggling or any prepared attempts.
Now he has passed that way see after him! there is not left any ves-
tige of despair or misanthropy or cunning or exclusiveness or the ig-
nominy of a nativity or color or delusion of hell or the necessity of

hell . . . and no man thenceforward shall be degraded for igno-
rance or weakness or sin.

The greatest poet hardly knows pettiness or triviality. If he
breathes into any thing that was before thought small it dilates with
the grandeur and life of the universe. He is a seer . . . he is individ-
ual . . . he is complete in himself . . . the others are as good as he,
only he sees it and they do not. He is not one of the chorus . . . he
does not stop for any regulations . . . he is the president of regula-
tion. What the eyesight does to the rest he does to the rest. Who
knows the curious mystery of the eyesight? The other senses cor-
roborate themselves, but this is removed from any proof but its own
and foreruns the identities of the spiritual world. A single glance of
it mocks all the investigations of man and all the instruments and
books of the earth and all reasoning. What is marvellous? what is
unlikely? what is impossible or baseless or vague? after you have
once just opened the space of a peachpit and given audience to far
and near and to the sunset and had all things enter with electric
swiftness softly and duly without confusion or jostling or jam.

The land and sea, the animals fishes and birds, the sky of heaven
and the orbs, the forests mountains and rivers, are not small
themes . . . but folks expect of the poet to indicate more than the
beauty and dignity which always attach to dumb real objects . . .
they expect him to indicate the path between reality and their
souls. Men and women perceive the beauty well enough . . . prob-
ably as well as he. The passionate tenacity of hunters, woodmen,
early risers, cultivators of gardens and orchards and fields, the love
of healthy women for the manly form, seafaring persons, drivers of
horses, the passion for light and the open air, all is an old varied
sign of the unfailing perception of beauty and of a residence of the
poetic in outdoor people. They can never be assisted by poets to
perceive . . . some may but they never can. The poetic quality is not
marshalled in rhyme or uniformity or abstract addresses to things
nor in melancholy complaints or good precepts, but is the life of
these and much else and is in the soul. The profit of rhyme is that
it drops seeds of a sweeter and more luxuriant rhyme, and of uni-
formity that it conveys itself into its own roots in the ground out of
sight. The rhyme and uniformity of perfect poems show the free
growth of metrical laws and bud from them as unerringly and

loosely as lilacs or roses on a bush, and take shapes as compact as the shapes of chestnuts and oranges and melons and pears, and shed the perfume impalpable to form. The fluency and ornaments of the finest poems or music or orations or recitations are not independent but dependent. All beauty comes from beautiful blood and a beautiful brain. If the greatnesses are in conjunction in a man or woman it is enough . . . the fact will prevail through the universe . . . but the gaggery and gilt of a million years will not prevail. Who troubles himself about his ornaments or fluency is lost. This is what you shall do:[4] Love the earth and sun and the animals, despise riches, give alms to every one that asks, stand up for the stupid and crazy, devote your income and labor to others, hate tyrants, argue not concerning God, have patience and indulgence toward the people, take off your hat to nothing known or unknown or to any man or number of men, go freely with powerful uneducated persons and with the young and with the mothers of families, read these leaves in the open air every season of every year of your life, re-examine all you have been told at school or church or in any book, dismiss whatever insults your own soul, and your very flesh shall be a great poem and have the richest fluency not only in its words but in the silent lines of its lips and face and between the lashes of your eyes and in every motion and joint of your body. . . . The poet shall not spend his time in unneeded work. He shall know that the ground is always ready ploughed and manured . . . others may not know it but he shall. He shall go directly to the creation. His trust shall master the trust of everything he touches . . . and shall master all attachment.

The known universe has one complete lover and that is the greatest poet. He consumes an eternal passion and is indifferent which chance happens and which possible contingency of fortune or misfortune and persuades daily and hourly his delicious pay. What balks or breaks others is fuel for his burning progress to contact and amorous joy. Other proportions of the reception of pleasure dwindle to nothing to his proportions. All expected from heaven or from the highest he is rapport with in the sight of the daybreak or a scene of the winter woods or the presence of children playing or with his arm round the neck of a man or woman. His love above all love has leisure and expanse . . . he leaves room ahead of himself. He is no irresolute or suspicious lover . . . he is sure . . . he scorns intervals. His experience and the showers and thrills are not for nothing. Nothing can jar him . . . suffering and darkness cannot—death and fear cannot. To him complaint and jealousy and envy are corpses buried and rotten in the earth . . . he saw them buried. The sea is not surer of the shore or the shore of the sea than he is of the fruition of his love and of all perfection and beauty.

The fruition of beauty is no chance of hit or miss . . . it is inevitable as life . . . it is exact and plumb as gravitation. From the eyesight proceeds another eyesight and from the hearing proceeds another hearing and from the voice proceeds another voice eternally curious of the harmony of things with man. To these respond perfections not only in the committees that were supposed to stand for the rest but in the rest themselves just the same. These understand the law of perfection in masses and floods . . . that its finish is to each for itself and onward from itself . . . that it is profuse and impartial . . . that there is not a minute of the light or dark nor an acre of the earth or sea without it—nor any direction of the sky nor any trade or employment nor any turn of events. This is the reason that about the proper expression of beauty there is precision and balance . . . one part does not need to be thrust above another. The best singer is not the one who has the most lithe and powerful organ . . . the pleasure of poems is not in them that take the handsomest measure and similes and sound.

Without effort and without exposing in the least how it is done the greatest poet brings the spirit of any or all events and passions and scenes and persons some more and some less to bear on your individual character as you hear or read. To do this well is to compete with the laws that pursue and follow time. What is the purpose must surely be there and the clue of it must be there . . . and the faintest indication is the indication of the best and then becomes the clearest indication. Past and present and future are not disjoined but joined. The greatest poet forms the consistence of what is to be from what has been and is. He drags the dead out of their coffins and stands them again on their feet . . . he says to the past, Rise and walk before me that I may realize you. He learns the lesson . . . he places himself where the future becomes present.

The greatest poet does not only dazzle his rays over character and scenes and passions . . . he finally ascends and finishes all . . . he exhibits the pinnacles that no man can tell what they are for or what is beyond . . . he glows a moment on the extremest verge. He is most wonderful in his last half-hidden smile or frown . . . by that flash of the moment of parting the one that sees it shall be encouraged or terrified afterwards for many years. The greatest poet does not moralize or make applications of morals . . . he knows the soul. The soul has that measureless pride which consists in never acknowledging any lessons but its own. But it has sympathy as measureless as its pride and the one balances the other and neither can stretch too far while it stretches in company with the other. The inmost secrets of art sleep with the twain. The greatest poet has lain close betwixt both and they are vital in his style and thoughts.

The art of art, the glory of expression and the sunshine of the light of letters is simplicity. Nothing is better than simplicity . . . nothing can make up for excess or for the lack of definiteness. To carry on the heave of impulse and pierce intellectual depths and give all subjects their articulations are powers neither common nor very uncommon. But to speak in literature with the perfect rectitude and insouciance of the movements of animals and the unimpeachableness of the sentiment of trees in the woods and grass by the roadside is the flawless triumph of art. If you have looked on him who has achieved it you have looked on one of the masters of the artists of all nations and times. You shall not contemplate the flight of the graygull over the bay or the mettlesome action of the blood horse or the tall leaning of sunflowers on their stalk or the appearance of the sun journeying through heaven or the appearance of the moon afterward with any more satisfaction than you shall contemplate him. The greatest poet has less a marked style and is more the channel of thoughts and things without increase or diminution, and is the free channel of himself. He swears to his art, I will not be meddlesome, I will not have in my writing any elegance or effect or originality to hang in the way between me and the rest like curtains. I will have nothing hang in the way, not the richest curtains. What I tell I tell for precisely what it is. Let who may exalt or startle or fascinate or soothe I will have purposes as health or heat or snow has and be as regardless of observation.

What I experience or portray shall go from my composition without a shred of my composition. You shall stand by my side and look in the mirror with me.

The old red blood and stainless gentility of great poets will be proved by their unconstraint. A heroic person walks at his ease through and out of that custom or precedent or authority that suits him not. Of the traits of the brotherhood of writers savans musicians inventors and artists nothing is finer than silent defiance advancing from new free forms. In the need of poems philosophy politics mechanism science behaviour, the craft of art, an appropriate native grand-opera, shipcraft, or any craft, he is greatest forever and forever who contributes the greatest original practical example. The cleanest expression is that which finds no sphere worthy of itself and makes one.

The messages of great poets to each man and woman are, Come to us on equal terms, Only then can you understand us, We are no better than you, What we enclose you enclose, What we enjoy you may enjoy. Did you suppose there could be only one Supreme? We affirm there can be unnumbered Supremes, and that one does not countervail another any more than one eyesight countervails another . . . and that men can be good or grand only of the consciousness of their supremacy within them. What do you think is the grandeur of storms and dismemberments and the deadliest battles and wrecks and the wildest fury of the elements and the power of the sea and the motion of nature and of the throes of human desires and dignity and hate and love? It is that something in the soul which says, Rage on, Whirl on, I tread master here and everywhere, Master of the spasms of the sky and of the shatter of the sea, Master of nature and passion and death, And of all terror and all pain.

The American bards shall be marked for generosity and affection and for encouraging competitors . . . They shall be kosmos . . . without monopoly or secrecy . . . glad to pass any thing to any one . . . hungry for equals night and day. They shall not be careful of riches and privilege . . . they shall be riches and privilege . . . they shall perceive who the most affluent man is. The most affluent man is he that confronts all the shows he sees by equivalents out of the stronger wealth of himself. The American bard shall delineate no class of persons nor one or two out of the strata of interests nor love most nor truth most nor the soul most nor the body most . . . and not be for the eastern states more than the western or the northern states more than the southern.

Exact science and its practical movements are no checks on the greatest poet but always his encouragement and support. The outset and remembrance are there . . . there the arms that lifted him first and brace him best . . . there he returns after all his goings and comings. The sailor and traveler . . . the anatomist chemist astronomer geologist phrenologist spiritualist mathematician historian and lexicographer are not poets, but they are the lawgivers of poets and their construction underlies the structure of every perfect poem. No matter what rises or is uttered they sent the seed of the conception of it . . . of them and by them stand the visible proofs of souls . . . always of their fatherstuff must be begotten the sinewy races of bards. If there shall be love and content between the father and the son and if the greatness of the son is the exuding of the greatness of the father there shall be love between the poet and the man of demonstrable science. In the beauty of poems are the tuft and final applause of science.

Great is the faith of the flush of knowledge and of the investigation of the depths of qualities and things. Cleaving and circling here swells the soul of the poet yet is president of itself always. The depths are fathomless and therefore calm. The innocence and nakedness are resumed . . . they are neither modest nor immodest. The whole theory of the special and supernatural and all that was twined with it or educed out of it departs as a dream. What has ever happened . . . what happens and whatever may or shall happen, the vital laws enclose all . . . they are sufficient for any case and for all cases . . . none to be hurried or retarded . . . any miracle of affairs or persons inadmissible in the vast clear scheme where every motion and every spear of grass and the frames and spirits of men and women and all that concerns them are unspeakably perfect miracles all referring to all and each distinct and in its place. It is also not consistent with the reality of the soul to admit that there is anything in the known universe more divine than men and women.

Men and women and the earth and all upon it are simply to be taken as they are, and the investigation of their past and present and future shall be unintermitted and shall be done with perfect candor.

Upon this basis philosophy speculates ever looking toward the poet, ever regarding the eternal tendencies of all toward happiness never inconsistent with what is clear to the senses and to the soul. For the eternal tendencies of all toward happiness make the only point of sane philosophy. Whatever comprehends less than that . . . whatever is less than the laws of light and of astronomical motion . . . or less than the laws that follow the thief the liar the glutton and the drunkard through this life and doubtless afterward . . . or less than vast stretches of time or the slow formation of density or the patient upheaving of strata — is of no account. Whatever would put God in a poem or system of philosophy as contending against some being or influence is also of no account. Sanity and ensemble characterise the great master . . . spoilt in one principle all is spoilt. The great master has nothing to do with miracles. He sees health for himself in being one of the mass . . . he sees the hiatus in singular eminence. To the perfect shape comes common ground. To be under the general law is great for that is to correspond with it. The master knows that he is unspeakably great and that all are unspeakably great . . . that nothing for instance is greater than to conceive children and bring them up well . . . that to be is just as great as to perceive or tell.

In the make of the great masters the idea of political liberty is indispensable. Liberty takes the adherence of heroes wherever men and women exist . . . but never takes any adherence or welcome from the rest more than from poets. They are the voice and exposition of liberty. They out of ages are worthy the grand idea . . . to them it is confided and they must sustain it. Nothing has precedence of it and nothing can warp or degrade it. The attitude of great poets is to cheer up slaves and horrify despots. The turn of their necks, the sound of their feet, the motions of their wrists, are full of hazard to the one and hope to the other. Come nigh them awhile and though they neither speak or advise you shall learn the faithful American lesson. Liberty is poorly served by men whose good intent is quelled from one failure or two failures or any number of failures, or from the casual indifference or ingratitude of the people, or from the sharp show of the tushes of power, or the bringing to bear soldiers and cannon or any penal statutes. Liberty relies upon itself, invites no one, promises nothing, sits in calmness and light, is positive and composed, and knows no discouragement. The battle rages with many a loud alarm and frequent advance and retreat . . . the enemy triumphs . . . the prison, the handcuffs, the iron necklace and anklet, the scaffold, garrote and leadballs do their work . . . the cause is asleep . . . the strong throats are choked with their own blood . . . the young men drop their eyelashes toward the ground when they pass each other . . . and is liberty gone out of that place? No never. When liberty goes it is not the first to go nor the second or third to go . . . it waits for all the rest to go . . . it is the last . . . When the memories of the old martyrs are faded utterly away . . . when the large names of patriots are laughed at in the public halls from the lips of the orators . . . when the boys are no more christened after the same but christened after tyrants and traitors instead . . . when the laws of the free are grudgingly permitted and laws for informers and bloodmoney are sweet to the taste of the people . . . when I and you walk abroad upon the earth stung with compassion at the sight of numberless brothers answering our equal friendship and calling no man master—and when we are elated with noble joy at the sight of slaves . . . when the soul retires in the cool communion of the night and surveys its experience and has much extasy over the word and deed that put back a helpless innocent person into the gripe of the gripers or into any cruel inferiority . . . when those in all parts of these states who could easier realize the true American character but do not yet—when the swarms of cringers, suckers, doughfaces, lice of politics, planners of sly involutions for their own preferment to city offices or state legislatures or the judiciary or congress or the presidency, obtain a response of love and natural deference from the people whether they get the offices or no . . . when it is better to be a bound booby and rogue in office at a high salary than the poorest free mechanic or farmer with his hat unmoved from his head and firm eyes and a candid and generous heart . . . and when servility by town or state or the federal government or any oppression on a large scale or small scale can be tried on without its own punishment following duly after in exact proportion against the smallest chance of escape . . . or rather when all life and all the souls of men and women are discharged from any part of the earth—then only shall the instinct of liberty be discharged from that part of the earth.

As the attributes of the poets of the kosmos concentre in the real body and soul and in the pleasure of things they possess the superiority of genuineness over all fiction and romance. As they emit themselves facts are showered over with light . . . the daylight is lit with more volatile light . . . also the deep between the setting and rising sun goes deeper many fold. Each precise object or condition or combination or process exhibits a beauty . . . the multiplication table its—old age its—the carpenter's trade its—the grand-opera its . . . the hugehulled cleanshaped New-York clipper at sea under steam or full sail gleams with unmatched beauty . . . the American circles and large harmonies of government gleam with theirs . . . and the commonest definite intentions and actions with theirs. The poets of the kosmos advance through all interpositions and coverings and turmoils and stratagems to first principles. They are of use . . . they dissolve poverty from its need and riches from its conceit. You large proprietor they say shall not realize or perceive more than any one else. The owner of the library is not he who holds a legal title to it having bought and paid for it. Any one and every one is owner of the library who can read the same through all the varieties of tongues and subjects and styles, and in whom they enter with ease and take residence and force toward paternity and maternity, and make supple and powerful and rich and large. . . . These American states strong and healthy and accomplished shall receive no pleasure from violations of natural models and must not permit them. In paintings or mouldings or carvings in mineral or wood, or in the illustrations of books or newspapers, or in any comic or tragic prints, or in the patterns of woven stuffs or any thing to beautify rooms or furniture or costumes, or to put upon cornices or monuments or on the prows or sterns of ships, or to put anywhere before the human eye indoors or out, that which distorts honest shapes or which creates unearthly beings or places or contingencies is a nuisance and revolt. Of the human form especially it is so great it must never be made ridiculous. Of ornaments to a work nothing outre can be allowed . . . but those ornaments can be allowed that conform to the perfect facts of the open air and that flow out of the nature of the work and come irrepressibly from it and are necessary to the completion of the work. Most works are most beautiful without ornament. . . . Exaggerations will be revenged in human physiology.

Clean and vigorous children are jetted and conceived only in those communities where the models of natural forms are public every day. . . . Great genius and the people of these states must never be demeaned to romances. As soon as histories are properly told there is no more need of romances.

The great poets are also to be known by the absence in them of tricks and by the justification of perfect personal candor. Then folks echo a new cheap joy and a divine voice leaping from their brains: How beautiful is candor! All faults may be forgiven of him who has perfect candor. Henceforth let no man of us lie, for we have seen that openness wins the inner and outer world and that there is no single exception, and that never since our earth gathered itself in a mass have deceit or subterfuge or prevarication attracted its smallest particle or the faintest tinge of a shade—and that through the enveloping wealth and rank of a state or the whole republic of states a sneak or sly person shall be discovered and despised . . . and that the soul has never been once fooled and never can be fooled . . . and thrift without the loving nod of the soul is only a fœtid puff . . . and there never grew up in any of the continents of the globe nor upon any planet or satellite or star, nor upon the asteroids, nor in any part of ethereal space, nor in the midst of density, nor under the fluid wet of the sea, nor in that condition which precedes the birth of babes, nor at any time during the changes of life, nor in that condition that follows what we term death, nor in any stretch of abeyance or action afterward of vitality, nor in any process of formation or reformation anywhere, a being whose instinct hated the truth.

Extreme caution or prudence, the soundest organic health, large hope and comparison and fondness for women and children, large alimentiveness and destructiveness and causality, with a perfect sense of the oneness of nature and the propriety of the same spirit applied to human affairs . . . these are called up of the float of the brain of the world to be parts of the greatest poet from his birth out of his mother's womb and from her birth out of her mother's. Caution seldom goes far enough. It has been thought that the prudent citizen was the citizen who applied himself to solid gains and did well for himself and his family and completed a lawful life without debt or crime. The greatest poet sees and admits these economies as he sees the economies of food and sleep, but has higher notions of prudence than to think he gives much when he gives a few slight attentions at the latch of the gate. The premises of the prudence of life are not the hospitality of it or the ripeness and harvest of it. Beyond the independence of a little sum laid aside for burial-money, and of a few clapboards around and shingles overhead on a lot of American soil owned, and the easy dollars that supply the year's plain clothing and meals, the melancholy prudence of the abandonment of such a great being as a man is to the toss and pallor of years of moneymaking with all their scorching days and icy nights and all their stifling deceits and underhanded dodgings, or infinitesimals of parlors, or shameless stuffing while others starve . . . and all the loss of the bloom and odor of the earth and of the flowers and atmosphere and of the sea and of the true taste of the women and men you pass or have to do with in youth or middle age, and the issuing sickness and desperate revolt at the close of a life without elevation or naivete, and the ghastly chatter of a death without serenity or majesty, is the great fraud upon modern civilization and forethought, blotching the surface and system which civilization undeniably drafts, and moistening with tears the immense features it spreads and spreads with such velocity before the reached kisses of the soul . . . Still the right explanation remains to be made about prudence. The prudence of the mere wealth and respectability of the most esteemed life appears too faint for the eye to observe at all when little and large alike drop quietly aside at the thought of the prudence suitable for immortality. What is wisdom that fills the thinness of a year or seventy or eighty years to wisdom spaced out by ages and coming back at a certain time with strong reinforcements and rich presents and the clear faces of wedding-guests as far as you can look in every direction running gaily toward you? Only the soul is of itself . . . all else has reference to what ensues. All that a person does or thinks is of consequence. Not a move can a man or woman make that affects him or her in a day or a month or any part of the direct lifetime or the hour of death but the same affects him or her onward afterward through the indirect lifetime. The indirect is always as great and real as the direct. The spirit receives from the body just as much as it gives to the body. Not one name of word or deed . . . not of venereal sores or discolorations . . . not the privacy of the onanist . . . not of the putrid veins of gluttons or rumdrinkers . . . not peculation or cunning or betrayal or murder . . . no serpentine poison of those that seduce women . . . not the foolish yielding of women . . . not prostitution . . . not of any depravity of young men . . . not of the attainment of gain by discreditable means . . . not any nastiness of appetite . . . not any harshness of officers to men or judges to prisoners or fathers to sons or sons to fathers or husbands to wives or bosses to their boys . . . not of greedy looks or malignant wishes . . . nor any of the wiles practised by people upon themselves . . . ever is or ever can be stamped on the programme but it is duly realized and returned, and that returned in further performances . . . and they returned again. Nor can the push of charity or personal force ever be any thing else than the profoundest reason, whether it brings arguments to hand or no. No specification is necessary . . . to add or subtract or divide is in vain. Little or big, learned or unlearned, white or black, legal or illegal, sick or well, from the first inspiration down the windpipe to the last expiration out of it, all that a male or female does that is vigorous and benevolent and clean is so much sure profit to him or her in the unshakable order of the universe and through the whole scope of it forever. If the savage or felon is wise it is well . . . if the greatest poet or savan is wise it is simply the same . . . if the President or chief justice is wise it is the same . . . if the young mechanic or farmer is wise it is no more or less . . . if the prostitute is wise it is no more nor less. The interest will come round . . . all will come round. All the best actions of war and peace . . . all help given to relatives and strangers and the poor and old and sorrowful and young children and widows and the sick, and to all shunned persons . . . all furtherance of fugitives and of the escape of slaves . . . all the self-denial that stood steady and aloof on wrecks and saw others take the seats of the boats . . . all offering of substance or life for the good old cause, or for a friend's sake or opinion's sake . . . all pains of enthusiasts scoffed at by their neighbors . . . all the vast sweet love and precious suffering of mothers . . . all honest men baffled in strifes recorded or unrecorded . . . all the grandeur and good of the few ancient nations whose fragments of annals we inherit . . . and all the good of the hundreds of far mightier and more ancient nations unknown to us by name or date or location . . . all that was ever manfully begun, whether it succeeded or not . . . all that has at any time been well suggested out of the divine heart of man or by the divinity of his mouth or by the shaping of his great hands . . . and all that is well thought or done this day on any part of the surface of the globe . . . or on any of the wandering stars or fixed stars by those there as we are here . . . or that is henceforth to be well thought or done by you whoever you are, or by any one—these singly and wholly inured at their time and inure now and will inure always to the identities from which they sprung or shall spring . . . Did you guess any of them lived only its moment? The world does not so exist . . . no parts palpable or impalpable so exist . . . no result exists now without being from its long antecedent result, and that from its antecedent, and so backward without the farthest mentionable spot coming a bit nearer the beginning than any other spot. . . . Whatever satisfies the soul is truth. The prudence of the greatest poet answers at last the craving and glut of the soul, is not contemptuous of less ways of prudence if they conform to its ways, puts off nothing, permits no let-up for its own case or any case, has no particular sabbath or judgment-day, divides not the living from the dead or the righteous from the unrighteous, is satisfied with the present, matches every thought or act by its correlative, knows no possible forgiveness or deputed atonement . . . knows that the young man who composedly periled his life and lost it has done exceeding well for himself, while the man who has not periled his life and retains it to old age in riches and ease has perhaps achieved nothing for himself worth mentioning . . . and that only that person has no great prudence to learn who has learnt to prefer real longlived things, and favors body and soul the same, and perceives the indirect assuredly following the direct, and what evil or good he does leaping onward and waiting to meet him again—and who in his spirit in any emergency whatever neither hurries or avoids death.

The direct trial of him who would be the greatest poet is today. If he does not flood himself with the immediate age as with vast oceanic tides . . . and if he does not attract his own land body and soul to himself and hang on its neck with incomparable love and plunge his semitic muscle into its merits and demerits . . . and if he be not himself the age transfigured . . . and if to him is not opened the eternity which gives similitude to all periods and locations and processes and animate and inanimate forms, and which is the bond of time, and rises up from its inconceivable vagueness and infiniteness in the swimming shape of today, and is held by the ductile anchors of life, and makes the present spot the passage from what was to what shall be, and commits itself to the representation of this wave of an hour and this one of the sixty beautiful children of the wave— let him merge in the general run and wait his development. . . . Still the final test of poems or any character or work remains. The prescient poet projects himself centuries ahead and judges performer or performance after the changes of time. Does it live through them? Does it still hold on untired? Will the same style and the direction of genius to similar points be satisfactory now? Has no new discovery in science or arrival at superior planes of thought and judgment and behaviour fixed him or his so that either can be looked down upon? Have the marches of tens and hundreds and thousands of years made willing detours to the right hand and the left hand for his sake? Is he beloved long and long after he is buried? Does the young man think often of him? and the young woman think often of him? and do the middleaged and the old think of him?

A great poem is for ages and ages in common and for all degrees and complexions and all departments and sects and for a woman as much as a man and a man as much as a woman. A great poem is no finish to a man or woman but rather a beginning. Has any one fancied he could sit at last under some due authority and rest satisfied with explanations and realize and be content and full? To no such terminus does the greatest poet bring . . . he brings neither cessation or sheltered fatness and ease. The touch of him tells in action. Whom he takes he takes with firm sure grasp into live regions previously unattained . . . thenceforward is no rest . . . they see the space and ineffable sheen that turn the old spots and lights into dead vacuums. The companion of him beholds the birth and progress of stars and learns one of the meanings. Now there shall be a man cohered out of tumult and chaos . . . the elder encourages the younger and shows him how . . . they two shall launch off fearlessly together till the new world fits an orbit for itself and looks unabashed on the lesser orbits of the stars and sweeps through the ceaseless rings and shall never be quiet again.

There will soon be no more priests. Their work is done. They may wait awhile . . . perhaps a generation or two . . . dropping off by degrees. A superior breed shall take their place . . . the gangs of kosmos and prophets en masse shall take their place. A new order shall arise and they shall be the priests of man, and every man shall be his own priest. The churches built under their umbrage shall be the churches of men and women. Through the divinity of themselves shall the kosmos and the new breed of poets be interpreters of men and women and of all events and things. They shall find their inspiration in real objects today, symptoms of the past and future. . . . They shall not deign to defend immortality or God or the perfection of things or liberty or the exquisite beauty and reality of the soul. They shall arise in America and be responded to from the remainder of the earth.

The English language befriends the grand American expression . . . it is brawny enough and limber and full enough. On the tough stock of a race who through all change of circumstances was never without the idea of political liberty, which is the animus of all liberty, it has attracted the terms of daintier and gayer and subtler and more elegant tongues. It is the powerful language of resistance . . . it is the dialect of common sense. It is the speech of the proud and melancholy races and of all who aspire. It is the chosen tongue to express growth faith self-esteem freedom justice equality friendliness amplitude prudence decision and courage. It is the medium that shall well nigh express the inexpressible.

No great literature nor any like style of behaviour or oratory or social intercourse or household arrangements or public institutions or the treatment by bosses of employed people, nor executive detail or detail of the army or navy, nor spirit of legislation or courts or police or tuition or architecture or songs or amusements or the costumes of young men, can long elude the jealous and passionate instinct of American standards. Whether or no the sign appears from the mouths of the people, it throbs a live interrogation in every freeman's and freewoman's heart after that which passes by or this built to remain. Is it uniform with my country? Are its disposals without ignominious distinctions? Is it for the evergrowing communes of brothers and lovers, large, well-united, proud beyond the old models, generous beyond all models? Is it something grown fresh out of the fields or drawn from the sea for use to me today here? I know that what answers for me an American must answer for any individual or nation that serves for a part of my materials. Does this answer? or is it without reference to universal needs? or sprung of the needs of the less developed society of special ranks? or old needs of pleasure overlaid by modern science and forms? Does this acknowledge liberty with audible and absolute acknowledgement, and set slavery at nought for life and death? Will it help breed one goodshaped and wellhung man, and a woman to be his perfect and independent mate? Does it improve manners? Is it for the nursing of the young of the republic? Does it solve readily with the sweet milk of the nipples of the breasts of the mother of many children? Has it too the old ever-fresh forbearance and impartiality? Does it look with the same love on the last born and on those hardening toward stature, and on the errant, and on those who disdain all strength of assault outside of their own?

The poems distilled from other poems will probably pass away. The coward will surely pass away. The expectation of the vital and great can only be satisfied by the demeanor of the vital and great.

The swarms of the polished deprecating and reflectors and the polite float off and leave no remembrance. America prepares with composure and goodwill for the visitors that have sent word. It is not intellect that is to be their warrant and welcome. The talented, the artist, the ingenious, the editor, the statesman, the erudite . . . they are not unappreciated . . . they fall in their place and do their work. The soul of the nation also does its work. No disguise can pass on it . . . no disguise can conceal from it. It rejects none, it permits all. Only toward as good as itself and toward the like of itself will it advance half-way. An individual is as superb as a nation when he has the qualities which make a superb nation. The soul of the largest and wealthiest and proudest nation may well go half-way to meet that of its poets. The signs are effectual. There is no fear of mistake. If the one is true the other is true. The proof of a poet is that his country absorbs him as affectionately as he has absorbed it.[5]

LEAVES OF GRASS

[Song of Myself]

I CELEBRATE myself,
And what I assume you shall assume,
For every atom belonging to me as good belongs to you.

I loafe and invite my soul,
I lean and loafe at my ease . . . . observing a spear of summer
    grass.

Houses and rooms are full of perfumes . . . . the shelves are
    crowded with perfumes,
I breathe the fragrance myself, and know it and like it,
The distillation would intoxicate me also, but I shall not let it.

The atmosphere is not a perfume . . . . it has no taste of the
    distillation . . . . it is odorless,
It is for my mouth forever . . . . I am in love with it,
I will go to the bank by the wood and become undisguised and
    naked,
I am mad for it to be in contact with me.

The smoke of my own breath,
Echoes, ripples, and buzzed whispers . . . . loveroot, silkthread,
    crotch and vine,[6]
My respiration and inspiration . . . . the beating of my heart . . . .
    the passing of blood and air through my lungs,
The sniff of green leaves and dry leaves, and of the shore and
    darkcolored sea-rocks, and of hay in the barn,
The sound of the belched words of my voice . . . . words loosed to
    the eddies of the wind,
A few light kisses . . . . a few embraces . . . . a reaching around of
    arms,

The play of shine and shade on the trees as the supple boughs
    wag,
The delight alone or in the rush of the streets, or along the fields
    and hillsides,
The feeling of health . . . . the full-noon trill . . . . the song of me
    rising from bed and meeting the sun.

Have you reckoned a thousand acres much? Have you reckoned
    the earth much?
Have you practiced so long to learn to read?
Have you felt so proud to get at the meaning of poems?

Stop this day and night with me and you shall possess the origin
    of all poems,
You shall possess the good of the earth and sun . . . . there are
    millions of suns left,
You shall no longer take things at second or third hand . . . . nor
    look through the eyes of the dead . . . . nor feed on the
    spectres in books,
You shall not look through my eyes either, nor take things
    from me,
You shall listen to all sides and filter them from yourself.

I have heard what the talkers were talking . . . . the talk of the
    beginning and the end,
But I do not talk of the beginning or the end.

There was never any more inception than there is now,
Nor any more youth or age than there is now;
And will never be any more perfection than there is now,
Nor any more heaven or hell than there is now.

Urge and urge and urge,
Always the procreant urge of the world.

Out of the dimness opposite equals advance . . . . Always
    substance and increase,

Always a knit of identity . . . . always distinction . . . . always a
    breed of life.

To elaborate is no avail . . . . Learned and unlearned feel that it
    is so.

Sure as the most certain sure . . . . plumb in the uprights, well
    entretied, braced in the beams,[7]
Stout as a horse, affectionate, haughty, electrical,
I and this mystery here we stand.

Clear and sweet is my soul . . . . and clear and sweet is all that is
    not my soul.

Lack one lacks both . . . . and the unseen is proved by the seen,
Till that becomes unseen and receives proof in its turn.

Showing the best and dividing it from the worst, age vexes age,
Knowing the perfect fitness and equanimity of things, while they
    discuss I am silent, and go bathe and admire myself.

Welcome is every organ and attribute of me, and of any man
    hearty and clean,
Not an inch nor a particle of an inch is vile, and none shall be
    less familiar than the rest.

I am satisfied . . . . I see, dance, laugh, sing;
As God comes a loving bedfellow and sleeps at my side all night
    and close on the peep of the day,
And leaves for me baskets covered with white towels bulging the
    house with their plenty,
Shall I postpone my acceptation and realization and scream at
    my eyes,
That they turn from gazing after and down the road,
And forthwith cipher and show me to a cent,
Exactly the contents of one, and exactly the contents of two, and
    which is ahead?

Trippers and askers surround me,
People I meet . . . . the effect upon me of my early life . . . . of the
    ward* and city I live in . . . . of the nation,
The latest news . . . . discoveries, inventions, societies . . . . authors
    old and new,
My dinner, dress, associates, looks, business, compliments, dues,
The real or fancied indifference of some man or woman I love,
The sickness of one of my folks—or of myself . . . . or ill-doing . . . .
    or loss or lack of money . . . . or depressions or exaltations,
They come to me days and nights and go from me again,
But they are not the Me myself.[8]

Apart from the pulling and hauling stands what I am,
Stands amused, complacent, compassionating, idle, unitary,
Looks down, is erect, bends an arm on an impalpable certain rest,
Looks with its sidecurved head curious what will come next,
Both in and out of the game, and watching and wondering at it.

Backward I see in my own days where I sweated through fog with
    linguists and contenders,
I have no mockings or arguments . . . . I witness and wait.

I believe in you my soul . . . . the other I am must not abase itself
    to you,
And you must not be abased to the other.

Loafe with me on the grass . . . . loose the stop from your throat,
Not words, not music or rhyme I want . . . . not custom or lecture,
    not even the best,
Only the lull I like, the hum of your valved voice.

I mind how we lay in June, such a transparent summer
    morning;
You settled your head athwart my hips and gently turned over
    upon me,

---

*In Whitman's time, New York City was divided into sections called wards; the
"Bloody Sixth" ward was the most infamous.

And parted the shirt from my bosom-bone, and plunged your
     tongue to my barestript heart,
And reached till you felt my beard, and reached till you held my
     feet.

Swiftly arose and spread around me the peace and joy and
     knowledge that pass all the art and argument of the earth;
And I know that the hand of God is the elderhand of my own,
And I know that the spirit of God is the eldest brother of my
     own,
And that all the men ever born are also my brothers . . . . and
     the women my sisters and lovers,
And that a kelson of the creation is love;
And limitless are leaves stiff or drooping in the fields,
And brown ants in the little wells beneath them,
And mossy scabs of the wormfence, and heaped stones, and elder
     and mullen and pokeweed.[9]

A child said, What is the grass? fetching it to me with full
     hands;
How could I answer the child? . . . . I do not know what it is any
     more than he.

I guess it must be the flag of my disposition, out of hopeful green
     stuff woven.

Or I guess it is the handkerchief of the Lord,
A scented gift and remembrancer designedly dropped,
Bearing the owner's name someway in the corners, that we may
     see and remark, and say Whose?

Or I guess the grass is itself a child . . . . the produced babe of the
     vegetation.

Or I guess it is a uniform hieroglyphic,
And it means, Sprouting alike in broad zones and narrow
     zones,
Growing among black folks as among white,

Kanuck, Tuckahoe, Congressman, Cuff,* I give them the same,
    I receive them the same.

And now it seems to me the beautiful uncut hair of graves.

Tenderly will I use you curling grass,
It may be you transpire from the breasts of young men,
It may be if I had known them I would have loved them;
It may be you are from old people and from women, and from
    offspring taken soon out of their mothers' laps,
And here you are the mothers' laps.

This grass is very dark to be from the white heads of old
    mothers,
Darker than the colorless beards of old men,
Dark to come from under the faint red roofs of mouths.

O I perceive after all so many uttering tongues!
And I perceive they do not come from the roofs of mouths for
    nothing.

I wish I could translate the hints about the dead young men and
    women,
And the hints about old men and mothers, and the offspring
    taken soon out of their laps.

What do you think has become of the young and old men?
And what do you think has become of the women and children?

They are alive and well somewhere;
The smallest sprout shows there is really no death,
And if ever there was it led forward life, and does not wait at the
    end to arrest it,
And ceased the moment life appeared.

---

*Whitman lists different types of people, from Kanucks (French Canadians) to
Tuckahoes (coastal Virginians) to congressmen to Cuffs (African day-name for a
male born on a Friday).

All goes onward and outward . . . . and nothing collapses,
And to die is different from what any one supposed, and luckier.

Has any one supposed it lucky to be born?
I hasten to inform him or her it is just as lucky to die, and I
　　know it.

I pass death with the dying, and birth with the new-washed
　　babe . . . . and am not contained between my hat and boots,
And peruse manifold objects, no two alike, and every one good,
The earth good, and the stars good, and their adjuncts all good.

I am not an earth nor an adjunct of an earth,
I am the mate and companion of people, all just as immortal and
　　fathomless as myself;
They do not know how immortal, but I know.

Every kind for itself and its own . . . . for me mine male and
　　female,
For me all that have been boys and that love women,
For me the man that is proud and feels how it stings to be
　　slighted,
For me the sweetheart and the old maid . . . . for me mothers and
　　the mothers of mothers,
For me lips that have smiled, eyes that have shed tears,
For me children and the begetters of children.

Who need be afraid of the merge?
Undrape . . . . you are not guilty to me, nor stale nor discarded,
I see through the broadcloth and gingham whether or no,
And am around, tenacious, acquisitive, tireless . . . . and can never
　　be shaken away.

The little one sleeps in its cradle,
I lift the gauze and look a long time, and silently brush away flies
　　with my hand.

The youngster and the redfaced girl turn aside up the bushy hill,
I peeringly view them from the top.

The suicide sprawls on the bloody floor of the bedroom,
It is so .... I witnessed the corpse .... there the pistol had
    fallen.[10]

The blab of the pave .... the tires of carts and sluff of bootsoles
    and talk of the promenaders,
The heavy omnibus, the driver with his interrogating thumb, the
    clank of the shod horses on the granite floor,
The carnival of sleighs, the clinking and shouted jokes and pelts
    of snowballs;
The hurrahs for popular favorites .... the fury of roused mobs,
The flap of the curtained litter—the sick man inside, borne to the
    hospital,
The meeting of enemies, the sudden oath, the blows and fall,
The excited crowd—the policeman with his star quickly working
    his passage to the centre of the crowd;
The impassive stones that receive and return so many echoes,
The souls moving along .... are they invisible while the least
    atom of the stones is visible?
What groans of overfed or half-starved who fall on the flags
    sunstruck or in fits,
What exclamations of women taken suddenly, who hurry home
    and give birth to babes,
What living and buried speech is always vibrating here .... what
    howls restrained by decorum,
Arrests of criminals, slights, adulterous offers made, acceptances,
    rejections with convex lips,
I mind them or the resonance of them .... I come again and
    again.

The big doors of the country-barn stand open and ready,
The dried grass of the harvest-time loads the slow-drawn wagon,
The clear light plays on the brown gray and green intertinged,
The armfuls are packed to the sagging mow:
I am there .... I help .... I came stretched atop of the load,
I felt its soft jolts .... one leg reclined on the other,
I jump from the crossbeams, and seize the clover and timothy,
And roll head over heels, and tangle my hair full of wisps.

Alone far in the wilds and mountains I hunt,
Wandering amazed at my own lightness and glee,
In the late afternoon choosing a safe spot to pass the night,
Kindling a fire and broiling the freshkilled game,
Soundly falling asleep on the gathered leaves, my dog and gun by
    my side.

The Yankee clipper is under her three skysails . . . . she cuts the
    sparkle and scud,
My eyes settle the land . . . . I bend at her prow or shout joyously
    from the deck.

The boatmen and clamdiggers arose early and stopped for me,
I tucked my trowser-ends in my boots and went and had a good
    time,
You should have been with us that day round the chowder-
    kettle.

I saw the marriage of the trapper in the open air in the far-
    west . . . . the bride was a red girl,
Her father and his friends sat near by crosslegged and dumbly
    smoking . . . . they had moccasins to their feet and large thick
    blankets hanging from their shoulders;
On a bank lounged the trapper . . . . he was dressed mostly in
    skins . . . . his luxuriant beard and curls protected his neck,
One hand rested on his rifle . . . . the other hand held firmly the
    wrist of the red girl,
She had long eyelashes . . . . her head was bare . . . . her coarse
    straight locks descended upon her voluptuous limbs and
    reached to her feet.

The runaway slave came to my house and stopped outside,
I heard his motions crackling the twigs of the woodpile,
Through the swung half-door of the kitchen I saw him limpsey
    and weak,
And went where he sat on a log, and led him in and assured him,
And brought water and filled a tub for his sweated body and
    bruised feet,

And gave him a room that entered from my own, and gave him
    some coarse clean clothes,
And remember perfectly well his revolving eyes and his
    awkwardness,
And remember putting plasters on the galls of his neck and
    ankles;
He staid with me a week before he was recuperated and passed
    north,
I had him sit next me at table . . . . my firelock leaned in the
    corner.

Twenty-eight young men bathe by the shore,
Twenty-eight young men, and all so friendly,
Twenty-eight years of womanly life, and all so lonesome.

She owns the fine house by the rise of the bank,
She hides handsome and richly drest aft the blinds of the
    window.

Which of the young men does she like the best?
Ah the homeliest of them is beautiful to her.

Where are you off to, lady? for I see you,
You splash in the water there, yet stay stock still in your room.

Dancing and laughing along the beach came the twenty-ninth
    bather,
The rest did not see her, but she saw them and loved them.

The beards of the young men glistened with wet, it ran from their
    long hair,
Little streams passed all over their bodies.

An unseen hand also passed over their bodies,
It descended tremblingly from their temples and ribs.

The young men float on their backs, their white bellies swell to
    the sun . . . . they do not ask who seizes fast to them,

They do not know who puffs and declines with pendant and
    bending arch,
They do not think whom they souse with spray.[11]

The butcher-boy puts off his killing-clothes, or sharpens his knife
    at the stall in the market,
I loiter enjoying his repartee and his shuffle and breakdown.[12]

Blacksmiths with grimed and hairy chests environ the anvil,
Each has his main-sledge . . . . they are all out . . . . there is a great
    heat in the fire.

From the cinder-strewed threshold I follow their movements,
The lithe sheer of their waists plays even with their massive arms,
Overhand the hammers roll—overhand so slow—overhand so sure,
They do not hasten, each man hits in his place.

The negro holds firmly the reins of his four horses . . . . the block
    swags underneath on its tied-over chain,
The negro that drives the huge dray of the stoneyard . . . . steady
    and tall he stands poised on one leg on the stringpiece,
His blue shirt exposes his ample neck and breast and loosens over
    his hipband,
His glance is calm and commanding . . . . he tosses the slouch of
    his hat away from his forehead,
The sun falls on his crispy hair and moustache . . . . falls on the
    black of his polish'd and perfect limbs.

I behold the picturesque giant and love him . . . . and I do not
    stop there,
I go with the team also.

In me the caresser of life wherever moving . . . . backward as well
    as forward slueing,
To niches aside and junior bending.

Oxen that rattle the yoke or halt in the shade, what is that you
    express in your eyes?
It seems to me more than all the print I have read in my life.

My tread scares the wood-drake and wood-duck on my distant and
    daylong ramble,
They rise together, they slowly circle around.
. . . . I believe in those winged purposes,
And acknowledge the red yellow and white playing within me,
And consider the green and violet and the tufted crown
    intentional;
And do not call the tortoise unworthy because she is not
    something else,
And the mocking bird in the swamp never studied the gamut, yet
    trills pretty well to me,
And the look of the bay mare shames silliness out of me.

The wild gander leads his flock through the cool night,
Ya-honk! he says, and sounds it down to me like an invitation;
The pert may suppose it meaningless, but I listen closer,
I find its purpose and place up there toward the November sky.

The sharphoofed moose of the north, the cat on the housesill,
    the chickadee, the prairie-dog,
The litter of the grunting sow as they tug at her teats,
The brood of the turkeyhen, and she with her halfspread wings,
I see in them and myself the same old law.

The press of my foot to the earth springs a hundred affections,
They scorn the best I can do to relate them.

I am enamoured of growing outdoors,
Of men that live among cattle or taste of the ocean or woods,
Of the builders and steerers of ships, of the wielders of axes and
    mauls, of the drivers of horses,
I can eat and sleep with them week in and week out.

What is commonest and cheapest and nearest and easiest is Me,
Me going in for my chances, spending for vast returns,
Adorning myself to bestow myself on the first that will take me,
Not asking the sky to come down to my goodwill,
Scattering it freely forever.

The pure contralto sings in the organloft,

The carpenter dresses his plank . . . . the tongue of his foreplane
      whistles its wild ascending lisp,

The married and unmarried children ride home to their
      thanksgiving dinner,

The pilot seizes the king-pin, he heaves down with a strong arm,

The mate stands braced in the whaleboat, lance and harpoon are
      ready,

The duck-shooter walks by silent and cautious stretches,

The deacons are ordained with crossed hands at the altar,

The spinning-girl retreats and advances to the hum of the big
      wheel,

The farmer stops by the bars of a Sunday and looks at the oats
      and rye,

The lunatic is carried at last to the asylum a confirmed case,

He will never sleep any more as he did in the cot in his mother's
      bedroom;*

The jour printer with gray head and gaunt jaws works at his
      case,

He turns his quid of tobacco, his eyes get blurred with the
      manuscript;

The malformed limbs are tied to the anatomist's table,

What is removed drops horribly in a pail;

The quadroon girl is sold at the stand . . . . the drunkard nods by
      the barroom stove,

The machinist rolls up his sleeves . . . . the policeman travels his
      beat . . . . the gatekeeper marks who pass,

The young fellow drives the express-wagon . . . . I love him
      though I do not know him;

The half-breed straps on his light boots to compete in the race,

The western turkey-shooting draws old and young . . . . some lean
      on their rifles, some sit on logs,

Out from the crowd steps the marksman and takes his position
      and levels his piece;

---

*Possibly a reference to Whitman's brother Jeff, who was mentally ill and confined
to an asylum.

The groups of newly-come immigrants cover the wharf or levee,
The woollypates hoe in the sugarfield, the overseer views them
  from his saddle;
The bugle calls in the ballroom, the gentlemen run for their
  partners, the dancers bow to each other;
The youth lies awake in the cedar-roofed garret and harks to the
  musical rain,
The Wolverine sets traps on the creek that helps fill the Huron,
The reformer ascends the platform, he spouts with his mouth and
  nose,
The company returns from its excursion, the darkey brings up the
  rear and bears the well-riddled target,
The squaw wrapt in her yellow-hemmed cloth is offering
  moccasins and beadbags for sale,
The connoisseur peers along the exhibition-gallery with halfshut
  eyes bent sideways,
The deckhands make fast the steamboat, the plank is thrown for
  the shoregoing passengers,
The young sister holds out the skein, the elder sister winds it off
  in a ball and stops now and then for the knots,
The one-year wife is recovering and happy, a week ago she bore
  her first child,
The cleanhaired Yankee girl works with her sewing-machine or in
  the factory or mill,
The nine months' gone is in the parturition chamber, her
  faintness and pains are advancing;
The pavingman leans on his twohanded rammer—the reporter's
  lead flies swiftly over the notebook—the signpainter is
  lettering with red and gold,
The canal-boy trots on the towpath—the bookkeeper counts at his
  desk—the shoemaker waxes his thread,
The conductor beats time for the band and all the performers
  follow him,
The child is baptised—the convert is making the first professions,
The regatta is spread on the bay . . . . how the white sails sparkle!
The drover watches his drove, he sings out to them that would stray,
The pedlar sweats with his pack on his back—the purchaser
  higgles about the odd cent,

The camera and plate are prepared, the lady must sit for her
 daguerreotype,[13]
The bride unrumples her white dress, the minutehand of the
 clock moves slowly,
The opium eater reclines with rigid head and just-opened lips,[14]
The prostitute draggles her shawl, her bonnet bobs on her tipsy
 and pimpled neck,
The crowd laugh at her blackguard oaths, the men jeer and wink
 to each other,
(Miserable! I do not laugh at your oaths nor jeer you,)
The President holds a cabinet council, he is surrounded by the
 great secretaries,
On the piazza walk five friendly matrons with twined arms;
The crew of the fish-smack pack repeated layers of halibut in the
 hold,
The Missourian crosses the plains toting his wares and his
 cattle,
The fare-collector goes through the train—he gives notice by the
 jingling of loose change,
The floormen are laying the floor—the tinners are tinning the
 roof—the masons are calling for mortar,
In single file each shouldering his hod pass onward the laborers;
Seasons pursuing each other the indescribable crowd is
 gathered . . . . it is the Fourth of July . . . . what salutes of
 cannon and small arms!
Seasons pursuing each other the plougher ploughs and the
 mower mows and the wintergrain falls in the ground;
Off on the lakes the pikefisher watches and waits by the hole in
 the frozen surface,
The stumps stand thick round the clearing, the squatter strikes
 deep with his axe,
The flatboatmen make fast toward dusk near the cottonwood or
 pekantrees,
The coon-seekers go now through the regions of the Red river, or
 through those drained by the Tennessee, or through those of
 the Arkansas,
The torches shine in the dark that hangs on the Chattahoochee
 or Altamahaw;

Patriarchs sit at supper with sons and grandsons and great
    grandsons around them,
In walls of adobie, in canvas tents, rest hunters and trappers after
    their day's sport.

The city sleeps and the country sleeps,
The living sleep for their time . . . . the dead sleep for their time,
The old husband sleeps by his wife and the young husband sleeps
    by his wife;
And those one and all tend inward to me, and I tend outward to
    them,
And such as it is to be of these more or less I am.

I am of old and young, of the foolish as much as the wise,
Regardless of others, ever regardful of others,
Maternal as well as paternal, a child as well as a man,
Stuffed with the stuff that is coarse, and stuffed with the stuff that
    is fine,
One of the great nations, the nation of many nations—the
    smallest the same and the largest the same,
A southerner soon as a northerner, a planter nonchalant and
    hospitable,
A Yankee bound my own way . . . . ready for trade . . . . my joints
    the limberest joints on earth and the sternest joints on earth,
A Kentuckian walking the vale of the Elkhorn in my deerskin
    leggings,
A boatman over the lakes or bays or along coasts . . . . a Hoosier, a
    Badger, a Buckeye,*
A Louisianian or Georgian, a poke-easy from sandhills and pines,
At home on Canadian snowshoes or up in the bush, or with
    fishermen off Newfoundland,
At home in the fleet of iceboats, sailing with the rest and tacking,
At home on the hills of Vermont or in the woods of Maine or the
    Texan ranch,
Comrade of Californians . . . . comrade of free northwesterners,
    loving their big proportions,

---

*Nicknames for people from Indiana, Wisconsin, and Ohio.

Comrade of raftsmen and coalmen—comrade of all who shake
    hands and welcome to drink and meat;
A learner with the simplest, a teacher of the thoughtfulest,
A novice beginning experient of myriads of seasons,
Of every hue and trade and rank, of every caste and religion,
Not merely of the New World but of Africa Europe or Asia . . . . a
    wandering savage,
A farmer, mechanic, or artist . . . . a gentleman, sailor, lover or
    quaker,
A prisoner, fancy-man, rowdy, lawyer, physician or priest.

I resist anything better than my own diversity,
And breathe the air and leave plenty after me,
And am not stuck up, and am in my place.

The moth and the fisheggs are in their place,
The suns I see and the suns I cannot see are in their place,
The palpable is in its place and the impalpable is in its place.

These are the thoughts of all men in all ages and lands, they are
    not original with me,
If they are not yours as much as mine they are nothing or next to
    nothing,
If they do not enclose everything they are next to nothing,
If they are not the riddle and the untying of the riddle they are
    nothing,
If they are not just as close as they are distant they are nothing.

This is the grass that grows wherever the land is and the water is,
This is the common air that bathes the globe.

This is the breath of laws and songs and behaviour,
This is the tasteless water of souls . . . . this is the true
    sustenance,
It is for the illiterate . . . . it is for the judges of the supreme
    court . . . . it is for the federal capitol and the state
    capitols,
It is for the admirable communes of literary men and composers
    and singers and lecturers and engineers and savans,

It is for the endless races of working people and farmers and
    seamen.

This is the trill of a thousand clear cornets and scream of the
    octave flute and strike of triangles.

I play not a march for victors only . . . . I play great marches for
    conquered and slain persons.

Have you heard that it was good to gain the day?
I also say it is good to fall . . . . battles are lost in the same spirit
    in which they are won.

I sound triumphal drums for the dead . . . . I fling through my
    embouchures* the loudest and gayest music to them,
Vivas to those who have failed, and to those whose war-vessels
    sank in the sea, and those themselves who sank in the sea,
And to all generals that lost engagements, and all overcome
    heroes, and the numberless unknown heroes equal to the
    greatest heroes known.

This is the meal pleasantly set . . . . this is the meat and drink for
    natural hunger,
It is for the wicked just the same as the righteous . . . . I make
    appointments with all,
I will not have a single person slighted or left away,
The keptwoman and sponger and thief are hereby invited . . . .
    the heavy-lipped slave is invited . . . . the venerealee is invited,
There shall be no difference between them and the rest.

This is the press of a bashful hand . . . . this is the float and odor
    of hair,

---

*Mouthpieces of wind instruments; also, in the singular, the shape the mouth
makes when blowing. The term is derived from the French word of the same
spelling that means "mouth" or "mouthpiece." Whitman was fond of using foreign
terminology (particularly French expressions) in his work—a seeming irony for this
self-declared "American Adam" of poetry.

This is the touch of my lips to yours . . . . this is the murmur of
    yearning,
This is the far-off depth and height reflecting my own face,
This is the thoughtful merge of myself and the outlet again.

Do you guess I have some intricate purpose?
Well I have . . . . for the April rain has, and the mica on the side
    of a rock has.

Do you take it I would astonish?
Does the daylight astonish? or the early redstart twittering through
    the woods?
Do I astonish more than they?

This hour I tell things in confidence,
I might not tell everybody but I will tell you.

Who goes there! hankering, gross, mystical, nude?
How is it I extract strength from the beef I eat?

What is a man anyhow? What am I? and what are you?
All I mark as my own you shall offset it with your own,
Else it were time lost listening to me.

I do not snivel that snivel the world over,
That months are vacuums and the ground but wallow
    and filth,
That life is a suck and a sell, and nothing remains at the end but
    threadbare crape and tears.

Whimpering and truckling fold with powders for invalids . . . .
    conformity goes to the fourth-removed,
I cock my hat as I please indoors or out.[15]

Shall I pray? Shall I venerate and be ceremonious?
I have pried through the strata and analyzed to a hair,
And counselled with doctors and calculated close and found no
    sweeter fat than sticks to my own bones.

In all people I see myself, none more and not one a barleycorn
    less,
And the good or bad I say of myself I say of them.

And I know I am solid and sound,
To me the converging objects of the universe perpetually flow,
All are written to me, and I must get what the writing means.

And I know I am deathless,
I know this orbit of mine cannot be swept by a carpenter's
    compass,
I know I shall not pass like a child's carlacue* cut with a burnt
    stick at night.

I know I am august,
I do not trouble my spirit to vindicate itself or be understood,
I see that the elementary laws never apologize,
I reckon I behave no prouder than the level I plant my house by
    after all.

I exist as I am, that is enough,
If no other in the world be aware I sit content,
And if each and all be aware I sit content.

One world is aware, and by far the largest to me, and that is myself,
And whether I come to my own today or in ten thousand or ten
    million years,
I can cheerfully take it now, or with equal cheerfulness I can wait.

My foothold is tenoned and mortised in granite,
I laugh at what you call dissolution,
And I know the amplitude of time.

I am the poet of the body,
And I am the poet of the soul.

---

*That is, a curlicue; a writerly flourish.

The pleasures of heaven are with me, and the pains of hell are
　　with me,
The first I graft and increase upon myself . . . . the latter I
　　translate into a new tongue.

I am the poet of the woman the same as the man,
And I say it is as great to be a woman as to be a man,
And I say there is nothing greater than the mother of men.

I chant a new chant of dilation or pride,
We have had ducking and deprecating about enough,
I show that size is only development.

Have you outstript the rest? Are you the President?
It is a trifle . . . . they will more than arrive there every one, and
　　still pass on.

I am he that walks with the tender and growing night;
I call to the earth and sea half-held by the night.

Press close barebosomed night! Press close magnetic nourishing
　　night!
Night of south winds! Night of the large few stars!
Still nodding night! Mad naked summer night!

Smile O voluptuous coolbreathed earth!
Earth of the slumbering and liquid trees!
Earth of departed sunset! Earth of the mountains misty-topt!
Earth of the vitreous pour of the full moon just tinged with blue!
Earth of shine and dark mottling the tide of the river!
Earth of the limpid gray of clouds brighter and clearer for my
　　sake!
Far-swooping elbowed earth! Rich apple-blossomed earth!
Smile, for your lover comes!

Prodigal! you have given me love! . . . . therefore I to you give
　　love!
O unspeakable passionate love!

Thruster holding me tight and that I hold tight!
We hurt each other as the bridegroom and the bride hurt each
    other.

You sea! I resign myself to you also . . . . I guess what you mean,
I behold from the beach your crooked inviting fingers,
I believe you refuse to go back without feeling of me;
We must have a turn together . . . . I undress . . . . hurry me out of
    sight of the land,
Cushion me soft . . . . rock me in billowy drowse,
Dash me with amorous wet . . . . I can repay you.

Sea of stretched ground-swells!
Sea breathing broad and convulsive breaths! .
Sea of the brine of life! Sea of unshovelled and always-ready graves!
Howler and scooper of storms! Capricious and dainty sea!
I am integral with you . . . . I too am of one phase and of all phases.

Partaker of influx and efflux . . . . extoller of hate and conciliation,
Extoller of amies* and those that sleep in each others' arms.

I am he attesting sympathy;
Shall I make my list of things in the house and skip the house
    that supports them?

I am the poet of commonsense and of the demonstrable and of
    immortality;
And am not the poet of goodness only . . . . I do not decline to be
    the poet of wickedness also.

Washes and razors for foofoos . . . . for me freckles and a bristling
    beard.

What blurt is it about virtue and about vice?
Evil propels me, and reform of evil propels me . . . . I stand
    indifferent,

---

*Friends; another example of Whitman's fondness for French expressions.

My gait is no faultfinder's or rejecter's gait,
I moisten the roots of all that has grown.

Did you fear some scrofula* out of the unflagging pregnancy?
Did you guess the celestial laws are yet to be worked over and
    rectified?

I step up to say that what we do is right and what we affirm is
    right . . . . and some is only the ore of right,
Witnesses of us . . . . one side a balance and the antipodal side a
    balance,
Soft doctrine as steady help as stable doctrine,
Thoughts and deeds of the present our rouse and early start.

This minute that comes to me over the past decillions,
There is no better than it and now.

What behaved well in the past or behaves well today is not such a
    wonder,
The wonder is always and always how there can be a mean man
    or an infidel.

Endless unfolding of words of ages!
And mine a word of the modern . . . . a word en masse.

A word of the faith that never balks,
One time as good as another time . . . . here or henceforward it is
    all the same to me.

A word of reality . . . . materialism first and last imbuing.

Hurrah for positive science! Long live exact demonstration!
Fetch stonecrop and mix it with cedar and branches of lilac;†

---

*Tubercular swelling of the neck glands; an example of the poet's interest in med-
icine and medical terminology, to be tested and expanded during his years as a
Civil War nurse.
†Whitman is describing the making of an elixir, as an example of "positive sci-
ence"; stonecrop is a plant used in curative medicines.

This is the lexicographer or chemist . . . . this made a grammar of
    the old cartouches,*
These mariners put the ship through dangerous unknown
    seas,
This is the geologist, and this works with the scalpel, and this is a
    mathematician.

Gentlemen I receive you, and attach and clasp hands
    with you,
The facts are useful and real . . . . they are not my dwelling I
    enter by them to an area of the dwelling.

I am less the reminder of property or qualities, and more the
    reminder of life,
And go on the square for my own sake and for other's
    sake,
And make short account of neuters and geldings, and favor men
    and women fully equipped,
And beat the gong of revolt, and stop with fugitives and them that
    plot and conspire.

Walt Whitman, an American, one of the roughs, a kosmos,[16]
Disorderly fleshy and sensual . . . . eating drinking and
    breeding,
No sentimentalist . . . . no stander above men and women or
    apart from them . . . . no more modest than immodest.

Unscrew the locks from the doors!
Unscrew the doors themselves from their jambs![17]

Whoever degrades another degrades me . . . . and whatever is
    done or said returns at last to me,
And whatever I do or say I also return.

---

*An ancient Egyptian ornamental figure, typically oval or oblong, that carries a de-
sign, inscription, or name; Whitman developed his knowledge of Egyptian culture
during years of visiting the Museum of Egyptian Antiquities on Broadway.

Through me the afflatus* surging and surging . . . . through me
    the current and index.

I speak the password primeval . . . . I give the sign of democracy;
By God! I will accept nothing which all cannot have their
    counterpart of on the same terms.

Through me many long dumb voices,
Voices of the interminable generations of slaves,
Voices of prostitutes and of deformed persons,
Voices of the diseased and despairing, and of thieves and dwarfs,
Voices of cycles of preparation and accretion,
And of the threads that connect the stars—and of wombs, and of
    the fatherstuff,
And of the rights of them the others are down upon,
Of the trivial and flat and foolish and despised,
Of fog in the air and beetles rolling balls of dung.

Through me forbidden voices,
Voices of sexes and lusts . . . . voices veiled, and I remove the veil,
Voices indecent by me clarified and transfigured.

I do not press my finger across my mouth,
I keep as delicate around the bowels as around the head and
    heart,
Copulation is no more rank to me than death is.

I believe in the flesh and the appetites,
Seeing hearing and feeling are miracles, and each part and tag of
    me is a miracle.

Divine am I inside and out, and I make holy whatever I touch or
    am touched from;
The scent of these arm-pits is aroma finer than prayer,
This head is more than churches or bibles or creeds.

---

*Inspiration.

If I worship any particular thing it shall be some of the spread of
    my body;
Translucent mould of me it shall be you,
Shaded ledges and rests, firm masculine coulter,* it shall be you,
Whatever goes to the tilth† of me it shall be you,
You my rich blood, your milky stream pale strippings of my life;
Breast that presses against other breasts it shall be you,
My brain it shall be your occult convolutions,
Root of washed sweet-flag, timorous pond-snipe, nest of guarded
    duplicate eggs, it shall be you,
Mixed tussled hay of head and beard and brawn it shall be you,
Trickling sap of maple, fibre of manly wheat, it shall be you;
Sun so generous it shall be you,
Vapors lighting and shading my face it shall be you,
You sweaty brooks and dews it shall be you,
Winds whose soft-tickling genitals rub against me it shall be you,
Broad muscular fields, branches of liveoak, loving lounger in my
    winding paths, it shall be you,
Hands I have taken, face I have kissed, mortal I have ever
    touched, it shall be you.

I dote on myself . . . . there is that lot of me, and all so luscious,
Each moment and whatever happens thrills me with joy.

I cannot tell how my ankles bend . . . . nor whence the cause of
    my faintest wish,
Nor the cause of the friendship I emit . . . . nor the cause of the
    friendship I take again.

To walk up my stoop is unaccountable . . . . I pause to consider if
    it really be,
That I eat and drink is spectacle enough for the great authors and
    schools,

---

*That is, the male genitals; the coulter is the prong that directs a plow into the turf.
In this section, Whitman mixes references to farming and nature with descriptions
of male genitals and sexuality.
†Cultivation.

A morning-glory at my window satisfies me more than the
metaphysics of books.

To behold the daybreak!
The little light fades the immense and diaphanous shadows,
The air tastes good to my palate.

Hefts of the moving world at innocent gambols, silently rising,
freshly exuding,
Scooting obliquely high and low.

Something I cannot see puts upward libidinous prongs,
Seas of bright juice suffuse heaven.

The earth by the sky staid with . . . . the daily close of their junction,
The heaved challenge from the east that moment over my head,
The mocking taunt, See then whether you shall be master!

Dazzling and tremendous how quick the sunrise would kill me,
If I could not now and always send sunrise out of me.

We also ascend dazzling and tremendous as the sun,
We found our own my soul in the calm and cool of the daybreak.

My voice goes after what my eyes cannot reach,
With the twirl of my tongue I encompass worlds and volumes of
worlds.

Speech is the twin of my vision . . . . it is unequal to measure itself.
It provokes me forever,
It says sarcastically, Walt, you understand enough . . . . why don't
you let it out then?

Come now I will not be tantalized . . . . you conceive too much of
articulation.

Do you not know how the buds beneath are folded?
Waiting in gloom protected by frost,

The dirt receding before my prophetical screams,
I underlying causes to balance them at last,
My knowledge my live parts . . . . it keeping tally with the
      meaning of things,
Happiness . . . . which whoever hears me let him or her set out in
      search of this day.

My final merit I refuse you . . . . I refuse putting from me the best
   I am.

Encompass worlds but never try to encompass me,
I crowd your noisiest talk by looking toward you.

Writing and talk do not prove me,
I carry the plenum of proof and every thing else in my face,
With the hush of my lips I confound the topmost skeptic.

I think I will do nothing for a long time but listen,
And accrue what I hear into myself . . . . and let sounds contribute
      toward me.

I hear the bravuras[18] of birds . . . . the bustle of growing wheat . . . .
      gossip of flames . . . . clack of sticks cooking my meals.

I hear the sound of the human voice . . . . a sound I love,
I hear all sounds as they are tuned to their uses . . . . sounds of the
      city and sounds out of the city . . . . sounds of the day and
      night;
Talkative young ones to those that like them . . . . the recitative of
      fish-pedlars and fruit-pedlars . . . . the loud laugh of
      workpeople at their meals,
The angry base of disjointed friendship . . . . the faint tones of the
      sick,
The judge with hands tight to the desk, his shaky lips
      pronouncing a death-sentence,
The heave'e'yo of stevedores unlading ships by the wharves . . . .
      the refrain of the anchor-lifters;

The ring of alarm-bells . . . . the cry of fire . . . . the whirr of swift-
    streaking engines and hose-carts with premonitory tinkles
    and colored lights,
The steam-whistle . . . . the solid roll of the train of approaching
    cars;
The slow-march played at night at the head of the association,
They go to guard some corpse . . . . the flag-tops are draped with
    black muslin.

I hear the violincello or man's heart complaint,
And hear the keyed cornet or else the echo of sunset.

I hear the chorus . . . . it is a grand-opera . . . . this indeed is music!

A tenor large and fresh as the creation fills me,
The orbic flex of his mouth is pouring and filling me full.

I hear the trained soprano . . . . she convulses me like the climax
    of my love-grip;
The orchestra whirls me wider than Uranus flies,
It wrenches unnamable ardors from my breast,
It throbs me to gulps of the farthest down horror,
It sails me . . . . I dab with bare feet . . . . they are licked by the
    indolent waves,
I am exposed . . . . cut by bitter and poisoned hail,
Steeped amid honeyed morphine . . . . my windpipe squeezed in
    the fakes of death,
Let up again to feel the puzzle of puzzles,
And that we call Being.

To be in any form, what is that?
If nothing lay more developed the quahaug* and its callous shell
    were enough.

---

*A clam; note in the next line Whitman's segue from the clam shell to the "shell"
of the human body.

Mine is no callous shell,
I have instant conductors all over me whether I pass or stop,
They seize every object and lead it harmlessly through me.[19]

I merely stir, press, feel with my fingers, and am happy,
To touch my person to some one else's is about as much as I can
    stand.

Is this then a touch? . . . . quivering me to a new identity,
Flames and ether making a rush for my veins,
Treacherous tip of me reaching and crowding to help them,
My flesh and blood playing out lightning, to strike what is hardly
    different from myself,
On all sides prurient provokers stiffening my limbs,
Straining the udder of my heart for its withheld drip,
Behaving licentious toward me, taking no denial,
Depriving me of my best as for a purpose,
Unbuttoning my clothes and holding me by the bare waist,
Deluding my confusion with the calm of the sunlight and pasture
    fields,
Immodestly sliding the fellow-senses away,
They bribed to swap off with touch, and go and graze at the edges
    of me,
No consideration, no regard for my draining strength or my
    anger,
Fetching the rest of the herd around to enjoy them awhile,
Then all uniting to stand on a headland and worry me.

The sentries desert every other part of me,
They have left me helpless to a red marauder,
They all come to the headland to witness and assist against me.

I am given up by traitors;
I talk wildly . . . . I have lost my wits . . . . I and nobody else am
    the greatest traitor,
I went myself first to the headland . . . . my own hands carried me
    there.

You villain touch! what are you doing? . . . . my breath is tight in
  its throat;
Unclench your floodgates! you are too much for me.

Blind loving wrestling touch! Sheathed hooded sharptoothed
  touch!
Did it make you ache so leaving me?

Parting tracked by arriving . . . . perpetual payment of the
  perpetual loan,
Rich showering rain, and recompense richer afterward.

Sprouts take and accumulate . . . . stand by the curb prolific and
  vital,
Landscapes projected masculine full-sized and golden.

All truths wait in all things,
They neither hasten their own delivery nor resist it,
They do not need the obstetric forceps of the surgeon,
The insignificant is as big to me as any,
What is less or more than a touch?

Logic and sermons never convince,
The damp of the night drives deeper into my soul.

Only what proves itself to every man and woman is so,
Only what nobody denies is so.

A minute and a drop of me settle my brain;
I believe the soggy clods shall become lovers and lamps,
And a compend of compends is the meat of a man or
  woman,
And a summit and flower there is the feeling they have for each
  other,
And they are to branch boundlessly out of that lesson until it
  becomes omnific,
And until every one shall delight us, and we them.

I believe a leaf of grass is no less than the journeywork of the stars,
And the pismire* is equally perfect, and a grain of sand, and the
    egg of the wren,
And the tree-toad is a chef-d'œuvre for the highest,
And the running blackberry would adorn the parlors of heaven,
And the narrowest hinge in my hand puts to scorn all machinery,
And the cow crunching with depressed head surpasses any statue,
And a mouse is miracle enough to stagger sextillions of infidels,
And I could come every afternoon of my life to look at the
    farmer's girl boiling her iron tea-kettle and baking shortcake.

I find I incorporate gneiss and coal and long-threaded moss and
    fruits and grains and esculent roots,
And am stucco'd with quadrupeds and birds all over,
And have distanced what is behind me for good reasons,
And call any thing close again when I desire it.

In vain the speeding or shyness,
In vain the plutonic rocks send their old heat against my approach,
In vain the mastodon retreats beneath its own powdered bones,
In vain objects stand leagues off and assume manifold shapes,
In vain the ocean settling in hollows and the great monsters lying
    low,
In vain the buzzard houses herself with the sky,
In vain the snake slides through the creepers and logs,
In vain the elk takes to the inner passes of the woods,
In vain the razorbilled auk sails far north to Labrador,
I follow quickly . . . . I ascend to the nest in the fissure of the cliff.

I think I could turn and live awhile with the animals . . . . they are
    so placid and self-contained,
I stand and look at them sometimes half the day long.

They do not sweat and whine about their condition,
They do not lie awake in the dark and weep for their sins,

---

*Ant.

They do not make me sick discussing their duty to God,
Not one is dissatisfied . . . . not one is demented with the mania of
     owning things,
Not one kneels to another nor to his kind that lived thousands of
     years ago,
Not one is respectable or industrious over the whole earth.

So they show their relations to me and I accept them;
They bring me tokens of myself . . . . they evince them plainly in
     their possession.

I do not know where they got those tokens,
I must have passed that way untold times ago and negligently
     dropt them,
Myself moving forward then and now and forever,
Gathering and showing more always and with velocity,
Infinite and omnigenous and the like of these among them;
Not too exclusive toward the reachers of my remembrancers,
Picking out here one that shall be my amie,
Choosing to go with him on brotherly terms.

A gigantic beauty of a stallion, fresh and responsive to my
     caresses,
Head high in the forehead and wide between the ears,
Limbs glossy and supple, tail dusting the ground,
Eyes well apart and full of sparkling wickedness . . . . ears finely
     cut and flexibly moving.

His nostrils dilate . . . . my heels embrace him . . . . his well built
     limbs tremble with pleasure . . . . we speed around and return.

I but use you a moment and then I resign you stallion . . . . and
     do not need your paces, and outgallop them,
And myself as I stand or sit pass faster than you.

Swift wind! Space! My Soul! Now I know it is true what I
     guessed at;
What I guessed when I loafed on the grass,

What I guessed while I lay alone in my bed .... and again
    as I walked the beach under the paling stars of the
    morning.

My ties and ballasts leave me .... I travel .... I sail .... my
    elbows rest in the sea-gaps,
I skirt the sierras .... my palms cover continents,
I am afoot with my vision.

By the city's quadrangular houses .... in log-huts, or camping
    with lumbermen,
Along the ruts of the turnpike .... along the dry gulch and rivulet
    bed,
Hoeing my onion-patch, and rows of carrots and parsnips . : . .
    crossing savannas .... trailing in forests,
Prospecting .... gold-digging .... girdling the trees of a new
    purchase,
Scorched ankle-deep by the hot sand .... hauling my boat down
    the shallow river;
Where the panther walks to and fro on a limb overhead ....
    where the buck turns furiously at the hunter,
Where the rattlesnake suns his flabby length on a rock .... where
    the otter is feeding on fish,
Where the alligator in his tough pimples sleeps by the bayou,
Where the black bear is searching for roots or honey .... where
    the beaver pats the mud with his paddle-tail;
Over the growing sugar .... over the cottonplant .... over the
    rice in its low moist field;
Over the sharp-peaked farmhouse with its scalloped scum and
    slender shoots from the gutters;
Over the western persimmon .... over the longleaved corn and
    the delicate blue-flowered flax;
Over the white and brown buckwheat, a hummer and a buzzer
    there with the rest,
Over the dusky green of the rye as it ripples and shades in the
    breeze;
Scaling mountains .... pulling myself cautiously up .... holding
    on by low scragged limbs,

Walking the path worn in the grass and beat through the leaves of
  the brush;
Where the quail is whistling betwixt the woods and the wheatlot,
Where the bat flies in the July eve . . . . where the great goldbug
  drops through the dark;
Where the flails keep time on the barn floor,
Where the brook puts out of the roots of the old tree and flows to
  the meadow,
Where cattle stand and shake away flies with the tremulous
  shuddering of their hides,
Where the cheese-cloth hangs in the kitchen, and andirons straddle
  the hearth-slab, and cobwebs fall in festoons from the rafters;
Where triphammers crash . . . . where the press is whirling its
  cylinders;[20]
Wherever the human heart beats with terrible throes out of
  its ribs;
Where the pear-shaped balloon is floating aloft . . . . floating in it
  myself and looking composedly down;
Where the life-car is drawn on the slipnoose . . . . where the heat
  hatches pale-green eggs in the dented sand,
Where the she-whale swims with her calves and never forsakes
  them,
Where the steamship trails hindways its long pennant of smoke,
Where the ground-shark's fin cuts like a black chip out of the
  water,
Where the half-burned brig is riding on unknown currents,
Where shells grow to her slimy deck, and the dead are corrupting
  below;
Where the striped and starred flag is borne at the head of the
  regiments;
Approaching Manhattan, up by the long-stretching island,
Under Niagara, the cataract falling like a veil over my countenance;
Upon a door-step . . . . upon the horse-block of hard wood
  outside,
Upon the race-course, or enjoying pic-nics or jigs or a good game
  of base-ball,[21]
At he-festivals with blackguard jibes and ironical license and
  bull-dances and drinking and laughter,

At the cider-mill, tasting the sweet of the brown sqush . . . .
    sucking the juice through a straw,
At apple-peelings, wanting kisses for all the red fruit I find,
At musters and beach-parties and friendly bees and huskings and
    house-raisings;
Where the mockingbird sounds his delicious gurgles, and cackles
    and screams and weeps,
Where the hay-rick stands in the barnyard, and the dry-stalks are
    scattered, and the brood cow waits in the hovel,
Where the bull advances to do his masculine work, and the stud
    to the mare, and the cock is treading the hen,
Where the heifers browse, and the geese nip their food with short
    jerks;
Where the sundown shadows lengthen over the limitless and
    lonesome prairie,
Where the herds of buffalo make a crawling spread of the square
    miles far and near;
Where the hummingbird shimmers . . . . where the neck of the
    longlived swan is curving and winding;
Where the laughing-gull scoots by the slappy shore and laughs
    her near-human laugh;
Where beehives range on a gray bench in the garden half-hid by
    the high weeds;
Where the band-necked partridges roost in a ring on the ground
    with their heads out;
Where burial coaches enter the arched gates of a cemetery;
Where winter wolves bark amid wastes of snow and icicled trees;
Where the yellow-crowned heron comes to the edge of the marsh
    at night and feeds upon small crabs;
Where the splash of swimmers and divers cools the warm noon;
Where the katydid works her chromatic reed on the walnut-tree
    over the well;
Through patches of citrons and cucumbers with silver-wired leaves,
Through the salt-lick or orange glade . . . . or under conical firs;
Through the gymnasium . . . . through the curtained saloon . . . .
    through the office or public hall;
Pleased with the native and pleased with the foreign . . . . pleased
    with the new and old,

Pleased with women, the homely as well as the handsome,

Pleased with the quakeress as she puts off her bonnet and talks
      melodiously,

Pleased with the primitive tunes of the choir of the whitewashed
      church,

Pleased with the earnest words of the sweating Methodist
      preacher, or any preacher . . . . looking seriously at the camp-
      meeting;

Looking in at the shop-windows in Broadway the whole
      forenoon . . . . pressing the flesh of my nose to the thick plate-
      glass,

Wandering the same afternoon with my face turned up to the
      clouds;

My right and left arms round the sides of two friends and I in the
      middle;

Coming home with the bearded and dark-cheeked bush-boy . . . .
      riding behind him at the drape of the day;

Far from the settlements studying the print of animals' feet, or the
      moccasin print;

By the cot in the hospital reaching lemonade to a feverish patient,

By the coffined corpse when all is still, examining with a candle;

Voyaging to every port to dicker and adventure;

Hurrying with the modern crowd, as eager and fickle as any,

Hot toward one I hate, ready in my madness to knife him;

Solitary at midnight in my back yard, my thoughts gone from me
      a long while,

Walking the old hills of Judea with the beautiful gentle god by my
      side;

Speeding through space . . . . speeding through heaven and the
      stars,

Speeding amid the seven satellites and the broad ring and the
      diameter of eighty thousand miles,

Speeding with tailed meteors . . . . throwing fire-balls like the rest,

Carrying the crescent child that carries its own full mother in its
      belly:

Storming enjoying planning loving cautioning,

Backing and filling, appearing and disappearing,

I tread day and night such roads.

I visit the orchards of God and look at the spheric product,
And look at quintillions ripened, and look at quintillions green.

I fly the flight of the fluid and swallowing soul,
My course runs below the soundings of plummets.

I help myself to material and immaterial,
No guard can shut me off, no law can prevent me.

I anchor my ship for a little while only,
My messengers continually cruise away or bring their returns to me.

I go hunting polar furs and the seal . . . . leaping chasms with a
    pike-pointed staff . . . . clinging to topples of brittle and blue.

I ascend to the foretruck . . . . I take my place late at night in the
    crow's nest . . . . we sail through the arctic sea . . . . it is plenty
    light enough,
Through the clear atmosphere I stretch around on the wonderful
    beauty,
The enormous masses of ice pass me and I pass them . . . . the
    scenery is plain in all directions,
The white-topped mountains point up in the distance . . . . I fling
    out my fancies toward them;
We are about approaching some great battlefield in which we are
    soon to be engaged,
We pass the colossal outposts of the encampment . . . . we pass
    with still feet and caution;
Or we are entering by the suburbs some vast and ruined city . . . .
    the blocks and fallen architecture more than all the living
    cities of the globe.

I am a free companion . . . . I bivouac* by invading watchfires.

I turn the bridegroom out of bed and stay with the bride myself,
And tighten her all night to my thighs and lips.

---

*A camp, often temporary, out in the open.

My voice is the wife's voice, the screech by the rail of the stairs,
They fetch my man's body up dripping and drowned.

I understand the large hearts of heroes,
The courage of present times and all times;
How the skipper saw the crowded and rudderless wreck of
     the steamship, and death chasing it up and down the
     storm,[22]
How he knuckled tight and gave not back one inch, and was
     faithful of days and faithful of nights,
And chalked in large letters on a board, Be of good cheer, We will
     not desert you;
How he saved the drifting company at last,
How the lank loose-gowned women looked when boated from the
     side of their prepared graves,
How the silent old-faced infants, and the lifted sick, and the
     sharp-lipped unshaved men;
All this I swallow and it tastes good . . . . I like it well, and it
     becomes mine,
I am the man . . . . I suffered . . . . I was there.

The disdain and calmness of martyrs,
The mother condemned for a witch and burnt with dry wood,
     and her children gazing on;
The hounded slave that flags in the race and leans by the fence,
     blowing and covered with sweat,
The twinges that sting like needles his legs and neck,
The murderous buckshot and the bullets,
All these I feel or am.

I am the hounded slave . . . . I wince at the bite of the dogs,
Hell and despair are upon me . . . . crack and again crack the
     marksmen,
I clutch the rails of the fence . . . . my gore dribs thinned with the
     ooze of my skin,
I fall on the weeds and stones,
The riders spur their unwilling horses and haul close,
They taunt my dizzy ears . . . . they beat me violently over the
     head with their whip-stocks.

Agonies are one of my changes of garments;
I do not ask the wounded person how he feels .... I myself
    become the wounded person,
My hurt turns livid upon me as I lean on a cane and observe.

I am the mashed fireman with breastbone broken[23] .... tumbling
    walls buried me in their debris,
Heat and smoke I inspired .... I heard the yelling shouts of my
    comrades,
I heard the distant click of their picks and shovels;
They have cleared the beams away .... they tenderly lift me forth.

I lie in the night air in my red shirt .... the pervading hush is for
    my sake,
Painless after all I lie, exhausted but not so unhappy,
White and beautiful are the faces around me .... the heads are
    bared of their fire-caps,
The kneeling crowd fades with the light of the torches.

Distant and dead resuscitate,
They show as the dial or move as the hands of me .... and I am
    the clock myself.

I am an old artillerist, and tell of some fort's bombardment ....
    and am there again.

Again the reveille of drummers .... again the attacking cannon
    and mortars and howitzers,
Again the attacked send their cannon responsive.

I take part .... I see and hear the whole,
The cries and curses and roar .... the plaudits for well aimed
    shots,
The ambulanza slowly passing and trailing its red drip,
Workmen searching after damages and to make indispensable
    repairs,
The fall of grenades through the rent roof .... the fan-shaped
    explosion,
The whizz of limbs heads stone wood and iron high in the air.

Again gurgles the mouth of my dying general . . . . he furiously
    waves with his hand,
He gasps through the clot . . . . Mind not me . . . . mind . . . . the
    entrenchments.

I tell not the fall of Alamo[24] . . . . not one escaped to tell the fall of
    Alamo,
The hundred and fifty are dumb yet at Alamo.

Hear now the tale of a jetblack sunrise,
Hear of the murder in cold blood of four hundred and twelve
    young men.

Retreating they had formed in a hollow square with their baggage
    for breastworks,
Nine hundred lives out of the surrounding enemy's nine times
    their number was the price they took in advance,
Their colonel was wounded and their ammunition gone,
They treated for an honorable capitulation, received writing
    and seal, gave up their arms, and marched back prisoners
    of war.

They were the glory of the race of rangers,
Matchless with a horse, a rifle, a song, a supper or a courtship,
Large, turbulent, brave, handsome, generous, proud and
    affectionate,
Bearded, sunburnt, dressed in the free costume of hunters,
Not a single one over thirty years of age.

The second Sunday morning they were brought out in squads
    and massacred . . . . it was beautiful early summer,
The work commenced about five o'clock and was over
    by eight.

None obeyed the command to kneel,
Some made a mad and helpless rush . . . . some stood stark and
    straight,
A few fell at once, shot in the temple or heart . . . . the living and
    dead lay together,

The maimed and mangled dug in the dirt . . . . the new-comers
    saw them there;
Some half-killed attempted to crawl away,
These were dispatched with bayonets or battered with the blunts
    of muskets;
A youth not seventeen years old seized his assassin till two more
    came to release him,
The three were all torn, and covered with the boy's blood.

At eleven o'clock began the burning of the bodies;
And that is the tale of the murder of the four hundred and twelve
    young men,
And that was a jetblack sunrise.

Did you read in the seabooks of the oldfashioned frigate-fight?[25]
Did you learn who won by the light of the moon and stars?

Our foe was no skulk in his ship, I tell you,
His was the English pluck, and there is no tougher or truer, and
    never was, and never will be;
Along the lowered eve he came, horribly raking us.

We closed with him . . . . the yards entangled . . . . the cannon
    touched,
My captain lashed fast with his own hands.

We had received some eighteen-pound shots under the water,
On our lower-gun-deck two large pieces had burst at the first fire,
    killing all around and blowing up overhead.

Ten o'clock at night, and the full moon shining and the leaks on
    the gain, and five feet of water reported,
The master-at-arms loosing the prisoners confined in the after-
    hold to give them a chance for themselves.

The transit to and from the magazine was now stopped by the
    sentinels,

They saw so many strange faces they did not know whom to
    trust.

Our frigate was afire . . . . the other asked if we demanded
    quarters? if our colors were struck and the fighting done?

I laughed content when I heard the voice of my little captain,
We have not struck, he composedly cried, We have just begun
    our part of the fighting.

Only three guns were in use,
One was directed by the captain himself against the enemy's
    mainmast,
Two well-served with grape and canister silenced his musketry
    and cleared his decks.

The tops alone seconded the fire of this little battery, especially
    the maintop,
They all held out bravely during the whole of the action.

Not a moment's cease,
The leaks gained fast on the pumps . . . . the fire eat toward the
    powder-magazine,
One of the pumps was shot away . . . . it was generally thought we
    were sinking.

Serene stood the little captain,
He was not hurried . . . . his voice was neither high nor low,
His eyes gave more light to us than our battle-lanterns.

Toward twelve at night, there in the beams of the moon they
    surrendered to us.

Stretched and still lay the midnight,
Two great hulls motionless on the breast of the darkness,
Our vessel riddled and slowly sinking . . . . preparations to pass to
    the one we had conquered,

The captain on the quarter deck coldly giving his orders through
    a countenance white as a sheet,
Near by the corpse of the child that served in the cabin,
The dead face of an old salt with long white hair and carefully
    curled whiskers,
The flames spite of all that could be done flickering aloft and below,
The husky voices of the two or three officers yet fit for duty,
Formless stacks of bodies and bodies by themselves . . . . dabs of
    flesh upon the masts and spars,
The cut of cordage and dangle of rigging . . . . the slight shock of
    the soothe of waves,
Black and impassive guns, and litter of powder-parcels, and the
    strong scent,
Delicate sniffs of the seabreeze . . . . smells of sedgy grass and fields
    by the shore . . . . death-messages given in charge to survivors,
The hiss of the surgeon's knife and the gnawing teeth of his saw,
The wheeze, the cluck, the swash of falling blood . . . . the short
    wild scream, the long dull tapering groan,
These so . . . . these irretrievable.

O Christ! My fit is mastering me!
What the rebel said gaily adjusting his throat to the rope-noose,
What the savage at the stump, his eye-sockets empty, his mouth
    spirting whoops and defiance,
What stills the traveler come to the vault at Mount Vernon,
What sobers the Brooklyn boy as he looks down the shores of the
    Wallabout and remembers the prison ships,
What burnt the gums of the redcoat at Saratoga when he
    surrendered his brigades,
These become mine and me every one, and they are but little,
I become as much more as I like.

I become any presence or truth of humanity here,
And see myself in prison shaped like another man,
And feel the dull unintermitted pain.

For me the keepers of convicts shoulder their carbines and keep
    watch,
It is I let out in the morning and barred at night.

Not a mutineer walks handcuffed to the jail, but I am handcuffed
    to him and walk by his side,
I am less the jolly one there, and more the silent one with sweat
    on my twitching lips.

Not a youngster is taken for larceny, but I go too and am tried
    and sentenced.

Not a cholera patient lies at the last gasp, but I also lie at the last
    gasp,
My face is ash-colored, my sinews gnarl . . . . away from me
    people retreat.

Askers embody themselves in me, and I am embodied in them,
I project my hat and sit shamefaced and beg.

I rise extatic through all, and sweep with the true gravitation,
The whirling and whirling is elemental within me.

Somehow I have been stunned. Stand back!
Give me a little time beyond my cuffed head and slumbers and
    dreams and gaping,
I discover myself on a verge of the usual mistake.

That I could forget the mockers and insults!
That I could forget the trickling tears and the blows of the
    bludgeons and hammers!
That I could look with a separate look on my own crucifixion and
    bloody crowning!

I remember . . . . I resume the overstaid fraction,
The grave of rock multiplies what has been confided to it . . . . or
    to any graves,
The corpses rise . . . . the gashes heal . . . . the fastenings roll
    away.

I troop forth replenished with supreme power, one of an average
    unending procession,

We walk the roads of Ohio and Massachusetts and Virginia and
    Wisconsin and New York and New Orleans and Texas and
    Montreal and San Francisco and Charleston and Savannah
    and Mexico,
Inland and by the seacoast and boundary lines . . . . and we pass
    the boundary lines.

Our swift ordinances are on their way over the whole earth,
The blossoms we wear in our hats are the growth of two thousand
    years.

Eleves* I salute you,
I see the approach of your numberless gangs . . . . I see you
    understand yourselves and me,
And know that they who have eyes are divine, and the blind and
    lame are equally divine,
And that my steps drag behind yours yet go before them,
And are aware how I am with you no more than I am with
    everybody.

The friendly and flowing savage . . . . Who is he?
Is he waiting for civilization or past it and mastering it?

Is he some southwesterner raised outdoors? Is he Canadian?
Is he from the Mississippi country? or from Iowa, Oregon or
    California? or from the mountain? or prairie life or bush-life?
    or from the sea?

Wherever he goes men and women accept and desire him,
They desire he should like them and touch them and speak to
    them and stay with them.

Behaviour lawless as snow-flakes . . . . words simple as grass . . . .
    uncombed head and laughter and naivete;
Slowstepping feet and the common features, and the common
    modes and emanations,

---

*Another instance of Whitman's use of French, this time the word for "pupil."

They descend in new forms from the tips of his fingers,
They are wafted with the odor of his body or breath . . . . they fly
   out of the glance of his eyes.

Flaunt of the sunshine I need not your bask . . . . lie over,
You light surfaces only . . . . I force the surfaces and the depths
   also.

Earth! you seem to look for something at my hands,
Say old topknot! what do you want?

Man or woman! I might tell how I like you, but cannot,
And might tell what it is in me and what it is in you, but cannot,
And might tell the pinings I have . . . . the pulse of my nights and
   days.

Behold I do not give lectures or a little charity,
What I give I give out of myself.

You there, impotent, loose in the knees, open your scarfed chops
   till I blow grit within you,
Spread your palms and lift the flaps of your pockets,
I am not to be denied . . . . I compel . . . . I have stores plenty and
   to spare,
And any thing I have I bestow.

I do not ask who you are . . . . that is not important to me,
You can do nothing and be nothing but what I will infold you.

To a drudge of the cottonfields or emptier of privies I lean . . . . on
   his right cheek I put the family kiss,
And in my soul I swear I never will deny him.

On women fit for conception I start bigger and nimbler babes,
This day I am jetting the stuff of far more arrogant republics.

To any one dying . . . . thither I speed and twist the knob of the
   door,

Turn the bedclothes toward the foot of the bed,
Let the physician and the priest go home.

I seize the descending man . . . . I raise him with resistless will.

O despairer, here is my neck,
By God! you shall not go down! Hang your whole weight upon
    me.

I dilate you with tremendous breath . . . . I buoy you up;
Every room of the house do I fill with an armed force . . . . lovers
    of me, bafflers of graves:
Sleep! I and they keep guard all night;
Not doubt, not decease shall dare to lay finger upon you,
I have embraced you, and henceforth possess you to myself,
And when you rise in the morning you will find what I tell you
    is so.

I am he bringing help for the sick as they pant on their backs,
And for strong upright men I bring yet more needed help.

I heard what was said of the universe,
Heard it and heard of several thousand years;
It is middling well as far as it goes . . . . but is that all?

Magnifying and applying come I,[26]
Outbidding at the start the old cautious hucksters,
The most they offer for mankind and eternity less than a spirt of
    my own seminal wet,
Taking myself the exact dimensions of Jehovah and laying them
    away,
Lithographing Kronos and Zeus his son, and Hercules his
    grandson,
Buying drafts of Osiris and Isis and Belus and Brahma and
    Adonai,
In my portfolio placing Manito loose, and Allah on a leaf, and the
    crucifix engraved,
With Odin, and the hideous-faced Mexitli, and all idols and images,

Honestly taking them all for what they are worth, and not a cent
more,
Admitting they were alive and did the work of their day,
Admitting they bore mites as for unfledged birds who have now to
rise and fly and sing for themselves,
Accepting the rough deific sketches to fill out better in
myself . . . . bestowing them freely on each man and woman
I see,
Discovering as much or more in a framer framing a house,
Putting higher claims for him there with his rolled-up sleeves,
driving the mallet and chisel;
Not objecting to special revelations . . . . considering a curl of
smoke or a hair on the back of my hand as curious as any
revelation;
Those ahold of fire-engines and hook-and-ladder ropes more to
me than the gods of the antique wars,
Minding their voices peal through the crash of destruction,
Their brawny limbs passing safe over charred laths . . . . their
white foreheads whole and unhurt out of the flames;
By the mechanic's wife with her babe at her nipple interceding
for every person born;
Three scythes at harvest whizzing in a row from three lusty angels
with shirts bagged out at their waists;
The snag-toothed hostler with red hair redeeming sins past and to
come,
Selling all he possesses and traveling on foot to fee lawyers for his
brother and sit by him while he is tried for forgery:
What was strewn in the amplest strewing the square rod about
me, and not filling the square rod then;
The bull and the bug never worshipped half enough,
Dung and dirt more admirable than was dreamed,
The supernatural of no account . . . . myself waiting my time to
be one of the supremes,
The day getting ready for me when I shall do as much good as the
best, and be as prodigious,
Guessing when I am it will not tickle me much to receive puffs
out of pulpit or print;
By my life-lumps! becoming already a creator!

Putting myself here and now to the ambushed womb of the shadows!

. . . . A call in the midst of the crowd,
My own voice, orotund sweeping and final.

Come my children,
Come my boys and girls, and my women and household and intimates,
Now the performer launches his nerve . . . . he has passed his prelude on the reeds within.

Easily written loosefingered chords! I feel the thrum of their climax and close.

My head evolves on my neck,
Music rolls, but not from the organ . . . . folks are around me, but they are no household of mine.

Ever the hard and unsunk ground,
Ever the eaters and drinkers . . . . ever the upward and downward sun . . . . ever the air and the ceaseless tides,
Ever myself and my neighbors, refreshing and wicked and real,
Ever the old inexplicable query . . . . ever that thorned thumb— that breath of itches and thirsts,
Ever the vexer's hoot! hoot! till we find where the sly one hides and bring him forth;
Ever love . . . . ever the sobbing liquid of life,
Ever the bandage under the chin . . . . ever the trestles of death.

Here and there with dimes on the eyes walking,[27]
To feed the greed of the belly the brains liberally spooning,
Tickets buying or taking or selling, but in to the feast never once going;
Many sweating and ploughing and thrashing, and then the chaff for payment receiving,
A few idly owning, and they the wheat continually claiming.

This is the city . . . . and I am one of the citizens;
Whatever interests the rest interests me . . . . politics, churches,
    newspapers, schools,
Benevolent societies, improvements, banks, tariffs, steamships,
    factories, markets,
Stocks and stores and real estate and personal estate.

They who piddle and patter here in collars and tailed coats . . . .
    I am aware who they are . . . . and that they are not worms or
    fleas,
I acknowledge the duplicates of myself under all the scrape-lipped
    and pipe-legged concealments.

The weakest and shallowest is deathless with me,
What I do and say the same waits for them,
Every thought that flounders in me the same flounders in them.

I know perfectly well my own egotism,
And know my omnivorous words, and cannot say any less,
And would fetch you whoever you are flush with myself.

My words are words of a questioning, and to indicate reality;
This printed and bound book . . . . but the printer and the
    printing-office boy?
The marriage estate and settlement . . . . but the body and mind
    of the bridegroom? also those of the bride?
The panorama of the sea . . . . but the sea itself?
The well-taken photographs . . . . but your wife or friend close and
    solid in your arms?
The fleet of ships of the line and all the modern
    improvements . . . . but the craft and pluck of the admiral?
The dishes and fare and furniture . . . . but the host and hostess,
    and the look out of their eyes?
The sky up there . . . . yet here or next door or across the way?
The saints and sages in history . . . . but you yourself?
Sermons and creeds and theology . . . . but the human brain, and
    what is called reason, and what is called love, and what is
    called life?

I do not despise you priests;
My faith is the greatest of faiths and the least of faiths,
Enclosing all worship ancient and modern, and all between
ancient and modern,
Believing I shall come again upon the earth after five thousand
years,
Waiting responses from oracles . . . . honoring the gods . . . .
saluting the sun,
Making a fetish of the first rock or stump . . . . powowing with
sticks in the circle of obis,*
Helping the lama or brahmin as he trims the lamps of the
idols,
Dancing yet through the streets in a phallic procession . . . . rapt
and austere in the woods, a gymnosophist,†
Drinking mead from the skull-cup . . . . to shasta and vedas
admirant . . . . minding the koran,‡
Walking the teokallis,§ spotted with gore from the stone and
knife—beating the serpent-skin drum;
Accepting the gospels, accepting him that was crucified, knowing
assuredly that he is divine,
To the mass kneeling—to the puritan's prayer rising—sitting
patiently in a pew,
Ranting and frothing in my insane crisis—waiting dead-like till
my spirit arouses me;
Looking forth on pavement and land, and outside of pavement
and land,
Belonging to the winders of the circuit of circuits.

One of that centripetal and centrifugal gang,
I turn and talk like a man leaving charges before a journey.

---

*Reference to African witchcraft practiced in the New World.
†Member of an ascetic ancient Hindu sect; gymnosophists did not wear clothing
and practiced meditation.
‡Shastras ("shastas" is a misspelling) and Vedas are sacred Hindu texts; the Koran
is the holy book of Muslims.
§Aztec temples.

Down-hearted doubters, dull and excluded,
Frivolous sullen moping angry affected disheartened atheistical,
I know every one of you, and know the unspoken interrogatories,
By experience I know them.

How the flukes splash!
How they contort rapid as lightning, with spasms and spouts of
    blood!

Be at peace bloody flukes of doubters and sullen mopers,
I take my place among you as much as among any;
The past is the push of you and me and all precisely the same,
And the day and night are for you and me and all,
And what is yet untried and afterward is for you and me and all.

I do not know what is untried and afterward,
But I know it is sure and alive and sufficient.

Each who passes is considered, and each who stops is considered,
    and not a single one can it fail.

It cannot fail the young man who died and was buried,
Nor the young woman who died and was put by his side,
Nor the little child that peeped in at the door and then drew back
    and was never seen again,
Nor the old man who has lived without purpose, and feels it with
    bitterness worse than gall,
Nor him in the poorhouse tubercled by rum and the bad disorder,
Nor the numberless slaughtered and wrecked . . . . nor the brutish
    koboo,* called the ordure of humanity,
Nor the sacs merely floating with open mouths for food to slip in,
Nor any thing in the earth, or down in the oldest graves of the earth,
Nor any thing in the myriads of spheres, nor one of the myriads of
    myriads that inhabit them,
Nor the present, nor the least wisp that is known.

---

*Slang for a native of Sumatra.

It is time to explain myself . . . . let us stand up.

What is known I strip away . . . . I launch all men and women
　　forward with me into the unknown.

The clock indicates the moment . . . . but what does eternity
　　indicate?
Eternity lies in bottomless reservoirs . . . . its buckets are rising
　　forever and ever,
They pour and they pour and they exhale away.

We have thus far exhausted trillions of winters and summers;
There are trillions ahead, and trillions ahead of them.

Births have brought us richness and variety,
And other births will bring us richness and variety.

I do not call one greater and one smaller,
That which fills its period and place is equal to any.

Were mankind murderous or jealous upon you my brother or my
　　sister?
I am sorry for you . . . . they are not murderous or jealous upon me;
All has been gentle with me . . . . I keep no account with
　　lamentation;
What have I to do with lamentation?

I am an acme of things accomplished, and I an encloser of things
　　to be.

My feet strike an apex of the apices of the stairs,
On every step bunches of ages, and larger bunches between the
　　steps,
All below duly traveled—and still I mount and mount.

Rise after rise bow the phantoms behind me,
Afar down I see the huge first Nothing, the vapor from the nostrils
　　of death,

I know I was even there . . . . I waited unseen and always,
And slept while God carried me through the lethargic mist,
And took my time . . . . and took no hurt from the fœtid
    carbon.[28]

Long I was hugged close . . . . long and long.

Immense have been the preparations for me,
Faithful and friendly the arms that have helped me.

Cycles ferried my cradle, rowing and rowing like cheerful
    boatmen;
For room to me stars kept aside in their own rings,
They sent influences to look after what was to hold me.

Before I was born out of my mother generations guided me,
My embryo has never been torpid . . . . nothing could overlay it;
For it the nebula cohered to an orb . . . . the long slow strata piled
    to rest it on . . . . vast vegetables gave it sustenance,
Monstrous sauroids transported it in their mouths and deposited it
    with care.

All forces have been steadily employed to complete and delight me,
Now I stand on this spot with my soul.

Span of youth! Ever-pushed elasticity! Manhood balanced and
    florid and full!

My lovers suffocate me!
Crowding my lips, and thick in the pores of my skin,
Jostling me through streets and public halls . . . . coming naked to
    me at night,
Crying by day Ahoy from the rocks of the river . . . . swinging and
    chirping over my head,
Calling my name from flowerbeds or vines or tangled underbrush,
Or while I swim in the bath . . . . or drink from the pump at the
    corner . . . . or the curtain is down at the opera . . . . or I
    glimpse at a woman's face in the railroad car;

Lighting on every moment of my life,
Bussing my body with soft and balsamic busses,
Noiselessly passing handfuls out of their hearts and giving them to
     be mine.

Old age superbly rising! Ineffable grace of dying days!

Every condition promulges not only itself . . . . it promulges what
     grows after and out of itself,
And the dark hush promulges as much as any.

I open my scuttle at night and see the far-sprinkled systems,
And all I see, multiplied as high as I can cipher, edge but the rim
     of the farther systems.

Wider and wider they spread, expanding and always expanding,
Outward and outward and forever outward.

My sun has his sun, and round him obediently wheels,
He joins with his partners a group of superior circuit,
And greater sets follow, making specks of the greatest inside them.

There is no stoppage, and never can be stoppage;
If I and you and the worlds and all beneath or upon their
     surfaces, and all the palpable life, were this moment reduced
     back to a pallid float, it would not avail in the long run,
We should surely bring up again where we now stand,
And as surely go as much farther, and then farther and farther.

A few quadrillions of eras, a few octillions of cubic leagues, do
     not hazard the span, or make it impatient,
They are but parts . . . . any thing is but a part.

See ever so far . . . . there is limitless space outside of that,
Count ever so much . . . . there is limitless time around that.

Our rendezvous is fitly appointed . . . . God will be there and wait
     till we come.

I know I have the best of time and space—and that I was never
    measured, and never will be measured.

I tramp a perpetual journey,
My signs are a rain-proof coat and good shoes and a staff cut from
    the woods;
No friend of mine takes his ease in my chair,
I have no chair, nor church nor philosophy;
I lead no man to a dinner-table or library or exchange,
But each man and each woman of you I lead upon a
    knoll,
My left hand hooks you round the waist,
My right hand points to landscapes of continents, and a plain
    public road.

Not I, not any one else can travel that road for you,
You must travel it for yourself.

It is not far . . . . it is within reach,
Perhaps you have been on it since you were born, and did not
    know,
Perhaps it is every where on water and on land.

Shoulder your duds, and I will mine, and let us hasten forth;
Wonderful cities and free nations we shall fetch as we go.

If you tire, give me both burdens, and rest the chuff of your hand
    on my hip,
And in due time you shall repay the same service to me;
For after we start we never lie by again.

This day before dawn I ascended a hill and looked at the crowded
    heaven,
And I said to my spirit, When we become the enfolders of those
    orbs and the pleasure and knowledge of every thing in them,
    shall we be filled and satisfied then?
And my spirit said No, we level that lift to pass and continue
    beyond.

You are also asking me questions, and I hear you;
I answer that I cannot answer . . . . you must find out for yourself.

Sit awhile wayfarer,
Here are biscuits to eat and here is milk to drink,
But as soon as you sleep and renew yourself in sweet clothes I will
    certainly kiss you with my goodbye kiss and open the gate for
    your egress hence.

Long enough have you dreamed contemptible dreams,
Now I wash the gum from your eyes,
You must habit yourself to the dazzle of the light and of every
    moment of your life.

Long have you timidly waded, holding a plank by the shore,
Now I will you to be a bold swimmer,
To jump off in the midst of the sea, and rise again and nod to me
    and shout, and laughingly dash with your hair.

I am the teacher of athletes,
He that by me spreads a wider breast than my own proves the
    width of my own,
He most honors my style who learns under it to destroy the
    teacher.

The boy I love, the same becomes a man not through derived
    power but in his own right,
Wicked, rather than virtuous out of conformity or fear,
Fond of his sweetheart, relishing well his steak,
Unrequited love or a slight cutting him worse than a wound cuts,
First rate to ride, to fight, to hit the bull's eye, to sail a skiff, to
    sing a song or play on the banjo,
Preferring scars and faces pitted with smallpox over all latherers
    and those that keep out of the sun.

I teach straying from me, yet who can stray from me?
I follow you whoever you are from the present hour;
My words itch at your ears till you understand them.

I do not say these things for a dollar, or to fill up the time while I
   wait for a boat;
It is you talking just as much as myself . . . . I act as the tongue
   of you,
It was tied in your mouth . . . . in mine it begins to be loosened.

I swear I will never mention love or death inside a house,
And I swear I never will translate myself at all, only to him or her
   who privately stays with me in the open air.

If you would understand me go to the heights or water-shore,
The nearest gnat is an explanation and a drop or the motion of
   waves a key,
The maul the oar and the handsaw second my words.

No shuttered room or school can commune with me,
But roughs and little children better than they.

The young mechanic is closest to me . . . . he knows me pretty well,
The woodman that takes his axe and jug with him shall take me
   with him all day,
The farmboy ploughing in the field feels good at the sound of my
   voice,
In vessels that sail my words must sail . . . . I go with fishermen
   and seamen, and love them,
My face rubs to the hunter's face when he lies down alone in his
   blanket,
The driver thinking of me does not mind the jolt of his wagon,
The young mother and old mother shall comprehend me,
The girl and the wife rest the needle a moment and forget where
   they are,
They and all would resume what I have told them.

I have said that the soul is not more than the body,
And I have said that the body is not more than the soul,
And nothing, not God, is greater to one than one's-self is,
And whoever walks a furlong without sympathy walks to his own
   funeral, dressed in his shroud,

And I or you pocketless of a dime may purchase the pick of the
    earth,
And to glance with an eye or show a bean in its pod confounds
    the learning of all times,
And there is no trade or employment but the young man
    following it may become a hero,
And there is no object so soft but it makes a hub for the wheeled
    universe,
And any man or woman shall stand cool and supercilious before
    a million universes.

And I call to mankind, Be not curious about God,
For I who am curious about each am not curious about God,
No array of terms can say how much I am at peace about God
    and about death.

I hear and behold God in every object, yet I understand God not
    in the least,
Nor do I understand who there can be more wonderful than myself.

Why should I wish to see God better than this day?
I see something of God each hour of the twenty-four, and each
    moment then,
In the faces of men and women I see God, and in my own face in
    the glass;
I find letters from God dropped in the street, and every one is
    signed by God's name,
And I leave them where they are, for I know that others will
    punctually come forever and ever.

And as to you death, and you bitter hug of mortality . . . . it is idle
    to try to alarm me.

To his work without flinching the accoucheur* comes,
I see the elderhand pressing receiving supporting,

---

*Midwife (French); two lines below, "exquisite flexible doors" have been interpreted
to mean the vaginal canal. See also the poem "Unfolded Out of the Folds" (p. 533).

I recline by the sills of the exquisite flexible doors . . . . and mark
    the outlet, and mark the relief and escape.

And as to you corpse I think you are good manure, but that does
    not offend me,
I smell the white roses sweetscented and growing,
I reach to the leafy lips . . . . I reach to the polished breasts of
    melons,

And as to you life, I reckon you are the leavings of many deaths,
No doubt I have died myself ten thousand times before.

I hear you whispering there O stars of heaven,
O suns . . . . O grass of graves . . . . O perpetual transfers and
    promotions . . . . if you do not say anything how can I say
    anything?

Of the turbid pool that lies in the autumn forest,
Of the moon that descends the steeps of the soughing twilight,
Toss, sparkles of day and dusk . . . . toss on the black stems that
    decay in the muck,
Toss to the moaning gibberish of the dry limbs.

I ascend from the moon . . . . I ascend from the night,
And perceive of the ghastly glitter the sunbeams reflected,
And debouch to the steady and central from the offspring great or
    small.

There is that in me . . . . I do not know what it is . . . . but I know
    it is in me.

Wrenched and sweaty . . . . calm and cool then my body becomes;
I sleep . . . . I sleep long.

I do not know it . . . . it is without name . . . . it is a word
    unsaid,
It is not in any dictionary or utterance or symbol.

Something it swings on more than the earth I swing on,
To it the creation is the friend whose embracing awakes me.

Perhaps I might tell more . . . . Outlines! I plead for my brothers
     and sisters.

Do you see O my brothers and sisters?
It is not chaos or death . . . . it is form and union and plan . . . . it
     is eternal life . . . . it is happiness.

The past and present wilt . . . . I have filled them and emptied
     them,
And proceed to fill my next fold of the future.

Listener up there! Here you . . . . what have you to confide to me?
Look in my face while I snuff the sidle of evening,
Talk honestly, for no one else hears you, and I stay only a minute
     longer.

Do I contradict myself?
Very well then . . . . I contradict myself;
I am large . . . . I contain multitudes.

I concentrate toward them that are nigh . . . . I wait on the door-
     slab.

Who has done his day's work and will soonest be through with his
     supper?
Who wishes to walk with me?

Will you speak before I am gone? Will you prove already too late?

The spotted hawk swoops by and accuses me . . . . he complains
     of my gab and my loitering.

I too am not a bit tamed . . . . I too am untranslatable,
I sound my barbaric yawp over the roofs of the world.[29]

The last scud of day holds back for me,
It flings my likeness after the rest and true as any on the shadowed
    wilds,
It coaxes me to the vapor and the dusk.

I depart as air . . . . I shake my white locks at the runaway sun,
I effuse my flesh in eddies and drift it in lacy jags.

I bequeath myself to the dirt to grow from the grass I love,
If you want me again look for me under your bootsoles.

You will hardly know who I am or what I mean,
But I shall be good health to you nevertheless,
And filter and fibre your blood.

Failing to fetch me at first keep encouraged,
Missing me one place search another,
I stop some where waiting for you[30]

LEAVES OF GRASS

[A Song for Occupations]

COME closer to me,
Push close my lovers and take the best I possess,
Yield closer and closer and give me the best you possess.

This is unfinished business with me . . . . how is it with you?
I was chilled with the cold types and cylinder and wet paper
    between us.

I pass so poorly with paper and types[31] . . . . I must pass with the
    contact of bodies and souls.

I do not thank you for liking me as I am, and liking the touch of
    me . . . . I know that it is good for you to do so.

Were all educations practical and ornamental well displayed out
    of me, what would it amount to?
Were I as the head teacher or charitable proprietor or wise
    statesman, what would it amount to?
Were I to you as the boss employing and paying you, would that
    satisfy you?

The learned and virtuous and benevolent, and the usual terms;
A man like me, and never the usual terms.

Neither a servant nor a master am I,
I take no sooner a large price than a small price . . . . I will have
    my own whoever enjoys me,
I will be even with you, and you shall be even with me.

If you are a workman or workwoman I stand as nigh as the
    nighest that works in the same shop,
If you bestow gifts on your brother or dearest friend, I demand as
    good as your brother or dearest friend,
If your lover or husband or wife is welcome by day or night, I
    must be personally as welcome;
If you have become degraded or ill, then I will become so for
    your sake;
If you remember your foolish and outlawed deeds, do you think I
    cannot remember my foolish and outlawed deeds?
If you carouse at the table I say I will carouse at the opposite side
    of the table;
If you meet some stranger in the street and love him or her, do I
    not often meet strangers in the street and love them?
If you see a good deal remarkable in me I see just as much
    remarkable in you.

Why what have you thought of yourself?
Is it you then that thought yourself less?

Is it you that thought the President greater than you? or the rich
    better off than you? or the educated wiser than you?

Because you are greasy or pimpled—or that you was once drunk,
    or a thief, or diseased, or rheumatic, or a prostitute—or are so
    now—or from frivolity or impotence—or that you are no
    scholar, and never saw your name in print . . . . do you give in
    that you are any less immortal?

Souls of men and women! it is not you I call unseen, unheard,
    untouchable and untouching;
It is not you I go argue pro and con about, and to settle whether
    you are alive or no;
I own publicly who you are, if nobody else owns . . . . and see and
    hear you, and what you give and take;
What is there you cannot give and take?

I see not merely that you are polite or whitefaced . . . . married or
    single . . . . citizens of old states or citizens of new states . . . .
    eminent in some profession . . . . a lady or gentleman in a
    parlor . . . . or dressed in the jail uniform . . . . or pulpit
    uniform,
Not only the free Utahan, Kansian, or Arkansian . . . . not only the
    free Cuban . . . not merely the slave . . . . not Mexican native,
    or Flatfoot, or negro from Africa,
Iroquois eating the warflesh—fishtearer in his lair of rocks and
    sand . . . . Esquimaux in the dark cold snowhouse . . . .
    Chinese with his transverse eyes . . . . Bedowee—or wandering
    nomad—or tabounschik* at the head of his droves,
Grown, half-grown, and babe—of this country and every country,
    indoors and outdoors I see . . . . and all else is behind or
    through them.

---

*Whitman takes liberties with spellings in this passage: *Esquimaux* is his plural of
"Eskimo"; *Bedowee* designates "Bedouin"; and *tabounschik* is a slang term for Middle Eastern nomads.

The wife—and she is not one jot less than the husband,
The daughter—and she is just as good as the son,
The mother—and she is every bit as much as the father.

Offspring of those not rich—boys apprenticed to trades,
Young fellows working on farms and old fellows working on farms;
The naive . . . . the simple and hardy . . . . he going to the polls
      to vote . . . . he who has a good time, and he who has a bad
      time;
Mechanics, southerners, new arrivals, sailors, mano'warsmen,
      merchantmen, coasters,
All these I see . . . . but nigher and farther the same I see;
None shall escape me, and none shall wish to escape me.

I bring what you much need, yet always have,
I bring not money or amours or dress or eating . . . . but I bring as
      good;
And send no agent or medium . . . . and offer no representative of
      value—but offer the value itself.

There is something that comes home to one now and perpetually,
It is not what is printed or preached or discussed . . . . it eludes
      discussion and print,
It is not to be put in a book . . . . it is not in this book,
It is for you whoever you are . . . . it is no farther from you than
      your hearing and sight are from you,
It is hinted by nearest and commonest and readiest . . . . it is not
      them, though it is endlessly provoked by them . . . . What is
      there ready and near you now?

You may read in many languages and read nothing about it;
You may read the President's message and read nothing about it
      there;
Nothing in the reports from the state department or treasury
      department . . . . or in the daily papers, or the weekly papers,
Or in the census returns or assessors' returns or prices current or
      any accounts of stock.

The sun and stars that float in the open air . . . . the appleshaped
    earth and we upon it . . . . surely the drift of them is
    something grand;
I do not know what it is except that it is grand, and that it is
    happiness,
And that the enclosing purport of us here is not a speculation,
    or bon-mot or reconnoissance,
And that it is not something which by luck may turn out well for
    us, and without luck must be a failure for us,
And not something which may yet be retracted in a certain
    contingency.

The light and shade—the curious sense of body and identity—the
    greed that with perfect complaisance devours all things—the
    endless pride and outstretching of man—unspeakable joys
    and sorrows,
The wonder every one sees in every one else he sees . . . . and the
    wonders that fill each minute of time forever and each acre of
    surface and space forever,
Have you reckoned them as mainly for a trade or farmwork? or for
    the profits of a store? or to achieve yourself a position? or to
    fill a gentleman's leisure or a lady's leisure?

Have you reckoned the landscape took substance and form that it
    might be painted in a picture?
Or men and women that they might be written of, and songs sung?
Or the attraction of gravity and the great laws and harmonious
    combinations and the fluids of the air as subjects for the
    savans?
Or the brown land and the blue sea for maps and charts?
Or the stars to be put in constellations and named fancy names?
Or that the growth of seeds is for agricultural tables or agriculture
    itself?

Old institutions . . . . these arts libraries legends collections—and
    the practice handed along in manufactures . . . . will we rate
    them so high?

Will we rate our prudence and business so high? .... I have no
     objection,
I rate them as high as the highest .... but a child born of a
     woman and man I rate beyond all rate.

We thought our Union grand and our Constitution grand;
I do not say they are not grand and good—for they are,
I am this day just as much in love with them as you,
But I am eternally in love with you and with all my fellows upon
     the earth.

We consider the bibles and religions divine .... I do not say they
     are not divine,
I say they have all grown out of you and may grow out of you
     still,
It is not they who give the life .... it is you who give the life;
Leaves are not more shed from the trees or trees from the earth
     than they are shed out of you.

The sum of all known value and respect I add up in you whoever
     you are;
The President is up there in the White House for you .... it is
     not you who are here for him,
The Secretaries act in their bureaus for you .... not you here for
     them,
The Congress convenes every December for you,
Laws, courts, the forming of states, the charters of cities, the going
     and coming of commerce and mails are all for you.

All doctrines, all politics and civilization exurge from you,
All sculpture and monuments and anything inscribed anywhere
     are tallied in you,
The gist of histories and statistics as far back as the records reach
     is in you this hour—and myths and tales the same;
If you were not breathing and walking here where would they all
     be?
The most renowned poems would be ashes .... orations and
     plays would be vacuums.

All architecture is what you do to it when you look upon it;
Did you think it was in the white or gray stone? or the lines of the
arches and cornices?

All music is what awakens from you when you are reminded by
the instruments,
It is not the violins and the cornets . . . . it is not the oboe nor the
beating drums—nor the notes of the baritone singer singing
his sweet romanza . . . . nor those of the men's chorus, nor
those of the women's chorus,
It is nearer and farther than they.

Will the whole come back then?
Can each see the signs of the best by a look in the lookingglass? Is
there nothing greater or more?
Does all sit there with you and here with me?

The old forever new things . . . . you foolish child! . . . . the closest
simplest things—this moment with you,
Your person and every particle that relates to your person,
The pulses of your brain waiting their chance and
encouragement at every deed or sight;
Anything you do in public by day, and anything you do in secret
betweendays,
What is called right and what is called wrong . . . . what you
behold or touch . . . . what causes your anger or wonder,
The anklechain of the slave, the bed of the bedhouse, the cards of
the gambler, the plates of the forger;
What is seen or learned in the street, or intuitively learned,
What is learned in the public school—spelling, reading, writing
and ciphering . . . . the blackboard and the teacher's diagrams:
The panes of the windows and all that appears through them . . . .
the going forth in the morning and the aimless spending of
the day;
(What is it that you made money? what is it that you got what you
wanted?)
The usual routine . . . . the workshop, factory, yard, office, store,
or desk;

The jaunt of hunting or fishing, or the life of hunting or fishing,
Pasturelife, foddering, milking and herding, and all the personnel
    and usages;
The plum-orchard and apple-orchard . . . . gardening . . . .
    seedlings, cuttings, flowers and vines,
Grains and manures . . marl, clay, loam . . the subsoil plough . . the
    shovel and pick and rake and hoe . . irrigation and draining;
The currycomb . . the horse-cloth . . the halter and bridle and
    bits . . the very wisps of straw,
The barn and barn-yard . . the bins and mangers . . the mows and
    racks:
Manufactures . . commerce . . engineering . . the building of
    cities, and every trade carried on there . . and the implements
    of every trade,
The anvil and tongs and hammer . . the axe and wedge . . the
    square and mitre and jointer and smoothingplane;
The plumbob and trowel and level . . the wall-scaffold, and the
    work of walls and ceilings . . or any mason-work:
The ship's compass . . the sailor's tarpaulin . . the stays and
    lanyards, and the ground-tackle for anchoring or mooring,
The sloop's tiller . . the pilot's wheel and bell . . the yacht or fish-
    smack . . the great gay-pennanted three-hundred-foot
    steamboat under full headway, with her proud fat breasts and
    her delicate swift-flashing paddles;
The trail and line and hooks and sinkers . . the seine, and hauling
    the seine;
Smallarms and rifles . . . . the powder and shot and caps and
    wadding . . . . the ordnance for war . . . . the carriages:
Everyday objects . . . . the housechairs, the carpet, the bed and
    the counterpane of the bed, and him or her sleeping at night,
    and the wind blowing, and the indefinite noises:
The snowstorm or rainstorm . . . . the tow-trowsers . . . . the lodge-
    hut in the woods, and the still-hunt:
City and country . . fireplace and candle . . gaslight and heater
    and aqueduct;
The message of the governor, mayor, or chief of police . . . . the
    dishes of breakfast or dinner or supper;

The bunkroom, the fire-engine, the string-team, and the car or
    truck behind;

The paper I write on or you write on . . and every word we
    write . . and every cross and twirl of the pen . . and the
    curious way we write what we think . . . . yet very faintly;

The directory, the detector, the ledger . . . . the books in ranks or
    the bookshelves . . . . the clock attached to the wall,

The ring on your finger . . the lady's wristlet . . the hammers
    of stonebreakers or coppersmiths . . the druggist's vials and
    jars;

The etui of surgical instruments, and the etui of oculist's or
    aurist's instruments, or dentist's instruments;

Glassblowing, grinding of wheat and corn . . casting, and what is
    cast . . tinroofing, shingledressing,

Shipcarpentering, flagging of sidewalks by flaggers . .
    dockbuilding, fishcuring, ferrying;

The pump, the piledriver, the great derrick . . the coalkiln and
    brickkiln,

Ironworks or whiteleadworks . . the sugarhouse . . steam-saws, and
    the great mills and factories;

The cottonbale . . the stevedore's hook . . the saw and buck of the
    sawyer . . the screen of the coalscreener . . the mould of the
    moulder . . the workingknife of the butcher;

The cylinder press . . the handpress . . the frisket and tympan . .
    the compositor's stick and rule,

The implements for daguerreotyping . . . . the tools of the rigger
    or grappler or sailmaker or blockmaker,

Goods of guttapercha or papiermache . . . . colors and
    brushes . . . . glaziers' implements,

The veneer and gluepot . . the confectioner's ornaments . . the
    decanter and glasses . . the shears and flatiron;

The awl and kneestrap . . the pint measure and quart measure . .
    the counter and stool . . the writingpen of quill or metal;

Billiards and tenpins . . . . the ladders and hanging ropes of the
    gymnasium, and the manly exercises;

The designs for wallpapers or oilcloths or carpets . . . . the fancies
    for goods for women . . . . the bookbinder's stamps;

Leatherdressing, coachmaking, boilermaking, ropetwisting,
    distilling, signpainting, limeburning, coopering,
    cottonpicking,
The walkingbeam of the steam-engine . . the throttle and
    governors, and the up and down rods,
Stavemachines and planingmachines . . . . the cart of the
    carman . . the omnibus . . the ponderous dray;
The snowplough and two engines pushing it . . . . the ride in the
    express train of only one car . . . . the swift go through a
    howling storm:
The bearhunt or coonhunt . . . . the bonfire of shavings in the
    open lot in the city . . the crowd of children watching;
The blows of the fighting-man . . the upper cut and one-two-three;
The shopwindows . . . . the coffins in the sexton's wareroom . . . .
    the fruit on the fruitstand . . . . the beef on the butcher's stall,
The bread and cakes in the bakery . . . . the white and red pork in
    the pork-store;
The milliner's ribbons . . the dressmaker's patterns . . . . the tea-
    table . . the homemade sweetmeats:
The column of wants in the one-cent paper . . the news by
    telegraph . . . . the amusements and operas and shows:
The cotton and woolen and linen you wear . . . . the money you
    make and spend;
Your room and bedroom . . . . your piano-forte . . . . the stove and
    cookpans,
The house you live in . . . . the rent . . . . the other tenants . . . .
    the deposit in the savings-bank . . . . the trade at the grocery,
The pay on Saturday night . . . . the going home, and the
    purchases;
In them the heft of the heaviest . . . . in them far more than you
    estimated, and far less also,
In them, not yourself . . . . you and your soul enclose all things,
    regardless of estimation,
In them your themes and hints and provokers . . if not, the whole
    earth has no themes or hints or provokers, and never had.

I do not affirm what you see beyond is futile . . . . I do not advise
    you to stop,

I do not say leadings you thought great are not great,
But I say that none lead to greater or sadder or happier than those
　　lead to.

Will you seek afar off? You surely come back at last,
In things best known to you finding the best or as good as the
　　best,
In folks nearest to you finding also the sweetest and strongest and
　　lovingest,
Happiness not in another place, but this place . . not for another
　　hour, but this hour,
Man in the first you see or touch . . . . always in your friend or
　　brother or nighest neighbor . . . . Woman in your mother or
　　lover or wife,[32]
And all else thus far known giving place to men and women.

When the psalm sings instead of the singer,
When the script preaches instead of the preacher,
When the pulpit descends and goes instead of the carver that
　　carved the supporting desk,
When the sacred vessels or the bits of the eucharist, or the lath
　　and plast, procreate as effectually as the young silversmiths or
　　bakers, or the masons in their overalls,
When a university course convinces like a slumbering woman
　　and child convince,
When the minted gold in the vault smiles like the
　　nightwatchman's daughter,
When warrantee deeds loafe in chairs opposite and are my
　　friendly companions,
I intend to reach them my hand and make as much of them as I
　　do of men and women.

LEAVES OF GRASS

[To Think of Time]

To think of Time . . . . to think through the retrospection,
To think of today . . and the ages continued henceforward.
Have you guessed you yourself would not continue? Have you
 dreaded those earth-beetles?
Have you feared the future would be nothing to you?

Is today nothing? Is the beginningless past nothing?
If the future is nothing they are just as surely nothing.

To think that the sun rose in the east . . . . that men and women
 were flexible and real and alive . . . . that every thing was real
 and alive;
To think that you and I did not see feel think nor bear our part,
To think that we are now here and bear our part.

Not a day passes . . not a minute or second without an
 accouchement;
Not a day passes . . not a minute or second without a corpse.

When the dull nights are over, and the dull days also,
When the soreness of lying so much in bed is over,
When the physician, after long putting off, gives the silent and
 terrible look for an answer,
When the children come hurried and weeping, and the brothers
 and sisters have been sent for,
When medicines stand unused on the shelf, and the camphor-
 smell has pervaded the rooms,
When the faithful hand of the living does not desert the hand of
 the dying,
When the twitching lips press lightly on the forehead of the
 dying,

When the breath ceases and the pulse of the heart ceases,
Then the corpse-limbs stretch on the bed, and the living look
    upon them,
They are palpable as the living are palpable.

The living look upon the corpse with their eyesight,
But without eyesight lingers a different living and looks curiously
    on the corpse.

To think that the rivers will come to flow, and the snow fall, and
    fruits ripen . . and act upon others as upon us now . . . . yet
    not act upon us;
To think of all these wonders of city and country . . and others
    taking great interest in them . . and we taking small interest
    in them.

To think how eager we are in building our houses,
To think others shall be just as eager . . and we quite indifferent.

I see one building the house that serves him a few years . . . . or
    seventy or eighty years at most;
I see one building the house that serves him longer than that.

Slowmoving and black lines creep over the whole earth . . . . they
    never cease . . . . they are the burial lines,
He that was President was buried, and he that is now President
    shall surely be buried.

Cold dash of waves at the ferrywharf,
Posh and ice in the river . . . . half-frozen mud in the streets,
A gray discouraged sky overhead . . . . the short last daylight of
    December,
A hearse and stages . . . . other vehicles give place,
The funeral of an old stagedriver . . . . the cortege mostly drivers.

Rapid the trot to the cemetery,
Duly rattles the deathbell . . . . the gate is passed . . . . the grave is
    halted at . . . . the living alight . . . . the hearse uncloses,

The coffin is lowered and settled . . . . the whip is laid on the
    coffin,
The earth is swiftly shovelled in . . . . a minute . . no one moves or
    speaks . . . . it is done,
He is decently put away . . . . is there anything more?

He was a goodfellow,
Freemouthed, quicktempered, not badlooking, able to take his
    own part,
Witty, sensitive to a slight, ready with life or death for a friend,
Fond of women, . . played some . . eat hearty and drank
    hearty,
Had known what it was to be flush . . grew lowspirited toward the
    last . . sickened . . was helped by a contribution,
Died aged forty-one years . . and that was his funeral.

Thumb extended or finger uplifted,
Apron, cape, gloves, strap . . . . wetweather clothes . . . . whip
    carefully chosen . . . . boss, spotter, starter, and hostler,
Somebody loafing on you, or you loafing on somebody . . . .
    headway . . . . man before and man behind,
Good day's work or bad day's work . . . . pet stock or mean
    stock . . . . first out or last out . . . . turning in at night,
To think that these are so much and so nigh to other drivers . . . .
    and he there takes no interest in them.

The markets, the government, the workingman's wages . . . . to
    think what account they are through our nights and days;
To think that other workingmen will make just as great account of
    them . . yet we make little or no account.

The vulgar and the refined . . . . what you call sin and what you
    call goodness . . to think how wide a difference;
To think the difference will still continue to others, yet we lie
    beyond the difference.

To think how much pleasure there is!
Have you pleasure from looking at the sky? Have you pleasure
    from poems?

Do you enjoy yourself in the city? or engaged in business? or
    planning a nomination and election? or with your wife and
    family?
Or with your mother and sisters? or in womanly housework? or
    the beautiful maternal cares?

These also flow onward to others . . . . you and I flow onward;
But in due time you and I shall take less interest in them.

Your farm and profits and crops . . . . to think how engrossed you are;
To think there will still be farms and profits and crops . . yet for
    you of what avail?

What will be will be well—for what is is well,
To take interest is well, and not to take interest shall be well.

The sky continues beautiful . . . . the pleasure of men with
    women shall never be sated . . nor the pleasure of women
    with men . . nor the pleasure from poems;
The domestic joys, the daily housework or business, the building
    of houses—they are not phantasms . . they have weight and
    form and location;
The farms and profits and crops . . the markets and wages and
    government . . they also are not phantasms;
The difference between sin and goodness is no apparition;
The earth is not an echo . . . . man and his life and all the things
    of his life are well-considered.

You are not thrown to the winds . . you gather certainly and safely
    around yourself,
Yourself! Yourself! Yourself forever and ever!

It is not to diffuse you that you were born of your mother and
    father—it is to identify you,
It is not that you should be undecided, but that you should be
    decided;
Something long preparing and formless is arrived and formed
    in you,
You are thenceforth secure, whatever comes or goes.

The threads that were spun are gathered . . . . the weft crosses the
    warp . . . . the pattern is systematic.

The preparations have every one been justified;
The orchestra have tuned their instruments sufficiently . . . . the
    baton has given the signal.

The guest that was coming . . . . he waited long for reasons . . . .
    he is now housed,
He is one of those who are beautiful and happy . . . . he is one of
    those that to look upon and be with is enough.

The law of the past cannot be eluded,
The law of the present and future cannot be eluded,
The law of the living cannot be eluded . . . . it is eternal,
The law of promotion and transformation cannot be eluded,
The law of heroes and good-doers cannot be eluded,
The law of drunkards and informers and mean persons cannot be
    eluded.

Slowmoving and black lines go ceaselessly over the earth,
Northerner goes carried and southerner goes carried . . . and they
    on the Atlantic side and they on the Pacific, and they
    between, and all through the Mississippi country . . . . and all
    over the earth.

The great masters and kosmos are well as they go . . . . the heroes
    and good-doers are well,
The known leaders and inventors and the rich owners and pious
    and distinguished may be well,
But there is more account than that . . . . there is strict account
    of all.

The interminable hordes of the ignorant and wicked are not
    nothing,
The barbarians of Africa and Asia are not nothing,
The common people of Europe are not nothing . . . . the
    American aborigines are not nothing,
A zambo or a foreheadless Crowfoot or a Camanche is not nothing,

The infected in the immigrant hospital are not nothing . . . . the
    murderer or mean person is not nothing,
The perpetual succession of shallow people are not nothing as
    they go,
The prostitute is not nothing . . . . the mocker of religion is not
    nothing as he goes.

I shall go with the rest . . . . we have satisfaction:
I have dreamed that we are not to be changed so much . . . . nor
    the law of us changed;
I have dreamed that heroes and good-doers shall be under the
    present and past law,
And that murderers and drunkards and liars shall be under the
    present and past law;
For I have dreamed that the law they are under now is enough.

And I have dreamed that the satisfaction is not so much
    changed . . . . and that there is no life without satisfaction;
What is the earth? what are body and soul without satisfaction?

I shall go with the rest,
We cannot be stopped at a given point . . . . that is no
    satisfaction;
To show us a good thing or a few good things for a space of
    time—that is no satisfaction;
We must have the indestructible breed of the best, regardless of
    time.

If otherwise, all these things came but to ashes of dung;
If maggots and rats ended us, then suspicion and treachery and
    death.

Do you suspect death? If I were to suspect death I should die
    now,
Do you think I could walk pleasantly and well-suited toward
    annihilation?

Pleasantly and well-suited I walk,
Whither I walk I cannot define, but I know it is good,

The whole universe indicates that it is good,
The past and the present indicate that it is good.

How beautiful and perfect are the animals! How perfect is my
　　soul!
How perfect the earth, and the minutest thing upon it!
What is called good is perfect, and what is called sin is just as
　　perfect;
The vegetables and minerals are all perfect . . and the
　　imponderable fluids are perfect;
Slowly and surely they have passed on to this, and slowly and
　　surely they will yet pass on.

O my soul! if I realize you I have satisfaction,
Animals and vegetables! if I realize you I have satisfaction,
Laws of the earth and air! if I realize you I have satisfaction.

I cannot define my satisfaction . . yet it is so,
I cannot define my life . . yet it is so.

I swear I see now that every thing has an eternal soul!
The trees have, rooted in the ground . . . . the weeds of the sea
　　have . . . . the animals.

I swear I think there is nothing but immortality!
That the exquisite scheme is for it, and the nebulous float is for it,
　　and the cohering is for it,
And all preparation is for it . . and identity is for it . . and life and
　　death are for it.

LEAVES OF GRASS

[The Sleepers]

I WANDER all night in my vision,
Stepping with light feet . . . . swiftly and noiselessly stepping and
    stopping,
Bending with open eyes over the shut eyes of sleepers;
Wandering and confused . . . . lost to myself . . . . ill-assorted . . . .
    contradictory,
Pausing and gazing and bending and stopping.

How solemn they look there, stretched and still;
How quiet they breathe, the little children in their cradles.

The wretched features of ennuyees, the white features of corpses,
    the livid faces of drunkards, the sick-gray faces of onanists,*
The gashed bodies on battlefields, the insane in their strong-
    doored rooms, the sacred idiots,
The newborn emerging from gates and the dying emerging from
    gates,
The night pervades them and enfolds them.

The married couple sleep calmly in their bed, he with his palm
    on the hip of the wife, and she with her palm on the hip of
    the husband,
The sisters sleep lovingly side by side in their bed,
The men sleep lovingly side by side in theirs,
And the mother sleeps with her little child carefully wrapped.

The blind sleep, and the deaf and dumb sleep,
The prisoner sleeps well in the prison . . . . the runaway son sleeps,

---

*Masturbators (from the biblical tale of Onan in Genesis 38).

The murderer that is to be hung next day . . . . how does he sleep?
And the murdered person . . . . how does he sleep?

The female that loves unrequited sleeps,
And the male that loves unrequited sleeps;
The head of the moneymaker that plotted all day sleeps,
And the enraged and treacherous dispositions sleep.

I stand with drooping eyes by the worstsuffering and restless,
I pass my hands soothingly to and fro a few inches from them;
The restless sink in their beds . . . . they fitfully sleep.

The earth recedes from me into the night,
I saw that it was beautiful . . . . and I see that what is not the earth
    is beautiful.

I go from bedside to bedside . . . . I sleep close with the other
    sleepers, each in turn;
I dream in my dream all the dreams of the other dreamers,
And I become the other dreamers.

I am a dance . . . . Play up there! the fit is whirling me fast.

I am the everlaughing . . . . it is new moon and twilight,
I see the hiding of douceurs* . . . . I see nimble ghosts whichever
    way I look,
Cache† and cache again deep in the ground and sea, and where it
    is neither ground or sea.

Well do they do their jobs, those journeymen divine,
Only from me can they hide nothing and would not if they
    could;
I reckon I am their boss, and they make me a pet besides,
And surround me, and lead me and run ahead when I walk,

---

*Plural of "sweetness" (French).
†Hiding place.

And lift their cunning covers and signify me with stretched arms,
    and resume the way;
Onward we move, a gay gang of blackguards with mirthshouting
    music and wildflapping pennants of joy.

I am the actor and the actress[33] . . . . the voter . . the politician,
The emigrant and the exile . . the criminal that stood in the box,
He who has been famous, and he who shall be famous after today,
The stammerer . . . . the wellformed person . . the wasted or
    feeble person.

I am she who adorned herself and folded her hair expectantly,
My truant lover has come and it is dark.

Double yourself and receive me darkness,
Receive me and my lover too . . . . he will not let me go with-
    out him.

I roll myself upon you as upon a bed . . . . I resign myself to the
    dusk.

He whom I call answers me and takes the place of my lover,
He rises with me silently from the bed.

Darkness you are gentler than my lover . . . . his flesh was sweaty
    and panting,
I feel the hot moisture yet that he left me.

My hands are spread forth . . I pass them in all directions,
I would sound up the shadowy shore to which you are journeying.

Be careful, darkness . . . . already, what was it touched me?
I thought my lover had gone . . . . else darkness and he are one,
I hear the heart-beat . . . . I follow . . I fade away.

O hotcheeked and blushing! O foolish hectic!
O for pity's sake, no one must see me now! . . . . my clothes were
    stolen while I was abed,
Now I am thrust forth, where shall I run?

Pier that I saw dimly last night when I looked from the windows,
Pier out from the main, let me catch myself with you and
    stay . . . . I will not chafe you;
I feel ashamed to go naked about the world,
And am curious to know where my feet stand . . . . and what is
    this flooding me, childhood or manhood . . . . and the hunger
    that crosses the bridge between.

The cloth laps a first sweet eating and drinking,
Laps life-swelling yolks . . . . laps ear of rose-corn, milky and just
    ripened:
The white teeth stay, and the boss-tooth advances in darkness,
And liquor is spilled on lips and bosoms by touching glasses, and
    the best liquor afterward.[34]

I descend my western course . . . . my sinews are flaccid,
Perfume and youth course through me, and I am their wake.

It is my face yellow and wrinkled instead of the old woman's,
I sit low in a strawbottom chair and carefully darn my grandson's
    stockings.

It is I too . . . . the sleepless widow looking out on the winter
    midnight,
I see the sparkles of starshine on the icy and pallid earth.

A shroud I see—and I am the shroud . . . . I wrap a body and lie
    in the coffin;
It is dark here underground . . . . it is not evil or pain here . . . . it
    is blank here, for reasons.

It seems to me that everything in the light and air ought to be
    happy;
Whoever is not in his coffin and the dark grave, let him know he
    has enough.

I see a beautiful gigantic swimmer swimming naked through the
    eddies of the sea,[35]

His brown hair lies close and even to his head . . . . he strikes out
    with courageous arms . . . . he urges himself with his legs.

I see his white body . . . . I see his undaunted eyes;
I hate the swift-running eddies that would dash him headforemost
    on the rocks.

What are you doing you ruffianly red-trickled waves?
Will you kill the courageous giant? Will you kill him in the prime
    of his middle age?

Steady and long he struggles;
He is baffled and banged and bruised . . . . he holds out while his
    strength holds out,
The slapping eddies are spotted with his blood . . . . they bear him
    away . . . . they roll him and swing him and turn him:
His beautiful body is borne in the circling eddies . . . . it is
    continually bruised on rocks,
Swiftly and out of sight is borne the brave corpse.

I turn but do not extricate myself;
Confused . . . . a pastreading . . . . another, but with darkness yet.

The beach is cut by the razory ice-wind . . . . the wreck-guns
    sounds,
The tempest lulls and the moon comes floundering through the
    drifts.

I look where the ship helplessly heads end on . . . . I hear the
    burst as she strikes . . I hear the howls of dismay . . . . they
    grow fainter and fainter.

I cannot aid with my wringing fingers;
I can but rush to the surf and let it drench me and freeze
    upon me.

I search with the crowd . . . . not one of the company is washed to
    us alive;

In the morning I help pick up the dead and lay them in rows in
    a barn.

Now of the old war-days[36] . . the defeat at Brooklyn;
Washington stands inside the lines . . he stands on the entrenched
    hills amid a crowd of officers,
His face is cold and damp . . . . he cannot repress the weeping
    drops . . . . he lifts the glass perpetually to his eyes . . . . the
    color is blanched from his cheeks,
He sees the slaughter of the southern braves confided to him by
    their parents.

The same at last and at last when peace is declared,
He stands in the room of the old tavern . . . . the wellbeloved
    soldiers all pass through.

The officers speechless and slow draw near in their turns,
The chief encircles their necks with his arm and kisses them on
    the cheek,
He kisses lightly the wet cheeks one after another . . . . he shakes
    hands and bids goodbye to the army.

Now I tell what my mother told me today as we sat at dinner
    together,[37]
Of when she was a nearly grown girl living home with her parents
    on the old homestead.

A red squaw came one breakfastime to the old homestead,
On her back she carried a bundle of rushes for rushbottoming
    chairs;
Her hair straight shiny coarse black and profuse halfenveloped
    her face,
Her step was free and elastic . . . . her voice sounded exquisitely as
    she spoke.

My mother looked in delight and amazement at the stranger,
She looked at the beauty of her tallborne face and full and pliant
    limbs,

The more she looked upon her she loved her,
Never before had she seen such wonderful beauty and purity;
She made her sit on a bench by the jamb of the fireplace . . . . she
　　cooked food for her,
She had no work to give her but she gave her remembrance and
　　fondness.

The red squaw staid all the forenoon, and toward the middle of
　　the afternoon she went away;
O my mother was loth to have her go away,
All the week she thought of her . . . . she watched for her many a
　　month,
She remembered her many a winter and many a summer,
But the red squaw never came nor was heard of there again.

Now Lucifer was not dead . . . . or if he was I am his sorrowful
　　terrible heir;[38]
I have been wronged . . . . I am oppressed . . . . I hate him that
　　oppresses me,
I will either destroy him, or he shall release me.

Damn him! how he does defile me,
How he informs against my brother and sister and takes pay for
　　their blood,
How he laughs when I look down the bend after the steamboat
　　that carries away my woman.

Now the vast dusk bulk that is the whale's bulk . . . . it seems
　　mine,
Warily, sportsman! though I lie so sleepy and sluggish, my tap is
　　death.

A show of the summer softness . . . . a contact of something
　　unseen . . . . an amour of the light and air;
I am jealous and overwhelmed with friendliness,
And will go gallivant with the light and the air myself,
And have an unseen something to be in contact with them
　　also.

O love and summer! you are in the dreams and in me,
Autumn and winter are in the dreams . . . . the farmer goes with
   his thrift,
The droves and crops increase . . . . the barns are wellfilled.

Elements merge in the night . . . . ships make tacks in
   the dreams . . . . the sailor sails . . . . the exile returns
   home,
The fugitive returns unharmed . . . . the immigrant is back
   beyond months and years;
The poor Irishman lives in the simple house of his childhood,
   with the wellknown neighbors and faces,
They warmly welcome him . . . . he is barefoot again . . . . he
   forgets he is welloff;
The Dutchman voyages home, and the Scotchman and
   Welchman voyage home . . and the native of the
   Mediterranean voyages home;
To every port of England and France and Spain enter wellfilled
   ships;
The Swiss foots it toward his hills . . . . the Prussian goes his way,
   and the Hungarian his way, and the Pole goes his way,
The Swede returns, and the Dane and Norwegian return.

The homeward bound and the outward bound,
The beautiful lost swimmer, the ennuyee, the onanist, the female
   that loves unrequited, the moneymaker,
The actor and actress . . those through with their parts and those
   waiting to commence,
The affectionate boy, the husband and wife, the voter, the
   nominee that is chosen and the nominee that has
   failed,
The great already known, and the great anytime after to day,
The stammerer, the sick, the perfectformed, the homely,
The criminal that stood in the box, the judge that sat and
   sentenced him, the fluent lawyers, the jury, the audience,
The laugher and weeper, the dancer, the midnight widow, the red
   squaw,

The consumptive, the erysipalite,* the idiot, he that is wronged,
The antipodes, and every one between this and them in the dark,
I swear they are averaged now . . . . one is no better than the other,
The night and sleep have likened them and restored them.

I swear they are all beautiful,
Every one that sleeps is beautiful . . . . every thing in the dim
      night is beautiful,
The wildest and bloodiest is over and all is peace.

Peace is always beautiful,
The myth of heaven indicates peace and night.

The myth of heaven indicates the soul;
The soul is always beautiful . . . . it appears more or it appears
      less . . . . it comes or lags behind,
It comes from its embowered garden and looks pleasantly on itself
      and encloses the world;
Perfect and clean the genitals previously jetting, and perfect and
      clean the womb cohering,
The head wellgrown and proportioned and plumb, and the
      bowels and joints proportioned and plumb.

The soul is always beautiful,
The universe is duly in order . . . . every thing is in its place,
What is arrived is in its place, and what waits is in its place;
The twisted skull waits . . . . the watery or rotten blood waits,
The child of the glutton or venerealee waits long, and the child
      of the drunkard waits long, and the drunkard himself waits
      long,
The sleepers that lived and died wait . . . . the far advanced are to go
      on in their turns, and the far behind are to go on in their turns,
The diverse shall be no less diverse, but they shall flow and
      unite . . . . they unite now.

---

*Victim of a skin disease called erysipelas.

The sleepers are very beautiful as they lie unclothed,
They flow hand in hand over the whole earth from east to west as
    they lie unclothed;
The Asiatic and African are hand in hand . . the European and
    American are hand in hand,
Learned and unlearned are hand in hand . . and male and female
    are hand in hand;
The bare arm of the girl crosses the bare breast of her lover . . . .
    they press close without lust . . . . his lips press her neck,
The father holds his grown or ungrown son in his arms with
    measureless love . . . . and the son holds the father in his arms
    with measureless love,
The white hair of the mother shines on the white wrist of the
    daughter,
The breath of the boy goes with the breath of the man . . . . friend
    is inarmed by friend,
The scholar kisses the teacher and the teacher kisses the
    scholar . . . . the wronged is made right,
The call of the slave is one with the master's call . . and the
    master salutes the slave,
The felon steps forth from the prison . . . . the insane
    becomes sane . . . . the suffering of sick persons is relieved,
The sweatings and fevers stop . . the throat that was unsound is
    sound . . the lungs of the consumptive are resumed . . the
    poor distressed head is free,
The joints of the rheumatic move as smoothly as ever, and
    smoother than ever,
Stiflings and passages open . . . . the paralysed become supple,
The swelled and convulsed and congested awake to themselves in
    condition,
They pass the invigoration of the night and the chemistry of the
    night and awake.

I too pass from the night;
I stay awhile away O night, but I return to you again and love you;
Why should I be afraid to trust myself to you?
I am not afraid . . . . I have been well brought forward by you;
I love the rich running day, but I do not desert her in whom I lay
    so long:

I know not how I came of you, and I know not where I go with
    you . . . . but I know I came well and shall go well.

I will stop only a time with the night . . . . and rise betimes.

I will duly pass the day O my mother and duly return to you;[39]
Not you will yield forth the dawn again more surely than you will
    yield forth me again,
Not the womb yields the babe in its time more surely than I shall
    be yielded from you in my time.

LEAVES OF GRASS

[I Sing the Body Electric]

THE bodies of men and women engirth me, and I engirth
    them,
They will not let me off nor I them till I go with them and
    respond to them and love them.

Was it dreamed whether those who corrupted their own live
    bodies could conceal themselves?
And whether those who defiled the living were as bad as they who
    defiled the dead?[40]

The expression of the body of man or woman balks account,
The male is perfect and that of the female is perfect.

The expression of a wellmade man appears not only in his face,
It is in his limbs and joints also . . . . it is curiously in the joints of
    his hips and wrists,
It is in his walk . . the carriage of his neck . . the flex of his waist
    and knees . . . . dress does not hide him,
The strong sweet supple quality he has strikes through the cotton
    and flannel;

To see him pass conveys as much as the best poem . . perhaps
more,
You linger to see his back and the back of his neck and
shoulderside.

The sprawl and fulness of babes . . . . the bosoms and heads of
women . . . . the folds of their dress . . . . their style as we pass
in the street . . . . the contour of their shape downwards;
The swimmer naked in the swimmingbath . . seen as he swims
through the salt transparent greenshine, or lies on his back
and rolls silently with the heave of the water;
Framers bare-armed framing a house . . hoisting the beams in
their places . . or using the mallet and mortising-chisel,
The bending forward and backward of rowers in rowboats . . . . the
horseman in his saddle;
Girls and mothers and housekeepers in all their exquisite offices,
The group of laborers seated at noontime with their open dinner-
kettles, and their wives waiting,
The female soothing a child . . . . the farmer's daughter in the
garden or cowyard,
The woodman rapidly swinging his axe in the woods . . . . the
young fellow hoeing corn . . . . the sleighdriver guiding his six
horses through the crowd,
The wrestle of wrestlers . . . . two apprentice-boys, quite grown,
lusty, goodnatured, nativeborn, out on the vacant lot at
sundown after work,
The coats vests and caps thrown down . . the embrace of love and
resistance,
The upperhold and underhold—the hair rumpled over and
blinding the eyes;
The march of firemen in their own costumes—the play of the
masculine muscle through cleansetting trowsers and
waistbands,
The slow return from the fire . . . . the pause when the bell strikes
suddenly again—the listening on the alert,
The natural perfect and varied attitudes . . . . the bent head, the
curved neck, the counting:
Suchlike I love . . . . I loosen myself and pass freely . . . . and am
at the mother's breast with the little child,

And swim with the swimmer, and wrestle with wrestlers, and march
    in line with the firemen, and pause and listen and count.

I knew a man . . . . he was a common farmer . . . . he was the
    father of five sons . . . . and in them were the fathers of
    sons . . . . and in them were the fathers of sons.

This man was a wonderful vigor and calmness and beauty of
    person;
The shape of his head, the richness and breadth of his
    manners, the pale yellow and white of his hair and beard,
    the immeasurable meaning of his black eyes,
These I used to go and visit him to see . . . . He was wise also,
He was six feet tall . . . . he was over eighty years old . . . . his sons
    were massive clean bearded tanfaced and handsome,
They and his daughters loved him . . . all who saw him loved
    him . . . they did not love him by allowance . . . they loved
    him with personal love;
He drank water only . . . . the blood showed like scarlet through
    the clear brown skin of his face;
He was a frequent gunner and fisher . . . he sailed his boat
    himself . . . he had a fine one presented to him by a
    shipjoiner . . . . he had fowling pieces, presented to him by
    men that loved him;
When he went with his five sons and many grandsons to hunt or
    fish you would pick him out as the most beautiful and
    vigorous of the gang,
You would wish long and long to be with him . . . . you would
    wish to sit by him in the boat that you and he might touch
    each other.

I have perceived that to be with those I like is enough,
To stop in company with the rest at evening is enough,
To be surrounded by beautiful curious breathing laughing flesh is
    enough,
To pass among them . . to touch any one . . . . to rest my arm ever
    so lightly round his or her neck for a moment . . . . what is
    this then?
I do not ask any more delight . . . . I swim in it as in a sea.

There is something in staying close to men and women and
    looking on them and in the contact and odor of them that
    pleases the soul well,
All things please the soul, but these please the soul well.

This is the female form,
A divine nimbus exhales from it from head to foot,
It attracts with fierce undeniable attraction,
I am drawn by its breath as if I were no more than a helpless
    vapor . . . . all falls aside but myself and it,
Books, art, religion, time . . the visible and solid earth . . the
    atmosphere and the fringed clouds . . what was expected of
    heaven or feared of hell are now consumed,
Mad filaments, ungovernable shoots play out of it . . the response
    likewise ungovernable,
Hair, bosom, hips, bend of legs, negligent falling hands—all
    diffused . . . . mine too diffused,
Ebb stung by the flow, and flow stung by the ebb . . . . loveflesh
    swelling and deliciously aching,
Limitless limpid jets of love hot and enormous . . . . quivering
    jelly of love . . . . white-blow and delirious juice,
Bridegroom-night of love working surely and softly into the
    prostrate dawn,
Undulating into the willing and yielding day,
Lost in the cleave of the clasping and sweetfleshed day.

This is the nucleus . . . after the child is born of woman the man
    is born of woman,
This is the bath of birth . . . this is the merge of small and large
    and the outlet again.

Be not ashamed women . . your privilege encloses the rest . . it is
    the exit of the rest,
You are the gates of the body and you are the gates of the soul.

The female contains all qualities and tempers them . . . . she is in
    her place . . . . she moves with perfect balance,

She is all things duly veiled . . . . she is both passive and
    active . . . . she is to conceive daughters as well as sons and
    sons as well as daughters.

As I see my soul reflected in nature . . . . as I see through a mist
    one with inexpressible completeness and beauty . . . . see the
    bent head and arms folded over the breast . . . . the female
    I see,
I see the bearer of the great fruit which is immortality . . . . the
    good thereof is not tasted by roues, and never can be.

The male is not less the soul, nor more . . . . he too is in his place,
He too is all qualities . . . . he is action and power . . . . the flush of
    the known universe is in him,
Scorn becomes him well and appetite and defiance become him
    well,
The fiercest largest passions . . bliss that is utmost and sorrow that
    is utmost become him well . . . . pride is for him,
The fullspread pride of man is calming and excellent to the
    soul;
Knowledge becomes him . . . . he likes it always . . . . he brings
    everything to the test of himself,
Whatever the survey . . whatever the sea and the sail, he strikes
    soundings at last only here,
Where else does he strike soundings except here?

The man's body is sacred and the woman's body is sacred . . . . it
    is no matter who,
Is it a slave? Is it one of the dullfaced immigrants just landed on
    the wharf?

Each belongs here or anywhere just as much as the welloff . . . .
    just as much as you,
Each has his or her place in the procession.

All is a procession,
The universe is a procession with measured and beautiful motion.

Do you know so much that you call the slave or the dullfaced
    ignorant?
Do you suppose you have a right to a good sight . . . and he or she
    has no right to a sight?
Do you think matter has cohered together from its diffused
    float, and the soil is on the surface and water runs
    and vegetation sprouts for you . . . and not for him
    and her?

A slave at auction!
I help the auctioneer . . . . the sloven does not half know his business.

Gentlemen look on this curious creature,
Whatever the bids of the bidders they cannot be high enough for
    him,
For him the globe lay preparing quintillions of years without one
    animal or plant,
For him the revolving cycles truly and steadily rolled.

In that head the allbaffling brain,
In it and below it the making of the attributes of heroes.

Examine these limbs, red black or white . . . . they are very cunning
    in tendon and nerve;
They shall be stript that you may see them.

Exquisite senses, lifelit eyes, pluck, volition,
Flakes of breastmuscle, pliant backbone and neck, flesh not
    flabby, goodsized arms and legs,
And wonders within there yet.

Within there runs his blood . . . . the same old blood . . the same
    red running blood;
There swells and jets his heart . . . . There all passions and
    desires . . all reachings and aspirations:
Do you think they are not there because they are not expressed in
    parlors and lecture-rooms?

This is not only one man . . . . he is the father of those who shall
    be fathers in their turns,
In him the start of populous states and rich republics,
Of him countless immortal lives with countless embodiments and
    enjoyments.

How do you know who shall come from the offspring of his
    offspring through the centuries?
Who might you find you have come from yourself if you could
    trace back through the centuries?

A woman at auction,
She too is not only herself . . . . she is the teeming mother of
    mothers,
She is the bearer of them that shall grow and be mates to the
    mothers.

Her daughters or their daughters' daughters . . who knows who
    shall mate with them?
Who knows through the centuries what heroes may come from
    them?

In them and of them natal love . . . . in them the divine
    mystery . . . . the same old beautiful mystery.

Have you ever loved a woman?
Your mother . . . . is she living? . . . . Have you been much with
    her? and has she been much with you?
Do you not see that these are exactly the same to all in all nations
    and times all over the earth?

If life and the soul are sacred the human body is sacred;
And the glory and sweet of a man is the token of manhood
    untainted,
And in man or woman a clean strong firmfibred body is beautiful
    as the most beautiful face.

Have you seen the fool that corrupted his own live body? or the
    fool that corrupted her own live body?
For they do not conceal themselves, and cannot conceal
    themselves.

Who degrades or defiles the living human body is cursed,
Who degrades or defiles the body of the dead is not more
    cursed.

LEAVES OF GRASS

[Faces]

SAUNTERING the pavement or riding the country byroads here
    then are faces,
Faces of friendship, precision, caution, sauvity, ideality,
The spiritual prescient face, the always welcome common
    benevolent face,
The face of the singing of music, the grand faces of natural
    lawyers and judges broad at the backtop,
The faces of hunters and fishers, bulged at the brows . . . . the
    shaved blanched faces of orthodox citizens,
The pure extravagant yearning questioning artist's face,
The welcome ugly face of some beautiful soul . . . . the handsome
    detested or despised face,
The sacred faces of infants . . . . the illuminated face of the
    mother of many children,
The face of an amour . . . . the face of veneration,
The face as of a dream . . . . the face of an immobile rock,
The face withdrawn of its good and bad . . a castrated
    face,
A wild hawk . . his wings clipped by the clipper,
A stallion that yielded at last to the thongs and knife of the
    gelder.

Sauntering the pavement or crossing the ceaseless ferry, here then
    are faces;
I see them and complain not and am content with all.

Do you suppose I could be content with all if I thought them
    their own finale?
This now is too lamentable a face for a man;
Some abject louse asking leave to be . . cringing for it,
Some milknosed maggot blessing what lets it wrig to its hole.

This face is a dog's snout sniffing for garbage;
Snakes nest in that mouth . . I hear the sibilant threat.

This face is a haze more chill than the arctic sea,
Its sleepy and wobbling icebergs crunch as they go.

This is a face of bitter herbs . . . . this an emetic . . . . they need no
    label,
And more of the drugshelf . . laudanum, caoutchouc, or hog's
    lard.[41]

This face is an epilepsy advertising and doing business . . . . its
    wordless tongue gives out the unearthly cry,
Its veins down the neck distend . . . . its eyes roll till they show
    nothing but their whites,
Its teeth grit . . the palms of the hands are cut by the turned-in
    nails,
The man falls struggling and foaming to the ground while he
    speculates well.

This face is bitten by vermin and worms,
And this is some murderer's knife with a halfpulled scabbard.

This face owes to the sexton his dismalest fee,
An unceasing deathbell tolls there.

Those are really men! . . . . the bosses and tufts of the great round
    globe!

Features of my equals, would you trick me with your creased and
     cadaverous march?
Well then you cannot trick me.

I see your rounded never-erased flow,
I see neath the rims of your haggard and mean disguises.

Splay and twist as you like . . . . poke with the tangling fores of
     fishes or rats,
You'll be unmuzzled . . . . you certainly will.

I saw the face of the most smeared and slobbering idiot they had
     at the asylum,
And I knew for my consolation what they knew not;
I knew of the agents that emptied and broke my brother,[42]
The same wait to clear the rubbish from the fallen tenement;
And I shall look again in a score or two of ages,
And I shall meet the real landlord perfect and unharmed, every
     inch as good as myself.

The Lord advances and yet advances:
Always the shadow in front . . . . always the reached hand bringing
     up the laggards.

Out of this face emerge banners and horses . . . . O superb! I
     see what is coming,
I see the high pioneercaps . . . . I see the staves of runners clearing
     the way,
I hear victorious drums.

This face is a lifeboat;
This is the face commanding and bearded . . . . it asks no odds of
     the rest;
This face is flavored fruit ready for eating;
This face of a healthy honest boy is the programme of all good.

These faces bear testimony slumbering or awake,
They show their descent from the Master himself.

Off the word I have spoken I except not one . . . . red white or
    black, all are deific,
In each house is the ovum . . . . it comes forth after a thousand
    years.

Spots or cracks at the windows do not disturb me,
Tall and sufficient stand behind and make signs to me;
I read the promise and patiently wait.

This is a fullgrown lily's face,
She speaks to the limber-hip'd man near the garden pickets,
Come here, she blushingly cries . . . . Come nigh to me limber-
    hip'd man and give me your finger and thumb,
Stand at my side till I lean as high as I can upon you,
Fill me with albescent honey . . . . bend down to me,
Rub to me with your chafing beard . . rub to my breast and
    shoulders.

The old face of the mother of many children:
Whist! I am fully content.

Lulled and late is the smoke of the Sabbath morning,
It hangs low over the rows of trees by the fences,
It hangs thin by the sassafras, the wildcherry and the catbrier
    under them.

I saw the rich ladies in full dress at the soiree,
I heard what the run of poets were saying so long,
Heard who sprang in crimson youth from the white froth and the
    water-blue.

Behold a woman!
She looks out from her quaker cap . . . . her face is clearer and
    more beautiful than the sky.

She sits in an armchair under the shaded porch of the farm-
    house,
The sun just shines on her old white head.

Her ample gown is of creamhued linen,
Her grandsons raised the flax, and her granddaughters spun it
    with the distaff and the wheel.

The melodious character of the earth!
The finish beyond which philosophy cannot go and does not wish
    to go!
The justified mother of men!

[Song of the Answerer]

A YOUNG man came to me with a message from his brother,
How should the young man know the whether and when of his
    brother?
Tell him to send me the signs.

And I stood before the young man face to face, and took his right
    hand in my left hand and his left hand in my right hand,
And I answered for his brother and for men . . . . and I answered
    for the poet, and sent these signs.

Him all wait for . . . . him all yield up to . . . . his word is decisive
    and final,
Him they accept . . . . in him lave . . . . in him perceive
    themselves as amid light,
Him they immerse, and he immerses them.

Beautiful women, the haughtiest nations, laws, the landscape,
    people and animals,
The profound earth and its attributes, and the unquiet ocean,
All enjoyments and properties, and money, and whatever money
    will buy,
The best farms . . . . others toiling and planting, and he
    unavoidably reaps,
The noblest and costliest cities . . . . others grading and building,
    and he domiciles there;

Nothing for any one but what is for him . . . . near and far are
    for him,
The ships in the offing . . . . the perpetual shows and marches on
    land are for him if they are for any body.

He puts things in their attitudes,
He puts today out of himself with plasticity and love,
He places his own city, times, reminiscences, parents, brothers and
    sisters, associations employment and politics, so that the rest
    never shame them afterward, nor assume to command them.

He is the answerer,
What can be answered he answers, and what cannot be answered
    he shows how it cannot be answered.

A man is a summons and challenge,
It is vain to skulk . . . . Do you hear that mocking and laughter?
    Do you hear the ironical echoes?

Books friendships philosophers priests action pleasure pride beat
    up and down seeking to give satisfaction;
He indicates the satisfaction, and indicates them that beat up and
    down also.

Whichever the sex . . . whatever the season or place he may go
    freshly and gently and safely by day or by night,
He has the passkey of hearts . . . . to him the response of the
    prying of hands on the knobs.

His welcome is universal . . . . the flow of beauty is not more
    welcome or universal than he is,
The person he favors by day or sleeps with at night is blessed.

Every existence has its idiom . . . . every thing has an idiom and
    tongue;
He resolves all tongues into his own, and bestows it upon men . .
    and any man translates . . and any man translates himself
    also:

One part does not counteract another part . . . . He is the joiner . .
     he sees how they join.

He says indifferently and alike, How are you friend? to the
     President at his levee,
And he says Good day my brother, to Cudge* that hoes in the
     sugarfield;
And both understand him and know that his speech is right.

He walks with perfect ease in the capitol,
He walks among the Congress . . . . and one representative says to
     another, Here is our equal appearing and new.

Then the mechanics take him for a mechanic,
And the soldiers suppose him to be a captain . . . . and the sailors
     that he has followed the sea,
And the authors take him for an author . . . . and the artists for an
     artist,
And the laborers perceive he could labor with them and love them;
No matter what the work is, that he is one to follow it or has
     followed it,
No matter what the nation, that he might find his brothers and
     sisters there.

The English believe he comes of their English stock,
A Jew to the Jew he seems . . . . a Russ to the Russ . . . . usual and
     near . . removed from none.

Whoever he looks at in the traveler's coffeehouse claims him,
The Italian or Frenchman is sure, and the German is sure, and
     the Spaniard is sure . . . . and the island Cuban is sure.

The engineer, the deckhand on the great lakes or on the
     Mississippi or St. Lawrence or Sacramento or Hudson or
     Delaware claims him.

---

*Common name for an African-American laborer.

The gentleman of perfect blood acknowledges his perfect blood,
The insulter, the prostitute, the angry person, the beggar, see
    themselves in the ways of him . . . . he strangely transmutes
    them,
They are not vile any more . . . . they hardly know themselves,
    they are so grown.

You think it would be good to be the writer of melodious verses,
Well it would be good to be the writer of melodious verses;
But what are verses beyond the flowing character you could
    have? . . . . or beyond beautiful manners and behaviour?
Or beyond one manly or affectionate deed of an
    apprenticeboy? . . . . or old woman? . . or man that has been
    in prison or is likely to be in prison?

[Europe, The 72d and 73d Years of These States][43]

SUDDENLY out of its stale and drowsy lair, the lair of slaves,
Like lightning Europe le'pt forth . . . . half startled at itself,
Its feet upon the ashes and the rags . . . . Its hands tight to the
    throats of kings.

O hope and faith! O aching close of lives! O many a sickened heart!
Turn back unto this day, and make yourselves afresh.

And you, paid to defile the People . . . . you liars mark:
Not for numberless agonies, murders, lusts,
For court thieving in its manifold mean forms,
Worming from his simplicity the poor man's wages;
For many a promise sworn by royal lips, and broken, and laughed
    at in the breaking,
Then in their power not for all these did the blows strike of
    personal revenge . . or the heads of the nobles fall;
The People scorned the ferocity of kings.

But the sweetness of mercy brewed bitter destruction, and the
    frightened rulers come back:

Each comes in state with his train . . . . hangman, priest and tax-
    gatherer . . . . soldier, lawyer, jailer and sycophant.

Yet behind all, lo, a Shape,
Vague as the night, draped interminably, head front and form in
    scarlet folds,
Whose face and eyes none may see,
Out of its robes only this . . . . the red robes, lifted by the arm,
One finger pointed high over the top, like the head of a snake
    appears.

Meanwhile corpses lie in new-made graves . . . . bloody corpses of
    young men:
The rope of the gibbet hangs heavily . . . . the bullets of princes
    are flying . . . . the creatures of power laugh aloud,
And all these things bear fruits . . . . and they are good.

Those corpses of young men,
Those martyrs that hang from the gibbets . . . those hearts pierced
    by the gray lead,
Cold and motionless as they seem . . live elsewhere with
    unslaughter'd vitality.

They live in other young men, O kings,
They live in brothers, again ready to defy you:
They were purified by death . . . . they were taught and exalted.

Not a grave of the murdered for freedom but grows seed for
    freedom . . . . in its turn to bear seed,
Which the winds carry afar and re-sow, and the rains and the
    snows nourish.

Not a disembodied spirit can the weapons of tyrants let loose,
But it stalks invisibly over the earth . . whispering counseling
    cautioning.

Liberty let others despair of you . . . . I never despair of you.

Is the house shut? Is the master away?
Nevertheless be ready . . . . be not weary of watching,
He will soon return . . . . his messengers come anon.

[A Boston Ballad]⁴⁴

CLEAR the way there Jonathan!*
Way for the President's marshal! Way for the government
  cannon!
Way for the federal foot and dragoons . . . . and the phantoms
  afterward.

I rose this morning early to get betimes in Boston town;
Here's a good place at the corner . . . . I must stand and see the
  show.

I love to look on the stars and stripes . . . . I hope the fifes will play
  Yankee Doodle.

How bright shine the foremost with cutlasses,
Every man holds his revolver . . . . marching stiff through Boston
  town.

A fog follows . . . . antiques of the same come limping,
Some appear wooden-legged and some appear bandaged and
  bloodless.

Why this is a show! It has called the dead out of the earth,
The old graveyards of the hills have hurried to see;
Uncountable phantoms gather by flank and rear of it,
Cocked hats of mothy mould and crutches made of mist,
Arms in slings and old men leaning on young men's shoulders.

---

*Nickname for a Yankee or New Englander.

What troubles you, Yankee phantoms? What is all this chattering
of bare gums?
Does the ague convulse your limbs? Do you mistake your
crutches for firelocks, and level them?
If you blind your eyes with tears you will not see the President's
marshal,
If you groan such groans you might balk the government
cannon.

For shame old maniacs! . . . . Bring down those tossed arms, and
let your white hair be;
Here gape your smart grandsons . . . . their wives gaze at them
from the windows,
See how well-dressed . . . . see how orderly they conduct
themselves.

Worse and worse . . . . Can't you stand it? Are you retreating?
Is this hour with the living too dead for you?

Retreat then! Pell-mell! . . . . Back to the hills, old limpers!
I do not think you belong here anyhow.

But there is one thing that belongs here . . . . Shall I tell you what
it is, gentlemen of Boston?

I will whisper it to the Mayor . . . . he shall send a committee to
England,
They shall get a grant from the Parliament, and go with a cart to
the royal vault.
Dig out King George's coffin . . . . unwrap him quick from the
graveclothes . . . . box up his bones for a journey:
Find a swift Yankee clipper . . . . here is freight for you
blackbellied clipper,
Up with your anchor! shake out your sails! . . . . steer straight
toward Boston bay.

Now call the President's marshal again, and bring out the
government cannon,

"Out of the mines"—About 41 years old, c.1860, photo probably taken by
J. W. Black in Boston, Massachusetts. Courtesy of the Bayley-Whitman
Collection of Ohio Wesleyan University, Delaware, Ohio, and the Walt
Whitman Birthplace Association, Huntington, New York. Saunders #2.

And fetch home the roarers from Congress, and make another
    procession and guard it with foot and dragoons.

Here is a centrepiece for them:
Look! all orderly citizens . . . . look from the windows women.

The committee open the box and set up the regal ribs and glue
    those that will not stay,
And clap the skull on top of the ribs, and clap a crown on top of
    the skull.[45]

You have got your revenge old buster! . . . . The crown is come to
    its own and more than its own.

Stick your hands in your pockets Jonathan . . . . you are a made
    man from this day,
You are mighty cute . . . . and here is one of your bargains.

===

[There Was a Child Went Forth]

THERE was a child went forth every day,
And the first object he looked upon and received with wonder or
    pity or love or dread, that object he became,
And that object became part of him for the day or a certain part
    of the day . . . . or for many years or stretching cycles of years.

The early lilacs became part of this child,
And grass, and white and red morningglories, and white and red
    clover, and the song of the phœbe-bird,
And the March-born lambs, and the sow's pink-faint litter, and the
    mare's foal, and the cow's calf, and the noisy brood of the
    barnyard or by the mire of the pondside . . and the fish
    suspending themselves so curiously below there . . and the
    beautiful curious liquid . . and the water-plants with their
    graceful flat heads . . all became part of him.

And the field-sprouts of April and May became part of him . . . .
wintergrain sprouts, and those of the light-yellow corn, and of
the esculent roots of the garden,
And the appletrees covered with blossoms, and the fruit
afterward . . . . and woodberries . . and the commonest weeds
by the road;
And the old drunkard staggering home from the outhouse of the
tavern whence he had lately risen,
And the schoolmistress that passed on her way to the school . .
and the friendly boys that passed . . and the quarrelsome
boys . . and the tidy and freshcheeked girls . . and the barefoot
negro boy and girl,
And all the changes of city and country wherever he went.

His own parents . . he that had propelled the fatherstuff at night,
and fathered him . . and she that conceived him in her womb
and birthed him . . . . they gave this child more of themselves
than that,
They gave him afterward every day . . . . they and of them became
part of him.

The mother at home quietly placing the dishes on the
suppertable,
The mother with mild words . . . . clean her cap and gown . . . . a
wholesome odor falling off her person and clothes as she
walks by:
The father, strong, selfsufficient, manly, mean, angered,
unjust,
The blow, the quick loud word, the tight bargain, the crafty
lure,[46]
The family usages, the language, the company, the furniture . . . .
the yearning and swelling heart,
Affection that will not be gainsayed . . . . The sense of what is
real . . . . the thought if after all it should prove unreal,
The doubts of daytime and the doubts of nighttime . . . the
curious whether and how,
Whether that which appears so is so . . . . Or is it all flashes and
specks?

Men and women crowding fast in the streets . . if they are not
    flashes and specks what are they?
The streets themselves, and the facades of houses . . . . the goods
    in the windows,
Vehicles . . teams . . the tiered wharves, and the huge crossing at
    the ferries;
The village on the highland seen from afar at sunset . . . . the river
    between,
Shadows . . aureola and mist . . light falling on roofs and gables of
    white or brown, three miles off,
The schooner near by sleepily dropping down the tide . . the little
    boat slacktowed astern,
The hurrying tumbling waves and quickbroken crests and
    slapping;
The strata of colored clouds . . . . the long bar of maroontint
    away solitary by itself . . . . the spread of purity it lies
    motionless in,
The horizon's edge, the flying seacrow, the fragrance of saltmarsh
    and shoremud;
These became part of that child who went forth every day, and
    who now goes and will always go forth every day,
And these become of him or her that peruses them now.

[Who Learns My Lesson Complete]

WHO learns my lesson complete?
Boss and journeyman and apprentice? . . . . churchman and
    atheist?
The stupid and the wise thinker . . . . parents and offspring . . . .
    merchant and clerk and porter and customer . . . . editor,
    author, artist and schoolboy?

Draw nigh and commence,
It is no lesson . . . . it lets down the bars to a good lesson,
And that to another . . . . and every one to another still.

The great laws take and effuse without argument,
I am of the same style, for I am their friend,
I love them quits and quits . . . . I do not halt and make salaams.

I lie abstracted and hear beautiful tales of things and the reasons
    of things,
They are so beautiful I nudge myself to listen.

I cannot say to any person what I hear . . . . I cannot say it to
    myself . . . . it is very wonderful.

It is no little matter, this round and delicious globe, moving so
    exactly in its orbit forever and ever, without one jolt or the
    untruth of a single second;
I do not think it was made in six days, nor in ten thousand years,
    nor ten decillions of years,
Nor planned and built one thing after another, as an architect
    plans and builds a house.

I do not think seventy years is the time of a man or woman,
Nor that seventy millions of years is the time of a man or
    woman,
Nor that years will ever stop the existence of me or any one else.

Is it wonderful that I should be immortal? as every one is
    immortal,
I know it is wonderful . . . . but my eyesight is equally
    wonderful . . . . and how I was conceived in my mother's
    womb is equally wonderful,
And how I was not palpable once but am now . . . . and was born
    on the last day of May 1819 . . . . and passed from a babe in
    the creeping trance of three summers and three winters to
    articulate and walk . . . . are all equally wonderful.

And that I grew six feet high . . . . and that I have become a man
    thirty-six years old in 1855[47] . . . . and that I am here anyhow—
    are all equally wonderful;

And that my soul embraces you this hour, and we affect each
    other without ever seeing each other, and never perhaps to
    see each other, is every bit as wonderful:
And that I can think such thoughts as these is just as
    wonderful,
And that I can remind you, and you think them and know them
    to be true is just as wonderful,
And that the moon spins round the earth and on with the earth is
    equally wonderful,
And that they balance themselves with the sun and stars is equally
    wonderful.

Come I should like to hear you tell me what there is in yourself
    that is not just as wonderful,
And I should like to hear the name of anything between
    Sunday morning and Saturday night that is not just as
    wonderful.

[Great Are the Myths]

GREAT are the myths . . . . I too delight in them,
Great are Adam and Eve . . . . I too look back and accept them;
Great the risen and fallen nations, and their poets, women, sages,
    inventors, rulers, warriors and priests.

Great is liberty! Great is equality! I am their follower,
Helmsmen of nations, choose your craft . . . . where you sail
    I sail,
Yours is the muscle of life or death . . . . yours is the perfect
    science . . . . in you I have absolute faith.

Great is today, and beautiful,
It is good to live in this age . . . . there never was any better.

Great are the plunges and throes and triumphs and falls of
    democracy,

Great the reformers with their lapses and screams,
Great the daring and venture of sailors on new explorations.

Great are yourself and myself,
We are just as good and bad as the oldest and youngest
    or any,
What the best and worst did we could do,
What they felt . . do not we feel it in ourselves?
What they wished . . do we not wish the same?

Great is youth, and equally great is old age . . . . great are the day
    and night;
Great is wealth and great is poverty . . . . great is expression and
    great is silence.

Youth large lusty and loving . . . . youth full of grace and force and
    fascination,
Do you know that old age may come after you with equal grace
    and force and fascination?

Day fullblown and splendid . . . . day of the immense sun, and
    action and ambition and laughter,
The night follows close, with millions of suns, and sleep and
    restoring darkness.

Wealth with the flush hand and fine clothes and
    hospitality:
But then the soul's wealth—which is candor and knowledge and
    pride and enfolding love:
Who goes for men and women showing poverty richer than
    wealth?

Expression of speech . . in what is written or said forget not that
    silence is also expressive,
That anguish as hot as the hottest and contempt as cold as the
    coldest may be without words,
That the true adoration is likewise without words and without
    kneeling.

Great is the greatest nation .. the nation of clusters of equal
     nations.

Great is the earth, and the way it became what it is,
Do you imagine it is stopped at this? . . . . and the increase
     abandoned?
Understand then that it goes as far onward from this as this is
     from the times when it lay in covering waters and gases.

Great is the quality of truth in man,
The quality of truth in man supports itself through all
     changes,
It is inevitably in the man . . . . He and it are in love, and never
     leave each other.

The truth in man is no dictum . . . . it is vital as eyesight,
If there be any soul there is truth . . . . if there be man or woman
     there is truth . . . . If there be physical or moral there is
     truth,
If there be equilibrium or volition there is truth . . . . if there be
     things at all upon the earth there is truth.

O truth of the earth! O truth of things! I am determined to press
     the whole way toward you,
Sound your voice! I scale mountains or dive in the sea
     after you.

Great is language . . . . it is the mightiest of the sciences,
It is the fulness and color and form and diversity of the earth . . . .
     and of men and women . . . . and of all qualities and
     processes;
It is greater than wealth . . . . it is greater than buildings or ships or
     religions or paintings or music.

Great is the English speech . . . . What speech is so great as the
     English?
Great is the English brood . . . . What brood has so vast a destiny
     as the English?

It is the mother of the brood that must rule the earth with the
    new rule,
The new rule shall rule as the soul rules, and as the love and
    justice and equality that are in the soul rule.

Great is the law . . . . Great are the old few landmarks of the law . . . .
    they are the same in all times and shall not be disturbed.
Great are marriage, commerce, newspapers, books, freetrade,
    railroads, steamers, international mails and telegraphs and
    exchanges.

Great is Justice;
Justice is not settled by legislators and laws . . . . it is in the soul,
It cannot be varied by statutes any more than love or pride or the
    attraction of gravity can,
It is immutable . . it does not depend on majorities . . . . majorities
    or what not come at last before the same passionless and
    exact tribunal.

For justice are the grand natural lawyers and perfect judges . . . . it
    is in their souls,
It is well assorted . . . . they have not studied for nothing . . . . the
    great includes the less,
They rule on the highest grounds . . . . they oversee all eras and
    states and administrations,

The perfect judge fears nothing . . . . he could go front to front
    before God,
Before the perfect judge all shall stand back . . . . life and death
    shall stand back . . . . heaven and hell shall stand back.

Great is goodness;
I do not know what it is any more than I know what health is . . . .
    but I know it is great.

Great is wickedness . . . . I find I often admire it just as much as I
    admire goodness:
Do you call that a paradox? It certainly is a paradox.

The eternal equilibrium of things is great, and the eternal
    overthrow of things is great,
And there is another paradox.

Great is life . . and real and mystical . . wherever and whoever,
Great is death . . . . Sure as life holds all parts together, death
    holds all parts together;
Sure as the stars return again after they merge in the light, death
    is great as life.

Leaves of Grass

Including
>SANDS AT SEVENTY... *1st Annex*,
>GOOD-BYE MY FANCY... *2d Annex*,
>A BACKWARD GLANCE O'ER TRAVEL'D ROADS,
>*and Portrait from Life.*

COME, said my Soul,[1]
Such verses for my Body let us write, (for we are one,)
That should I after death invisibly return,
Or, long, long hence, in other spheres,
There to some group of mates the chants resuming,
(Tallying Earth's soil, trees, winds, tumultuous waves,)
Ever with pleas'd smile I may keep on,
Ever and ever yet the verses owning—as, first, I here and now,
Signing for Soul and Body, set to them my name,

Walt Whitman

PHILADELPHIA
DAVID McKAY, PUBLISHER
23 SOUTH NINTH STREET
1891-'2

Walt Whitman 1887

"Laughing philosopher" — 68 years old, 1887, photo taken by George C. Cox
in New York, New York. Courtesy of the Library of Congress,
Charles E. Feinberg Collection. Saunders #95.

CONTENTS

"Death-bed" Edition, 1891–1892

INSCRIPTIONS 165

    One's-Self I Sing 165
    A I Ponder'd in Silence 165
    In Cabin'd Ships at Sea 166
    To Foreign Lands 167
    To a Historian 167
    To Thee Old Cause 168
    Eidólons 168
    For Him I Sing 171
    When I Read the Book 172
    Beginning My Studies 172
    Beginners 172
    To the States 173
    On Journeys Through the States 173
    To a Certain Cantatrice 173
    Me Imperturbe 174
    Savantism 174
    The Ship Starting 175
    I Hear America Singing 175
    What Place Is Besieged? 176
    Still Though the One I Sing 176
    Shut Not Your Doors 176
    Poets to Come 176
    To You 177
    Thou Reader 177

Starting from Paumanok 177

Song of Myself 190

CHILDREN OF ADAM 252

    To the Garden the World 252
    From Pent-up Aching Rivers 252

I Sing the Body Electric. 254
A Woman Waits for Me 263
Spontaneous Me 264
One Hour to Madness and Joy. 267
Out of the Rolling Ocean the Crowd. 268
Ages and Ages Returning at Intervals 268
We Two, How Long We Were Fool'd. 269
O Hymen! O Hymenee! 269
I Am He That Aches with Love 270
Native Moments 270
Once I Pass'd Through a Populous City. 270
I Heard You Solemn-Sweet Pipes of the Organ 271
Facing West from California's Shores 271
As Adam Early in the Morning. 272

CALAMUS 274

In Paths Untrodden 274
Scented Herbage of My Breast. 274
Whoever You Are Holding Me Now in Hand 276
For You O Democracy. 278
These I Singing in Spring 278
Not Heaving from My Ribb'd Breast Only. 280
Of the Terrible Doubt of Appearances. 280
The Base of All Metaphysics 281
Recorders Ages Hence 282
When I Heard at the Close of the Day. 283
Are You the New Person Drawn toward Me? 283
Roots and Leaves Themselves Alone 284
Not Heat Flames up and Consumes 284
Trickle Drops. 285
City of Orgies. 285
Behold This Swarthy Face 286
I Saw in Louisiana a Live-Oak Growing. 286
To a Stranger 287
This Moment Yearning and Thoughtful 287
I Hear It Was Charged Against Me 288
The Prairie-Grass Dividing 288
When I Peruse the Conquer'd Fame 289
We Two Boys Together Clinging 289

A Promise to California 289
Here the Frailest Leaves of Me 290
No Labor-saving Machine 290
A Glimpse 290
A Leaf for Hand in Hand 291
Earth, My Likeness. 291
I Dream'd in a Dream 291
What Think You I Take My Pen in Hand? 292
To the East and to the West 292
Sometimes with One I Love. 292
To a Western Boy. 293
Fast-anchor'd Eternal O Love! 293
Among the Multitude 293
O You Whom I Often and Silently Come 293
That Shadow My Likeness. 294
Full of Life Now 294
Salut au Monde! 294
Song of the Open Road 305
Crossing Brooklyn Ferry. 316
Song of the Answerer 322
Our Old Feuillage 327
A Song of Joys 332
Song of the Broad-Axe 339
Song of the Exposition 351
Song of the Redwood-Tree. 361
A Song for Occupations. 365
A Song of the Rolling Earth. 373
Youth, Day, Old Age and Night. 379

BIRDS OF PASSAGE 380

Song of the Universal. 380
Pioneers! O Pioneers!. 382
To You. 387
France, The 18th Year of these States. 389
Myself and Mine. 390
Year of Meteors (1859–60) 392
With Antecedents 393

A Broadway Pageant. 395

Sea-Drift 400

Out of the Cradle Endlessly Rocking 400
As I Ebb'd with the Ocean of Life 406
Tears 409
To the Man-of-War-Bird 410
Aboard at a Ship's Helm 411
On the Beach at Night 411
The World Below the Brine 412
On the Beach at Night Alone 413
Song for All Seas, All Ships 414
Patroling Barnegat 415
After the Sea-Ship 415

By the Roadside 417

A Boston Ballad (1854) 417
Europe, The 72d and 73d Years of These States 419
A Hand-Mirror 421
Gods 421
Germs 422
Thoughts 422
When I Heard the Learn'd Astronomer 423
Perfections 423
O Me! O Life! 423
To a President 424
I Sit and Look Out 424
To Rich Givers 425
The Dalliance of the Eagles 425
Roaming in Thought 426
A Farm Picture 426
A Child's Amaze 426
The Runner 426
Beautiful Women 427
Mother and Babe 427
Thought 427
Visor'd 427
Thought 427
Gliding o'er All 428
Hast Never Come to Thee an Hour 428

Thought. 428
To Old Age 428
Locations and Times 428
Offerings 429
To the States, To Identify the 16th, 17th, or
    18th Presidentiad 429

DRUM-TAPS 430

First O Songs for a Prelude 430
Eighteen Sixty-One 432
Beat! Beat! Drums! 433
From Paumanok Starting I Fly like a Bird 434
Song of the Banner at Daybreak 435
Rise O Days from Your Fathomless Deeps 441
Virginia—The West 444
City of Ships 444
The Centenarian's Story 445
Cavalry Crossing a Ford. 449
Bivouac on a Mountain Side. 450
An Army Corps on the March 450
By the Bivouac's Fitful Flame 451
Come Up from the Fields Father 451
Vigil Strange I Kept on the Field One Night 453
A March in the Ranks Hard-Prest, and
    the Road Unknown 454
A Sight in Camp in the Daybreak Gray and Dim 455
As Toilsome I Wander'd Virginia's Woods 456
Not the Pilot 457
Year That Trembled and Reel'd Beneath Me. 457
The Wound-Dresser. 457
Long, Too Long America 460
Give Me the Splendid Silent Sun 461
Dirge for Two Veterans 462
Over the Carnage Rose Prophetic a Voice 464
I Saw Old General at Bay 465
The Artilleryman's Vision 465
Ethiopia Saluting the Colors. 466
Not Youth Pertains to Me 467
Race of Veterans 467

World Take Good Notice. 468
O Tan-faced Prairie-Boy 468
Look Down Fair Moon 468
Reconciliation 468
How Solemn as One by One. 469
As I Lay with My Head in Your Lap Camerado. 469
Delicate Cluster 470
To a Certain Civilian. 470
Lo, Victress on the Peaks 471
Spirit Whose Work Is Done 471
Adieu to a Soldier. 472
Turn O Libertad 473
To the Leaven'd Soil They Trod. 473

MEMORIES OF PRESIDENT LINCOLN 475

When Lilacs Last in the Dooryard Bloom'd. 475
O Captain! My Captain! 484
Hush'd Be the Camps To-day. 485
This Dust Was Once the Man. 485

By Blue Ontario's Shore. 485

Reversals. 501

AUTUMN RIVULETS 502

As Consequent, *Etc.*. 502
The Return of the Heroes 503
There Was a Child Went Forth 509
Old Ireland. 511
The City Dead-House. 511
This Compost. 512
To a Foil'd European Revolutionaire 514
Unnamed Lands. 516
Song of Prudence. 517
The Singer in the Prison 520
Warble for Lilac-Time 522
Outlines for a Tomb. 523
Out from Behind This Mask 525
Vocalism 526
To Him That Was Crucified 528

You Felons on Trial in Courts 528
Laws for Creations 529
To a Common Prostitute 530
I Was Looking a Long While 530
Thought 531
Miracles 531
Sparkles from the Wheel 532
To a Pupil 533
Unfolded Out of the Folds 533
What Am I After All 534
Kosmos 534
Others May Praise What They Like 535
Who Learns My Lesson Complete? 535
Tests 537
The Torch 537
O Star of France (1870–71) 537
The Ox-tamer 539
An Old Man's Thought of School 540
Wandering at Morn 540
Italian Music in Dakota 541
With All Thy Gifts 542
My Picture-Gallery 542
The Prairie States 542

Proud Music of the Storm 543

Passage to India 549

Prayer of Columbus 558

The Sleepers 560

Transpositions 570

To Think of Time 570

WHISPERS OF HEAVENLY DEATH 577

Darest Thou Now O Soul 577
Whispers of Heavenly Death 577
Chanting the Square Deific 578
Of Him I Love Day and Night 580
Yet, Yet, Ye Downcast Hours 581
As if a Phantom Caress'd Me 582

Assurances 582
Quicksand Years. 583
That Music Always Round Me 583
What Ship Puzzled at Sea 584
A Noiseless Patient Spider 584
O Living Always, Always Dying 584
To One Shortly to Die 585
Night on the Prairies 585
Thought. 586
The Last Invocation. 587
A I Watch'd the Ploughman Ploughing 587
Pensive and Faltering. 587

Thou Mother with Thy Equal Brood 588

A Paumanok Picture 594

From Noon to Starry Night 595

Thou Orb Aloft Full-Dazzling. 595
Faces 596
The Mystic Trumpeter 600
To a Locomotive in Winter 603
O Magnet-South 604
Mannahatta. 606
All Is Truth 607
A Riddle Song 608
Excelsior 609
Ah Poverties, Wincings, and Sulky Retreats 610
Thoughts 610
Mediums 611
Weave In, My Hardy Life 611
Spain, 1873–74 612
By Broad Potomac's Shore 612
From Far Dakota's Cañons. 613
Old War-Dreams 614
Thick-sprinkled Bunting. 615
What Best I See in Thee 615
Spirit That Form'd This Scene. 616
As I Walk These Broad Majestic Days 616
A Clear Midnight. 617

SONGS OF PARTING 618

As the Time Draws Nigh 618
Years of the Modern 618
Ashes of Soldiers 620
Thoughts 621
Song at Sunset 623
As at Thy Portals Also Death 625
My Legacy 626
Pensive on Her Dead Gazing 626
Camps of Green 627
The Sobbing of the Bells 628
As They Draw to a Close 629
Joy, Shipmate, Joy! 629
The Untold Want 629
Portals 630
These Carols 630
Now Finalé to the Shore 630
So Long! 630

FIRST ANNEX: SANDS AT SEVENTY 635

Mannahatta 635
Paumanok 635
From Montauk Point 635
To Those Who've Fail'd 636
A Carol Closing Sixty-nine 636
The Bravest Soldiers 636
A Font of Type 637
A I Sit Writing Here 637
My Canary Bird 637
Queries to My Seventieth Year 637
The Wallabout Martyrs 638
The First Dandelion 638
America 638
Memories 639
To-day and Thee 639
After the Dazzle of Day 639
Abraham Lincoln, Born Feb. 12, 1809 639
Out of May's Shows Selected 640

Halcyon Days 640
Fancies at Navesink 640

    The Pilot in the Mist 640
    Had I the Choice. 641
    You Tides with Ceaseless Swell 641
    Last of Ebb, and Daylight Waning. 641
    And Yet Not You Alone 642
    Proudly the Flood Comes In. 642
    By That Long Scan of Waves 642
    Then Last of All 643

Election Day, November, 1884. 643
With Husky-Haughty Lips, O Sea!. 644
Death of General Grant. 645
Red Jacket (From Aloft) 645
Washington's Monument, February, 1885 646
Of That Blithe Throat of Thine. 646
Broadway. 647
To Get the Final Lilt of Songs 647
Old Salt Kossabone 648
The Dead Tenor 648
Continuities. 649
Yonnondio. 649
Life 650
"Going Somewhere" 650
Small the Theme of My Chant 651
True Conquerors 651
The United States to Old World Critics. 652
The Calming Thought of All 652
Thanks in Old Age. 652
Life and Death. 653
The Voice of the Rain 653
Soon Shall the Winter's Foil Be Here 653
While Not the Past Forgetting 654
The Dying Veteran 654
Stronger Lessons 655
A Prairie Sunset. 655
Twenty Years 656
Orange Buds by Mail from Florida 656

Twilight 657
You Lingering Sparse Leaves of Me 657
Not Meagre, Latent Boughs Alone 657
The Dead Emperor 657
As the Greek's Signal Flame 658
The Dismantled Ship 658
Now Precedent Songs, Farewell 658
An Evening Lull 659
Old Age's Lambent Peaks 659
After the Supper and Talk 660

SECOND ANNEX: GOOD-BYE MY FANCY 661

Preface Note to 2d Annex 661
Sail Out for Good, Eidólon Yacht! 663
Lingering Last Drops 663
Good-Bye My Fancy 664
On, On the Same, Ye Jocund Twain! 664
My 71st Year 665
Apparitions 665
The Pallid Wreath 665
An Ended Day 666
Old Age's Ship & Crafty Death's 667
To the Pending Year 667
Shakspere-Bacon's Cipher 667
Long, Long Hence 668
Bravo, Paris Exposition! 668
Interpolation Sounds 668
To the Sun-set Breeze 669
Old Chants 670
A Christmas Greeting 671
Sounds of the Winter 671
A Twilight Song 672
When the Full-Grown Poet Came 672
Osceola 673
A Voice from Death 674
A Persian Lesson 675
The Commonplace 676
"The Rounded Catalogue Divine Complete" 676
Mirages 677

L. of G.'s Purport 678
The Unexpress'd 678
Grand Is the Seen 679
Unseen Buds 679
Good-Bye my Fancy! 679

A Backward Glance o'er Travel'd Roads 681

INTRODUCTION
TO "DEATH-BED" EDITION

———— •◆• ————

In the thirty-six years between the First Edition of *Leaves of Grass* and the so-called "Death-bed" Edition, Whitman's original collection of twelve poems grew to more than 400 poems. Each of the original twelve appeared in some form in the "Death-bed" Edition. Other poems were created from lines extracted from other works: "Youth, Day, Old Age and Night," for example, is comprised of lines 19 through 22 of "[Great Are the Myths]."* The 1860 poem "States!" was excluded from the final edition of *Leaves*; instead it formed the basis for "Over the Carnage Rose Prophetic a Voice" and "For You, O Democracy." Most of the new poems were inspired by national events as much as by Walt's personal history. Just as he had prophesied in the 1855 preface, the poet's spirit "responds to his country's spirit." Whitman's *Leaves of Grass* was an ever-developing idea, itself a song that evolved as organically as its title suggests, along with the singer and his subject.

For those interested in the complex publication history of Whitman's poems, the section "Publication Information" at the end of this book provides dates and title changes. Below is a list of editions Whitman published during his lifetime:

1855 (First Edition): Two impressions the same year, the later one with preliminary leaves including three of Whitman's very positive, anonymous self-reviews.

---

*Titles of First Edition poems are presented in brackets. Whitman did not title the twelve poems in the First Edition but gave them titles as he included them in subsequent editions (see "Publication Information").

1856 (Second Edition): A single impression, including Emerson's congratulatory letter in a promotional section entitled "Leaves-Droppings."

1860–1861 (Third Edition): Two impressions of the same text, which included special titled groupings of poems ("clusters") for the first time.

1865 (*Drum-Taps*): A separate book of poems on the Civil War, not initially part of *Leaves of Grass* but an important later addition and defining collection.

1865–1866 (*Sequel to Drum-Taps*): Bound in with *Drum-Taps* after Lincoln's death.

1867 (Fourth Edition): *Leaves of Grass* poems, plus the annexes "Drum-Taps," "Sequel to Drum-Taps," and "Songs before Parting."

1871, 1872, 1876 (Fifth Edition): The Fifth Edition was published in Washington, D.C., in 1871 with ten new poems, and republished again later that year with the separately paginated section *Passage to India*, also published as a separate volume that year. The 1872 impression contains the annexes "Passage to India" and "After All, Not to Create Only." The 1876 impression came out in two variants: *Leaves of Grass: Author's Edition, with Portraits and Intercalations* and *Leaves of Grass: Author's Edition, with Portraits from Life*; a companion volume entitled *Two Rivulets* accompanied both Author's Editions.

1881, 1882, 1883, 1884, 1888, 1889, 1891–1892 (Sixth Edition): The 1881 plates were used in all subsequent impressions of *Leaves of Grass* during Whitman's lifetime, though each of these editions has some individuating features (such as annexes, covers, or altered poem titles).

Most readers are introduced to the "Death-bed" Edition as "the" Whitman text and are confounded by the book's actual prior history. Why did Whitman revise *Leaves of Grass* so frequently? Here was a man who *needed* to sell his work, without family money, rich friends, or another substantial income; here was a newspaper editor and journalist who was skilled at (and even enjoyed) the task of editing; here was a poet striving to write a people's poetry, always ready to respond to new stimuli and revise his definitions. The year before his death, however, Whitman apparently realized that he would have to put his various editions in some preferential order. He thus gave his blessing to the "Death-bed" Edition, published as indicated on the title page in "1891–'2." "As there are now several editions of L. of G., different texts and dates, I wish to say that I prefer and recommend this present one," Whitman notes on the verso of the title page. The "Death-bed" Edition thereby became the staple of Whitman anthologies.

The editors of the authoritative *Leaves of Grass: A Textual Variorum of the Printed Poems* (see "For Further Reading") note that there is a major problem with accepting Whitman's pronouncement: The text approved by Whitman was not necessarily the same one that later bore his letter of approval. About a hundred presentation copies of the "approved" edition that were issued were actually the uncorrected 1888 *Leaves of Grass* poems; later, the corrected 1889 plates were issued with the same green cloth binding used for the uncorrected 1888 plates (for more details, see volume I of the *Variorum*, pp. xxiv–xxv). To avoid problems and confusion, the current edition is based on the *Variorum* text, still the definitive example of Whitman's actual "Death-bed" *Leaves of Grass*.

There are many benefits to beginning one's study of Whitman with the 1891–1892 edition. These are, after all, the poems Whitman thought best represented a lifetime of writing. Helpful features not included in some prior editions (such as section numbers) make long poems easier to read and study. Several major "clusters" of poems are maintained, important prose pieces (such as "A Backward Glance o'er Travel'd Roads") are included, and two annexes ("Sands at Seventy" and "Good-Bye My Fancy") are added for the first time. It is a large, impressive collection that resists chronological order and often groups poems by "idea."

—Karen Karbiener

INSCRIPTIONS

ONE'S-SELF I SING

One's-self I sing, a simple separate person,
Yet utter the word Democratic, the word En-Masse.[2]

Of physiology from top to toe I sing,
Not physiognomy alone nor brain alone is worthy for the Muse, I
    say the Form complete is worthier far,
The Female equally with the Male I sing.

Of Life immense in passion, pulse, and power,
Cheerful, for freest action form'd under the laws divine,
The Modern Man I sing.

AS I PONDER'D IN SILENCE

As I ponder'd in silence,
Returning upon my poems, considering, lingering long,
A Phantom arose before me with distrustful aspect,
Terrible in beauty, age, and power,
The genius of poets of old lands,
As to me directing like flame its eyes,
With finger pointing to many immortal songs,
And menacing voice, *What singest thou?* it said,
Know'st thou not there is but one theme for ever-enduring bards?
And that is the theme of War, the fortune of battles,
The making of perfect soldiers.

Be it so, then I answer'd,
*I too haughty Shade also sing war, and a longer and greater one
     than any,*
*Waged in my book with varying fortune, with flight, advance and
     retreat, victory deferr'd and wavering,*
*(Yet methinks certain, or as good as certain, at the last,) the field
     the world,*
For life and death, for the Body and for the eternal Soul,
Lo, I too am come, chanting the chant of battles,
I above all promote brave soldiers.

IN CABIN'D SHIPS AT SEA

In cabin'd ships at sea,
The boundless blue on every side expanding,
With whistling winds and music of the waves, the large imperious
     waves,
Or some lone bark buoy'd on the dense marine,
Where joyous full of faith, spreading white sails,
She cleaves the ether mid the sparkle and the foam of day, or
     under many a star at night,
By sailors young and old haply will I, a reminiscence of the land,
     be read,
In full rapport at last.

Here are our thoughts, voyagers' thoughts,
Here not the land, firm land, alone appears, may then by them be
     said,
*The sky o'erarches here, we feel the undulating deck beneath our
     feet,*
We feel the long pulsation, ebb and flow of endless motion,
*The tones of unseen mystery, the vague and vast suggestions of the
     briny world, the liquid-flowing syllables,*
*The perfume, the faint creaking of the cordage, the melancholy
     rhythm,*
The boundless vista and the horizon far and dim are all here,
And this is ocean's poem.

Then falter not O book, fulfil your destiny,
You not a reminiscence of the land alone,
You too as a lone bark cleaving the ether, purpos'd I know not
    whither, yet ever full of faith,
Consort to every ship that sails, sail you!
Bear forth to them folded my love, (dear mariners, for you I fold it
    here in every leaf;)
Speed on my book! spread your white sails my little bark athwart
    the imperious waves,
Chant on, sail on, bear o'er the boundless blue from me to every
    sea,
This song for mariners and all their ships.

TO FOREIGN LANDS

I heard that you ask'd for something to prove this puzzle the New
    World,
And to define America, her athletic Democracy,
Therefore I send you my poems that you behold in them what
    you wanted.

TO A HISTORIAN

You who celebrate bygones,
Who have explored the outward, the surfaces of the races, the life
    that has exhibited itself,
Who have treated of man as the creature of politics, aggregates,
    rulers and priests,
I, habitan of the Alleghanies,* treating of him as he is in himself
    in his own rights,
Pressing the pulse of the life that has seldom exhibited itself, (the
    great pride of man in himself,)

---

*Like English poet William Blake (1757–1827), Whitman often made up words and
spellings. "Habitan" is his variant of "inhabitant"; he also personalized the spelling
of the Alleghenies, America's oldest mountain range.

Chanter of Personality, outlining what is yet to be,
I project the history of the future.

TO THEE OLD CAUSE

To thee old cause!
Thou peerless, passionate, good cause,
Thou stern, remorseless, sweet idea,
Deathless throughout the ages, races, lands,
After a strange sad war, great war for thee,
(I think all war through time was really fought, and ever will be
    really fought, for thee,)
These chants for thee, the eternal march of thee.

(A war O soldiers not for itself alone,
Far, far more stood silently waiting behind, now to advance in this
    book.)

Thou orb of many orbs!
Thou seething principle! thou well-kept, latent germ! thou
    centre!
Around the idea of thee the war revolving,
With all its angry and vehement play of causes,
(With vast results to come for thrice a thousand years,)
These recitatives for thee,—my book and the war are one,
Merged in its spirit I and mine, as the contest hinged on thee,
As a wheel on its axis turns, this book unwitting to itself,
Around the idea of thee.

EIDÓLONS*

I met a seer,
Passing the hues and objects of the world,

---

*Images (Greek); as Whitman explains in his manuscript "Notebook on Words" (lo-
cated in the Feinberg Collection at the New York Public Library): "Ei-dó-lon (Gr)
phantom—the *image* of a Helen of Troy instead of a real flesh and blood woman."

The fields of art and learning, pleasure, sense,
  To glean eidólons.

  Put in thy chants said he,
No more the puzzling hour nor day, nor segments, parts,
  put in,
Put first before the rest as light for all and entrance-song of all,
  That of eidólons.
  Ever the dim beginning,
Ever the growth, the rounding of the circle,
Ever the summit and the merge at last, (to surely start again,)
  Eidólons! eidólons!

  Ever the mutable,
Ever materials, changing, crumbling, re-cohering,
Ever the ateliers, the factories divine,
  Issuing eidólons.

  Lo, I or you,
Or woman, man, or state, known or unknown,
We seeming solid wealth, strength, beauty build,
  But really build eidólons.

  The ostent evanescent,
The substance of an artist's mood or savan's studies long,
Or warrior's, martyr's, hero's toils,
  To fashion his eidólon.

  Of every human life,
(The units gather'd, posted, not a thought, emotion, deed,
  left out,)
The whole or large or small summ'd, added up,
  In its eidólon.

  The old, old urge,
Based on the ancient pinnacles, lo, newer, higher pinnacles,
From science and the modern still impell'd,
  The old, old urge, eidólons.

The present now and here,
America's busy, teeming, intricate whirl,
Of aggregate and segregate for only thence releasing,
  To-day's eidólons.

These with the past,
Of vanish'd lands, of all the reigns of kings across the sea,
Old conquerors, old campaigns, old sailors' voyages,
  Joining eidólons.

Densities, growth, façades,
Strata of mountains, soils, rocks, giant trees,
Far-born, far-dying, living long, to leave,
  Eidólons everlasting.

Exalté, rapt, ecstatic,
The visible but their womb of birth,
Of orbic tendencies to shape and shape and shape,
  The mighty earth-eidólon.

All space, all time,
(The stars, the terrible perturbations of the suns,
Swelling, collapsing, ending, serving their longer, shorter use,)
  Fill'd with eidólons only.

The noiseless myriads,
The infinite oceans where the rivers empty,
The separate countless free identities, like eyesight,
  The true realities, eidólons.

Not this the world,
Nor these the universes, they the universes,
Purport and end, ever the permanent life of life,
  Eidólons, eidólons.

Beyond thy lectures learn'd professor,
Beyond thy telescope or spectroscope observer keen, beyond all
  mathematics,

Beyond the doctor's surgery, anatomy, beyond the chemist with
     his chemistry,
     The entities of entities, eidólons.

     Unfix'd yet fix'd,
Ever shall be, ever have been and are,
Sweeping the present to the infinite future,
     Eidólons, eidólons, eidólons.

     The prophet and the bard,
Shall yet maintain themselves, in higher stages yet,
Shall mediate to the Modern, to Democracy, interpret yet to
     them,
     God and eidólons.

     And thee my soul,
Joys, ceaseless exercises, exaltations,
Thy yearning amply fed at last, prepared to meet,
     Thy mates, eidólons.

     Thy body permanent,
The body lurking there within thy body,
The only purport of the form thou art, the real I myself,
     An image, an eidólon.

     Thy very songs not in thy songs,
No special strains to sing, none for itself,
But from the whole resulting, rising at last and floating,
     A round full-orb'd eidólon.

FOR HIM I SING

For him I sing,
I raise the present on the past,
(As some perennial tree out of its roots, the present on the past,)
With time and space I him dilate and fuse the immortal laws,
To make himself by them the law unto himself.

WHEN I READ THE BOOK

When I read the book, the biography famous,
And is this then (said I) what the author calls a man's life?
And so will some one when I am dead and gone write my life?
(As if any man really knew aught of my life,
Why even I myself I often think know little or nothing of my real
    life,
Only a few hints, a few diffused faint clews and indirections
I seek for my own use to trace out here.)

BEGINNING MY STUDIES

Beginning my studies the first step pleas'd me so much,
The mere fact consciousness, these forms, the power of motion,
The least insect or animal, the senses, eyesight, love,
The first step I say awed me and pleas'd me so much,
I have hardly gone and hardly wish'd to go any farther,
But stop and loiter all the time to sing it in ecstatic songs.

BEGINNERS

How they are provided for upon the earth, (appearing at
    intervals,)
How dear and dreadful they are to the earth,
How they inure to themselves as much as to any—what a paradox
    appears their age,
How people respond to them, yet know them not,
How there is something relentless in their fate all times,
How all times mischoose the objects of their adulation and
    reward,
And how the same inexorable price must still be paid for the
    same great purchase.

TO THE STATES

To the States or any one of them, or any city of the States, *Resist
  much, obey little,*
Once unquestioning obedience, once fully enslaved,
Once fully enslaved, no nation, state, city of this earth, ever
  afterward resumes its liberty.

ON JOURNEYS THROUGH THE STATES

On journeys through the States we start,
(Ay through the world, urged by these songs,
Sailing henceforth to every land, to every sea,)
We willing learners of all, teachers of all, and lovers of all.

We have watch'd the seasons dispensing themselves and
  passing on,
And have said, Why should not a man or woman do as much as
  the seasons, and effuse as much?

We dwell a while in every city and town,
We pass through Kanada, the North-east, the vast valley of the
  Mississippi, and the Southern States,
We confer on equal terms with each of the States,
We make trial of ourselves and invite men and women to hear,
We say to ourselves, Remember, fear not, be candid, promulge
  the body and the soul,
Dwell a while and pass on, be copious, temperate, chaste,
  magnetic,[3]
And what you effuse may then return as the seasons return,
And may be just as much as the seasons.

TO A CERTAIN CANTATRICE[4]

Here, take this gift,
I was reserving it for some hero, speaker, or general,

One who should serve the good old cause, the great idea, the
    progress and freedom of the race,
Some brave confronter of despots, some daring rebel;
But I see that what I was reserving belongs to you just as much as
    to any.

ME IMPERTURBE*

Me imperturbe, standing at ease in Nature,
Master of all or mistress of all, aplomb in the midst of irrational
    things,
Imbued as they, passive, receptive, silent as they,
Finding my occupation, poverty, notoriety, foibles, crimes, less
    important than I thought,
Me toward the Mexican sea, or in the Mannahatta† or the
    Tennessee, or far north or inland,
A river man, or a man of the woods or of any farm-life of these
    States or of the coast, or the lakes or Kanada,
Me wherever my life is lived, O to be self-balanced for
    contingencies,
To confront night, storms, hunger, ridicule, accidents, rebuffs, as
    the trees and animals do.

SAVANTISM‡

Thither as I look I see each result and glory retracing itself and
    nestling close, always obligated,
Thither hours, months, years—thither trades, compacts,
    establishments, even the most minute,

---

*The title, which looks like Latin but isn't, is another example of Whitman's individualized use of language. The meaning is "I am imperturbable."

†Algonquian name for Manhattan Island. Whitman's favorite brother, Thomas Jefferson Whitman, named his daughter Manahatta [sic]; she was born in 1860, the same year "Me Imperturbe" was first included in *Leaves of Grass*.

‡Whitman's term for the gifted vision of a seer-prophet.

Thither every-day life, speech, utensils, politics, persons,
  estates;
Thither we also, I with my leaves and songs, trustful, admirant,
As a father to his father going takes his children along
  with him.

THE SHIP STARTING

Lo, the unbounded sea,
On its breast a ship starting, spreading all sails, carrying even her
  moonsails,
The pennant is flying aloft as she speeds she speeds so stately
  below emulous waves press forward,
They surround the ship with shining curving motions
  and foam.

I HEAR AMERICA SINGING[5]

I hear America singing, the varied carols I hear,
Those of mechanics, each one singing his as it should be blithe
  and strong,
The carpenter singing his as he measures his plank or beam,
The mason singing his as he makes ready for work, or leaves off
  work,
The boatman singing what belongs to him in his boat, the
  deckhand singing on the steamboat deck,
The shoemaker singing as he sits on his bench, the hatter singing
  as he stands,
The wood-cutter's song, the ploughboy's on his way in the
  morning, or at noon intermission or at sundown,
The delicious singing of the mother, or of the young wife at work,
  or of the girl sewing or washing,
Each singing what belongs to him or her and to none else,
The day what belongs to the day—at night the party of young
  fellows, robust, friendly,
Singing with open mouths their strong melodious songs.

WHAT PLACE IS BESIEGED?

What place is besieged, and vainly tries to raise the siege?
Lo, I send to that place a commander, swift, brave, immortal,
And with him horse and foot, and parks of artillery,
And artillery-men, the deadliest that ever fired gun.

STILL THOUGH THE ONE I SING

Still though the one I sing,
(One, yet of contradictions made,) I dedicate to Nationality,
I leave in him revolt, (O latent right of insurrection! O
    quenchless, indispensable fire!)

SHUT NOT YOUR DOORS

Shut not your doors to me proud libraries,
For that which was lacking on all your well-fill'd shelves, yet
    needed most, I bring,
Forth from the war emerging, a book I have made,
The words of my book nothing, the drift of it every thing,
A book separate, not link'd with the rest nor felt by the intellect,
But you ye untold latencies will thrill to every page.

POETS TO COME

Poets to come! orators, singers, musicians to come!
Not to-day is to justify me and answer what I am for,
But you, a new brood, native, athletic, continental, greater than
    before known,
Arouse! for you must justify me.

I myself but write one or two indicative words for the future,
I but advance a moment only to wheel and hurry back in the
    darkness.

I am a man who, sauntering along without fully stopping, turns a
    casual look upon you and then averts his face,
Leaving it to you to prove and define it,
Expecting the main things from you.

TO YOU

Stranger, if you passing meet me and desire to speak to me, why
    should you not speak to me?
And why should I not speak to you?

THOU READER

Thou reader throbbest life and pride and love the same as I,
Therefore for thee the following chants.

STARTING FROM PAUMANOK*

— 1 —

Starting from fish-shape Paumanok where I was born,
Well-begotten, and rais'd by a perfect mother,
After roaming many lands, lover of populous pavements,
Dweller in Mannahatta my city, or on southern savannas,
Or a soldier camp'd or carrying my knapsack and gun, or a miner
    in California,
Or rude in my home in Dakota's woods, my diet meat, my drink
    from the spring,
Or withdrawn to muse and meditate in some deep recess,
Far from the clank of crowds intervals passing rapt and happy,

---

*"Paumanok" is the Algonquian name for Long Island, where Whitman indeed got
his start: He was born in Huntington, Suffolk County, and his birthplace is now a
state historic site.

Aware of the fresh free giver the flowing Missouri, aware of
    mighty Niagara,
Aware of the buffalo herds grazing the plains, the hirsute and
    strong-breasted bull,
Of earth, rocks, Fifth-month* flowers experienced, stars, rain,
    snow, my amaze,
Having studied the mocking-bird's tones and the flight of the
    mountain-hawk,
And heard at dawn the unrivall'd one, the hermit thrush from the
    swamp-cedars,
Solitary, singing in the West, I strike up for a New World.

— 2 —

Victory, union, faith, identity, time,
The indissoluble compacts, riches, mystery,
Eternal progress, the kosmos, and the modern reports.

This then is life,
Here is what has come to the surface after so many throes and
    convulsions.

How curious! how real!
Underfoot the divine soil, overhead the sun.

See revolving the globe,
The ancestor-continents away group'd together,
The present and future continents north and south, with the
    isthmus between.

See, vast trackless spaces,
As in a dream they change, they swiftly fill,
Countless masses debouch upon them,

---

*Quaker designation for May. Whitman was proud of his family's Quaker ties; he
wrote essays on Quakers Elias Hicks and George Fox for his prose miscellany *No-
vember Boughs* (1888).

They are now cover'd with the foremost people, arts, institutions,
   known.

See, projected through time,
For me an audience interminable.

With firm and regular step they wend, they never stop,
Successions of men, Americanos, a hundred millions,
One generation playing its part and passing on,
Another generation playing its part and passing on in its turn,
With faces turn'd sideways or backward towards me to listen,
With eyes retrospective towards me.

– 3 –

Americanos! conquerors! marches humanitarian!
Foremost! century marches! Libertad! masses!
For you a programme of chants.

Chants of the prairies,
Chants of the long-running Mississippi, and down to the Mexican
   sea,
Chants of Ohio, Indiana, Illinois, Iowa, Wisconsin and Minnesota,
Chants going forth from the centre from Kansas, and thence
   equidistant,
Shooting in pulses of fire ceaseless to vivify all.

– 4 –

Take my leaves America, take them South and take them North,
Make welcome for them everywhere, for they are your own
   offspring,
Surround them East and West, for they would surround you,
And you precedents, connect lovingly with them, for they
   connect lovingly with you.

I conn'd old times,
I sat studying at the feet of the great masters,

Now if eligible O that the great masters might return and
    study me.

In the name of these States shall I scorn the antique?
Why these are the children of the antique to justify it.

– 5 –

Dead poets, philosophs, priests,
Martyrs, artists, inventors, governments long since,
Language-shapers on other shores,
Nations once powerful, now reduced, withdrawn, or desolate,
I dare not proceed till I respectfully credit what you have left
    wafted hither,
I have perused it, own it is admirable, (moving awhile
    among it,)
Think nothing can ever be greater, nothing can ever deserve
    more than it deserves,
Regarding it all intently a long while, then dismissing it,
I stand in my place with my own day here.

Here lands female and male,
Here the heir-ship and heiress-ship of the world, here the flame
    of materials,
Here spirituality the translatress, the openly-avow'd,
The ever-tending, the finale of visible forms,
The satisfier, after due long-waiting now advancing,
Yes here comes my mistress the soul.

– 6 –

The soul,
Forever and forever—longer than soil is brown and solid—longer
    than water ebbs and flows.

I will make the poems of materials, for I think they are to be the
    most spiritual poems,
And I will make the poems of my body and of mortality,

For I think I shall then supply myself with the poems of my soul
    and of immortality.

I will make a song for these States that no one State may under
    any circumstances be subjected to another State,
And I will make a song that there shall be comity by day and by
    night between all the States, and between any two of them,
And I will make a song for the ears of the President, full of
    weapons with menacing points,
And behind the weapons countless dissatisfied faces;
And a song make I of the One form'd out of all,
The fang'd and glittering One whose head is over all,
Resolute warlike One including and over all,
(However high the head of any else that head is over all.)

I will acknowledge contemporary lands,
I will trail the whole geography of the globe and salute
    courteously every city large and small,
And employments! I will put in my poems that with you is
    heroism upon land and sea,
And I will report all heroism from an American point of view.

I will sing the song of companionship,
I will show what alone must finally compact these,
I believe these are to found their own ideal of manly love,
    indicating it in me,
I will therefore let flame from me the burning fires that were
    threatening to consume me,
I will lift what has too long kept down those smouldering fires,
I will give them complete abandonment,
I will write the evangel-poem of comrades and of love,
For who but I should understand love with all its sorrow and joy?
And who but I should be the poet of comrades?

– 7 –

I am the credulous man of qualities, ages, races,
I advance from the people in their own spirit,
Here is what sings unrestricted faith.

Omnes! omnes! let others ignore what they may,
I make the poem of evil also, I commemorate that part
    also,
I am myself just as much evil as good, and my nation is—and
     I say there is in fact no evil,
(Or if there is I say it is just as important to you, to the land or to
     me, as any thing else.)

I too, following many and follow'd by many, inaugurate a religion,
     I descend into the arena,
(It may be I am destin'd to utter the loudest cries there, the
     winner's pealing shouts,
Who knows? they may rise from me yet, and soar above every
     thing.)

Each is not for its own sake,
I say the whole earth and all the stars in the sky are for religion's
     sake.

I say no man has ever yet been half devout enough,
None has ever yet adored or worship'd half enough,
None has begun to think how divine he himself is, and how
     certain the future is.

I say that the real and permanent grandeur of these States must
     be their religion,
Otherwise there is no real and permanent grandeur;
(Nor character nor life worthy the name without
     religion,
Nor land nor man or woman without religion.)

– 8 –

What are you doing young man?
Are you so earnest, so given up to literature, science, art,
     amours?
These ostensible realities, politics, points?
Your ambition or business whatever it may be?

It is well—against such I say not a word, I am their poet also,
But behold! such swiftly subside, burnt up for religion's sake,
For not all matter is fuel to heat, impalpable flame, the essential
    life of the earth,
Any more than such are to religion.

– 9 –

What do you seek so pensive and silent?
What do you need camerado?[6]
Dear son do you think it is love?

Listen dear son—listen America, daughter or son,
It is a painful thing to love a man or woman to excess, and yet it
    satisfies, it is great,
But there is something else very great, it makes the whole coincide,
It, magnificent, beyond materials, with continuous hands sweeps
    and provides for all.

– 10 –

Know you, solely to drop in the earth the germs of a greater
    religion,
The following chants each for its kind I sing.

My comrade!
For you to share with me two greatnesses, and a third one rising
    inclusive and more resplendent,
The greatness of Love and Democracy, and the greatness of
    Religion.

Melange mine own, the unseen and the seen,
Mysterious ocean where the streams empty,
Prophetic spirit of materials shifting and flickering around me,
Living beings, identities now doubtless near us in the air that we
    know not of,
Contact daily and hourly that will not release me,
These selecting, these in hints demanded of me.

Not he with a daily kiss onward from childhood kissing me,
Has winded and twisted around me that which holds me
 to him,
Any more than I am held to the heavens and all the spiritual
 world,
After what they have done to me, suggesting themes.

O such themes—equalities! O divine average!
Warblings under the sun, usher'd as now, or at noon,
 or setting,
Strains musical flowing through ages, now reaching hither,
I take to your reckless and composite chords, add to them, and
 cheerfully pass them forward.

— 11 —

As I have walk'd in Alabama my morning walk,
I have seen where the she-bird the mocking-bird sat on her nest
 in the briers hatching her brood.

I have seen the he-bird also,
I have paus'd to hear him near at hand inflating his throat and
 joyfully singing.

And while I paus'd it came to me that what he really sang for was
 not there only,
Nor for his mate nor himself only, nor all sent back by the
 echoes,
But subtle, clandestine, away beyond,
A charge transmitted and gift occult for those being born.

— 12 —

Democracy! near at hand to you a throat is now inflating itself
 and joyfully singing.

Ma femme! for the brood beyond us and of us,
For those who belong here and those to come,

I exultant to be ready for them will now shake out carols stronger
    and haughtier than have ever yet been heard upon earth.
I will make the songs of passion to give them their way,

And your songs outlaw'd offenders, for I scan you with kindred
    eyes, and carry you with me the same as any.

I will make the true poem of riches,
To earn for the body and the mind whatever adheres and goes
    forward and is not dropt by death;
I will effuse egotism and show it underlying all, and I will be the
    bard of personality,
And I will show of male and female that either is but the equal of
    the other,
And sexual organs and acts! do you concentrate in me, for I am
    determin'd to tell you with courageous clear voice to prove
    you illustrious,
And I will show that there is no imperfection in the present, and
    can be none in the future,
And I will show that whatever happens to anybody it may be
    turn'd to beautiful results,
And I will show that nothing can happen more beautiful than
    death,
And I will thread a thread through my poems that time and
    events are compact,
And that all the things of the universe are perfect miracles, each
    as profound as any.

I will not make poems with reference to parts,
But I will make poems, songs, thoughts, with reference to
    ensemble,
And I will not sing with reference to a day, but with reference to
    all days,
And I will not make a poem nor the least part of a poem but has
    reference to the soul,
Because having look'd at the objects of the universe, I find there
    is no one nor any particle of one but has reference to the
    soul.

– 13 –

Was somebody asking to see the soul?
See, your own shape and countenance, persons, substances,
     beasts, the trees, the running rivers, the rocks and sands.

All hold spiritual joys and afterwards loosen them;
How can the real body ever die and be buried?

Of your real body and any man's or woman's real body,
Item for item it will elude the hands of the corpse-cleaners and
     pass to fitting spheres,
Carrying what has accrued to it from the moment of birth to the
     moment of death.

Not the types set up by the printer return their impression, the
     meaning, the main concern,
Any more than a man's substance and life or a woman's substance
     and life return in the body and the soul,
Indifferently before death and after death.

Behold, the body includes and is the meaning, the main concern,
     and includes and is the soul;
Whoever you are, how superb and how divine is your body, or any
     part of it!

– 14 –

Whoever you are, to you endless announcements!

Daughter of the lands did you wait for your poet?
Did you wait for one with a flowing mouth and indicative hand?
Toward the male of the States, and toward the female of the
     States,
Exulting words, words to Democracy's lands.

Interlink'd, food-yielding lands!
Land of coal and iron! land of gold! land of cotton, sugar, rice!

Land of wheat, beef, pork! land of wool and hemp! land of the
apple and the grape!

Land of the pastoral plains, the grass-fields of the world! land of
those sweet-air'd interminable plateaus!

Land of the herd, the garden, the healthy house of adobie!

Lands where the north-west Columbia winds, and where the
south-west Colorado winds!

Land of the eastern Chesapeake! land of the Delaware!

Land of Ontario, Erie, Huron, Michigan!

Land of the Old Thirteen! Massachusetts land! land of Vermont
and Connecticut!

Land of the ocean shores! land of sierras and peaks!

Land of boatmen and sailors! fishermen's land!

Inextricable lands! the clutch'd together! the passionate ones!

The side by side! the elder and younger brothers! the bony-
limb'd!

The great women's land! the feminine! the experienced sisters
and the inexperienced sisters!

Far breath'd land! Arctic braced! Mexican breez'd! the diverse!
the compact!

The Pennsylvanian! the Virginian! the double Carolinian!

O all and each well-loved by me! my intrepid nations! O I at any
rate include you all with perfect love!

I cannot be discharged from you! not from one any sooner than
another!

O death! O for all that, I am yet of you unseen this hour with
irrepressible love,

Walking New England, a friend, a traveler,

Splashing my bare feet in the edge of the summer ripples on
Paumanok's sands,

Crossing the prairies, dwelling again in Chicago, dwelling in
every town,

Observing shows, births, improvements, structures, arts,

Listening to orators and oratresses in public halls,

Of and through the States as during life, each man and woman
my neighbor,

The Louisianian, the Georgian, as near to me, and I as near to
him and her,

The Mississippian and Arkansian yet with me, and I yet with any
    of them,
Yet upon the plains west of the spinal river, yet in my house of
    adobie,
Yet returning eastward, yet in the Seaside State or in Maryland,
Yet Kanadian cheerily braving the winter, the snow and ice
    welcome to me,
Yet a true son either of Maine or of the Granite State, or the
    Narragansett Bay State, or the Empire State,
Yet sailing to other shores to annex the same, yet welcoming every
    new brother,
Hereby applying these leaves to the new ones from the hour they
    unite with the old ones,
Coming among the new ones myself to be their companion and
    equal, coming personally to you now,
Enjoining you to acts, characters, spectacles, with me.

– 15 –

With me with firm holding, yet haste, haste on.

For your life adhere to me,
(I may have to be persuaded many times before I consent to give
    myself really to you, but what of that?
Must not Nature be persuaded many times?)

No dainty dolce affettuoso* I,
Bearded, sun-burnt, gray-neck'd, forbidding, I have arrived,
To be wrestled with as I pass for the solid prizes of the universe,
For such I afford whoever can persevere to win them.

– 16 –

On my way a moment I pause,
Here for you! and here for America!

---

*Musical terms, from the Italian, for "sweet" and "sentimental, affected person."

Still the present I raise aloft, still the future of the States I
    harbinge glad and sublime,
And for the past I pronounce what the air holds of the red
    aborigines.

The red aborigines,
Leaving natural breaths, sounds of rain and winds, calls as of birds
    and animals in the woods, syllabled to us for names,
Okonee, Koosa, Ottawa, Monongahela, Sauk, Natchez,
    Chattahoochee, Kaqueta, Oronoco,
Wabash, Miami, Saginaw, Chippewa, Oshkosh, Walla-Walla,
Leaving such to the States they melt, they depart, charging the
    water and the land with names.

– 17 –

Expanding and swift, henceforth,
Elements, breeds, adjustments, turbulent, quick and audacious,
A world primal again, vistas of glory incessant and branching,
A new race dominating previous ones and grander far, with new
    contests,
New politics, new literatures and religions, new inventions and arts.

These, my voice announcing—I will sleep no more but arise,
You oceans that have been calm within me! how I feel you,
    fathomless, stirring, preparing unprecedented waves and
    storms.

– 18 –

See, steamers steaming through my poems,
See, in my poems immigrants continually coming and landing,
See, in arriere, the wigwam, the trail, the hunter's hut, the flat-
    boat, the maize leaf, the claim, the rude fence, and the
    backwoods village,
See, on the one side the Western Sea and on the other the
    Eastern Sea, how they advance and retreat upon my poems as
    upon their own shores,

See, pastures and forests in my poems—see, animals wild and
    tame—see, beyond the Kaw, countless herds of buffalo
    feeding on short curly grass,
See, in my poems, cities, solid, vast, inland, with paved streets, with
    iron and stone edifices, ceaseless vehicles, and commerce,
See, the many-cylinder'd steam printing-press—see, the electric
    telegraph stretching across the continent,
See, through Atlantica's depths pulses American Europe
    reaching, pulses of Europe duly return'd,
See, the strong and quick locomotive as it departs, panting,
    blowing the steam-whistle,
See, ploughmen ploughing farms—see, miners digging mines—
    see, the numberless factories,
See, mechanics busy at their benches with tools—see from
    among them superior judges, philosophs, Presidents, emerge,
    drest in working dresses,
See, lounging through the shops and fields of the States, me
    well-belov'd, close-held by day and night,
Hear the loud echoes of my songs there—read the hints come
    at last.

– 19 –

O camerado close! O you and me at last, and us two only.[7]
O a word to clear one's path ahead endlessly!
O something ecstatic and undemonstrable! O music wild!
O now I triumph—and you shall also;
O hand in hand—O wholesome pleasure—O one more desirer
    and lover!
O to haste firm holding—to haste, haste on with me.

SONG OF MYSELF[8]

– 1 –

I celebrate myself, and sing myself,
And what I assume you shall assume
For every atom belonging to me as good belongs to you.

I loafe and invite my soul,
I lean and loafe at my ease observing a spear of summer grass.

My tongue, every atom of my blood, form'd from this soil, this
    air,
Born here of parents born here from parents the same, and their
    parents the same,
I, now thirty-seven years old in perfect health begin,
Hoping to cease not till death.

Creeds and schools in abeyance,
Retiring back a while sufficed at what they are, but never
    forgotten,
I harbor for good or bad, I permit to speak at every hazard,
Nature without check with original energy.

— 2 —

Houses and rooms are full of perfumes, the shelves are crowded
    with perfumes,
I breathe the fragrance myself and know it and like it,
The distillation would intoxicate me also, but I shall not let it.

The atmosphere is not a perfume, it has no taste of the
    distillation, it is odorless,
It is for my mouth forever, I am in love with it,
I will go to the bank by the wood and become undisguised
    and naked,
I am mad for it to be in contact with me.

The smoke of my own breath,
Echoes, ripples, buzz'd whispers, love-root, silk-thread, crotch
    and vine,
My respiration and inspiration, the beating of my heart, the
    passing of blood and air through my lungs,
The sniff of green leaves and dry leaves, and of the shore and
    dark-color'd sea rocks, and of hay in the barn,
The sound of the belch'd words of my voice loos'd to the eddies of
    the wind,

A few light kisses, a few embraces, a reaching around of arms,
The play of shine and shade on the trees as the supple
　　　boughs wag,
The delight alone or in the rush of the streets, or along the fields
　　　and hill-sides,
The feeling of health, the full-noon trill, the song of me rising
　　　from bed and meeting the sun.

Have you reckon'd a thousand acres much? have you reckon'd the
　　　earth much?
Have you practis'd so long to learn to read?
Have you felt so proud to get at the meaning of poems?

Stop this day and night with me and you shall possess the origin
　　　of all poems,
You shall possess the good of the earth and sun, (there are
　　　millions of suns left,)
You shall no longer take things at second or third hand, nor look
　　　through the eyes of the dead, nor feed on the spectres in
　　　books,
You shall not look through my eyes either, nor take things
　　　from me,
You shall listen to all sides and filter them from your self.

– 3 –

I have heard what the talkers were talking, the talk of the
　　　beginning and the end,
But I do not talk of the beginning or the end.

There was never any more inception than there is now,
Nor any more youth or age than there is now,
And will never be any more perfection than there is now,
Nor any more heaven or hell than there is now.

Urge and urge and urge,
Always the procreant urge of the world.

Out of the dimness opposite equals advance, always substance
and increase, always sex,
Always a knit of identity, always distinction, always a breed of life.

To elaborate is no avail, learn'd and unlearn'd feel that it is so.

Sure as the most certain sure, plumb in the uprights, well
entretied, braced in the beams,
Stout as a horse, affectionate, haughty, electrical,
I and this mystery here we stand.

Clear and sweet is my soul, and clear and sweet is all that is
not my soul.

Lack one lacks both, and the unseen is proved by the seen,
Till that becomes unseen and receives proof in its turn.

Showing the best and dividing it from the worst age vexes age,
Knowing the perfect fitness and equanimity of things, while they
discuss I am silent, and go bathe and admire myself.

Welcome is every organ and attribute of me, and of any man
hearty and clean,
Not an inch nor a particle of an inch is vile, and none shall be
less familiar than the rest.

I am satisfied—I see, dance, laugh, sing;
As the hugging and loving bed-fellow sleeps at my side through the
night, and withdraws at the peep of the day with stealthy tread,
Leaving me baskets cover'd with white towels swelling the house
with their plenty,
Shall I postpone my acceptation and realization and scream at
my eyes,
That they turn from gazing after and down the road,
And forthwith cipher and show me to a cent,
Exactly the value of one and exactly the value of two, and
which is ahead?

– 4 –

Trippers and askers surround me,
People I meet, the effect upon me of my early life or the ward
    and city I live in, or the nation,
The latest dates, discoveries, inventions, societies, authors old
    and new,
My dinner, dress, associates, looks, compliments, dues,
The real or fancied indifference of some man or woman I love,
The sickness of one of my folks or of myself, or ill-doing or loss
    or lack of money, or depressions or exaltations,
Battles, the horrors of fratricidal war, the fever of doubtful news,
    the fitful events;
These come to me days and nights and go from me again,
But they are not the Me myself.

Apart from the pulling and hauling stands what I am,
Stands amused, complacent, compassionating, idle, unitary,
Looks down, is erect, or bends an arm on an impalpable
    certain rest,
Looking with side-curved head curious what will come next,
Both in and out of the game and watching and wondering at it.

Backward I see in my own days where I sweated through fog with
    linguists and contenders,
I have no mockings or arguments, I witness and wait.

– 5 –

I believe in you my soul, the other I am must not abase itself to you,
And you must not be abased to the other.

Loafe with me on the grass, loose the stop from your throat,
Not words, not music or rhyme I want, not custom or lecture, not
    even the best,
Only the lull I like, the hum of your valvéd voice.

I mind how once we lay such a transparent summer morning,

How you settled your head athwart my hips and gently turn'd over
    upon me,
And parted the shirt from my bosom-bone, and plunged your
    tongue to my bare-stript heart,
And reach'd till you felt my beard, and reach'd till you held my feet.

Swiftly arose and spread around me the peace and knowledge that
    pass all the argument of the earth,
And I know that the hand of God is the promise of my own,
And I know that the spirit of God is the brother of my own,
And that all the men ever born are also my brothers, and the
    women my sisters and lovers,
And that a kelson of the creation is love,
And limitless are leaves stiff or drooping in the fields,
And brown ants in the little wells beneath them,
And mossy scabs of the worm fence, heap'd stones, elder, mullein
    and poke-weed.

– 6 –

A child said *What is the grass?* fetching it to me with full hands;
How could I answer the child? I do not know what it is any more
    than he.

I guess it must be the flag of my disposition, out of hopeful green
    stuff woven.

Or I guess it is the handkerchief of the Lord,
A scented gift and remembrancer designedly dropt,
Bearing the owner's name someway in the corners, that we may
    see and remark, and say *Whose?*

Or I guess the grass is itself a child, the produced babe of the
    vegetation.

Or I guess it is a uniform hieroglyphic,
And it means, Sprouting alike in broad zones and narrow zones,
Growing among black folks as among white,

Kanuck, Tuckahoe, Congressman, Cuff, I give them the same,
    I receive them the same.

And now it seems to me the beautiful uncut hair of graves.

Tenderly will I use you curling grass,
It may be you transpire from the breasts of young men,
It may be if I had known them I would have loved them,
It may be you are from old people, or from offspring taken soon
    out of their mothers' laps,
And here you are the mothers' laps.

This grass is very dark to be from the white heads of old
    mothers,
Darker than the colorless beards of old men,
Dark to come from under the faint red roofs of mouths.

O I perceive after all so many uttering tongues,
And I perceive they do not come from the roofs of mouths for
    nothing.

I wish I could translate the hints about the dead young men
    and women,
And the hints about old men and mothers, and the offspring
    taken soon out of their laps.

What do you think has become of the young and old men?
And what do you think has become of the women and
    children?

They are alive and well somewhere,
The smallest sprout shows there is really no death,
And if ever there was it led forward life, and does not wait at the
    end to arrest it,
And ceas'd the moment life appear'd.

All goes onward and outward, nothing collapses,
And to die is different from what any one supposed, and luckier.

– 7 –

Has any one supposed it lucky to be born?
I hasten to inform him or her it is just as lucky to die, and I
    know it.

I pass death with the dying and birth with the new-wash'd babe,
    and am not contain'd between my hat and boots,
And peruse manifold objects, no two alike and every one good,
The earth good and the stars good, and their adjuncts all good.

I am not an earth nor an adjunct of an earth,
I am the mate and companion of people, all just as immortal and
    fathomless as myself,
(They do not know how immortal, but I know.)

Every kind for itself and its own, for me mine male and female,
For me those that have been boys and that love women,
For me the man that is proud and feels how it stings to be
    slighted,
For me the sweet-heart and the old maid, for me mothers and the
    mothers of mothers,
For me lips that have smiled, eyes that have shed tears,
For me children and the begetters of children.

Undrape! you are not guilty to me, nor stale nor discarded,
I see through the broadcloth and gingham whether or no,
And am around, tenacious, acquisitive, tireless, and cannot be
    shaken away.

– 8 –

The little one sleeps in its cradle,
I lift the gauze and look a long time, and silently brush away flies
    with my hand.

The youngster and the red-faced girl turn aside up the bushy hill,
I peeringly view them from the top.

The suicide sprawls on the bloody floor of the bedroom,
I witness the corpse with its dabbled hair, I note where the pistol
    has fallen.

The blab of the pave, tires of carts, sluff of boot-soles, talk of the
    promenaders,
The heavy omnibus, the driver with his interrogating thumb,
    the clank of the shod horses on the granite floor,
The snow-sleighs, clinking, shouted jokes, pelts of snowballs,
The hurrahs for popular favorites, the fury of rous'd mobs,
The flap of the curtain'd litter, a sick man inside borne to the
    hospital,
The meeting of enemies, the sudden oath, the blows and fall,
The excited crowd, the policeman with his star quickly working
    his passage to the centre of the crowd,
The impassive stones that receive and return so many echoes,
What groans of over-fed or half-starv'd who fall sun-struck or
    in fits,
What exclamations of women taken suddenly who hurry home
    and give birth to babes,
What living and buried speech is always vibrating here, what
    howls restrain'd by decorum,
Arrests of criminals, slights, adulterous offers made, acceptances,
    rejections with convex lips,
I mind them or the show or resonance of them—I come and
    I depart.

– 9 –

The big doors of the country barn stand open and ready,
The dried grass of the harvest-time loads the slow-drawn wagon,
The clear light plays on the brown gray and green intertinged,
The armfuls are pack'd to the sagging mow.

I am there, I help, I came stretch'd atop of the load,
I felt its soft jolts, one leg reclined on the other,
I jump from the cross-beams and seize the clover and timothy,
And roll head over heels and tangle my hair full of wisps.

– 10 –

Alone far in the wilds and mountains I hunt,
Wandering amazed at my own lightness and glee,
In the late afternoon choosing a safe spot to pass the night,
Kindling a fire and broiling the fresh-kill'd game,
Falling asleep on the gather'd leaves with my dog and gun by
    my side.

The Yankee clipper is under her sky-sails, she cuts the sparkle
    and scud,
My eyes settle the land, I bend at her prow or shout joyously from
    the deck.

The boatmen and clam-diggers arose early and stopt for me,
I tuck'd my trouser-ends in my boots and went and had a good
    time;
You should have been with us that day round the chowder-kettle.

I saw the marriage of the trapper in the open air in the far west,
    the bride was a red girl,
Her father and his friends sat near cross-legged and dumbly
    smoking, they had moccasins to their feet and large thick
    blankets hanging from their shoulders,
On a bank lounged the trapper, he was drest mostly in skins,
    his luxuriant beard and curls protected his neck, he held
    his bride by the hand,
She had long eyelashes, her head was bare, her coarse straight
    locks descended upon her voluptuous limbs and reach'd
    to her feet.

The runaway slave came to my house and stopt outside,
I heard his motions crackling the twigs of the woodpile,
Through the swung half-door of the kitchen I saw him limpsy
    and weak,
And went where he sat on a log and led him in and assured him,
And brought water and fill'd a tub for his sweated body and
    bruis'd feet,

And gave him a room that enter'd from my own, and gave him
     some coarse clean clothes,
And remember perfectly well his revolving eyes and his
     awkwardness,
And remember putting plasters on the galls of his neck and ankles;
He staid with me a week before he was recuperated and
     pass'd north,
I had him sit next me at table, my fire-lock lean'd in the corner.

— 11 —

Twenty-eight young men bathe by the shore,
Twenty-eight young men and all so friendly;
Twenty-eight years of womanly life and all so lonesome.

She owns the fine house by the rise of the bank,
She hides handsome and richly drest aft the blinds of the window.

Which of the young men does she like the best?
Ah the homeliest of them is beautiful to her.

Where are you off to, lady? for I see you,
You splash in the water there, yet stay stock still in your room.

Dancing and laughing along the beach came the twenty-ninth
     bather,
The rest did not see her, but she saw them and loved them.

The beards of the young men glisten'd with wet, it ran from their
     long hair,
Little streams pass'd all over their bodies.

An unseen hand also pass'd over their bodies,
It descended tremblingly from their temples and ribs.

The young men float on their backs, their white bellies bulge to
     the sun, they do not ask who seizes fast to them,

They do not know who puffs and declines with pendant and
    bending arch,
They do not think whom they souse with spray.

— 12 —

The butcher-boy puts off his killing-clothes, or sharpens his knife
    at the stall in the market,
I loiter enjoying his repartee and his shuffle and breakdown.

Blacksmiths with grimed and hairy chests environ the anvil,
Each has his main-sledge, they are all out, there is a great heat
    in the fire.

From the cinder-strew'd threshold I follow their movements,
The lithe sheer of their waists plays even with their massive
    arms,
Overhand the hammers swing, overhand so slow, overhand
    so sure,
They do not hasten, each man hits in his place.

— 13 —

The negro holds firmly the reins of his four horses, the block
    swags underneath on its tied-over chain,
The negro that drives the long dray of the stone-yard, steady and
    tall he stands pois'd on one leg on the string-piece,
His blue shirt exposes his ample neck and breast and loosens over
    his hip-band,
His glance is calm and commanding, he tosses the slouch of his
    hat away from his forehead,
The sun falls on his crispy hair and mustache, falls on the black
    of his polish'd and perfect limbs.

I behold the picturesque giant and love him, and I do not
    stop there,
I go with the team also.

In me the caresser of life wherever moving, backward as well as
    forward sluing,
To niches aside and junior bending, not a person or object
    missing,
Absorbing all to myself and for this song.

Oxen that rattle the yoke and chain or halt in the leafy shade,
    what is that you express in your eyes?
It seems to me more than all the print I have read in my life.

My tread scares the wood-drake and wood-duck on my distant and
    day-long ramble,
They rise together, they slowly circle around.

I believe in those wing'd purposes,
And acknowledge red, yellow, white, playing within me,
And consider green and violet and the tufted crown
    intentional,
And do not call the tortoise unworthy because she is not
    something else,
And the jay in the woods never studied the gamut, yet trills pretty
    well to me,
And the look of the bay mare shames silliness out of me.

— 14 —

The wild gander leads his flock through the cool night,
Ya honk he says, and sounds it down to me like an
    invitation,
The pert may suppose it meaningless, but I listening close,
Find its purpose and place up there toward the wintry sky.

The sharp-hoof'd moose of the north, the cat on the house-sill,
    the chickadee, the prairie-dog,
The litter of the grunting sow as they tug at her teats,
The brood of the turkey-hen and she with her half-spread
    wings,
I see in them and myself the same old law.

The press of my foot to the earth springs a hundred affections,
They scorn the best I can do to relate them.

I am enamour'd of growing out-doors,
Of men that live among cattle or taste of the ocean or woods,
Of the builders and steerers of ships and the wielders of axes and
     mauls, and the drivers of horses,
I can eat and sleep with them week in and week out.

What is commonest, cheapest, nearest, easiest, is Me,
Me going in for my chances, spending for vast returns,
Adorning myself to bestow myself on the first that will take me,
Not asking the sky to come down to my good will,
Scattering it freely forever.

– 15 –

The pure contralto sings in the organ loft,
The carpenter dresses his plank, the tongue of his foreplane
     whistles its wild ascending lisp,
The married and unmarried children ride home to their
     Thanksgiving dinner,
The pilot seizes the king-pin, he heaves down with a strong arm,
The mate stands braced in the whale-boat, lance and harpoon
     are ready,
The duck-shooter walks by silent and cautious stretches,
The deacons are ordain'd with cross'd hands at the altar,
The spinning-girl retreats and advances to the hum of the big wheel,
The farmer stops by the bars as he walks on a First-day loafe and
     looks at the oats and rye,
The lunatic is carried at last to the asylum a confirm'd case,
(He will never sleep any more as he did in the cot in his mother's
     bed-room;)
The jour printer with gray head and gaunt jaws works at his case,
He turns his quid of tobacco while his eyes blurr with the
     manuscript;
The malform'd limbs are tied to the surgeon's table,
What is removed drops horribly in a pail;

The quadroon girl is sold at the auction-stand, the drunkard nods
     by the bar-room stove,
The machinist rolls up his sleeves, the policeman travels his beat,
     the gate-keeper marks who pass,
The young fellow drives the express-wagon, (I love him, though I
     do not know him;)
The half-breed straps on his light boots to compete in the race,
The western turkey-shooting draws old and young, some lean on
     their rifles, some sit on logs,
Out from the crowds steps the marksman, takes his position,
     levels his piece;
The groups of newly-come immigrants cover the wharf or levee,
As the woolly-pates hoe in the sugar-field, the overseer views them
     from his saddle,
The bugle calls in the ball-room, the gentlemen run for their
     partners, the dancers bow to each other,
The youth lies awake in the cedar-roof'd garret and harks to the
     musical rain,
The Wolverine sets traps on the creek that helps fill the Huron,
The squaw wrapt in her yellow-hemm'd cloth is offering
     moccasins and bead-bags for sale,
The connoisseur peers along the exhibition-gallery with half-shut
     eyes bent sideways,
As the deck-hands make fast the steamboat the plank is thrown for
     the shore-going passengers,
The young sister holds out the skein while the elder sister winds it
     off in a ball, and stops now and then for the knots,
The one-year wife is recovering and happy having a week ago
     borne her first child,
The clean-hair'd Yankee girl works with her sewing-machine or in
     the factory or mill,
The paving-man leans on his two-handed rammer, the reporter's
     lead flies swiftly over the note-book, the sign-painter is
     lettering with blue and gold,
The canal boy trots on the tow-path, the book-keeper counts at his
     desk, the shoemaker waxes his thread,
The conductor beats time for the band and all the performers
     follow him,

The child is baptized, the convert is making his first
    professions,
The regatta is spread on the bay, the race is begun, (how the
    white sails sparkle!)
The drover watching his drove sings out to them that
    would stray,
The pedler sweats with his pack on his back (the purchaser
    higgling about the odd cent;)
The bride unrumples her white dress, the minute-hand of the
    clock moves slowly,
The opium-eater reclines with rigid head and just
    open'd lips,
The prostitute draggles her shawl, her bonnet bobs on her tipsy
    and pimpled neck,
The crowd laugh at her blackguard oaths, the men jeer and wink
    to each other,
(Miserable! I do not laugh at your oaths nor jeer you;)
The President holding a cabinet council is surrounded by the
    great Secretaries,
On the piazza walk three matrons stately and friendly with
    twined arms,
The crew of the fish-smack pack repeated layers of halibut in the
    hold,
The Missourian crosses the plains toting his wares and his
    cattle,
As the fare-collector goes through the train he gives notice by the
    jingling of loose change,
The floor-men are laying the floor, the tinners are tinning the
    roof, the masons are calling for mortar,
In single file each shouldering his hod pass onward the
    laborers;
Seasons pursuing each other the indescribable crowd is gather'd,
    it is the fourth of Seventh-month, (what salutes of cannon
    and small arms!)
Seasons pursuing each other the plougher ploughs, the mower
    mows, and the winter-grain falls in the ground;
Off on the lakes the pike-fisher watches and waits by the hole in
    the frozen surface,

The stumps stand thick round the clearing, the squatter strikes
    deep with his axe,
Flatboatmen make fast towards dusk near the cotton-wood or
    pecan-trees,
Coon-seekers go through the regions of the Red river or
    through those drain'd by the Tennessee, or through those
    of the Arkansas,
Torches shine in the dark that hangs on the Chattahoochee or
    Altamahaw,
Patriarchs sit at supper with sons and grandsons and
    great-grandsons around them,
In walls of adobie, in canvas tents, rest hunters and trappers after
    their day's sport,
The city sleeps and the country sleeps,
The living sleep for their time, the dead sleep for their time,
The old husband sleeps by his wife and the young husband sleeps
    by his wife;
And these tend inward to me, and I tend outward to them,
And such as it is to be of these more or less I am,
And of these one and all I weave the song of myself.

– 16 –

I am of old and young, of the foolish as much as the wise,
Regardless of others, ever regardful of others,
Maternal as well as paternal, a child as well as a man,
Stuff'd with the stuff that is coarse and stuff'd with the stuff
    that is fine,
One of the Nation of many nations, the smallest the same and
    the largest the same,
A Southerner soon as a Northerner, a planter nonchalant and
    hospitable down by the Oconee I live,
A Yankee bound my own way ready for trade, my joints the
    limberest joints on earth and the sternest joints on earth,
A Kentuckian walking the vale of the Elkhorn in my deerskin
    leggings, a Louisianian or Georgian,
A boatman over lakes or bays or along coasts, a Hoosier, Badger,
    Buckeye;

At home on Kanadian snow-shoes or up in the bush, or with
    fishermen off Newfoundland,
At home in the fleet of ice-boats, sailing with the rest and
    tacking,
At home on the hills of Vermont or in the woods of Maine, or the
    Texan ranch,
Comrade of Californians, comrade of free North-Westerners,
    (loving their big proportions,)
Comrade of raftsmen and coalmen, comrade of all who shake
    hands and welcome to drink and meat,
A learner with the simplest, a teacher of the thoughtfullest,
A novice beginning yet experient of myriads of seasons,
Of every hue and caste am I, of every rank and religion,
A farmer, mechanic, artist, gentleman, sailor, quaker,
Prisoner, fancy-man, rowdy, lawyer, physician, priest.

I resist any thing better than my own diversity,
Breathe the air but leave plenty after me,
And am not stuck up, and am in my place.

(The moth and the fish-eggs are in their place,
The bright suns I see and the dark suns I cannot see are in
    their place,
The palpable is in its place and the impalpable is in its place.)

– 17 –

These are really the thoughts of all men in all ages and lands,
    they are not original with me,
If they are not yours as much as mine they are nothing, or next
    to nothing,
If they are not the riddle and the untying of the riddle they are
    nothing,
If they are not just as close as they are distant they are nothing.

This is the grass that grows wherever the land is and the
    water is,
This the common air that bathes the globe.

– 18 –

With music strong I come, with my cornets and my drums,
I play not marches for accepted victors only, I play marches for
    conquer'd and slain persons.

Have you heard that it was good to gain the day?
I also say it is good to fall, battles are lost in the same spirit
    in which they are won.

I beat and pound for the dead,
I blow through my embouchures my loudest and gayest for them.

Vivas to those who have fail'd!
And to those whose war-vessels sank in the sea!
And to those themselves who sank in the sea!
And to all generals that lost engagements, and all overcome heroes!
And the numberless unknown heroes equal to the greatest heroes
    known!

– 19 –

This is the meal equally set, this the meat for natural hunger,
It is for the wicked just the same as the righteous, I make
    appointments with all,
I will not have a single person slighted or left away,
The kept-woman, sponger, thief, are hereby invited;
The heavy-lipp'd slave is invited, the venerealee is invited;
There shall be no difference between them and the rest.

This is the press of a bashful hand, this the float and odor of hair,
This the touch of my lips to yours, this the murmur of yearning,
This the far-off depth and height reflecting my own face,
This the thoughtful merge of myself, and the outlet again.

Do you guess I have some intricate purpose?
Well I have, for the Fourth month showers have, and the mica on
    the side of a rock has.

Do you take it I would astonish?
Does the daylight astonish? does the early redstart twittering
    through the woods?
Do I astonish more than they?

This hour I tell things in confidence,
I might not tell everybody, but I will tell you.

— 20 —

Who goes there? hankering, gross, mystical, nude;
How is it I extract strength from the beef I eat?

What is a man anyhow? what am I? what are you?

All I mark as my own you shall offset it with your own,
Else it were time lost listening to me.

I do not snivel that snivel the world over,
That months are vacuums and the ground but wallow and filth.

Whimpering and truckling fold with powders for invalids,
    conformity goes to the fourth-remov'd,
I wear my hat as I please indoors or out.

Why should I pray? why should I venerate and be ceremonious?

Having pried through the strata, analyzed to a hair, counsel'd
    with doctors and calculated close,
I find no sweeter fat than sticks to my own bones.

In all people I see myself, none more and not one a barley-corn
    less,
And the good or bad I say of myself I say of them.

I know I am solid and sound,
To me the converging objects of the universe perpetually flow,
All are written to me, and I must get what the writing means.

I know I am deathless,
I know this orbit of mine cannot be swept by a carpenter's
 compass,
I know I shall not pass like a child's carlacue cut with a burnt
 stick at night.

I know I am august,
I do not trouble my spirit to vindicate itself or be understood,
I see that the elementary laws never apologize,
(I reckon I behave no prouder than the level I plant my house by,
 after all.)

I exist as I am, that is enough,
If no other in the world be aware I sit content,
And if each and all be aware I sit content.

One world is aware and by far the largest to me, and that is
 myself,
And whether I come to my own to-day or in ten thousand or ten
 million years,
I can cheerfully take it now, or with equal cheerfulness I
 can wait.

My foothold is tenon'd and mortis'd in granite,
I laugh at what you call dissolution,
And I know the amplitude of time.

— 21 —

I am the poet of the Body and I am the poet of the Soul,
The pleasures of heaven are with me and the pains of hell are
 with me,
The first I graft and increase upon myself, the latter I translate
 into a new tongue.

I am the poet of the woman the same as the man,
And I say it is as great to be a woman as to be a man,
And I say there is nothing greater than the mother of men.

I chant the chant of dilation or pride,
We have had ducking and deprecating about enough,
I show that size is only development.

Have you outstript the rest? are you the President?
It is a trifle, they will more than arrive there every one, and still
    pass on.

I am he that walks with the tender and growing night,
I call to the earth and sea half-held by the night.

Press close bare-bosom'd night—press close magnetic nourishing
    night!
Night of south winds—night of the large few stars!
Still nodding night—mad naked summer night.

Smile O voluptuous cool-breath'd earth!
Earth of the slumbering and liquid trees!
Earth of departed sunset—earth of the mountains misty-topt!
Earth of the vitreous pour of the full moon just tinged with
    blue!
Earth of shine and dark mottling the tide of the river!
Earth of the limpid gray of clouds brighter and clearer for my sake!
Far-swooping elbow'd earth—rich apple-blossom'd earth!
Smile, for your lover comes.

Prodigal, you have given me love—therefore I to you give love!
O unspeakable passionate love.

— 22 —

You sea! I resign myself to you also—I guess what you mean,
I behold from the beach your crooked inviting fingers,
I believe you refuse to go back without feeling of me,
We must have a turn together, I undress, hurry me out of sight of
    the land,
Cushion me soft, rock me in billowy drowse,
Dash me with amorous wet, I can repay you.

Sea of stretch'd ground-swells,
Sea breathing broad and convulsive breaths,
Sea of the brine of life and of unshovell'd yet always-ready
    graves,
Howler and scooper of storms, capricious and dainty sea,
I am integral with you, I too am of one phase and of all
    phases.

Partaker of influx and efflux I, extoller of hate and
    conciliation,
Extoller of amies and those that sleep in each others' arms.

I am he attesting sympathy,
(Shall I make my list of things in the house and skip the house
    that supports them?)

I am not the poet of goodness only, I do not decline to be the
    poet of wickedness also.

What blurt is this about virtue and about vice?
Evil propels me and reform of evil propels me, I stand
    indifferent,
My gait is no fault-finder's or rejecter's gait,
I moisten the roots of all that has grown.

Did you fear some scrofula out of the unflagging pregnancy?
Did you guess the celestial laws are yet to be work'd over and
    rectified?

I find one side a balance and the antipodal side a balance,
Soft doctrine as steady help as stable doctrine,
Thoughts and deeds of the present our rouse and early start.

This minute that comes to me over the past decillions,
There is no better than it and now.

What behaved well in the past or behaves well to-day is not such
    a wonder,

The wonder is always and always how there can be a mean man
    or an infidel.

— 23 —

Endless unfolding of words of ages!
And mine a word of the modern, the word En-Masse.

A word of the faith that never balks,
Here or henceforward it is all the same to me, I accept Time
    absolutely.

It alone is without flaw, it alone rounds and completes all,
That mystic baffling wonder alone completes all.

I accept Reality and dare not question it,
Materialism first and last imbuing.

Hurrah for positive science! long live exact demonstration!
Fetch stonecrop mixt with cedar and branches of lilac,
This is the lexicographer, this the chemist, this made a grammar
    of the old cartouches,
These mariners put the ship through dangerous unknown
    seas,
This is the geologist, this works with the scalpel, and this is a
    mathematician.

Gentlemen, to you the first honors always!
Your facts are useful, and yet they are not my dwelling,
I but enter by them to an area of my dwelling.

Less the reminders of properties told my words,
And more the reminders they of life untold, and of freedom and
    extrication,
And make short account of neuters and geldings, and favor men
    and women fully equipt,
And beat the gong of revolt, and stop with fugitives and them that
    plot and conspire.

− 24 −

Walt Whitman, a kosmos, of Manhattan the son,[9]
Turbulent, fleshy, sensual, eating, drinking and breeding,
No sentimentalist, no stander above men and women or apart
      from them,
No more modest than immodest.

Unscrew the locks from the doors!
Unscrew the doors themselves from their jambs!

Whoever degrades another degrades me,
And whatever is done or said returns at last to me.

Through me the afflatus surging and surging, through me the
      current and index.

I speak the pass-word primeval, I give the sign of democracy,
By God! I will accept nothing which all cannot have their
      counter-part of on the same terms.

Through me many long dumb voices,
Voices of the interminable generations of prisoners and slaves,
Voices of the diseas'd and despairing and of thieves and dwarfs,
Voices of cycles of preparation and accretion,
And of the threads that connect the stars, and of wombs and of
      the father-stuff,
And of the rights of them the others are down upon,
Of the deform'd, trivial, flat, foolish, despised,
Fog in the air, beetles rolling balls of dung.

Through me forbidden voices,
Voices of sexes and lusts, voices veil'd and I remove the veil,
Voices indecent by me clarified and transfigur'd.

I do not press my fingers across my mouth,
I keep as delicate around the bowels as around the head and heart,
Copulation is no more rank to me than death is.

I believe in the flesh and the appetites,
Seeing, hearing, feeling, are miracles, and each part and tag of
    me is a miracle.

Divine am I inside and out, and I make holy whatever I touch or
    am touch'd from,
The scent of these arm-pits aroma finer than prayer,
This head more than churches, bibles, and all the creeds.

If I worship one thing more than another it shall be the spread of
    my own body, or any part of it,
Translucent mould of me it shall be you!
Shaded ledges and rests it shall be you!
Firm masculine colter it shall be you!
Whatever goes to the tilth of me it shall be you!
You my rich blood! your milky stream pale strippings of my life!
Breast that presses against other breasts it shall be you!
My brain it shall be your occult convolutions!
Root of wash'd sweet-flag! timorous pond-snipe! nest of guarded
    duplicate eggs! it shall be you!
Mix'd tussled hay of head, beard, brawn, it shall be you!
Trickling sap of maple, fibre of manly wheat, it shall be you!
Sun so generous it shall be you!
Vapors lighting and shading my face it shall be you!
You sweaty brooks and dews it shall be you!
Winds whose soft-tickling genitals rub against me it shall
    be you!
Broad muscular fields, branches of live oak, loving lounger in my
    winding paths, it shall be you!
Hands I have taken, face I have kiss'd, mortal I have ever touch'd,
    it shall be you.

I dote on myself, there is that lot of me and all so luscious,
Each moment and whatever happens thrills me with joy,
I cannot tell how my ankles bend, nor whence the cause of my
    faintest wish,
Nor the cause of the friendship I emit, nor the cause of the
    friendship I take again.

That I walk up my stoop, I pause to consider if it really be,
A morning-glory at my window satisfies me more than the
     metaphysics of books.

To behold the day-break!
The little light fades the immense and diaphanous shadows,
The air tastes good to my palate.

Hefts of the moving world at innocent gambols silently rising,
     freshly exuding,
Scooting obliquely high and low.

Something I cannot see puts upward libidinous prongs,
Seas of bright juice suffuse heaven.

The earth by the sky staid with, the daily close of their junction,
The heav'd challenge from the east that moment over my head,
The mocking taunt, See then whether you shall be master!

– 25 –

Dazzling and tremendous how quick the sun-rise would kill me,
If I could not now and always send sun-rise out of me.

We also ascend dazzling and tremendous as the sun,
We found our own O my soul in the calm and cool of the
     day-break.

My voice goes after what my eyes cannot reach,
With the twirl of my tongue I encompass worlds and volumes of
     worlds.

Speech is the twin of my vision, it is unequal to measure itself,
It provokes me forever, it says sarcastically,
Walt you contain enough, why don't you let it out then?

Come now I will not be tantalized, you conceive too much of
     articulation,

Do you not know O speech how the buds beneath you are folded?
Waiting in gloom, protected by frost,
The dirt receding before my prophetical screams,
I underlying causes to balance them at last,
My knowledge my live parts, it keeping tally with the meaning of
　　all things,
Happiness, (which whoever hears me let him or her set out in
　　search of this day.)

My final merit I refuse you, I refuse putting from me what I
　　really am,
Encompass worlds, but never try to encompass me,
I crowd your sleekest and best by simply looking toward you.

Writing and talk do not prove me,
I carry the plenum of proof and every thing else in my face,
With the hush of my lips I wholly confound the skeptic.

– 26 –

Now I will do nothing but listen,
To accrue what I hear into this song, to let sounds contribute
　　toward it.

I hear bravuras of birds, bustle of growing wheat, gossip of flames,
　　clack of sticks cooking my meals,
I hear the sound I love, the sound of the human voice,
I hear all sounds running together, combined, fused or
　　following,
Sounds of the city and sounds out of the city, sounds of the day
　　and night,
Talkative young ones to those that like them, the loud laugh of
　　work-people at their meals,
The angry base of disjointed friendship, the faint tones of the sick,
The judge with hands tight to the desk, his pallid lips
　　pronouncing a death-sentence,
The heave'e'yo of stevedores unlading ships by the wharves, the
　　refrain of the anchor lifters,

The ring of alarm-bells, the cry of fire, the whirr of swift-streaking
    engines and hose-carts with premonitory tinkles and color'd
    lights,
The steam-whistle, the solid roll of the train of approaching cars,
The slow march play'd at the head of the association marching
    two and two,
(They go to guard some corpse, the flag-tops are draped with
    black muslin.)

I hear the violoncello, ('tis the young man's heart's complaint,)
I hear the key'd cornet, it glides quickly in through my ears,
It shakes mad-sweet pangs through my belly and breast.

I hear the chorus, it is a grand opera,
Ah this indeed is music—this suits me.

A tenor large and fresh as the creation fills me,
The orbic flex of his mouth is pouring and filling me full.

I hear the train'd soprano (what work with hers is this?)[10]
The orchestra whirls me wider than Uranus flies,
It wrenches such ardors from me I did not know I possess'd
    them,
It sails me, I dab with bare feet, they are lick'd by the indolent
    waves,
I am cut by bitter and angry hail, I lose my breath,
Steep'd amid honey'd morphine, my windpipe throttled in fakes
    of death,
At length let up again to feel the puzzle of puzzles,
And that we call Being.

– 27 –

To be in any form, what is that?
(Round and round we go, all of us, and ever come back
    thither,)
If nothing lay more develop'd the quahaug in its callous shell
    were enough.

Mine is no callous shell,
I have instant conductors all over me whether I pass or stop,
They seize every object and lead it harmlessly through me.

I merely stir, press, feel with my fingers, and am happy,
To touch my person to some one else's is about as much as I
     can stand.

– 28 –

Is this then a touch? quivering me to a new identity,
Flames and ether making a rush for my veins,
Treacherous tip of me reaching and crowding to help them,
My flesh and blood playing out lightning to strike what is hardly
     different from myself,
On all sides prurient provokers stiffening my limbs,
Straining the udder of my heart for its withheld drip,
Behaving licentious toward me, taking no denial,
Depriving me of my best as for a purpose,
Unbuttoning my clothes, holding me by the bare waist,
Deluding my confusion with the calm of the sunlight and
     pasture-fields,
Immodestly sliding the fellow-senses away,
They bribed to swap off with touch and go and graze at the edges
     of me,
No consideration, no regard for my draining strength or my anger,
Fetching the rest of the herd around to enjoy them a while,
Then all uniting to stand on a headland and worry me.

The sentries desert every other part of me,
They have left me helpless to a red marauder,
They all come to the headland to witness and assist against me.

I am given up by traitors,
I talk wildly, I have lost my wits, I and nobody else am the
     greatest traitor,
I went myself first to the headland, my own hands carried me
     there.

You villain touch! what are you doing? my breath is tight in its
    throat,
Unclench your floodgates, you are too much for me.

– 29 –

Blind loving wrestling touch, sheath'd hooded sharptooth'd
    touch!
Did it make you ache so, leaving me?

Parting track'd by arriving, perpetual payment of perpetual loan,
Rich showering rain, and recompense richer afterward.

Sprouts take and accumulate, stand by the curb prolific and vital,
Landscapes projected masculine, full-sized and golden.

– 30 –

All truths wait in all things,
They neither hasten their own delivery nor resist it,
They do not need the obstetric forceps of the surgeon,
The insignificant is as big to me as any,
(What is less or more than a touch?)

Logic and sermons never convince,
The damp of the night drives deeper into my soul.

(Only what proves itself to every man and woman is so,
Only what nobody denies is so.)

A minute and a drop of me settle my brain,
I believe the soggy clods shall become lovers and lamps,
And a compend of compends is the meat of a man or woman,
And a summit and flower there is the feeling they have for each
    other,
And they are to branch boundlessly out of that lesson until it
    becomes omnific,
And until one and all shall delight us, and we them.

– 31 –

I believe a leaf of grass is no less than the journey-work of the
    stars,
And the pismire is equally perfect, and a grain of sand, and the
    egg of the wren,
And the tree-toad is a chef-d'œuvre for the highest,
And the running blackberry would adorn the parlors of heaven,
And the narrowest hinge in my hand puts to scorn all
    machinery,
And the cow crunching with depress'd head surpasses any
    statue,
And a mouse is miracle enough to stagger sextillions of infidels.

I find I incorporate gneiss, coal, long-threaded moss, fruits, grains,
    esculent roots,
And am stucco'd with quadrupeds and birds all over,
And have distanced what is behind me for good reasons,
But call any thing back again when I desire it.

In vain the speeding or shyness,
In vain the plutonic rocks send their old heat against my
    approach,
In vain the mastodon retreats beneath its own powder'd bones,
In vain objects stand leagues off and assume manifold shapes,
In vain the ocean settling in hollows and the great monsters
    lying low,
In vain the buzzard houses herself with the sky,
In vain the snake slides through the creepers and logs,
In vain the elk takes to the inner passes of the woods,
In vain the razor-bill'd auk sails far north to Labrador,
I follow quickly, I ascend to the nest in the fissure of the cliff.

– 32 –

I think I could turn and live with animals, they are so placid and
    self-contain'd,
I stand and look at them long and long.

They do not sweat and whine about their condition,
They do not lie awake in the dark and weep for their sins,
They do not make me sick discussing their duty to God,
Not one is dissatisfied, not one is demented with the mania of
    owning things,
Not one kneels to another, nor to his kind that lived thousands of
    years ago,
Not one is respectable or unhappy over the whole earth.

So they show their relations to me and I accept them,
They bring me tokens of myself, they evince them plainly in their
    possession.

I wonder where they get those tokens,
Did I pass that way huge times ago and negligently drop
    them?
Myself moving forward then and now and forever,
Gathering and showing more always and with velocity,
Infinite and omnigenous, and the like of these among them,
Not too exclusive toward the reachers of my remembrancers,
Picking out here one that I love, and now go with him on
    brotherly terms.

A gigantic beauty of a stallion, fresh and responsive to my
    caresses,
Head high in the forehead, wide between the ears,
Limbs glossy and supple, tail dusting the ground,
Eyes full of sparkling wickedness, ears finely cut, flexibly
    moving.

His nostrils dilate as my heels embrace him,
His well-built limbs tremble with pleasure as we race around and
    return.

I but use you a minute, then I resign you, stallion,
Why do I need your paces when I myself out-gallop them?
Even as I stand or sit passing faster than you.

− 33 −

Space and Time! now I see it is true, what I guess'd at,
What I guess'd when I loaf'd on the grass,
What I guess'd while I lay alone in my bed,
And again as I walk'd the beach under the paling stars of the
    morning.

My ties and ballasts leave me, my elbows rest in sea-gaps,
I skirt sierras, my palms cover continents,
I am afoot with my vision.

By the city's quadrangular houses — in log huts, camping with
    lumbermen,
Along the ruts of the turnpike, along the dry gulch and rivulet bed,
Weeding my onion-patch or hoeing rows of carrots and parsnips,
    crossing savannas, trailing in forests,
Prospecting, gold-digging, girdling the trees of a new purchase,
Scorch'd ankle-deep by the hot sand, hauling my boat down the
    shallow river,
Where the panther walks to and fro on a limb overhead, where
    the buck turns furiously at the hunter,
Where the rattlesnake suns his flabby length on a rock, where the
    otter is feeding on fish,
Where the alligator in his tough pimples sleeps by the bayou,
Where the black bear is searching for roots or honey, where the
    beaver pats the mud with his paddle-shaped tail;
Over the growing sugar, over the yellow-flower'd cotton plant,
    over the rice in its low moist field,
Over the sharp-peak'd farm house, with its scallop'd scum and
    slender shoots from the gutters,
Over the western persimmon, over the long-leav'd corn, over the
    delicate blue-flower flax,
Over the white and brown buckwheat, a hummer and buzzer
    there with the rest,
Over the dusky green of the rye as it ripples and shades in the
    breeze;

Scaling mountains, pulling myself cautiously up, holding on by
    low scragged limbs,
Walking the path worn in the grass and beat through the leaves of
    the brush,
Where the quail is whistling betwixt the woods and the wheat-lot,
Where the bat flies in the Seventh-month eve, where the great
    gold-bug drops through the dark,
Where the brook puts out of the roots of the old tree and flows to
    the meadow,
Where cattle stand and shake away flies with the tremulous
    shuddering of their hides,
Where the cheese-cloth hangs in the kitchen, where andirons
    straddle the hearth-slab, where cobwebs fall in festoons from
    the rafters;
Where trip-hammers crash, where the press is whirling its cylinders,
Wherever the human heart beats with terrible throes under its ribs,
Where the pear-shaped balloon is floating aloft, (floating in it
    myself and looking composedly down,)
Where the life-car is drawn on the slip-noose, where the heat
    hatches pale-green eggs in the dented sand,
Where the she-whale swims with her calf and never forsakes it,
Where the steam-ship trails hind-ways its long pennant of smoke,
Where the fin of the shark cuts like a black chip out of the
    water,
Where the half-burn'd brig is riding on unknown currents,
Where shells grow to her slimy deck, where the dead are
    corrupting below;
Where the dense-starr'd flag is borne at the head of the regiments,
Approaching Manhattan up by the long-stretching island,
Under Niagara, the cataract falling like a veil over my
    countenance,
Upon a door-step, upon the horse-block of hard wood outside,
Upon the race-course, or enjoying picnics or jigs or a good game
    of base-ball,
At he-festivals, with blackguard gibes, ironical license, bull-
    dances, drinking, laughter,
At the cider-mill tasting the sweets of the brown mash, sucking
    the juice through a straw,

At apple-peelings wanting kisses for all the red fruit I find,
At musters, beach-parties, friendly bees, huskings, house-raisings;
Where the mocking-bird sounds his delicious gurgles, cackles,
    screams, weeps,
Where the hay-rick stands in the barn-yard, where the dry-stalks
    are scatter'd, where the brood-cow waits in the hovel,
Where the bull advances to do his masculine work, where the
    stud to the mare, where the cock is treading the hen,
Where the heifers browse, where geese nip their food with short
    jerks,
Where sun-down shadows lengthen over the limitless and
    lonesome prairie,
Where herds of buffalo make a crawling spread of the square
    miles far and near,
Where the humming-bird shimmers, where the neck of the long-
    lived swan is curving and winding,
Where the laughing-gull scoots by the shore, where she laughs
    her near-human laugh,
Where bee-hives range on a gray bench in the garden half hid by
    the high weeds,
Where band-neck'd partridges roost in a ring on the ground with
    their heads out,
Where burial coaches enter the arch'd gates of a cemetery,
Where winter wolves bark amid wastes of snow and icicled trees,
Where the yellow-crown'd heron comes to the edge of the marsh
    at night and feeds upon small crabs,
Where the splash of swimmers and divers cools the warm noon,
Where the katy-did works her chromatic reed on the walnut-tree
    over the well,
Through patches of citrons and cucumbers with silver-wired leaves,
Through the salt-lick or orange glade, or under conical firs,
Through the gymnasium, through the curtain'd saloon, through
    the office or public hall;
Pleas'd with the native and pleas'd with the foreign, pleas'd with
    the new and old,
Pleas'd with the homely woman as well as the handsome,
Pleas'd with the quakeress as she puts off her bonnet and talks
    melodiously,

Pleas'd with the tune of the choir of the whitewash'd church,
Pleas'd with the earnest words of the sweating Methodist
    preacher, impress'd seriously at the camp meeting;
Looking in at the shop windows of Broadway the whole forenoon,
    flatting the flesh of my nose on the thick plate glass,
Wandering the same afternoon with my face turn'd up to the
    clouds, or down a lane or along the beach,
My right and left arms round the sides of two friends, and I in the
    middle;
Coming home with the silent and dark-cheek'd bush boy, (behind
    me he rides at the drape of the day,)
Far from the settlements studying the print of animals' feet, or the
    moccasin print,
By the cot in the hospital reaching lemonade to a feverish patient,
Nigh the coffin'd corpse when all is still, examining with a candle;
Voyaging to every port to dicker and adventure,
Hurrying with the modern crowd as eager and fickle as any,
Hot toward one I hate, ready in my madness to knife him,
Solitary at midnight in my back yard, my thoughts gone from me
    a long while,
Walking the old hills of Judæa with the beautiful gentle God by
    my side,
Speeding through space, speeding through heaven and the stars,
Speeding amid the seven satellites and the broad ring, and the
    diameter of eighty thousand miles,
Speeding with tail'd meteors, throwing fire-balls like the rest,
Carrying the crescent child that carries its own full mother in its
    belly,
Storming, enjoying, planning, loving, cautioning,
Backing and filling, appearing and disappearing,
I tread day and night such roads.

I visit the orchards of spheres and look at the product,
And look at quintillions ripen'd and look at quintillions green.

I fly those flights of a fluid and swallowing soul,
My course runs below the soundings of plummets.

I help myself to material and immaterial,
No guard can shut me off, no law prevent me.

I anchor my ship for a little while only,
My messengers continually cruise away or bring their returns
　　to me.

I go hunting polar furs and the seal, leaping chasms with a pike-
　　pointed staff, clinging to topples of brittle and blue.

I ascend to the foretruck,
I take my place late at night in the crow's-nest,
We sail the arctic sea, it is plenty light enough,
Through the clear atmosphere I stretch around on the wonderful
　　beauty,
The enormous masses of ice pass me and I pass them, the scenery
　　is plain in all directions,
The white-topt mountains show in the distance, I fling out my
　　fancies toward them,
We are approaching some great battle-field in which we are soon
　　to be engaged,
We pass the colossal outposts of the encampment, we pass with
　　still feet and caution,
Or we are entering by the suburbs some vast and ruin'd city,
The blocks and fallen architecture more than all the living cities
　　of the globe.

I am a free companion, I bivouac by invading watchfires,
I turn the bridegroom out of bed and stay with the bride
　　myself,
I tighten her all night to my thighs and lips.

My voice is the wife's voice, the screech by the rail of the stairs,
They fetch my man's body up dripping and drown'd.

I understand the large hearts of heroes,
The courage of present times and all times,

How the skipper saw the crowded and rudderless wreck of the
    steam-ship, and Death chasing it up and down the storm,
How he knuckled tight and gave not back an inch, and was
    faithful of days and faithful of nights,
And chalk'd in large letters on a board, *Be of good cheer, we will
    not desert you;*
How he follow'd with them and tack'd with them three days and
    would not give it up,
How he saved the drifting company at last,
How the lank loose-gown'd women look'd when boated from the
    side of their prepared graves,
How the silent old-faced infants and the lifted sick, and the sharp-
    lipp'd unshaved men;
All this I swallow, it tastes good, I like it well, it becomes mine,
I am the man, I suffer'd, I was there.

The disdain and calmness of martyrs,
The mother of old, condemn'd for a witch, burnt with dry wood,
    her children gazing on,
The hounded slave that flags in the race, leans by the fence,
    blowing, cover'd with sweat,
The twinges that sting like needles his legs and neck, the
    murderous buckshot and the bullets,
All these I feel or am.

I am the hounded slave, I wince at the bite of the dogs,
Hell and despair are upon me, crack and again crack the
    marksmen,
I clutch the rails of the fence, my gore dribs, thinn'd with the
    ooze of my skin,
I fall on the weeds and stones,
The riders spur their unwilling horses, haul close,
Taunt my dizzy ears and beat me violently over the head with
    whip-stocks.

Agonies are one of my changes of garments,
I do not ask the wounded person how he feels, I myself become
    the wounded person,
My hurts turn livid upon me as I lean on a cane and observe.

I am the mash'd fireman with breast-bone broken,
Tumbling walls buried me in their debris,
Heat and smoke I inspired, I heard the yelling shouts of my
    comrades,
I heard the distant click of their picks and shovels,
They have clear'd the beams away, they tenderly lift me
    forth.

I lie in the night air in my red shirt, the pervading hush is for my
    sake,
Painless after all I lie exhausted but not so unhappy,
White and beautiful are the faces around me, the heads are bared
    of their fire-caps,
The kneeling crowd fades with the light of the torches.

Distant and dead resuscitate,
They show as the dial or move as the hands of me, I am the clock
    myself.

I am an old artillerist, I tell of my fort's bombardment,
I am there again.

Again the long roll of the drummers,
Again the attacking cannon, mortars,
Again to my listening ears the cannon responsive.

I take part, I see and hear the whole,
The cries, curses, roar, the plaudits for well-aim'd shots,
The ambulanza slowly passing trailing its red drip,
Workmen searching after damages, making indispensable
    repairs,
The fall of grenades through the rent roof, the fan-shaped
    explosion,
The whizz of limbs, heads, stone, wood, iron, high in the air.

Again gurgles the mouth of my dying general, he furiously waves
    with his hand,
He gasps through the clot *Mind not me — mind — the
entrenchments.*

– 34 –

Now I tell what I knew in Texas in my early youth,
(I tell not the fall of Alamo,
Not one escaped to tell the fall of Alamo,
The hundred and fifty are dumb yet at Alamo,)
'Tis the tale of the murder in cold blood of four hundred and
    twelve young men.

Retreating they had form'd in a hollow square with their baggage
    for breastworks,
Nine hundred lives out of the surrounding enemys, nine times
    their number, was the price they took in advance,
Their colonel was wounded and their ammunition gone,
They treated for an honorable capitulation, receiv'd writing and
    seal, gave up their arms and march'd back prisoners of war.

They were the glory of the race of rangers,
Matchless with horse, rifle, song, supper, courtship,
Large, turbulent, generous, handsome, proud, and affectionate,
Bearded, sunburnt, drest in the free costume of hunters,
Not a single one over thirty years of age.

The second First-day morning they were brought out in squads
    and massacred, it was beautiful early summer,
The work commenced about five o'clock and was over by
    eight.

None obey'd the command to kneel,
Some made a mad and helpless rush, some stood stark and
    straight,
A few fell at once, shot in the temple or heart, the living and dead
    lay together,
The maim'd and mangled dug in the dirt, the new-comers saw
    them there,
Some half-kill'd attempted to crawl away,
These were despatch'd with bayonets or batter'd with the blunts of
    muskets,

A youth not seventeen years old seiz'd his assassin till two more
      came to release him,
The three were all torn and cover'd with the boy's blood.

At eleven o'clock began the burning of the bodies;
That is the tale of the murder of the four hundred and twelve
      young men.

− 35 −

Would you hear of an old-time sea fight?
Would you learn who won by the light of the moon and stars?
List to the yarn, as my grandmother's father the sailor told it to me.

Our foe was no skulk in his ship I tell you, (said he,)
His was the surly English pluck, and there is no tougher or truer,
      and never was, and never will be;
Along the lower'd eve he came horribly raking us.

We closed with him, the yards entangled, the cannon touch'd,
My captain lash'd fast with his own hands.

We had receiv'd some eighteen pound shots under the water,
On our lower-gun-deck two large pieces had burst at the first fire,
      killing all around and blowing up overhead.

Fighting at sun-down, fighting at dark,
Ten o'clock at night, the full moon well up, our leaks on the gain,
      and five feet of water reported,
The master-at-arms loosing the prisoners confined in the after-
      hold to give them a chance for themselves.

The transit to and from the magazine is now stopt by the sentinels,
They see so many strange faces they do not know whom to trust.

Our frigate takes fire,
The other asks if we demand quarter?
If our colors are struck and the fighting done?

Now I laugh content, for I hear the voice of my little captain,
We have not struck, he composedly cries, *we have just begun our
     part of the fighting.*

Only three guns are in use,
One is directed by the captain himself against the enemy's
     main-mast,
Two well serv'd with grape and canister silence his musketry and
     clear his decks.

The tops alone second the fire of this little battery, especially the
     main-top,
They hold out bravely during the whole of the action.

Not a moment's cease,
The leaks gain fast on the pumps, the fire eats toward the powder-
     magazine.

One of the pumps has been shot away, it is generally thought we
     are sinking.

Serene stands the little captain,
He is not hurried, his voice is neither high nor low,
His eyes give more light to us than our battle-lanterns.

Toward twelve there in the beams of the moon they surrender to us.

– 36 –

Stretch'd and still lies the midnight,
Two great hulls motionless on the breast of the darkness,
Our vessel riddled and slowly sinking, preparations to pass to the
     one we have conquer'd,
The captain on the quarter-deck coldly giving his orders through
     a countenance white as a sheet,
Near by the corpse of the child that serv'd in the cabin,
The dead face of an old salt with long white hair and carefully
     curl'd whiskers,

The flames spite of all that can be done flickering aloft and
    below,
The husky voices of the two or three officers yet fit for duty,
Formless stacks of bodies and bodies by themselves, dabs of flesh
    upon the masts and spars,
Cut of cordage, dangle of rigging, slight shock of the soothe of
    waves,
Black and impassive guns, litter of powder-parcels, strong scent,
A few large stars overhead, silent and mournful shining,
Delicate sniffs of sea-breeze, smells of sedgy grass and fields by
    the shore, death-messages given in charge to survivors,
The hiss of the surgeon's knife, the gnawing teeth of his saw,
Wheeze, cluck, swash of falling blood, short wild scream, and
    long, dull, tapering groan,
These so, these irretrievable.

― 37 ―

You laggards there on guard! look to your arms!
In at the conquer'd doors they crowd! I am possess'd!
Embody all presences outlaw'd or suffering,
See myself in prison shaped like another man,
And feel the dull unintermitted pain.[11]

For me the keepers of convicts shoulder their carbines and keep
    watch,
It is I let out in the morning and barr'd at night.

Not a mutineer walks handcuff'd to jail but I am handcuff'd to
    him and walk by his side,
(I am less the jolly one there, and more the silent one with sweat
    on my twitching lips.)

Not a youngster is taken for larceny but I go up too, and am tried
    and sentenced.

Not a cholera patient lies at the last gasp but I also lie at the last
    gasp,

My face is ash-color'd, my sinews gnarl, away from me people
     retreat.

Askers embody themselves in me and I am embodied in them,
I project my hat, sit shame-faced, and beg.

– 38 –

Enough! enough! enough![12]
Somehow I have been stunn'd. Stand back!
Give me a little time beyond my cuff'd head, slumbers, dreams,
     gaping,
I discover myself on the verge of a usual mistake.

That I could forget the mockers and insults!
That I could forget the trickling tears and the blows of the
     bludgeons and hammers!
That I could look with a separate look on my own crucifixion and
     bloody crowning.

I remember now,
I resume the overstaid fraction,
The grave of rock multiplies what has been confided to it, or to
     any graves,
Corpses rise, gashes heal, fastenings roll from me.

I troop forth replenish'd with supreme power, one of an average
     unending procession,
Inland and sea-coast we go, and pass all boundary lines,
Our swift ordinances on their way over the whole earth,
The blossoms we wear in our hats the growth of thousands of years.

Eleves, I salute you! come forward!
Continue your annotations, continue your questionings.

– 39 –

The friendly and flowing savage, who is he?
Is he waiting for civilization, or past it and mastering it?

Is he some Southwesterner rais'd out-doors? is he Kanadian?
Is he from the Mississippi country? Iowa, Oregon, California?
The mountains? prairie life, bush life? or sailor from the sea?

Wherever he goes men and women accept and desire him,
They desire he should like them, touch them, speak to them, stay
    with them.

Behavior lawless as snow-flakes, words simple as grass, uncomb'd
    head, laughter, and naiveté,
Slow-stepping feet, common features, common modes and
    emanations,
They descend in new forms from the tips of his fingers,
They are wafted with the odor of his body or breath, they fly out
    of the glance of his eyes.

– 40 –

Flaunt of the sunshine I need not your bask—lie over!
You light surfaces only, I force surfaces and depths also.

Earth! you seem to look for something at my hands,
Say, old top-knot, what do you want?

Man or woman, I might tell how I like you, but cannot,
And might tell what it is in me and what it is in you, but
    cannot,
And might tell that pining I have, that pulse of my nights
    and days.

Behold, I do not give lectures or a little charity,
When I give I give myself.

You there, impotent, loose in the knees,
Open your scarf'd chops till I blow grit within you,
Spread your palms and lift the flaps of your pockets,
I am not to be denied, I compel, I have stores plenty and to
    spare,
And any thing I have I bestow.

I do not ask who you are, that is not important to me,
You can do nothing and be nothing but what I will infold you.

To cotton-field drudge or cleaner of privies I lean,
On his right cheek I put the family kiss,
And in my soul I swear I never will deny him.

On women fit for conception I start bigger and nimbler babes,
(This day I am jetting the stuff of far more arrogant republics.)

To any one dying, thither I speed and twist the knob of the door,
Turn the bed-clothes toward the foot of the bed,
Let the physician and the priest go home.

I seize the descending man and raise him with resistless will,
O despairer, here is my neck,
By God, you shall not go down! hang your whole weight upon me.

I dilate you with tremendous breath, I buoy you up,
Every room of the house do I fill with an arm'd force,
Lovers of me, bafflers of graves.

Sleep—I and they keep guard all night,
Not doubt, not decease shall dare to lay finger upon you,
I have embraced you, and henceforth possess you to myself,
And when you rise in the morning you will find what I tell you
    is so.

– 41 –

I am he bringing help for the sick as they pant on their backs,
And for strong upright men I bring yet more needed help.
I heard what was said of the universe,
Heard it and heard it of several thousand years;
It is middling well as far as it goes—but is that all?

Magnifying and applying come I,
Outbidding at the start the old cautious hucksters,

Taking myself the exact dimensions of Jehovah,
Lithographing Kronos, Zeus his son, and Hercules his grandson,
Buying drafts of Osiris, Isis, Belus, Brahma, Buddha,
In my portfolio placing Manito loose, Allah on a leaf, the crucifix
 engraved,
With Odin and the hideous-faced Mexitli and every idol and
 image,
Taking them all for what they are worth and not a cent more,
Admitting they were alive and did the work of their days,
(They bore mites as for unfledg'd birds who have now to rise and
 fly and sing for themselves,)
Accepting the rough deific sketches to fill out better in myself,
 bestowing them freely on each man and woman I see,
Discovering as much or more in a framer framing a house,
Putting higher claims for him there with his roll'd-up sleeves
 driving the mallet and chisel,
Not objecting to special revelations, considering a curl of smoke
 or a hair on the back of my hand just as curious as any
 revelation,
Lads ahold of fire-engines and hook-and-ladder ropes no less to
 me than the gods of the antique wars,
Minding their voices peal through the crash of destruction,
Their brawny limbs passing safe over charr'd laths, their white
 foreheads whole and unhurt out of the flames;
By the mechanic's wife with her babe at her nipple interceding
 for every person born,
Three scythes at harvest whizzing in a row from three lusty angels
 with shirts bagg'd out at their waists,
The snag-tooth'd hostler with red hair redeeming sins past and to
 come,
Selling all he possesses, traveling on foot to fee lawyers for his
 brother and sit by him while he is tried for forgery;
What was strewn in the amplest strewing the square rod about
 me, and not filling the square rod then,
The bull and the bug never worshipp'd half enough,
Dung and dirt more admirable than was dream'd,
The supernatural of no account, myself waiting my time to be
 one of the supremes,

The day getting ready for me when I shall do as much good as the
    best, and be as prodigious;
By my life-lumps! becoming already a creator,
Putting myself here and now to the ambush'd womb of the
    shadows.

– 42 –

A call in the midst of the crowd,
My own voice, orotund sweeping and final.

Come my children,
Come my boys and girls, my women, household and intimates,
Now the performer launches his nerve, he has pass'd his prelude
    on the reeds within.

Easily written loose finger'd chords—I feel the thrum of your
    climax and close.

My head slues round on my neck,
Music rolls, but not from the organ,
Folks are around me, but they are no household of mine.

Ever the hard unsunk ground,
Ever the eaters and drinkers, ever the upward and downward sun,
    ever the air and the ceaseless tides,
Ever myself and my neighbors, refreshing, wicked, real,
Ever the old inexplicable query, ever that thorn'd thumb, that
    breath of itches and thirsts,
Ever the vexer's *hoot! hoot!* till we find where the sly one hides
    and bring him forth,
Ever love, ever the sobbing liquid of life,
Ever the bandage under the chin, ever the trestles of death.

Here and there with dimes on the eyes walking,
To feed the greed of the belly the brains liberally spooning,
Tickets buying, taking, selling, but in to the feast never once
    going,

Many sweating, ploughing, thrashing, and then the chaff for
    payment receiving,
A few idly owning, and they the wheat continually claiming.

This is the city and I am one of the citizens,
Whatever interests the rest interests me, politics, wars, markets,
    newspapers, schools,
The mayor and councils, banks, tariffs, steamships, factories,
    stocks, stores, real estate and personal estate.

The little plentiful manikins skipping around in collars and tail'd
    coats,
I am aware who they are, (they are positively not worms or
    fleas,)
I acknowledge the duplicates of myself, the weakest and
    shallowest is deathless with me,
What I do and say the same waits for them,
Every thought that flounders in me the same flounders in them.

I know perfectly well my own egotism,
Know my omnivorous lines and must not write any less,
And would fetch you whoever you are flush with myself.

Not words of routine this song of mine,
But abruptly to question, to leap beyond yet nearer bring;
This printed and bound book—but the printer and the printing-
    office boy?
The well-taken photographs—but your wife or friend close and
    solid in your arms?
The black ship mail'd with iron, her mighty guns in her turrets—
    but the pluck of the captain and engineers?
In the houses the dishes and fare and furniture—but the host and
    hostess, and the look out of their eyes?
The sky up there—yet here or next door, or across the way?
The saints and sages in history—but you yourself?
Sermons, creeds, theology—but the fathomless human
    brain,
And what is reason? and what is love? and what is life?

- 43 -

I do not despise you priests, all time, the world over,
My faith is the greatest of faiths and the least of faiths,
Enclosing worship ancient and modern and all between ancient
    and modern,
Believing I shall come again upon the earth after five thousand
    years,
Waiting responses from oracles, honoring the gods, saluting the
    sun,
Making a fetich of the first rock or stump, powowing with sticks
    in the circle of obis,
Helping the llama or brahmin as he trims the lamps of the idols,
Dancing yet through the streets in a phallic procession, rapt and
    austere in the woods a gymnosophist,
Drinking mead from the skull-cup, to Shastas and Vedas
    admirant, minding the Koran,
Walking the teokallis, spotted with gore from the stone and knife,
    beating the serpent-skin drum,
Accepting the Gospels, accepting him that was crucified, knowing
    assuredly that he is divine,
To the mass kneeling or the puritan's prayer rising, or sitting
    patiently in a pew,
Ranting and frothing in my insane crisis, or waiting dead-like till
    my spirit arouses me,
Looking forth on pavement and land, or outside of pavement and
    land,
Belonging to the winders of the circuit of circuits.

One of that centripetal and centrifugal gang I turn and talk like a
    man leaving charges before a journey.

Down-hearted doubters dull and excluded,
Frivolous, sullen, moping, angry, affected, dishearten'd,
    atheistical,
I know every one of you, I know the sea of torment, doubt,
    despair and unbelief.

How the flukes splash!
How they contort rapid as lightning, with spasms and spouts of
    blood!

Be at peace bloody flukes of doubters and sullen mopers,
I take my place among you as much as among any,
The past is the push of you, me, all, precisely the same,
And what is yet untried and afterward is for you, me, all, precisely
    the same.

I do not know what is untried and afterward,
But I know it will in its turn prove sufficient, and cannot fail.

Each who passes is consider'd, each who stops is consider'd, not a
    single one can it fail.

It cannot fail the young man who died and was buried,
Nor the young woman who died and was put by his side,
Nor the little child that peep'd in at the door, and then drew back
    and was never seen again,
Nor the old man who has lived without purpose, and feels it with
    bitterness worse than gall,
Nor him in the poor house tubercled by rum and the bad disorder,
Nor the numberless slaughter'd and wreck'd, nor the brutish
    koboo call'd the ordure of humanity,
Nor the sacs merely floating with open mouths for food to slip in,
Nor any thing in the earth, or down in the oldest graves of the earth,
Nor any thing in the myriads of spheres, nor the myriads of
    myriads that inhabit them.
Nor the present, nor the least wisp that is known.

- 44 -

It is time to explain myself—let us stand up.

What is known I strip away,
I launch all men and women forward with me into the Unknown.

The clock indicates the moment—but what does eternity
     indicate?

We have thus far exhausted trillions of winters and summers,
There are trillions ahead, and trillions ahead of them.

Births have brought us richness and variety,
And other births will bring us richness and variety.

I do not call one greater and one smaller,
That which fills its period and place is equal to any.

Were mankind murderous or jealous upon you, my brother, my
     sister?
I am sorry for you, they are not murderous or jealous upon me,
All has been gentle with me, I keep no account with lamentation,
(What have I to do with lamentation?)

I am an acme of things accomplish'd, and I an encloser of things
     to be.

My feet strike an apex of the apices of the stairs,
On every step bunches of ages, and larger bunches between
     the steps,
All below duly travel'd, and still I mount and mount.

Rise after rise bow the phantoms behind me,
Afar down I see the huge first Nothing, I know I was even there,
I waited unseen and always, and slept through the lethargic mist,
And took my time, and took no hurt from the fetid carbon.

Long I was hugg'd close—long and long.

Immense have been the preparations for me,
Faithful and friendly the arms that have help'd me.

Cycles ferried my cradle, rowing and rowing like cheerful
     boatmen,

For room to me stars kept aside in their own rings,
They sent influences to look after what was to hold me.

Before I was born out of my mother generations guided me,
My embryo has never been torpid, nothing could overlay it.

For it the nebula cohered to an orb,
The long slow strata piled to rest it on,
Vast vegetables gave it sustenance,
Monstrous sauroids transported it in their mouths and deposited it
    with care.

All forces have been steadily employ'd to complete and delight me,
Now on this spot I stand with my robust soul.

– 45 –

O span of youth! ever-push'd elasticity!
O manhood, balanced, florid and full.

My lovers suffocate me,
Crowding my lips, thick in the pores of my skin,
Jostling me through streets and public halls, coming naked to me
    at night,
Crying by day *Ahoy!* from the rocks of the river, swinging and
    chirping over my head,
Calling my name from flower-beds, vines, tangled underbrush,
Lighting on every moment of my life,
Bussing my body with soft balsamic busses,
Noiselessly passing handfuls out of their hearts and giving them to
    be mine.

Old age superbly rising! O welcome, ineffable grace of dying
    days!

Every condition promulges not only itself, it promulges what
    grows after and out of itself,
And the dark hush promulges as much as any.

I open my scuttle at night and see the far-sprinkled systems,
And all I see, multiplied as high as I can cipher edge but the rim
    of the farther systems.

Wider and wider they spread, expanding, always expanding,
Outward and outward and forever outward.

My sun has his sun and round him obediently wheels,
He joins with his partners a group of superior circuit,
And greater sets follow, making specks of the greatest inside them.

There is no stoppage and never can be stoppage,
If I, you, and the worlds, and all beneath or upon their surfaces,
    were this moment reduced back to a pallid float, it would not
    avail in the long run,
We should surely bring up again where we now stand,
And surely go as much farther, and then farther and farther.

A few quadrillions of eras, a few octillions of cubic leagues, do
    not hazard the span or make it impatient,
They are but parts, anything is but a part.

See ever so far, there is limitless space outside of that,
Count ever so much, there is limitless time around that.

My rendezvous is appointed, it is certain,
The Lord will be there and wait till I come on perfect terms,
The great Camerado, the lover true for whom I pine will be there.[13]

– 46 –

I know I have the best of time and space, and was never measured
    and never will be measured.

I tramp a perpetual journey, (come listen all!)
My signs are a rain-proof coat, good shoes, and a staff cut from
    the woods,

No friend of mine takes his ease in my chair,
I have no chair, no church, no philosophy,
I lead no man to a dinner-table, library, exchange,
But each man and each woman of you I lead upon a knoll,
My left hand hooking you round the waist,
My right hand pointing to landscapes of continents and the
     public road.

Not I, not any one else can travel that road for you,
You must travel it for yourself.

It is not far, it is within reach,
Perhaps you have been on it since you were born and did not
     know,
Perhaps it is everywhere on water and on land.
Shoulder your duds dear son, and I will mine, and let us hasten
     forth,
Wonderful cities and free nations we shall fetch as we go.

If you tire, give me both burdens, and rest the chuff of your hand
     on my hip,
And in due time you shall repay the same service to me,
For after we start we never lie by again.

This day before dawn I ascended a hill and look'd at the crowded
     heaven,
And I said to my spirit *When we become the enfolders of those
     orbs, and the pleasure and knowledge of every thing in them,
     shall we be fill'd and satisfied then?*
And my spirit said No, *we but level that lift to pass and continue
     beyond.*

You are also asking me questions and I hear you,
I answer that I cannot answer, you must find out for yourself.

Sit a while dear son,
Here are biscuits to eat and here is milk to drink,

But as soon as you sleep and renew yourself in sweet clothes, I
    kiss you with a good-by kiss and open the gate for your egress
    hence.

Long enough have you dream'd contemptible dreams,
Now I wash the gum from your eyes,
You must habit yourself to the dazzle of the light and of every
    moment of your life.

Long have you timidly waded holding a plank by the shore,
Now I will you to be a bold swimmer,
To jump off in the midst of the sea, rise again, nod to me, shout,
    and laughingly dash with your hair.

47

I am the teacher of athletes,
He that by me spreads a wider breast than my own proves the
    width of my own,
He most honors my style who learns under it to destroy the teacher.

The boy I love, the same becomes a man not through derived
    power, but in his own right,
Wicked rather than virtuous out of conformity or fear,
Fond of his sweetheart, relishing well his steak,
Unrequited love or a slight cutting him worse than sharp steel
    cuts,
First-rate to ride, to fight, to hit the bull's eye, to sail a skiff, to
    sing a song or play on the banjo,
Preferring scars and the beard and faces pitted with small-pox
    over all latherers,
And those well-tann'd to those that keep out of the sun.

I teach straying from me, yet who can stray from me?
I follow you whoever you are from the present hour,
My words itch at your ears till you understand them.

I do not say these things for a dollar or to fill up the time while I
    wait for a boat,

(It is you talking just as much as myself, I act as the tongue
    of you,
Tied in your mouth, in mine it begins to be loosen'd.)

I swear I will never again mention love or death inside a
    house,
And I swear I will never translate myself at all, only to him or her
    who privately stays with me in the open air.

If you would understand me go to the heights or water-shore,
The nearest gnat is an explanation, and a drop or motion of waves
    a key,
The maul, the oar, the hand-saw, second my words.

No shutter'd room or school can commune with me,
But roughs and little children better than they.

The young mechanic is closest to me, he knows me well,
The woodman that takes his axe and jug with him shall take me
    with him all day,
The farm-boy ploughing in the field feels good at the sound of
    my voice,
In vessels that sail my words sail, I go with fishermen and seamen
    and love them.

The soldier camp'd or upon the march is mine,
On the night ere the pending battle many seek me, and I do not
    fail them,
On that solemn night (it may be their last) those that know me
    seek me.

My face rubs to the hunter's face when he lies down alone in his
    blanket,
The driver thinking of me does not mind the jolt of his
    wagon,
The young mother and old mother comprehend me,
The girl and the wife rest the needle a moment and forget where
    they are,
They and all would resume what I have told them.

– 48 –

I have said that the soul is not more than the body,
And I have said that the body is not more than the soul,
And nothing, not God, is greater to one than one's self is,
And whoever walks a furlong without sympathy walks to his own
    funeral drest in his shroud,
And I or you pocketless of a dime may purchase the pick of the
    earth,
And to glance with an eye or show a bean in its pod confounds
    the learning of all times,
And there is no trade or employment but the young man
    following it may become a hero,
And there is no object so soft but it makes a hub for the wheel'd
    universe,
And I say to any man or woman, Let your soul stand cool and
    composed before a million universes.

And I say to mankind, Be not curious about God,
For I who am curious about each am not curious about God,
(No array of terms can say how much I am at peace about God
    and about death.)

I hear and behold God in every object, yet understand God not
    in the least,
Nor do I understand who there can be more wonderful than
    myself.

Why should I wish to see God better than this day?
I see something of God each hour of the twenty-four, and each
    moment then,
In the faces of men and women I see God, and in my own face in
    the glass,
I find letters from God dropt in the street, and every one is sign'd
    by God's name,
And I leave them where they are, for I know that wheresoe'er
    I go,
Others will punctually come for ever and ever.

− 49 −

And as to you Death, and you bitter hug of mortality, it is idle to
    try to alarm me.

To his work without flinching the accoucheur comes,
I see the elder-hand pressing receiving supporting,
I recline by the sills of the exquisite flexible doors,
And mark the outlet, and mark the relief and escape.

And as to you Corpse I think you are good manure, but that does
    not offend me,
I smell the white roses sweet-scented and growing,
I reach to the leafy lips, I reach to the polish'd breasts of
    melons.

And as to you Life I reckon you are the leavings of many
    deaths,
(No doubt I have died myself ten thousand times before.)

I hear you whispering there O stars of heaven,
O suns—O grass of graves—O perpetual transfers and
    promotions,
If you do not say any thing how can I say any thing?

Of the turbid pool that lies in the autumn forest,
Of the moon that descends the steeps of the soughing
    twilight,
Toss, sparkles of day and dusk—toss on the black stems that decay
    in the muck,
Toss to the moaning gibberish of the dry limbs.

I ascend from the moon, I ascend from the night,
I perceive that the ghastly glimmer is noonday sunbeams
    reflected,
And debouch to the steady and central from the offspring great or
    small.

– 50 –

There is that in me—I do not know what it is—but I know it is
   in me.

Wrench'd and sweaty—calm and cool then my body becomes,
I sleep—I sleep long.

I do not know it—it is without name—it is a word unsaid,
It is not in any dictionary, utterance, symbol.

Something it swings on more than the earth I swing on,
To it the creation is the friend whose embracing awakes me.

Perhaps I might tell more. Outlines! I plead for my brothers and
   sisters.

Do you see O my brothers and sisters?
It is not chaos or death—it is form, union, plan—it is eternal
   life—it is Happiness.

– 51 –

The past and present wilt—I have fill'd them, emptied them.
And proceed to fill my next fold of the future.

Listener up there! what have you to confide to me?
Look in my face while I snuff the sidle of evening,
(Talk honestly, no one else hears you, and I stay only a minute
   longer.)

Do I contradict myself?
Very well then I contradict myself,
(I am large, I contain multitudes.)

I concentrate toward them that are nigh, I wait on the
   door-slab.

Who has done his day's work? who will soonest be through with
    his supper?
Who wishes to walk with me?

Will you speak before I am gone? will you prove already
    too late?

– 52 –

The spotted hawk swoops by and accuses me, he complains of my
    gab and my loitering.

I too am not a bit tamed, I too am untranslatable,
I sound my barbaric yawp over the roofs of the world.

The last scud of day holds back for me,
It flings my likeness after the rest and true as any on the shadow'd
    wilds,
It coaxes me to the vapor and the dusk.

I depart as air, I shake my white locks at the runaway sun,
I effuse my flesh in eddies, and drift it in lacy jags.

I bequeath myself to the dirt to grow from the grass I love,
If you want me again look for me under your boot-soles.

You will hardly know who I am or what I mean,
But I shall be good health to you nevertheless,
And filter and fibre your blood.

Failing to fetch me at first keep encouraged,
Missing me one place search another,
I stop somewhere waiting for you.[14]

CHILDREN OF ADAM[15]

———◆———

TO THE GARDEN THE WORLD

To the garden the world anew ascending,
Potent mates, daughters, sons, preluding,
The love, the life of their bodies, meaning and being,
Curious here behold my resurrection after slumber,
The revolving cycles in their wide sweep having brought me
    again,
Amorous, mature, all beautiful to me, all wondrous,
My limbs and the quivering fire that ever plays through them, for
    reasons, most wondrous,
Existing I peer and penetrate still,
Content with the present, content with the past,
By my side or back of me Eve following,
Or in front, and I following her just the same.

FROM PENT-UP ACHING RIVERS

From pent-up aching rivers,
From that of myself without which I were nothing,
From what I am determin'd to make illustrious, even if I stand
    sole among men,
From my own voice resonant, singing the phallus,
Singing the song of procreation,
Singing the need of superb children and therein superb grown
    people,
Singing the muscular urge and the blending,
Singing the bedfellow's song, (O resistless yearning!
O for any and each the body correlative attracting!

O for you whoever you are your correlative body! O it, more than
    all else, you delighting!)
From the hungry gnaw that eats me night and day,
From native moments, from bashful pains, singing them,
Seeking something yet unfound though I have diligently sought it
    many a long year,
Singing the true song of the soul fitful at random,
Renascent with grossest Nature or among animals,
Of that, of them and what goes with them my poems informing,
Of the smell of apples and lemons, of the pairing of birds,
Of the wet of woods, of the lapping of waves,
Of the mad pushes of waves upon the land, I them chanting,
The overture lightly sounding, the strain anticipating,
The welcome nearness, the sight of the perfect body,
The swimmer swimming naked in the bath, or motionless on his
    back lying and floating,
The female form approaching, I pensive, love-flesh tremulous
    aching,
The divine list for myself or you or for any one making,
The face, the limbs, the index from head to foot, and what it
    arouses,
The mystic deliria, the madness amorous, the utter abandonment,
(Hark close and still what I now whisper to you,
I love you, O you entirely possess me,
O that you and I escape from the rest and go utterly off, free and
    lawless,
Two hawks in the air, two fishes swimming in the sea not more
    lawless than we;)
The furious storm through me careering, I passionately trembling,
The oath of the inseparableness of two together, of the woman
    that loves me and whom I love more than my life, that oath
    swearing,
(O I willingly stake all for you,
O let me be lost if it must be so!
O you and I! what is it to us what the rest do or think?
What is all else to us? only that we enjoy each other and exhaust
    each other if it must be so;)
From the master, the pilot I yield the vessel to,

The general commanding me, commanding all, from him
    permission taking,
From time the programme hastening, (I have loiter'd too long as
    it is.)
From sex, from the warp and from the woof,[16]
From privacy, from frequent repinings alone,
From plenty of persons near and yet the right person not near,
From the soft sliding of hands over me and thrusting of fingers
    through my hair and beard,
From the long sustain'd kiss upon the mouth or bosom,
From the close pressure that makes me or any man drunk,
    fainting with excess,
From what the divine husband knows, from the work of
    fatherhood,
From exultation, victory and relief, from the bedfellow's embrace
    in the night,
From the act-poems of eyes, hands, hips and bosoms,
From the cling of the trembling arm,
From the bending curve and the clinch,
From side by side the pliant coverlet off-throwing,
From the one so unwilling to have me leave, and me just as
    unwilling to leave,
(Yet a moment O tender waiter,* and I return,)
From the hour of shining stars and dropping dews,
From the night a moment I emerging flitting out,
Celebrate you act divine and you children prepared for,
And you stalwart loins.

I SING THE BODY ELECTRIC[17]

– 1 –

I sing the body electric,
The armies of those I love engirth me and I engirth them,

---

*That is, one who waits.

They will not let me off till I go with them, respond to them,
And discorrupt them, and charge them full with the charge of
  the soul.

Was it doubted that those who corrupt their own bodies conceal
    themselves?
And if those who defile the living are as bad as they who defile
  the dead?
And if the body does not do fully as much as the soul?
And if the body were not the soul, what is the soul?

— 2 —

The love of the body of man or woman balks account, the body
    itself balks account,
That of the male is perfect, and that of the female is perfect.

The expression of the face balks account,
But the expression of a well-made man appears not only in his
  face,
It is in his limbs and joints also, it is curiously in the joints of his
  hips and wrists,
It is in his walk, the carriage of his neck, the flex of his waist and
  knees, dress does not hide him,
The strong sweet quality he has strikes through the cotton and
  broadcloth,
To see him pass conveys as much as the best poem, perhaps more,
You linger to see his back, and the back of his neck and shoulder-
  side.

The sprawl and fulness of babes, the bosoms and heads of
    women, the folds of their dress, their style as we pass in the
    street, the contour of their shape downwards,
The swimmer naked in the swimming-bath, seen as he swims
    through the transparent green-shine, or lies with his face up
    and rolls silently to and fro in the heave of the water,
The bending forward and backward of rowers in row-boats, the
  horseman in his saddle,

Girls, mothers, house-keepers, in all their performances,
The group of laborers seated at noon-time with their open dinner-
kettles, and their wives waiting,
The female soothing a child, the farmer's daughter in the garden
or cow-yard,
The young fellow hoeing corn, the sleigh-driver driving his six
horses through the crowd,
The wrestle of wrestlers, two apprentice-boys, quite grown, lusty,
good-natured, native-born, out on the vacant lot at sundown
after work,
The coats and caps thrown down, the embrace of love and
resistance,
The upper-hold and under-hold, the hair rumpled over and
blinding the eyes;
The march of firemen in their own costumes, the play of
masculine muscle through clean-setting trowsers and waist-
straps,
The slow return from the fire, the pause when the bell strikes
suddenly again, and the listening on the alert,
The natural, perfect, varied attitudes, the bent head, the curv'd
neck and the counting;
Such-like I love—I loosen myself, pass freely, am at the mother's
breast with the little child,
Swim with the swimmers, wrestle with wrestlers, march in line
with the firemen, and pause, listen, count.

— 3 —

I knew a man, a common farmer, the father of five sons,
And in them the fathers of sons, and in them the fathers of sons.
This man was of wonderful vigor, calmness, beauty of person,
The shape of his head, the pale yellow and white of his hair and
beard, the immeasurable meaning of his black eyes, the
richness and breadth of his manners,
These I used to go and visit him to see, he was wise also,
He was six feet tall, he was over eighty years old, his sons were
massive, clean, bearded, tan-faced, handsome,
They and his daughters loved him, all who saw him loved him,

They did not love him by allowance, they loved him with
    personal love,
He drank water only, the blood show'd like scarlet through the
    clear-brown skin of his face,
He was a frequent gunner and fisher, he sail'd his boat himself,
    he had a fine one presented to him by a ship-joiner, he had
    fowling-pieces presented to him by men that loved him,
When he went with his five sons and many grand-sons to hunt or
    fish, you would pick him out as the most beautiful and
    vigorous of the gang,
You would wish long and long to be with him, you would wish to
    sit by him in the boat that you and he might touch each
    other.

– 4 –

I have perceiv'd that to be with those I like is enough,
To stop in company with the rest at evening is enough,
To be surrounded by beautiful, curious, breathing, laughing flesh
    is enough,
To pass among them or touch any one, or rest my arm ever so
    lightly round his or her neck for a moment, what is this then?
I do not ask any more delight, I swim in it as in a sea.

There is something in staying close to men and women and
    looking on them, and in the contact and odor of them, that
    pleases the soul well,
All things please the soul, but these please the soul well.

– 5 –

This is the female form,
A divine nimbus exhales from it from head to foot,
It attracts with fierce undeniable attraction,
I am drawn by its breath as if I were no more than a helpless
    vapor, all falls aside but myself and it,
Books, art, religion, time, the visible and solid earth, and what
    was expected of heaven or fear'd of hell, are now consumed,

Mad filaments, ungovernable shoots play out of it, the response
     likewise ungovernable,
Hair, bosom, hips, bend of legs, negligent falling hands all
     diffused, mine too diffused,
Ebb stung by the flow and flow stung by the ebb, love-flesh
     swelling and deliciously aching,
Limitless limpid jets of love hot and enormous, quivering jelly of
     love, white-blow and delirious juice,
Bridegroom night of love working surely and softly into the
     prostrate dawn,
Undulating into the willing and yielding day,
Lost in the cleave of the clasping and sweet-flesh'd day.

This the nucleus—after the child is born of woman, man is born
     of woman,
This the bath of birth, this the merge of small and large, and the
     outlet again.

Be not ashamed women, your privilege encloses the rest, and is
     the exit of the rest,
You are the gates of the body, and you are the gates of the soul.

The female contains all qualities and tempers them,
She is in her place and moves with perfect balance,
She is all things duly veil'd, she is both passive and active,
She is to conceive daughters as well as sons, and sons as well as
     daughters.

As I see my soul reflected in Nature,
As I see through a mist, One with inexpressible completeness,
     sanity, beauty,
See the bent head and arms folded over the breast, the Female
     I see.

– 6 –

The male is not less the soul nor more, he too is in his place,
He too is all qualities, he is action and power,

The flush of the known universe is in him,
Scorn becomes him well, and appetite and defiance become him
    well,
The wildest largest passions, bliss that is utmost, sorrow that is
    utmost become him well, pride is for him,
The full-spread pride of man is calming and excellent to the
    soul,
Knowledge becomes him, he likes it always, he brings every thing
    to the test of himself,
Whatever the survey, whatever the sea and the sail he strikes
    soundings at last only here,
(Where else does he strike soundings except here?)

The man's body is sacred and the woman's body is sacred,
No matter who it is, it is sacred—is it the meanest one in the
    laborers' gang?
Is it one of the dull-faced immigrants just landed on the wharf?
Each belongs here or anywhere just as much as the well-off, just
    as much as you,
Each has his or her place in the procession.

(All is a procession,
The universe is a procession with measured and perfect motion.)

Do you know so much yourself that you call the meanest
    ignorant?
Do you suppose you have a right to a good sight, and he or she
    has no right to a sight?
Do you think matter has cohered together from its diffuse float,
    and the soil is on the surface, and water runs and vegetation
    sprouts,
For you only, and not for him and her?

— 7 —

A man's body at auction,
(For before the war I often go to the slave-mart and watch the
    sale,)

I help the auctioneer, the sloven does not half know his
    business.

Gentlemen look on this wonder,
Whatever the bids of the bidders they cannot be high enough
    for it,
For it the globe lay preparing quintillions of years without one
    animal or plant,
For it the revolving cycles truly and steadily roll'd.

In this head the all-baffling brain,
In it and below it the makings of heroes.

Examine these limbs, red, black, or white, they are cunning in
    tendon and nerve,
They shall be stript that you may see them.

Exquisite senses, life-lit eyes, pluck, volition,
Flakes of breast-muscle, pliant backbone and neck, flesh not
    flabby, good-sized arms and legs,
And wonders within there yet.

Within there runs blood,
The same old blood! the same red-running blood!
There swells and jets a heart, there all passions, desires, reachings,
    aspirations,
(Do you think they are not there because they are not express'd in
    parlors and lecture-rooms?)

This is not only one man, this the father of those who shall be
    fathers in their turns,
In him the start of populous states and rich republics,
Of him countless immortal lives with countless embodiments and
    enjoyments.

How do you know who shall come from the offspring of his
    offspring through the centuries?
(Who might you find you have come from yourself, if you could
    trace back through the centuries?)

– 8 –

A woman's body at auction,
She too is not only herself, she is the teeming mother of mothers,
She is the bearer of them that shall grow and be mates to the
      mothers.

Have you ever loved the body of a woman?
Have you ever loved the body of a man?
Do you not see that these are exactly the same to all in all nations
      and times all over the earth?

If any thing is sacred the human body is sacred,
And the glory and sweet of a man is the token of manhood
      untainted,
And in man or woman a clean, strong, firm-fibred body, is more
      beautiful than the most beautiful face.

Have you seen the fool that corrupted his own live body? or the
      fool that corrupted her own live body?
For they do not conceal themselves, and cannot conceal
      themselves.[18]

– 9 –

O my body! I dare not desert the likes of you in other men and
      women, nor the likes of the parts of you,
I believe the likes of you are to stand or fall with the likes of the
      soul, (and that they are the soul,)
I believe the likes of you shall stand or fall with my poems, and
      that they are my poems,
Man's, woman's, child's, youth's, wife's, husband's, mother's,
      father's, young man's, young woman's poems,
Head, neck, hair, ears, drop and tympan of the ears,
Eyes, eye-fringes, iris of the eye, eyebrows, and the waking or
      sleeping of the lids,
Mouth, tongue, lips, teeth, roof of the mouth, jaws, and the jaw-
      hinges,
Nose, nostrils of the nose, and the partition,

Cheeks, temples, forehead, chin, throat, back of the neck,
    neck-slue,
Strong shoulders, manly beard, scapula, hind-shoulders, and the
    ample side-round of the chest,
Upper-arm, armpit, elbow-socket, lower-arm, arm-sinews, arm-
    bones,
Wrist and wrist-joints, hand, palm, knuckles, thumb, forefinger,
    finger-joints, finger-nails,
Broad breast-front, curling hair of the breast, breast-bone,
    breast-side,
Ribs, belly, backbone, joints of the backbone,
Hips, hip-sockets, hip-strength, inward and outward round,
    man-balls, man-root,
Strong set of thighs, well carrying the trunk above,
Leg-fibres, knee, knee-pan, upper-leg, under-leg,
Ankles, instep, foot-ball, toes, toe-joints, the heel;
All attitudes, all the shapeliness, all the belongings of my or your
    body or of any one's body, male or female,
The lung-sponges, the stomach-sac, the bowels sweet and
    clean,
The brain in its folds inside the skull-frame,
Sympathies, heart-valves, palate-valves, sexuality, maternity,
Womanhood, and all that is a woman, and the man that comes
    from woman,
The womb, the teats, nipples, breast-milk, tears, laughter,
    weeping, love-looks, love-perturbations and risings,
The voice, articulation, language, whispering, shouting aloud,
Food, drink, pulse, digestion, sweat, sleep, walking, swimming,
Poise on the hips, leaping, reclining, embracing, arm-curving and
    tightening,
The continual changes of the flex of the mouth, and around the
    eyes,
The skin, the sunburnt shade, freckles, hair,
The curious sympathy one feels when feeling with the hand the
    naked meat of the body,
The circling rivers the breath, and breathing it in and out,
The beauty of the waist, and thence of the hips, and thence
    downward toward the knees,

The thin red jellies within you or within me, the bones and the
    marrow in the bones,
The exquisite realization of health;
O I say these are not the parts and poems of the body only, but of
    the soul,
O I say now these are the soul!

A WOMAN WAITS FOR ME

A woman waits for me, she contains all, nothing is lacking,
Yet all were lacking if sex were lacking, or if the moisture of the
    right man were lacking.

Sex contains all, bodies, souls,
Meanings, proofs, purities, delicacies, results, promulgations,
Songs, commands, health, pride, the maternal mystery, the
    seminal milk,
All hopes, benefactions, bestowals, all the passions, loves,
    beauties, delights of the earth,
All the governments, judges, gods, follow'd persons of the earth,
These are contain'd in sex as parts of itself and justifications of itself.

Without shame the man I like knows and avows the deliciousness
    of his sex,
Without shame the woman I like knows and avows hers.

Now I will dismiss myself from impassive women,
I will go stay with her who waits for me, and with those women
    that are warm-blooded and sufficient for me,
I see that they understand me and do not deny me,
I see that they are worthy of me, I will be the robust husband of
    those women.

They are not one jot less than I am,
They are tann'd in the face by shining suns and blowing winds,
Their flesh has the old divine suppleness and strength,
They know how to swim, row, ride, wrestle, shoot, run, strike,
    retreat, advance, resist, defend themselves,[19]

They are ultimate in their own right—they are calm, clear, well-
      possess'd of themselves.

I draw you close to me, you women,
I cannot let you go, I would do you good,
I am for you, and you are for me, not only for our own sake, but
      for others' sakes,
Envelop'd in you sleep greater heroes and bards,
They refuse to awake at the touch of any man but me.

It is I, you women, I make my way,
I am stern, acrid, large, undissuadable, but I love you,
I do not hurt you any more than is necessary for you,
I pour the stuff to start sons and daughters fit for these States,
      I press with slow rude muscle,
I brace myself effectually, I listen to no entreaties,
I dare not withdraw till I deposit what has so long accumulated
      within me.[20]

Through you I drain the pent-up rivers of myself,
In you I wrap a thousand onward years,
On you I graft the grafts of the best-beloved of me and America,
The drops I distil upon you shall grow fierce and athletic girls,
      new artists, musicians, and singers,
The babes I beget upon you are to beget babes in their turn,
I shall demand perfect men and women out of my love-spendings,
I shall expect them to interpenetrate with others, as I and you
      interpenetrate now,
I shall count on the fruits of the gushing showers of them, as I
      count on the fruits of the gushing showers I give now,
I shall look for loving crops from the birth, life, death,
      immortality, I plant so lovingly now.

SPONTANEOUS ME

Spontaneous me, Nature,
The loving day, the mounting sun, the friend I am happy with,

The arm of my friend hanging idly over my shoulder,
The hillside whiten'd with blossoms of the mountain ash,
The same late in autumn, the hues of red, yellow, drab, purple,
    and light and dark green,
The rich coverlet of the grass, animals and birds, the private
    untrimm'd bank, the primitive apples, the pebble-stones,
Beautiful dripping fragments, the negligent list of one after
    another as I happen to call them to me or think of them,
The real poems, (what we call poems being merely pictures,)
The poems of the privacy of the night, and of men like me,
This poem drooping shy and unseen that I always carry, and that
    all men carry,
(Know once for all, avow'd on purpose, wherever are men like
    me, are our lusty lurking masculine poems,)
Love-thoughts, love-juice, love-odor, love-yielding, love-climbers,
    and the climbing sap,
Arms and hands of love, lips of love, phallic thumb of love,
    breasts of love, bellies press'd and glued together with love,
Earth of chaste love, life that is only life after love,
The body of my love, the body of the woman I love, the body of
    the man, the body of the earth,
Soft forenoon airs that blow from the south-west,
The hairy wild-bee that murmurs and hankers up and down, that
    gripes the full-grown lady-flower, curves upon her with
    amorous firm legs, takes his will of her, and holds himself
    tremulous and tight till he is satisfied;
The wet of woods through the early hours,
Two sleepers at night lying close together as they sleep, one
    with an arm slanting down across and below the waist of
    the other,
The smell of apples, aromas from crush'd sage-plant, mint,
    birch-bark,
The boy's longings, the glow and pressure as he confides to me
    what he was dreaming,
The dead leaf whirling its spiral whirl and falling still and content
    to the ground,
The no-form'd stings that sights, people, objects, sting me
    with,

The hubb'd sting of myself, stinging me as much as it ever can
      any one,
The sensitive, orbic, underlapp'd brothers, that only privileged
      feelers may be intimate where they are,
The curious roamer the hand roaming all over the body, the
      bashful withdrawing of flesh where the fingers soothingly
      pause and edge themselves,
The limpid liquid within the young man,
The vex'd corrosion so pensive and so painful,
The torment, the irritable tide that will not be at rest,
The like of the same I feel, the like of the same in others,
The young man that flushes and flushes, and the young woman
      that flushes and flushes,
The young man that wakes deep at night, the hot hand seeking to
      repress what would master him,
The mystic amorous night, the strange half-welcome pangs,
      visions, sweats,
The pulse pounding through palms and trembling encircling
      fingers, the young man all color'd, red, ashamed, angry;
The souse upon me of my lover the sea, as I lie willing and
      naked,
The merriment of the twin babes that crawl over the grass in
      the sun, the mother never turning her vigilant eyes from
      them,
The walnut-trunk, the walnut-husks, and the ripening or ripen'd
      long-round walnuts,
The continence of vegetables, birds, animals,
The consequent meanness of me should I skulk or find myself
      indecent, while birds and animals never once skulk or find
      themselves indecent,
The great chastity of paternity, to match the great chastity of
      maternity,
The oath of procreation I have sworn, my Adamic and fresh
      daughters,
The greed that eats me day and night with hungry gnaw, till I
      saturate what shall produce boys to fill my place when I am
      through,
The wholesome relief, repose, content,

And this bunch pluck'd at random from myself,
It has done its work—I toss it carelessly to fall where it may.[21]

ONE HOUR TO MADNESS AND JOY

One hour to madness and joy! O furious! O confine me not!
(What is this that frees me so in storms?
What do my shouts amid lightnings and raging winds mean?)

O to drink the mystic deliria deeper than any other man!
O savage and tender achings! (I bequeath them to you my
     children,
I tell them to you, for reasons, O bridegroom and bride.)

O to be yielded to you whoever you are, and you to be yielded to
     me in defiance of the world!
O to return to Paradise! O bashful and feminine!
O to draw you to me, to plant on you for the first time the lips of
     a determin'd man.

O the puzzle, the thrice-tied knot, the deep and dark pool, all
     untied and illumin'd!
O to speed where there is space enough and air enough at last!
To be absolv'd from previous ties and conventions, I from mine
     and you from yours!
To find a new unthought-of nonchalance with the best of
     Nature!
To have the gag remov'd from one's mouth!
To have the feeling to-day or any day I am sufficient as I am.

O something unprov'd! something in a trance!
To escape utterly from others' anchors and holds!
To drive free! to love free! to dash reckless and dangerous!
To court destruction with taunts, with invitations!
To ascend, to leap to the heavens of the love indicated to me!
To rise thither with my inebriate soul!
To be lost if it must be so!

To feed the remainder of life with one hour of fulness and
    freedom!
With one brief hour of madness and joy.

OUT OF THE ROLLING OCEAN THE CROWD

Out of the rolling ocean the crowd came a drop gently to me,
Whispering *I love you, before long I die,*
I have travel'd a long way merely to look on you to touch you,
For I could not die till I once look'd on you,
For I fear'd I might afterward lose you.

Now we have met, we have look'd, we are safe,
Return in peace to the ocean my love,
I too am part of that ocean my love, we are not so much
    separated,
Behold the great rondure, the cohesion of all, how perfect!
But as for me, for you, the irresistible sea is to separate us,
As for an hour carrying us diverse, yet cannot carry us diverse
    forever;
Be not impatient—a little space—know you I salute the air, the
    ocean and the land,
Every day at sundown for your dear sake my love.

AGES AND AGES RETURNING AT INTERVALS

Ages and ages returning at intervals,
Undestroy'd, wandering immortal,
Lusty, phallic, with the potent original loins, perfectly sweet,
I, chanter of Adamic songs,
Through the new garden the West, the great cities calling,
Deliriate, thus prelude what is generated, offering these, offering
    myself,
Bathing myself, bathing my songs in Sex,
Offspring of my loins.

WE TWO, HOW LONG WE WERE FOOL'D

We two, how long we were fool'd,
Now transmuted, we swiftly escape as Nature escapes,
We are Nature, long have we been absent, but now we return,
We become plants, trunks, foliage, roots, bark,
We are bedded in the ground, we are rocks,
We are oaks, we grow in the openings side by side,
We browse, we are two among the wild herds spontaneous
      as any,
We are two fishes swimming in the sea together,
We are what locust blossoms are, we drop scent around lanes
      mornings and evenings,
We are also the coarse smut of beasts, vegetables, minerals,
We are two predatory hawks, we soar above and look down,
We are two resplendent suns, we it is who balance ourselves orbic
      and stellar, we are as two comets,
We prowl fang'd and four-footed in the woods, we spring on prey,
We are two clouds forenoons and afternoons driving overhead,
We are seas mingling, we are two of those cheerful waves rolling
      over each other and interwetting each other,
We are what the atmosphere is, transparent, receptive, pervious,
      impervious,
We are snow, rain, cold, darkness, we are each product and
      influence of the globe,
We have circled and circled till we have arrived home again,
      we two,
We have voided all but freedom and all but our own joy.

O HYMEN! O HYMENEE!

O hymen! O hymenee! why do you tantalize me thus?
O why sting me for a swift moment only?
Why can you not continue? O why do you now cease?
Is it because if you continued beyond the swift moment you
      would soon certainly kill me?

I AM HE THAT ACHES WITH LOVE

I am he that aches with amorous love;
Does the earth gravitate? does not all matter, aching, attract all
    matter?
So the body of me to all I meet or know.

NATIVE MOMENTS

Native moments—when you come upon me—ah you are here
    now,
Give me now libidinous joys only,
Give me the drench of my passions, give me life coarse and rank,
To-day I go consort with Nature's darlings, to-night too,
I am for those who believe in loose delights, I share the midnight
    orgies of young men,
I dance with the dancers and drink with the drinkers,
The echoes ring with our indecent calls, I pick out some low
    person for my dearest friend,
He shall be lawless, rude, illiterate, he shall be one condemn'd by
    others for deeds done,
I will play a part no longer, why should I exile myself from my
    companions?
O you shunn'd persons, I at least do not shun you,
I come forthwith in your midst, I will be your poet,
I will be more to you than to any of the rest.

ONCE I PASS'D THROUGH A POPULOUS CITY[22]

Once I pass'd through a populous city imprinting my brain for
    future use with its shows, architecture, customs, traditions,
Yet now of all that city I remember only a woman I casually met
    there who detain'd me for love of me,
Day by day and night by night we were together—all else has
    long been forgotten by me,
I remember I say only that woman who passionately clung to me,

Again we wander, we love, we separate again,
Again she holds me by the hand, I must not go,
I see her close beside me with silent lips sad and tremulous.

I HEARD YOU SOLEMN-SWEET PIPES
OF THE ORGAN

I heard you solemn-sweet pipes of the organ as last Sunday morn
    I pass'd the church,
Winds of autumn, as I walk'd the woods at dusk I heard your
    long-stretch'd sighs up above so mournful,
I heard the perfect Italian tenor singing at the opera, I heard the
    soprano in the midst of the quartet singing;
Heart of my love! you too I heard murmuring low through one of
    the wrists around my head,
Heard the pulse of you when all was still ringing little bells last
    night under my ear.

FACING WEST FROM CALIFORNIA'S SHORES

Facing west from California's shores,
Inquiring, tireless, seeking what is yet unfound,
I, a child, very old, over waves, towards the house of maternity,
    the land of migrations, look afar,
Look off the shores of my Western sea, the circle almost
    circled;
For starting westward from Hindustan, from the vales of
    Kashmere,
From Asia, from the north, from the God, the sage, and the
    hero,
From the south, from the flowery peninsulas and the spice
    islands,
Long having wander'd since, round the earth having wander'd,
Now I face home again, very pleas'd and joyous,
(But where is what I started for so long ago?
And why is it yet unfound?)

AS ADAM EARLY IN THE MORNING

As Adam early in the morning,
Walking forth from the bower refresh'd with sleep,
Behold me where I pass, hear my voice, approach,
Touch me, touch the palm of your hand to my body as I pass,
Be not afraid of my body.

"Walt Whitman & his rebel soldier friend Pete Doyle"—46 years old, 1865,
photo taken in Washington D.C. Courtesy of the Library of Congress,
Charles E. Feinberg Collection. Saunders #29.

CALAMUS[23]

IN PATHS UNTRODDEN

In paths untrodden,
In the growth by margins of pond-waters,
Escaped from the life that exhibits itself,
From all the standards hitherto publish'd, from the pleasures, profits, conformities,
Which too long I was offering to feed my soul,
Clear to me now standards not yet publish'd, clear to me that my soul,
That the soul of the man I speak for rejoices in comrades,
Here by myself away from the clank of the world,
Tallying and talk'd to here by tongues aromatic,
No longer abash'd, (for in this secluded spot I can respond as I would not dare elsewhere,)
Strong upon me the life that does not exhibit itself, yet contains all the rest,
Resolv'd to sing no songs to-day but those of manly attachment,
Projecting them along that substantial life,
Bequeathing hence types of athletic love,
Afternoon this delicious Ninth-month in my forty-first year,
I proceed for all who are or have been young men,
To tell the secret of my nights and days,
To celebrate the need of comrades.

SCENTED HERBAGE OF MY BREAST

Scented herbage of my breast,
Leaves from you I glean, I write, to be perused best afterwards,

Tomb-leaves, body-leaves growing up above me above death,
Perennial roots, tall leaves, O the winter shall not freeze you
   delicate leaves,
Every year shall you bloom again, out from where you retired you
   shall emerge again;
O I do not know whether many passing by will discover you or
   inhale your faint odor, but I believe a few will;
O slender leaves! O blossoms of my blood! I permit you to tell in
   your own way of the heart that is under you,
O I do not know what you mean there underneath yourselves,
   you are not happiness,
You are often more bitter than I can bear, you burn and sting
   me,
Yet you are beautiful to me you faint tinged roots, you make me
   think of death,
Death is beautiful from you, (what indeed is finally beautiful
   except death and love?)
O I think it is not for life I am chanting here my chant of lovers,
   I think it must be for death,
For how calm, how solemn it grows to ascend to the atmosphere
   of lovers,
Death or life I am then indifferent, my soul declines to prefer,
(I am not sure but the high soul of lovers welcomes death most,)
Indeed O death, I think now these leaves mean precisely the
   same as you mean,
Grow up taller sweet leaves that I may see! grow up out of my
   breast!
Spring away from the conceal'd heart there!
Do not fold yourself so in your pink-tinged roots timid leaves!
Do not remain down there so ashamed, herbage of my breast!
Come I am determin'd to unbare this broad breast of mine, I have
   long enough stifled and choked;
Emblematic and capricious blades I leave you, now you serve me
   not,
I will say what I have to say by itself,
I will sound myself and comrades only, I will never again utter a
   call only their call,
I will raise with it immortal reverberations through the States,

I will give an example to lovers to take permanent shape and will
    through the States,
Through me shall the words be said to make death exhilarating,
Give me your tone therefore O death, that I may accord with it,
Give me yourself, for I see that you belong to me now above
    all, and are folded inseparably together, you love and death
    are,
Nor will I allow you to balk me any more with what I was calling
    life,
For now it is convey'd to me that you are the purports essential,
That you hide in these shifting forms of life, for reasons, and that
    they are mainly for you,
That you beyond them come forth to remain, the real reality,
That behind the mask of materials you patiently wait, no matter
    how long,
That you will one day perhaps take control of all,
That you will perhaps dissipate this entire show of appearance,
That may-be you are what it is all for, but it does not last so very
    long,
But you will last very long.

WHOEVER YOU ARE HOLDING ME NOW IN HAND[24]

Whoever you are holding me now in hand,
Without one thing all will be useless,
I give you fair warning before you attempt me further,
I am not what you supposed, but far different.

Who is he that would become my follower?
Who would sign himself a candidate for my affections?

The way is suspicious, the result uncertain, perhaps destructive,
You would have to give up all else, I alone would expect to be
    your sole and exclusive standard,
Your novitiate would even then be long and exhausting,
The whole past theory of your life and all conformity to the lives
    around you would have to be abandon'd,

Therefore release me now before troubling yourself any further,
    let go your hand from my shoulders,
Put me down and depart on your way.

Or else by stealth in some wood for trial,
Or back of a rock in the open air,
(For in any roof'd room of a house I emerge not, nor in company,
And in libraries I lie as one dumb, a gawk, or unborn, or dead,)
But just possibly with you on a high hill, first watching lest any
    person for miles around approach unawares,
Or possibly with you sailing at sea, or on the beach of the sea or
    some quiet island,
Here to put your lips upon mine I permit you,
With the comrade's long-dwelling kiss or the new husband's kiss,
For I am the new husband and I am the comrade.

Or if you will, thrusting me beneath your clothing,
Where I may feel the throbs of your heart or rest upon your hip,
Carry me when you go forth over land or sea;
For thus merely touching you is enough, is best,
And thus touching you would I silently sleep and be carried
    eternally.

But these leaves conning you con at peril,
For these leaves and me you will not understand,
They will elude you at first and still more afterward, I will
    certainly elude you,
Even while you should think you had unquestionably caught me,
    behold!
Already you see I have escaped from you.

For it is not for what I have put into it that I have written this
    book,
Nor is it by reading it you will acquire it,
Nor do those know me best who admire me and vauntingly praise
    me,
Nor will the candidates for my love (unless at most a very few)
    prove victorious,

Nor will my poems do good only, they will do just as much evil,
    perhaps more,
For all is useless without that which you may guess at many times
    and not hit, that which I hinted at;
Therefore release me and depart on your way.

FOR YOU O DEMOCRACY

Come, I will make the continent indissoluble,
I will make the most splendid race the sun ever shone upon,
I will make divine magnetic lands,
        With the love of comrades,
            With the life-long love of comrades.

I will plant companionship thick as trees along all the rivers of
    America, and along the shores of the great lakes, and all over
    the prairies,
I will make inseparable cities with their arms about each
    other's necks.
            By the love of comrades,
                By the manly love of comrades.

For you these from me, O Democracy, to serve you ma
    femme!
For you, for you I am trilling these songs.

THESE I SINGING IN SPRING

These I singing in spring collect for lovers,
(For who but I should understand lovers and all their sorrow and
    joy?
And who but I should be the poet of comrades?)
Collecting I traverse the garden the world, but soon I pass the gates,
Now along the pond-side, now wading in a little, fearing not
    the wet,

Now by the post-and-rail fences where the old stones thrown
    there, pick'd from the fields, have accumulated,
(Wild-flowers and vines and weeds come up through the stones
    and partly cover them, beyond these I pass,)
Far, far in the forest, or sauntering later in summer, before I think
    where I go,
Solitary, smelling the earthy smell, stopping now and then in the
    silence,
Alone I had thought, yet soon a troop gathers around me,
Some walk by my side and some behind, and some embrace my
    arms or neck,
They the spirits of dear friends dead or alive, thicker they come, a
    great crowd, and I in the middle,
Collecting, dispensing, singing, there I wander with them,
Plucking something for tokens, tossing toward whoever is
    near me,
Here, lilac, with a branch of pine,
Here, out of my pocket, some moss which I pull'd off a live-oak in
    Florida as it hung trailing down,[25]
Here, some pinks and laurel leaves, and a handful of sage,
And here what I now draw from the water, wading in the pond-
    side,
(O here I last saw him that tenderly loves me, and returns again
    never to separate from me,
And this, O this shall henceforth be the token of comrades, this
    calamus-root shall,
Interchange it youths with each other! let none render it back!)
And twigs of maple and a bunch of wild orange and chestnut,
And stems of currants and plum-blows, and the aromatic cedar,
These I compass'd around by a thick cloud of spirits,
Wandering, point to or touch as I pass, or throw them loosely
    from me,
Indicating to each one what he shall have, giving something to
    each;
But what I drew from the water by the pond-side, that I reserve,
I will give of it, but only to them that love as I myself am capable
    of loving.

NOT HEAVING FROM MY RIBB'D BREAST ONLY

Not heaving from my ribb'd breast only,
Not in sighs at night in rage dissatisfied with myself,
Not in those long-drawn, ill-supprest sighs,
Not in many an oath and promise broken,
Not in my wilful and savage soul's volition,
Not in the subtle nourishment of the air,
Not in this beating and pounding at my temples and wrists,
Not in the curious systole and diastole within which will one day
     cease,
Not in many a hungry wish told to the skies only,
Not in cries, laughter, defiances, thrown from me when alone far
     in the wilds,
Not in husky pantings through clinch'd teeth,
Not in sounded and resounded words, chattering words, echoes,
     dead words,
Not in the murmurs of my dreams while I sleep,
Nor the other murmurs of these incredible dreams of every day,
Nor in the limbs and senses of my body that take you and dismiss
     you continually—not there,
Not in any or all of them O adhesiveness![26] O pulse of my life!
Need I that you exist and show yourself any more than in these
     songs.

OF THE TERRIBLE DOUBT OF APPEARANCES

Of the terrible doubt of appearances,
Of the uncertainty after all, that we may be deluded,
That may-be reliance and hope are but speculations after all,
That may-be identity beyond the grave is a beautiful fable only,
May-be the things I perceive, the animals, plants, men, hills,
     shining and flowing waters,
The skies of day and night, colors, densities, forms, may-be these
     are (as doubtless they are) only apparitions, and the real
     something has yet to be known,

(How often they dart out of themselves as if to confound me and
    mock me!
How often I think neither I know, nor any man knows, aught of
    them,)
May-be seeming to me what they are (as doubtless they indeed
    but seem) as from my present point of view, and might
    prove (as of course they would) nought of what they
    appear, or nought anyhow, from entirely changed points
    of view;
To me these and the like of these are curiously answer'd by my
    lovers, my dear friends,
When he whom I love travels with me or sits a long while holding
    me by the hand,
When the subtle air, the impalpable, the sense that words and
    reason hold not, surround us and pervade us,
Then I am charged with untold and untellable wisdom, I am
    silent, I require nothing further,
I cannot answer the question of appearances or that of identity
    beyond the grave,
But I walk or sit indifferent, I am satisfied,
He ahold of my hand has completely satisfied me.

THE BASE OF ALL METAPHYSICS[27]

And now gentlemen,
A word I give to remain in your memories and minds,
As base and finale too for all metaphysics.

(So to the students the old professor,
At the close of his crowded course.)

Having studied the new and antique, the Greek and Germanic
    systems,
Kant having studied and stated, Fichte and Schelling and
    Hegel,
Stated the lore of Plato, and Socrates greater than Plato,

And greater than Socrates sought and stated, Christ divine having
　　studied long,
I see reminiscent to-day those Greek and Germanic systems,
See the philosophies all, Christian churches and tenets see,
Yet underneath Socrates clearly see, and underneath Christ the
　　divine I see,
The dear love of man for his comrade, the attraction of friend to
　　friend,
Of the well-married husband and wife, of children and parents,
Of city for city and land for land.

RECORDERS AGES HENCE

Recorders ages hence,
Come, I will take you down underneath this impassive exterior,
　　I will tell you what to say of me,
Publish my name and hang up my picture as that of the tenderest
　　lover,
The friend the lover's portrait, of whom his friend his lover was
　　fondest,
Who was not proud of his songs, but of the measureless ocean of
　　love within him, and freely pour'd it forth,
Who often walk'd lonesome walks thinking of his dear friends, his
　　lovers,
Who pensive away from one he lov'd often lay sleepless and
　　dissatisfied at night,
Who knew too well the sick, sick dread lest the one he lov'd
　　might secretly be indifferent to him,
Whose happiest days were far away through fields, in woods, on
　　hills, he and another wandering hand in hand, they twain
　　apart from other men,
Who oft as he saunter'd the streets curv'd with his arm the
　　shoulder of his friend, while the arm of his friend rested upon
　　him also.

WHEN I HEARD AT THE CLOSE OF THE DAY

When I heard at the close of the day how my name had been
    receiv'd with plaudits in the capitol, still it was not a happy
    night for me that follow'd,
And else when I carous'd, or when my plans were accomplish'd,
    still I was not happy,
But the day when I rose at dawn from the bed of perfect health,
    refresh'd, singing, inhaling the ripe breath of autumn,
When I saw the full moon in the west grow pale and disappear in
    the morning light,
When I wander'd alone over the beach, and undressing bathed,
    laughing with the cool waters, and saw the sun rise,
And when I thought how my dear friend my lover was on his way
    coming, O then I was happy,
O then each breath tasted sweeter, and all that day my food
    nourish'd me more, and the beautiful day pass'd well,
And the next came with equal joy, and with the next at evening
    came my friend,
And that night while all was still I heard the waters roll slowly
    continually up the shores,
I heard the hissing rustle of the liquid and sands as directed to me
    whispering to congratulate me,
For the one I love most lay sleeping by me under the same cover
    in the cool night,
In the stillness in the autumn moonbeams his face was inclined
    toward me,
And his arm lay lightly around my breast—and that night I was
    happy.

ARE YOU THE NEW PERSON DRAWN TOWARD ME?

Are you the new person drawn toward me?
To begin with take warning, I am surely far different from what
    you suppose;
Do you suppose you will find in me your ideal?
Do you think it so easy to have me become your lover?

Do you think the friendship of me would be unalloy'd
    satisfaction?
Do you think I am trusty and faithful?
Do you see no further than this façade, this smooth and tolerant
    manner of me?
Do you suppose yourself advancing on real ground toward a real
    heroic man?
Have you no thought O dreamer that it may be all maya, illusion?

ROOTS AND LEAVES THEMSELVES ALONE

Roots and leaves themselves alone are these,
Scents brought to men and women from the wild woods and
    pond-side,
Breast-sorrel and pinks of love, fingers that wind around tighter
    than vines,
Gushes from the throats of birds hid in the foliage of trees as the
    sun is risen,
Breezes of land and love set from living shores to you on the
    living sea, to you O sailors!
Frost-mellow'd berries and Third-month twigs offer'd fresh to
    young persons wandering out in the fields when the winter
    breaks up,
Love-buds put before you and within you whoever you are,
Buds to be unfolded on the old terms,
If you bring the warmth of the sun to them they will open and
    bring form, color, perfume, to you,
If you become the aliment and the wet they will become flowers,
    fruits, tall branches and trees.

NOT HEAT FLAMES UP AND CONSUMES

Not heat flames up and consumes,
Not sea-waves hurry in and out,
Not the air delicious and dry, the air of ripe summer, bears lightly
    along white down-balls of myriads of seeds,

Wafted, sailing gracefully, to drop where they may;
Not these, O none of these more than the flames of me,
    consuming, burning for his love whom I love,
O none more than I hurrying in and out;
Does the tide hurry, seeking something, and never give up?
    O I the same,
O nor down-balls nor perfumes, nor the high rain-emitting
    clouds, are borne through the open air,
Any more than my soul is borne through the open air,
Wafted in all directions O love, for friendship, for you.

TRICKLE DROPS

Trickle drops! my blue veins leaving!
O drops of me! trickle, slow drops,
Candid from me falling, drip, bleeding drops,
From wounds made to free you whence you were prison'd,
From my face, from my forehead and lips,
From my breast, from within where I was conceal'd, press forth
    red drops, confession drops,
Stain every page, stain every song I sing, every word I say, bloody
    drops,
Let them know your scarlet heat, let them glisten,
Saturate them with yourself all ashamed and wet,
Glow upon all I have written or shall write, bleeding drops,
Let it all be seen in your light, blushing drops.

CITY OF ORGIES

City of orgies, walks and joys,
City whom that I have lived and sung in your midst will one day
    make you illustrious,
Not the pageants of you, not your shifting tableaus, your
    spectacles, repay me,
Not the interminable rows of your houses, nor the ships at the
    wharves,

Nor the processions in the streets, nor the bright windows with
    goods in them,
Nor to converse with learn'd persons, or bear my share in the
    soiree or feast;
Not those, but as I pass O Manhattan, your frequent and swift
    flash of eyes offering me love,
Offering response to my own—these repay me,
Lovers, continual lovers, only repay me.

BEHOLD THIS SWARTHY FACE

Behold this swarthy face, these gray eyes,
This beard, the white wool unclipt upon my neck,
My brown hands and the silent manner of me without charm;
Yet comes one a Manhattanese and ever at parting kisses me
    lightly on the lips with robust love,
And I on the crossing of the street or on the ship's deck give a kiss
    in return,
We observe that salute of American comrades land and sea,
We are those two natural and nonchalant persons.

I SAW IN LOUISIANA A LIVE-OAK GROWING[28]

I saw in Louisiana a live-oak growing,
All alone stood it and the moss hung down from the branches,
Without any companion it grew there uttering joyous leaves of
    dark green,
And its look, rude, unbending, lusty, made me think of
    myself,
But I wonder'd how it could utter joyous leaves standing alone
    there without its friend near, for I knew I could not,
And I broke off a twig with a certain number of leaves upon it,
    and twined around it a little moss,
And brought it away, and I have placed it in sight in my room,
It is not needed to remind me as of my own dear friends,
(For I believe lately I think of little else than of them,)

Yet it remains to me a curious token, it makes me think of manly
  love;
For all that, and though the live-oak glistens there in Louisiana
  solitary in a wide flat space,
Uttering joyous leaves all its life without a friend a lover
  near,
I know very well I could not.

TO A STRANGER

Passing stranger! you do not know how longingly I look upon
  you,
You must be he I was seeking, or she I was seeking, (it comes to
  me as of a dream,)
I have somewhere surely lived a life of joy with you,
All is recall'd as we flit by each other, fluid, affectionate, chaste,
  matured,
You grew up with me, were a boy with me or a girl with me,
I ate with you and slept with you, your body has become not
  yours only nor left my body mine only,
You give me the pleasure of your eyes, face, flesh, as we pass, you
  take of my beard, breast, hands, in return,
I am not to speak to you, I am to think of you when I sit alone or
  wake at night alone,
I am to wait, I do not doubt I am to meet you again,
I am to see to it that I do not lose you.

THIS MOMENT YEARNING AND THOUGHTFUL

This moment yearning and thoughtful sitting alone,
It seems to me there are other men in other lands yearning and
  thoughtful,
It seems to me I can look over and behold them in Germany,
  Italy, France, Spain,
Or far, far away, in China, or in Russia or Japan, talking other
  dialects,

And it seems to me if I could know those men I should become
    attached to them as I do to men in my own lands,
O I know we should be brethren and lovers,
I know I should be happy with them.

I HEAR IT WAS CHARGED AGAINST ME

I hear it was charged against me that I sought to destroy
    institutions,
But really I am neither for nor against institutions,
(What indeed have I in common with them? or what with the
    destruction of them?)
Only I will establish in the Mannahatta and in every city of these
    States inland and seaboard,
And in the fields and woods, and above every keel little or large
    that dents the water,
Without edifices or rules or trustees or any argument,
The institution of the dear love of comrades.

THE PRAIRIE-GRASS DIVIDING

The prairie-grass dividing, its special odor breathing,
I demand of it the spiritual corresponding,
Demand the most copious and close companionship of men,
Demand the blades to rise of words, acts, beings,
Those of the open atmosphere, coarse, sunlit, fresh, nutritious,
Those that go their own gait, erect, stepping with freedom and
    command, leading not following,
Those with a never-quell'd audacity, those with sweet and lusty
    flesh clear of taint,
Those that look carelessly in the faces of Presidents and
    governors, as to say *Who are you?*
Those of earth-born passion, simple, never constrain'd, never
    obedient,
Those of inland America.

WHEN I PERUSE THE CONQUER'D FAME

When I peruse the conquer'd fame of heroes and the victories of
　　mighty generals, I do not envy the generals,
Nor the President in his Presidency, nor the rich in his great
　　house,
But when I hear of the brotherhood of lovers, how it was with
　　them,
How together through life, through dangers, odium, unchanging,
　　long and long,
Through youth and through middle and old age, how unfaltering,
　　how affectionate and faithful they were,
Then I am pensive—I hastily walk away fill'd with the bitterest
　　envy.

WE TWO BOYS TOGETHER CLINGING

We two boys together clinging,
One the other never leaving,
Up and down the roads going, North and South excursions making,
Power enjoying, elbows stretching, fingers clutching,
Arm'd and fearless, eating, drinking, sleeping, loving,
No law less than ourselves owning, sailing, soldiering, thieving,
　　threatening,
Misers, menials, priests alarming, air breathing, water drinking,
　　on the turf or the sea beach dancing,
Cities wrenching, ease scorning, statutes mocking, feebleness
　　chasing,
Fulfilling our foray.

A PROMISE TO CALIFORNIA

A promise to California,
Or inland to the great pastoral Plains, and on to Puget Sound and
　　Oregon;

Sojourning east a while longer, soon I travel toward you, to
    remain, to teach robust American love,
For I know very well that I and robust love belong among you,
    inland, and along the Western sea;
For these States tend inland and toward the Western sea, and I
    will also.

HERE THE FRAILEST LEAVES OF ME

Here the frailest leaves of me and yet my strongest lasting,
Here I shade and hide my thoughts, I myself do not expose
    them,
And yet they expose me more than all my other poems.

NO LABOR-SAVING MACHINE

No labor-saving machine,
Nor discovery have I made,
Nor will I be able to leave behind me any wealthy bequest to
    found a hospital or library,
Nor reminiscence of any deed of courage for America,
Nor literary success nor intellect, nor book for the book-shelf,
But a few carols vibrating through the air I leave,
For comrades and lovers.

A GLIMPSE[29]

A glimpse through an interstice caught,
Of a crowd of workmen and drivers in a bar-room around the
    stove late of a winter night, and I unremark'd seated in a
    corner,
Of a youth who loves me and whom I love, silently approaching
    and seating himself near, that he may hold me by the hand,
A long while amid the noises of coming and going, of drinking
    and oath and smutty jest,

There we two, content, happy in being together, speaking little,
  perhaps not a word.

A LEAF FOR HAND IN HAND

A leaf for hand in hand;
You natural persons old and young!
You on the Mississippi and on all the branches and bayous of the
  Mississippi!
You friendly boatmen and mechanics! you roughs!
You twain! and all processions moving along the streets!
I wish to infuse myself among you till I see it common for you to
  walk hand in hand.

EARTH, MY LIKENESS

Earth, my likeness,
Though you look so impassive, ample and spheric there,
I now suspect that is not all;
I now suspect there is something fierce in you eligible to burst
  forth,
For an athlete is enamour'd of me, and I of him,
But toward him there is something fierce and terrible in me
  eligible to burst forth,
I dare not tell it in words, not even in these songs.

I DREAM'D IN A DREAM[30]

I dream'd in a dream I saw a city invincible to the attacks of the
  whole of the rest of the earth,
I dream'd that was the new city of Friends,
Nothing was greater there than the quality of robust love, it led
  the rest,
It was seen every hour in the actions of the men of that city,
And in all their looks and words.

WHAT THINK YOU I TAKE MY PEN IN HAND?

What think you I take my pen in hand to record?
The battle ship, perfect-model'd, majestic, that I saw pass the
  offing to-day under full sail?
The splendors of the past day? or the splendor of the night that
  envelops me?
Or the vaunted glory and growth of the great city spread around
  me?—no;
But merely of two simple men I saw to-day on the pier in the
  midst of the crowd, parting the parting of dear friends,
The one to remain hung on the other's neck and passionately
  kiss'd him,
While the one to depart tightly prest the one to remain in his
  arms.

TO THE EAST AND TO THE WEST

To the East and to the West,
To the man of the Seaside State and of Pennsylvania,
To the Kanadian of the north, to the Southerner I love,
These with perfect trust to depict you as myself, the germs are in
  all men,
I believe the main purport of these States is to found a superb
  friendship, exalté, previously unknown,
Because I perceive it waits, and has been always waiting, latent in
  all men.

SOMETIMES WITH ONE I LOVE

Sometimes with one I love I fill myself with rage for fear I effuse
  unreturn'd love,
But now I think there is no unreturn'd love, the pay is certain one
  way or another,
(I loved a certain person ardently and my love was not return'd,
Yet out of that I have written these songs.)

TO A WESTERN BOY

Many things to absorb I teach to help you become eleve of mine;
Yet if blood like mine circle not in your veins,
If you be not silently selected by lovers and do not silently select
    lovers,
Of what use is it that you seek to become eleve of mine?

FAST-ANCHOR'D ETERNAL O LOVE!

Fast-anchor'd eternal O love! O woman I love!
O bride! O wife! more resistless than I can tell, the thought of you!
Then separate, as disembodied or another born,
Ethereal, the last athletic reality, my consolation,
I ascend, I float in the regions of your love O man,
O sharer of my roving life.

AMONG THE MULTITUDE

Among the men and women the multitude,
I perceive one picking me out by secret and divine signs,
Acknowledging none else, not parent, wife, husband, brother,
    child, any nearer than I am,
Some are baffled, but that one is not—that one knows me.

Ah lover and perfect equal,
I meant that you should discover me so by faint indirections,
And I when I meet you mean to discover you by the like in you.

O YOU WHOM I OFTEN AND SILENTLY COME

O you whom I often and silently come where you are that I may
    be with you,
As I walk by your side or sit near, or remain in the same room
    with you,

Little you know the subtle electric fire that for your sake is playing
     within me.

THAT SHADOW MY LIKENESS

That shadow my likeness that goes to and fro seeking a livelihood,
     chattering, chaffering,
How often I find myself standing and looking at it where it flits,
How often I question and doubt whether that is really me;
But among my lovers and caroling these songs,
O I never doubt whether that is really me.

FULL OF LIFE NOW

Full of life now, compact, visible,
I, forty years old the eighty-third year of the States,
To one a century hence or any number of centuries hence,
To you yet unborn these, seeking you.

When you read these I that was visible am become invisible,
Now it is you, compact, visible, realizing my poems, seeking
     me,
Fancying how happy you were if I could be with you and become
     your comrade;
Be it as if I were with you. (Be not too certain but I am now with
     you.)

SALUT AU MONDE!

— 1 —

O take my hand Walt Whitman!
Such gliding wonders! such sights and sounds!
Such join'd unended links, each hook'd to the next,
Each answering all, each sharing the earth with all.

What widens within you Walt Whitman?
What waves and soils exuding?
What climes? what persons and cities are here?
Who are the infants, some playing, some slumbering?
Who are the girls? who are the married women?
Who are the groups of old men going slowly with their arms
    about each other's necks?
What rivers are these? what forests and fruits are these?
What are the mountains call'd that rise so high in the mists?
What myriads of dwellings are they fill'd with dwellers?

− 2 −

Within me latitude widens, longitude lengthens,
Asia, Africa, Europe, are to the east—America is provided for in
    the west,
Banding the bulge of the earth winds the hot equator,
Curiously north and south turn the axis-ends,
Within me is the longest day, the sun wheels in slanting rings, it
    does not set for months,
Stretch'd in due time within me the midnight sun just rises above
    the horizon and sinks again,
Within me zones, seas, cataracts, forests, volcanoes, groups,
Malaysia, Polynesia, and the great West Indian islands.

− 3 −

What do you hear Walt Whitman?

I hear the workman singing and the farmer's wife singing,
I hear in the distance the sounds of children and of animals early
    in the day,
I hear emulous shouts of Australians pursuing the wild horse,
I hear the Spanish dance with castanets in the chestnut shade, to
    the rebeck and guitar,
I hear continual echoes from the Thames,
I hear fierce French liberty songs,
I hear of the Italian boat-sculler the musical recitative of old poems,

I hear the locusts in Syria as they strike the grain and grass with
    the showers of their terrible clouds,
I hear the Coptic refrain toward sundown, pensively falling on the
    breast of the black venerable vast mother the Nile,
I hear the chirp of the Mexican muleteer, and the bells of the
    mule,
I hear the Arab muezzin calling from the top of the mosque,
I hear the Christian priests at the altars of their churches, I hear
    the responsive bass and soprano,
I hear the cry of the Cossack, and the sailor's voice putting to sea
    at Okotsk,*
I hear the wheeze of the slave-coffle† as the slaves march on, as
    the husky gangs pass on by twos and threes, fasten'd together
    with wrist-chains and ankle-chains,
I hear the Hebrew reading his records and psalms,
I hear the rhythmic myths of the Greeks, and the strong legends
    of the Romans,
I hear the tale of the divine life and bloody death of the beautiful
    God the Christ,
I hear the Hindoo teaching his favorite pupil the loves, wars,
    adages, transmitted safely to this day from poets who wrote
    three thousand years ago.

– 4 –

What do you see Walt Whitman?
Who are they you salute, and that one after another salute you?

I see a great round wonder rolling through space,
I see diminute farms, hamlets, ruins, graveyards, jails, factories,
    palaces, hovels, huts of barbarians, tents of nomads upon the
    surface,
I see the shaded part on one side where the sleepers are sleeping,
    and the sunlit part on the other side,

---

*Siberian seaport; more commonly spelled Okhotsk.
†Slave caravan.

I see the curious rapid change of the light and shade,
I see distant lands, as real and near to the inhabitants of them as
my land is to me.

I see plenteous waters,
I see mountain peaks, I see the sierras of Andes where they range,
I see plainly the Himalayas, Chian Shahs, Altays, Ghauts,
I see the giant pinnacles of Elbruz, Kazbek, Bazardjusi,
I see the Styrian Alps, and the Karnac Alps,
I see the Pyrenees, Balks, Carpathians, and to the north the
Dofrafields, and off at sea mount Hecla,*
I see Vesuvius and Etna, the mountains of the Moon, and the
Red mountains of Madagascar,
I see the Lybian, Arabian, and Asiatic deserts,
I see huge dreadful Arctic and Antarctic icebergs,
I see the superior oceans and the inferior ones, the Atlantic and
Pacific, the sea of Mexico, the Brazilian sea, and the sea of
Peru,
The waters of Hindustan, the China sea, and the gulf of Guinea,
The Japan waters, the beautiful bay of Nagasaki landlock'd in its
mountains,
The spread of the Baltic, Caspian, Bothnia, the British shores,
and the bay of Biscay,
The clear-sunn'd Mediterranean, and from one to another of its
islands,
The White sea, and the sea around Greenland.

I behold the mariners of the world,
Some are in storms, some in the night with the watch on the
look-out,
Some drifting helplessly, some with contagious diseases.

I behold the sail and steamships of the world, some in clusters in
port, some on their voyages,

---

*In the previous four lines, the poet tours mountain ranges in China, Siberia,
India, Austria, Italy, and Iceland.

Some double the cape of Storms, some cape Verde, others capes
    Guardafui, Bon, or Bajadore,
Others Dondra head, others pass the straits of Sunda, others cape
    Lopatka, others Behring's straits,
Others cape Horn, others sail the gulf of Mexico or along Cuba
    or Hayti, others Hudson's bay or Baffin's bay,
Others pass the straits of Dover, others enter the Wash, others the
    firth of Solway, others round cape Clear, others the Land's End,
Others traverse the Zuyder Zee or the Scheld,
Others as comers and goers at Gibraltar or the Dardanelles,
Others sternly push their way through the northern winter-packs,
Others descend or ascend the Obi or the Lena,
Others the Niger or the Congo, others the Indus, the
    Burampooter and Cambodia,
Others wait steam'd up ready to start in the ports of Australia,
Wait at Liverpool, Glasgow, Dublin, Marseilles, Lisbon, Naples,
    Hamburg, Bremen, Bordeaux, the Hague, Copenhagen,
Wait at Valparaiso, Rio Janeiro, Panama.

− 5 −

I see the tracks of the railroads[31] of the earth,
I see them in Great Britain, I see them in Europe,
I see them in Asia and in Africa.

I see the electric telegraphs of the earth,
I see the filaments of the news of the wars, deaths, losses, gains,
    passions, of my race.

I see the long river-stripes of the earth,
I see the Amazon and the Paraguay,
I see the four great rivers of China, the Amour, the Yellow River,
    the Yiang-tse, and the Pearl,
I see where the Seine flows, and where the Danube, the Loire,
    the Rhone, and the Guadalquiver flow,
I see the windings of the Volga, the Dnieper, the Oder,
I see the Tuscan going down the Arno, and the Venetian along
    the Po,
I see the Greek seaman sailing out of Egina bay.

– 6 –

I see the site of the old empire of Assyria, and that of Persia, and
   that of India,
I see the falling of the Ganges over the high rim of Saukara.

I see the place of the idea of the Deity incarnated by avatars in
   human forms,
I see the spots of the successions of priests on the earth, oracles,
   sacrifices, brahmins, sabians, llamas, monks, muftis, exhorters,
I see where druids walk'd the groves of Mona, I see the mistletoe
   and vervain,*
I see the temples of the deaths of the bodies of Gods, I see the old
   signifiers.

I see Christ eating the bread of his last supper in the midst of
   youths and old persons,
I see where the strong divine young man the Hercules toil'd
   faithfully and long and then died,
I see the place of the innocent rich life and hapless fate of the
   beautiful nocturnal son, the full-limb'd Bacchus,
I see Kneph, blooming, drest in blue, with the crown of feathers
   on his head,
I see Hermes, unsuspected, dying, well-belov'd, saying to the
   people *Do not weep for me,*
This is not my true country, I have lived banish'd from my true
   country, I now go back there,
I return to the celestial sphere where every one goes in his turn.

– 7 –

I see the battle-fields of the earth, grass grows upon them and
   blossoms and corn,
I see the tracks of ancient and modern expeditions.

---

*The poet "sees" Druids at the groves of Mona, an ancient sacred site in Anglesey,
an island off the coast of northwestern Wales; the plants mistletoe and vervain are
associated with practices of the Druids.

I see the nameless masonries, venerable messages of the unknown
    events, heroes, records of the earth.

I see the places of the sagas,
I see pine-trees and fir-trees torn by northern blasts,
I see granite bowlders and cliffs, I see green meadows and lakes,
I see the burial-cairns of Scandinavian warriors,
I see them raised high with stones by the marge of restless oceans,
    that the dead men's spirits when they wearied of their quiet
    graves might rise up through the mounds and gaze on the
    tossing billows, and be refresh'd by storms, immensity, liberty,
    action.

I see the steppes of Asia,
I see the tumuli of Mongolia, I see the tents of Kalmucks and
    Baskirs,
I see the nomadic tribes with herds of oxen and cows,
I see the table-lands notch'd with ravines, I see the jungles and
    deserts,
I see the camel, the wild steed, the bustard, the fat-tail'd sheep,
    the antelope, and the burrowing wolf.

I see the highlands of Abyssinia,
I see flocks of goats feeding, and see the fig-tree, tamarind, date,
And see fields of teff-wheat and places of verdure and gold.

I see the Brazilian vaquero,
I see the Bolivian ascending mount Sorata,
I see the Wacho crossing the plains, I see the incomparable rider
    of horses with his lasso on his arm,
I see over the pampas the pursuit of wild cattle for their hides.

– 8 –

I see the regions of snow and ice,
I see the sharp-eyed Samoiede and the Finn,
I see the seal-seeker in his boat poising his lance,
I see the Siberian on his slight-built sledge drawn by dogs,

I see the porpoise-hunters, I see the whale-crews of the south
    Pacific and the north Atlantic,
I see the cliffs, glaciers, torrents, valleys, of Switzerland—I mark
    the long winters and the isolation.

I see the cities of the earth and make myself at random a part of
    them,
I am a real Parisian,
I am a habitan of Vienna, St. Petersburg, Berlin, Constantinople,
I am of Adelaide, Sidney, Melbourne,
I am of London, Manchester, Bristol, Edinburgh, Limerick,
I am of Madrid, Cadiz, Barcelona, Oporto, Lyons, Brussels,
    Berne, Frankfort, Stuttgart, Turin, Florence,
I belong in Moscow, Cracow, Warsaw, or northward in
    Christiania or Stockholm, or in Siberian Irkutsk, or in some
    street in Iceland,
I descend upon all those cities, and rise from them again.

— 10 —

I see vapors exhaling from unexplored countries,
I see the savage types, the bow and arrow, the poison'd splint, the
    fetich, and the obi.

I see African and Asiatic towns,
I see Algiers, Tripoli, Derne, Mogadore, Timbuctoo, Monrovia,
I see the swarms of Pekin, Canton, Benares, Delhi, Calcutta,
    Tokio,
I see the Kruman in his hut, and the Dahoman and Ashantee-
    man in their huts,
I see the Turk smoking opium in Aleppo,
I see the picturesque crowds at the fairs of Khiva and those of
    Herat,
I see Teheran, I see Muscat and Medina and the intervening
    sands, I see the caravans toiling onward,
I see Egypt and the Egyptians, I see the pyramids and obelisks,
I look on chisell'd histories, records of conquering kings,
    dynasties, cut in slabs of sand-stone, or on granite-blocks,

I see at Memphis mummy-pits containing mummies embalm'd,
 swathed in linen cloth, lying there many centuries,
I look on the fall'n Theban, the large-ball'd eyes, the side-
 drooping neck, the hands folded across the breast.

I see all the menials of the earth, laboring,
I see all the prisoners in the prisons,
I see the defective human bodies of the earth,
The blind, the deaf and dumb, idiots, hunchbacks, lunatics,
The pirates, thieves, betrayers, murderers, slave-makers of the earth,
The helpless infants, and the helpless old men and women.

I see male and female everywhere,
I see the serene brotherhood of philosophs,
I see the constructiveness of my race,
I see the results of the perseverance and industry of my race,
I see ranks, colors, barbarisms, civilizations, I go among them,
 I mix indiscriminately,
And I salute all the inhabitants of the earth.

      – 11 –

You whoever you are!
You daughter or son of England!
You of the mighty Slavic tribes and empires! you Russ in Russia!
You dim-descended, black, divine-soul'd African, large, fine-
 headed, nobly-form'd, superbly destin'd, on equal terms
 with me!
You Norwegian! Swede! Dane! Icelander! you Prussian!
You Spaniard of Spain! you Portuguese!
You Frenchwoman and Frenchman of France!
You Belge! you liberty-lover of the Netherlands! (you stock
 whence I myself have descended;)
You sturdy Austrian! you Lombard! Hun! Bohemian! farmer of
 Styria!
You neighbor of the Danube!
You working-man of the Rhine, the Elbe, or the Weser! you
 working-woman too!

You Sardinian! you Bavarian! Swabian! Saxon! Wallachian!
     Bulgarian!
You Roman! Neapolitan! you Greek!
You lithe matador in the arena at Seville!
You mountaineer living lawlessly on the Taurus or Caucasus!
You Bokh horse-herd watching your mares and stallions feeding!
You beautiful-bodied Persian at full speed in the saddle shooting
     arrows to the mark!
You Chinaman and Chinawoman of China! you Tartar of
     Tartary!
You women of the earth subordinated at your tasks!
You Jew journeying in your old age through every risk to stand
     once on Syrian ground!
You other Jews waiting in all lands for your Messiah!
You thoughtful Armenian pondering by some stream of the
     Euphrates! you peering amid the ruins of Nineveh! you
     ascending mount Ararat!
You foot-worn pilgrim welcoming the far-away sparkle of the
     minarets of Mecca!
You sheiks along the stretch from Suez to Bab-el-mandeb ruling
     your families and tribes!
You olive-grower tending your fruit on fields of Nazareth,
     Damascus, or Lake Tiberias!
You Thibet trader on the wide inland or bargaining in the shops
     of Lassa!
You Japanese man or woman! you liver in Madagascar, Ceylon,
     Sumatra, Borneo!
All you continentals of Asia, Africa, Europe, Australia, indifferent
     of place!
All you on the numberless islands of the archipelagoes of the
     sea!
And you of centuries hence when you listen to me!
And you each and everywhere whom I specify not, but include
     just the same!
Health to you! good will to you all, from me and America sent!
Each of us inevitable,
Each of us limitless—each of us with his or her right upon the
     earth,

Each of us allow'd the eternal purports of the earth,
Each of us here as divinely as any is here.

— 12 —

You Hottentot with clicking palate! you woolly-hair'd hordes!
You own'd persons dropping sweat-drops or blood-drops!
You human forms with the fathomless ever-impressive
    countenances of brutes!
You poor koboo whom the meanest of the rest look down
    upon for all your glimmering language and
    spirituality!
You dwarf'd Kamtschatkan, Greenlander, Lapp!
You Austral negro, naked, red, sooty, with protrusive lip,
    groveling, seeking your food!
You Caffre, Berber, Soudanese!
You haggard, uncouth, untutor'd Bedowee!
You plague-swarms in Madras, Nankin, Kaubul, Cairo!
You benighted roamer of Amazonia! you Patagonian! you
    Feejeeman!
I do not prefer others so very much before you either,
I do not say one word against you, away back there where you
    stand,
(You will come forward in due time to my side.)

— 13 —

My spirit has pass'd in compassion and determination around the
    whole earth,
I have look'd for equals and lovers and found them ready for me
    in all lands,
I think some divine rapport has equalized me with them.

You vapors, I think I have risen with you, moved away to distant
    continents, and fallen down there, for reasons,
I think I have blown with you you winds;
You waters I have finger'd every shore with you,

I have run through what any river or strait of the globe has run
    through,
I have taken my stand on the bases of peninsulas and on the high
    embedded rocks, to cry thence:

Salut au monde!
What cities the light or warmth penetrates I penetrate those cities
    myself,
All islands to which birds wing their way I wing my way myself.

Toward you all, in America's name,
I raise high the perpendicular hand, I make the signal,
To remain after me in sight forever,
For all the haunts and homes of men.

SONG OF THE OPEN ROAD[32]

— 1 —

Afoot and light-hearted I take to the open road,
Healthy, free, the world before me,
The long brown path before me leading wherever I choose.

Henceforth I ask not good-fortune, I myself am good-fortune,
Henceforth I whimper no more, postpone no more, need nothing,
Done with indoor complaints, libraries, querulous criticisms,
Strong and content I travel the open road.

The earth, that is sufficient,
I do not want the constellations any nearer,
I know they are very well where they are,
I know they suffice for those who belong to them.

(Still here I carry my old delicious burdens,
I carry them, men and women, I carry them with me wherever
    I go,

I swear it is impossible for me to get rid of them
I am fill'd with them, and I will fill them in return.)

— 2 —

You road I enter upon and look around, I believe you are not all
    that is here,
I believe that much unseen is also here.

Here the profound lesson of reception, nor preference nor denial,
The black with his woolly head, the felon, the diseas'd, the
    illiterate person, are not denied;
The birth, the hasting after the physician, the beggar's
    tramp, the drunkard's stagger, the laughing party of
    mechanics,
The escaped youth, the rich person's carriage, the fop, the
    eloping couple,
The early market-man, the hearse, the moving of furniture into
    the town, the return back from the town,
They pass, I also pass, any thing passes, none can be
    interdicted,
None but are accepted, none but shall be dear to me.

— 3 —

You air that serves me with breath to speak!
You objects that call from diffusion my meanings and give them
    shape!
You light that wraps me and all things in delicate equable showers!
You paths worn in the irregular hollows by the roadsides!
I believe you are latent with unseen existences, you are so dear to
    me.

You flagg'd walks of the cities! you strong curbs at the edges!
You ferries! you planks and posts of wharves! you timber-lined
    sides! you distant ships!
You rows of houses! you window-pierc'd façades! you roofs!
You porches and entrances! you copings and iron guards!

You windows whose transparent shells might expose so much!
You doors and ascending steps! you arches!
You gray stones of interminable pavements! you trodden
    crossings!
From all that has touch'd you I believe you have imparted to
    yourselves, and now would impart the same secretly to me,
From the living and the dead you have peopled your impassive
    surfaces, and the spirits thereof would be evident and
    amicable with me.

– 4 –

The earth expanding right hand and left hand,
The picture alive, every part in its best light,
The music falling in where it is wanted, and stopping where it is
    not wanted,
The cheerful voice of the public road, the gay fresh sentiment of
    the road.

O highway I travel, do you say to me Do not leave me?
Do you say *Venture not—if you leave me you are lost?*
Do you say *I am already prepared, I am well-beaten and undenied,*
    adhere to me?
O public road, I say back I am not afraid to leave you, yet I love you,
You express me better than I can express myself,
You shall be more to me than my poem.

I think heroic deeds were all conceiv'd in the open air, and all
    free poems also,
I think I could stop here myself and do miracles,
I think whatever I shall meet on the road I shall like, and whoever
    beholds me shall like me,
I think whoever I see must be happy.

– 5 –

From this hour I ordain myself loos'd of limits and imaginary
    lines,

Going where I list, my own master total and absolute,
Listening to others, considering well what they say,
Pausing, searching, receiving, contemplating,
Gently, but with undeniable will, divesting myself of the holds
    that would hold me.

I inhale great draughts of space,
The east and the west are mine, and the north and the south are
    mine.

I am larger, better than I thought,
I did not know I held so much goodness.

All seems beautiful to me,
I can repeat over to men and women You have done such good to
    me I would do the same to you,
I will recruit for myself and you as I go,
I will scatter myself among men and women as I go,
I will toss a new gladness and roughness among them,
Whoever denies me it shall not trouble me,
Whoever accepts me he or she shall be blessed and shall
    bless me.

– 6 –

Now if a thousand perfect men were to appear it would not
    amaze me,
Now if a thousand beautiful forms of women appear'd it would
    not astonish me.

Now I see the secret of the making of the best persons,
It is to grow in the open air and to eat and sleep with the
    earth.

Here a great personal deed has room,
(Such a deed seizes upon the hearts of the whole race of men,
Its effusion of strength and will overwhelms law and mocks all
    authority and all argument against it.)

Here is the test of wisdom,
Wisdom is not finally tested in schools,
Wisdom cannot be pass'd from one having it to another not
    having it,
Wisdom is of the soul, is not susceptible of proof, is its own proof,
Applies to all stages and objects and qualities and is content,
Is the certainty of the reality and immortality of things, and the
    excellence of things;
Something there is in the float[33] of the sight of things that
    provokes it out of the soul.

Now I re-examine philosophies and religions,
They may prove well in lecture-rooms, yet not prove at all under the
    spacious clouds and along the landscape and flowing currents.

Here is realization,
Here is a man tallied—he realizes here what he has in him,
The past, the future, majesty, love—if they are vacant of you, you
    are vacant of them.

Only the kernel of every object nourishes;
Where is he who tears off the husks for you and me?
Where is he that undoes stratagems and envelopes for you and me?

Here is adhesiveness, it is not previously fashion'd, it is apropos;
Do you know what it is as you pass to be loved by strangers?
Do you know the talk of those turning eye-balls?

— 7 —

Here is the efflux of the soul,
The efflux of the soul comes from within through embower'd
    gates, ever provoking questions,
These yearnings why are they? these thoughts in the darkness why
    are they?
Why are there men and women that while they are nigh me the
    sunlight expands my blood?
Why when they leave me do my pennants of joy sink flat and lank?

Why are there trees I never walk under but large and melodious
    thoughts descend upon me?
(I think they hang there winter and summer on those trees and
    always drop fruit as I pass;)
What is it I interchange so suddenly with strangers?
What with some driver as I ride on the seat by his side?
What with some fisherman drawing his seine by the shore as I
    walk by and pause?
What gives me to be free to a woman's and man's goodwill? what
    gives them to be free to mine?

– 8 –

The efflux of the soul is happiness, here is happiness,
I think it pervades the open air, waiting at all times,
Now it flows unto us, we are rightly charged.

Here rises the fluid and attaching character,
The fluid and attaching character is the freshness and sweetness
    of man and woman,
(The herbs of the morning sprout no fresher and sweeter every
    day out of the roots of themselves, than it sprouts fresh and
    sweet continually out of itself.)

Toward the fluid and attaching character exudes the sweat of the
    love of young and old,
From it falls distill'd the charm that mocks beauty and
    attainments,
Toward it heaves the shuddering longing ache of contact.

– 9 –

Allons! whoever you are come travel with me!
Traveling with me you find what never tires.

The earth never tires,
The earth is rude, silent, incomprehensible at first, Nature is rude
    and incomprehensible at first,

Be not discouraged, keep on, there are divine things well envelop'd,
I swear to you there are divine things more beautiful than words
    can tell.

Allons! we must not stop here,
However sweet these laid-up stores, however convenient this
    dwelling we cannot remain here,
However shelter'd this port and however calm these waters we
    must not anchor here,
However welcome the hospitality that surrounds us we are
    permitted to receive it but a little while.

– 10 –

Allons! the inducements shall be greater,
We will sail pathless and wild seas,
We will go where winds blow, waves dash, and the Yankee clipper
    speeds by under full sail.

Allons! with power, liberty, the earth, the elements,
Health, defiance, gayety, self-esteem, curiosity;
Allons! from all formules!
From your formules, O bat-eyed and materialistic priests.

The stale cadaver blocks up the passage—the burial waits no
    longer.

Allons! yet take warning!
He traveling with me needs the best blood, thews, endurance,
None may come to the trial till he or she bring courage and
    health,
Come not here if you have already spent the best of yourself,
Only those may come who come in sweet and determin'd bodies,
No diseas'd person, no rum-drinker or venereal taint is permitted
    here.

(I and mine do not convince by arguments, similes, rhymes,
We convince by our presence.)

– 11 –

Listen! I will be honest with you,
I do not offer the old smooth prizes, but offer rough new prizes,
These are the days that must happen to you:
You shall not heap up what is call'd riches,
You shall scatter with lavish hand all that you earn or achieve,
You but arrive at the city to which you were destin'd, you hardly
    settle yourself to satisfaction before you are call'd by an
    irresistible call to depart,
You shall be treated to the ironical smiles and mockings of those
    who remain behind you,
What beckonings of love you receive you shall only answer with
    passionate kisses of parting,
You shall not allow the hold of those who spread their reach'd
    hands toward you.

– 12 –

Allons! after the great Companions, and to belong to them!
They too are on the road—they are the swift and majestic men—
    they are the greatest women,
Enjoyers of calms of seas and storms of seas,
Sailors of many a ship, walkers of many a mile of land,
Habitués of many distant countries, habitués of far-distant
    dwellings,
Trusters of men and women, observers of cities, solitary toilers,
Pausers and contemplators of tufts, blossoms, shells of the shore,
Dancers at wedding-dances, kissers of brides, tender helpers of
    children, bearers of children,
Soldiers of revolts, standers by gaping graves, lowerers-down of
    coffins,
Journeyers over consecutive seasons, over the years, the curious
    years each emerging from that which preceded it,
Journeyers as with companions, namely their own diverse phases,
Forth-steppers from the latent unrealized baby-days,
Journeyers gayly with their own youth, journeyers with their
    bearded and well-grain'd manhood,

Journeyers with their womanhood, ample, unsurpass'd, content,
Journeyers with their own sublime old age of manhood or
      womanhood,
Old age, calm, expanded, broad with the haughty breadth of the
      universe,
Old age, flowing free with the delicious near-by freedom of
      death.

— 13 —

Allons! to that which is endless as it was beginningless,
To undergo much, tramps of days, rests of nights,
To merge all in the travel they tend to, and the days and nights
      they tend to,
Again to merge them in the start of superior journeys,
To see nothing anywhere but what you may reach it and
      pass it,
To conceive no time, however distant, but what you may reach it
      and pass it,
To look up or down no road but it stretches and waits for you,
      however long but it stretches and waits for you,
To see no being, not God's or any, but you also go thither,
To see no possession but you may possess it, enjoying all without
      labor or purchase, abstracting the feast yet not abstracting one
      particle of it,
To take the best of the farmer's farm and the rich man's elegant
      villa, and the chaste blessings of the well-married couple, and
      the fruits of orchards and flowers of gardens,
To take to your use out of the compact cities as you pass
      through,
To carry buildings and streets with you afterward wherever
      you go,
To gather the minds of men out of their brains as you encounter
      them, to gather the love out of their hearts,
To take your lovers on the road with you, for all that you leave
      them behind you,
To know the universe itself as a road, as many roads, as roads for
      traveling souls.

All parts away for the progress of souls,
All religion, all solid things, arts, governments—all that was or is
    apparent upon this globe or any globe, falls into niches and
    corners before the procession of souls along the grand roads
    of the universe.

Of the progress of the souls of men and women along the grand
    roads of the universe, all other progress is the needed emblem
    and sustenance.

Forever alive, forever forward,
Stately, solemn, sad, withdrawn, baffled, mad, turbulent, feeble,
    dissatisfied,
Desperate, proud, fond, sick, accepted by men, rejected by
    men,
They go! they go! I know that they go, but I know not where
    they go,
But I know that they go toward the best—toward something great.

Whoever you are, come forth! or man or woman come forth!
You must not stay sleeping and dallying there in the house,
    though you built it, or though it has been built for you.

Out of the dark confinement! out from behind the screen!
It is useless to protest, I know all and expose it.

Behold through you as bad as the rest,
Through the laughter, dancing, dining, supping, of people,
Inside of dresses and ornaments, inside of those wash'd and
    trimm'd faces,
Behold a secret silent loathing and despair.

No husband, no wife, no friend, trusted to hear the confession,
Another self, a duplicate of every one, skulking and hiding it
    goes,
Formless and wordless through the streets of the cities, polite and
    bland in the parlors,
In the cars of railroads, in steamboats, in the public assembly,

Home to the houses of men and women, at the table, in the
    bedroom, everywhere,
Smartly attired, countenance smiling, form upright, death under
    the breast-bones, hell under the skull-bones,
Under the broadcloth and gloves, under the ribbons and artificial
    flowers,
Keeping fair with the customs, speaking not a syllable of itself,
Speaking of any thing else but never of itself.

– 14 –

Allons! through struggles and wars!
The goal that was named cannot be countermanded.

Have the past struggles succeeded?
What has succeeded? yourself? your nation? Nature?
Now understand me well—it is provided in the essence of
    things that from any fruition of success, no matter what,
    shall come forth something to make a greater struggle
    necessary.

My call is the call of battle, I nourish active rebellion,
He going with me must go well arm'd,
He going with me goes often with spare diet, poverty, angry
    enemies, desertions.

– 15 –

Allons! the road is before us!
It is safe—I have tried it—my own feet have tried it well—be not
    detain'd!
Let the paper remain on the desk unwritten, and the book on the
    shelf unopen'd!
Let the tools remain in the workshop! let the money remain
    unearn'd!
Let the school stand! mind not the cry of the teacher!
Let the preacher preach in his pulpit! let the lawyer plead in the
    court, and the judge expound the law.

Camerado, I give you my hand!
I give you my love more precious than money,
I give you myself before preaching or law;
Will you give me yourself? will you come travel with me?
Shall we stick by each other as long as we live?

CROSSING BROOKLYN FERRY[34]

– 1 –

Flood-tide below me! I see you face to face!
Clouds of the west—sun there half an hour high*—I see you also
     face to face.

Crowds of men and women attired in the usual costumes, how
     curious you are to me!
On the ferry-boats the hundreds and hundreds that cross,
     returning home, are more curious to me than you suppose,
And you that shall cross from shore to shore years hence are
     more to me, and more in my meditations, than you might
     suppose.

– 2 –

The impalpable sustenance of me from all things at all hours of
     the day,
The simple, compact, well-join'd scheme, myself disintegrated,
     every one disintegrated yet part of the scheme,
The similitudes of the past and those of the future,
The glories strung like beads on my smallest sights and hearings,
     on the walk in the street and the passage over the river,
The current rushing so swiftly and swimming with me far away,

---

*Depending upon the time of year, the poet is looking on a late-afternoon or an
early-evening sky—in other words, he is returning home to Brooklyn after a day's
labor in Manhattan. The poem's original title was "Sun-down Poem," and Whitman
sets this scene by placing the sun "there"—that is, in the west—"half an hour high."

The others that are to follow me, the ties between me and them,
The certainty of others, the life, love, sight, hearing of others.

Others will enter the gates of the ferry and cross from shore to shore,
Others will watch the run of the flood-tide,
Others will see the shipping of Manhattan north and west, and
    the heights of Brooklyn to the south and east,
Others will see the islands large and small;
Fifty years hence, others will see them as they cross, the sun half
    an hour high,
A hundred years hence, or ever so many hundred years hence,
    others will see them,
Will enjoy the sunset, the pouring in of the flood-tide, the falling-
    back to the sea of the ebb-tide.

– 3 –

It avails not, time nor place—distance avails not,
I am with you, you men and women of a generation, or ever so
    many generations hence,
Just as you feel when you look on the river and sky, so I felt,
Just as any of you is one of a living crowd, I was one of a crowd,
Just as you are refresh'd by the gladness of the river and the bright
    flow, I was refresh'd,
Just as you stand and lean on the rail, yet hurry with the swift
    current, I stood yet was hurried,
Just as you look on the numberless masts of ships and the thick-
    stemm'd pipes of steamboats, I look'd.

I too many and many a time cross'd the river of old,
Watched the Twelfth-month sea-gulls, saw them high in the air
    floating with motionless wings, oscillating their bodies,
Saw how the glistening yellow lit up parts of their bodies and left
    the rest in strong shadow,
Saw the slow-wheeling circles and the gradual edging toward the
    south,
Saw the reflection of the summer sky in the water,
Had my eyes dazzled by the shimmering track of beams,

Look'd at the fine centrifugal spokes of light round the shape of
    my head in the sunlit water,*
Look'd on the haze on the hills southward and south-westward,
Look'd on the vapor as it flew in fleeces tinged with violet,
Look'd toward the lower bay to notice the vessels arriving,
Saw their approach, saw aboard those that were near me,
Saw the white sails of schooners and sloops, saw the ships at anchor,
The sailors at work in the rigging or out astride the spars,
The round masts, the swinging motion of the hulls, the slender
    serpentine pennants,
The large and small steamers in motion, the pilots in their pilot-
    houses,
The white wake left by the passage, the quick tremulous whirl of
    the wheels,
The flags of all nations, the falling of them at sunset,
The scallop-edged waves in the twilight, the ladled cups, the
    frolicsome crests and glistening,
The stretch afar growing dimmer and dimmer, the gray walls of
    the granite storehouses by the docks,
On the river the shadowy group, the big steam-tug closely flank'd
    on each side by the barges, the hay-boat, the belated lighter,
On the neighboring shore the fires from the foundry chimneys
    burning high and glaringly into the night,
Casting their flicker of black contrasted with wild red and yellow
    light over the tops of houses, and down into the clefts of streets.

— 4 —

These and all else were to me the same as they are to you,
I loved well those cities, loved well the stately and rapid river,
The men and women I saw were all near to me,
Others the same—others who look back on me because I look'd
    forward to them,
(The time will come, though I stop here to-day and to-night.)

---

*The poet sees his reflection illuminated by the sun behind him, causing the "halo
effect" described here.

– 5 –

What is it then between us?
What is the count of the scores or hundreds of years between us?

Whatever it is, it avails not—distance avails not, and place avails not,
I too lived, Brooklyn of ample hills was mine,
I too walk'd the streets of Manhattan island, and bathed in the
     waters around it,
I too felt the curious abrupt questionings stir within me,
In the day among crowds of people sometimes they came upon
     me,
In my walks home late at night or as I lay in my bed they came
     upon me,
I too had been struck from the float forever held in solution,
I too had receiv'd identity by my body,
That I was I knew was of my body, and what I should be I knew I
     should be of my body.

– 6 –

It is not upon you alone the dark patches fall,[35]
The dark threw its patches down upon me also,
The best I had done seem'd to me blank and suspicious,
My great thoughts as I supposed them, were they not in reality
     meagre?
Nor is it you alone who know what it is to be evil,
I am he who knew what it was to be evil,
I too knitted the old knot of contrariety,
Blabb'd, blush'd, resented, lied, stole, grudg'd,
Had guile, anger, lust, hot wishes I dared not speak,
Was wayward, vain, greedy, shallow, sly, cowardly, malignant,
The wolf, the snake, the hog, not wanting in me,
The cheating look, the frivolous word, the adulterous wish, not
     wanting,
Refusals, hates, postponements, meanness, laziness, none of these
     wanting,
Was one with the rest, the days and haps of the rest,

Was call'd by my nighest name by clear loud voices of young men
  as they saw me approaching or passing,
Felt their arms on my neck as I stood, or the negligent leaning of
  their flesh against me as I sat,
Saw many I loved in the street or ferry-boat or public assembly,
  yet never told them a word,
Lived the same life with the rest, the same old laughing, gnawing,
  sleeping,
Play'd the part that still looks back on the actor or actress,
The same old role, the role that is what we make it, as great as
  we like,
Or as small as we like, or both great and small.

– 7 –

Closer yet I approach you,
What thought you have of me now, I had as much of you — I laid
  in my stores in advance,
I consider'd long and seriously of you before you were born.

Who was to know what should come home to me?
Who knows but I am enjoying this?
Who knows, for all the distance, but I am as good as looking at
  you now, for all you cannot see me?

– 8 –

Ah, what can ever be more stately and admirable to me than
  mast-hemm'd Manhattan?
River and sunset and scallop-edg'd waves of flood-tide?
The sea-gulls oscillating their bodies, the hay-boat in the twilight,
  and the belated lighter?
What gods can exceed these that clasp me by the hand, and with
  voices I love call me promptly and loudly by my nighest
  name as I approach?
What is more subtle than this which ties me to the woman or
  man that looks in my face?
Which fuses me into you now, and pours my meaning into you?

We understand then do we not?
What I promis'd without mentioning it, have you not accepted?
What the study could not teach—what the preaching could not
accomplish is accomplish'd, is it not?

– 9 –

Flow on, river! flow with the flood-tide, and ebb with the
ebb-tide!
Frolic on, crested and scallop-edg'd waves!
Gorgeous clouds of the sunset! drench with your splendor me, or
the men and women generations after me!
Cross from shore to shore, countless crowds of passengers!
Stand up, tall masts of Mannahatta! stand up, beautiful hills of
Brooklyn!
Throb, baffled and curious brain! throw out questions and
answers!
Suspend here and everywhere, eternal float of solution!
Gaze, loving and thirsting eyes, in the house or street or public
assembly!
Sound out, voices of young men! loudly and musically call me by
my nighest name!
Live, old life! play the part that looks back on the actor or actress!
Play the old role, the role that is great or small according as one
makes it!
Consider, you who peruse me, whether I may not in unknown
ways be looking upon you;
Be firm, rail over the river, to support those who lean idly, yet
haste with the hasting current;
Fly on, sea-birds! fly sideways, or wheel in large circles high in
the air;
Receive the summer sky, you water, and faithfully hold it till all
downcast eyes have time to take it from you!
Diverge, fine spokes of light, from the shape of my head, or any
one's head, in the sunlit water!
Come on, ships from the lower bay! pass up or down, white-sail'd
schooners, sloops, lighters!
Flaunt away, flags of all nations! be duly lower'd at sunset!

Burn high your fires, foundry chimneys! cast black shadows at
    nightfall! cast red and yellow light over the tops of the houses!
Appearances, now or henceforth, indicate what you are,
You necessary film, continue to envelop the soul,
About my body for me, and your body for you, be hung out
    divinest aromas,
Thrive, cities—bring your freight, bring your shows, ample and
    sufficient rivers,
Expand, being than which none else is perhaps more spiritual,
Keep your places, objects than which none else is more lasting.

You have waited, you always wait, you dumb, beautiful
    ministers,[36]
We receive you with free sense at last, and are insatiate
    henceforward,
Not you any more shall be able to foil us, or withhold yourselves
    from us,
We use you, and do not cast you aside—we plant you
    permanently within us,
We fathom you not—we love you—there is perfection in you
    also,
You furnish your parts toward eternity,
Great or small, you furnish your parts toward the soul.

SONG OF THE ANSWERER

− 1 −

Now list to my morning's romanza, I tell the signs of the
    Answerer,
To the cities and farms I sing as they spread in the sunshine
    before me.

A young man comes to me bearing a message from his brother,
How shall the young man know the whether and when of his
    brother?
Tell him to send me the signs.

And I stand before the young man face to face, and take his right
    hand in my left hand and his left hand in my right hand,
And I answer for his brother and for men, and I answer for him
    that answers for all, and send these signs.

Him all wait for, him all yield up to, his word is decisive and final,
Him they accept, in him lave, in him perceive themselves as
    amid light,
Him they immerse and he immerses them.

Beautiful women, the haughtiest nations, laws, the landscape,
    people, animals,
The profound earth and its attributes and the unquiet ocean, (so
    tell I my morning's romanza,)
All enjoyments and properties and money, and whatever money
    will buy,
The best farms, others toiling and planting and he unavoidably
    reaps,
The noblest and costliest cities, others grading and building and
    he domiciles there,
Nothing for any one but what is for him, near and far are for him,
    the ships in the offing,
The perpetual shows and marches on land are for him if they are
    for anybody.

He puts things in their attitudes,
He puts to-day out of himself with plasticity and love,
He places his own times, reminiscences, parents, brothers and
    sisters, associations, employment, politics, so that the rest
    never shame them afterward, nor assume to command them.

He is the Answerer,
What can be answer'd he answers, and what cannot be answer'd
    he shows how it cannot be answer'd.

A man is a summons and challenge,
(It is vain to skulk—do you hear that mocking and laughter? do
    you hear the ironical echoes?)

Books, friendships, philosophers, priests, action, pleasure, pride,
    beat up and down seeking to give satisfaction,
He indicates the satisfaction, and indicates them that beat up and
    down also.

Whichever the sex, whatever the season or place, he may go
    freshly and gently and safely by day or by night,
He has the pass-key of hearts, to him the response of the prying of
    hands on the knobs.

His welcome is universal, the flow of beauty is not more welcome
    or universal than he is,
The person he favors by day or sleeps with at night is blessed.

Every existence has its idiom, every thing has an idiom and
    tongue,
He resolves all tongues into his own and bestows it upon men,
    and any man translates, and any man translates himself also,
One part does not counteract another part, he is the joiner, he
    sees how they join.

He says indifferently and alike *How are you friend?* to the
    President at his levee,
And he says *Good-day my brother,* to Cudge that hoes in the
    sugar-field,
And both understand him and know that his speech is right.

He walks with perfect ease in the capitol,
He walks among the Congress, and one Representative says to
    another, *Here is our equal appearing and new.*

Then the mechanics take him for a mechanic,
And the soldiers suppose him to be a soldier, and the sailors that
    he has follow'd the sea,
And the authors take him for an author, and the artists for an
    artist,
And the laborers perceive he could labor with them and love them,

No matter what the work is, that he is the one to follow it or has
    follow'd it,
No matter what the nation, that he might find his brothers and
    sisters there.

The English believe he comes of their English stock,
A Jew to the Jew he seems, a Russ to the Russ, usual and near,
    removed from none.

Whoever he looks at in the traveler's coffee-house claims him,
The Italian or Frenchman is sure, the German is sure, the
    Spaniard is sure, and the island Cuban is sure,
The engineer, the deck-hand on the great lakes, or on the
    Mississippi or St. Lawrence or Sacramento, or Hudson or
    Paumanok sound, claims him.

The gentleman of perfect blood acknowledges his perfect blood,
The insulter, the prostitute, the angry person, the beggar, see
    themselves in the ways of him, he strangely transmutes
    them,
They are not vile any more, they hardly know themselves they are
    so grown.

— 2 —

The indications and tally of time,
Perfect sanity shows the master among philosophs,
Time, always without break, indicates itself in parts,
What always indicates the poet is the crowd of the pleasant
    company of singers, and their words,
The words of the singers are the hours or minutes of the light or
    dark, but the words of the maker of poems are the general
    light and dark,
The maker of poems settles justice, reality, immortality,
His insight and power encircle things and the human race,
He is the glory and extract thus far of things and of the human
    race.

The singers do not beget, only the Poet begets,
The singers are welcom'd, understood, appear often enough, but
    rare has the day been, likewise the spot, of the birth of the
    maker of poems, the Answerer,
(Not every century nor every five centuries has contain'd such a
    day, for all its names.)

The singers of successive hours of centuries may have ostensible
    names, but the name of each of them is one of the singers,
The name of each is, eye-singer, ear-singer, head-singer, sweet-
    singer, night-singer, parlor-singer, love-singer, weird-singer, or
    something else.

All this time and at all times wait the words of true poems,
The words of true poems do not merely please,
The true poets are not followers of beauty but the august masters
    of beauty;
The greatness of sons is the exuding of the greatness of mothers
    and fathers,
The words of true poems are the tuft and final applause of
    science.

Divine instinct, breadth of vision, the law of reason, health,
    rudeness of body, withdrawnness,
Gayety, sun-tan, air-sweetness, such are some of the words of
    poems.

The sailor and traveler underlie the maker of poems, the
    Answerer,
The builder, geometer, chemist, anatomist, phrenologist, artist, all
    these underlie the maker of poems, the Answerer.

The words of the true poems give you more than poems,
They give you to form for yourself poems, religions, politics, war,
    peace, behavior, histories, essays, daily life, and every thing
    else,
They balance ranks, colors, races, creeds, and the sexes,
They do not seek beauty, they are sought,

Forever touching them or close upon them follows beauty,
    longing, fain, love-sick.

They prepare for death, yet are they not the finish, but rather the
    outset,
They bring none to his or her terminus or to be content and
    full,
Whom they take they take into space to behold the birth of stars,
    to learn one of the meanings,
To launch off with absolute faith, to sweep through the ceaseless
    rings and never be quiet again.

OUR OLD FEUILLAGE*

Always our old feuillage!
Always Florida's green peninsula—always the priceless delta of
    Louisiana—always the cotton-fields of Alabama and Texas,
Always California's golden hills and hollows, and the silver
    mountains of New Mexico—always soft-breath'd Cuba,
Always the vast slope drain'd by the Southern sea, inseparable
    with the slopes drain'd by the Eastern and Western seas,
The area the eighty-third year of these States, the three and a half
    millions of square miles,
The eighteen thousand miles of sea-coast and bay-coast on the
    main, the thirty thousand miles of river navigation,
The seven millions of distinct families and the same number of
    dwellings—always these, and more, branching forth into
    numberless branches,
Always the free range and diversity—always the continent of
    Democracy;
Always the prairies, pastures, forests, vast cities, travelers, Kanada,
    the snows;
Always these compact lands tied at the hips with the belt stringing
    the huge oval lakes;

---

*The French word for "foliage"—yet another reference to "leaves."

Always the West with strong native persons, the increasing density
there, the habitans, friendly, threatening, ironical, scorning
invaders;
All sights, South, North, East—all deeds, promiscuously done at
all times,
All characters, movements, growths, a few noticed, myriads
unnoticed,
Through Mannahatta's streets I walking, these things gathering,
On interior rivers by night in the glare of pine knots, steamboats
wooding up,
Sunlight by day on the valley of the Susquehanna, and on the
valleys of the Potomac and Rappahannock and the valleys of
the Roanoke and Delaware,
In their northerly wilds beasts of prey haunting the Adirondacks
the hills or lapping the Saginaw waters to drink,
In a lonesome inlet a sheldrake lost from the flock sitting on the
water rocking silently,
In farmers' barns oxen in the stable, their harvest labor done they
rest standing, they are too tired,
Afar on arctic ice the she-walrus lying drowsily while her cubs
play around,
The hawk sailing where men have not yet sail'd, the farthest polar
sea, ripply, crystalline, open, beyond the floes,
White drift spooning ahead where the ship in the tempest
dashes,
On solid land what is done in cities as the bells strike midnight
together,
In primitive woods the sounds there also sounding, the howl of
the wolf, the scream of the panther, and the hoarse bellow of
the elk,
In winter beneath the hard blue ice of Moosehead lake, in
summer visible through the clear waters, the great trout
swimming,
In lower latitudes in warmer air in the Carolinas the large black
buzzard floating slowly high beyond the tree tops,
Below, the red cedar festoon'd with tylandria, the pines and
cypresses growing out of the white sand that spreads far and
flat,

Rude boats descending the big Pedee, climbing plants, parasites
     with color'd flowers and berries enveloping huge trees,
The waving drapery on the live-oak trailing long and low,
     noiselessly waved by the wind,
The camp of Georgia wagoners just after dark, the supper-fires
     and the cooking and eating by whites and negroes,
Thirty or forty great wagons, the mules, cattle, horses, feeding
     from troughs,
The shadows, gleams, up under the leaves of the old sycamore-
     trees, the flames with the black smoke from the pitch-pine
     curling and rising;
Southern fishermen fishing, the sounds and inlets of North
     Carolina's coast, the shad-fishery and the herring-fishery, the
     large sweep-seines, the windlasses on shore work'd by horses,
     the clearing, curing, and packing houses;
Deep in the forest in piney woods turpentine dropping from the
     incisions in the trees, there are the turpentine works,
There are the negroes at work in good health, the ground in all
     directions is cover'd with pine straw;
In Tennessee and Kentucky slaves busy in the coalings, at the
     forge, by the furnace-blaze, or at the corn-shucking,
In Virginia, the planter's son returning after a long absence,
     joyfully welcom'd and kiss'd by the aged mulatto nurse,
On rivers boatmen safely moor'd at nightfall in their boats under
     shelter of high banks,
Some of the younger men dance to the sound of the banjo or
     fiddle, others sit on the gunwale smoking and talking;
Late in the afternoon the mocking-bird, the American mimic,
     singing in the Great Dismal Swamp,
There are the greenish waters, the resinous odor, the plenteous
     moss, the cypress-tree, and the juniper-tree;
Northward, young men of Mannahatta, the target company from
     an excursion returning home at evening, the musket-muzzles
     all bear bunches of flowers presented by women;
Children at play, or on his father's lap a young boy fallen asleep,
     (how his lips move! how he smiles in his sleep!)
The scout riding on horseback over the plains west of the
     Mississippi, he ascends a knoll and sweeps his eyes around;

California life, the miner, bearded, dress'd in his rude costume,
    the stanch California friendship, the sweet air, the graves one
    in passing meets solitary just aside the horse-path;
Down in Texas the cotton-field, the negro-cabins, drivers driving
    mules or oxen before rude carts, cotton bales piled on banks
    and wharves;
Encircling all, vast-darting up and wide, the American Soul, with
    equal hemispheres, one Love, one Dilation or Pride;
In arriere the peace-talk with the Iroquois the aborigines, the
    calumet, the pipe of good-will, arbitration, and indorsement,
The sachem blowing the smoke first toward the sun and then
    toward the earth,
The drama of the scalp-dance enacted with painted faces and
    guttural exclamations,
The setting out of the war-party, the long and stealthy march,
The single file, the swinging hatchets, the surprise and slaughter
    of enemies;
All the acts, scenes, ways, persons, attitudes of these States,
    reminiscences, institutions,
All these States compact, every square mile of these States
    without excepting a particle;
Me pleas'd, rambling in lanes and country fields, Paumanok's
    fields,
Observing the spiral flight of two little yellow butterflies shuffling
    between each other, ascending high in the air,
The darting swallow, the destroyer of insects, the fall traveler
    southward but returning northward early in the spring,
The country boy at the close of the day driving the herd of cows
    and shouting to them as they loiter to browse by the
    roadside,
The city wharf, Boston, Philadelphia, Baltimore, Charleston, New
    Orleans, San Francisco,
The departing ships when the sailors heave at the capstan;
Evening—me in my room—the setting sun,
The setting summer sun shining in my open window, showing the
    swarm of flies, suspended, balancing in the air in the centre of
    the room, darting athwart, up and down, casting swift shadows
    in specks on the opposite wall where the shine is;

The athletic American matron speaking in public to crowds of
    listeners,
Males, females, immigrants, combinations, the copiousness, the
    individuality of the States, each for itself—the money-makers,
Factories, machinery, the mechanical forces, the windlass, lever,
    pulley, all certainties,
The certainty of space, increase, freedom, futurity,
In space the sporades, the scatter'd islands, the stars—on the firm
    earth, the lands, my lands,
O lands! all so dear to me—what you are, (whatever it is,) I
    putting it at random in these songs, become a part of that,
    whatever it is,
Southward there, I screaming, with wings slow flapping,
    with the myriads of gulls wintering along the coasts of
    Florida,
Otherways there atwixt the banks of the Arkansaw, the Rio
    Grande, the Nueces, the Brazos, the Tombigbee, the Red
    River, the Saskatchawan or the Osage, I with the spring
    waters laughing and skipping and running,
Northward, on the sands, on some shallow bay of Paumanok, I
    with parties of snowy herons wading in the wet to seek worms
    and aquatic plants,
Retreating, triumphantly twittering, the king-bird, from piercing
    the crow with its bill, for amusement—and I triumphantly
    twittering,
The migrating flock of wild geese alighting in autumn to refresh
    themselves, the body of the flock feed, the sentinels outside
    move around with erect heads watching, and are from time to
    time reliev'd by other sentinels—and I feeding and taking
    turns with the rest,
In Kanadian forests the moose, large as an ox, corner'd by
    hunters, rising desperately on his hind feet, and plunging
    with his fore-feet, the hoofs as sharp as knives—and I,
    plunging at the hunters, corner'd and desperate,
In the Mannahatta, streets, piers, shipping, store-houses, and the
    countless workmen working in the shops,
And I too of the Mannahatta, singing thereof—and no less in
    myself than the whole of the Mannahatta in itself,

Singing the song of These, my ever-united lands—my body no
    more inevitably united, part to part, and made out of a
    thousand diverse contributions one identity, any more than
    my lands are inevitably united and made ONE IDENTITY;
Nativities, climates, the grass of the great pastoral Plains,
Cities, labors, death, animals, products, war, good and evil—
    these me,
These affording, in all their particulars, the old feuillage to me
    and to America, how can I do less than pass the clew of the
    union of them, to afford the like to you?
Whoever you are! how can I but offer you divine leaves, that you
    also be eligible as I am?
How can I but as here chanting, invite you for yourself to collect
    bouquets of the incomparable feuillage of these States?

A SONG OF JOYS

O to make the most jubilant song!
Full of music—full of manhood, womanhood, infancy!
Full of common employments—full of grain and trees.

O for the voices of animals—O for the swiftness and balance of
    fishes!
O for the dropping of raindrops in a song!
O for the sunshine and motion of waves in a song!

O the joy of my spirit—it is uncaged—it darts like lightning!
It is not enough to have this globe or a certain time,
I will have thousands of globes and all time.

O the engineer's joys! to go with a locomotive!
To hear the hiss of steam, the merry shriek, the steam-whistle, the
    laughing locomotive!
To push with resistless way and speed off in the distance.

O the gleesome saunter over fields and hillsides!
The leaves and flowers of the commonest weeds, the moist fresh
    stillness of the woods,

The exquisite smell of the earth at daybreak, and all through the
    forenoon.

O the horseman's and horsewoman's joys!
The saddle, the gallop, the pressure upon the seat, the cool
    gurgling by the ears and hair.

O the fireman's joys!
I hear the alarm at dead of night,
I hear bells, shouts! I pass the crowd, I run!
The sight of the flames maddens me with pleasure.

O the joy of the strong-brawn'd fighter, towering in the arena in
    perfect condition, conscious of power, thirsting to meet his
    opponent.

O the joy of that vast elemental sympathy which only the human
    soul is capable of generating and emitting in steady and
    limitless floods.

O the mother's joys!
The watching, the endurance, the precious love, the anguish, the
    patiently yielded life.

O the joy of increase, growth, recuperation,
The joy of soothing and pacifying, the joy of concord and
    harmony.

O to go back to the place where I was born,
To hear the birds sing once more,
To ramble about the house and barn and over the fields once
    more,
And through the orchard and along the old lanes once more.

O to have been brought up on bays, lagoons, creeks, or along the
    coast,
To continue and be employ'd there all my life,
The briny and damp smell, the shore, the salt weeds exposed at
    low water,

The work of fishermen, the work of the eel-fisher and clam-
    fisher;
I come with my clam-rake and spade, I come with my eel-spear,
Is the tide out? I join the group of clam-diggers on the flats,
I laugh and work with them, I joke at my work like a mettlesome
    young man;
In winter I take my eel-basket and eel-spear and travel out on foot
    on the ice—I have a small axe to cut holes in the ice,
Behold me well-clothed going gayly or returning in the afternoon,
    my brood of tough boys accompanying me,
My brood of grown and part-grown boys, who love to be with no
    one else so well as they love to be with me,
By day to work with me, and by night to sleep with me.

Another time in warm weather out in a boat, to lift the lobster-pots
    where they are sunk with heavy stones, (I know the buoys,)
O the sweetness of the Fifth-month morning upon the water as I
    row just before sunrise toward the buoys,
I pull the wicker pots up slantingly, the dark green lobsters are
    desperate with their claws as I take them out, I insert wooden
    pegs in the joints of their pincers,
I go to all the places one after another, and then row back to the
    shore,
There in a huge kettle of boiling water the lobsters shall be boil'd
    till their color becomes scarlet.

Another time mackerel-taking,
Voracious, mad for the hook, near the surface, they seem to fill
    the water for miles;
Another time fishing for rock-fish in Chesapeake bay, I one of the
    brown-faced crew;
Another time trailing for blue-fish off Paumanok, I stand with
    braced body,
My left foot is on the gunwale, my right arm throws far out the
    coils of slender rope,
In sight around me the quick veering and darting of fifty skiffs, my
    companions.

O boating on the rivers,
The voyage down the St. Lawrence, the superb scenery, the
    steamers,
The ships sailing, the Thousand Islands, the occasional timber-
    raft and the raftsmen with long-reaching sweep-oars,
The little huts on the rafts, and the stream of smoke when they
    cook supper at evening.

(O something pernicious and dread!
Something far away from a puny and pious life!
Something unproved! something in a trance!
Something escaped from the anchorage and driving free.)

O to work in mines, or forging iron,
Foundry casting, the foundry itself, the rude high roof, the ample
    and shadow'd space,
The furnace, the hot liquid pour'd out and running.

O to resume the joys of the soldier!
To feel the presence of a brave commanding officer—to feel his
    sympathy!
To behold his calmness—to be warm'd in the rays of his smile!
To go to battle—to hear the bugles play and the drums beat!
To hear the crash of artillery—to see the glittering of the bayonets
    and musket-barrels in the sun!
To see men fall and die and not complain!
To taste the savage taste of blood—to be so devilish!
To gloat so over the wounds and deaths of the enemy.

O the whaleman's joys! O I cruise my old cruise again!
I feel the ship's motion under me, I feel the Atlantic breezes
    fanning me,
I hear the cry again sent down from the mast head,
    There—she blows!
Again I spring up the rigging to look with the rest—we descend,
    wild with excitement,
I leap in the lower'd boat, we row toward our prey where he lies,

We approach stealthy and silent, I see the mountainous mass,
    lethargic, basking,
I see the harpooner standing up, I see the weapon dart from his
    vigorous arm;
O swift again far out in the ocean the wounded whale, settling,
    running to windward, tows me,
Again I see him rise to breathe, we row close again,
I see a lance driven through his side, press'd deep, turn'd in the
    wound,
Again we back off, I see him settle again, the life is leaving him fast,
As he rises he spouts blood, I see him swim in circles narrower
    and narrower, swiftly cutting the water—I see him die,
He gives one convulsive leap in the centre of the circle, and then
    falls flat and still in the bloody foam.

O the old manhood of me, my noblest joy of all!
My children and grand-children, my white hair and beard,
My largeness, calmness, majesty, out of the long stretch of my life.

O ripen'd joy of womanhood! O happiness at last!
I am more than eighty years of age, I am the most venerable
    mother,
How clear is my mind—how all people draw nigh to me!
What attractions are these beyond any before? what bloom more
    than the bloom of youth?
What beauty is this that descends upon me and rises out of me?

O the orator's joys!
To inflate the chest, to roll the thunder of the voice out from the
    ribs and throat,
To make the people rage, weep, hate, desire, with yourself,
To lead America—to quell America with a great tongue.

O the joy of my soul leaning pois'd on itself, receiving identity
    through materials and loving them, observing characters and
    absorbing them,
My soul vibrated back to me from them, from sight, hearing,
    touch, reason, articulation, comparison, memory, and the like,

The real life of my senses and flesh transcending my senses and
        flesh,
My body done with materials, my sight done with my material
        eyes,
Proved to me this day beyond cavil that it is not my material eyes
        which finally see,
Nor my material body which finally loves, walks, laughs, shouts,
        embraces, procreates.

O the farmer's joys!
Ohioan's, Illinoisian's, Wisconsinese', Kanadian's, Iowan's,
        Kansian's, Missourian's, Oregonese' joys!
To rise at peep of day and pass forth nimbly to work,
To plough land in the fall for winter-sown crops,
To plough land in the spring for maize,
To train orchards, to graft the trees, to gather apples in the fall.

O to bathe in the swimming-bath, or in a good place along shore,
To splash the water! to walk ankle-deep, or race naked along the
        shore.

O to realize space!
The plenteousness of all, that there are no bounds,
To emerge and be of the sky, of the sun and moon and flying
        clouds, as one with them.

O the joy of a manly self-hood!
To be servile to none, to defer to none, not to any tyrant known or
        unknown,
To walk with erect carriage, a step springy and elastic,
To look with calm gaze or with a flashing eye,
To speak with a full and sonorous voice out of a broad chest,
To confront with your personality all the other personalities of the
        earth.

Know'st thou the excellent joys of youth?
Joys of the dear companions and of the merry word and laughing
        face?

Joy of the glad light-beaming day, joy of the wide-breath'd
    games?
Joy of sweet music, joy of the lighted ball-room and the
    dancers?
Joy of the plenteous dinner, strong carouse and drinking?

Yet O my soul supreme!
Know'st thou the joys of pensive thought?
Joys of the free and lonesome heart, the tender, gloomy heart?
Joys of the solitary walk, the spirit bow'd yet proud, the suffering
    and the struggle?
The agonistic throes, the ecstasies, joys of the solemn musings day
    or night?
Joys of the thought of Death, the great spheres Time and Space?
Prophetic joys of better, loftier love's ideals, the divine wife, the
    sweet, eternal, perfect comrade?
Joys all thine own undying one, joys worthy thee O soul.

O while I live to be the ruler of life, not a slave,
To meet life as a powerful conqueror,
No fumes, no ennui, no more complaints or scornful criticisms,
To these proud laws of the air, the water and the ground, proving
    my interior soul impregnable,
And nothing exterior shall ever take command of me.

For not life's joys alone I sing, repeating—the joy of death!
The beautiful touch of Death, soothing and benumbing a few
    moments, for reasons,
Myself discharging my excrementitious body to be burn'd, or
    render'd to powder, or buried,
My real body doubtless left to me for other spheres,
My voided body nothing more to me, returning to the
    purifications, further offices, eternal uses of the earth.

O to attract by more than attraction!
How it is I know not—yet behold! the something which obeys
    none of the rest,
It is offensive, never defensive—yet how magnetic it draws.

O to struggle against great odds, to meet enemies undaunted!
To be entirely alone with them, to find how much one can stand!
To look strife, torture, prison, popular odium, face to face!
To mount the scaffold, to advance to the muzzles of guns with
    perfect nonchalance!
To be indeed a God!

O to sail to sea in a ship!
To leave this steady unendurable land,
To leave the tiresome sameness of the streets, the sidewalks and
    the houses,
To leave you O you solid motionless land, and entering a ship,
To sail and sail and sail!

O to have life henceforth a poem of new joys!
To dance, clap hands, exult, shout, skip, leap, roll on, float on!
To be a sailor of the world bound for all ports,
A ship itself, (see indeed these sails I spread to the sun and air,)
A swift and swelling ship full of rich words, full of joys.

SONG OF THE BROAD-AXE

– 1 –

Weapon shapely, naked, wan,[37]
Head from the mother's bowels drawn,
Wooded flesh and metal bone, limb only one and lip only one,
Gray-blue leaf by red-heat grown, helve produced from a little
    seed sown,
Resting the grass amid and upon,
To be lean'd and to lean on.

Strong shapes and attributes of strong shapes, masculine trades,
    sights and sounds,
Long varied train of an emblem, dabs of music,
Fingers of the organist skipping staccato over the keys of the great
    organ.

– 2 –

Welcome are all earth's lands, each for its kind,
Welcome are lands of pine and oak,
Welcome are lands of the lemon and fig,
Welcome are lands of gold,
Welcome are lands of wheat and maize, welcome those of the
    grape,
Welcome are lands of sugar and rice,
Welcome the cotton-lands, welcome those of the white potato
    and sweet potato,
Welcome are mountains, flats, sands, forests, prairies,
Welcome the rich borders of rivers, table-lands, openings,
Welcome the measureless grazing-lands, welcome the teeming
    soil of orchards, flax, honey, hemp;
Welcome just as much the other more hard-faced lands,
Lands rich as lands of gold or wheat and fruit lands,
Lands of mines, lands of the manly and rugged ores,
Lands of coal, copper, lead, tin, zinc,
Lands of iron — lands of the make of the axe.

– 3 –

The log at the wood-pile, the axe supported by it,
The sylvan hut, the vine over the doorway, the space clear'd for a
    garden,
The irregular tapping of rain down on the leaves after the storm is
    lull'd,
The wailing and moaning at intervals, the thought of the sea,
The thought of ships struck in the storm and put on their beam
    ends, and the cutting away of masts,
The sentiment of the huge timbers of old-fashion'd houses and
    barns,
The remember'd print or narrative, the voyage at a venture of
    men, families, goods,
The disembarkation, the founding of a new city,
The voyage of those who sought a New England and found it, the
    outset anywhere,

The settlements of the Arkansas, Colorado, Ottawa, Willamette,
The slow progress, the scant fare, the axe, rifle, saddlebags;
The beauty of all adventurous and daring persons,
The beauty of wood-boys and wood-men with their clear
    untrimm'd faces,
The beauty of independence, departure, actions that rely on
    themselves,
The American contempt for statutes and ceremonies, the
    boundless impatience of restraint,
The loose drift of character, the inkling through random types,
    the solidification;
The butcher in the slaughter-house, the hands aboard schooners
    and sloops, the raftsman, the pioneer,
Lumbermen in their winter camp, daybreak in the woods,
    stripes of snow on the limbs of trees, the occasional
    snapping,
The glad clear sound of one's own voice, the merry song, the
    natural life of the woods, the strong day's work,
The blazing fire at night, the sweet taste of supper, the talk, the
    bed of hemlock-boughs and the bear-skin;
The house-builder at work in cities or anywhere,
The preparatory jointing, squaring, sawing, mortising,
The hoist-up of beams, the push of them in their places, laying
    them regular,
Setting the studs by their tenons in the mortises according as they
    were prepared,
The blows of mallets and hammers, the attitudes of the men,
    their curv'd limbs,
Bending, standing, astride the beams, driving in pins, holding on
    by posts and braces,
The hook'd arm over the plate, the other arm wielding the axe,
The floor-men forcing the planks close to be nail'd,
Their postures bringing their weapons downward on the bearers,
The echoes resounding through the vacant building;
The huge storehouse carried up in the city well under way,
The six framing-men, two in the middle and two at each end,
    carefully bearing on their shoulders a heavy stick for a cross-
    beam,

The crowded line of masons with trowels in their right hands rapidly
    laying the long side-wall, two hundred feet from front to rear,
The flexible rise and fall of backs, the continual click of the
    trowels striking the bricks,
The bricks one after another each laid so workmanlike in its
    place, and set with a knock of the trowel-handle,
The piles of materials, the mortar on the mortar-boards, and the
    steady replenishing by the hod-men;
Spar-makers in the spar-yard, the swarming row of well-grown
    apprentices,
The swing of their axes on the square-hew'd log shaping it toward
    the shape of a mast,
The brisk short crackle of the steel driven slantingly into the pine,
The butter-color'd chips flying off in great flakes and slivers,
The limber motion of brawny young arms and hips in easy
    costumes,
The constructor of wharves, bridges, piers, bulk-heads, floats, stays
    against the sea;
The city fireman, the fire that suddenly bursts forth in the close-
    pack'd square,
The arriving engines, the hoarse shouts, the nimble stepping and
    daring,
The strong command through the fire trumpets, the falling in
    line, the rise and fall of the arms forcing the water,
The slender, spasmic, blue-white jets, the bringing to bear of the
    hooks and ladders and their execution,
The crash and cut away of connecting wood-work, or through
    floors if the fire smoulders under them,
The crowd with their lit faces watching, the glare and dense
    shadows;
The forger at his forge-furnace and the user of iron after him,
The maker of the axe large and small, and the welder and
    temperer,
The chooser breathing his breath on the cold steel and trying the
    edge with his thumb,
The one who clean-shapes the handle and sets it firmly in the
    socket;
The shadowy processions of the portraits of the past users also,

The primal patient mechanics, the architects and engineers,
The far-off Assyrian edifice and Mizra* edifice,
The Roman lictors† preceding the consuls,
The antique European warrior with his axe in combat,
The uplifted arm, the clatter of blows on the helmeted head,
The death-howl, the limpsy tumbling body, the rush of friend and
    foe thither,
The siege of revolted lieges determin'd for liberty,
The summons to surrender, the battering at castle gates, the truce
    and parley,
The sack of an old city in its time,
The bursting in of mercenaries and bigots tumultuously and
    disorderly,
Roar, flames, blood, drunkenness, madness,
Goods freely rifled from houses and temples, screams of women
    in the gripe of brigands,
Craft and thievery of camp-followers, men running, old persons
    despairing,
The hell of war, the cruelties of creeds,
The list of all executive deeds and words just or unjust,
The power of personality just or unjust.

− 4 −

Muscle and pluck forever!
What invigorates life invigorates death,
And the dead advance as much as the living advance,
And the future is no more uncertain than the present,
For the roughness of the earth and of man encloses as much as
    the delicatesse of the earth and of man,
And nothing endures but personal qualities.

What do you think endures?
Do you think a great city endures?

---

*Ancient name for Egypt.
†Minor Roman officials who cleared the way for chief magistrates.

Or a teeming manufacturing state? or a prepared constitution? or
    the best built steamships?
Or hotels of granite and iron? or any chef-d'œuvres of
    engineering, forts, armaments?

Away! these are not to be cherish'd for themselves,
They fill their hour, the dancers dance, the musicians play for
    them,
The show passes, all does well enough of course,
All does very well till one flash of defiance.

A great city is that which has the greatest men and women,
If it be a few ragged huts it is still the greatest city in the whole
    world.

– 5 –

The place where a great city stands is not the place of stretch'd
    wharves, docks, manufactures, deposits of produce merely,
Nor the place of ceaseless salutes of new-comers or the anchor-
    lifters of the departing,
Nor the place of the tallest and costliest buildings or shops selling
    goods from the rest of the earth,
Nor the place of the best libraries and schools, nor the place
    where money is plentiest,
Nor the place of the most numerous population.

Where the city stands with the brawniest breed of orators and
    bards,
Where the city stands that is belov'd by these, and loves them in
    return and understands them,
Where no monuments exist to heroes but in the common words
    and deeds,
Where thrift is in its place, and prudence is in its place,
Where the men and women think lightly of the laws,
Where the slave ceases, and the master of slaves ceases,
Where the populace rise at once against the never-ending
    audacity of elected persons,

Where fierce men and women pour forth as the sea to the whistle
    of death pours its sweeping and unript waves,
Where outside authority enters always after the precedence of
    inside authority,
Where the citizen is always the head and ideal, and President,
    Mayor, Governor and what not, are agents for pay,
Where children are taught to be laws to themselves, and to
    depend on themselves,
Where equanimity is illustrated in affairs,
Where speculations on the soul are encouraged,
Where women walk in public processions in the streets the same
    as the men,
Where they enter the public assembly and take places the same
    as the men;
Where the city of the faithfulest friends stands,
Where the city of the cleanliness of the sexes stands,
Where the city of the healthiest fathers stands,
Where the city of the best-bodied mothers stands,
There the great city stands.

– 6 –

How beggarly appear arguments before a defiant deed!
How the floridness of the materials of cities shrivels before a
    man's or woman's look!

All waits or goes by default till a strong being appears;
A strong being is the proof of the race and of the ability of the
    universe,
When he or she appears materials are overaw'd,
The dispute on the soul stops,
The old customs and phrases are confronted, turn'd back, or laid
    away.

What is your money-making now? what can it do now?
What is your respectability now?
What are your theology, tuition, society, traditions, statute-books,
    now?

Where are your jibes of being now?
Where are your cavils about the soul now?

– 7 –

A sterile landscape covers the ore, there is as good as the best for
　　all the forbidding appearance,
There is the mine, there are the miners,
The forge-furnace is there, the melt is accomplish'd, the
　　hammers-men are at hand with their tongs and hammers,
What always served and always serves is at hand.

Than this nothing has better served, it has served all,
Served the fluent-tongued and subtle-sensed Greek, and long ere
　　the Greek,
Served in building the buildings that last longer than any,
Served the Hebrew, the Persian, the most ancient
　　Hindustanee,
Served the mound-raiser on the Mississippi, served those whose
　　relics remain in Central America,
Served Albic temples in woods or on plains, with unhewn pillars
　　and the druids,
Served the artificial clefts, vast, high, silent, on the snow-cover'd
　　hills of Scandinavia,
Served those who time out of mind made on the granite
　　walls rough sketches of the sun, moon, stars, ships, ocean
　　waves,
Served the paths of the irruptions of the Goths, served the pastoral
　　tribes and nomads,
Served the long distant Kelt, served the hardy pirates of the
　　Baltic,
Served before any of those the venerable and harmless men of
　　Ethiopia,
Served the making of helms for the galleys of pleasure and the
　　making of those for war,
Served all great works on land and all great works on the sea,
For the mediæval ages and before the mediæval ages,
Served not the living only then as now, but served the dead.

– 8 –

I see the European headsman,
He stands mask'd, clothed in red, with huge legs and strong
    naked arms,
And leans on a ponderous axe.

(Whom have you slaughter'd lately European headsman?
Whose is that blood upon you so wet and sticky?)

I see the clear sunsets of the martyrs,
I see from the scaffolds the descending ghosts,
Ghosts of dead lords, uncrown'd ladies, impeach'd ministers,
    rejected kings,
Rivals, traitors, poisoners, disgraced chieftains and the rest.

I see those who in any land have died for the good cause,
The seed is spare, nevertheless the crop shall never run out,
(Mind you O foreign kings, O priests, the crop shall never run out.)

I see the blood wash'd entirely away from the axe,
Both blade and helve are clean,
They spirt no more the blood of European nobles, they clasp no
    more the necks of queens.

I see the headsman withdraw and become useless,
I see the scaffold untrodden and mouldy, I see no longer any axe
    upon it,
I see the mighty and friendly emblem of the power of my own
    race, the newest, largest race.

– 9 –

(America! I do not vaunt my love for you,
I have what I have.)

The axe leaps!
The solid forest gives fluid utterances,

They tumble forth, they rise and form,
Hut, tent, landing, survey,
Flail, plough, pick, crowbar, spade,
Shingle, rail, prop, wainscot, jamb, lath, panel, gable,
Citadel, ceiling, saloon, academy, organ, exhibition-house,
    library,
Cornice, trellis, pilaster, balcony, window, turret, porch,
Hoe, rake, pitchfork, pencil, wagon, staff, saw, jack-plane, mallet,
    wedge, rounce,
Chair, tub, hoop, table, wicket, vane, sash, floor,
Work-box, chest, string'd instrument, boat, frame, and what not,
Capitols of States, and capitol of the nation of States,
Long stately rows in avenues, hospitals for orphans or for the poor
    or sick,
Manhattan steamboats and clippers taking the measure of all seas.

The shapes arise!
Shapes of the using of axes anyhow, and the users and all that
    neighbors them,
Cutters down of wood and haulers of it to the Penobscot or
    Kennebec,
Dwellers in cabins among the California mountains or by the
    little lakes or on the Columbia,
Dwellers south on the banks of the Gila or Rio Grande friendly
    gatherings, the characters and fun,
Dwellers along the St. Lawrence, or north in Kanada, or down by
    the Yellowstone, dwellers on coasts and off coasts,
Seal-fishers, whalers, arctic seamen breaking passages through
    the ice.

The shapes arise!
Shapes of factories, arsenals, foundries, markets,
Shapes of the two-threaded tracks of railroads,
Shapes of the sleepers of bridges, vast frameworks, girders, arches,
Shapes of the fleets of barges, tows, lake and canal craft, river
    craft,
Ship-yards and dry-docks along the Eastern and Western seas, and
    in many a bay and by-place,

The live-oak kelsons, the pine planks, the spars, the hackmatack-
    roots for knees,*
The ships themselves on their ways, the tiers of scaffolds, the
    workmen busy outside and inside,
The tools lying around, the great auger and little auger, the adze,
    bolt, line, square, gouge, and bead-plane.

— 10 —

The shapes arise!
The shape measur'd, saw'd, jack'd, join'd, stain'd,
The coffin-shape for the dead to lie within in his shroud,
The shape got out in posts, in the bedstead posts, in the posts of
    the bride's bed,
The shape of the little trough, the shape of the rockers beneath,
    the shape of the babe's cradle,
The shape of the floor-planks, the floor-planks for dancers' feet,
The shape of the planks of the family home, the home of the
    friendly parents and children,
The shape of the roof of the home of the happy young man and
    woman, the roof over the well-married young man and
    woman,
The roof over the supper joyously cook'd by the chaste wife, and
    joyously eaten by the chaste husband, content after his day's
    work.

The shapes arise!
The shape of the prisoner's place in the court-room, and of him
    or her seated in the place,
The shape of the liquor-bar lean'd against by the young rum-
    drinker and the old rum-drinker,
The shape of the shamed and angry stairs trod by sneaking foot-
    steps,

*The structural supports (keelsons) of this ship are built from one of Whitman's
most significant plant types, the live oak (see endnote 23 to the "Calamus" cluster).
The supports that bear strain (the knees) are made from the tamarack or American
larch tree.

The shape of the sly settee, and the adulterous unwholesome
    couple,
The shape of the gambling-board with its devilish winnings and
    losings,
The shape of the step-ladder for the convicted and sentenced
    murderer, the murderer with haggard face and pinion'd arms,
The sheriff at hand with his deputies, the silent and white-lipp'd
    crowd, the dangling of the rope.

The shapes arise!
Shapes of doors giving many exits and entrances,
The door passing the dissever'd friend flush'd and in haste,
The door that admits good news and bad news,
The door whence the son left home confident and puff'd up,
The door he enter'd again from a long and scandalous absence,
    diseas'd, broken down, without innocence, without means.

— 11 —

Her shape arises,
She less guarded than ever, yet more guarded than ever,
The gross and soil'd she moves among do not make her gross and
    soil'd,
She knows the thoughts as she passes, nothing is conceal'd from her,
She is none the less considerate or friendly therefor,
She is the best belov'd, it is without exception, she has no reason
    to fear and she does not fear,
Oaths, quarrels, hiccupp'd songs, smutty expressions, are idle to
    her as she passes,
She is silent, she is possess'd of herself, they do not offend her,
She receives them as the laws of Nature receive them, she is strong,
She too is a law of Nature—there is no law stronger than she is.

— 12 —

The main shapes arise!
Shapes of Democracy total, result of centuries,
Shapes ever projecting other shapes,

Shapes of turbulent manly cities,
Shapes of the friends and home-givers of the whole earth,
Shapes bracing the earth and braced with the whole earth.

SONG OF THE EXPOSITION

— 1 —

(Ah little recks the laborer,
How near his work is holding him to God,
The loving Laborer through space and time.)

After all not to create only, or found only,
But to bring perhaps from afar what is already founded,
To give it our own identity, average, limitless, free,
To fill the gross the torpid bulk with vital religious fire,
Not to repel or destroy so much as accept, fuse, rehabilitate,
To obey as well as command, to follow more than to lead,
These also are the lessons of our New World;
While how little the New after all, how much the Old, Old
    World!
Long and long has the grass been growing,
Long and long has the rain been falling,
Long has the globe been rolling round.

— 2 —

Come Muse migrate from Greece and Ionia,
Cross out please those immensely overpaid accounts,
That matter of Troy and Achilles' wrath, and Æneas', Odysseus'
    wanderings,
Placard "Removed" and "To Let" on the rocks of your snowy
    Parnassus,
Repeat at Jerusalem, place the notice high on Jaffa's gate and on
    Mount Moriah,
The same on the walls of your German, French and Spanish
    castles and Italian collections,

For know a better, fresher, busier sphere, a wide, untried domain
   awaits, demands you.

– 3 –

Responsive to our summons,
Or rather to her long-nurs'd inclination,
Join'd with an irresistible, natural gravitation,
She comes! I hear the rustling of her gown,
I scent the odor of her breath's delicious fragrance,
I mark her step divine, her curious eyes a-turning, rolling,
Upon this very scene.

The dame of dames! can I believe then
Those ancient temples, sculptures classic, could none of them
   retain her?
Nor shades of Virgil and Dante, nor myriad memories,
   poems, old associations, magnetize and hold on to her?
But that she's left them all—and here?

Yes, if you will allow me to say so,
I, my friends, if you do not, can plainly see her,
The same undying soul of earth's, activity's, beauty's, heroism's
   expression,
Out from her evolutions hither come, ended the strata of her
   former themes,
Hidden and cover'd by to-day's, foundation of to-day's
Ended, deceas'd through time, her voice by Castaly's fountain,
Silent the broken-lipp'd Sphynx in Egypt, silent all those century-
   baffling tombs,
Ended for aye the epics of Asia's, Europe's helmeted warriors,
   ended the primitive call of the muses
Calliope's call forever closed, Clio, Melpomene, Thalia dead,
Ended the stately rhythmus of Una and Oriana, ended the quest
   of the holy Graal,
Jerusalem a handful of ashes blown by the wind, extinct,
The Crusaders' streams of shadowy midnight troops sped with the
   sunrise,

Amadis, Tancred, utterly gone, Charlemagne, Roland, Oliver gone,
Palmerin, ogre, departed, vanish'd the turrets that Usk from its
       waters reflected,
Arthur vanish'd with all his knights, Merlin and Lancelot and
       Galahad, all gone, dissolv'd utterly like an exhalation;
Pass'd! pass'd! for us, forever pass'd, that once so mighty world,
       now void, inanimate, phantom world,
Embroider'd, dazzling, foreign world, with all its gorgeous
       legends, myths,
Its kings and castles proud, its priests and warlike lords and
       courtly dames,
Pass'd to its charnel vault, coffin'd with crown and armor on,
Blazon'd with Shakspere's purple page,
And dirged by Tennyson's sweet sad rhyme.[38]

I say I see, my friends, if you do not, the illustrious emigré,
       (having it is true in her day, although the same, changed,
       journey'd considerable,)
Making directly for this rendezvous, vigorously clearing a path for
       herself, striding through the confusion,
By thud of machinery and shrill steam-whistle undismay'd,
Bluff'd not a bit by drain-pipe, gasometers, artificial fertilizers,
Smiling and pleas'd with palpable intent to stay,
She's here, install'd amid the kitchen ware!

– 4 –

But hold—don't I forget my manners?
To introduce the stranger, (what else indeed do I live to chant
       for?) to thee Columbia;
In liberty's name welcome immortal! clasp hands,
And ever henceforth sisters dear be both.

Fear not O Muse! truly new ways and days receive, surround you,
I candidly confess a queer, queer race, of novel fashion,
And yet the same old human race, the same within, without,
Faces and hearts the same, feelings the same, yearnings the same,
The same old love, beauty and use the same.

– 5 –

We do not blame thee elder World, nor really separate ourselves
    from thee,
(Would the son separate himself from the father?)
Looking back on thee, seeing thee to thy duties, grandeurs,
    through past ages bending, building,
We build to ours to-day.

Mightier than Egypt's tombs,
Fairer than Grecia's, Roma's temples,
Prouder than Milan's statued, spired cathedral,
More picturesque than Rhenish castle-keeps,
We plan even now to raise, beyond them all,
Thy great cathedral sacred industry, no tomb,
A keep for life for practical invention.

As in a waking vision,
E'en while I chant I see it rise, I scan and prophesy outside and in,
Its manifold ensemble.

Around a palace,* loftier, fairer, ampler than any yet,
Earth's modern wonder, history's seven outstripping,
High rising tier on tier with glass and iron façades,
Gladdening the sun and sky, enhued in cheerfulest hues,
Bronze, lilac, robin's-egg, marine and crimson,
Over whose golden roof shall flaunt, beneath thy banner
    Freedom,
The banners of the States and flags of every land,
A brood of lofty, fair, but lesser palaces shall cluster.

Somewhere within their walls shall all that forwards perfect
    human life be started,
Tried, taught, advanced, visibly exhibited.

---

*New York City's Crystal Palace, a wonder itself and an exhibition area for the latest discoveries and inventions; it opened in 1853 and was destroyed by fire in 1858.

Not only all the world of works, trade, products,
But all the workmen of the world here to be represented.

Here shall you trace in flowing operation,
In every state of practical, busy movement, the rills of civilization,
Materials here under your eye shall change their shape as if by
     magic,
The cotton shall be pick'd almost in the very field,
Shall be dried, clean'd, ginn'd, baled, spun into thread and cloth
     before you,
You shall see hands at work at all the old processes and all the
     new ones,
You shall see the various grains and how flour is made and then
     bread baked by the bakers,
You shall see the crude ores of California and Nevada passing on
     and on till they become bullion,
You shall watch how the printer sets type, and learn what a
     composing-stick is,
You shall mark in amazement the Hoe press whirling its
     cylinders, shedding the printed leaves steady and fast,
The photograph, model, watch, pin, nail, shall be created
     before you.

In large calm halls, a stately museum shall teach you the infinite
     lessons of minerals,
In another, woods, plants, vegetation shall be illustrated—in
     another animals, animal life and development.

One stately house shall be the music house,
Others for other arts—learning, the sciences, shall all be here,
None shall be slighted, none but shall here be honor'd, help'd,
     exampled.

– 6 –

(This, this and these, America, shall be *your* pyramids and obelisks,
Your Alexandrian Pharos, gardens of Babylon,
Your temple at Olympia.)

The male and female many laboring not,
Shall ever here confront the laboring many,
With precious benefits to both, glory to all,
To thee America, and thee eternal Muse.

And here shall ye inhabit powerful Matrons!
In your vast state vaster than all the old,
Echoed through long, long centuries to come,
To sound of different, prouder songs, with stronger themes,
Practical, peaceful life, the people's life, the People themselves,
Lifted, illumin'd, bathed in peace—elate, secure in peace.

– 7 –

Away with themes of war! away with war itself!
Hence from my shuddering sight to never more return that show
    of blacken'd, mutilated corpses!
That hell unpent and raid of blood, fit for wild tigers or for lop-
    tongued wolves, not reasoning men,
And in its stead speed industry's campaigns,
With thy undaunted armies, engineering,
Thy pennants labor, loosen'd to the breeze,
Thy bugles sounding loud and clear.

Away with old romance![39]
Away with novels, plots and plays of foreign courts,
Away with love-verses sugar'd in rhyme, the intrigues, amours of
    idlers,
Fitted for only banquets of the night where dancers to late music
    slide,
The unhealthy pleasures, extravagant dissipations of the few,
With perfumes, heat and wine, beneath the dazzling chandeliers.

To you ye reverent sane sisters,*
I raise a voice for far superber themes for poets and for art,

---

*The nine Muses, ancient sister goddesses who were guiding spirits for an array of
arts and sciences.

To exalt the present and the real,
To teach the average man the glory of his daily walk and
    trade,
To sing in songs how exercise and chemical life are never to be
    baffled,
To manual work for each and all, to plough, hoe, dig,
To plant and tend the tree, the berry, vegetables, flowers,
For every man to see to it that he really do something, for every
    woman too;
To use the hammer and the saw, (rip, or cross-cut,)
To cultivate a turn for carpentering, plastering, painting,
To work as tailor, tailoress, nurse, hostler, porter,
To invent a little, something ingenious, to aid the washing,
    cooking, cleaning,
And hold it no disgrace to take a hand at them themselves.

I say I bring thee Muse to-day and here,
All occupations, duties broad and close,
Toil, healthy toil and sweat, endless, without cessation,
The old, old practical burdens, interests, joys,
The family, parentage, childhood, husband and wife,
The house-comforts, the house itself and all its belongings,
Food and its preservation, chemistry applied to it,
Whatever forms the average, strong, complete, sweet-blooded
    man or woman, the perfect longeve personality,
And helps its present life to health and happiness, and shapes its
    soul,
For the eternal real life to come.

With latest connections, works, the inter-transportation of the
    world,
Steam-power, the great express lines, gas, petroleum,
These triumphs of our time, the Atlantic's delicate cable,
The Pacific railroad, the Suez canal, the Mont Cenis and
    Gothard and Hoosac tunnels, the Brooklyn bridge,[40]
This earth all spann'd with iron rails, with lines of steamships
    threading every sea,
Our own rondure, the current globe I bring.

– 8 –

And thou America,
Thy offspring towering e'er so high, yet higher, Thee above all
     towering,
With Victory on thy left, and at thy right hand Law;
Thou Union holding all, fusing, absorbing, tolerating all,
Thee, ever thee, I sing.

Thou, also thou, a World,
With all thy wide geographies, manifold, different, distant,
Rounded by thee in one—one common orbic language,
One common indivisible destiny for All.

And by the spells which ye vouchsafe to those your ministers in
     earnest,
I here personify and call my themes, to make them pass
     before ye.

Behold, America! (and thou, ineffable guest and sister!)
For thee come trooping up thy waters and thy lands;
Behold! thy fields and farms, thy far-off woods and mountains,
As in procession coming.

Behold, the sea itself,
And on its limitless, heaving breast, the ships;
See, where their white sails, bellying in the wind, speckle the
     green and blue,
See, the steamers coming and going, steaming in or out of
     port,
See, dusky and undulating, the long pennants of smoke.

Behold, in Oregon, far in the north and west,
Or in Maine, far in the north and east, thy cheerful axemen,
Wielding all day their axes.

Behold, on the lakes, thy pilots at their wheels, thy oarsmen,
How the ash writhes under those muscular arms!

There by the furnace, and there by the anvil,
Behold thy sturdy blacksmiths swinging their sledges,
Overhand so steady, overhand they turn and fall with joyous
    clank,
Like a tumult of laughter.

Mark the spirit of invention everywhere, thy rapid patents,
Thy continual workshops, foundries, risen or rising,
See, from their chimneys how the tall flame-fires stream.

Mark, thy interminable farms, North, South,
Thy wealthy daughter-states, Eastern and Western,
The varied products of Ohio, Pennsylvania, Missouri, Georgia,
    Texas, and the rest,
Thy limitless crops, grass, wheat, sugar, oil, corn, rice, hemp, hops,
Thy barns all fill'd, the endless freight-train and the bulging store-
    house,
The grapes that ripen on thy vines, the apples in thy orchards,
Thy incalculable lumber, beef, pork, potatoes, thy coal, thy gold
    and silver,
The inexhaustible iron in thy mines.

All thine O sacred Union!
Ships, farms, shops, barns, factories, mines,
City and State, North, South, item and aggregate,
We dedicate, dread Mother, all to thee!

Protectress absolute, thou! bulwark of all!
For well we know that while thou givest each and all, (generous
    as God,)
Without thee neither all nor each, nor land, home,
Nor ship, nor mine, nor any here this day secure,
Nor aught, nor any day secure.

- 9 -

And thou, the Emblem waving over all!
Delicate beauty, a word to thee, (it may be salutary,)

Remember thou hast not always been as here to-day so
    comfortably ensovereign'd,
In other scenes than these have I observ'd thee flag,
Not quite so trim and whole and freshly blooming in folds of
    stainless silk,
But I have seen thee bunting, to tatters torn upon thy splinter'd
    staff,
Or clutch'd to some young color-bearer's breast with desperate
    hands,
Savagely struggled for, for life or death, fought over long,
'Mid cannons' thunder-crash and many a curse and groan and
    yell, and rifle-volleys cracking sharp,
And moving masses as wild demons surging, and lives as nothing
    risk'd,
For thy mere remnant grimed with dirt and smoke and sopp'd in
    blood,
For sake of that, my beauty, and that thou might'st dally as now
    secure up there,
Many a good man have I seen go under.

Now here and these and hence in peace, all thine O Flag!
And here and hence for thee, O universal Muse! and thou for
    them!
And here and hence O Union, all the work and workmen
    thine!
None separate from thee—henceforth One only, we and
    thou,
(For the blood of the children, what is it, only the blood
    maternal?
And lives and works, what are they all at last, except the roads to
    faith and death?)

While we rehearse our measureless wealth, it is for thee, dear
    Mother,
We own it all and several to-day indissoluble in thee;
Think not our chant, our show, merely for products gross
    or lucre—it is for thee, the soul in thee, electric,
    spiritual!

Our farms, inventions, crops, we own in thee! cities and States in
     thee!
Our freedom all in thee! our very lives in thee!

SONG OF THE REDWOOD-TREE[41]

— 1 —

A California song,
A prophecy and indirection, a thought impalpable to breathe as air,
A chorus of dryads, fading, departing, or hamadryads departing,*
A murmuring, fateful, giant voice, out of the earth and sky,
Voice of a mighty dying tree in the redwood forest dense.

Farewell my brethren,
Farewell O earth and sky, farewell ye neighboring waters,
My time has ended, my term has come.

Along the northern coast,
Just back from the rock-bound shore and the caves,
In the saline air from the sea in the Mendocino country,
With the surge for base and accompaniment low and hoarse,
With crackling blows of axes sounding musically driven by strong
     arms,
Riven deep by the sharp tongues of the axes, there in the redwood
     forest dense,
I heard the mighty tree its death-chant chanting.

The choppers heard not, the camp shanties echoed not,
The quick-ear'd teamsters and chain and jack-screw men heard not,
As the wood-spirits came from their haunts of a thousand years to
     join the refrain,
But in my soul I plainly heard.

---

*Dryads and hamadryads are wood nymphs—in this case, the voices of the red-
wood trees of the title.

Murmuring out of its myriad leaves,
Down from its lofty top rising two hundred feet high,
Out of its stalwart trunk and limbs, out of its foot-thick bark,
That chant of the seasons and time, chant not of the past only but
    the future.

You untold life of me,
And all you venerable and innocent joys,
Perennial hardy life of me with joys 'mid rain and many a summer
    sun,
And the white snows and night and the wild winds;
O the great patient rugged joys, my soul's strong joys unreck'd by
    man,
(For know I bear the soul befitting me, I too have consciousness,
    identity,
And all the rocks and mountains have, and all the earth,)
Joys of the life befitting me and brothers mine,
Our time, our term has come.

Nor yield we mournfully majestic brothers,
We who have grandly fill'd our time;
With Nature's calm content, with tacit huge delight,
We welcome what we wrought for through the past,
And leave the field for them.

For them predicted long,
For a superber race, they too to grandly fill their time,
For them we abdicate, in them ourselves ye forest kings!
In them these skies and airs, these mountain peaks, Shasta,
    Nevadas,
These huge precipitous cliffs, this amplitude, these valleys, far
    Yosemite,
To be in them absorb'd, assimilated.

Then to a loftier strain,
Still prouder, more ecstatic rose the chant,
As if the heirs, the deities of the West,
Joining with master-tongue bore part.

Not wan from Asia's fetiches,
Nor red from Europe's old dynastic slaughter-house,
(Area of murder-plots of thrones, with scent left yet of wars and
    scaffolds everywhere,)
But come from Nature's long and harmless throes, peacefully
    builded thence,
These virgin lands, lands of the Western shore,
To the new culminating man, to you, the empire new,
You promis'd long, we pledge, we dedicate.

You occult deep volitions,
You average spiritual manhood, purpose of all, pois'd on yourself,
    giving not taking law,
You womanhood divine, mistress and source of all, whence life and
    love and aught that comes from life and love,
You unseen moral essence of all the vast materials of America, (age
    upon age working in death the same as life,)
You that, sometimes known, oftener unknown, really shape
    and mould the New World, adjusting it to Time and
    Space,
You hidden national will lying in your abysms, conceal'd but ever
    alert,
You past and present purposes tenaciously pursued, may be
    unconscious of yourselves,
Unswerv'd by all the passing errors, perturbations of the
    surface;
You vital, universal, deathless germs, beneath all creeds, arts,
    statutes, literatures,
Here build your homes for good, establish here, these areas entire,
    lands of the Western shore,
We pledge, we dedicate to you.

For man of you, your characteristic race,
Here may he hardy, sweet, gigantic grow, here tower proportionate
    to Nature,
Here climb the vast pure spaces unconfined, uncheck'd by wall or
    roof,
Here laugh with storm or sun, here joy, here patiently inure,

Here heed himself, unfold himself, (not others' formulas heed,) here
    fill his time,
To duly fall, to aid, unreck'd at last,
To disappear, to serve.

Thus on the northern coast,
In the echo of teamsters' calls and the clinking chains, and the
    music of choppers' axes,
The falling trunk and limbs, the crash, the muffled shriek, the
    groan,
Such words combined from the redwood tree, as of voices
    ecstatic, ancient and rustling,
The century-lasting, unseen dryads, singing, withdrawing,
All their recesses of forests and mountains leaving,
From the Cascade range to the Wahsatch, or Idaho far, or
    Utah,
To the deities of the modern henceforth yielding,
The chorus and indications, the vistas of coming humanity, the
    settlements, features all,
In the Mendocino woods I caught.

– 2 –

The flashing and golden pageant of California,
The sudden and gorgeous drama, the sunny and ample lands,
The long and varied stretch from Puget sound to Colorado south,
Lands bathed in sweeter, rarer, healthier air, valleys and
    mountain cliffs,
The fields of Nature long prepared and fallow, the silent, cyclic
    chemistry,
The slow and steady ages plodding, the unoccupied surface
    ripening, the rich ores forming beneath;
At last the New arriving, assuming, taking possession,
A swarming and busy race settling and organizing everywhere,
Ships coming in from the whole round world, and going out to
    the whole world,
To India and China and Australia and the thousand island
    paradises of the Pacific,

Populous cities, the latest inventions, the steamers on the rivers,
    the railroads, with many a thrifty farm, with machinery,
And wool and wheat and the grape, and diggings of yellow
    gold.

– 3 –

But more in you than these, lands of the Western shore,
(These but the means, the implements, the standing-ground,)
I see in you, certain to come, the promise of thousands of years,
    till now deferr'd,
Promis'd to be fulfill'd, our common kind, the race.

The new society at last, proportionate to Nature,
In man of you, more than your mountain peaks or stalwart trees
    imperial,
In woman more, far more, than all your gold or vines, or even
    vital air.

Fresh come, to a new world indeed, yet long prepared,
I see the genius of the modern, child of the real and ideal,
Clearing the ground for broad humanity, the true America, heir
    of the past so grand,
To build a grander future.

A SONG FOR OCCUPATIONS

– 1 –

A song for occupations!
In the labor of engines and trades and the labor of fields I find the
    developments,
And find the eternal meanings.

Workmen and Workwomen!
Were all educations practical and ornamental well display'd out of
    me, what would it amount to?

Were I as the head teacher, charitable proprietor, wise statesman,
  what would it amount to?
Were I to you as the boss employing and paying you, would that
  satisfy you?

The learn'd, virtuous, benevolent, and the usual terms,
A man like me and never the usual terms.

Neither a servant nor a master I,
I take no sooner a large price than a small price, I will have my
  own whoever enjoys me,
I will be even with you and you shall be even with me.

If you stand at work in a shop I stand as nigh as the nighest in the
  same shop,
If you bestow gifts on your brother or dearest friend I demand as
  good as your brother or dearest friend,
If your lover, husband, wife, is welcome by day or night, I must be
  personally as welcome,
If you become degraded, criminal, ill, then I become so for your
  sake,
If you remember your foolish and outlaw'd deeds, do you
  think I cannot remember my own foolish and outlaw'd
  deeds?
If you carouse at the table I carouse at the opposite side of the
  table,
If you meet some stranger in the streets and love him or her, why
  I often meet strangers in the street and love them.

Why what have you thought of yourself?
Is it you then that thought yourself less?
Is it you that thought the President greater than you?
Or the rich better off than you? or the educated wiser than you?

(Because you are greasy or pimpled, or were once drunk, or a
  thief,
Or that you are diseas'd, or rheumatic, or a prostitute,

Or from frivolity or impotence, or that you are no scholar and
    never saw your name in print,
Do you give in that you are any less immortal?)

— 2 —

Souls of men and women! it is not you I call unseen, unheard,
    untouchable and untouching,
It is not you I go argue pro and con about, and to settle whether
    you are alive or no,
I own publicly who you are, if nobody else owns.

Grown, half-grown and babe, of this country and every country,
    in-doors and out-doors, one just as much as the other, I see,
And all else behind or through them.

The wife, and she is not one jot less than the husband,
The daughter, and she is just as good as the son,
The mother, and she is every bit as much as the father.

Offspring of ignorant and poor, boys apprenticed to trades,
Young fellows working on farms and old fellows working on farms,
Sailor-men, merchant-men, coasters, immigrants,
All these I see, but nigher and farther the same I see,
None shall escape me and none shall wish to escape me.

I bring what you much need yet always have,
Not money, amours, dress, eating, erudition, but as good,
I send no agent or medium, offer no representative of value, but
    offer the value itself.

There is something that comes to one now and perpetually,
It is not what is printed, preach'd, discussed, it eludes discussion
    and print,
It is not to be put in a book, it is not in this book,
It is for you whoever you are, it is no farther from you than your
    hearing and sight are from you,

It is hinted by nearest, commonest, readiest, it is ever provoked by
    them.

You may read in many languages, yet read nothing about it,
You may read the President's message and read nothing about it
    there,
Nothing in the reports from the State department or Treasury
    department, or in the daily papers or weekly papers,
Or in the census or revenue returns, prices current, or any
    accounts of stock.

– 3 –

The sun and stars that float in the open air,
The apple-shaped earth and we upon it, surely the drift of them is
    something grand,
I do not know what it is except that it is grand, and that it is
    happiness,
And that the enclosing purport of us here is not a speculation or
    bon-mot or reconnoissance,
And that it is not something which by luck may turn out well for
    us, and without luck must be a failure for us,
And not something which may yet be retracted in a certain
    contingency.

The light and shade, the curious sense of body and identity,
    the greed that with perfect complaisance devours all
    things,
The endless pride and outstretching of man, unspeakable joys
    and sorrows,
The wonder every one sees in every one else he sees, and the
    wonders that fill each minute of time forever,
What have you reckon'd them for, camerado?
Have you reckon'd them for your trade or farm-work? or for the
    profits of your store?
Or to achieve yourself a position? or to fill a gentleman's leisure,
    or a lady's leisure?

Have you reckon'd that the landscape took substance and form
    that it might be painted in a picture?
Or men and women that they might be written of, and songs sung?
Or the attraction of gravity, and the great laws and harmonious
    combinations and the fluids of the air, as subjects for the
    savans?
Or the brown land and the blue sea for maps and charts?
Or the stars to be put in constellations and named fancy names?
Or that the growth of seeds is for agricultural tables, or agriculture
    itself?

Old institutions, these arts, libraries, legends, collections, and the
    practice handed along in manufactures, will we rate them so
    high?
Will we rate our cash and business high? I have no objection,
I rate them as high as the highest—then a child born of a woman
    and man I rate beyond all rate.

We thought our Union grand, and our Constitution grand,
I do not say they are not grand and good, for they are,
I am this day just as much in love with them as you,
Then I am in love with You, and with all my fellows upon the
    earth.

We consider bibles and religions divine—I do not say they are not
    divine,
I say they have all grown out of you, and may grow out of you still,
It is not they who give the life, it is you who give the life,
Leaves are not more shed from the trees, or trees from the earth,
    than they are shed out of you.

− 4 −

The sum of all known reverence I add up in you whoever you
    are,
The President is there in the White House for you, it is not you
    who are here for him,

The Secretaries act in their bureaus for you, not you here for
  them,
The Congress convenes every Twelfth-month for you,
Laws, courts, the forming of States, the charters of cities, the
  going and coming of commerce and mails, are all for you.

List close my scholars dear,
Doctrines, politics and civilization exurge from you,
Sculpture and monuments and any thing inscribed anywhere are
  tallied in you,
The gist of histories and statistics as far back as the records reach
  is in you this hour, and myths and tales the same,
If you were not breathing and walking here, where would they
  all be?
The most renown'd poems would be ashes, orations and plays
  would be vacuums.

All architecture is what you do to it when you look upon it,
(Did you think it was in the white or gray stone? or the lines of
  the arches and cornices?)

All music is what awakes from you when you are reminded by the
  instruments,
It is not the violins and the cornets, it is not the oboe nor the
  beating drums, nor the score of the baritone singer singing
  his sweet romanza, nor that of the men's chorus, nor that of
  the women's chorus,
It is nearer and farther than they.

– 5 –

Will the whole come back then?
Can each see signs of the best by a look in the looking-glass? is
  there nothing greater or more?
Does all sit there with you, with the mystic unseen soul?

Strange and hard that paradox true I give,
Objects gross and the unseen soul are one.

House-building, measuring, sawing the boards,

Blacksmithing, glass-blowing, nail-making, coopering, tin-roofing, shingle-dressing,

Ship-joining, dock-building, fish-curing, flagging of sidewalks by flaggers,

The pump, the pile-driver, the great derrick, the coal-kiln and brick-kiln,

Coal-mines and all that is down there, the lamps in the darkness, echoes, songs, what meditations, what vast native thoughts looking through smutch'd faces,

Iron-works, forge-fires in the mountains or by river-banks, men around feeling the melt with huge crowbars, lumps of ore, the due combining of ore, limestone, coal,

The blast-furnace and the puddling-furnace, the loup-lump at the bottom of the melt at last, the rolling-mill, the stumpy bars of pig-iron, the strong clean-shaped T-rail for railroads,

Oil-works, silk-works, white-lead works, the sugar-house, steam-saws, the great mills and factories,

Stone-cutting, shapely trimmings for façades or window or door-lintels, the mallet, the tooth-chisel, the jib to protect the thumb,

The calking-iron, the kettle of boiling vault-cement, and the fire under the kettle,

The cotton-bale, the stevedore's hook, the saw and buck of the sawyer, the mould of the moulder, the working-knife of the butcher, the ice-saw, and all the work with ice,

The work and tools of the rigger, grappler, sail-maker, block-maker,

Goods of gutta-percha,* papier-maché, colors, brushes, brush-making, glazier's implements,

The veneer and glue-pot, the confectioner's ornaments, the decanter and glasses, the shears and flat-iron,

The awl and knee-strap, the pint measure and quart measure, the counter and stool, the writing-pen of quill or metal, the making of all sorts of edged tools,

---

*A rubber-like gum.

The brewery, brewing, the malt, the vats, every thing that is done
    by brewers, wine-makers, vinegar-makers,
Leather-dressing, coach-making, boiler-making, rope-twisting,
    distilling, sign-painting, lime-burning, cotton-picking, electro-
    plating, electrotyping, stereotyping,
Stave-machines, planing-machines, reaping-machines, ploughing-
    machines, thrashing-machines, steamwagons,
The cart of the carman, the omnibus, the ponderous dray,
Pyrotechny, letting off color'd fireworks at night, fancy figures and
    jets;
Beef on the butcher's stall, the slaughter-house of the butcher, the
    butcher in his killing-clothes,
The pens of live pork, the killing-hammer, the hog-hook,
    the scalder's tub, gutting, the cutter's cleaver, the
    packer's maul, and the plenteous winterwork of pork-
    packing,
Flour-works, grinding of wheat, rye, maize, rice, the barrels and
    the half and quarter barrels, the loaded barges, the high piles
    on wharves and levees,
The men and the work of the men on ferries, railroads, coasters,
    fish-boats, canals;
The hourly routine of your own or any man's life, the shop, yard,
    store, or factory,
These shows all near you by day and night—workman! whoever
    you are, your daily life!
In that and them the heft of the heaviest—in that and them far
    more than you estimated, (and far less also,)
In them realities for you and me, in them poems for you
    and me,
In them, not yourself—you and your soul enclose all things,
    regardless of estimation,
In them the development good—in them all themes, hints,
    possibilities.

I do not affirm that what you see beyond is futile, I do not advise
    you to stop,
I do not say leadings you thought great are not great,
But I say that none lead to greater than these lead to.

– 6 –

Will you seek afar off? you surely come back at last,
In things best known to you finding the best, or as good as the best,
In folks nearest to you finding the sweetest, strongest, lovingest,
Happiness, knowledge, not in another place but this place, not for
    another hour but this hour,
Man in the first you see or touch, always in friend, brother,
    nighest neighbor—woman in mother, sister, wife,
The popular tastes and employments taking precedence in poems
    or anywhere,
You workwomen and workmen of these States having your own
    divine and strong life,
And all else giving place to men and women like you.

When the psalm sings instead of the singer,
When the script preaches instead of the preacher,
When the pulpit descends and goes instead of the carver that
    carved the supporting desk,
When I can touch the body of books by night or by day, and
    when they touch my body back again,
When a university course convinces like a slumbering woman
    and child convince,
When the minted gold in the vault smiles like the night-
    watchman's daughter,
When warrantee deeds loafe in chairs opposite and are my
    friendly companions,
I intend to reach them my hand, and make as much of them as I
    do of men and women like you.

A SONG OF THE ROLLING EARTH

– 1 –

A song of the rolling earth, and of words according,
Were you thinking that those were the words, those upright lines?
    those curves, angles, dots?

No, those are not the words, the substantial words are in the
    ground and sea,
They are in the air, they are in you.

Were you thinking that those were the words, those delicious
    sounds out of your friends' mouths?
No, the real words are more delicious than they.

Human bodies are words, myriads of words,
(In the best poems re-appears the body, man's or woman's, well-
    shaped, natural, gay,
Every part able, active, receptive, without shame or the need of
    shame.)

Air, soil, water, fire—those are words,
I myself am a word with them—my qualities interpenetrate with
    theirs—my name is nothing to them,
Though it were told in the three thousand languages, what would
    air, soil, water, fire, know of my name?

A healthy presence, a friendly or commanding gesture, are words,
    sayings, meanings,
The charms that go with the mere looks of some men and
    women, are sayings and meanings also.

The workmanship of souls is by those inaudible words of the earth,
The masters know the earth's words and use them more than
    audible words.

Amelioration is one of the earth's words,
The earth neither lags nor hastens,
It has all attributes, growths, effects, latent in itself from the jump,
It is not half beautiful only, defects and excrescences show just as
    much as perfections show.

The earth does not withhold, it is generous enough,
The truths of the earth continually wait, they are not so conceal'd
    either,
They are calm, subtle, untransmissible by print,

They are imbued through all things conveying themselves willingly,
Conveying a sentiment and invitation, I utter and utter,
I speak not, yet if you hear me not of what avail am I to you?
To bear, to better, lacking these of what avail am I?

(Accouche! accouchez!*
Will you rot your own fruit in yourself there?
Will you squat and stifle there?)

The earth does not argue,
Is not pathetic, has no arrangements,
Does not scream, haste, persuade, threaten, promise,
Makes no discriminations, has no conceivable failures,
Closes nothing, refuses nothing, shuts none out,
Of all the powers, objects, states, it notifies, shuts none out.

The earth does not exhibit itself nor refuse to exhibit itself,
     possesses still underneath,
Underneath the ostensible sounds, the august chorus of heroes,
     the wail of slaves,
Persuasions of lovers, curses, gasps of the dying, laughter of young
     people, accents of bargainers,
Underneath these possessing words that never fail.

To her children the words of the eloquent dumb great mother
     never fail,
The true words do not fail, for motion does not fail and reflection
     does not fail,
Also the day and night do not fail, and the voyage we pursue does
     not fail.

Of the interminable sisters,[42]
Of the ceaseless cotillons of sisters,
Of the centripetal and centrifugal sisters, the elder and younger
     sisters,
The beautiful sister we know dances on with the rest.

---

*Give birth! (French).

With her ample back towards every beholder,
With the fascinations of youth and the equal fascinations of age,
Sits she whom I too love like the rest, sits undisturb'd,
Holding up in her hand what has the character of a mirror, while
    her eyes glance back from it,
Glance as she sits, inviting none, denying none,
Holding a mirror day and night tirelessly before her own face.

Seen at hand or seen at a distance,
Duly the twenty-four appear in public every day,
Duly approach and pass with their companions or a companion,
Looking from no countenances of their own, but from the
    countenances of those who are with them,
From the countenances of children or women or the manly
    countenance,
From the open countenances of animals or from inanimate
    things,
From the landscape or waters or from the exquisite apparition of
    the sky,
From our countenances, mine and yours, faithfully returning
    them,
Every day in public appearing without fail, but never twice with
    the same companions.

Embracing man, embracing all, proceed the three hundred and
    sixty-five resistlessly round the sun;
Embracing all, soothing, supporting, follow close three hundred
    and sixty-five offsets of the first, sure and necessary as they.

Tumbling on steadily, nothing dreading,
Sunshine, storm, cold, heat, forever withstanding, passing,
    carrying,
The soul's realization and determination still inheriting,
The fluid vacuum around and ahead still entering and dividing,
No balk retarding, no anchor anchoring, on no rock striking,
Swift, glad, content, unbereav'd, nothing losing,
Of all able and ready at any time to give strict account,
The divine ship sails the divine sea.

− 2 −

Whoever you are! motion and reflection are especially for you,
The divine ship sails the divine sea for you.

Whoever you are! you are he or she for whom the earth is solid
     and liquid,
You are he or she for whom the sun and moon hang in the sky,
For none more than you are the present and the past,
For none more than you is immortality.

Each man to himself and each woman to herself, is the word of
     the past and present, and the true word of immortality;
No one can acquire for another—not one,
Not one can grow for another—not one.

The song is to the singer, and comes back most to him,
The teaching is to the teacher, and comes back most to him,
The murder is to the murderer, and comes back most to him,
The theft is to the thief, and comes back most to him,
The love is to the lover, and comes back most to him,
The gift is to the giver, and comes back most to him—it cannot fail,
The oration is to the orator, the acting is to the actor and actress
     not to the audience,
And no man understands any greatness or goodness but his own,
     or the indication of his own.

− 3 −

I swear the earth shall surely be complete to him or her who shall
     be complete,
The earth remains jagged and broken only to him or her who
     remains jagged and broken.

I swear there is no greatness or power that does not emulate those
     of the earth,
There can be no theory of any account unless it corroborate the
     theory of the earth,

No politics, song, religion, behavior, or what not, is of account,
    unless it compare with the amplitude of the earth,
Unless it face the exactness, vitality, impartiality, rectitude of the
    earth.

I swear I begin to see love with sweeter spasms than that which
    responds love,
It is that which contains itself, which never invites and never refuses.

I swear I begin to see little or nothing in audible words,
All merges toward the presentation of the unspoken meanings
    of the earth,
Toward him who sings the songs of the body and of the truths
    of the earth,
Toward him who makes the dictionaries of words that print
    cannot touch.

I swear I see what is better than to tell the best,
It is always to leave the best untold.

When I undertake to tell the best I find I cannot,
My tongue is ineffectual on its pivots,
My breath will not be obedient to its organs,
I become a dumb man.

The best of the earth cannot be told anyhow, all or any is best,
It is not what you anticipated, it is cheaper, easier, nearer,
Things are not dismiss'd from the places they held before,
The earth is just as positive and direct as it was before,
Facts, religions, improvements, politics, trades, are as real as before,
But the soul is also real, it too is positive and direct,
No reasoning, no proof has establish'd it,
Undeniable growth has establish'd it.

– 4 –

These to echo the tones of souls and the phrases of souls,
(If they did not echo the phrases of souls what were they then?
If they had not reference to you in especial what were they then?)

I swear I will never henceforth have to do with the faith that tells
    the best,
I will have to do only with that faith that leaves the best untold.

Say on, sayers! sing on, singers!
Delve! mould! pile the words of the earth!
Work on, age after age, nothing is to be lost,
It may have to wait long, but it will certainly come in use,
When the materials are all prepared and ready, the architects
    shall appear.

I swear to you the architects shall appear without fail,
I swear to you they will understand you and justify you,
The greatest among them shall be he who best knows you, and
    encloses all and is faithful to all,
He and the rest shall not forget you, they shall perceive that you
    are not an iota less than they,
You shall be fully glorified in them.

YOUTH, DAY, OLD AGE AND NIGHT

Youth, large, lusty, loving—youth full of grace, force, fascination,
Do you know that Old Age may come after you with equal grace,
    force, fascination?

Day full-blown and splendid—day of the immense sun, action,
    ambition, laughter,
The Night follows close with millions of suns, and sleep and
    restoring darkness.

BIRDS OF PASSAGE

SONG OF THE UNIVERSAL

– 1 –

Come said the Muse,
Sing me a song no poet yet has chanted,
Sing me the universal.

In this broad earth of ours,
Amid the measureless grossness and the slag,
Enclosed and safe within its central heart,
Nestles the seed perfection.

By every life a share or more or less,
None born but it is born, conceal'd or unconceal'd the seed is
        waiting.

– 2 –

Lo! keen-eyed towering science,
As from tall peaks the modern overlooking,
Successive absolute fiats issuing.

Yet again, lo! the soul, above all science,
For it has history gather'd like husks around the globe,
For it the entire star-myriads roll through the sky.

In spiral routes by long detours,
(As a much-tacking ship upon the sea,)
For it the partial to the permanent flowing,
For it the real to the ideal tends.

For it the mystic evolution,
Not the right only justified, what we call evil also justified.

Forth from their masks, no matter what,
From the huge festering trunk, from craft and guile and tears,
Health to emerge and joy, joy universal.

Out of the bulk, the morbid and the shallow,
Out of the bad majority, the varied countless frauds of men and
    states,
Electric, antiseptic yet, cleaving, suffusing all,
Only the good is universal.

– 3 –

Over the mountain-growths disease and sorrow,
An uncaught bird is ever hovering, hovering,
High in the purer, happier air.

From imperfection's murkiest cloud,
Darts always forth one ray of perfect light,
One flash of heaven's glory.

To fashion's, custom's discord,
To the mad Babel-din, the deafening orgies,
Soothing each lull a strain is heard, just heard,
From some far shore the final chorus sounding.

O the blest eyes, the happy hearts,
That see, that know the guiding thread so fine,
Along the mighty labyrinth.

– 4 –

And thou America,
For the scheme's culmination, its thought and its reality,
For these (not for thyself) thou hast arrived.

Thou too surroundest all,
Embracing carrying welcoming all, thou too by pathways broad
　　and new,
To the ideal tendest.

The measur'd faiths of other lands, the grandeurs of the past,
Are not for thee, but grandeurs of thine own,
Deific faiths and amplitudes, absorbing, comprehending all,
All eligible to all.

All, all for immortality,
Love like the light silently wrapping all,
Nature's amelioration blessing all,
The blossoms, fruits of ages, orchards divine and certain,
Forms, objects, growths, humanities, to spiritual images ripening.

Give me O God to sing that thought,
Give me, give him or her I love this quenchless faith,
In Thy ensemble, whatever else withheld withhold not from us,
Belief in plan of Thee enclosed in Time and Space,
Health, peace, salvation universal.

Is it a dream?
Nay but the lack of it the dream,
And failing it life's lore and wealth a dream,
And all the world a dream.

PIONEERS! O PIONEERS!

Come my tan-faced children,
Follow well in order, get your weapons ready,
Have you your pistols? have you your sharp-edged axes?
　　　　Pioneers! O pioneers!

For we cannot tarry here,
We must march my darlings, we must bear the brunt of
　　　　danger,

We the youthful sinewy races, all the rest on us depend,
        Pioneers! O pioneers!

       O you youths, Western youths,
So impatient, full of action, full of manly pride and friendship,
Plain I see you Western youths, see you tramping with the foremost,
        Pioneers! O pioneers!

       Have the elder races halted?
Do they droop and end their lesson, wearied over there
        beyond the seas?
We take up the task eternal, and the burden and the lesson,
        Pioneers! O pioneers!

       All the past we leave behind,
We debouch* upon a newer mightier world, varied world,
Fresh and strong the world we seize, world of labor and the march,
        Pioneers! O pioneers!

       We detachments steady throwing,
Down the edges, through the passes, up the mountains steep,
Conquering, holding, daring, venturing as we go the unknown ways,
        Pioneers! O pioneers!

       We primeval forests felling,
We the rivers stemming, vexing we and piercing deep the
        mines within,
We the surface broad surveying, we the virgin soil upheaving,
        Pioneers! O pioneers!

       Colorado men are we,
From the peaks gigantic, from the great sierras and the
        high plateaus,
From the mine and from the gully, from the hunting trail we come,
        Pioneers! O pioneers!

---

*Whitman's misused French, meaning "emerge."

From Nebraska, from Arkansas,
Central inland race are we, from Missouri, with the con-
    tinental blood intervein'd,
All the hands of comrades clasping, all the Southern, all
    the Northern,
        Pioneers! O pioneers!

O resistless restless race!
O beloved race in all! O my breast aches with tender love
    for all!
O I mourn and yet exult, I am rapt with love for all,
        Pioneers! O pioneers!

Raise the mighty mother mistress,
Waving high the delicate mistress, over all the starry mis-
    tress, (bend your heads all,)
Raise the fang'd and warlike mistress, stern, impassive,
    weapon'd mistress,
        Pioneers! O pioneers!

See my children, resolute children,
By those swarms upon our rear we must never yield or
    falter,
Ages back in ghostly millions frowning there behind us
    urging,
        Pioneers! O pioneers!

On and on the compact ranks,
With accessions ever waiting, with the places of the dead
    quickly fill'd,
Through the battle, through defeat, moving yet and never
    stopping,
        Pioneers! O pioneers!

O to die advancing on!
Are there some of us to droop and die? has the hour
    come?

Then upon the march we fittest die, soon and sure the gap
        is fill'd,
        Pioneers! O pioneers!

        All the pulses of the world,
Falling in they beat for us, with the Western movement
        beat,
Holding single or together, steady moving to the front, all
        for us,
        Pioneers! O pioneers!

        Life's involv'd and varied pageants,
All the forms and shows, all the workmen at their work,
All the seamen and the landsmen, all the masters with their slaves,
        Pioneers! O pioneers!

        All the hapless silent lovers,
All the prisoners in the prisons, all the righteous and the wicked,
All the joyous, all the sorrowing, all the living, all the dying,
        Pioneers! O pioneers!

        I too with my soul and body,
We, a curious trio, picking, wandering on our way,
Through these shores amid the shadows, with the appari-
        tions pressing,
        Pioneers! O pioneers!

        Lo, the darting bowling orb!
Lo, the brother orbs around, all the clustering suns and planets,
All the dazzling days, all the mystic nights with dreams,
        Pioneers! O pioneers!

        These are of us, they are with us,
All for primal needed work, while the followers there in
        embryo wait behind,
We to-day's procession heading, we the route for travel clearing,
        Pioneers! O pioneers!

O you daughters of the West!
O you young and elder daughters! O you mothers and
      you wives!
Never must you be divided, in our ranks you move united,
      Pioneers! O pioneers!

Minstrels latent on the prairies!
(Shrouded bards of other lands, you may rest, you have
      done your work,)
Soon I hear you coming warbling, soon you rise and
      tramp amid us,
      Pioneers! O pioneers!

Not for delectations sweet,
Not the cushion and the slipper, not the peaceful and the
      studious,
Not the riches safe and palling, not for us the tame enjoyment,
      Pioneers! O pioneers!

Do the feasters gluttonous feast?
Do the corpulent sleepers sleep? have they lock'd and
      bolted doors?
Still be ours the diet hard, and the blanket on the ground,
      Pioneers! O pioneers!

Has the night descended?
Was the road of late so toilsome? did we stop discouraged
      nodding on our way?
Yet a passing hour I yield you in your tracks to pause
      oblivious,
      Pioneers! O pioneers!

Till with sound of trumpet,
Far, far off the daybreak call—hark! how loud and clear I
      hear it wind,
Swift! to the head of the army!—swift! spring to your places,
      Pioneers! O pioneers!

TO YOU

Whoever you are, I fear you are walking the walks of dreams,
I fear these supposed realities are to melt from under your feet
    and hands,
Even now your features, joys, speech, house, trade, manners,
    troubles, follies, costume, crimes, dissipate away from you,
Your true soul and body appear before me,
They stand forth out of affairs, out of commerce, shops, work,
    farms, clothes, the house, buying, selling, eating, drinking,
    suffering, dying.

Whoever you are, now I place my hand upon you, that you be my
    poem,
I whisper with my lips close to your ear,
I have loved many women and men, but I love none better than
    you.

O I have been dilatory and dumb,
I should have made my way straight to you long ago,
I should have blabb'd nothing but you, I should have chanted
    nothing but you.

I will leave all and come and make the hymns of you,
None has understood you, but I understand you,
None has done justice to you, you have not done justice to yourself,
None but has found you imperfect, I only find no imperfection in
    you,
None but would subordinate you, I only am he who will never
    consent to subordinate you,
I only am he who places over you no master, owner, better, God,
    beyond what waits intrinsically in yourself.

Painters have painted their swarming groups and the centre-figure
    of all,
From the head of the centre-figure spreading a nimbus of gold-
    color'd light,
But I paint myriads of heads, but paint no head without its
    nimbus of gold-color'd light,

From my hand from the brain of every man and woman it
    streams, effulgently flowing forever.

O I could sing such grandeurs and glories about you!
You have not known what you are, you have slumber'd upon
    yourself all your life,
Your eyelids have been the same as closed most of the time,
What you have done returns already in mockeries,
(Your thrift, knowledge, prayers, if they do not return in
    mockeries, what is their return?)

The mockeries are not you,
Underneath them and within them I see you lurk,
I pursue you where none else has pursued you,
Silence, the desk, the flippant expression, the night, the
    accustom'd routine, if these conceal you from others or from
    yourself, they do not conceal you from me,
The shaved face, the unsteady eye, the impure complexion, if
    these balk others they do not balk me,
The pert apparel, the deform'd attitude, drunkenness, greed,
    premature death, all these I part aside.

There is no endowment in man or woman that is not tallied in
    you,
There is no virtue, no beauty in man or woman, but as good is in
    you,
No pluck, no endurance in others, but as good is in you,
No pleasure waiting for others, but an equal pleasure waits for you.

As for me, I give nothing to any one except I give the like
    carefully to you,
I sing the songs of the glory of none, not God, sooner than I sing
    the songs of the glory of you.

Whoever you are! claim your own at any hazard!
These shows of the East and West are tame compared to you,
These immense meadows, these interminable rivers, you are im-
    mense and interminable as they,

These furies, elements, storms, motions of Nature, throes of
      apparent dissolution, you are he or she who is master or
      mistress over them,
Master or mistress in your own right over Nature, elements, pain,
      passion, dissolution.

The hopples fall from your ankles, you find an unfailing sufficiency,
Old or young, male or female, rude, low, rejected by the rest,
      whatever you are promulges itself,
Through birth, life, death, burial, the means are provided,
      nothing is scanted,
Through angers, losses, ambition, ignorance, ennui, what you are
      picks its way.

FRANCE, THE 18TH YEAR OF THESE STATES[43]

A great year and place,
A harsh discordant natal scream out-sounding, to touch the
      mother's heart closer than any yet.*

I walk'd the shores of my Eastern sea,
Heard over the waves the little voice,
Saw the divine infant where she woke mournfully wailing,
      amid the roar of cannon, curses, shouts, crash of falling
      buildings,
Was not so sick from the blood in the gutters running, nor from
      the single corpses, nor those in heaps, nor those borne away
      in the tumbrils,
Was not so desperate at the battues of death—was not so shock'd
      at the repeated fusillades of the guns.

Pale, silent, stern, what could I say to that long-accrued retribution?
Could I wish humanity different?

---

*The mother, or "ma femme" (French for "my wife") of the last lines, is Democ-
racy personified; the newborn infant is liberated France.

Could I wish the people made of wood and stone?
Or that there be no justice in destiny or time?

O Liberty! O mate for me!
Here too the blaze, the grape-shot and the axe, in reserve, to fetch
    them out in case of need,
Here too, though long represt, can never be destroy'd,
Here too could rise at last murdering and ecstatic,
Here too demanding full arrears of vengeance.

Hence I sign this salute over the sea,
And I do not deny that terrible red birth and baptism,
But remember the little voice that I heard wailing, and wait with
    perfect trust, no matter how long,
And from to-day sad and cogent I maintain the bequeath'd cause,
    as for all lands,
And I send these words to Paris with my love,
And I guess some chansonniers there will understand them,
For I guess there is latent music yet in France, floods of it,
O I hear already the bustle of instruments, they will soon be
    drowning all that would interrupt them,
O I think the east wind brings a triumphal and free march,
It reaches hither, it swells me to joyful madness,
I will run transpose it in words, to justify it,
I will yet sing a song for you ma femme.

MYSELF AND MINE

Myself and mine gymnastic ever,
To stand the cold or heat, to take good aim with a gun, to sail a
    boat, to manage horses, to beget superb children,
To speak readily and clearly, to feel at home among common
    people,
And to hold our own in terrible positions on land and sea.

Not for an embroiderer,
(There will always be plenty of embroiderers, I welcome them also,)

But for the fibre of things and for inherent men and
    women.

Not to chisel ornaments,
But to chisel with free stroke the heads and limbs of plenteous
    supreme Gods, that the States may realize them walking and
    talking.

Let me have my own way,
Let others promulge the laws, I will make no account of the laws,
Let others praise eminent men and hold up peace, I hold up
    agitation and conflict,
I praise no eminent man, I rebuke to his face the one that was
    thought most worthy.

(Who are you? and what are you secretly guilty of all your life?
Will you turn aside all your life? will you grub and chatter all
    your life?
And who are you, blabbing by rote, years, pages, languages,
    reminiscences,
Unwitting to-day that you do not know how to speak properly a
    single word?)

Let others finish specimens, I never finish specimens,
I start them by exhaustless laws as Nature does, fresh and modern
    continually.

I give nothing as duties,
What others give as duties I give as living impulses,
(Shall I give the heart's action as a duty?)

Let others dispose of questions, I dispose of nothing, I arouse
    unanswerable questions,
Who are they I see and touch, and what about them?
What about these likes of myself that draw me so close by tender
    directions and indirections?

I call to the world to distrust the accounts of my friends, but listen
    to my enemies, as I myself do,

I charge you forever reflect those who would expound me, for I
    cannot expound myself,
I charge that there be no theory or school founded out of me,
I charge you to leave all free, as I have left all free.

After me, vista!
O I see life is not short, but immeasurably long,
I henceforth tread the world chaste, temperate, an early riser, a
    steady grower,
Every hour the semen of centuries, and still of centuries.

I must follow up these continual lessons of the air, water, earth,
I perceive I have no time to lose.

YEAR OF METEORS (1859–60)[44]

Year of meteors! brooding year!
I would bind in words retrospective some of your deeds and signs,
I would sing your contest for the 19th Presidentiad,*
I would sing how an old man, tall, with white hair, mounted the
    scaffold in Virginia,†
(I was at hand, silent I stood with teeth shut close, I watch'd,
I stood very near you old man when cool and indifferent, but
    trembling with age and your unheal'd wounds you mounted
    the scaffold;)
I would sing in my copious song your census returns of the States,
The tables of population and products, I would sing of your ships
    and their cargoes,
The proud black ships of Manhattan arriving, some fill'd with
    immigrants, some from the isthmus with cargoes of gold,
Songs thereof would I sing, to all that hitherward comes would I
    welcome give,

---

*Abraham Lincoln ran against Stephen Douglas and became the sixteenth presi-
dent of the United States; Whitman refers here to the nineteenth term of the pres-
idency.
†Abolitionist John Brown was hung for treason in Charles Town, Virginia (now
West Virginia), on December 2, 1859.

And you would I sing, fair stripling! welcome to you from me,
 young prince of England!*
(Remember you surging Manhattan's crowds as you pass'd with
 your cortege of nobles?
There in the crowds stood I, and singled you out with attachment;)
Nor forget I to sing of the wonder, the ship as she swam up my bay,
Well-shaped and stately the Great Eastern swam up my bay, she
 was 600 feet long,†
Her moving swiftly surrounded by myriads of small craft I forget
 not to sing;
Nor the comet that came unannounced out of the north flaring
 in heaven,
Nor the strange huge meteor-procession dazzling and clear
 shooting over our heads,
(A moment, a moment long it sail'd its balls of unearthly light
 over our heads,
Then departed, dropped in the night, and was gone;)
Of such, and fitful as they, I sing—with gleams from them would
 I gleam and patch these chants,
Your chants, O year all mottled with evil and good—year of
 forebodings!
Year of comets and meteors transient and strange—lo! even here
 one equally transient and strange!
As I flit through you hastily, soon to fall and be gone, what is this
 chant,
What am I myself but one of your meteors?

WITH ANTECEDENTS

— 1 —

With antecedents,
With my fathers and mothers and the accumulations of past
 ages,

---

*Edward, prince of Wales, visited New York City on October 11, 1860.
†The British steamship *The Great Eastern* made her first transatlantic crossing to
New York in 1860.

With all which, had it not been, I would not now be here, as I am,
With Egypt, India, Phenicia, Greece and Rome,
With the Kelt, the Scandinavian, the Alb and the Saxon,
With antique maritime ventures, laws, artisanship, wars and
     journeys,
With the poet, the skald, the saga, the myth, and the oracle,
With the sale of slaves, with enthusiasts, with the troubadour, the
     crusader, and the monk,
With those old continents whence we have come to this new
     continent,
With the fading kingdoms and kings over there,
With the fading religions and priests,
With the small shores we look back to from our own large and
     present shores,
With countless years drawing themselves onward and arrived at
     these years,
You and me arrived—America arrived and making this year,
This year! sending itself ahead countless years to come.

— 2 —

O but it is not the years—it is I, it is You,
We touch all laws and tally all antecedents,
We are the skald, the oracle, the monk and the knight, we easily
     include them and more,
We stand amid time beginningless and endless, we stand amid
     evil and good,
All swings around us, there is as much darkness as light,
The very sun swings itself and its system of planets around us,
Its sun, and its again, all swing around us.

As for me, (torn, stormy, amid these vehement days,)
I have the idea of all, and am all and believe in all,
I believe materialism is true and spiritualism is true, I reject no part.

(Have I forgotten any part? any thing in the past?
Come to me whoever and whatever, till I give you recognition.)

I respect Assyria, China, Teutonia, and the Hebrews,
I adopt each theory, myth, god, and demi-god,
I see that the old accounts, bibles, genealogies, are true, without
    exception,
I assert that all past days were what they must have been,
And that they could no-how have been better than they were,
And that to-day is what it must be, and that America is,
And that to-day and America could no-how be better than they are.

− 3 −

In the name of these States and in your and my name, the Past,
And in the name of these States and in your and my name, the
    Present time.

I know that the past was great and the future will be great,
And I know that both curiously conjoint in the present time,
(For the sake of him I typify, for the common average man's sake,
    your sake if you are he,)
And that where I am or you are this present day, there is the
    centre of all days, all races,
And there is the meaning to us of all that has ever come of races
    and days, or ever will come.

A BROADWAY PAGEANT[45]

− 1 −

Over the Western sea hither from Niphon come,
Courteous, the swart-cheek'd two-sworded envoys,
Leaning back in their open barouches, bare-headed, impassive,
Ride to-day through Manhattan.

Libertad! I do not know whether others behold what I behold,
In the procession along with the nobles of Niphon, the errand-
    bearers,

Bringing up the rear, hovering above, around, or in the ranks
     marching,
But I will sing you a song of what I behold Libertad.

When million-footed Manhattan unpent descends to her
     pavements,
When the thunder-cracking guns arouse me with the proud roar
     I love,
When the round-mouth'd guns out of the smoke and smell I love
     spit their salutes,
When the fire-flashing guns have fully alerted me, and heaven-
     clouds canopy my city with a delicate thin haze,
When gorgeous the countless straight stems, the forests at the
     wharves, thicken with colors,
When every ship richly drest carries her flag at the peak,
When pennants trail and street-festoons hang from the windows,
When Broadway is entirely given up to foot-passengers and foot-
     standers, when the mass is densest,
When the façades of the houses are alive with people, when eyes
     gaze riveted tens of thousands at a time,
When the guests from the islands advance, when the pageant
     moves forward visible,
When the summons is made, when the answer that waited
     thousands of years answers,
I too arising, answering, descend to the pavements, merge with
     the crowd, and gaze with them.

— 2 —

Superb-faced Manhattan!
Comrade Americanos! to us, then at last the Orient comes.

To us, my city,
Where our tall-topt marble and iron beauties range on opposite
     sides, to walk in the space between,
To-day our Antipodes* comes.

---

*Opposites.

The Originatress comes,
The nest of languages, the bequeather of poems, the race
    of eld,
Florid with blood, pensive, rapt with musings, hot with passion,
Sultry with perfume, with ample and flowing garments,
With sunburnt visage, with intense soul and glittering eyes,
The race of Brahma comes.

See my cantabile!* these and more are flashing to us from the
    procession,
As it moves changing, a kaleidoscope divine it moves changing
    before us.

For not the envoys nor the tann'd Japanee from his
    island only,
Lithe and silent the Hindoo appears, the Asiatic continent itself
    appears, the past, the dead,
The murky night-morning of wonder and fable inscrutable,
The envelop'd mysteries, the old and unknown hive-bees,
The north, the sweltering south, eastern Assyria, the Hebrews,
    the ancient of ancients,
Vast desolated cities, the gliding present, all of these and more
    are in the pageant-procession.

Geography, the world, is in it,
The Great Sea, the brood of islands, Polynesia, the coast
    beyond,
The coast you henceforth are facing—you Libertad! from your
    Western golden shores,
The countries there with their populations, the millions en-masse
    are curiously here,
The swarming market-places, the temples with idols ranged along
    the sides or at the end, bonze, brahmin, and llama,
Mandarin, farmer, merchant, mechanic, and fisherman,

---

*Smooth, lyrical, flowing, song-like piece; the word is more commonly used as an
adjective.

The singing-girl and the dancing-girl, the ecstatic persons, the
  secluded emperors,
Confucius himself, the great poets and heroes, the warriors, the
  castes, all,
Trooping up, crowding from all directions, from the Altay
  mountains,
From Thibet, from the four winding and far-flowing rivers of China,
From the southern peninsulas and the demi-continental islands
  from Malaysia,
These and whatever belongs to them palpable show forth to me,
  and are seiz'd by me,
And I am seiz'd by them, and friendlily held by them,
Till as here them all I chant, Libertad! for themselves and
  for you.

For I too raising my voice join the ranks of this pageant,
I am the chanter, I chant aloud over the pageant,
I chant the world on my Western sea,
I chant copious the islands beyond, thick as stars in the sky,
I chant the new empire grander than any before, as in a vision it
  comes to me,
I chant America the mistress, I chant a greater supremacy,
I chant projected a thousand blooming cities yet in time on those
  groups of sea-islands,
My sail-ships and steam-ships threading the archipelagoes,
My stars and stripes fluttering in the wind,
Commerce opening, the sleep of ages having done its work, races
  reborn, refresh'd,
Lives, works resumed—the object I know not—but the old, the
  Asiatic renew'd as it must be,
Commencing from this day surrounded by the world.

– 3 –

And you Libertad of the world!
You shall sit in the middle well-pois'd thousands and thousands of
  years,

As to-day from one side the nobles of Asia come to you,
As to-morrow from the other side the queen of England sends her
    eldest son to you.*

The sign is reversing, the orb is enclosed,
The ring is circled, the journey is done,
The box-lid is but perceptibly open'd, nevertheless the perfume
    pours copiously out of the whole box.

Young Libertad! with the venerable Asia, the all-mother,
Be considerate with her now and ever hot Libertad, for you
    are all,
Bend your proud neck to the long-off mother now sending
    messages over the archipelagoes to you,
Bend your proud neck low for once, young Libertad.

Were the children straying westward so long? so wide the
    tramping?
Were the precedent dim ages debouching westward from Paradise
    so long?
Were the centuries steadily footing it that way, all the while
    unknown, for you, for reasons?

They are justified, they are accomplish'd, they shall now be turn'd
    the other way also, to travel toward you thence,
They shall now also march obediently eastward for your sake
    Libertad.

---

*As in "Year of Meteors," Whitman refers to the visit of Edward, prince of Wales,
to New York in 1860.

SEA-DRIFT[46]

OUT OF THE CRADLE ENDLESSLY ROCKING[47]

Out of the cradle endlessly rocking,
Out of the mocking-bird's throat, the musical shuttle,
Out of the Ninth-month* midnight,
Over the sterile sands and the fields beyond, where the child
    leaving his bed wander'd alone, bareheaded, barefoot,
Down from the shower'd halo,
Up from the mystic play of shadows twining and twisting as if they
    were alive,
Out from the patches of briers and blackberries,
From the memories of the bird that chanted to me,
From your memories sad brother, from the fitful risings and
    fallings I heard,
From under that yellow half-moon late-risen and swollen as if
    with tears,
From those beginning notes of yearning and love there in the
    mist,
From the thousand responses of my heart never to cease,
From the myriad thence-arous'd words,
From the word[48] stronger and more delicious than any,
From such as now they start the scene revisiting,
As a flock, twittering, rising, or overhead passing,
Borne hither, ere all eludes me, hurriedly,
A man, yet by these tears a little boy again,
Throwing myself on the sand, confronting the waves,

---

*Quaker designation for September, but perhaps also an allusion to the culmina-
tion of a pregnancy.

I, chanter of pains and joys, uniter of here and hereafter,
Taking all hints to use them, but swiftly leaping beyond them,
A reminiscence sing.

Once Paumanok,
When the lilac-scent was in the air and Fifth-month grass was
    growing,
Up this seashore in some briers,
Two feather'd guests from Alabama, two together,
And their nest, and four light-green eggs spotted with brown,
And every day the he-bird to and fro near at hand,
And every day the she-bird crouch'd on her nest, silent, with
    bright eyes,
And every day I, a curious boy, never too close, never disturbing
    them,
Cautiously peering, absorbing, translating.

Shine! shine! shine![49]
Pour down your warmth, great sun!
While we bask, we two together.

Two together!
Winds blow south, or winds blow north,
Day come white, or night come black,
Home, or rivers and mountains from home,
Singing all time, minding no time,
While we two keep together.

Till of a sudden,
May-be kill'd, unknown to her mate,
One forenoon the she-bird crouch'd not on the nest,
Nor return'd that afternoon, nor the next,
Nor ever appear'd again.

And thenceforward all summer in the sound of the sea,
And at night under the full of the moon in calmer weather,
Over the hoarse surging of the sea,
Or flitting from brier to brier by day,

I saw, I heard at intervals the remaining one, the he-bird,
The solitary guest from Alabama.

Blow! blow! blow!
Blow up sea-winds along Paumanok's shore;
I wait and I wait till you blow my mate to me.

Yes, when the stars glisten'd,
All night long on the prong of a moss-scallop'd stake,
Down almost amid the slapping waves,
Sat the lone singer wonderful causing tears.

He call'd on his mate,
He pour'd forth the meanings which I of all men know.

Yes my brother I know,
The rest might not, but I have treasur'd every note,
For more than once dimly down to the beach gliding,
Silent, avoiding the moonbeams, blending myself with the shadows,
Recalling now the obscure shapes, the echoes, the sounds and
    sights after their sorts,
The white arms out in the breakers tirelessly tossing,
I, with bare feet, a child, the wind wafting my hair,
Listen'd long and long.

Listen'd to keep, to sing, now translating the notes,
Following you my brother.

Soothe! soothe! soothe!
Close on its wave soothes the wave behind,
And again another behind embracing and lapping, every one close,
But my love soothes not me, not me.

Low hangs the moon, it rose late,
It is lagging—O I think it is heavy with love, with love.

O madly the sea pushes upon the land,
With love, with love.

O night! do I not see my love fluttering out among the breakers?
What is that little black thing I see there in the white?

Loud! loud! loud!
Loud I call to you, my love!

High and clear I shoot my voice over the waves,
Surely you must know who is here, is here,
You must know who I am, my love.

Low-hanging moon!
What is that dusky spot in your brown yellow?
O it is the shape, the shape of my mate!
O moon do not keep her from me any longer.

Land! land! O land!
Whichever way I turn, O I think you could give me my mate back
      again if you only would,
For I am almost sure I see her dimly whichever way I look.

O rising stars!
Perhaps the one I want so much will rise, will rise with some of you.

O throat! O trembling throat!
Sound clearer through the atmosphere!
Pierce the woods, the earth,
Somewhere listening to catch you must be the one I want.

Shake out carols!
Solitary here, the night's carols!
Carols of lonesome love! death's carols!
Carols under that lagging, yellow, waning moon!
O under that moon where she droops almost down into the sea!
O reckless despairing carols.

But soft! sink low!
Soft! let me just murmur,
And do you wait a moment you husky-nois'd sea,

For somewhere I believe I heard my mate responding to me,
So faint, I must be still, be still to listen,
But not altogether still, for then she might not come immediately
    to me.

Hither my love!
Here I am! here!
With this just-sustain'd note I announce myself to you,
This gentle call is for you my love, for you.

Do not be decoy'd elsewhere,
That is the whistle of the wind, it is not my voice,
That is the fluttering, the fluttering of the spray,
Those are the shadows of leaves.

O darkness! O in vain!
O I am very sick and sorrowful.

O brown halo in the sky near the moon, drooping upon the sea!
O troubled reflection in the sea!
O throat! O throbbing heart!
And I singing uselessly, uselessly all the night.

O past! O happy life! O songs of joy!
In the air, in the woods, over fields,
Loved! loved! loved! loved! loved!
But my mate no more, no more with me!
We two together no more.

The aria sinking,
All else continuing, the stars shining,
The winds blowing, the notes of the bird continuous echoing,
With angry moans the fierce old mother incessantly moaning,
On the sands of Paumanok's shore gray and rustling,
The yellow half-moon enlarged, sagging down, drooping, the face
    of the sea almost touching,
The boy ecstatic, with his bare feet the waves, with his hair the at-
    mosphere dallying,

The love in the heart long pent, now loose, now at last
tumultuously bursting,
The aria's meaning, the ears, the soul, swiftly depositing,
The strange tears down the cheeks coursing,
The colloquy there, the trio, each uttering,
The undertone, the savage old mother incessantly crying,
To the boy's soul's questions sullenly timing, some drown'd secret
hissing,
To the outsetting bard.

Demon or bird! (said the boy's soul,)
Is it indeed toward your mate you sing? or is it really to me?
For I, that was a child, my tongue's use sleeping, now I have
heard you,
Now in a moment I know what I am for, I awake,
And already a thousand singers, a thousand songs, clearer, louder
and more sorrowful than yours,
A thousand warbling echoes have started to life within me, never
to die.

O you singer solitary, singing by yourself, projecting me,
O solitary me listening, never more shall I cease perpetuating you,
Never more shall I escape, never more the reverberations,
Never more the cries of unsatisfied love be absent from me,
Never again leave me to be the peaceful child I was before what
there in the night,
By the sea under the yellow and sagging moon,
The messenger there arous'd, the fire, the sweet hell within,
The unknown want, the destiny of me.

O give me the clew! (it lurks in the night here somewhere,)
O if I am to have so much, let me have more!

A word then, (for I will conquer it,)
The word final, superior to all,
Subtle, sent up—what is it?—I listen;
Are you whispering it, and have been all the time, you sea-waves?
Is that it from your liquid rims and wet sands?

Whereto answering, the sea,
Delaying not, hurrying not,
Whisper'd me through the night, and very plainly before
    daybreak,
Lisp'd to me the low and delicious word death,
And again death, death, death, death,
Hissing melodious, neither like the bird nor like my arous'd
    child's heart,
But edging near as privately for me rustling at my feet,
Creeping thence steadily up to my ears and laving me softly all
    over,
Death, death, death, death, death.[50]

Which I do not forget,
But fuse the song of my dusky demon and brother,
That he sang to me in the moonlight on Paumanok's gray beach,
With the thousand responsive songs at random,
My own songs awaked from that hour,
And with them the key, the word up from the waves,
The word of the sweetest song and all songs,
That strong and delicious word which, creeping to my feet,
(Or like some old crone rocking the cradle, swathed in sweet
    garments, bending aside,)
The sea whisper'd me.

AS I EBB'D WITH THE OCEAN OF LIFE[51]

– 1 –

As I ebb'd with the ocean of life,
As I wended the shores I know,
As I walk'd where the ripples continually wash you Paumanok,*
Where they rustle up hoarse and sibilant,

---

*Native American term for Long Island, the fish-shaped island where Whitman
was born. The poet later designates Paumanok as his male progenitor, and the sea
around it as his "mother."

Where the fierce old mother endlessly cries for her castaways,
I musing late in the autumn day, gazing off southward,
Held by this electric self out of the pride of which I utter
    poems,
Was seiz'd by the spirit that trails in the lines underfoot,
The rim, the sediment that stands for all the water and all the
    land of the globe.

Fascinated, my eyes reverting from the south, dropt, to follow
    those slender windrows,
Chaff, straw, splinters of wood, weeds, and the sea-gluten,
Scum, scales from shining rocks, leaves of salt-lettuce, left by the
    tide,
Miles walking, the sound of breaking waves the other side of me,
Paumanok there and then as I thought the old thought of
    likenesses,
These you presented to me you fish-shaped island,
As I wended the shores I know,
As I walk'd with that electric self seeking types.

— 2 —

As I wend to the shores I know not,
As I list to the dirge, the voices of men and women wreck'd,
As I inhale the impalpable breezes that set in upon me,
As the ocean so mysterious rolls toward me closer and closer,
I too but signify at the utmost a little wash'd up drift,
A few sands and dead leaves to gather,
Gather, and merge myself as part of the sands and drift.

O baffled, balk'd, bent to the very earth,
Oppress'd with myself that I have dared to open my mouth,
Aware now that amid all that blab whose echoes recoil upon me
    I have not once had the least idea who or what I am,
But that before all my arrogant poems the real Me stands yet
    untouch'd, untold, altogether unreach'd,
Withdrawn far, mocking me with mock-congratulatory signs
    and bows,

With peals of distant ironical laughter at every word I have
　　written,
Pointing in silence to these songs, and then to the sand beneath.

I perceive I have not really understood any thing, not a single
　　object, and that no man ever can,
Nature here in sight of the sea taking advantage of me to dart
　　upon me and sting me,
Because I have dared to open my mouth to sing at all.

— 3 —

You oceans both, I close with you,
We murmur alike reproachfully rolling sands and drift, knowing
　　not why,
These little shreds indeed standing for you and me and all.

You friable* shore with trails of debris,
You fish-shaped island, I take what is underfoot,
What is yours is mine my father.

I too Paumanok,
I too have bubbled up, floated the measureless float, and been
　　wash'd on your shores,
I too am but a trail of drift and debris,
I too leave little wrecks upon you, you fish-shaped island.

I throw myself upon your breast my father,
I cling to you so that you cannot unloose me,
I hold you so firm till you answer me something.

Kiss me my father,
Touch me with your lips as I touch those I love,
Breathe to me while I hold you close the secret of the murmuring
　　I envy.

*Brittle; easily crumbled; fragile.

– 4 –

Ebb, ocean of life, (the flow will return,)
Cease not your moaning you fierce old mother,
Endlessly cry for your castaways, but fear not, deny not me,
Rustle not up so hoarse and angry against my feet as I touch you
    or gather from you.

I mean tenderly by you and all,
I gather for myself and for this phantom looking down where we
    lead, and following me and mine.

Me and mine, loose windrows, little corpses,
Froth, snowy white, and bubbles,
(See, from my dead lips the ooze exuding at last,
See, the prismatic colors glistening and rolling,)
Tufts of straw, sands, fragments,
Buoy'd hither from many moods, one contradicting another,
From the storm, the long calm, the darkness, the swell,
Musing, pondering, a breath, a briny tear, a dab of liquid or soil,
Up just as much out of fathomless workings fermented and thrown,
A limp blossom or two, torn, just as much over waves floating,
    drifted at random,
Just as much for us that sobbing dirge of Nature,
Just as much whence we come that blare of the cloud-trumpets,
We, capricious, brought hither we know not whence, spread out
    before you,
You up there walking or sitting,
Whoever you are, we too lie in drifts at your feet.

TEARS

Tears! tears! tears!
In the night, in solitude, tears,
On the white shore dripping, dripping, suck'd in by the sand,
Tears, not a star shining, all dark and desolate,
Moist tears from the eyes of a muffled head;

O who is that ghost? that form in the dark, with tears?
What shapeless lump is that, bent, crouch'd there on the sand?
Streaming tears, sobbing tears, throes, choked with wild cries;
O storm, embodied, rising, careering with swift steps along the
　　beach!
O wild and dismal night storm, with wind—O belching and
　　desperate!
O shade so sedate and decorous by day, with calm countenance
　　and regulated pace,
But away at night as you fly, none looking—O then the
　　unloosen'd ocean,
Of tears! tears! tears!

TO THE MAN-OF-WAR-BIRD[52]

Thou who hast slept all night upon the storm,
Waking renew'd on thy prodigious pinions,
(Burst the wild storm? above it thou ascended'st,
And rested on the sky, thy slave that cradled thee,)
Now a blue point, far, far in heaven floating,
As to the light emerging here on deck I watch thee,
(Myself a speck, a point on the world's floating vast.)

Far, far at sea,
After the night's fierce drifts have strewn the shore with wrecks,
With re-appearing day as now so happy and serene,
The rosy and elastic dawn, the flashing sun,
The limpid spread of air cerulean,
Thou also re-appearest.

Thou born to match the gale, (thou art all wings,)
To cope with heaven and earth and sea and hurricane,
Thou ship of air that never furl'st thy sails,
Days, even weeks untired and onward, through spaces, realms
　　gyrating,
At dusk that look'st on Senegal, at morn America,
That sport'st amid the lightning-flash and thunder-cloud,

In them, in thy experiences, had'st thou my soul,
What joys! what joys were thine!

ABOARD AT A SHIP'S HELM

Aboard at a ship's helm,
A young steersman steering with care.

Through fog on a sea-coast dolefully ringing,
An ocean bell—O a warning bell, rock'd by the waves.

O you give good notice indeed, you bell by the sea-reefs ringing,
Ringing, ringing, to warn the ship from its wreck-place.

For as on the alert O steersman, you mind the loud admonition,
The bows turn, the freighted ship tacking speeds away under her
     gray sails,
The beautiful and noble ship with all her precious wealth speeds
     away gayly and safe.

But O the ship, the immortal ship! O ship aboard the ship!
Ship of the body, ship of the soul, voyaging, voyaging, voyaging.

ON THE BEACH AT NIGHT

On the beach at night,
Stands a child with her father,
Watching the east, the autumn sky.

Up through the darkness,
While ravening clouds, the burial clouds, in black masses spreading,
Lower sullen and fast athwart and down the sky,
Amid a transparent clear belt of ether yet left in the east,
Ascends large and calm the lord-star Jupiter,
And nigh at hand, only a very little above,
Swim the delicate sisters the Pleiades.

From the beach the child holding the hand of her father,
Those burial-clouds that lower victorious soon to devour all,
Watching, silently weeps.

Weep not, child,
Weep not, my darling,
With these kisses let me remove your tears,
The ravening clouds shall not long be victorious,
They shall not long possess the sky, they devour the stars only in
    apparition,
Jupiter shall emerge, be patient, watch again another night, the
    Pleiades shall emerge,
They are immortal, all those stars both silvery and golden shall
    shine out again,
The great stars and the little ones shall shine out again, they
    endure,
The vast immortal suns and the long-enduring pensive moons
    shall again shine.

Then dearest child mournest thou only for Jupiter?
Considerest thou alone the burial of the stars?

Something there is,
(With my lips soothing thee, adding I whisper,
I give thee the first suggestion, the problem and indirection,)
Something there is more immortal even than the stars,
(Many the burials, many the days and nights, passing away,)
Something that shall endure longer even than lustrous Jupiter,
Longer than sun or any revolving satellite,
Or the radiant sisters the Pleiades.

THE WORLD BELOW THE BRINE

The world below the brine,
Forests at the bottom of the sea, the branches and leaves,
Sea-lettuce, vast lichens, strange flowers and seeds, the thick
    tangle, openings, and pink turf,

Different colors, pale gray and green, purple, white, and gold, the
    play of light through the water,
Dumb swimmers there among the rocks, coral, gluten, grass,
    rushes, and the aliment of the swimmers,
Sluggish existences grazing there suspended, or slowly crawling
    close to the bottom,
The sperm-whale at the surface blowing air and spray, or
    disporting with his flukes,
The leaden-eyed shark, the walrus, the turtle, the hairy sea-
    leopard, and the sting-ray,
Passions there, wars, pursuits, tribes, sight in those ocean-depths,
    breathing that thick-breathing air, as so many do,
The change thence to the sight here, and to the subtle air
    breathed by beings like us who walk this sphere,
The change onward from ours to that of beings who walk other
    spheres.

ON THE BEACH AT NIGHT ALONE

On the beach at night alone,
As the old mother sways her to and fro singing her husky song,
As I watch the bright stars shining, I think a thought of the clef of
    the universes and of the future.[53]

A vast similitude interlocks all,
All spheres, grown, ungrown, small, large, suns, moons, planets,
All distances of place however wide,
All distances of time, all inanimate forms,
All souls, all living bodies though they be ever so different, or in
    different worlds,
All gaseous, watery, vegetable, mineral processes, the fishes, the
    brutes,
All nations, colors, barbarisms, civilizations, languages,
All identities that have existed or may exist on this globe, or any
    globe,
All lives and deaths, all of the past, present, future,
This vast similitude spans them, and always has spann'd,

And shall forever span them and compactly hold and enclose
    them.

SONG FOR ALL SEAS, ALL SHIPS

— 1 —

To-day a rude brief recitative,
Of ships sailing the seas, each with its special flag or ship-signal,
Of unnamed heroes in the ships—of waves spreading and
    spreading far as the eye can reach,
Of dashing spray, and the winds piping and blowing,
And out of these a chant for the sailors of all nations,
Fitful, like a surge.

Of sea-captains young or old, and the mates, and of all intrepid
    sailors,
Of the few, very choice, taciturn, whom fate can never surprise
    nor death dismay,
Pick'd sparingly without noise by thee old ocean, chosen by thee,
Thou sea that pickest and cullest the race in time, and unitest
    nations,
Suckled by thee, old husky nurse, embodying thee,
Indomitable, untamed as thee.

(Ever the heroes on water or on land, by ones or twos appearing,
Ever the stock preserv'd and never lost, though rare, enough for
    seed preserv'd.)

— 2 —

Flaunt out O sea your separate flags of nations!
Flaunt out visible as ever the various ship-signals!
But do you reserve especially for yourself and for the soul of man
    one flag above all the rest,
A spiritual woven signal for all nations, emblem of man elate
    above death,
Token of all brave captains and all intrepid sailors and mates,

And all that went down doing their duty,
Reminiscent of them, twined from all intrepid captains young
    or old,
A pennant universal, subtly waving all time, o'er all brave sailors,
All seas, all ships.

PATROLING BARNEGAT*

Wild, wild the storm, and the sea high running,
Steady the roar of the gale, with incessant undertone muttering,
Shouts of demoniac laughter fitfully piercing and pealing,
Waves, air, midnight, their savagest trinity lashing,
Out in the shadows there milk-white combs careering,
On beachy slush and sand spirts of snow fierce slanting,
Where through the murk the easterly death-wind breasting,
Through cutting swirl and spray watchful and firm advancing,
(That in the distance! is that a wreck? is the red signal flaring?)
Slush and sand of the beach tireless till daylight wending,
Steadily, slowly, through hoarse roar never remitting,
Along the midnight edge by those milk-white combs careering,
A group of dim, weird forms, struggling, the night confronting,
That savage trinity warily watching.

AFTER THE SEA-SHIP

After the sea-ship, after the whistling winds,
After the white-gray sails taut to their spars and ropes,
Below, a myriad myriad waves hastening, lifting up their necks,
Tending in ceaseless flow toward the track of the ship,
Waves of the ocean bubbling and gurgling, blithely prying,
Waves, undulating waves, liquid, uneven, emulous waves,
Toward that whirling current, laughing and buoyant, with curves,

---

*Barnegat is the name of a bay on the coast of New Jersey, east of Whitman's last
home in Camden.

Where the great vessel sailing and tacking displaced the surface,
Larger and smaller waves in the spread of the ocean yearnfully
    flowing,
The wake of the sea-ship after she passes, flashing and frolicsome
    under the sun,
A motley procession with many a fleck of foam and many
    fragments,
Following the stately and rapid ship, in the wake following.

BY THE ROADSIDE

A BOSTON BALLAD (1854)[54]

To get betimes in Boston town I rose this morning early,
Here's a good place at the corner, I must stand and see the show.

Clear the way there Jonathan!
Way for the President's marshal—way for the government
    cannon!
Way for the Federal foot and dragoons, (and the apparitions
    copiously tumbling.)

I love to look on the Stars and Stripes, I hope the fifes will play
    Yankee Doodle.
How bright shine the cutlasses of the foremost troops!
Every man holds his revolver, marching stiff through Boston
    town.

A fog follows, antiques of the same come limping,
Some appear wooden-legged, and some appear bandaged and
    bloodless.

Why this is indeed a show—it has called the dead out of the earth!
The old graveyards of the hills have hurried to see!
Phantoms! phantoms countless by flank and rear!
Cock'd hats of mothy mould—crutches made of mist!
Arms in slings—old men leaning on young men's shoulders.

What troubles you Yankee phantoms? what is all this chattering of
    bare gums?

Does the ague convulse your limbs? do you mistake your crutches
    for firelocks and level them?

If you blind your eyes with tears you will not see the President's
    marshal,
If you groan such groans you might balk the government cannon.

For shame old maniacs—bring down those toss'd arms, and let
    your white hair be,
Here gape your great grandsons, their wives gaze at them from the
    windows,
See how well dress'd, see how orderly they conduct themselves.

Worse and worse—can't you stand it? are you retreating?
Is this hour with the living too dead for you?

Retreat then—pell-mell!
To your graves—back—back to the hills old limpers!
I do not think you belong here anyhow.

But there is one thing that belongs here—shall I tell you what it
    is, gentlemen of Boston?

I will whisper it to the Mayor, he shall send a committee to
    England,
They shall get a grant from the Parliament, go with a cart to the
    royal vault,
Dig out King George's coffin, unwrap him quick from the grave-
    clothes, box up his bones for a journey,
Find a swift Yankee clipper—here is freight for you, black-bellied
    clipper,
Up with your anchor—shake out your sails—steer straight toward
    Boston bay.

Now call for the President's marshal again, bring out the
    government cannon,
Fetch home the roarers from Congress, make another procession,
    guard it with foot and dragoons.

This centre-piece for them;
Look, all orderly citizens—look from the windows, women!

The committee open the box, set up the regal ribs, glue those that
    will not stay,
Clap the skull on top of the ribs, and clap a crown on top of the
    skull.

You have got your revenge, old buster—the crown is come to its
    own, and more than its own.

Stick your hands in your pockets, Jonathan—you are a made man
    from this day,
You are mighty cute—and here is one of your bargains.

EUROPE, THE 72D AND 73D YEARS OF THESE STATES[55]

Suddenly out of its stale and drowsy lair, the lair of slaves,
Like lightning it le'pt forth half startled at itself,
Its feet upon the ashes and the rags, its hands tight to the throats
    of kings.

O hope and faith!
O aching dose of exiled patriots' lives!
O many a sicken'd heart!
Turn back unto this day and make yourselves afresh.

And you, paid to defile the People—you liars, mark!
Not for numberless agonies, murders, lusts,
For court thieving in its manifold mean forms, worming from his
    simplicity the poor man's wages,
For many a promise sworn by royal lips and broken and laugh'd at
    in the breaking,
Then in their power not for all these did the blows strike revenge,
    or the heads of the nobles fall;
The People scorn'd the ferocity of kings.

But the sweetness of mercy brew'd bitter destruction, and the
    frighten'd monarchs come back,
Each comes in state with his train, hangman, priest, tax-
    gatherer,
Soldier, lawyer, lord, jailer, and sycophant.

Yet behind all lowering stealing, lo, a shape,
Vague as the night, draped interminably, head, front and form, in
    scarlet folds,
Whose face and eyes none may see,
Out of its robes only this, the red robes lifted by the arm,
One finger crook'd pointed high over the top, like the head of a
    snake appears.

Meanwhile corpses lie in new-made graves, bloody corpses of
    young men,
The rope of the gibbet hangs heavily, the bullets of princes are
    flying, the creatures of power laugh aloud,
And all these things bear fruits, and they are good.

Those corpses of young men,
Those martyrs that hang from the gibbets, those hearts pierc'd by
    the gray lead,
Cold and motionless as they seem live elsewhere with
    unslaughter'd vitality.

They live in other young men O kings!
They live in brothers again ready to defy you,
They were purified by death, they were taught and exalted.

Not a grave of the murder'd for freedom but grows seed for
    freedom, in its turn to bear seed,
Which the winds carry afar and re-sow, and the rains and the
    snows nourish.

Not a disembodied spirit can the weapons of tyrants let loose,
But it stalks invisibly over the earth, whispering, counseling,
    cautioning.

Liberty, let others despair of you—I never despair of you.

Is the house shut? is the master away?
Nevertheless, be ready, be not weary of watching,
He will soon return, his messengers come anon.

A HAND-MIRROR[56]

Hold it up sternly—see this it sends back, (who is it? is it you?)
Outside fair costume, within ashes and filth,
No more a flashing eye, no more a sonorous voice or springy step,
Now some slave's eye, voice, hands, step,
A drunkard's breath, unwholesome eater's face, venerealee's
      flesh,
Lungs rotting away piecemeal, stomach sour and cankerous,
Joints rheumatic, bowels clogged with abomination,
Blood circulating dark and poisonous streams,
Words babble, hearing and touch callous,
No brain, no heart left, no magnetism of sex;
Such from one look in this looking-glass ere you go hence,
Such a result so soon—and from such a beginning!

GODS[57]

Lover divine and perfect Comrade,
Waiting content, invisible yet, but certain,
Be thou my God.

Thou, thou, the Ideal Man,
Fair, able, beautiful, content, and loving,
Complete in body and dilate in spirit,
Be thou my God.

O Death, (for Life has served its turn,)
Opener and usher to the heavenly mansion,
Be thou my God.

Aught, aught of mightiest, best I see, conceive, or know,
(To break the stagnant tie—thee, thee to free, O soul,)
Be thou my God.

All great ideas, the races' aspirations,
All heroisms, deeds of rapt enthusiasts,
Be ye my Gods.

Or Time and Space,
Or shape of Earth divine and wondrous,
Or some fair shape I viewing, worship,
Or lustrous orb of sun or star by night,
Be ye my Gods.

GERMS

Forms, qualities, lives, humanity, language, thoughts,
The ones known, and the ones unknown, the ones on the stars,
The stars themselves, some shaped, others unshaped,
Wonders as of those countries, the soil, trees, cities, inhabitants,
    whatever they may be,
Splendid suns, the moons and rings, the countless combinations
    and effects,
Such-like, and as good as such-like, visible here or anywhere,
    stand provided for in a handful of space, which I extend my
    arm and half enclose with my hand,
That containing the start of each and all, the virtue, the germs
    of all.

THOUGHTS

Of ownership—as if one fit to own things could not at pleasure
    enter upon all, and incorporate them into himself or herself;
Of vista—suppose some sight in arriere through the formative
    chaos, presuming the growth, fulness, life, now attain'd on
    the journey,

(But I see the road continued, and the journey ever continued;)
Of what was once lacking on earth, and in due time has become
    supplied—and of what will yet be supplied,
Because all I see and know I believe to have its main purport in
    what will yet be supplied.

WHEN I HEARD THE LEARN'D ASTRONOMER

When I heard the learn'd astronomer,
When the proofs, the figures, were ranged in columns
    before me,
When I was shown the charts and diagrams, to add, divide, and
    measure them,
When I sitting heard the astronomer where he lectured with
    much applause in the lecture-room,
How soon unaccountable I became tired and sick,
Till rising and gliding out I wander'd off by myself,
In the mystical moist night-air, and from time to time,
Look'd up in perfect silence at the stars.

PERFECTIONS

Only themselves understand themselves and the like of
    themselves,
As souls only understand souls.

O ME! O LIFE!

O me! O life! of the questions of these recurring,
Of the endless trains of the faithless, of cities fill'd with the
    foolish,
Of myself forever reproaching myself, (for who more foolish than
    I, and who more faithless?)
Of eyes that vainly crave the light, of the objects mean, of the
    struggle ever renew'd,

Of the poor results of all, of the plodding and sordid crowds I see
    around me,
Of the empty and useless years of the rest, with the rest me
    intertwined,
The question, O me! so sad, recurring—What good amid these,
    O me, O life?

Answer

That you are here—that life exists and identity,
That the powerful play goes on, and you may contribute
    a verse.

TO A PRESIDENT

All you are doing and saying is to America dangled mirages,
You have not learn'd of Nature—of the politics of Nature you
    have not learn'd the great amplitude, rectitude,
    impartiality,
You have not seen that only such as they are for these States,
And that what is less than they must sooner or later lift off from
    these States.

I SIT AND LOOK OUT

I sit and look out upon all the sorrows of the world, and upon all
    oppression and shame,
I hear secret convulsive sobs from young men at anguish with
    themselves, remorseful after deeds done,
I see in low life the mother misused by her children, dying,
    neglected, gaunt, desperate,
I see the wife misused by her husband, I see the treacherous
    seducer of young women,
I mark the ranklings of jealousy and unrequited love attempted to
    be hid, I see these sights on the earth,

I see the workings of battle, pestilence, tyranny, I see martyrs and
    prisoners,
I observe a famine at sea, I observe the sailors casting lots who
    shall be kill'd to preserve the lives of the rest,
I observe the slights and degradations cast by arrogant persons
    upon laborers, the poor, and upon negroes, and the like;
All these—all the meanness and agony without end I sitting look
    out upon,
See, hear, and am silent.

TO RICH GIVERS

What you give me I cheerfully accept,
A little sustenance, a hut and garden, a little money, as I
    rendezvous with my poems,
A traveler's lodging and breakfast as I journey through the
    States,—why should I be ashamed to own such gifts? why to
    advertise for them?
For I myself am not one who bestows nothing upon man and
    woman,
For I bestow upon any man or woman the entrance to all the gifts
    of the universe.

THE DALLIANCE OF THE EAGLES[58]

Skirting the river road, (my forenoon walk, my rest,)
Skyward in air a sudden muffled sound, the dalliance of
    the eagles,
The rushing amorous contact high in space together,
The clinching interlocking claws, a living, fierce, gyrating
    wheel,
Four beating wings, two beaks, a swirling mass tight grappling,
In tumbling turning clustering loops, straight downward
    falling,
Till o'er the river pois'd, the twain yet one, a moment's lull,

A motionless still balance in the air, then parting, talons
    loosing,
Upward again on slow-firm pinions slanting, their separate diverse
    flight,
She hers, he his, pursuing.

ROAMING IN THOUGHT[59]

(After reading HEGEL)

Roaming in thought over the Universe, I saw the little that is
    Good steadily hastening towards immortality,
And the vast all that is call'd Evil I saw hastening to merge itself
    and become lost and dead.

A FARM PICTURE

Through the ample open door of the peaceful country barn,
A sunlit pasture field with cattle and horses feeding,
And haze and vista, and the far horizon fading away.

A CHILD'S AMAZE

Silent and amazed even when a little boy,
I remember I heard the preacher every Sunday put God in his
    statements,
As contending against some being or influence.

THE RUNNER

On a flat road runs the well-train'd runner,
He is lean and sinewy with muscular legs,
He is thinly clothed, he leans forward as he runs,
With lightly closed fists and arms partially rais'd.

BEAUTIFUL WOMEN

Women sit or move to and fro, some old, some young,
The young are beautiful—but the old are more beautiful than the
young.

MOTHER AND BABE

I see the sleeping babe nestling the breast of its
mother,
The sleeping mother and babe—hush'd, I study them long
and long.

THOUGHT

Of obedience, faith, adhesiveness;
As I stand aloof and look there is to me something profoundly
affecting in large masses of men following the lead of those
who do not believe in men.

VISOR'D

A mask, a perpetual natural disguiser of herself,
Concealing her face, concealing her form,
Changes and transformations every hour, every moment,
Falling upon her even when she sleeps.

THOUGHT

Of Justice—as if Justice could be any thing but the same ample
law, expounded by natural judges and saviors,
As if it might be this thing or that thing, according to
decisions.

GLIDING O'ER ALL

Gliding o'er all, through all,
Through Nature, Time, and Space,
As a ship on the waters advancing,
The voyage of the soul—not life alone,
Death, many deaths I'll sing.

HAST NEVER COME TO THEE AN HOUR

Hast never come to thee an hour,
A sudden gleam divine, precipitating, bursting all these bubbles,
    fashions, wealth?
These eager business aims—books, politics, art, amours,
To utter nothingness?

THOUGHT

Of Equality—as if it harm'd me, giving others the same chances
    and rights as myself—as if it were not indispensable to my
    own rights that others possess the same.

TO OLD AGE

I see in you the estuary that enlarges and spreads itself grandly as
    it pours in the great sea.

LOCATIONS AND TIMES

Locations and times—what is it in me that meets them all,
    whenever and wherever, and makes me at home?
Forms, colors, densities, odors—what is it in me that corresponds
    with them?

OFFERINGS

A thousand perfect men and women appear,
Around each gathers a cluster of friends, and gay children and
    youths, with offerings.

TO THE STATES, TO IDENTIFY THE 16TH, 17TH, OR 18TH PRESIDENTIAD*

Why reclining, interrogating? why myself and all drowsing?
What deepening twilight—scum floating atop of the waters,
Who are they as bats and night-dogs askant in the capitol?
What a filthy Presidentiad! (O South, your torrid suns! O North,
    your arctic freezings!)
Are those really Congressmen? are those the great Judges? is that
    the President?
Then I will sleep awhile yet, for I see that these States sleep, for
    reasons;
(With gathering murk, with muttering thunder and lambent
    shoots we all duly awake,
South, North, East, West, inland and seaboard, we will surely
    awake.)

---

*The "16th, 17th, or 18th Presidentiad" refers to the terms of Millard Fillmore, Franklin Pierce, and James Buchanan (see endnote 3 to the First Edition).

DRUM-TAPS[60]

FIRST O SONGS FOR A PRELUDE

First O songs for a prelude,
Lightly strike on the stretch'd tympanum pride and joy in my city,
How she led the rest to arms, how she gave the cue,
How at once with lithe limbs unwaiting a moment she sprang,
(O superb! O Manhattan, my own, my peerless!
O strongest you in the hour of danger, in crisis! O truer than steel!)
How you sprang—how you threw off the costumes of peace with
      indifferent hand,
How your soft opera-music changed, and the drum and fife were
      heard in their stead,
How you led to the war, (that shall serve for our prelude, songs of
      soldiers,)
How Manhattan drum-taps led.

Forty years had I in my city seen soldiers parading,
Forty years as a pageant, till unawares the lady of this teeming and
      turbulent city,
Sleepless amid her ships, her houses, her incalculable wealth,
With her million children around her, suddenly,
At dead of night, at news from the south,
Incens'd struck with clinch'd hand the pavement.

A shock electric, the night sustain'd it,
Till with ominous hum our hive at daybreak pour'd out its myriads.

From the houses then and the workshops, and through all the
      doorways,
Leapt they tumultuous, and lo! Manhattan arming.

To the drum-taps prompt,
The young men falling in and arming,
The mechanics arming, (the trowel, the jack-plane, the black-
smith's hammer, tost aside with precipitation,)
The lawyer leaving his office and arming, the judge leaving the
court,
The driver deserting his wagon in the street, jumping down,
throwing the reins abruptly down on the horses' backs,
The salesman leaving the store, the boss, book-keeper, porter, all
leaving;
Squads gather everywhere by common consent and arm,
The new recruits, even boys, the old men show them how to wear
their accoutrements, they buckle the straps carefully,
Outdoors arming, indoors arming, the flash of the musket-
barrels,
The white tents cluster in camps, the arm'd sentries around, the
sunrise cannon and again at sunset,
Arm'd regiments arrive every day, pass through the city, and
embark from the wharves,
(How good they look as they tramp down to the river, sweaty, with
their guns on their shoulders!
How I love them! how I could hug them, with their brown faces
and their clothes and knapsacks cover'd with dust!)
The blood of the city up—arm'd! arm'd! the cry
everywhere,
The flags flung out from the steeples of churches and from all the
public buildings and stores,
The tearful parting, the mother kisses her son, the son kisses his
mother,
(Loth is the mother to part, yet not a word does she speak to
detain him,)
The tumultuous escort, the ranks of policemen preceding,
clearing the way,
The unpent enthusiasm, the wild cheers of the crowd for their
favorites,
The artillery, the silent cannons bright as gold, drawn along,
rumble lightly over the stones,
(Silent cannons, soon to cease your silence,

Soon unlimber'd to begin the red business;)
All the mutter of preparation, all the determin'd arming,
The hospital service, the lint, bandages and medicines,
The women volunteering for nurses, the work begun for in
    earnest, no mere parade now;
War! an arm'd race is advancing! the welcome for battle, no
    turning away;
War! be it weeks, months, or years, an arm'd race is advancing to
    welcome it.

Mannahatta a-march—and it's O to sing it well!
It's O for a manly life in the camp.

And the sturdy artillery,
The guns bright as gold, the work for giants, to serve well the guns,
Unlimber them! (no more as the past forty years for salutes for
    courtesies merely,
Put in something now besides powder and wadding.)

And you lady of ships, you Mannahatta,
Old matron of this proud, friendly, turbulent city,
Often in peace and wealth you were pensive or covertly frown'd
    amid all your children,
But now you smile with joy exulting old Mannahatta.

EIGHTEEN SIXTY-ONE*

Arm'd year—year of the struggle,
No dainty rhymes or sentimental love verses for you terrible year,
Not you as some pale poetling seated at a desk lisping cadenzas
    piano,
But as a strong man erect, clothed in blue clothes, advancing,
    carrying a rifle on your shoulder,

---

*The poem's title was originally set in numerals ("1861"). Whitman often recalled hearing about the attack at Fort Sumter after attending a performance at New York's Academy of Music on April 13, 1861.

With well-gristled body and sunburnt face and hands, with a knife
  in the belt at your side,
As I heard you shouting loud, your sonorous voice ringing across
  the continent,
Your masculine voice O year, as rising amid the great cities,
Amid the men of Manhattan I saw you as one of the workmen,
  the dwellers in Manhattan,
Or with large steps crossing the prairies out of Illinois and
  Indiana,
Rapidly crossing the West with springy gait and descending the
  Alleghanies,
Or down from the great lakes or in Pennsylvania, or on deck
  along the Ohio river,
Or southward along the Tennessee or Cumberland rivers, or at
  Chattanooga on the mountain top,
Saw I your gait and saw I your sinewy limbs clothed in blue,
  bearing weapons, robust year,
Heard your determin'd voice launch'd forth again and again,
Year that suddenly sang by the mouths of the round-lipp'd
  cannon,
I repeat you, hurrying, crashing, sad, distracted year.

BEAT! BEAT! DRUMS!

Beat! beat! drums!—blow! bugles! blow!
Through the windows—through doors—burst like a ruthless force,
Into the solemn church, and scatter the congregation,
Into the school where the scholar is studying;
Leave not the bridegroom quiet—no happiness must he have now
  with his bride,
Nor the peaceful farmer any peace, ploughing his field or
  gathering his grain,
So fierce you whirr and pound you drums—so shrill you bugles
  blow.

Beat! beat! drums!—blow! bugles! blow!
Over the traffic of cities—over the rumble of wheels in the streets;

Are beds prepared for sleepers at night in the houses? no sleepers
　　must sleep in those beds,
No bargainers' bargains by day—no brokers or speculators—
　　would they continue?
Would the talkers be talking? would the singer attempt to
　　sing?
Would the lawyer rise in the court to state his case before the
　　judge?
Then rattle quicker, heavier drums—you bugles wilder blow.

Beat! beat! drums!—blow! bugles! blow!
Make no parley—stop for no expostulation,
Mind not the timid—mind not the weeper or prayer,
Mind not the old man beseeching the young man,
Let not the child's voice be heard, nor the mother's entreaties,
Make even the trestles to shake the dead where they lie awaiting
　　the hearses,
So strong you thump O terrible drums—so loud you bugles
　　blow.

FROM PAUMANOK STARTING I FLY LIKE A BIRD

From Paumanok starting I fly like a bird,
Around and around to soar to sing the idea of all,
To the north betaking myself to sing there arctic songs,
To Kanada till I absorb Kanada in myself, to Michigan then,
To Wisconsin, Iowa, Minnesota, to sing their songs, (they are
　　inimitable;)
Then to Ohio and Indiana to sing theirs, to Missouri and Kansas
　　and Arkansas to sing theirs,
To Tennessee and Kentucky, to the Carolinas and Georgia to sing
　　theirs,
To Texas and so along up toward California, to roam accepted
　　everywhere;
To sing first, (to the tap of the war-drum if need be,)
The idea of all, of the Western world one and inseparable,
And then the song of each member of these States.

SONG OF THE BANNER AT DAYBREAK[61]

Poet

O a new song, a free song,
Flapping, flapping, flapping, flapping, by sounds, by voices clearer,
By the wind's voice and that of the drum,
By the banner's voice and child's voice and sea's voice and father's
     voice,
Low on the ground and high in the air,
On the ground where father and child stand,
In the upward air where their eyes turn,
Where the banner at daybreak is flapping.

Words! book-words! what are you?
Words no more, for hearken and see,
My song is there in the open air, and I must sing,
With the banner and pennant a-flapping.

I'll weave the chord and twine in,
Man's desire and babe's desire, I'll twine them in, I'll put in life,
I'll put the bayonet's flashing point, I'll let bullets and slugs
     whizz,
(As one carrying a symbol and menace far into the future,
Crying with trumpet voice, *Arouse and beware! Beware and
     arouse!*)
I'll pour the verse with streams of blood, full of volition, full
     of joy,
Then loosen, launch forth, to go and compete,
With the banner and pennant a-flapping.

Pennant

Come up here, bard, bard,
Come up here, soul, soul,
Come up here, dear little child,
To fly in the clouds and winds with me, and play with the
     measureless light.

Child

Father what is that in the sky beckoning to me with long
    finger?
And what does it say to me all the while?

Father

Nothing my babe you see in the sky,
And nothing at all to you it says—but look you my babe,
Look at these dazzling things in the houses, and see you the
    money-shops opening,
And see you the vehicles preparing to crawl along the streets with
    goods;
These, ah these, how valued and toil'd for these!
How envied by all the earth.

Poet

Fresh and rosy red the sun is mounting high,
On floats the sea in distant blue careering through its channels,
On floats the wind over the breast of the sea setting in toward
    land,
The great steady wind from west or west-by-south,
Floating so buoyant with milk-white foam on the waters.

But I am not the sea nor the red sun,
I am not the wind with girlish laughter,
Not the immense wind which strengthens, not the wind which
    lashes,
Not the spirit that ever lashes its own body to terror and death,
But I am that which unseen comes and sings, sings, sings,
Which babbles in brooks and scoots in showers on the land,
Which the birds know in the woods mornings and evenings,
And the shore-sands know and the hissing wave, and that banner
    and pennant,
Aloft there flapping and flapping.

Child

O father it is alive—it is full of people—it has children,
O now it seems to me it is talking to its children,
I hear it—it talks to me—O it is wonderful!
O it stretches—it spreads and runs so fast—O my father,
It is so broad it covers the whole sky.

Father

Cease, cease, my foolish babe,
What you are saying is sorrowful to me, much it displeases me;
Behold with the rest again I say, behold not banners and pennants
     aloft,
But the well-prepared pavements behold, and mark the solid-
     wall'd houses.

Banner and Pennant

Speak to the child O bard out of Manhattan,
To our children all, or north or south of Manhattan,
Point this day, leaving all the rest, to us over all—and yet we know
     not why,
For what are we, mere strips of cloth profiting nothing,
Only flapping in the wind?

Poet

I hear and see not strips of cloth alone,
I hear the tramp of armies, I hear the challenging sentry,
I hear the jubilant shouts of millions of men, I hear Liberty!
I hear the drums beat and the trumpets blowing,
I myself move abroad swift-rising flying then,
I use the wings of the land-bird and use the wings of the sea-bird,
     and look down as from a height,
I do not deny the precious results of peace, I see populous cities
     with wealth incalculable,

I see numberless farms, I see the farmers working in their fields or
    barns,
I see mechanics working, I see buildings everywhere founded,
    going up, or finish'd,
I see trains of cars swiftly speeding along railroad tracks drawn by
    the locomotives,
I see the stores, depots, of Boston, Baltimore, Charleston, New
    Orleans,
I see far in the West the immense area of grain, I dwell awhile
    hovering,
I pass to the lumber forests of the North, and again to the
    Southern plantation, and again to California;
Sweeping the whole I see the countless profit, the busy
    gatherings, earn'd wages,
See the Identity formed out of thirty-eight spacious and haughty
    States, (and many more to come,)
See forts on the shores of harbors, see ships sailing in and out;
Then over all, (aye! aye!) my little and lengthen'd pennant shaped
    like a sword,
Runs swiftly up indicating war and defiance—and now the
    halyards have rais'd it,
Side of my banner broad and blue, side of my starry banner,
Discarding peace over all the sea and land.

Banner and Pennant

Yet louder, higher, stronger, bard! yet farther, wider cleave!
No longer let our children deem us riches and peace alone,
We may be terror and carnage, and are so now,
Not now are we any one of these spacious and haughty States,
    (nor any five, nor ten,)
Nor market nor depot we, nor money-bank in the city,
But these and all, and the brown and spreading land, and the
    mines below, are ours,
And the shores of the sea are ours, and the rivers great and
    small,
And the fields they moisten, and the crops and the fruits
    are ours,

Bays and channels and ships sailing in and out are ours—while
    we over all,
Over the area spread below, the three or four millions of square
    miles, the capitals,
The forty millions of people,—O bard! in life and death supreme,
We, even we, henceforth flaunt out masterful, high up above,
Not for the present alone, for a thousand years chanting through
    you,
This song to the soul of one poor little child.

Child

O my father I like not the houses,
They will never to me be any thing, nor do I like money,
But to mount up there I would like, O father dear, that banner
    I like,
That pennant I would be and must be.

Father

Child of mine you fill me with anguish,
To be that pennant would be too fearful,
Little you know what it is this day, and after this day, forever,
It is to gain nothing, but risk and defy every thing,
Forward to stand in front of wars—and O, such wars!—what have
    you to do with them?
With passions of demons, slaughter, premature death?

Banner

Demons and death then I sing,
Put in all, aye all will I, sword-shaped pennant for war,
And a pleasure new and ecstatic, and the prattled yearning of
    children,
Blent with the sounds of the peaceful land and the liquid wash of
    the sea,
And the black ships fighting on the sea envelop'd in smoke,
And the icy cool of the far, far north, with rustling cedars and pines,

And the whirr of drums and the sound of soldiers marching, and
    the hot sun shining south,
And the beach-waves combing over the beach on my Eastern
    shore, and my Western shore the same,
And all between those shores, and my ever running Mississippi
    with bends and chutes,
And my Illinois fields, and my Kansas fields, and my fields of
    Missouri,
The Continent, devoting the whole identity without reserving an
    atom,
Pour in! whelm that which asks, which sings, with all and the
    yield of all,
Fusing and holding, claiming, devouring the whole,
No more with tender lip, nor musical labial sound,
But out of the night emerging for good, our voice persuasive no
    more,
Croaking like crows here in the wind.

Poet

My limbs, my veins dilate, my theme is clear at last,
Banner so broad advancing out of the night, I sing you haughty
    and resolute,
I burst through where I waited long, too long, deafen'd and
    blinded,
My hearing and tongue are come to me, (a little child taught me,)
I hear from above O pennant of war your ironical call and demand,
Insensate! insensate! (yet I at any rate chant you,) O banner!
Not houses of peace indeed are you, nor any nor all their
    prosperity, (if need be, you shall again have every one of
    those houses to destroy them,
You thought not to destroy those valuable houses, standing fast,
    full of comfort, built with money,
May they stand fast, then? not an hour except you above them
    and all stand fast;)
O banner, not money so precious are you, not farm produce you,
    nor the material good nutriment,
Nor excellent stores, nor landed on wharves from the ships,

Not the superb ships with sail-power or steam-power, fetching and
    carrying cargoes,
Nor machinery, vehicles, trade, nor revenues—but you as
    henceforth I see you,
Running up out of the night, bringing your cluster of stars, (ever
    enlarging stars,)
Divider of daybreak you, cutting the air, touch'd by the sun,
    measuring the sky,
(Passionately seen and yearn'd for by one poor little child,
While others remain busy or smartly talking, forever teaching
    thrift, thrift;)
O you up there! O pennant! where you undulate like a snake
    hissing so curious,
Out of reach, an idea only, yet furiously fought for, risking bloody
    death, loved by me,
So loved—O you banner leading the day with stars brought from
    the night!
Valueless, object of eyes, over all and demanding all—(absolute
    owner of all)—O banner and pennant!
I too leave the rest—great as it is, it is nothing—houses, machines
    are nothing—I see them not,
I see but you, O warlike pennant! O banner so broad, with stripes,
    I sing you only,
Flapping up there in the wind.

RISE O DAYS FROM YOUR FATHOMLESS DEEPS

— 1 —

Rise O days from your fathomless deeps, till you loftier, fiercer
    sweep,
Long for my soul hungering gymnastic I devour'd what the earth
    gave me,
Long I roam'd the woods of the north, long I watch'd Niagara
    pouring,
I travel'd the prairies over and slept on their breast, I cross'd the
    Nevadas, I cross'd the plateaus,

I ascended the towering rocks along the Pacific, I sail'd out
    to sea,
I sail'd through the storm, I was refresh'd by the storm,
I watch'd with joy the threatening maws of the waves,
I mark'd the white combs where they career'd so high, curling
    over,
I heard the wind piping, I saw the black clouds,
Saw from below what arose and mounted, (O superb! O wild as
    my heart, and powerful!)
Heard the continuous thunder as it bellow'd after the lightning,
Noted the slender and jagged threads of lightning as sudden
    and fast amid the din they chased each other across
    the sky;
These, and such as these, I, elate, saw—saw with wonder, yet
    pensive and masterful,
All the menacing might of the globe uprisen around me,
Yet there with my soul I fed, I fed content, supercilious.

— 2 —

'Twas well, O soul—'twas a good preparation you gave me,
Now we advance our latent and ampler hunger to fill,
Now we go forth to receive what the earth and the sea never
    gave us,
Not through the mighty woods we go, but through the mightier
    cities,
Something for us is pouring now more than Niagara pouring,
Torrents of men, (sources and rills of the Northwest are you
    indeed inexhaustible?)
What, to pavements and homesteads here, what were those storms
    of the mountains and sea?
What, to passions I witness around me to-day? was the sea
    risen?
Was the wind piping the pipe of death under the black clouds?
Lo! from deeps more unfathomable, something more deadly and
    savage,
Manhattan rising, advancing with menacing front—Cincinnati,
    Chicago, unchain'd;

What was that swell I saw on the ocean? behold what comes
    here,
How it climbs with daring feet and hands—how it dashes!
How the true thunder bellows after the lightning—how bright the
    flashes of lightning!
How Democracy with desperate vengeful port strides on, shown
    through the dark by those flashes of lightning!
(Yet a mournful wail and low sob I fancied I heard through the
    dark,
In a lull of the deafening confusion.)

– 3 –

Thunder on! stride on, Democracy! strike with vengeful stroke!
And do you rise higher than ever yet O days, O cities!
Crash heavier, heavier yet O storms! you have done me good,
My soul prepared in the mountains absorbs your immortal strong
    nutriment,
Long had I walk'd my cities, my country roads through farms,
    only half satisfied,
One doubt nauseous undulating like a snake, crawl'd on the
    ground before me,
Continually preceding my steps, turning upon me oft, ironically
    hissing low;
The cities I loved so well I abandon'd and left, I sped to the
    certainties suitable to me,
Hungering, hungering, hungering, for primal energies and
    Nature's dauntlessness,
I refresh'd myself with it only, I could relish it only,
I waited the bursting forth of the pent fire—on the water and air I
    waited long;
But now I no longer wait, I am fully satisfied, I am glutted,
I have witness'd the true lightning, I have witness'd my cities
    electric,
I have lived to behold man burst forth and warlike America rise,
Hence I will seek no more the food of the northern solitary
    wilds,
No more the mountains roam or sail the stormy sea.

VIRGINIA—THE WEST

The noble sire fallen on evil days,
I saw with hand uplifted, menacing, brandishing,
(Memories of old in abeyance, love and faith in abeyance,)
The insane knife toward the Mother of All.

The noble son on sinewy feet advancing,
I saw, out of the land of prairies, land of Ohio's waters and of
    Indiana,
To the rescue the stalwart giant hurry his plenteous offspring,
Drest in blue, bearing their trusty rifles on their shoulders.

Then the Mother of All with calm voice speaking,
As to you Rebellious, (I seemed to hear her say,) why strive
    against me, and why seek my life?
When you yourself forever provide to defend me?
For you provided me Washington—and now these also.

CITY OF SHIPS[62]

City of ships!
(O the black ships! O the fierce ships!
O the beautiful sharp-bow'd steam-ships and sail-ships!)
City of the world! (for all races are here,
All the lands of the earth make contributions here;)
City of the sea! city of hurried and glittering tides!
City whose gleeful tides continually rush or recede, whirling in
    and out with eddies and foam!
City of wharves and stores—city of tall façades of marble and iron!
Proud and passionate city—mettlesome, mad, extravagant city!
Spring up O city—not for peace alone, but be indeed yourself,
    warlike!
Fear not—submit to no models but your own O city!
Behold me—incarnate me as I have incarnated you!
I have rejected nothing you offer'd me—whom you adopted
  ·   I have adopted,

Good or bad I never question you—I love all—I do not condemn
    any thing,
I chant and celebrate all that is yours—yet peace no more,
In peace I chanted peace, but now the drum of war is mine,
War, red war is my song through your streets, O city!

THE CENTENARIAN'S STORY[63]

*(Volunteer of 1861–2, at Washington Park, Brooklyn, assisting the
Centenarian.)*

Give me your hand old Revolutionary,
The hill-top is nigh, but a few steps, (make room gentlemen,)
Up the path you have follow'd me well, spite of your hundred and
    extra years,
You can walk old man, though your eyes are almost done,
Your faculties serve you, and presently I must have them serve me.

Rest, while I tell what the crowd around us means,
On the plain below recruits are drilling and exercising,
There is the camp, one regiment departs to-morrow,
Do you hear the officers giving their orders?
Do you hear the clank of the muskets?

Why what comes over you now old man?
Why do you tremble and clutch my hand so convulsively?
The troops are but drilling, they are yet surrounded with smiles,
Around them at hand the well-drest friends and the women,
While splendid and warm the afternoon sun shines down,
Green the midsummer verdure and fresh blows the dallying breeze,
O'er proud and peaceful cities and arm of the sea between.

But drill and parade are over, they march back to quarters,
Only hear that approval of hands! hear what a clapping!

As wending the crowds now part and disperse—but we old man,
Not for nothing have I brought you hither—we must remain,
You to speak in your turn, and I to listen and tell.

The Centenarian

When I clutch'd your hand it was not with terror,
But suddenly pouring about me here on every side,
And below there where the boys were drilling, and up the slopes
    they ran,
And where tents are pitch'd, and wherever you see south and
    south-east and south-west,
Over hills, across lowlands, and in the skirts of woods,
And along the shores, in mire (now fill'd over) came again and
    suddenly raged,
As eighty-five years a-gone no mere parade receiv'd with applause
    of friends,
But a battle which I took part in myself—aye, long ago as it is, I
    took part in it,
Walking then this hilltop, this same ground.

Aye, this is the ground,
My blind eyes even as I speak behold it re-peopled
    from graves,
The years recede, pavements and stately houses disappear,
Rude forts appear again, the old hoop'd guns are mounted,
I see the lines of rais'd earth stretching from river to bay,
I mark the vista of waters, I mark the uplands and slopes;
Here we lay encamp'd, it was this time in summer also.

As I talk I remember all, I remember the Declaration,
It was read here, the whole army paraded, it was read to us
    here,
By his staff surrounded the General stood in the middle, he held
    up his unsheath'd sword,
It glitter'd in the sun in full sight of the army.

'Twas a bold act then—the English war-ships had just arrived,
We could watch down the lower bay where they lay at anchor,
And the transports swarming with soldiers.

A few days more and they landed, and then the battle.

Twenty thousand were brought against us,
A veteran force furnish'd with good artillery.

I tell not now the whole of the battle,
But one brigade early in the forenoon order'd forward to engage
    the red-coats,
Of that brigade I tell, and how steadily it march'd,
And how long and well it stood confronting death.

Who do you think that was marching steadily sternly confronting
    death?
It was the brigade of the youngest men, two thousand strong,
Rais'd in Virginia and Maryland, and most of them known
    personally to the General.

Jauntily forward they went with quick step toward Gowanus' waters,
Till of a sudden unlook'd for by defiles through the woods, gain'd
    at night,
The British advancing, rounding in from the east, fiercely playing
    their guns,
That brigade of the youngest was cut off and at the enemy's mercy.

The General watch'd them from this hill,
They made repeated desperate attempts to burst their environment,
Then drew close together, very compact, their flag flying in the
    middle,
But O from the hills how the cannon were thinning and thinning
    them!

It sickens me yet, that slaughter!
I saw the moisture gather in drops on the face of the General.
I saw how he wrung his hands in anguish.

Meanwhile the British manœuvr'd to draw us out for a pitch'd battle,
But we dared not trust the chances of a pitch'd battle.

We fought the fight in detachments,
Sallying forth we fought at several points, but in each the luck
    was against us,

Our foe advancing, steadily getting the best of it, push'd us back
    to the works on this hill,
Till we turn'd menacing here, and then he left us.

That was the going out of the brigade of the youngest men, two
    thousand strong,
Few return'd, nearly all remain in Brooklyn.

That and here my General's first battle,
No women looking on nor sunshine to bask in, it did not
    conclude with applause,
Nobody clapp'd hands here then.

But in darkness in mist on the ground under a chill rain,
Wearied that night we lay foil'd and sullen,
While scornfully laugh'd many an arrogant lord off against us
    encamp'd,
Quite within hearing, feasting, clinking wineglasses together over
    their victory.

So dull and damp and another day,
But the night of that, mist lifting, rain ceasing,
Silent as a ghost while they thought they were sure of him, my
    General retreated.

I saw him at the river-side,
Down by the ferry lit by torches, hastening the embarcation;
My General waited till the soldiers and wounded were all pass'd
    over,
And then, (it was just ere sunrise,) these eyes rested on him for
    the last time.

Every one else seem'd fill'd with gloom,
Many no doubt thought of capitulation.

But when my General pass'd me,
As he stood in his boat and look'd toward the coming sun,
I saw something different from capitulation.

Terminus

Enough, the Centenarian's story ends,
The two, the past and present, have interchanged,
I myself as connecter, as chansonnier of a great future, am now
    speaking.

And is this the ground Washington trod?
And these waters I listlessly daily cross, are these the waters he
    cross'd,
As resolute in defeat as other generals in their proudest triumphs?

I must copy the story, and send it eastward and westward,
I must preserve that look as it beam'd on you rivers of Brooklyn.

See—as the annual round returns the phantoms return,
It is the 27th of August and the British have landed,
The battle begins and goes against us, behold through the smoke
    Washington's face,
The brigade of Virginia and Maryland have march'd forth to
    intercept the enemy,
They are cut off, murderous artillery from the hills plays upon
    them,
Rank after rank falls, while over them silently droops the flag,
Baptized that day in many a young man's bloody wounds,
In death, defeat, and sisters', mothers' tears.

Ah, hills and slopes of Brooklyn! I perceive you are more valuable
    than your owners supposed;
In the midst of you stands an encampment very old,
Stands forever the camp of that dead brigade.

CAVALRY CROSSING A FORD

A line in long array where they wind betwixt green islands,
They take a serpentine course, their arms flash in the sun—hark
    to the musical clank,

Behold the silvery river, in it the splashing horses loitering stop to
    drink,
Behold the brown-faced men, each group, each person a picture,
    the negligent rest on the saddles,
Some emerge on the opposite bank, others are just entering the
    ford—while,
Scarlet and blue and snowy white,
The guidon flags flutter gayly in the wind.

BIVOUAC ON A MOUNTAIN SIDE*

I see before me now a traveling army halting,
Below a fertile valley spread, with barns and the orchards of
    summer,
Behind, the terraced sides of a mountain, abrupt, in places rising
    high,
Broken, with rocks, with clinging cedars, with tall shapes dingily
    seen,
The numerous camp-fires scatter'd near and far, some away up on
    the mountain,
The shadowy forms of men and horses, looming, large-sized,
    flickering,
And over all the sky—the sky! far, far out of reach, studded,
    breaking out, the eternal stars.

AN ARMY CORPS ON THE MARCH

With its cloud of skirmishers in advance,
With now the sound of a single shot snapping like a whip, and
    now an irregular volley,
The swarming ranks press on and on, the dense brigades
    press on,
Glittering dimly, toiling under the sun—the dust-cover'd men,

---

*A "bivouac" is a temporary encampment, often in the open.

In columns rise and fall to the undulations of the ground,
With artillery interspers'd—the wheels rumble, the horses sweat,
As the army corps advances.

BY THE BIVOUAC'S FITFUL FLAME

By the bivouac's fitful flame,
A procession winding around me, solemn and sweet and slow—
    but first I note,
The tents of the sleeping army, the fields' and woods' dim
    outline,
The darkness lit by spots of kindled fire, the silence,
Like a phantom far or near an occasional figure moving,
The shrubs and trees, (as I lift my eyes they seem to be stealthily
    watching me,)
While wind in procession thoughts, O tender and wondrous
    thoughts,
Of life and death, of home and the past and loved, and of those
    that are far away;
A solemn and slow procession there as I sit on the ground,
By the bivouac's fitful flame.

COME UP FROM THE FIELDS FATHER

Come up from the fields father, here's a letter from our Pete,
And come to the front door mother, here's a letter from thy dear
    son.

Lo, 'tis autumn,
Lo, where the trees, deeper green, yellower and redder,
Cool and sweeten Ohio's villages with leaves fluttering in the
    moderate wind,
Where apples ripe in the orchards hang and grapes on the trellis'd
    vines,
(Smell you the smell of the grapes on the vines?
Smell you the buckwheat where the bees were lately buzzing?)

Above all, lo, the sky so calm, so transparent after the rain, and
    with wondrous clouds,
Below too, all calm, all vital and beautiful, and the farm prospers
    well.

Down in the fields all prospers well,
But now from the fields come father, come at the daughter's call,
And come to the entry mother, to the front door come right
    away.

Fast as she can she hurries, something ominous, her steps
    trembling,
She does not tarry to smooth her hair nor adjust her cap.

Open the envelope quickly,
O this is not our son's writing, yet his name is sign'd,
O a strange hand writes for our dear son, O stricken mother's
    soul!
All swims before her eyes, flashes with black, she catches the
    main words only,
Sentences broken, *gunshot wound in the breast, cavalry skirmish,*
    taken to hospital.
At present low, but will soon be better.

Ah now the single figure to me,
Amid all teeming and wealthy Ohio with all its cities and farms,
Sickly white in the face and dull in the head, very faint,
By the jamb of a door leans.

Grieve not so, dear mother, (the just-grown daughter speaks
    through her sobs,
The little sisters huddle around speechless and dismay'd,)
See, dearest mother, the letter says Pete will soon be better.

Alas poor boy, he will never be better, (nor may-be needs to be
    better, that brave and simple soul,)
While they stand at home at the door he is dead already,
The only son is dead.

But the mother needs to be better,
She with thin form presently drest in black,
By day her meals untouch'd, then at night fitfully sleeping, often
    waking,
In the midnight waking, weeping, longing with one deep
    longing,
O that she might withdraw unnoticed, silent from life escape and
    withdraw,
To follow, to seek, to be with her dear dead son.

VIGIL STRANGE I KEPT ON THE FIELD
ONE NIGHT

Vigil strange I kept on the field one night;
When you my son and my comrade dropt at my side that day,
One look I but gave which your dear eyes return'd with a look I
    shall never forget,
One touch of your hand to mine O boy, reach'd up as you lay on
    the ground,
Then onward I sped in the battle, the even-contested battle,
Till late in the night reliev'd to the place at last again I made my
    way,
Found you in death so cold dear comrade, found your body son
    of responding kisses, (never again on earth responding,)
Bared your face in the starlight, curious the scene, cool blew the
    moderate night-wind,
Long there and then in vigil I stood, dimly around me the battle-
    field spreading,
Vigil wondrous and vigil sweet there in the fragrant silent night,
But not a tear fell, not even a long-drawn sigh, long, long I gazed,
Then on the earth partially reclining sat by your side leaning my
    chin in my hands,
Passing sweet hours, immortal and mystic hours with you dearest
    comrade— not a tear, not a word,
Vigil of silence, love and death, vigil for you my son and my
    soldier,
As onward silently stars aloft, eastward new ones upward stole,

Vigil final for you brave boy, (I could not save you, swift was your
     death,
I faithfully loved you and cared for you living, I think we shall
     surely meet again,)
Till at latest lingering of the night, indeed just as the dawn
     appear'd,
My comrade I wrapt in his blanket, envelop'd well his form,
Folded the blanket well, tucking it carefully over head and
     carefully under feet,
And there and then and bathed by the rising sun, my son in his
     grave, in his rude-dug grave I deposited,
Ending my vigil strange with that, vigil of night and battle-field dim,
Vigil for boy of responding kisses, (never again on earth
     responding,)
Vigil for comrade swiftly slain, vigil I never forget, how as day
     brighten'd,
I rose from the chill ground and folded my soldier well in his
     blanket,
And buried him where he fell.

A MARCH IN THE RANKS HARD-PREST, AND THE ROAD UNKNOWN

A march in the ranks hard-prest, and the road unknown,
A route through a heavy wood with muffled steps in the darkness,
Our army foil'd with loss severe, and the sullen remnant
     retreating,
Till after midnight glimmer upon us the lights of a dim-lighted
     building,
We come to an open space in the woods, and halt by the dim-
     lighted building,
'Tis a large old church at the crossing roads, now an impromptu
     hospital,
Entering but for a minute I see a sight beyond all the pictures and
     poems ever made,
Shadows of deepest, deepest black, just lit by moving candles and
     lamps,

And by one great pitchy torch stationary with wild red flame and
    clouds of smoke,
By these, crowds, groups of forms vaguely I see on the floor, some
    in the pews laid down,
At my feet more distinctly a soldier, a mere lad, in danger of
    bleeding to death, (he is shot in the abdomen,)
I stanch the blood temporarily, (the youngster's face is white as
    a lily,)
Then before I depart I sweep my eyes o'er the scene fain to
    absorb it all,
Faces, varieties, postures beyond description, most in obscurity,
    some of them dead,
Surgeons operating, attendants holding lights, the smell of ether,
    the odor of blood,
The crowd, O the crowd of the bloody forms, the yard outside
    also fill'd,
Some on the bare ground, some on planks or stretchers, some in
    the death-spasm sweating,
An occasional scream or cry, the doctor's shouted orders or calls,
The glisten of the little steel instruments catching the glint of the
    torches,
These I resume as I chant, I see again the forms, I smell the odor,
Then hear outside the orders given, *Fall in, my men, fall in*;
But first I bend to the dying lad, his eyes open, a half-smile gives
    he me,
Then the eyes close, calmly close, and I speed forth to the
    darkness,
Resuming, marching, ever in darkness marching, on in the ranks,
The unknown road still marching.

A SIGHT IN CAMP IN THE DAYBREAK
GRAY AND DIM

A sight in camp in the daybreak gray and dim,
As from my tent I emerge so early sleepless,
As slow I walk in the cool fresh air the path near by the hospital
    tent,

Three forms I see on stretchers lying, brought out there untended
    lying,
Over each the blanket spread, ample brownish woolen blanket,
Gray and heavy blanket, folding, covering all.

Curious I halt and silent stand,
Then with light fingers I from the face of the nearest the first just
    lift the blanket;
Who are you elderly man so gaunt and grim, with well-gray'd
    hair, and flesh all sunken about the eyes?
Who are you my dear comrade?
Then to the second I step—and who are you my child and darling?
Who are you sweet boy with cheeks yet blooming?

Then to the third—a face nor child nor old, very calm, as of
    beautiful yellow-white ivory;
Young man I think I know you—I think this face is the face of the
    Christ himself,
Dead and divine and brother of all, and here again he lies.

AS TOILSOME I WANDER'D VIRGINIA'S WOODS

As toilsome I wander'd Virginia's woods,
To the music of rustling leaves kick'd by my feet, (for 'twas
    autumn,)
I mark'd at the foot of a tree the grave of a soldier;
Mortally wounded he and buried on the retreat, (easily all could I
    understand,)
The halt of a mid-day hour, when up! no time to lose—yet this
    sign left,
On a tablet scrawl'd and nail'd on the tree by the grave,
Bold, cautious, true, and my loving comrade.

Long, long I muse, then on my way go wandering,
Many a changeful season to follow, and many a scene of life,
Yet at times through changeful season and scene, abrupt, alone,
    or in the crowded street,

Comes before me the unknown soldier's grave, comes the
    inscription rude in Virginia's woods,
Bold, cautious, true, and my loving comrade.

NOT THE PILOT

Not the pilot has charged himself to bring his ship into port,
    though beaten back and many times baffled;
Not the pathfinder penetrating inland weary and long,
By deserts parch'd, snows chill'd, rivers wet, perseveres till he
    reaches his destination,
More than I have charged myself, heeded or unheeded, to
    compose a march for these States,
For a battle-call, rousing to arms if need be, years, centuries hence.

YEAR THAT TREMBLED AND REEL'D BENEATH ME

Year that trembled and reel'd beneath me!
Your summer wind was warm enough, yet the air I breathed
    froze me,
A thick gloom fell through the sunshine and darken'd me,
Must I change my triumphant songs? said I to myself,
Must I indeed learn to chant the cold dirges of the baffled?
And sullen hymns of defeat?

THE WOUND-DRESSER[64]

− 1 −

An old man bending I come among new faces,
Years looking backward resuming in answer to children,
Come tell us old man, as from young men and maidens that
    love me,
(Arous'd and angry, I'd thought to beat the alarum, and urge
    relentless war,

But soon my fingers fail'd me, my face droop'd and I resign'd
      myself,
To sit by the wounded and soothe them, or silently watch the dead;)
Years hence of these scenes, of these furious passions, these
      chances,
Of unsurpass'd heroes, (was one side so brave? the other was
      equally brave;)
Now be witness again, paint the mightiest armies of earth,
Of those armies so rapid so wondrous what saw you to tell us?
What stays with you latest and deepest? of curious panics,
Of hard-fought engagements or sieges tremendous what deepest
      remains?

— 2 —

O maidens and young men I love and that love me,
What you ask of my days those the strangest and sudden your
      talking recalls,
Soldier alert I arrive after a long march cover'd with sweat and dust,
In the nick of time I come, plunge in the fight, loudly shout in
      the rush of successful charge,
Enter the captur'd works—yet lo, like a swift-running river they
      fade,
Pass and are gone they fade—I dwell not on soldiers' perils or
      soldiers' joys,
(Both I remember well—many the hardships, few the joys, yet I
      was content.)

But in silence, in dreams' projections,
While the world of gain and appearance and mirth goes on,
So soon what is over forgotten, and waves wash the imprints off
      the sand,
With hinged knees returning I enter the doors, (while for you
      up there,
Whoever you are, follow without noise and be of strong heart.)

Bearing the bandages, water and sponge,
Straight and swift to my wounded I go,

Where they lie on the ground after the battle brought in,
Where their priceless blood reddens the grass the ground,
Or to the rows of the hospital tent, or under the roof'd hospital,
To the long rows of cots up and down each side I return,
To each and all one after another I draw near, not one do I
    miss,
An attendant follows holding a tray, he carries a refuse pail,
Soon to be fill'd with clotted rags and blood, emptied, and fill'd
    again.

I onward go, I stop,
With hinged knees and steady hand to dress wounds,
I am firm with each, the pangs are sharp yet unavoidable,
One turns to me his appealing eyes—poor boy! I never knew
    you,
Yet I think I could not refuse this moment to die for you, if that
    would save you.

− 3 −

On, on I go, (open doors of time! open hospital doors!)
The crush'd head I dress, (poor crazed hand tear not the bandage
    away,)
The neck of the cavalry-man with the bullet through and through
    I examine,
Hard the breathing rattles, quite glazed already the eye, yet life
    struggles hard,
(Come sweet death! be persuaded O beautiful death!
In mercy come quickly.)

From the stump of the arm, the amputated hand,
I undo the clotted lint, remove the slough, wash off the matter
    and blood,
Back on his pillow the soldier bends with curv'd neck and side-
    falling head,
His eyes are closed, his face is pale, he dares not look on the
    bloody stump,
And has not yet look'd on it.

I dress a wound in the side, deep, deep,
But a day or two more, for see the frame all wasted and sinking,
And the yellow-blue countenance see.

I dress the perforated shoulder, the foot with the bullet-wound,
Cleanse the one with a gnawing and putrid gangrene, so
    sickening, so offensive,
While the attendant stands behind aside me holding the tray and
    pail.

I am faithful, I do not give out,
The fractur'd thigh, the knee, the wound in the abdomen,
These and more I dress with impassive hand, (yet deep in my
    breast a fire, a burning flame.)

−4−

Thus in silence in dreams' projections,
Returning, resuming, I thread my way through the hospitals,
The hurt and wounded I pacify with soothing hand,
I sit by the restless all the dark night, some are so young,
Some suffer so much, I recall the experience sweet and sad,
(Many a soldier's loving arms about this neck have cross'd and
    rested,
Many a soldier's kiss dwells on these bearded lips.)

LONG, TOO LONG AMERICA

Long, too long America,
Traveling roads all even and peaceful you learn'd from joys and
    prosperity only,
But now, ah now, to learn from crises of anguish, advancing,
    grappling with direst fate and recoiling not,
And now to conceive and show to the world what your children
    en-masse really are,
(For who except myself has yet conceiv'd what your children en-
    masse really are?)

GIVE ME THE SPLENDID SILENT SUN

– 1 –

Give me the splendid silent sun with all his beams full-dazzling,
Give me juicy autumnal fruit ripe and red from the orchard,
Give me a field where the unmow'd grass grows,
Give me an arbor, give me the trellis'd grape,
Give me fresh corn and wheat, give me serene-moving animals
    teaching content,
Give me nights perfectly quiet as on high plateaus west of the
    Mississippi, and I looking up at the stars,
Give me odorous at sunrise a garden of beautiful flowers where I
    can walk undisturb'd,
Give me for marriage a sweet-breath'd woman of whom I should
    never tire,
Give me a perfect child, give me away aside from the noise of the
    world a rural domestic life,
Give me to warble spontaneous songs recluse by myself, for my
    own ears only,
Give me solitude, give me Nature, give me again O Nature your
    primal sanities!
These demanding to have them, (tired with ceaseless excitement,
    and rack'd by the war-strife,)
These to procure incessantly asking, rising in cries from my heart,
While yet incessantly asking still I adhere to my city,
Day upon day and year upon year O city, walking your streets,
Where you hold me enchain'd a certain time refusing to give
    me up,
Yet giving to make me glutted, enrich'd of soul, you give me
    forever faces;
(O I see what I sought to escape, confronting, reversing my cries,
I see my own soul trampling down what it ask'd for.)

– 2 –

Keep your splendid silent sun,
Keep your woods O Nature, and the quiet places by the woods,

Keep your fields of clover and timothy, and your cornfields and
    orchards,
Keep the blossoming buckwheat fields where the Ninth-month
    bees hum;
Give me faces and streets—give me these phantoms incessant and
    endless along the trottoirs!
Give me interminable eyes—give me women—give me comrades
    and lovers by the thousand!
Let me see new ones every day—let me hold new ones by the
    hand every day!
Give me such shows—give me the streets of Manhattan!
Give me Broadway, with the soldiers marching—give me the
    sound of the trumpets and drums!
(The soldiers in companies or regiments—some starting away,
    flush'd and reckless,
Some, their time up, returning with thinn'd ranks, young, yet very
    old, worn, marching, noticing nothing;)
Give me the shores and wharves heavy-fringed with black ships!
O such for me! O an intense life, full to repletion and varied!
The life of the theatre, bar-room, huge hotel, for me!
The saloon of the steamer! the crowded excursion for me! the
    torchlight procession!
The dense brigade bound for the war, with high piled military
    wagons following;
People, endless, streaming, with strong voices, passions,
    pageants,
Manhattan streets with their powerful throbs, with beating drums
    as now,
The endless and noisy chorus, the rustle and clank of muskets,
    (even the sight of the wounded,)
Manhattan crowds, with their turbulent musical chorus,
Manhattan faces and eyes forever for me.

DIRGE FOR TWO VETERANS[65]

    The last sunbeam
Lightly falls from the finish'd Sabbath,

On the pavement here, and there beyond it is looking,
    Down a new-made double grave.

    Lo, the moon ascending,
Up from the east the silvery round moon,
Beautiful over the house-tops, ghastly, phantom moon,
    Immense and silent moon.

    I see a sad procession,
And I hear the sound of coming full-key'd bugles,
All the channels of the city streets they're flooding,
    As with voices and with tears.

    I hear the great drums pounding,
And the small drums steady whirring,
And every blow of the great convulsive drums,
    Strikes me through and through.

    For the son is brought with the father,
(In the foremost ranks of the fierce assault they fell,
Two veterans son and father dropt together,
    And the double grave awaits them.)

    Now nearer blow the bugles,
And the drums strike more convulsive,
And the daylight o'er the pavement quite has faded,
    And the strong dead-march enwraps me.

    In the eastern sky up-buoying,
The sorrowful vast phantom moves illumin'd,
('Tis some mother's large transparent face,
    In heaven brighter growing.)

    O strong dead-march you please me!
O moon immense with your silvery face you soothe me!
O my soldiers twain! O my veterans passing to burial!
    What I have I also give you.

The moon gives you light,
And the bugles and the drums give you music,
And my heart, O my soldiers, my veterans,
    My heart gives you love.

OVER THE CARNAGE ROSE
PROPHETIC A VOICE

Over the carnage rose prophetic a voice,
Be not dishearten'd, affection shall solve the problems of freedom
    yet,
Those who love each other shall become invincible,
They shall yet make Columbia victorious.

Sons of the Mother of All, you shall yet be victorious,
You shall yet laugh to scorn the attacks of all the remainder of the
    earth.

No danger shall balk Columbia's lovers,
If need be a thousand shall sternly immolate themselves for one.

One from Massachusetts shall be a Missourian's comrade,
From Maine and from hot Carolina, and another an Oregonese,
    shall be friends triune,
More precious to each other than all the riches of the earth.

To Michigan, Florida perfumes shall tenderly come,
Not the perfumes of flowers, but sweeter, and wafted beyond death.

It shall be customary in the houses and streets to see manly
    affection,
The most dauntless and rude shall touch face to face lightly,
The dependence of Liberty shall be lovers,
The continuance of Equality shall be comrades.

These shall tie you and band you stronger than hoops of iron,
I, ecstatic, O partners! O lands! with the love of lovers tie you.

(Were you looking to be held together by lawyers?
Or by an agreement on a paper? or by arms?
Nay, nor the world, nor any living thing, will so cohere.)

I SAW OLD GENERAL AT BAY

I saw old General at bay,
(Old as he was, his gray eyes yet shone out in battle like stars,)
His small force was now completely hemm'd in, in his works,
He call'd for volunteers to run the enemy's lines, a desperate
    emergency,
I saw a hundred and more step forth from the ranks, but two or
    three were selected,
I saw them receive their orders aside, they listen'd with care, the
    adjutant was very grave,
I saw them depart with cheerfulness, freely risking their lives.

THE ARTILLERYMAN'S VISION[66]

While my wife at my side lies slumbering, and the wars are over
    long,
And my head on the pillow rests at home, and the vacant
    midnight passes,
And through the stillness, through the dark, I hear, just hear, the
    breath of my infant,
There in the room as I wake from sleep this vision presses upon me;
The engagement opens there and then in fantasy unreal,
The skirmishers begin, they crawl cautiously ahead, I hear the
    irregular snap! snap!
I hear the sounds of the different missiles, the short *t-h-t! t-h-t!* of
    the rifle balls,
I see the shells exploding leaving small white clouds, I hear the
    great shells shrieking as they pass,
The grape like the hum and whirr of wind through the trees,
    (tumultuous now the contest rages,)
All the scenes at the batteries rise in detail before me again,

The crashing and smoking, the pride of the men in their
    pieces,
The chief-gunner ranges and sights his piece and selects a fuse
    of the right time,
After firing I see him lean aside and look eagerly off to note the
    effect;
Elsewhere I hear the cry of a regiment charging, (the young
    colonel leads himself this time with brandish'd sword,)
I see the gaps cut by the enemy's volleys, (quickly fill'd up, no
    delay,)
I breathe the suffocating smoke, then the flat clouds hover low
    concealing all;
Now a strange lull for a few seconds, not a shot fired on either
    side,
Then resumed the chaos louder than ever, with eager calls and
    orders of officers,
While from some distant part of the field the wind wafts to my
    ears a shout of applause, (some special success,)
And ever the sound of the cannon far or near, (rousing even in
    dreams a devilish exultation and all the old mad joy in the
    depths of my soul,)
And ever the hastening of infantry shifting positions, batteries,
    cavalry, moving hither and thither,
(The falling, dying, I heed not, the wounded dripping and red
    I heed not, some to the rear are hobbling,)
Grime, heat, rush, aide-de-camps galloping by or on a
    full run,
With the patter of small arms, the warning *s-s-t* of the rifles, (these
    in my vision I hear or see,)
And bombs bursting in air, and at night the vari-color'd rockets.

ETHIOPIA SALUTING THE COLORS

Who are you dusky woman, so ancient hardly human,
With your woolly-white and turban'd head, and bare bony feet?
Why rising by the roadside here, do you the colors greet?

('Tis while our army lines Carolina's sands and pines,
Forth from thy hovel door thou Ethiopia com'st to me,
As under doughty Sherman I march toward the sea.)

Me master years a hundred since from my parents sunder'd,
A little child, they caught me as the savage beast is caught,
Then hither me across the sea the cruel slaver brought.

No further does she say, but lingering all the day,
Her high-borne turban'd head she wags, and rolls her darkling
    eye,
And courtesies to the regiments, the guidons moving by.

What is it fateful woman, so blear, hardly human?
Why wag your head with turban bound, yellow, red and green?
Are the things so strange and marvelous you see or have seen?

NOT YOUTH PERTAINS TO ME

Not youth pertains to me,
Nor delicatesse, I cannot beguile the time with talk,
Awkward in the parlor, neither a dancer nor elegant,
In the learn'd coterie sitting constrain'd and still, for learning
    inures not to me,
Beauty, knowledge, inure not to me—yet there are two or three
    things inure to me,
I have nourish'd the wounded and sooth'd many a dying soldier,
And at intervals waiting or in the midst of camp,
Composed these songs.

RACE OF VETERANS

Race of veterans—race of victors!
Race of the soil, ready for conflict—race of the conquering march!
(No more credulity's race, abiding-temper'd race,)

Race henceforth owning no law but the law of itself,
Race of passion and the storm.

WORLD TAKE GOOD NOTICE

World take good notice, silver stars fading,
Milky hue ript, weft of white detaching,
Coals thirty-eight, baleful and burning,
Scarlet, significant, hands off warning,
Now and henceforth flaunt from these shores.

O TAN-FACED PRAIRIE-BOY

O tan-faced prairie-boy,
Before you came to camp came many a welcome gift,
Praises and presents came and nourishing food, till at last among
    the recruits,
You came, taciturn, with nothing to give—we but look'd on each
    other,
When lo! more than all the gifts of the world you gave me.

LOOK DOWN FAIR MOON

Look down fair moon and bathe this scene,
Pour softly down night's nimbus floods on faces ghastly, swollen,
    purple,
On the dead on their backs with arms toss'd wide,
Pour down your unstinted nimbus sacred moon.

RECONCILIATION

Word over all, beautiful as the sky,
Beautiful that war and all its deeds of carnage must in time be
    utterly lost,

That the hands of the sisters Death and Night incessantly softly
    wash again, and ever again, this soil'd world;
For my enemy is dead, a man divine as myself is dead,
I look where he lies white-faced and still in the coffin—I draw near,
Bend down and touch lightly with my lips the white face in the
    coffin.

HOW SOLEMN AS ONE BY ONE

(Washington City, 1865)

How solemn as one by one,
As the ranks returning worn and sweaty, as the men file by where
    I stand,
As the faces the masks appear, as I glance at the faces studying the
    masks,
(As I glance upward out of this page studying you, dear friend,
    whoever you are,)
How solemn the thought of my whispering soul to each in the
    ranks, and to you,
I see behind each mask that wonder a kindred soul,
O the bullet could never kill what you really are, dear friend,
Nor the bayonet stab what you really are;
The soul! yourself I see, great as any, good as the best,
Waiting secure and content, which the bullet could never kill,
Nor the bayonet stab O friend.

AS I LAY WITH MY HEAD IN YOUR LAP CAMERADO

As I lay with my head in your lap camerado,
The confession I made I resume, what I said to you and the open
    air I resume,
I know I am restless and make others so,
I know my words are weapons full of danger, full of death,
For I confront peace, security, and all the settled laws, to unsettle
    them,

I am more resolute because all have denied me than I could ever
    have been had all accepted me,
I heed not and have never heeded either experience, cautions,
    majorities, nor ridicule,
And the threat of what is call'd hell is little or nothing to me,
And the lure of what is call'd heaven is little or nothing to me;
Dear camerado! I confess I have urged you onward with me,
    and still urge you, without the least idea what is our
    destination,
Or whether we shall be victorious, or utterly quell'd and
    defeated.

DELICATE CLUSTER[67]

Delicate cluster! flag of teeming life!
Covering all my lands—all my seashores lining!
Flag of death! (how I watch'd you through the smoke of battle
    pressing!
How I heard you flap and rustle, cloth defiant!)
Flag cerulean—sunny flag, with the orbs of night dappled!
Ah my silvery beauty—ah my wooly white and crimson!
Ah to sing the song of you, my matron mighty!
My sacred one, my mother.

TO A CERTAIN CIVILIAN

Did you ask dulcet rhymes from me?
Did you seek the civilian's peaceful and languishing rhymes?
Did you find what I sang erewhile so hard to follow?
Why I was not singing erewhile for you to follow, to understand—
    nor am I now;
(I have been born of the same as the war was born,
The drum-corps' rattle is ever to me sweet music, I love well the
    martial dirge,
With slow wail and convulsive throb leading the officer's
    funeral;)

What to such as you anyhow such a poet as I? therefore leave my
    works,
And go lull yourself with what you can understand, and with
    piano-tunes,
For I lull nobody, and you will never understand me.

LO, VICTRESS ON THE PEAKS[68]

Lo, Victress on the peaks,
Where thou with mighty brow regarding the world,
(The world O Libertad, that vainly conspired against thee,)
Out of its countless beleaguering toils, after thwarting them all,
Dominant, with the dazzling sun around thee,
Flauntest now unharm'd in immortal soundness and bloom—lo,
    in these hours supreme,
No poem proud, I chanting bring to thee, nor mastery's rapturous
    verse,
But a cluster containing night's darkness and blood-dripping
    wounds,
And psalms of the dead.

SPIRIT WHOSE WORK IS DONE

(Washington City, 1865)

Spirit whose work is done—spirit of dreadful hours!
Ere departing fade from my eyes your forests of bayonets;
Spirit of gloomiest fears and doubts, (yet onward ever unfaltering
    pressing,)
Spirit of many a solemn day and many a savage scene—electric
    spirit,
That with muttering voice through the war now closed, like a
    tireless phantom flitted,
Rousing the land with breath of flame, while you beat and beat
    the drum,
Now as the sound of the drum, hollow and harsh to the last,
    reverberates round me,

As your ranks, your immortal ranks, return, return from the
    battles,
As the muskets of the young men yet lean over their shoulders,
As I look on the bayonets bristling over their shoulders,
As those slanted bayonets, whole forests of them appearing
    in the distance, approach and pass on, returning homeward,
Moving with steady motion, swaying to and fro to the right and
    left,
Evenly lightly rising and falling while the steps keep time;
    Spirit of hours I knew, all hectic red one day, but pale as
    death next day,
Touch my mouth ere you depart, press my lips close,
Leave me your pulses of rage—bequeath them to me—fill me
    with currents convulsive,
Let them scorch and blister out of my chants when you are
    gone,
Let them identify you to the future in these songs.

ADIEU TO A SOLDIER

Adieu O soldier,
You of the rude campaigning, (which we shared,)
The rapid march, the life of the camp,
The hot contention of opposing fronts, the long manœuvre,
Red battles with their slaughter, the stimulus, the strong terrific
    game,
Spell of all brave and manly hearts, the trains of time through you
    and like of you all fill'd,
With war and war's expression.

Adieu dear comrade,
Your mission is fulfill'd—but I, more warlike,
Myself and this contentious soul of mine,
Still on our own campaigning bound,
Through untried roads with ambushes opponents lined,
Through many a sharp defeat and many a crisis, often baffled,

Here marching, ever marching on, a war fight out—aye here,
To fiercer, weightier battles give expression.

TURN O LIBERTAD

Turn O Libertad, for the war is over,
From it and all henceforth expanding, doubting no more,
    resolute, sweeping the world,
Turn from lands retrospective recording proofs of the past,
From the singers that sing the trailing glories of the past,
From the chants of the feudal world, the triumphs of kings,
    slavery, caste,
Turn to the world, the triumphs reserv'd and to come—give up
    that backward world,
Leave to the singers of hitherto, give them the trailing past,
But what remains remains for singers for you—wars to come are
    for you,
(Lo, how the wars of the past have duly inured to you, and the
    wars of the present also inure;)
Then turn, and be not alarm'd O Libertad—turn your undying
    face,
To where the future, greater than all the past,
Is swiftly, surely preparing for you.

TO THE LEAVEN'D SOIL THEY TROD[69]

To the leaven'd soil they trod calling I sing for the last,
(Forth from my tent emerging for good, loosing, untying the tent-
    ropes,)
In the freshness the forenoon air, in the far-stretching circuits and
    vistas again to peace restored,
To the fiery fields emanative and the endless vistas beyond, to the
    South and the North,
To the leaven'd soil of the general Western world to attest my
    songs,

To the Alleghanian hills and the tireless Mississippi,
To the rocks I calling sing, and all the trees in the woods,
To the plains of the poems of heroes, to the prairies spreading
    wide,
To the far-off sea and the unseen winds, and the sane
    impalpable air;
And responding they answer all, (but not in words,)
The average earth, the witness of war and peace, acknowledges
    mutely,
The prairie draws me close, as the father to bosom broad the son,
The Northern ice and rain that began me nourish me to the end,
But the hot sun of the South is to fully ripen my songs.

MEMORIES OF PRESIDENT LINCOLN

WHEN LILACS LAST IN THE DOORYARD BLOOM'D[70]

— 1 —

When lilacs last in the dooryard bloom'd,
And the great star early droop'd in the western sky in the night,
I mourn'd, and yet shall mourn with ever-returning spring.

Ever-returning spring, trinity sure to me you bring,
Lilac blooming perennial and drooping star in the west,
And thought of him I love.

— 2 —

O powerful western fallen star!
O shades of night—O moody, tearful night!
O great star disappear'd—O the black murk that hides the star!
O cruel hands that hold me powerless—O helpless soul of me!
O harsh surrounding cloud that will not free my soul.

— 3 —

In the dooryard fronting an old farm-house near the white-wash'd
    palings,
Stands the lilac-bush tall-growing with heart-shaped leaves of rich
    green,
With many a pointed blossom rising delicate, with the perfume
    strong I love,
With every leaf a miracle—and from this bush in the dooryard,

With delicate-color'd blossoms and heart-shaped leaves of rich
    green,
A sprig with its flower I break.

– 4 –

In the swamp in secluded recesses,
A shy and hidden bird is warbling a song.

Solitary the thrush,
The hermit withdrawn to himself, avoiding the settlements,
    Sings by himself a song.

Song of the bleeding throat,
Death's outlet song of life, (for well dear brother I know,
If thou wast not granted to sing thou would'st surely die.)

– 5 –

Over the breast of the spring, the land, amid cities,
Amid lanes and through old woods, where lately the violets
    peep'd from the ground, spotting the gray debris,
Amid the grass in the fields each side of the lanes, passing the
    endless grass,
Passing the yellow-spear'd wheat, every grain from its shroud in
    the dark-brown fields uprisen,
Passing the apple-tree blows of white and pink in the orchards,
Carrying a corpse to where it shall rest in the grave,
Night and day journeys a coffin.[71]

– 6 –

Coffin that passes through lanes and streets,
Through day and night with the great cloud darkening the land,
With the pomp of the inloop'd flags with the cities draped in
    black,
With the show of the States themselves as of crape-veil'd women
    standing,

With processions long and winding and the flambeaus of the
    night,
With the countless torches lit, with the silent sea of faces and the
    unbared heads,
With the waiting depot, the arriving coffin, and the sombre faces,
With dirges through the night, with the thousand voices rising
    strong and solemn,
With all the mournful voices of the dirges pour'd around the coffin,
The dim-lit churches and the shuddering organs—where amid
    these you journey,
With the tolling tolling bells' perpetual clang,
Here, coffin that slowly passes,
I give you my sprig of lilac.

– 7 –

(Nor for you, for one alone,
Blossoms and branches green to coffins all I bring,
For fresh as the morning, thus would I chant a song for you O
    sane and sacred death.

All over bouquets of roses,
O death, I cover you over with roses and early lilies,
But mostly and now the lilac that blooms the first,
Copious I break, I break the sprigs from the bushes,
With loaded arms I come, pouring for you,
For you and the coffins all of you O death.)

– 8 –

O western orb sailing the heaven,
Now I know what you must have meant as a month since
    I walk'd,
As I walk'd in silence the transparent shadowy night,
As I saw you had something to tell as you bent to me night after
    night,
As you droop'd from the sky low down as if to my side, (while the
    other stars all look'd on,)

As we wander'd together the solemn night, (for something I know
    not what kept me from sleep,)
As the night advanced, and I saw on the rim of the west how full
    you were of woe,
As I stood on the rising ground in the breeze in the cool
    transparent night,
As I watch'd where you pass'd and was lost in the netherward
    black of the night,
As my soul in its trouble dissatisfied sank, as where you sad orb,
Concluded, dropt in the night, and was gone.

— 9 —

Sing on there in the swamp,
O singer bashful and tender, I hear your notes, I hear
    your call,
I hear, I come presently, I understand you,
But a moment I linger, for the lustrous star has detain'd me,
The star my departing comrade holds and detains me.

— 10 —

O how shall I warble myself for the dead one there I loved?
And how shall I deck my song for the large sweet soul that has
    gone?
And what shall my perfume be for the grave of him I love?

Sea-winds blown from east and west,
Blown from the Eastern sea and blown from the Western sea, till
    there on the prairies meeting,
These and with these and the breath of my chant,
I'll perfume the grave of him I love.

— 11 —

O what shall I hang on the chamber walls?
And what shall the pictures be that I hang on the walls,
To adorn the burial-house of him I love?

Pictures of growing spring and farms and homes,
With the Fourth-month eve at sundown, and the gray smoke lucid
    and bright,
With floods of the yellow gold of the gorgeous, indolent, sinking
    sun, burning, expanding the air,
With the fresh sweet herbage under foot, and the pale green
    leaves of the trees prolific,
In the distance the flowing glaze, the breast of the river, with a
    wind-dapple here and there,
With ranging hills on the banks, with many a line against the sky,
    and shadows,
And the city at hand with dwellings so dense, and stacks of
    chimneys,
And all the scenes of life and the workshops, and the workmen
    homeward returning.

— 12 —

Lo, body and soul—this land,
My own Manhattan with spires, and the sparkling and hurrying
    tides, and the ships,
The varied and ample land, the South and the North in the light,
    Ohio's shores and flashing Missouri,
And ever the far-spreading prairies cover'd with grass and corn.

Lo, the most excellent sun so calm and haughty,
The violet and purple morn with just-felt breezes,
The gentle soft-born measureless light,
The miracle spreading bathing all, the fulfill'd noon,
The coming eve delicious, the welcome night and the stars,
Over my cities shining all, enveloping man and land.

— 13 —

Sing on, sing on you gray-brown bird,
Sing from the swamps, the recesses, pour your chant from the
    bushes,
Limitless out of the dusk, out of the cedars and pines.

Sing on dearest brother, warble your reedy song,
Loud human song, with voice of uttermost woe.

O liquid and free and tender!
O wild and loose to my soul—O wondrous singer!
You only I hear—yet the star holds me, (but will soon depart,)
Yet the lilac with mastering odor holds me.

— 14 —

Now while I sat in the day and look'd forth,
In the close of the day with its light and the fields of spring, and
    the farmers preparing their crops,
In the large unconscious scenery of my land with its lakes and
    forests,
In the heavenly aerial beauty, (after the perturb'd winds and the
    storms,)
Under the arching heavens of the afternoon swift passing, and the
    voices of children and women,
The many-moving sea-tides, and I saw the ships how they sail'd,
And the summer approaching with richness, and the fields all
    busy with labor,
And the infinite separate houses, how they all went on, each with
    its meals and minutia of daily usages,
And the streets how their throbbings throbb'd, and the cities
    pent—lo, then and there,
Falling upon them all and among them all, enveloping me with
    the rest,
Appear'd the cloud, appealed the long black trail,
And I knew death, its thought, and the sacred knowledge of
    death.

Then with the knowledge of death as walking one side of me,
And the thought of death close-walking the other side of me,
And I in the middle as with companions, and as holding the
    hands of companions,
I fled forth to the hiding receiving night that talks not,

Down to the shores of the water, the path by the swamp in the
    dimness,
To the solemn shadowy cedars and ghostly pines so still.

And the singer so shy to the rest receiv'd me,
The gray-brown bird I know receiv'd us comrades three,
And he sang the carol of death, and a verse for him
    I love.

From deep secluded recesses,
From the fragrant cedars and the ghostly pines so still,
Came the carol of the bird.

And the charm of the carol rapt me,
As I held as if by their hands my comrades in the night,
And the voice of my spirit tallied the song of the bird.

Come lovely and soothing death,[72]
Undulate round the world, serenely arriving, arriving,
In the day, in the night, to all, to each,
Sooner or later delicate death.

Prais'd be the fathomless universe,
For life and joy, and for objects and knowledge curious,
And for love, sweet love—but praise! praise! praise!
For the sure-enwinding arms of cool-enfolding death.
Dark mother always gliding near with soft feet,
Have none chanted for thee a chant of fullest welcome?
Then I chant it for thee, I glorify thee above all,
I bring thee a song that when thou must indeed come, come
    unfalteringly.

Approach strong deliveress,
When it is so, when thou hast taken them I joyously sing
    the dead,
Lost in the loving floating ocean of thee,
Laved in the flood of thy bliss O death.

From me to thee glad serenades,
Dances for thee I propose saluting thee, adornments and feastings
*   for thee,*
And the sights of the open landscape and the high-spread sky are
*   fitting,*
And life and the fields, and the huge and thoughtful night.

The night in silence under many a star,
The ocean shore and the husky whispering wave whose voice
*   I know,*
And the soul turning to thee O vast and well-veil'd death,
And the body gratefully nestling close to thee.

Over the tree-tops I float thee a song,
Over the rising and sinking waves, over the myriad fields and the
*   prairies wide,*
Over the dense-pack'd cities all and the teeming wharves and ways,
I float this carol with joy, with joy to thee O death.

— 15 —

To the tally of my soul,
Loud and strong kept up the gray-brown bird,
With pure deliberate notes spreading filling the night.

Loud in the pines and cedars dim,
Clear in the freshness moist and the swamp-perfume,
And I with my comrades there in the night.

While my sight that was bound in my eyes unclosed,
As to long panoramas of visions.

And I saw askant the armies,
I saw as in noiseless dreams hundreds of battle-flags,
Borne through the smoke of the battles and pierc'd with missiles I
    saw them,
And carried hither and yon through the smoke, and torn and
    bloody,

And at last but a few shreds left on the staffs, (and all in silence,)
And the staffs all splinter'd and broken.

I saw battle-corpses, myriads of them,
And the white skeletons of young men, I saw them,
I saw the debris and debris of all the slain soldiers of the war,
But I saw they were not as was thought,
They themselves were fully at rest, they suffer'd not,
The living remain'd and suffer'd, the mother suffer'd,
And the wife and the child and the musing comrade suffer'd,
And the armies that remain'd suffer'd.

– 16 –

Passing the visions, passing the night,
Passing, unloosing the hold of my comrades' hands,
Passing the song of the hermit bird and the tallying song of my
    soul,
Victorious song, death's outlet song, yet varying ever-altering song,
As low and wailing, yet clear the notes, rising and falling, flooding
    the night,
Sadly sinking and fainting, as warning and warning, and yet again
    bursting with joy,
Covering the earth and filling the spread of the heaven,
As that powerful psalm in the night I heard from recesses,
Passing, I leave thee lilac with heart-shaped leaves,
I leave thee there in the door-yard, blooming, returning with spring.

I cease from my song for thee,
From my gaze on thee in the west, fronting the west, communing
    with thee,
O comrade lustrous with silver face in the night.

Yet each to keep and all, retrievements out of the night,
The song, the wondrous chant of the gray-brown bird,
And the tallying chant, the echo arous'd in my soul,
With the lustrous and drooping star with the countenance full
    of woe,

With the holders holding my hand nearing the call of the bird,
Comrades mine and I in the midst, and their memory ever to
    keep, for the dead I loved so well,
For the sweetest, wisest soul of all my days and lands—and this for
    his dear sake,
Lilac and star and bird twined with the chant of my soul,
There in the fragrant pines and the cedars dusk and dim.

O CAPTAIN! MY CAPTAIN![73]

O Captain! my Captain! our fearful trip is done,
The ship has weather'd every rack, the prize we sought is won,
The port is near, the bells I hear, the people all exulting,
While follow eyes the steady keel, the vessel grim and daring;
        But O heart! heart! heart!
         O the bleeding drops of red,
           Where on the deck my Captain lies,
            Fallen cold and dead.

O Captain! my Captain! rise up and hear the bells;
Rise up—for you the flag is flung—for you the bugle trills,
For you bouquets and ribbon'd wreaths—for you the shores
    a-crowding,
For you they call, the swaying mass, their eager faces turning;
        Here Captain! dear father!
       This arm beneath your head!
        It is some dream that on the deck,
          You've fallen cold and dead.

My Captain does not answer, his lips are pale and still,
My father does not feel my arm, he has no pulse nor will,
The ship is anchor'd safe and sound, its voyage closed and done,
From fearful trip the victor ship comes in with object won;
        Exult O shores, and ring O bells!
        But I with mournful tread,
         Walk the deck my Captain lies,
          Fallen cold and dead.

HUSH'D BE THE CAMPS TO-DAY

(May 4, 1865)

Hush'd be the camps to-day,
And soldiers let us drape our war-worn weapons,
And each with musing soul retire to celebrate,
Our dear commander's death.

No more for him life's stormy conflicts,
Nor victory, nor defeat—no more time's dark events,
Charging like ceaseless clouds across the sky.
But sing poet in our name,
Sing of the love we bore him—because you, dweller in camps,
    know it truly.

As they invault the coffin there,
Sing—as they close the doors of earth upon him—one verse,
For the heavy hearts of soldiers.

THIS DUST WAS ONCE THE MAN

This dust was once the man,
Gentle, plain, just and resolute, under whose cautious hand,
Against the foulest crime in history known in any land or age,
Was saved the Union of these States.

BY BLUE ONTARIO'S SHORE[74]

– 1 –

By blue Ontario's shore,
As I mused of these warlike days and of peace return'd, and the
    dead that return no more,
A Phantom gigantic superb, with stern visage accosted me,

Chant me the poem, it said, *that comes from the soul of America,*
     chant me the carol of victory,
And strike up the marches of Libertad, marches more powerful yet,
And sing me before you go the song of the throes of Democracy.

(Democracy, the destin'd conqueror, yet treacherous lip-smiles
     everywhere,
And death and infidelity at every step.)

— 2 —

A Nation announcing itself,
I myself make the only growth by which I can be appreciated,
I reject none, accept all, then reproduce all in my own forms.

A breed whose proof is in time and deeds,
What we are we are, nativity is answer enough to objections,
We wield ourselves as a weapon is wielded,
We are powerful and tremendous in ourselves,
We are executive in ourselves, we are sufficient in the variety of
     ourselves,
We are the most beautiful to ourselves and in ourselves,
We stand self-pois'd in the middle, branching thence over the world,
From Missouri, Nebraska, or Kansas, laughing attacks to scorn.

Nothing is sinful to us outside of ourselves,
Whatever appears, whatever does not appear, we are beautiful or
     sinful in ourselves only.

(O Mother—O Sisters dear!
If we are lost, no victor else has destroy'd us,
It is by ourselves we go down to eternal night.)

— 3 —

Have you thought there could be but a single supreme?
There can be any number of supremes—one does not countervail
     another any more than one eyesight countervails another, or
     one life countervails another.

All is eligible to all,
All is for individuals, all is for you,
No condition is prohibited, not God's or any.

All comes by the body, only health puts you rapport with the
    universe.

Produce great Persons, the rest follows.

– 4 –

Piety and conformity to them that like,
Peace, obesity, allegiance, to them that like,
I am he who tauntingly compels men, women, nations,
Crying, Leap from your seats and contend for your lives!

I am he who walks the States with a barb'd tongue, questioning
    every one I meet,
Who are you that wanted only to be told what you knew before?
Who are you that wanted only a book to join you in your nonsense?

(With pangs and cries as thine own O bearer of many children,
These clamors wild to a race of pride I give.)

O lands, would you be freer than all that has ever been before?
If you would be freer than all that has been before, come listen
    to me.

Fear grace, elegance, civilization, delicatesse,
Fear the mellow sweet, the sucking of honey-juice,
Beware the advancing mortal ripening of Nature,
Beware what precedes the decay of the ruggedness of states
    and men.

– 5 –

Ages, precedents, have long been accumulating undirected
    materials,
America brings builders, and brings its own styles.

The immortal poets of Asia and Europe have done their work and
pass'd to other spheres,
A work remains, the work of surpassing all they have done.

America, curious toward foreign characters, stands by its own at
all hazards,
Stands removed, spacious, composite, sound, initiates the true use
of precedents,
Does not repel them or the past or what they have produced
under their forms,
Takes the lesson with calmness, perceives the corpse slowly borne
from the house,
Perceives that it waits a little while in the door, that it was fittest
for its days,
That its life has descended to the stalwart and well-shaped heir
who approaches,
And that he shall be fittest for his days.

Any period one nation must lead,
One land must be the promise and reliance of the future.

These States are the amplest poem,
Here is not merely a nation but a teeming Nation of nations,
Here the doings of men correspond with the broadcast doings of
the day and night,
Here is what moves in magnificent masses careless of particulars,
Here are the roughs, beards, friendliness, combativeness, the soul
loves,
Here the flowing trains, here the crowds, equality, diversity, the
soul loves.

– 6 –

Land of lands and bards to corroborate!
Of them standing among them, one lifts to the light a west-bred
face,
To him the hereditary countenance bequeath'd both mother's and
father's,

His first parts substances, earth, water, animals, trees,
Built of the common stock, having room for far and near,
Used to dispense with other lands, incarnating this land,
Attracting it body and soul to himself, hanging on its neck with
     incomparable love,
Plunging his seminal muscle into its merits and demerits,
Making its cities, beginnings, events, diversities, wars, vocal in
     him,
Making its rivers, lakes, bays, embouchure in him,
Mississippi with yearly freshets and changing chutes, Columbia,
     Niagara, Hudson, spending themselves lovingly in him,
If the Atlantic coast stretch or the Pacific coast stretch, he
     stretching with them North or South,
Spanning between them East and West, and touching whatever is
     between them,
Growths growing from him to offset the growths of pine, cedar,
     hemlock, live oak, locust, chestnut, hickory, cottonwood,
     orange, magnolia,
Tangles as tangled in him as any canebrake or swamp,
He likening sides and peaks of mountains, forests coated with
     northern transparent ice,
Off him pasturage sweet and natural as savanna, upland, prairie,
Through him flights, whirls, screams, answering those of the fish-
     hawk, mocking-bird, night-heron, and eagle,
His spirit surrounding his country's spirit, unclosed to good and
     evil,
Surrounding the essences of real things, old times and present
     times,
Surrounding just found shores, islands, tribes of red aborigines,
Weather-beaten vessels, landings, settlements, embryo stature and
     muscle,
The haughty defiance of the Year One, war, peace, the formation
     of the Constitution,
The separate States, the simple elastic scheme, the immigrants,
The Union always swarming with blatherers and always sure and
     impregnable,
The unsurvey'd interior, log-houses, clearings, wild animals,
     hunters, trappers,

Surrounding the multiform agriculture, mines, temperature, the
    gestation of new States,
Congress convening every Twelfth-month, the members duly
    coming up from the uttermost parts,
Surrounding the noble character of mechanics and farmers,
    especially the young men,
Responding their manners, speech, dress, friendships, the gait
    they have of persons who never knew how it felt to stand in
    the presence of superiors,
The freshness and candor of their physiognomy, the copiousness
    and decision of their phrenology,
The picturesque looseness of their carriage, their fierceness when
    wrong'd,
The fluency of their speech, their delight in music, their curiosity,
    good temper and open-handedness, the whole composite make,
The prevailing ardor and enterprise, the large amativeness,
The perfect equality of the female with the male, the fluid
    movement of the population,
The superior marine, free commerce, fisheries, whaling, gold-
    digging,
Wharf-hemm'd cities, railroad and steamboat lines intersecting all
    points,
Factories, mercantile life, labor-saving machinery, the Northeast,
    Northwest, Southwest,
Manhattan firemen, the Yankee swap, southern plantation life,
Slavery—the murderous, treacherous conspiracy to raise it upon
    the ruins of all the rest,
On and on to the grapple with it—Assassin! then your life or ours
    be the stake, and respite no more.

– 7 –

(Lo, high toward heaven, this day,
Libertad, from the conqueress' field return'd,
I mark the new aureola around your head,
No more of soft astral, but dazzling and fierce,
With war's flames and the lambent lightnings playing,
And your port immovable where you stand,

With still the inextinguishable glance and the clinch'd and lifted
    fist,
And your foot on the neck of the menacing one, the scorner
    utterly crush'd beneath you,
The menacing arrogant one that strode and advanced with his
    senseless scorn, bearing the murderous knife,
The wide-swelling one, the braggart that would yesterday do so
    much,
To-day a carrion dead and damn'd, the despised of all the earth,
An offal rank, to the dunghill maggots spurn'd.)

– 8 –

Others take finish, but the Republic is ever constructive and ever
    keeps vista,
Others adorn the past, but you O days of the present, I adorn you,
O days of the future I believe in you—I isolate myself for your sake,
O America because you build for mankind I build for you,
O well-beloved stone-cutters, I lead them who plan with decision
    and science,
Lead the present with friendly hand toward the future.

(Bravas to all impulses sending sane children to the next age!
But damn that which spends itself with no thought of the stain,
    pains, dismay, feebleness, it is bequeathing.)

– 9 –

I listened to the Phantom by Ontario's shore,
I heard the voice arising demanding bards,
By them all native and grand, by them alone can these States be
    fused into the compact organism of a Nation.

To hold men together by paper and seal or by compulsion is no
    account;
That only holds men together which aggregates all in a living
    principle, as the hold of the limbs of the body or the fibres of
    plants.

Of all races and eras these States with veins full of poetical stuff
    most need poets, and are to have the greatest, and use them
    the greatest,
Their Presidents shall not be their common referee so much as
    their poets shall.

(Soul of love and tongue of fire!
Eye to pierce the deepest deeps and sweep the world!
Ah Mother, prolific and full in all besides, yet how long barren,
    barren?)

— 10 —

Of these States the poet is the equable man,
Not in him but off from him things are grotesque, eccentric, fail
    of their full returns,
Nothing out of its place is good, nothing in its place is bad,
He bestows on every object or quality its fit proportion, neither
    more nor less,
He is the arbiter of the diverse, he is the key,
He is the equalizer of his age and land,
He supplies what wants supplying, he checks what wants
    checking,
In peace out of him speaks the spirit of peace, large, rich, thrifty,
    building populous towns, encouraging agriculture, arts,
    commerce, lighting the study of man, the soul, health,
    immortality, government,
In war he is the best backer of the war, he fetches artillery as good
    as the engineer's, he can make every word he speaks draw
    blood,
The years straying toward infidelity he withholds by his steady
    faith,
He is no arguer, he is judgment, (Nature accepts him
    absolutely,)
He judges not as the judge judges but as the sun falling round a
    helpless thing,
As he sees the farthest he has the most faith,
His thoughts are the hymns of the praise of things,

In the dispute on God and eternity he is silent,
He sees eternity less like a play with a prologue and
    denouement,
He sees eternity in men and women, he does not see men and
    women as dreams or dots.

For the great Idea, the idea of perfect and free individuals,
For that, the bard walks in advance, leader of leaders,
The attitude of him cheers up slaves and horrifies foreign despots.

Without extinction is Liberty, without retrograde is Equality,
They live in the feelings of young men and the best women,
(Not for nothing have the indomitable heads of the earth been
    always ready to fall for Liberty.)

— 11 —

For the great Idea,
That, O my brethren, that is the mission of poets.

Songs of stern defiance ever ready,
Songs of the rapid arming and the march,
The flag of peace quick-folded, and instead the flag we know,
Warlike flag of the great Idea.

(Angry cloth I saw there leaping!
I stand again in leaden rain your flapping folds saluting,
I sing you over all, flying beckoning through the fight—O the
    hard-contested fight!
The cannons ope their rosy-flashing muzzles—the hurtled balls
    scream,
The battle-front forms amid the smoke—the volleys pour
    incessant from the line,
Hark, the ringing word *Charge!*—now the tussle and the furious
    maddening yells,
Now the corpses tumble curl'd upon the ground,
Cold, cold in death, for precious life of you,
Angry cloth I saw there leaping.)

– 12 –

Are you he who would assume a place to teach or be a poet here
　　in the States?
The place is august, the terms obdurate.

Who would assume to teach here may well prepare himself body
　　and mind,
He may well survey, ponder, arm, fortify, harden, make lithe
　　himself,
He shall surely be question'd beforehand by me with many and
　　stern questions.
Who are you indeed who would talk or sing to America?
Have you studied out the land, its idioms and men?
Have you learn'd the physiology, phrenology, politics, geography,
　　pride, freedom, friendship of the land? its substratums and
　　objects?
Have you consider'd the organic compact of the first day of the
　　first year of Independence, sign'd by the Commissioners,
　　ratified by the States, and read by Washington at the head
　　of the army?
Have you possess'd yourself of the Federal Constitution?
Do you see who have left all feudal processes and poems behind
　　them, and assumed the poems and processes of Democracy?
Are you faithful to things? do you teach what the land and sea, the
　　bodies of men, womanhood, amativeness, heroic angers,
　　teach?
Have you sped through fleeting customs, popularities?
Can you hold your hand against all seductions, follies, whirls,
　　fierce contentions? are you very strong? are you really of the
　　whole People?
Are you not of some coterie? some school or mere religion?
Are you done with reviews and criticisms of life? animating now
　　to life itself?
Have you vivified yourself from the maternity of these States?
Have you too the old ever-fresh forbearance and impartiality?
Do you hold the like love for those hardening to maturity? for the
　　last born? little and big? and for the errant?

What is this you bring my America?
Is it uniform with my country?
Is it not something that has been better told or done before?
Have you not imported this or the spirit of it in some ship?
Is it not a mere tale? a rhyme? a prettiness?—is the good old
    cause in it?
Has it not dangled long at the heels of the poets, politicians,
    literats, of enemies' lands?
Does it not assume that what is notoriously gone is still here?
Does it answer universal needs? will it improve manners?
Does it sound with trumpet-voice the proud victory of the Union
    in that secession war?
Can your performance face the open fields and the seaside?
Will it absorb into me as I absorb food, air, to appear again in my
    strength, gait, face?
Have real employments contributed to it? original makers, not
    mere amanuenses?
Does it meet modern discoveries, calibres, facts, face to face?
What does it mean to American persons, progresses, cities?
    Chicago, Kanada, Arkansas?
Does it see behind the apparent custodians the real custodians
    standing, menacing, silent, the mechanics, Manhattanese,
    Western men, Southerners, significant alike in their apathy,
    and in the promptness of their love?
Does it see what finally befalls, and has always finally befallen,
    each temporizer, patcher, outsider, partialist, alarmist, infidel,
    who has ever ask'd any thing of America?
What mocking and scornful negligence?
The track strew'd with the dust of skeletons,
By the roadside others disdainfully toss'd.

– 13 –

Rhymes and rhymers pass away, poems distill'd from poems pass
    away,
The swarms of reflectors and the polite pass, and leave ashes,
Admirers, importers, obedient persons, make but the soil of
    literature,

America justifies itself, give it time, no disguise can deceive it or
     conceal from it, it is impassive enough,
Only toward the likes of itself will it advance to meet them,
If its poets appear it will in due time advance to meet them, there
     is no fear of mistake,
(The proof of a poet shall be sternly deferr'd till his country
     absorbs him as affectionately as he has absorb'd it.)

He masters whose spirit masters, he tastes sweetest who results
     sweetest in the long run,
The blood of the brawn beloved of time is unconstraint;
In the need of songs, philosophy, an appropriate native grand-
     opera, shipcraft, any craft,
He or she is greatest who contributes the greatest original
     practical example.

Already a nonchalant breed, silently emerging, appears on the
     streets,
People's lips salute only doers, lovers, satisfiers, positive knowers,
There will shortly be no more priests, I say their work is done,
Death is without emergencies here, but life is perpetual
     emergencies here,
Are your body, days, manners, superb? after death you shall be
     superb,
Justice, health, self-esteem, clear the way with irresistible
     power;
How dare you place any thing before a man?

– 14 –

Fall behind me States!
A man before all—myself, typical, before all.

Give me the pay I have served for,
Give me to sing the songs of the great Idea, take all the rest,
I have loved the earth, sun, animals, I have despised riches,
I have given alms to every one that ask'd, stood up for the stupid
     and crazy, devoted my income and labor to others,

Hated tyrants, argued not concerning God, had patience and
    indulgence toward the people, taken off my hat to nothing
    known or unknown,
Gone freely with powerful uneducated persons and with the
    young, and with the mothers of families,
Read these leaves to myself in the open air, tried them by trees,
    stars, rivers,
Dismiss'd whatever insulted my own soul or defiled my body,
Claim'd nothing to myself which I have not carefully claim'd for
    others on the same terms,
Sped to the camps, and comrades found and accepted from every
    State,
(Upon this breast has many a dying soldier lean'd to breathe his
    last,
This arm, this hand, this voice, have nourish'd, rais'd, restored,
To life recalling many a prostrate form;)
I am willing to wait to be understood by the growth of the taste of
    myself,
Rejecting none, permitting all.

(Say O Mother, have I not to your thought been faithful?
Have I not through life kept you and yours before me?)

– 15 –

I swear I begin to see the meaning of these things,
It is not the earth, it is not America who is so great,
It is I who am great or to be great, it is You up there, or any one,
It is to walk rapidly through civilizations, governments,
    theories,
Through poems, pageants, shows, to form individuals.

Underneath all, individuals,
I swear nothing is good to me now that ignores individuals,
The American compact is altogether with individuals,
The only government is that which makes minute of individuals,
The whole theory of the universe is directed unerringly to one
    single individual—namely to You.

(Mother! with subtle sense severe, with the naked sword in your
    hand,
I saw you at last refuse to treat but directly with individuals.)

– 16 –

Underneath all, Nativity,
I swear I will stand by my own nativity, pious or impious so be it;
I swear I am charm'd with nothing except nativity,
Men, women, cities, nations, are only beautiful from nativity.

Underneath all is the Expression of love for men and women,
(I swear I have seen enough of mean and impotent modes of
    expressing love for men and women,
After this day I take my own modes of expressing love for men
    and women.)

I swear I will have each quality of my race in myself,
(Talk as you like, he only suits these States whose manners favor
    the audacity and sublime turbulence of the States.)

Underneath the lessons of things, spirits, Nature, governments,
    ownerships, I swear I perceive other lessons,
Underneath all to me is myself, to you yourself, (the same
    monotonous old song.)

– 17 –

O I see flashing that this America is only you and me,
Its power, weapons, testimony, are you and me,
Its crimes, lies, thefts, defections, are you and me,
Its Congress is you and me, the officers, capitols, armies, ships,
    are you and me,
Its endless gestations of new States are you and me,
The war, (that war so bloody and grim, the war I will henceforth
    forget), was you and me,
Natural and artificial are you and me,
Freedom, language, poems, employments, are you and me,
Past, present, future, are you and me.

I dare not shirk any part of myself,
Not any part of America good or bad,
Not to build for that which builds for mankind,
Not to balance ranks, complexions, creeds, and the sexes,
Not to justify science nor the march of equality,
Nor to feed the arrogant blood of the brawn belov'd of time.

I am for those that have never been master'd,
For men and women whose tempers have never been master'd,
For those whom laws, theories, conventions, can never
    master.

I am for those who walk abreast with the whole earth,
Who inaugurate one to inaugurate all.

I will not be outfaced by irrational things,
I will penetrate what it is in them that is sarcastic upon me,
I will make cities and civilizations defer to me,
This is what I have learnt from America—it is the amount, and it
    I teach again.

(Democracy, while weapons were everywhere aim'd at your
    breast,
I saw you serenely give birth to immortal children, saw in dreams
    your dilating form,
Saw you with spreading mantle covering the world.)

– 18 –

I will confront these shows of the day and night,
I will know if I am to be less than they,
I will see if I am not as majestic as they,
I will see if I am not as subtle and real as they,
I will see if I am to be less generous than they,
I will see if I have no meaning, while the houses and ships have
    meaning,
I will see if the fishes and birds are to be enough for themselves,
    and I am not to be enough for myself.

I match my spirit against yours you orbs, growths, mountains,
    brutes,
Copious as you are I absorb you all in myself, and become the
    master myself,
America isolated yet embodying all, what is it finally except
    myself?
These States, what are they except myself?

I know now why the earth is gross, tantalizing, wicked, it is for my
    sake,
I take you specially to be mine, you terrible, rude forms.

(Mother, bend down, bend close to me your face,
I know not what these plots and wars and deferments are for,
I know not fruition's success, but I know that through war and
    crime your work goes on, and must yet go on.)

– 19 –

Thus by blue Ontario's shore,
While the winds fann'd me and the waves came trooping
    toward me,
I thrill'd with the power's pulsations, and the charm of my theme
    was upon me,
Till the tissues that held me parted their ties upon me.

And I saw the free souls of poets,
The loftiest bards of past ages strode before me,
Strange large men, long unwaked, undisclosed, were disclosed
    to me.

– 20 –

O my rapt verse, my call, mock me not!
Not for the bards of the past, not to invoke them have I launch'd
    you forth,
Not to call even those lofty bards here by Ontario's shores,
Have I sung so capricious and loud my savage song.

Bards for my own land only I invoke,
(For the war the war is over, the field is clear'd,)
Till they strike up marches henceforth triumphant and onward,
To cheer O Mother your boundless expectant soul.

Bards of the great Idea! bards of the peaceful inventions! (for the
　　war, the war is over!)
Yet bards of latent armies, a million soldiers waiting ever-ready,
Bards with songs as from burning coals or the lightning's fork'd
　　stripes!
Ample Ohio's, Kanada's bards—bards of California! inland
　　bards—bards of the war!
You by my charm I invoke.

REVERSALS[75]

Let that which stood in front go behind,
Let that which was behind advance to the front,
Let bigots, fools, unclean persons, offer new propositions,
Let the old propositions be postponed,
Let a man seek pleasure everywhere except in himself,
Let a woman seek happiness everywhere except in herself.

AUTUMN RIVULETS[76]

AS CONSEQUENT, ETC.[77]

As consequent from store of summer rains,
Or wayward rivulets in autumn flowing,
Or many a herb-lined brook's reticulations,
Or subterranean sea-rills making for the sea,
Songs of continued years I sing.

Life's ever-modern rapids first, (soon, soon to blend,
With the old streams of death.)

Some threading Ohio's farm-fields or the woods,
Some down Colorado's cañons from sources of perpetual snow,
Some half-hid in Oregon, or away southward in Texas,
Some in the north finding their way to Erie, Niagara, Ottawa,
Some to Atlantica's bays, and so to the great salt brine.

In you whoe'er you are my book perusing,
In I myself, in all the world, these currents flowing,
All, all toward the mystic ocean tending.

Currents for starting a continent new,
Overtures sent to the solid out of the liquid,
Fusion of ocean and land, tender and pensive waves,
(Not safe and peaceful only, waves rous'd and ominous too,
Out of the depths the storm's abysmic waves, who knows whence?
Raging over the vast, with many a broken spar and tatter'd sail.)

Or from the sea of Time, collecting vasting all, I bring,
A windrow-drift of weeds and shells.

O little shells, so curious-convolute, so limpid-cold and voiceless,
Will you not little shells to the tympans of temples held,
Murmurs and echoes still call up, eternity's music faint and far,
Wafted inland, sent from Atlantica's rim, strains for the soul of the
    prairies,
Whisper'd reverberations, chords for the ear of the West joyously
    sounding,
Your tidings old, yet ever new and untranslatable,
Infinitesimals out of my life, and many a life,
(For not my life and years alone I give—all, all I give,)
These waifs from the deep, cast high and dry,
Wash'd on America's shores?

THE RETURN OF THE HEROES

— 1 —

For the lands and for these passionate days and for myself,
Now I awhile retire to thee O soil of autumn fields,
Reclining on thy breast, giving myself to thee,
Answering the pulses of thy sane and equable heart,
Tuning a verse for thee.

O earth that hast no voice, confide to me a voice,
O harvest of my lands—O boundless summer growths,
O lavish brown parturient earth—O infinite teeming womb,
A song to narrate thee.

— 2 —

Ever upon this stage,
Is acted God's calm annual drama,
Gorgeous processions, songs of birds,
Sunrise that fullest feeds and freshens most the soul,
The heaving sea, the waves upon the shore, the musical, strong
    waves,
The woods, the stalwart trees, the slender, tapering trees,

The liliput countless armies of the grass,
The heat, the showers, the measureless pasturages,
The scenery of the snows, the winds' free orchestra,
The stretching light-hung roof of clouds, the clear cerulean and
    the silvery fringes,
The high dilating stars, the placid beckoning stars,
The moving flocks and herds, the plains and emerald meadows,
The shows of all the varied lands and all the growths and products.

– 3 –

Fecund America—to-day,
Thou art all over set in births and joys!
Thou groan'st with riches, thy wealth clothes thee as a swathing-
    garment,
Thou laughest loud with ache of great possessions,
A myriad twining life like interlacing vines binds all thy vast   .
    demesne,
As some huge ship freighted to water's edge thou ridest into port,
As rain falls from the heaven and vapors rise from earth, so have
    the precious values fallen upon thee and risen out of thee;
Thou envy of the globe! thou miracle!
Thou, bathed, choked, swimming in plenty,
Thou lucky Mistress of the tranquil barns,
Thou Prairie Dame that sittest in the middle and lookest out
    upon thy world, and lookest East and lookest West,
Dispensatress, that by a word givest a thousand miles, a million
    farms, and missest nothing,
Thou all-acceptress—thou hospitable, (thou only art hospitable as
    God is hospitable.)

– 4 –

When late I sang sad was my voice,
Sad were the shows around me with deafening noises of hatred
    and smoke of war;
In the midst of the conflict, the heroes, I stood,
Or pass'd with slow step through the wounded and dying.

But now I sing not war,
Nor the measur'd march of soldiers, nor the tents of camps,
Nor the regiments hastily coming up deploying in line of
    battle;
No more the sad, unnatural shows of war.

Ask'd room those flush'd immortal ranks, the first forth-stepping
    armies?
Ask room alas the ghastly ranks, the armies dread that
    follow'd.

(Pass, pass, ye proud brigades, with your tramping sinewy legs,
With your shoulders young and strong, with your knapsacks and
    your muskets;
How elate I stood and watch'd you, where starting off you
    march'd.

Pass—then rattle drums again,
For an army heaves in sight, O another gathering army,
Swarming, trailing on the rear, O you dread accruing army,
O you regiments so piteous, with your mortal diarrhœa, with your
    fever,
O my land's maim'd darlings, with the plenteous bloody bandage
    and the crutch,
Lo, your pallid army follows.)

− 5 −

But on these days of brightness,
On the far-stretching beauteous landscape, the roads and
    lanes, the high-piled farm-wagons, and the fruits and
    barns,
Should the dead intrude?

Ah the dead to me mar not, they fit well in Nature,
They fit very well in the landscape under the trees
    and grass,
And along the edge of the sky in the horizon's far margin.

Nor do I forget you Departed,
Nor in winter or summer my lost ones,
But most in the open air as now when my soul is rapt and at
    peace, like pleasing phantoms,
Your memories rising glide silently by me.

– 6 –

I saw the day the return of the heroes,
(Yet the heroes never surpass'd shall never return,
Them that day I saw not.)

I saw the interminable corps, I saw the processions of armies,
I saw them approaching, defiling by with divisions,
Streaming northward, their work done, camping awhile in
    clusters of mighty camps.

No holiday soldiers—youthful, yet veterans,
Worn, swart, handsome, strong, of the stock of homestead and
    workshop,
Harden'd of many a long campaign and sweaty march,
Inured on many a hard-fought bloody field.

A pause—the armies wait,
A million flush'd embattled conquerors wait,
The world too waits, then soft as breaking night and sure as
    dawn,
They melt, they disappear,

Exult O lands! victorious lands!
Not there your victory on those red shuddering fields,
But here and hence your victory.

Melt, melt away ye armies—disperse ye blue-clad soldiers,
Resolve ye back again, give up for good your deadly arms,
Other the arms the fields henceforth for you, or South or
    North,
With saner wars, sweet wars, life-giving wars.

− 7 −

Loud O my throat, and clear O soul!
The season of thanks and the voice of full-yielding,
The chant of joy and power for boundless fertility.

All till'd and untill'd fields expand before me,
I see the true arenas of my race, or first or last,
Man's innocent and strong arenas.

I see the heroes at other toils,
I see well-wielded in their hands the better weapons.

I see where the Mother of All,
With full-spanning eye gazes forth, dwells long,
And counts the varied gathering of the products.

Busy the far, the sunlit panorama,
Prairie, orchard, and yellow grain of the North,
Cotton and rice of the South and Louisianian cane,
Open unseeded fallows, rich fields of clover and timothy,
Kine and horses feeding, and droves of sheep and swine,
And many a stately river flowing and many a jocund brook,
And healthy uplands with herby-perfumed breezes,
And the good green grass, that delicate miracle the ever-recurring
    grass.

− 8 −

Toil on heroes! harvest the products!
Not alone on those warlike fields the Mother of All,
With dilated form and lambent eyes watch'd you.

Toil on heroes! toil well! handle the weapons well!
The Mother of All, yet here as ever she watches you.

Well-pleased America thou beholdest,
Over the fields of the West those crawling monsters,

The human-divine inventions, the labor-saving implements;
Beholdest moving in every direction imbued as with life the
 revolving hay-rakes,
The steam-power reaping-machines and the horse-power
 machines,
The engines, thrashers of grain and cleaners of grain, well
 separating the straw, the nimble work of the patent
 pitchfork,
Beholdest the newer saw-mill, the southern cotton-gin, and the
 rice-cleanser.
Beneath thy look O Maternal,
With these and else and with their own strong hands the heroes
 harvest.

All gather and all harvest,
Yet but for thee O Powerful, not a scythe might swing as now in
 security,
Not a maize-stalk dangle as now its silken tassels in peace.

Under thee only they harvest, even but a wisp of hay under thy
 great face only,
Harvest the wheat of Ohio, Illinois, Wisconsin, every barbed spear
 under thee,
Harvest the maize of Missouri, Kentucky, Tennessee, each ear in
 its light-green sheath,
Gather the hay to its myriad mows in the odorous tranquil
 barns,
Oats to their bins, the white potato, the buckwheat of Michigan,
 to theirs;
Gather the cotton in Mississippi or Alabama, dig and hoard
 the golden the sweet potato of Georgia and the Carolinas,
Clip the wool of California or Pennsylvania,
Cut the flax in the Middle States, or hemp or tobacco in the
 Borders,
Pick the pea and the bean, or pull apples from the trees or
 bunches of grapes from the vines,
Or aught that ripens in all these States or North or South,
Under the beaming sun and under thee.

THERE WAS A CHILD WENT FORTH

There was a child went forth every day,
And the first object he look'd upon, that object he became,
And that object became part of him for the day or a certain part
    of the day,
Or for many years or stretching cycles of years.

The early lilacs became part of this child,
And grass and white and red morning-glories, and white and red
    clover, and the song of the phœbe-bird,
And the Third-month lambs and the sow's pink-faint litter, and
    the mare's foal and the cow's calf,
And the noisy brood of the barnyard or by the mire of the pond-
    side,
And the fish suspending themselves so curiously below there, and
    the beautiful curious liquid,
And the water-plants with their graceful flat heads, all became
    part of him.

The field-sprouts of Fourth-month and Fifth-month became part
    of him,
Winter-grain sprouts and those of the light-yellow corn, and the
    esculent roots of the garden,
And the apple-trees cover'd with blossoms and the fruit afterward,
    and wood-berries, and the commonest weeds by the road,
And the old drunkard staggering home from the outhouse of the
    tavern whence he had lately risen,
And the schoolmistress that pass'd on her way to the school,
And the friendly boys that pass'd, and the quarrelsome boys,
And the tidy and fresh-cheek'd girls, and the barefoot negro boy
    and girl,
And all the changes of city and country wherever he went.

His own parents, he that had father'd him and she that had
    conceiv'd him in her womb and birth'd him,
They give this child more of themselves than that,
They gave him afterward every day, they became part of him.

The mother at home quietly placing the dishes on the supper-
table,
The mother with mild words, clean her cap and gown, a
wholesome odor falling off her person and clothes as she
walks by,
The father, strong, self-sufficient, manly, mean, anger'd,
unjust,
The blow, the quick loud word, the tight bargain, the crafty
lure,
The family usages, the language, the company, the furniture, the
yearning and swelling heart,
Affection that will not be gainsay'd, the sense of what is real, the
thought if after all it should prove unreal,
The doubts of day-time and the doubts of night-time, the curious
whether and how,
Whether that which appears so is so, or is it all flashes and
specks?
Men and women crowding fast in the streets, if they are not
flashes and specks what are they?
The streets themselves and the façades of houses, and goods in
the windows,
Vehicles, teams, the heavy-plank'd wharves, the huge crossing at
the ferries,
The village on the highland seen from afar at sunset, the river
between,
Shadows, aureola and mist, the light falling on roofs and gables of
white or brown two miles off,
The schooner near by sleepily dropping down the tide, the little
boat slack-tow'd astern,
The hurrying tumbling waves, quick-broken crests, slapping,
The strata of color'd clouds, the long bar of maroon-tint
away solitary by itself, the spread of purity it lies
motionless in,
The horizon's edge, the flying sea-crow, the fragrance of salt
marsh and shore mud,
These became part of that child who went forth every day, and
who now goes, and will always go forth every day.

OLD IRELAND[78]

Far hence amid an isle of wondrous beauty,
Crouching over a grave an ancient sorrowful mother,
Once a queen, now lean and tatter'd seated on the ground,
Her old white hair drooping dishevel'd round her shoulders,
At her feet fallen an unused royal harp,
Long silent, she too long silent, mourning her shrouded hope and
    heir,
Of all the earth her heart most full of sorrow because most full
    of love.

Yet a word ancient mother,
You need crouch there no longer on the cold ground with
    forehead between your knees,
O you need not sit there veil'd in your old white hair so
    dishevel'd,
For know you the one you mourn is not in that grave,
It was an illusion, the son you love was not really dead,
The Lord is not dead, he is risen again young and strong in
    another country,
Even while you wept there by your fallen harp by the grave,
What you wept for was translated, pass'd from the grave,
The winds favor'd and the sea sail'd it,
And now with rosy and new blood,
Moves to-day in a new country.

THE CITY DEAD-HOUSE

By the city dead-house by the gate,
As idly sauntering wending my way from the clangor,
I curious pause, for lo, an outcast form, a poor dead prostitute
    brought,
Her corpse they deposit unclaim'd, it lies on the damp brick
    pavement,
The divine woman, her body, I see the body, I look on it alone,

That house once full of passion and beauty, all else I notice not,
Nor stillness so cold, nor running water from faucet, nor odors
    morbific impress me,
But the house alone—that wondrous house—that delicate fair
    house—that ruin!
That immortal house more than all the rows of dwellings ever
    built!
Or white-domed capitol with majestic figure surmounted, or all
    the old high-spired cathedrals,
That little house alone more than them all—poor, desperate
    house!
Fair, fearful wreck—tenement of a soul—itself a soul,
Unclaim'd, avoided house—take one breath from my tremulous
    lips,
Take one tear dropt aside as I go for thought of you,
Dead house of love—house of madness and sin, crumbled,
    crush'd,
House of life, erewhile talking and laughing—but ah, poor house,
    dead even then,
Months, years, an echoing, garnish'd house—but dead, dead,
    dead.

THIS COMPOST

– 1 –

Something startles me where I thought I was safest,
I withdraw from the still woods I loved,
I will not go now on the pastures to walk,
I will not strip the clothes from my body to meet my lover the sea,
I will not touch my flesh to the earth as to other flesh to
    renew me.

O how can it be that the ground itself does not sicken?
How can you be alive you growths of spring?
How can you furnish health you blood of herbs, roots, orchards,
    grain?

Are they not continually putting distemper'd corpses within you?
Is not every continent work'd over and over with sour dead?

Where have you disposed of their carcasses?
Those drunkards and gluttons of so many generations?
Where have you drawn off all the foul liquid and meat?
I do not see any of it upon you to-day, or perhaps I am deceiv'd,
I will run a furrow with my plough, I will press my spade through
    the sod and turn it up underneath,
I am sure I shall expose some of the foul meat.

— 2 —

Behold this compost! behold it well!
Perhaps every mite has once form'd part of a sick person—yet
    behold!
The grass of spring covers the prairies,
The bean bursts noiselessly through the mould in the garden,
The delicate spear of the onion pierces upward,
The apple-buds cluster together on the apple-branches,
The resurrection of the wheat appears with pale visage out of its
    graves,
The tinge awakes over the willow-tree and the mulberry-tree,
The he-birds carol mornings and evenings while the she-birds sit
    on their nests,
The young of poultry break through the hatch'd eggs,
The new-born of animals appear, the calf is dropt from the cow,
    the colt from the mare,
Out of its little hill faithfully rise the potato's dark green leaves,
Out of its hill rises the yellow maize-stalk, the lilacs bloom in the
    dooryards,
The summer growth is innocent and disdainful above all those
    strata of sour dead.

What chemistry!
That the winds are really not infectious,
That this is no cheat, this transparent green-wash of the sea which
    is so amorous after me,

That it is safe to allow it to lick my naked body all over with its
    tongues,
That it will not endanger me with the fevers that have deposited
    themselves in it,
That all is clean forever and forever,
That the cool drink from the well tastes so good,
That blackberries are so flavorous and juicy,
That the fruits of the apple-orchard and the orange-orchard, that
    melons, grapes, peaches, plums, will none of them poison me,
That when I recline on the grass I do not catch any disease,
Though probably every spear of grass rises out of what was once a
    catching disease.

Now I am terrified at the Earth, it is that calm and patient,
It grows such sweet things out of such corruptions,
It turns harmless and stainless on its axis, with such endless
    successions of diseas'd corpses,
It distills such exquisite winds out of such infused fetor,
It renews with such unwitting looks its prodigal, annual,
    sumptuous crops,
It gives such divine materials to men, and accepts such leavings
    from them at last.

TO A FOIL'D EUROPEAN REVOLUTIONAIRE

Courage yet, my brother or my sister!
Keep on—Liberty is to be subserv'd whatever occurs;
That is nothing that is quell'd by one or two failures, or any
    number of failures,
Or by the indifference or ingratitude of the people, or by any
    unfaithfulness,
Or the show of the tushes of power, soldiers, cannon, penal statutes.

What we believe in waits latent forever through all the continents,
Invites no one, promises nothing, sits in calmness and light, is
    positive and composed, knows no discouragement,
Waiting patiently, waiting its time.

(Not songs of loyalty alone are these,
But songs of insurrection also,
For I am the sworn poet of every dauntless rebel the world over,
And he going with me leaves peace and routine behind him,
And stakes his life to be lost at any moment.)

The battle rages with many a loud alarm and frequent advance
    and retreat,
The infidel triumphs, or supposes he triumphs,
The prison, scaffold, garroté, handcuffs, iron necklace and lead-
    balls do their work,
The named and unnamed heroes pass to other spheres,
The great speakers and writers are exiled, they lie sick in distant
    lands,
The cause is asleep, the strongest throats are choked with their
    own blood,
The young men droop their eyelashes toward the ground when
    they meet;
But for all this Liberty has not gone out of the place, nor the
    infidel enter'd into full possession.
When liberty goes out of a place it is not the first to go, nor the
    second or third to go,
It waits for all the rest to go, it is the last.

When there are no more memories of heroes and martyrs,
And when all life and all the souls of men and women are
    discharged from any part of the earth,
Then only shall liberty or the idea of liberty be discharged from
    that part of the earth,
And the infidel come into full possession.

Then courage European revolter, revoltress!
For till all ceases neither must you cease.

I do not know what you are for, (I do not know what I am for
    myself, nor what any thing is for,)
But I will search carefully for it even in being foil'd,
In defeat, poverty, misconception, imprisonment—for they too
    are great.

Did we think victory great?
So it is—but now it seems to me, when it cannot be help'd, that
    defeat is great,
And that death and dismay are great.

UNNAMED LANDS

Nations ten thousand years before these States, and many times
    ten thousand years before these States,
Garner'd clusters of ages that men and women like us grew up
    and travel'd their course and pass'd on,
What vast-built cities, what orderly republics, what pastoral tribes
    and nomads,
What histories, rulers, heroes, perhaps transcending all others,
What laws, customs, wealth, arts, traditions,
What sort of marriage, what costumes, what physiology and
    phrenology,
What of liberty and slavery among them, what they thought of
    death and the soul,
Who were witty and wise, who beautiful and poetic, who brutish
    and undevelop'd,
Not a mark, not a record remains—and yet all remains.

O I know that those men and women were not for nothing, any
    more than we are for nothing,
I know that they belong to the scheme of the world every bit as
    much as we now belong to it.

Afar they stand, yet near to me they stand,
Some with oval countenances learn'd and calm,
Some naked and savage, some like huge collections of insects,
Some in tents, herdsmen, patriarchs, tribes, horsemen,
Some prowling through woods, some living peaceably on farms,
    laboring, reaping, filling barns,
Some traversing paved avenues, amid temples, palaces, factories,
    libraries, shows, courts, theatres, wonderful monuments.

Are those billions of men really gone?
Are those women of the old experience of the earth gone?
Do their lives, cities, arts, rest only with us?
Did they achieve nothing for good for themselves?

I believe of all those men and women that fill'd the unnamed
      lands, every one exists this hour here or elsewhere, invisible
      to us,
In exact proportion to what he or she grew from in life, and out of
      what he or she did, felt, became, loved, sinn'd, in life.

I believe that was not the end of those nations or any person of
      them, any more than this shall be the end of my nation, or of
      me;
Of their languages, governments, marriage, literature, products,
      games, wars, manners, crimes, prisons, slaves, heroes, poets,
I suspect their results curiously await in the yet unseen world,
      counterparts of what accrued to them in the seen world,
I suspect I shall meet them there,
I suspect I shall there find each old particular of those unnamed
      lands.

SONG OF PRUDENCE[79]

Manhattan's streets I saunter'd pondering,
On Time, Space, Reality—on such as these, and abreast with
      them Prudence.

The last explanation always remains to be made about
      prudence,
Little and large alike drop quietly aside from the prudence that
      suits immortality.

The soul is of itself,
All verges to it, all has reference to what ensues,
All that a person does, says, thinks, is of consequence,

Not a move can a man or woman make, that affects him or her in
 a day, month, any part of the direct lifetime, or the hour of
 death,
But the same affects him or her onward afterward through the
 indirect lifetime.

The indirect is just as much as the direct,
The spirit receives from the body just as much as it gives to the
 body, if not more.

Not one word or deed, not venereal sore, discoloration, privacy of
 the onanist,
Putridity of gluttons or rum-drinkers, peculation, cunning,
 betrayal, murder, seduction, prostitution,
But has results beyond death as really as before death.

Charity and personal force are the only investments worth any
 thing.

No specification is necessary, all that a male or female does, that is
 vigorous, benevolent, clean, is so much profit to him or her,
In the unshakable order of the universe and through the whole
 scope of it forever.

Who has been wise receives interest,
Savage, felon, President, judge, farmer, sailor, mechanic, literat,
 young, old, it is the same,
The interest will come round—all will come round.

Singly, wholly, to affect now, affected their time, will forever affect,
 all of the past and all of the present and all of the future,
All the brave actions of war and peace,
All help given to relatives, strangers, the poor, old, sorrowful,
 young children, widows, the sick, and to shunn'd persons,
All self-denial that stood steady and aloof on wrecks, and saw
 others fill the seats of the boats,
All offering of substance or life for the good old cause, or for a
 friend's sake, or opinion's sake,

All pains of enthusiasts scoff'd at by their neighbors,
All the limitless sweet love and precious suffering of mothers,
All honest men baffled in strifes recorded or unrecorded,
All the grandeur and good of ancient nations whose fragments we
    inherit,
All the good of the dozens of ancient nations unknown to us by
    name, date, location,
All that was ever manfully begun, whether it succeeded or no,
All suggestions of the divine mind of man or the divinity of his
    mouth, or the shaping of his great hands,
All that is well thought or said this day on any part of the globe,
    or on any of the wandering stars, or on any of the fix'd stars,
    by those there as we are here,
All that is henceforth to be thought or done by you whoever you
    are, or by any one,
These inure, have inured, shall inure, to the identities from which
    they sprang, or shall spring.

Did you guess any thing lived only its moment?
The world does not so exist, no parts palpable or impalpable so
    exist,
No consummation exists without being from some long previous
    consummation, and that from some other,
Without the farthest conceivable one coming a bit nearer the
    beginning than any.

Whatever satisfies souls is true;
Prudence entirely satisfies the craving and glut of souls,
Itself only finally satisfies the soul,
The soul has that measureless pride which revolts from every
    lesson but its own.

Now I breathe the word of the prudence that walks abreast with
    time, space, reality,
That answers the pride which refuses every lesson but its own.

What is prudence is indivisible,
Declines to separate one part of life from every part,

Divides not the righteous from the unrighteous or the living from
the dead,
Matches every thought or act by its correlative,
Knows no possible forgiveness or deputed atonement,
Knows that the young man who composedly peril'd his life
and lost it has done exceedingly well for himself without
doubt,
That he who never peril'd his life, but retains it to old age in
riches and ease, has probably achiev'd nothing for himself
worth mentioning,
Knows that only that person has really learn'd who has learn'd to
prefer results,
Who favors body and soul the same,
Who perceives the indirect assuredly following the direct,
Who in his spirit in any emergency whatever neither hurries nor
avoids death.

THE SINGER IN THE PRISON[80]

— 1 —

O sight of pity, shame and dole!
O fearful thought—a convict soul.

Rang the refrain along the hall, the prison,
Rose to the roof, the vaults of heaven above,
Pouring in floods of melody in tones so pensive sweet and strong
the like whereof was never heard,
Reaching the far-off sentry and the armed guards, who ceas'd their
pacing,
Making the hearer's pulses stop for ecstasy and awe.

— 2 —

The sun was low in the west one winter day,
When down a narrow aisle amid the thieves and outlaws of the
land,

(There by the hundreds seated, sear-faced murderers, wily
    counterfeiters,
Gather'd to Sunday church in prison walls, the keepers round,
Plenteous, well-armed, watching with vigilant eyes,)
Calmly a lady walk'd holding a little innocent child by either
    hand,
Whom seating on their stools beside her on the platform,
She, first preluding with the instrument a low and musical prelude,
In voice surpassing all, sang forth a quaint old hymn.

A soul confined by bars and bands,
Cries, help! O help! and wrings her hands,
Blinded her eyes, bleeding her breast,
Nor pardon finds, nor balm of rest.

Ceaseless she paces to and fro,
O heart-sick days! O nights of woe!
Nor hand of friend, nor loving face,
Nor favor comes, nor word of grace.

It was not I that sinn'd the sin,
The ruthless body dragg'd me in;
Though long I strove courageously,
The body was too much for me.

Dear prison'd soul bear up a space,
For soon or late the certain grace;
To set thee free and bear thee home,
The heavenly pardoner death shall come.

      Convict no more, nor shame, nor dole!
      Depart—a God enfranchis'd soul!

— 3 —

The singer ceas'd,
One glance swept from her clear calm eyes o'er all those upturn'd
    faces,

Strange sea of prison faces, a thousand varied, crafty, brutal,
    seam'd and beauteous faces,
Then rising, passing back along the narrow aisle between them,
While her gown touch'd them rustling in the silence,
She vanish'd with her children in the dusk.

While upon all, convicts and armed keepers ere they stirr'd,
(Convict forgetting prison, keeper his loaded pistol,)
A hush and pause fell down a wondrous minute,
With deep half-stifled sobs and sound of bad men bow'd and
    moved to weeping,
And youth's convulsive breathings, memories of home,
The mother's voice in lullaby, the sister's care, the happy childhood,
The long-pent spirit rous'd to reminiscence;
A wondrous minute then—but after in the solitary night, to many,
    many there,
Years after, even in the hour of death, the sad refrain, the tune,
    the voice, the words,
Resumed, the large calm lady walks the narrow aisle,
The wailing melody again, the singer in the prison sings,

O sight of pity, shame and dole!
O fearful thought—a convict soul.

WARBLE FOR LILAC-TIME

Warble me now for joy of lilac-time, (returning in reminiscence,)
Sort me O tongue and lips for Nature's sake, souvenirs of earliest
    summer,
Gather the welcome signs, (as children with pebbles or stringing
    shells,)
Put in April and May, the hylas croaking in the ponds, the elastic
    air,
Bees, butterflies, the sparrow with its simple notes,
Blue-bird and darting swallow, nor forget the high-hole flashing
    his golden wings,
The tranquil sunny haze, the clinging smoke, the vapor,

Shimmer of waters with fish in them, the cerulean above,
All that is jocund and sparkling, the brooks running,
The maple woods, the crisp February days and the sugar-making,
The robin where he hops, bright-eyed, brown-breasted,
With musical clear call at sunrise, and again at sunset,
Or flitting among the trees of the apple-orchard, building the nest
    of his mate,
The melted snow of March, the willow sending forth its yellow-
    green sprouts,
For spring-time is here! the summer is here! and what is this in it
    and from it?
Thou, soul, unloosen'd—the restlessness after I know not what;
Come, let us lag here no longer, let us be up and away!
O if one could but fly like a bird!
O to escape, to sail forth as in a ship!
To glide with thee O soul, o'er all, in all, as a ship o'er the waters;
Gathering these hints, the preludes, the blue sky, the grass, the
    morning drops of dew,
The lilac-scent, the bushes with dark green heart-shaped leaves,
Wood-violets, the little delicate pale blossoms called innocence,
Samples and sorts not for themselves alone, but for their atmo-
    sphere,
To grace the bush I love—to sing with the birds,
A warble for joy of lilac-time, returning in reminiscence.

OUTLINES FOR A TOMB

(G.P., Buried 1870)

– 1 –

What may we chant, O thou within this tomb?
What tablets, outlines, hang for thee, O millionaire?
The life thou lived'st we know not,
But that thou walk'dst thy years in barter, 'mid the haunts of
    brokers,
Nor heroism thine, nor war, nor glory.

— 2 —

Silent, my soul,
With drooping lids, as waiting, ponder'd,
Turning from all the samples, monuments of heroes.

While through the interior vistas,
Noiseless uprose, phantasmic, (as by night Auroras of the north,)
Lambent tableaus, prophetic, bodiless scenes,
Spiritual projections.
In one, among the city streets a laborer's home appear'd,
After his day's work done, cleanly, sweet-air'd, the gaslight burning,
The carpet swept and a fire in the cheerful stove.

In one, the sacred parturition scene,
A happy painless mother birth'd a perfect child.

In one, at a bounteous morning meal,
Sat peaceful parents with contented sons.

In one, by twos and threes, young people,
Hundreds concentring, walk'd the paths and streets and roads,
Toward a tall-domed school.

In one a trio beautiful,
Grandmother, loving daughter, loving daughter's daughter, sat,
Chatting and sewing.

In one, along a suite of noble rooms,
'Mid plenteous books and journals, paintings on the walls, fine
      statuettes,
Were groups of friendly journeymen, mechanics young and old,
Reading, conversing.

All, all the shows of laboring life,
City and country, women's, men's and children's,
Their wants provided for, hued in the sun and tinged for once
      with joy,

Marriage, the street, the factory, farm, the house-room, lodging-
    room,
Labor and toil, the bath, gymnasium, playground, library, college,
The student, boy or girl, led forward to be taught,
The sick cared for, the shoeless shod, the orphan father'd and
    mother'd,
The hungry fed, the houseless housed;
(The intentions perfect and divine,
The workings, details, haply human.)

– 3 –

O thou within this tomb,
From thee such scenes, thou stintless, lavish giver,
Tallying the gifts of earth, large as the earth,
Thy name an earth, with mountains, fields and tides.

Nor by your streams alone, you rivers,
By you, your banks Connecticut,
By you and all your teeming life old Thames,
By you Potomac laving the ground Washington trod, by you
    Patapsco,
You Hudson, you endless Mississippi—nor you alone,
But to the high seas launch, my thought, his memory.

OUT FROM BEHIND THIS MASK

(To Confront a Portrait)

– 1 –

Out from behind this bending rough-cut mask,
These lights and shades, this drama of the whole,
This common curtain of the face contain'd in me for me, in you
    for you, in each for each,
(Tragedies, sorrows, laughter, tears—O heaven!
The passionate teeming plays this curtain hid!)

This glaze of God's serenest purest sky,
This film of Satan's seething pit,
This heart's geography's map, this limitless small continent, this
    soundless sea;
Out from the convolutions of this globe,
This subtler astronomic orb than sun or moon, than Jupiter,
    Venus, Mars,
This condensation of the universe, (nay here the only
    universe,
Here the idea, all in this mystic handful wrapt;)
These burin'd eyes, flashing to you to pass to future time,
To launch and spin through space revolving sideling, from these
    to emanate,
To you whoe'er you are—a look.

— 2 —

A traveler of thoughts and years, of peace and war,
Of youth long sped and middle age declining,
(As the first volume of a tale perused and laid away, and this the
    second,
Songs, ventures, speculations, presently to close,)
Lingering a moment here and now, to you I opposite turn,
As on the road or at some crevice door by chance, or open'd
    window,
Pausing, inclining, baring my head, you specially I greet,
To draw and clinch your soul for once inseparably with mine,
Then travel travel on.

VOCALISM

— 1 —

Vocalism, measure, concentration, determination, and the divine
    power to speak words;
Are you full-lung'd and limber-lipp'd from long trial? from
    vigorous practice? from physique?

Do you move in these broad lands as broad as they?
Come duly to the divine power to speak words?
For only at last after many years, after chastity, friendship,
    procreation, prudence, and nakedness,
After treading ground and breasting river and lake,
After a loosen'd throat, after absorbing eras, temperaments, races,
    after knowledge, freedom, crimes,
After complete faith, after clarifyings, elevations, and removing
    obstructions,
After these and more, it is just possible there comes to a man, a
    woman, the divine power to speak words;
Then toward that man or that woman swiftly hasten all—none
    refuse, all attend,
Armies, ships, antiquities, libraries, paintings, machines, cities,
    hate, despair, amity, pain, theft, murder, aspiration, form in
    close ranks,
They debouch as they are wanted to march obediently through
    the mouth of that man or that woman.

– 2 –

O what is it in me that makes me tremble so at voices?
Surely whoever speaks to me in the right voice, him or her I shall
    follow,
As the water follows the moon, silently, with fluid steps, anywhere
    around the globe.

All waits for the right voices;
Where is the practis'd and perfect organ? where is the develop'd
    soul?
For I see every word utter'd thence has deeper, sweeter, new
    sounds, impossible on less terms.

I see brains and lips closed, tympans and temples unstruck,
Until that comes which has the quality to strike and to
    unclose,
Until that comes which has the quality to bring forth what lies
    slumbering forever ready in all words.

TO HIM THAT WAS CRUCIFIED

My spirit to yours dear brother,
Do not mind because many sounding your name do not
    understand you,
I do not sound your name, but I understand you,
I specify you with joy O my comrade to salute you, and to salute
    those who are with you, before and since, and those to come
    also,
That we all labor together transmitting the same charge and
    succession,
We few equals indifferent of lands, indifferent of times,
We, enclosers of all continents, all castes, allowers of all theologies,
Compassionaters, perceivers, rapport of men,
We walk silent among disputes and assertions, but reject not the
    disputers nor any thing that is asserted,
We hear the bawling and din, we are reach'd at by divisions,
    jealousies, recriminations on every side,
They close peremptorily upon us to surround us, my comrade,
Yet we walk unheld, free, the whole earth over, journeying up
    and down till we make our ineffaceable mark upon time and
    the diverse eras,
Till we saturate time and eras, that the men and women of
    races, ages to come, may prove brethren and lovers as
    we are.

YOU FELONS ON TRIAL IN COURTS

You felons on trial in courts,
You convicts in prison-cells, you sentenced assassins chain'd and
    handcuffed with iron,
Who am I too that I am not on trial or in prison?
Me ruthless and devilish as any, that my wrists are not chain'd
    with iron, or my ankles with iron?

You prostitutes flaunting over the trottoirs or obscene in your
    rooms,

Who am I that I should call you more obscene than myself?

O culpable! I acknowledge—I exposé!
(O admirers, praise not me—compliment not me—you make me
    wince,
I see what you do not—I know what you do not.)

Inside these breast-bones I lie smutch'd and choked,
Beneath this face that appears so impassive hell's tides continually
    run,
Lusts and wickedness are acceptable to me,
I walk with delinquents with passionate love,
I feel I am of them—I belong to those convicts and prostitutes
    myself,
And henceforth I will not deny them—for how can I deny
    myself?

LAWS FOR CREATIONS

Laws for creations,
For strong artists and leaders, for fresh broods of teachers and
    perfect literats for America,
For noble savans and coming musicians.

All must have reference to the ensemble of the world, and the
    compact truth of the world,
There shall be no subject too pronounced—all works shall
    illustrate the divine law of indirections.

What do you suppose creation is?
What do you suppose will satisfy the soul, except to walk free and
    own no superior?
What do you suppose I would intimate to you in a hundred ways,
    but that man or woman is as good as God?
And that there is no God any more divine than Yourself?
And that that is what the oldest and newest myths finally
    mean?

And that you or any one must approach creations through such
    laws?

TO A COMMON PROSTITUTE

Be composed—be at ease with me—I am Walt Whitman, liberal
    and lusty as Nature,
Not till the sun excludes you do I exclude you,
Not till the waters refuse to glisten for you and the leaves to
    rustle for you, do my words refuse to glisten and rustle
    for you.

My girl I appoint with you an appointment, and I charge you that
    you make preparation to be worthy to meet me,
And I charge you that you be patient and perfect till I come.

Till then I salute you with a significant look that you do not
    forget me.

I WAS LOOKING A LONG WHILE

I was looking a long while for Intentions,
For a clew to the history of the past for myself, and for these
    chants—and now I have found it,
It is not in those paged fables in the libraries, (them I neither
    accept nor reject,)
It is no more in the legends than in all else,
It is in the present—it is this earth to-day,
It is in Democracy—(the purport and aim of all the past,)
It is the life of one man or one woman to-day—the average man
    of to-day,
It is in languages, social customs, literatures, arts,
It is in the broad show of artificial things, ships, machinery,
    politics, creeds, modern improvements, and the interchange
    of nations,
All for the modern—all for the average man of to-day.

THOUGHT

Of persons arrived at high positions, ceremonies, wealth,
    scholarships, and the like;
(To me all that those persons have arrived at sinks away from
    them, except as it results to their bodies and souls,
So that often to me they appear gaunt and naked,
And often to me each one mocks the others, and mocks himself
    or herself,
And of each one the core of life, namely happiness, is full of the
    rotten excrement of maggots,
And often to me those men and women pass unwittingly the true
    realities of life, and go toward false realities,
And often to me they are alive after what custom has served them,
    but nothing more,
And often to me they are sad, hasty, unwaked sonnambules
    walking the dusk.)

MIRACLES

Why, who makes much of a miracle?
As to me I know of nothing else but miracles,
Whether I walk the streets of Manhattan,
Or dart my sight over the roofs of houses toward the sky,
Or wade with naked feet along the beach just in the edge of the
    water,
Or stand under trees in the woods,
Or talk by day with any one I love, or sleep in the bed at night
    with any one I love,
Or sit at table at dinner with the rest,
Or look at strangers opposite me riding in the car,
Or watch honey-bees busy around the hive of a summer
    forenoon,
Or animals feeding in the fields,
Or birds, or the wonderfulness of insects in the air,
Or the wonderfulness of the sundown, or of stars shining so quiet
    and bright,

Or the exquisite delicate thin curve of the new moon in spring;
These with the rest, one and all, are to me miracles,
The whole referring, yet each distinct and in its place.

To me every hour of the light and dark is a miracle,
Every cubic inch of space is a miracle,
Every square yard of the surface of the earth is spread with the same,
Every foot of the interior swarms with the same.

To me the sea is a continual miracle,
The fishes that swim—the rocks—the motion of the waves—the
    ships with men in them,
What stranger miracles are there?

SPARKLES FROM THE WHEEL

Where the city's ceaseless crowd moves on the livelong day,
Withdrawn I join a group of children watching, I pause aside with
    them.

By the curb toward the edge of the flagging,
A knife-grinder works at his wheel sharpening a great knife,
Bending over he carefully holds it to the stone, by foot and knee,
With measur'd tread he turns rapidly, as he presses with light but
    firm hand,
Forth issue then in copious golden jets,
Sparkles from the wheel.

The scene and all its belongings, how they seize and affect me,
The sad sharp-chinn'd old man with worn clothes and broad
    shoulder-band of leather,
Myself effusing and fluid, a phantom curiously floating, now here
    absorb'd and arrested,
The group, (an unminded point set in a vast surrounding,)
The attentive, quiet children, the loud, proud, restive base of the
    streets,
The low hoarse purr of the whirling stone, the light-press'd blade,

Diffusing, dropping, sideways-darting, in tiny showers of gold,
Sparkles from the wheel.

TO A PUPIL

Is reform needed? is it through you?
The greater the reform needed, the greater the Personality you
    need to accomplish it.

You! do you not see how it would serve to have eyes, blood,
    complexion, clean and sweet?
Do you not see how it would serve to have such a body and soul
    that when you enter the crowd an atmosphere of desire and
    command enters with you, and every one is impress'd with
    your Personality?

O the magnet! the flesh over and over!
Go, dear friend, if need be give up all else, and commence to-day
    to inure yourself to pluck, reality, self-esteem, definiteness,
    elevatedness,
Rest not till you rivet and publish yourself of your own Personality.

UNFOLDED OUT OF THE FOLDS[81]

Unfolded out of the folds of the woman man comes unfolded,
    and is always to come unfolded,
Unfolded only out of the superbest woman of the earth is to come
    the superbest man of the earth,
Unfolded out of the friendliest woman is to come the friendliest
    man,
Unfolded only out of the perfect body of a woman can a man be
    form'd of perfect body,
Unfolded only out of the inimitable poems of woman can come
    the poems of man, (only thence have my poems come;)
Unfolded out of the strong and arrogant woman I love, only
    thence can appear the strong and arrogant man I love,

Unfolded by brawny embraces from the well-muscled woman I
    love, only thence come the brawny embraces of the man,
Unfolded out of the folds of the woman's brain come all the folds
    of the man's brain, duly obedient,
Unfolded out of the justice of the woman all justice is unfolded,
Unfolded out of the sympathy of the woman is all sympathy;
A man is a great thing upon the earth and through eternity, but
    every jot of the greatness of man is unfolded out of woman;
First the man is shaped in the woman, he can then be shaped in
    himself.

WHAT AM I AFTER ALL

What am I after all but a child, pleas'd with the sound of my own
    name? repeating it over and over;
I stand apart to hear—it never tires me.

To you your name also;
Did you think there was nothing but two or three pronunciations
    in the sound of your name?

KOSMOS

Who includes diversity and is Nature,
Who is the amplitude of the earth, and the coarseness and
    sexuality of the earth, and the great charity of the earth, and
    the equilibrium also,
Who has not look'd forth from the windows the eyes for nothing,
    or whose brain held audience with messengers for nothing,
Who contains believers and disbelievers, who is the most majestic
    lover,
Who holds duly his or her triune proportion of realism,
    spiritualism, and of the æsthetic or intellectual,
Who having consider'd the body finds all its organs and parts good,
Who, out of the theory of the earth and of his or her body
    understands by subtle analogies all other theories,

The theory of a city, a poem, and of the large politics of these
    States;
Who believes not only in our globe with its sun and moon, but in
    other globes with their suns and moons,
Who, constructing the house of himself or herself, not for a day
    but for all time, sees races, eras, dates, generations,
The past, the future, dwelling there, like space, inseparable
    together.

OTHERS MAY PRAISE WHAT THEY LIKE

Others may praise what they like;
But I, from the banks of the running Missouri, praise nothing in
    art or aught else,
Till it has well inhaled the atmosphere of this river, also the
    western prairie-scent,
And exudes it all again.

WHO LEARNS MY LESSON COMPLETE?

Who learns my lesson complete?
Boss, journeyman, apprentice, churchman and atheist,
The stupid and the wise thinker, parents and offspring, merchant,
    clerk, porter and customer,
Editor, author, artist, and schoolboy—draw nigh and
    commence;
It is no lesson—it lets down the bars to a good lesson,
And that to another, and every one to another still.

The great laws take and effuse without argument,
I am of the same style, for I am their friend,
I love them quits and quits, I do not halt and make salaams.

I lie abstracted and hear beautiful tales of things and the reasons
    of things,
They are so beautiful I nudge myself to listen.

I cannot say to any person what I hear—I cannot say it to
    myself—it is very wonderful.

It is no small matter, this round and delicious globe moving so
    exactly in its orbit for ever and ever, without one jolt or the
    untruth of a single second,
I do not think it was made in six days, nor in ten thousand years,
    nor ten billions of years,
Nor plann'd and built one thing after another as an architect
    plans and builds a house.

I do not think seventy years is the time of a man or woman,
Nor that seventy millions of years is the time of a man or
    woman,
Nor that years will ever stop the existence of me, or any
    one else.

Is it wonderful that I should be immortal? as every one is
    immortal;
I know it is wonderful, but my eyesight is equally wonderful, and
    how I was conceived in my mother's womb is equally
    wonderful,
And pass'd from a babe in the creeping trance of a couple of
    summers and winters to articulate and walk—all this is
    equally wonderful.

And that my soul embraces you this hour, and we affect
    each other without ever seeing each other, and never
    perhaps to see each other, is every bit as wonderful.

And that I can think such thoughts as these is just as
    wonderful,
And that I can remind you, and you think them and know them
    to be true, is just as wonderful.
And that the moon spins round the earth and on with the earth, is
    equally wonderful,
And that they balance themselves with the sun and stars is equally
    wonderful.

TESTS

All submit to them where they sit, inner, secure, unapproachable
    to analysis in the soul,
Not traditions, not the outer authorities are the judges,
They are the judges of outer authorities and of all traditions,
They corroborate as they go only whatever corroborates
    themselves, and touches themselves;
For all that, they have it forever in themselves to corroborate far
    and near without one exception.

THE TORCH

On my Northwest coast in the midst of the night a fishermen's
    group stands watching,
Out on the lake that expands before them, others are spearing
    salmon,
The canoe, a dim shadowy thing, moves across the black water,
Bearing a torch ablaze at the prow.

O STAR OF FRANCE (1870-71)[82]

O star of France,
The brightness of thy hope and strength and fame,
Like some proud ship that led the fleet so long,
Beseems to-day a wreck driven by the gale, a mastless hulk,
And 'mid its teeming madden'd half-drown'd crowds,
Nor helm nor helmsman.

Dim smitten star,
Orb not of France alone, pale symbol of my soul, its dearest
    hopes,
The struggle and the daring, rage divine for liberty,
Of aspirations toward the far ideal, enthusiast's dreams of
    brotherhood,
Of terror to the tyrant and the priest.

Star crucified—by traitors sold,
Star panting o'er a land of death, heroic land,
Strange, passionate, mocking, frivolous land.

Miserable! yet for thy errors, vanities, sins, I will not now rebuke
    thee,
Thy unexampled woes and pangs have quell'd them all,
And left thee sacred.

In that amid thy many faults thou ever aimedst highly,
In that thou wouldst not really sell thyself however great the
    price,
In that thou surely wakedst weeping from thy drugg'd sleep,
In that alone among thy sisters thou, giantess, didst rend the ones
    that shamed thee,
In that thou couldst not, wouldst not, wear the usual chains,
This cross, thy livid face, thy pierced hands and feet,
The spear thrust in thy side.

O star! O ship of France, beat back and baffled long!
Bear up O smitten orb! O ship continue on!

Sure as the ship of all, the Earth itself,
Product of deathly fire and turbulent chaos,
Forth from its spasms of fury and its poisons,
Issuing at last in perfect power and beauty,
Onward beneath the sun following its course,
So thee O ship of France!

Finish'd the days, the clouds dispel'd,
The travail o'er, the long-sought extrication,
When lo! reborn, high o'er the European world,
(In gladness answering thence, as face afar to face, reflecting ours
    Columbia,)
Again thy star O France, fair lustrous star,
In heavenly peace, clearer, more bright than ever,
Shall beam immortal.

THE OX-TAMER

In a far-away northern county in the placid pastoral region,
Lives my farmer friend, the theme of my recitative, a famous
    tamer of oxen,
There they bring him the three-year-olds and the four-year-olds to
    break them,
He will take the wildest steer in the world and break him and
    tame him,
He will go fearless without any whip where the young bullock
    chafes up and down the yard,
The bullock's head tosses restless high in the air with raging
    eyes,
Yet see you! how soon his rage subsides—how soon this tamer
    tames him;
See you! on the farms hereabout a hundred oxen young and old,
    and he is the man who has tamed them,
They all know him, all are affectionate to him;
See you! some are such beautiful animals, so lofty looking;
Some are buff-color'd, some mottled, one has a
        white line running along his back, some are
        brindled,
Some have wide flaring horns (a good sign)—see you! the bright
    hides,
See, the two with stars on their foreheads—see, the round bodies
    and broad backs,
How straight and square they stand on their legs—what fine
    sagacious eyes!
How they watch their tamer—they wish him near them—how
    they turn to look after him!
What yearning expression! how uneasy they are when he moves
    away from them;
Now I marvel what it can be he appears to them, (books, politics,
    poems, depart—all else departs,)
I confess I envy only his fascination—my silent, illiterate friend,
Whom a hundred oxen love there in his life on farms,
In the northern county far, in the placid pastoral region.

AN OLD MAN'S THOUGHT OF SCHOOL

For the Inauguration of a Public School, Camden,
New Jersey, 1874

An old man's thought of school,
An old man gathering youthful memories and blooms that youth
　　itself cannot.

Now only do I know you,
O fair auroral skies—O morning dew upon the grass!

And these I see, these sparkling eyes,
These stores of mystic meaning, these young lives,
Building, equipping like a fleet of ships, immortal ships,
Soon to sail out over the measureless seas,
On the soul's voyage.

Only a lot of boys and girls?
Only the tiresome spelling, writing, ciphering classes?
Only a public school?
Ah more, infinitely more;
(As George Fox rais'd his warning cry, "Is it this pile of brick and
　　mortar, these dead floors, windows, rails, you call the church?
Why this is not the church at all—the church is living, ever living
　　souls.")

And you America,
Cast you the real reckoning for your present?
The lights and shadows of your future, good or evil?
To girlhood, boyhood look, the teacher and the school.

WANDERING AT MORN

Wandering at morn,
Emerging from the night from gloomy thoughts, thee in my
　　thoughts,

Yearning for thee harmonious Union! thee, singing bird divine!
Thee coil'd in evil times my country, with craft and black dismay,
    with every meanness, treason thrust upon thee,
This common marvel I beheld—the parent thrush I watch'd
    feeding its young,
The singing thrush whose tones of joy and faith ecstatic,
Fail not to certify and cheer my soul.

There ponder'd, felt I,
If worms, snakes, loathsome grubs, may to sweet spiritual songs be
    turn'd,
If vermin so transposed, so used and bless'd may be,
Then may I trust in you, your fortunes, days, my country;
Who knows but these may be the lessons fit for you?
From these your future song may rise with joyous trills,
Destin'd to fill the world.

ITALIAN MUSIC IN DAKOTA[83]

["The Seventeenth—the finest Regimental Band I ever heard."]

Through the soft evening air enwinding all,
Rocks, woods, fort, cannon, pacing sentries, endless wilds,
In dulcet streams, in flutes' and cornets' notes,
Electric, pensive, turbulent, artificial,
(Yet strangely fitting even here, meanings unknown before,
Subtler than ever, more harmony, as if born here, related here,
Not to the city's fresco'd rooms, not to the audience of the opera
    house,
Sounds, echoes, wandering strains, as really here at home,
Sonnambula's innocent love, trios with *Norma's* anguish,
And thy ecstatic chorus *Poliuto*;)
Ray'd in the limpid yellow slanting sundown,
Music, Italian music in Dakota.

While Nature, sovereign of this gnarl'd realm,
Lurking in hidden barbaric grim recesses,

Acknowledging rapport however far remov'd,
(As some old root or soil of earth its last-born flower or fruit,)
Listens well pleas'd.

WITH ALL THY GIFTS

With all thy gifts America,
Standing secure, rapidly tending, overlooking the world,
Power, wealth, extent, vouchsafed to thee—with these and like of
    these vouchsafed to thee,
What if one gift thou lackest? (the ultimate human problem
    never solving,)
The gift of perfect women fit for thee—what if that gift of gifts
    thou lackest?
The towering feminine of thee? the beauty, health, completion,
    fit for thee?
The mothers fit for thee?

MY PICTURE-GALLERY

In a little house keep I pictures suspended, it is not a fix'd house,
It is round, it is only a few inches from one side to the other;
Yet behold, it has room for all the shows of the world, all
    memories!
Here the tableaus of life, and here the groupings of death;
Here, do you know this? this is cicerone himself,
With finger rais'd he points to the prodigal pictures.

THE PRAIRIE STATES

A newer garden of creation, no primal solitude,
Dense, joyous, modern, populous millions, cities and farms,
With iron interlaced, composite, tied, many in one,
By all the world contributed—freedom's and law's and thrift's
    society,

The crown and teeming paradise, so far, of time's accumulations,
To justify the past.

PROUD MUSIC OF THE STORM[84]

— 1 —

Proud music of the storm,
Blast that careers so free, whistling across the prairies,
Strong hum of forest tree-tops—wind of the mountains,
Personified dim shapes—you hidden orchestras,
You serenades of phantoms with instruments alert,
Blending with Nature's rhythmus all the tongues of nations;
You chords left as by vast composers—you choruses,
You formless, free, religious dances—you from the Orient,
You undertone of rivers, roar of pouring cataracts,
You sounds from distant guns with galloping cavalry,
Echoes of camps with all the different bugle-calls,
Trooping tumultuous, filling the midnight late, bending me
        powerless,
Entering my lonesome slumber-chamber, why have you
        seiz'd me?

— 2 —

Come forward O my soul, and let the rest retire,
Listen, lose not, it is toward thee they tend,
Parting the midnight, entering my slumber-chamber,
For thee they sing and dance O soul.

A festival song,
The duet of the bridegroom and the bride, a marriage-march,
With lips of love, and hearts of lovers fill'd to the brim with
        love,
The red-flush'd cheeks and perfumes, the cortege swarming full
        of friendly faces young and old,
To flutes' clear notes and sounding harps' cantabile.

Now loud approaching drums,
Victoria! see'st thou in powder-smoke the banners torn but flying?
    the rout of the baffled?
Hearest those shouts of a conquering army?

(Ah soul, the sobs of women, the wounded groaning in agony,
The hiss and crackle of flames, the blacken'd ruins, the embers of
    cities,
The dirge and desolation of mankind.)

Now airs antique and mediæval fill me,
I see and hear old harpers with their harps at Welsh festivals,
I hear the minnesingers singing their lays of love,
I hear the minstrels, gleemen, troubadours, of the middle ages.

Now the great organ sounds,
Tremulous, while underneath, (as the hid footholds of the earth,
On which arising rest, and leaping forth depend,
All shapes of beauty, grace and strength, all hues we know,
Green blades of grass and warbling birds, children that gambol
    and play, the clouds of heaven above,)
The strong base stands, and its pulsations intermits not,
Bathing, supporting, merging all the rest, maternity of all the rest,
And with it every instrument in multitudes,
The players playing, all the world's musicians,
The solemn hymns and masses rousing adoration,
All passionate heart-chants, sorrowful appeals,
The measureless sweet vocalists of ages,
And for their solvent setting earth's own diapason,
Of winds and woods and mighty ocean waves,
A new composite orchestra, binder of years and climes, ten-fold
    renewer,
As of the far-back days the poets tell, the Paradiso,
The straying thence, the separation long, but now the wandering
    done,
The journey done, the journeyman come home,
And man and art with Nature fused again.
Tutti! for earth and heaven;
(The Almighty leader now for once has signal'd with his wand.)

The manly strophe of the husbands of the world,
And all the wives responding.

The tongues of violins,
(I think O tongues ye tell this heart, that cannot tell itself,
This brooding yearning heart, that cannot tell itself.)

— 3 —

Ah from a little child,
Thou knowest soul how to me all sounds became music,
My mother's voice in lullaby or hymn,
(The voice, O tender voices, memory's loving voices,
Last miracle of all, O dearest mother's, sister's, voices;)
The rain, the growing corn, the breeze among the long-leav'd corn,
The measur'd sea-surf beating on the sand,
The twittering bird, the hawk's sharp scream,
The wild-fowl's notes at night as flying low migrating north or
     south,
The psalm in the country church or mid the clustering trees, the
     open air camp-meeting,
The fiddler in the tavern, the glee, the long-strung sailor-song,
The lowing cattle, bleating sheep, the crowing cock at dawn.

All songs of current lands come sounding round me,
The German airs of friendship, wine and love,
Irish ballads, merry jigs and dances, English warbles,
Chansons of France, Scotch tunes, and o'er the rest,
Italia's peerless compositions.

Across the stage with pallor on her face, yet lurid passion,
Stalks Norma brandishing the dagger in her hand.

I see poor crazed Lucia's eyes' unnatural gleam,
Her hair down her back falls loose and dishevel'd.

I see where Ernani walking the bridal garden,
Amid the scent of night-roses, radiant, holding his bride by the hand,
Hears the infernal call, the death-pledge of the horn.

To crossing swords and gray hairs bared to heaven,
The clear electric base and baritone of the world,
The trombone duo, Libertad forever!

From Spanish chestnut trees' dense shade,
By old and heavy convent walls a wailing song,
Song of lost love, the torch of youth and life quench'd in despair,
Song of the dying swan, Fernando's heart is breaking.

Awaking from her woes at last retriev'd Amina sings,
Copious as stars and glad as morning light the torrents of
    her joy.

(The teeming lady comes,
The lustrious orb, Venus contralto, the blooming mother,
Sister of loftiest gods, Alboni's self I hear.)

— 4 —

I hear those odes, symphonies, operas,
I hear in the *William Tell* the music of an arous'd and angry
    people,
I hear Meyerbeer's *Huguenots*, the *Prophet*, or *Robert*,
Gounod's *Faust*, or Mozart's *Don Juan*.

I hear the dance-music of all nations,
The waltz, some delicious measure, lapsing, bathing me in bliss,
The bolero to tinkling guitars and clattering castanets.

I see religious dances old and new,
I hear the sound of the Hebrew lyre,
I see the crusaders marching bearing the cross on high, to the
    martial clang of cymbals,
I hear dervishes monotonously chanting, interspers'd with frantic
    shouts, as they spin around turning always towards Mecca,
I see the rapt religious dances of the Persians and the Arabs,
Again, at Eleusis, home of Ceres, I see the modern Greeks
    dancing,

I hear them clapping their hands as they bend their bodies,
I hear the metrical shuffling of their feet.
I see again the wild old Corybantian dance, the performers
    wounding each other,
I see the Roman youth to the shrill sound of flageolets throwing
    and catching their weapons,
As they fall on their knees and rise again.

I hear from the Mussulman mosque the muezzin calling,
I see the worshippers within, nor form nor sermon, argument nor
    word,
But silent, strange, devout, rais'd, glowing heads, ecstatic faces.

I hear the Egyptian harps of many strings,
The primitive chants of the Nile boatmen,
The sacred imperial hymns of China,
To the delicate sounds of the king, (the stricken wood and stone,)
Or to Hindu flutes and the fretting twang of the vina,
A band of bayaderes.

– 5 –

Now Asia, Africa leave me, Europe seizing inflates me,
To organs huge and bands I hear as from vast concourses of voices,
Luther's strong hymn *Eine feste Burg ist unser Gott,*
Rossini's *Stabat Mater dolorosa,*
Or floating in some high cathedral dim with gorgeous color'd
    windows,
The passionate *Agnus Dei* or *Gloria in Excelsis.*

Composers! mighty maestros!
And you, sweet singers of old lands, soprani, tenori, bassi!
To you a new bard caroling in the West,
Obeisant sends his love.

(Such led to thee O soul,
All senses, shows and objects, lead to thee,
But now it seems to me sound leads o'er all the rest.)

I hear the annual singing of the children in St. Paul's
    cathedral,
Or, under the high roof of some colossal hall, the symphonies,
    oratorios of Beethoven, Handel, or Haydn,
The *Creation* in billows of godhood laves me.

Give me to hold all sounds, (I madly struggling cry,)
Fill me with all the voices of the universe,
Endow me with their throbbings, Nature's also,
The tempests, waters, winds, operas and chants, marches and
    dances,
Utter, pour in, for I would take them all!

– 6 –

Then I woke softly,
And pausing, questioning awhile the music of my dream,
And questioning all those reminiscences, the tempest in its fury,
And all the songs of sopranos and tenors,
And those rapt oriental dances of religious fervor,
And the sweet varied instruments, and the diapason of organs,
And all the artless plaints of love and grief and death,
I said to my silent curious soul out of the bed of the slumber-
    chamber,
Come, for I have found the clue I sought so long,
Let us go forth refresh'd amid the day,
Cheerfully tallying life, walking the world, the real,
Nourish'd henceforth by our celestial dream.

And I said, moreover,
Haply what thou hast heard O soul was not the sound of winds,
Nor dream of raging storm, nor sea-hawk's flapping wings nor
    harsh scream,
Nor vocalism of sun-bright Italy,
Nor German organ majestic, nor vast concourse of voices, nor
    layers of harmonies,
Nor strophes of husbands and wives, nor sound of marching
    soldiers,

Nor flutes, nor harps, nor the bugle-calls of camps,
But to a new rhythmus fitted for thee,
Poems bridging the way from Life to Death, vaguely wafted in
　　night air, uncaught, unwritten,
Which let us go forth in the bold day and write.

PASSAGE TO INDIA[85]

− 1 −

Singing my days,
Singing the great achievements of the present,
Singing the strong light works of engineers,
Our modern wonders, (the antique ponderous Seven outvied,)
In the Old World the east the Suez canal,
The New by its mighty railroad spann'd,
The seas inlaid with eloquent gentle wires;
Yet first to sound, and ever sound, the cry with thee O soul,
The Past! the Past! the Past!

The Past—the dark unfathom'd retrospect!
The teeming gulf—the sleepers and the shadows!
The past—the infinite greatness of the past!
For what is the present after all but a growth out of the past?
(As a projectile form'd, impell'd, passing a certain line, still
　　keeps on,
So the present, utterly form'd, impell'd by the past.)

− 2 −

Passage O soul to India!
Eclaircise* the myths Asiatic, the primitive fables.

Not you alone proud truths of the world,

---

*Clarify (French).

Nor you alone ye facts of modern science,
But myths and fables of eld, Asia's, Africa's fables,
The far-darting beams of the spirit, the unloos'd dreams,
The deep diving bibles and legends,
The daring plots of the poets, the elder religions;
O you temples fairer than lilies pour'd over by the rising sun!
O you fables spurning the known, eluding the hold of the known,
      mounting to heaven!
You lofty and dazzling towers, pinnacled, red as roses, burnish'd
      with gold!
Towers of fables immortal fashion'd from mortal dreams!
You too I welcome and fully the same as the rest!
You too with joy I sing.

Passage to India!
Lo, soul, seest thou not God's purpose from the first?
The earth to be spann'd, connected by network,
The races, neighbors, to marry and be given in marriage,
The oceans to be cross'd, the distant brought near,
The lands to be welded together.

A worship new I sing,
You captains, voyagers, explorers, yours,
You engineers, you architects, machinists, yours,
You, not for trade or transportation only,
But in God's name, and for thy sake O soul.

– 3 –

Passage to India!
Lo soul for thee of tableaus twain,
I see in one the Suez canal initiated, open'd,
I see the procession of steamships, the Empress Eugenie's leading
      the van,
I mark from on deck the strange landscape, the pure sky, the level
      sand in the distance,
I pass swiftly the picturesque groups, the workmen gather'd,
The gigantic dredging machines.

In one again, different, (yet thine, all thine, O soul, the same,)
I see over my own continent the Pacific railroad surmounting
    every barrier,
I see continual trains of cars winding along the Platte carrying
    freight and passengers,
I hear the locomotives rushing and roaring, and the shrill steam-
    whistle,
I hear the echoes reverberate through the grandest scenery in the
    world,
I cross the Laramie plains, I note the rocks in grotesque shapes,
    the buttes,
I see the plentiful larkspur and wild onions, the barren, colorless,
    sage-deserts,
I see in glimpses afar or towering immediately above me the great
    mountains, I see the Wind river and the Wahsatch
    mountains,
I see the Monument mountain and the Eagle's Nest, I pass the
    Promontory, I ascend the Nevadas,
I scan the noble Elk mountain and wind around its base,
I see the Humboldt range, I thread the valley and cross the river,
I see the clear waters of lake Tahoe, I see forests of majestic pines,
Or crossing the great desert, the alkaline plains, I behold
    enchanting mirages of waters and meadows,
Marking through these and after all, in duplicate slender lines,
Bridging the three or four thousand miles of land travel,
Tying the Eastern to the Western sea,
The road between Europe and Asia.

(Ah Genoese thy dream! thy dream!
Centuries after thou art laid in thy grave,
The shore thou foundest verifies thy dream.)

— 4 —

Passage to India!
Struggles of many a captain, tales of many a sailor dead,
Over my mood stealing and spreading they come,
Like clouds and cloudlets in the unreach'd sky.

Along all history, down the slopes,
As a rivulet running, sinking now, and now again to the surface
    rising,
A ceaseless thought, a varied train—lo, soul, to thee, thy sight,
    they rise,
The plans, the voyages again, the expeditions;
Again Vasco de Gama sails forth,
Again the knowledge gain'd, the mariner's compass,
Lands found and nations born, thou born America,
For purpose vast, man's long probation fill'd,
Thou rondure of the world at last accomplish'd.

– 5 –

O vast Rondure, swimming in space,
Cover'd all over with visible power and beauty,
Alternate light and day and the teeming spiritual darkness,
Unspeakable high processions of sun and moon and countless
    stars above,
Below, the manifold grass and waters, animals, mountains, trees,
With inscrutable purpose, some hidden prophetic intention,
Now first it seems my thought begins to span thee.

Down from the gardens of Asia descending radiating,
Adam and Eve appear, then their myriad progeny after them,
Wandering, yearning, curious, with restless explorations,
With questionings, baffled, formless, feverish, with never-happy
    hearts,
With that sad incessant refrain, *Wherefore unsatisfied soul?* and
    Whither O mocking life?

Ah who shall soothe these feverish children?
Who justify these restless explorations?
Who speak the secret of impassive earth?
Who bind it to us? what is this separate Nature so unnatural?
What is this earth to our affections? (unloving earth, without a
    throb to answer ours,
Cold earth, the place of graves.)

Yet soul be sure the first intent remains, and shall be carried out,
Perhaps even now the time has arrived.

After the seas are all cross'd, (as they seem already cross'd,)
After the great captains and engineers have accomplish'd their
    work,
After the noble inventors, after the scientists, the chemist, the
    geologist, ethnologist,
Finally shall come the poet worthy that name,
The true son of God shall come singing his songs.

Then not your deeds only O voyagers, O scientists and inventors,
    shall be justified,
All these hearts as of fretted children shall be sooth'd,
All affection shall be fully responded to, the secret shall be told,
All these separations and gaps shall be taken up and hook'd and
    link'd together,
The whole earth, this cold, impassive, voiceless earth, shall be
    completely justified,
Trinitas divine shall be gloriously accomplish'd and compacted by
    the true son of God, the poet,
(He shall indeed pass the straits and conquer the mountains,
He shall double the cape of Good Hope to some purpose,)
Nature and Man shall be disjoin'd and diffused no more,
The true son of God shall absolutely fuse them.

– 6 –

Year at whose wide-flung door I sing!
Year of the purpose accomplish'd!
Year of the marriage of continents, climates and oceans!
(No mere doge of Venice now wedding the Adriatic,)
I see O year in you the vast terraqueous globe given and
    giving all,
Europe to Asia, Africa join'd, and they to the New World,
The lands, geographies, dancing before you, holding a festival
    garland,
As brides and bridegrooms hand in hand.

Passage to India!
Cooling airs from Caucasus far, soothing cradle of man,
The river Euphrates flowing, the past lit up again.

Lo soul, the retrospect brought forward,
The old, most populous, wealthiest of earth's lands,
The streams of the Indus and the Ganges and their many
        affluents,
(I my shores of America walking to-day behold, resuming all,)
The tale of Alexander on his warlike marches suddenly dying,
On one side China and on the other side Persia and Arabia,
To the south the great seas and the bay of Bengal,
The flowing literatures, tremendous epics, religions, castes,
Old occult Brahma interminably far back, the tender and junior
        Buddha,
Central and southern empires and all their belongings, possessors,
The wars of Tamerlane, the reign of Aurungzebe,
The traders, rulers, explorers, Moslems, Venetians, Byzantium,
        the Arabs, Portuguese,
The first travelers famous yet, Marco Polo, Batouta the Moor,
Doubts to be solv'd, the map incognita, blanks to be fill'd,
The foot of man unstay'd, the hands never at rest,
Thyself O soul that will not brook a challenge.

The mediæval navigators rise before me,
The world of 1492, with its awaken'd enterprise,
Something swelling in humanity now like the sap of the earth in
        spring,
The sunset splendor of chivalry declining.

And who art thou sad shade?
Gigantic, visionary, thyself a visionary,
With majestic limbs and pious beaming eyes,
Spreading around with every look of thine a golden world,
Enhuing it with gorgeous hues.

As the chief histrion,
Down to the footlights walks in some great scena,

Dominating the rest I see the Admiral himself,
(History's type of courage, action, faith,)
Behold him sail from Palos leading his little fleet,
His voyage behold, his return, his great fame,
His misfortunes, calumniators, behold him a prisoner, chain'd,
Behold his dejection, poverty, death.

(Curious in time I stand, noting the efforts of heroes,
Is the deferment long? bitter the slander, poverty, death?
Lies the seed unreck'd for centuries in the ground? lo, to God's
    due occasion,
Uprising in the night, it sprouts, blooms,
And fills the earth with use and beauty.)

– 7 –

Passage indeed O soul to primal thought,
Not lands and seas alone, thy own clear freshness,
The young maturity of brood and bloom,
To realms of budding bibles.

O soul, repressless, I with thee and thou with me,
Thy circumnavigation of the world begin,
Of man, the voyage of his mind's return,
To reason's early paradise,
Back, back to wisdom's birth, to innocent intuitions,
Again with fair creation.

– 8 –

O we can wait no longer,
We too take ship O soul,
Joyous we too launch out on trackless seas,
Fearless for unknown shores on waves of ecstasy to sail,
Amid the wafting winds, (thou pressing me to thee, I thee to me,
    O soul,)
Caroling free, singing our song of God,
Chanting our chant of pleasant exploration.

With laugh and many a kiss,
(Let others deprecate, let others weep for sin, remorse,
      humiliation,)
O soul thou pleasest me, I thee.

Ah more than any priest O soul we too believe in God,
But with the mystery of God we dare not dally.

O soul thou pleasest me, I thee,
Sailing these seas or on the hills, or waking in the night,
Thoughts, silent thoughts, of Time and Space and Death, like
      waters flowing,
Bear me indeed as through the regions infinite,
Whose air I breathe, whose ripples hear, lave me all over,
Bathe me O God in thee, mounting to thee,
I and my soul to range in range of thee.

O Thou transcendent,
Nameless, the fibre and the breath,
Light of the light, shedding forth universes, thou centre of them,
Thou mightier centre of the true, the good, the loving,
Thou moral, spiritual fountain—affection's source—thou
      reservoir,
(O pensive soul of me—O thirst unsatisfied—waitest not there?
Waitest not haply for us somewhere there the Comrade perfect?)
Thou pulse—thou motive of the stars, suns, systems,
That, circling, move in order, safe, harmonious,
Athwart the shapeless vastnesses of space,
How should I think, how breathe a single breath, how speak, if,
      out of myself,
I could not launch, to those, superior universes?

Swiftly I shrivel at the thought of God,
At Nature and its wonders, Time and Space and Death,
But that I, turning, call to thee O soul, thou actual Me,
And lo, thou gently masterest the orbs,
Thou matest Time, smilest content at Death,
And fillest, swellest full the vastnesses of Space.

Greater than stars or suns,
Bounding O soul thou journeyest forth;
What love than thine and ours could wider amplify?
What aspirations, wishes, outvie thine and ours O soul?
What dreams of the ideal? what plans of purity, perfection, strength?
What cheerful willingness for others' sake to give up all?
For others' sake to suffer all?

Reckoning ahead O soul when thou, the time achiev'd,
The seas all cross'd, weather'd the capes, the voyage done,
Surrounded, copest, frontest God, yieldest, the aim attain'd,
As fill'd with friendship, love complete, the Elder Brother found,
The Younger melts in fondness in his arms.

9

Passage to more than India!
Are thy wings plumed indeed for such far flights?
O soul, voyagest thou indeed on voyages like those?
Disportest thou on waters such as those?
Soundest below the Sanscrit and the Vedas?
Then have thy bent unleash'd.

Passage to you, your shores, ye aged fierce enigmas!
Passage to you, to mastership of you, ye strangling problems!
You, strew'd with the wrecks of skeletons, that, living, never
     reach'd you.

Passage to more than India!
O secret of the earth and sky!
Of you O waters of the sea! O winding creeks and rivers!
Of you O woods and fields! of you strong mountains of my land!
Of you O prairies! of you gray rocks!
O morning red! O clouds! O rain and snows!
O day and night, passage to you!

O sun and moon and all you stars! Sirius and Jupiter!
Passage to you!

Passage, immediate passage! the blood burns in my veins!
Away O soul! hoist instantly the anchor!
Cut the hawsers—haul out—shake out every sail!
Have we not stood here like trees in the ground long enough?
Have we not grovel'd here long enough, eating and drinking like
    mere brutes?
Have we not darken'd and dazed ourselves with books long
    enough?

Sail forth—steer for the deep waters only,
Reckless O soul, exploring, I with thee, and thou with me,
For we are bound where mariner has not yet dared to go,
And we will risk the ship, ourselves and all.

O my brave soul!
O farther farther sail!
O daring joy, but safe! are they not all the seas of God?
O farther, farther, farther sail!

PRAYER OF COLUMBUS[86]

A batter'd, wreck'd old man,
Thrown on this savage shore, far, far from home,
Pent by the sea and dark rebellious brows, twelve dreary months,
Sore, stiff with many toils, sicken'd and nigh to death,
I take my way along the island's edge,
Venting a heavy heart.

I am too full of woe!
Haply I may not live another day;
I cannot rest O God, I cannot eat or drink or sleep,
Till I put forth myself, my prayer, once more to Thee,
Breathe, bathe myself once more in Thee, commune with Thee,
Report myself once more to Thee.

Thou knowest my years entire, my life,
My long and crowded life of active work, not adoration merely;

Thou knowest the prayers and vigils of my youth,
Thou knowest my manhood's solemn and visionary meditations,
Thou knowest how before I commenced I devoted all to come to
     Thee,
Thou knowest I have in age ratified all those vows and strictly
     kept them,
Thou knowest I have not once lost nor faith nor ecstasy in Thee,
In shackles, prison'd, in disgrace, repining not,
Accepting all from Thee, as duly come from Thee.

All my emprises have been fill'd with Thee,
My speculations, plans, begun and carried on in thoughts of Thee,
Sailing the deep or journeying the land for Thee;
Intentions, purports, aspirations mine, leaving results to Thee.

O I am sure they really came from Thee,
The urge, the ardor, the unconquerable will,
The potent, felt, interior command, stronger than words,
A message from the Heavens whispering to me even in sleep,
These sped me on.

By me and these the work so far accomplish'd,
By me earth's elder cloy'd and stifled lands uncloy'd, unloos'd,
By me the hemispheres rounded and tied, the unknown to the
     known.

The end I know not, it is all in Thee,
Or small or great I know not—haply what broad fields, what
     lands,
Haply the brutish measureless human undergrowth I know,
Transplanted there may rise to stature, knowledge worthy Thee,
Haply the swords I know may there indeed be turn'd to reaping-
     tools,
Haply the lifeless cross I know, Europe's dead cross, may bud and
     blossom there.

One effort more, my altar this bleak sand;
That Thou O God my life hast lighted,

With ray of light, steady, ineffable, vouchsafed of Thee,
Light rare untellable, lighting the very light,
Beyond all signs, descriptions, languages;
For that O God, be it my latest word, here on my knees,
Old, poor, and paralyzed, I thank Thee.

My terminus near,
The clouds already closing in upon me,
The voyage balk'd, the course disputed, lost,
I yield my ships to Thee.

My hands, my limbs grow nerveless,
My brain feels rack'd, bewilder'd,
Let the old timbers part, I will not part,
I will cling fast to Thee, O God, though the waves buffet me,
Thee, Thee at least I know.

Is it the prophet's thought I speak, or am I raving?
What do I know of life? what of myself?
I know not even my own work past or present,
Dim ever-shifting guesses of it spread before me,
Of newer better worlds, their mighty parturition,
Mocking, perplexing me.

And these things I see suddenly, what mean they?
As if some miracle, some hand divine unseal'd my eyes,
Shadowy vast shapes smile through the air and sky,
And on the distant waves sail countless ships,
And anthems in new tongues I hear saluting me.

THE SLEEPERS[87]

— 1 —

I wander all night in my vision,
Stepping with light feet, swiftly and noiselessly stepping and
    stopping,
Bending with open eyes over the shut eyes of sleepers,

Wandering and confused, lost to myself, ill-assorted, contradictory,
Pausing, gazing, bending, and stopping.

How solemn they look there, stretch'd and still,
How quiet they breathe, the little children in their cradles.

The wretched features of ennuyés, the white features of
    corpses, the livid faces of drunkards, the sick-gray faces of
    onanists,
The gash'd bodies on battle-fields, the insane in their strong-
    door'd rooms, the sacred idiots, the new-born emerging from
    gates, and the dying emerging from gates,
The night pervades them and infolds them.

The married couple sleep calmly in their bed, he with his palm
    on the hip of the wife, and she with her palm on the hip of
    the husband,
The sisters sleep lovingly side by side in their bed,
The men sleep lovingly side by side in theirs,
And the mother sleeps with her little child carefully wrapt.

The blind sleep, and the deaf and dumb sleep,
The prisoner sleeps well in the prison, the runaway son sleeps,
The murderer that is to be hung next day, how does he sleep?
And the murder'd person, how does he sleep?

The female that loves unrequited sleeps,
And the male that loves unrequited sleeps,
The head of the money-maker that plotted all day sleeps,
And the enraged and treacherous dispositions, all, all sleep.

I stand in the dark with drooping eyes by the worst-suffering and
    the most restless,
I pass my hands soothingly to and fro a few inches from them,
The restless sink in their beds, they fitfully sleep.

Now I pierce the darkness, new beings appear,
The earth recedes from me into the night,

I saw that it was beautiful, and I see that what is not the earth is
   beautiful.

I go from bedside to bedside, I sleep close with the other sleepers
   each in turn,
I dream in my dream all the dreams of the other dreamers,
And I become the other dreamers.

I am a dance—play up there! the fit is whirling me fast!

I am the ever-laughing—it is new moon and twilight,
I see the hiding of douceurs, I see nimble ghosts whichever way I
   look,
Cache and cache again deep in the ground and sea, and where it
   is neither ground nor sea.

Well do they do their jobs those journeymen divine,
Only from me can they hide nothing, and would not if they could,
I reckon I am their boss and they make me a pet besides,
And surround me and lead me and run ahead when I walk,
To lift their cunning covers to signify me with stretch'd arms, and
   resume the way;
Onward we move, a gay gang of blackguards! with mirth-shouting
   music and wild-flapping pennants of joy!

I am the actor, the actress, the voter, the politician,
The emigrant and the exile, the criminal that stood in the box,
He who has been famous and he who shall be famous after to-day,
The stammerer, the well-form'd person, the wasted or feeble
   person.

I am she who adorn'd herself and folded her hair expectantly,
My truant lover has come, and it is dark.

Double yourself and receive me darkness,
Receive me and my lover too, he will not let me go without him.

I roll myself upon you as upon a bed, I resign myself to the dusk.

He whom I call answers me and takes the place of my lover,
He rises with me silently from the bed.

Darkness, you are gentler than my lover, his flesh was sweaty and
    panting,
I feel the hot moisture yet that he left me.

My hands are spread forth, I pass them in all directions,
I would sound up the shadowy shore to which you are
    journeying.

Be careful darkness! already what was it touch'd me?
I thought my lover had gone, else darkness and he are one,
I hear the heart-beat, I follow, I fade away.

— 2 —

I descend my western course, my sinews are flaccid,
Perfume and youth course through me and I am their wake.

It is my face yellow and wrinkled instead of the old woman's,
I sit low in a straw-bottom chair and carefully darn my grandson's
    stockings.

It is I too, the sleepless widow looking out on the winter
    midnight,
I see the sparkles of starshine on the icy and pallid earth.

A shroud I see and I am the shroud, I wrap a body and lie in the
    coffin,
It is dark here under ground, it is not evil or pain here, it is blank
    here, for reasons.

(It seems to me that every thing in the light and air ought to be
    happy,
Whoever is not in his coffin and the dark grave let him know he
    has enough.)

– 3 –

I see a beautiful gigantic swimmer swimming naked through the
    eddies of the sea,
His brown hair lies close and even to his head, he strikes out with
    courageous arms, he urges himself with his legs,
I see his white body, I see his undaunted eyes,
I hate the swift-running eddies that would dash him head-
    foremost on the rocks.

What are you doing you ruffianly red-trickled waves?
Will you kill the courageous giant? will you kill him in the prime
    of his middle age?

Steady and long he struggles,
He is baffled, bang'd, bruis'd, he holds out while his strength
    holds out,
The slapping eddies are spotted with his blood, they bear him
    away, they roll him, swing him, turn him,
His beautiful body is borne in the circling eddies, it is continually
    bruis'd on rocks,
Swiftly and out of sight is borne the brave corpse.

– 4 –

I turn but do not extricate myself,
Confused, a past-reading, another, but with darkness yet.

The beach is cut by the razory ice-wind, the wreck-guns sound,
The tempest lulls, the moon comes floundering through the
    drifts.

I look where the ship helplessly heads end on, I hear the burst as
    she strikes, I hear the howls of dismay, they grow fainter and
    fainter.

I cannot aid with my wringing fingers,
I can but rush to the surf and let it drench me and freeze upon me.

I search with the crowd, not one of the company is wash'd to us
 alive,
In the morning I help pick up the dead and lay them in rows in
 a barn.

– 5 –

Now of the older war-days, the defeat at Brooklyn,
Washington stands inside the lines, he stands on the intrench'd
 hills amid a crowd of officers,
His face is cold and damp, he cannot repress the weeping
 drops,
He lifts the glass perpetually to his eyes, the color is blanch'd
 from his cheeks,
He sees the slaughter of the southern braves confided to him by
 their parents.

The same at last and at last when peace is declared,
He stands in the room of the old tavern, the well-belov'd soldiers
 all pass through,
The officers speechless and slow draw near in their turns,
The chief encircles their necks with his arm and kisses them on
 the cheek,
He kisses lightly the wet cheeks one after another, he shakes
 hands and bids good-by to the army.

– 6 –

Now what my mother told me one day as we sat at dinner
 together,
Of when she was a nearly grown girl living home with her parents
 on the old homestead.

A red squaw came one breakfast-time to the old homestead,
On her back she carried a bundle of rushes for rush-bottoming
 chairs,
Her hair, straight, shiny, coarse, black, profuse, half-envelop'd her
 face,

Her step was free and elastic, and her voice sounded exquisitely as
    she spoke.

My mother look'd in delight and amazement at the
    stranger,
She look'd at the freshness of her tall-borne face and full and
    pliant limbs,
The more she look'd upon her she loved her,
Never before had she seen such wonderful beauty and purity,
She made her sit on a bench by the jamb of the fireplace, she
    cook'd food for her,
She had no work to give her, but she gave her remembrance and
    fondness.

The red squaw staid all the forenoon, and toward the middle of
    the afternoon she went away,
O my mother was loth to have her go away,
All the week she thought of her, she watch'd for her many a
    month,
She remember'd her many a winter and many a summer,
But the red squaw never came nor was heard of there
    again.

− 7 −

A show of the summer softness—a contact of something
    unseen—an amour of the light and air,
I am jealous and overwhelm'd with friendliness,
And will go gallivant with the light and air myself.

O love and summer, you are in the dreams and in me,
Autumn and winter are in the dreams, the farmer goes with his
    thrift,
The droves and crops increase, the barns are well-fill'd.

Elements merge in the night, ships make tacks in the dreams,
The sailor sails, the exile returns home,

The fugitive returns unharm'd, the immigrant is back beyond
    months and years,
The poor Irishman lives in the simple house of his childhood
    with the well-known neighbors and faces,
They warmly welcome him, he is barefoot again, he forgets he is
    well off,
The Dutchman voyages home, and the Scotchman and
    Welshman voyage home, and the native of the Mediterranean
    voyages home,
To every port of England, France, Spain, enter well-fill'd ships,
The Swiss foots it toward his hills, the Prussian goes his way, the
    Hungarian his way, and the Pole his way,
The Swede returns, and the Dane and Norwegian return.

The homeward bound and the outward bound,
The beautiful lost swimmer, the ennuyé, the onanist, the female
    that loves unrequited, the money-maker,
The actor and actress, those through with their parts and those
    waiting to commence,
The affectionate boy, the husband and wife, the voter, the
    nominee that is chosen and the nominee that has fail'd,
The great already known and the great any time after to-day,
The stammerer, the sick, the perfect-form'd, the homely,
The criminal that stood in the box, the judge that sat and
    sentenced him, the fluent lawyers, the jury, the audience,
The laugher and weeper, the dancer, the midnight widow, the red
    squaw,
The consumptive, the erysipalite, the idiot, he that is wrong'd,
The antipodes, and every one between this and them in the
    dark,
I swear they are averaged now—one is no better than the other,
The night and sleep have liken'd them and restored them.

I swear they are all beautiful,
Every one that sleeps is beautiful, every thing in the dim light is
    beautiful,
The wildest and bloodiest is over, and all is peace.

Peace is always beautiful,
The myth of heaven indicates peace and night.

The myth of heaven indicates the soul,
The soul is always beautiful, it appears more or it appears less, it
     comes or it lags behind,
It comes from its embower'd garden and looks pleasantly on itself
     and encloses the world,
Perfect and clean the genitals previously jetting, and perfect and
     clean the womb cohering,
The head well-grown proportion'd and plumb, and the bowels
     and joints proportion'd and plumb.

The soul is always beautiful,
The universe is duly in order, every thing is in its place,
What has arrived is in its place and what waits shall be in its
     place,
The twisted skull waits, the watery or rotten blood waits,
The child of the glutton or venerealee waits long, and the child
     of the drunkard waits long, and the drunkard himself waits
     long,
The sleepers that lived and died wait, the far advanced are to go
     on in their turns, and the far behind are to come on in their
     turns,
The diverse shall be no less diverse, but they shall flow and
     unite—they unite now.

– 8 –

The sleepers are very beautiful as they lie unclothed,
They flow hand in hand over the whole earth from east to west as
     they lie unclothed,
The Asiatic and African are hand in hand, the European and
     American are hand in hand,
Learn'd and unlearn'd are hand in hand, and male and female
     are hand in hand,
The bare arm of the girl crosses the bare breast of her lover, they
     press close without lust, his lips press her neck,

The father holds his grown or ungrown son in his arms with
    measureless love, and the son holds the father in his arms
    with measureless love,
The white hair of the mother shines on the white wrist of the
    daughter,
The breath of the boy goes with the breath of the man, friend is
    inarm'd by friend,
The scholar kisses the teacher and the teacher kisses the scholar,
    the wrong'd is made right,
The call of the slave is one with the master's call, and the master
    salutes the slave,
The felon steps forth from the prison, the insane becomes sane,
    the suffering of sick persons is reliev'd,
The sweatings and fevers stop, the throat that was unsound is
    sound, the lungs of the consumptive are resumed, the poor
    distress'd head is free,
The joints of the rheumatic move as smoothly as ever, and
    smoother than ever,
Stiflings and passages open, the paralyzed become supple,
The swell'd and convuls'd and congested awake to themselves in
    condition,
They pass the invigoration of the night and the chemistry of the
    night, and awake.

I too pass from the night,
I stay a while away O night, but I return to you again and
    love you.

Why should I be afraid to trust myself to you?
I am not afraid, I have been well brought forward by you,
I love the rich running day, but I do not desert her in whom I lay
    so long,
I know not how I came of you and I know not where I go with
    you, but I know I came well and shall go well.

I will stop only a time with the night, and rise betimes,
I will duly pass the day O my mother, and duly return
    to you.

TRANSPOSITIONS

Let the reformers descend from the stands where they are forever
    bawling—let an idiot or insane person appear on each of the
    stands;
Let judges and criminals be transposed—let the prison-keepers be
    put in prison—let those that were prisoners take the keys;
Let them that distrust birth and death lead the rest.

TO THINK OF TIME[88]

– 1 –

To think of time—of all that retrospection,
To think of to-day, and the ages continued henceforward.

Have you guess'd you yourself would not continue?
Have you dreaded these earth-beetles?
Have you fear'd the future would be nothing to you?

Is to-day nothing? is the beginningless past nothing?
If the future is nothing they are just as surely nothing.

To think that the sun rose in the east—that men and women were
    flexible, real, alive—that every thing was alive,
To think that you and I did not see, feel, think, nor bear
    our part,
To think that we are now here and bear our part.

– 2 –

Not a day passes, not a minute or second without an
    accouchement,
Not a day passes, not a minute or second without a corpse.

The dull nights go over and the dull days also,
The soreness of lying so much in bed goes over,

The physician after long putting off gives the silent and terrible
 look for an answer,
The children come hurried and weeping, and the brothers and
 sisters are sent for,
Medicines stand unused on the shelf, (the camphor-smell has
 long pervaded the rooms,)
The faithful hand of the living does not desert the hand of the
 dying,
The twitching lips press lightly on the forehead of the dying,
The breath ceases and the pulse of the heart ceases,
The corpse stretches on the bed and the living look upon it,
It is palpable as the living are palpable.

The living look upon the corpse with their eyesight,
But without eyesight lingers a different living and looks curiously
 on the corpse.

− 3 −

To think the thought of death merged in the thought of
 materials,
To think of all these wonders of city and country, and others
 taking great interest in them, and we taking no interest in
 them.

To think how eager we are in building our houses,
To think others shall be just as eager, and we quite indifferent.

(I see one building the house that serves him a few years, or
 seventy or eighty years at most,
I see one building the house that serves him longer than
 that.)

Slow-moving and black lines creep over the whole earth—they
 never cease—they are the burial lines,
He that was President was buried, and he that is now President
 shall surely be buried.

− 4 −

A reminiscence of the vulgar fate,
A frequent sample of the life and death of workmen,
Each after his kind.

Cold dash of waves at the ferry-wharf, posh and ice in the river,
    half-frozen mud in the streets,
A gray discouraged sky overhead, the short last daylight of
    December,
A hearse and stages, the funeral of an old Broadway stage-driver,
    the cortege mostly drivers.

Steady the trot to the cemetery, duly rattles the death-bell,
The gate is pass'd, the new-dug grave is halted at, the living alight,
    the hearse uncloses,
The coffin is pass'd out, lower'd and settled, the whip is laid on
    the coffin, the earth is swiftly shovel'd in,
The mound above is flatted with the spades—silence,
A minute—no one moves or speaks—it is done,
He is decently put away—is there any thing more?

He was a good fellow, free-mouth'd, quick-temper'd, not bad-
    looking,
Ready with life or death for a friend, fond of women, gambled,
    ate hearty, drank hearty,
Had known what it was to be flush, grew low-spirited toward the
    last, sicken'd, was help'd by a contribution,
Died, aged forty-one years—and that was his funeral.

Thumb extended, finger uplifted, apron, cape, gloves, strap, wet-
    weather clothes, whip carefully chosen,
Boss, spotter, starter, hostler, somebody loafing on you, you
    loafing on somebody, headway, man before and man
    behind,
Good day's work, bad day's work, pet stock, mean stock, first out,
    last out, turning-in at night,

To think that these are so much and so nigh to other drivers, and
    he there takes no interest in them.

– 5 –

The markets, the government, the working-man's wages, to think
    what account they are through our nights and days,
To think that other working-men will make just as great account
    of them, yet we make little or no account.

The vulgar and the refined, what you call sin and what you call
    goodness, to think how wide a difference,
To think the difference will still continue to others, yet we lie
    beyond the difference.

To think how much pleasure there is,
Do you enjoy yourself in the city? or engaged in business? or
    planning a nomination and election? or with your wife and
    family?
Or with your mother and sisters? or in womanly housework? or
    the beautiful maternal cares?
These also flow onward to others, you and I flow onward,
But in due time you and I shall take less interest in them.

Your farm, profits, crops—to think how engross'd you are,
To think there will still be farms, profits, crops, yet for you of what
    avail?

– 6 –

What will be will be well, for what is is well,
To take interest is well, and not to take interest shall be well.

The domestic joys, the daily housework or business, the building
    of houses are not phantasms, they have weight, form, location,
Farms, profits, crops, markets, wages, government, are none of
    them phantasms,

The difference between sin and goodness is no delusion,
The earth is not an echo, man and his life and all the things of
    his life are well-consider'd.

You are not thrown to the winds, you gather certainly and safely
    around yourself,
Yourself! yourself! yourself, for ever and ever!

– 7 –

It is not to diffuse you that you were born of your mother and
    father, it is to identify you,
It is not that you should be undecided, but that you should be
    decided,
Something long preparing and formless is arrived and form'd in
    you,
You are henceforth secure, whatever comes or goes.

The threads that were spun are gather'd, the weft crosses the
    warp, the pattern is systematic.

The preparations have every one been justified,
The orchestra have sufficiently tuned their instruments, the baton
    has given the signal.

The guest that was coming, he waited long, he is now
    housed,
He is one of those who are beautiful and happy, he is one of those
    that to look upon and be with is enough.

The law of the past cannot be eluded,
The law of the present and future cannot be eluded,
The law of the living cannot be eluded, it is eternal,
The law of promotion and transformation cannot be eluded,
The law of heroes and good-doers cannot be eluded,
The law of drunkards, informers, mean persons, not one iota
    thereof can be eluded.

– 8 –

Slow moving and black lines go ceaselessly over the earth,
Northerner goes carried and Southerner goes carried, and they on
    the Atlantic side and they on the Pacific,
And they between, and all through the Mississippi country, and
    all over the earth.

The great masters and kosmos are well as they go, the heroes and
    good-doers are well,
The known leaders and inventors and the rich owners and pious
    and distinguish'd may be well,
But there is more account than that, there is strict account
    of all.

The interminable hordes of the ignorant and wicked are not
    nothing,
The barbarians of Africa and Asia are not nothing,
The perpetual successions of shallow people are not nothing as
    they go.

Of and in all these things,
I have dream'd that we are not to be changed so much, nor the
    law of us changed,
I have dream'd that heroes and good-doers shall be under the
    present and past law,
And that murderers, drunkards, liars, shall be under the present
    and past law,
For I have dream'd that the law they are under now is enough.

And I have dream'd that the purpose and essence of the known
    life, the transient,
Is to form and decide identity for the unknown life, the permanent.

If all came but to ashes of dung,
If maggots and rats ended us, then Alarum! for we are betray'd,
Then indeed suspicion of death.

Do you suspect death? if I were to suspect death I should die now,
Do you think I could walk pleasantly and well-suited toward
    annihilation?

Pleasantly and well-suited I walk,
Whither I walk I cannot define, but I know it is good,
The whole universe indicates that it is good,
The past and the present indicate that it is good.

How beautiful and perfect are the animals!
How perfect the earth, and the minutest thing upon it!
What is called good is perfect, and what is called bad is just as
    perfect,
The vegetables and minerals are all perfect, and the
    imponderable fluids perfect;
Slowly and surely they have pass'd on to this, and slowly and
    surely they yet pass on.

– 9 –

I swear I think now that every thing without exception has an
    eternal soul!
The trees have, rooted in the ground! the weeds of the sea have!
    the animals!

I swear I think there is nothing but immortality!
That the exquisite scheme is for it, and the nebulous float is for it,
    and the cohering is for it!
And all preparation is for it—and identity is for it—and life and
    materials are altogether for it!

WHISPERS OF HEAVENLY DEATH[89]

DAREST THOU NOW O SOUL

Darest thou now O soul,
Walk out with me toward the unknown region,
Where neither ground is for the feet nor any path to follow?

No map there, nor guide,
Nor voice sounding, nor touch of human hand,
Nor face with blooming flesh, nor lips, nor eyes, are in that land.

I know it not O soul,
Nor dost thou, all is a blank before us,
All waits undream'd of in that region, that inaccessible land.

Till when the ties loosen,
All but the ties eternal, Time and Space,
Nor darkness, gravitation, sense, nor any bounds bounding us.

Then we burst forth, we float,
In Time and Space O soul, prepared for them,
Equal, equipt at last, (O joy! O fruit of all!) them to fulfil O soul.

WHISPERS OF HEAVENLY DEATH[90]

Whispers of heavenly death murmur'd I hear,
Labial gossip of night, sibilant chorals,
Footsteps gently ascending, mystical breezes wafted soft and low,
Ripples of unseen rivers, tides of a current flowing, forever
    flowing,

(Or is it the plashing of tears? the measureless waters of human
    tears?)

I see, just see skyward, great cloud masses,
Mournfully slowly they roll, silently swelling and mixing,
With at times a half-dimm'd sadden'd far-off star,
Appearing and disappearing.

(Some parturition rather, some solemn immortal birth;
On the frontiers to eyes impenetrable,
Some soul is passing over.)

CHANTING THE SQUARE DEIFIC[91]

— 1 —

Chanting the square deific, out of the One advancing, out of the
    sides,
Out of the old and new, out of the square entirely divine,
Solid, four-sided, (all the sides needed,) from this side Jehovah
    am I,
Old Brahm I, and I Saturnius am;
Not Time affects me—I am Time, old, modern as any,
Unpersuadable, relentless, executing righteous
    judgments,
As the Earth, the Father, the brown old Kronos, with laws,
Aged beyond computation, yet ever new, ever with those mighty
    laws rolling,
Relentless I forgive no man—whoever sins dies—I will have that
    man's life;
Therefore let none expect mercy—have the seasons, gravitation,
    the appointed days, mercy? no more have I,
But as the seasons and gravitation, and as all the appointed days
    that forgive not,
I dispense from this side judgments inexorable without the least
    remorse.

— 2 —

Consolator most mild, the promis'd one advancing,
With gentle hand extended, the mightier God am I,
Foretold by prophets and poets in their most rapt prophecies and
    poems,
From this side, lo! the Lord Christ gazes—lo! Hermes I—lo!
    mine is Hercules' face,
All sorrow, labor, suffering, I, tallying it, absorb in myself,
Many times have I been rejected, taunted, put in prison, and
    crucified, and many times shall be again,
All the world have I given up for my dear brothers' and sisters'
    sake, for the soul's sake,
Wending my way through the homes of men, rich or poor, with
    the kiss of affection,
For I am affection, I am the cheer-bringing God, with hope and
    all-enclosing charity,
With indulgent words as to children, with fresh and sane words,
    mine only,
Young and strong I pass knowing well I am destin'd myself to an
    early death;
But my charity has no death—my wisdom dies not, neither early
    nor late,
And my sweet love bequeath'd here and elsewhere never
    dies.

— 3 —

Aloof, dissatisfied, plotting revolt,
Comrade of criminals, brother of slaves,
Crafty, despised, a drudge, ignorant,
With sudra face and worn brow, black, but in the depths of my
    heart, proud as any,
Lifted now and always against whoever scorning assumes to
    rule me,
Morose, full of guile, full of reminiscences, brooding, with many
    wiles,

(Though it was thought I was baffled and dispel'd, and my wiles
    done, but that will never be,)
Defiant, I, Satan, still live, still utter words, in new lands duly
    appearing, (and old ones also,)
Permanent here from my side, warlike, equal with any, real
    as any,
Nor time nor change shall ever change me or my words.

− 4 −

Santa Spirita, breather, life,
Beyond the light, lighter than light,
Beyond the flames of hell, joyous, leaping easily above hell,
Beyond Paradise, perfumed solely with mine own perfume,
Including all life on earth, touching, including God, including
    Saviour and Satan,
Ethereal, pervading all, (for without me what were all? what were
    God?)
Essence of forms, life of the real identities, permanent, positive,
    (namely the unseen,)
Life of the great round world, the sun and stars, and of man, I,
    the general soul,
Here the square finishing, the solid, I the most solid,
Breathe my breath also through these songs.

OF HIM I LOVE DAY AND NIGHT[92]

Of him I love day and night I dream'd I heard he was
    dead,
And I dream'd I went where they had buried him I love, but he
    was not in that place,
And I dream'd I wander'd searching among burial-places to find
    him,
And I found that every place was a burial-place;
The houses full of life were equally full of death, (this house is
    now,)

The streets, the shipping, the places of amusement, the Chicago,
    Boston, Philadelphia, the Mannahatta, were as full of the
    dead as of the living,
And fuller, O vastly fuller of the dead than of the living;
And what I dream'd I will henceforth tell to every person and age,
And I stand henceforth bound to what I dream'd,
And now I am willing to disregard burial-places and dispense with
    them,
And if the memorials of the dead were put up indifferently
    everywhere, even in the room where I eat or sleep, I should
    be satisfied,
And if the corpse of any one I love, or if my own corpse, be
    duly render'd to powder and pour'd in the sea, I shall be
    satisfied,
Or if it be distributed to the winds I shall be satisfied.

YET, YET, YE DOWNCAST HOURS

Yet, yet, ye downcast hours, I know ye also,
Weights of lead, how ye clog and cling at my ankles,
Earth to a chamber of mourning turns—I hear the o'erweening,
    mocking voice,
Matter is conqueror—matter, triumphant only, continues onward.

Despairing cries float ceaselessly toward me,
The call of my nearest lover, putting forth, alarm'd, uncertain,
The sea I am quickly to sail, come tell me,
Come tell me where I am speeding, tell me my destination.

I understand your anguish, but I cannot help you,
I approach, hear, behold, the sad mouth, the look out of the eyes,
    your mute inquiry,
Whither I go from the bed I recline on, come tell me;
Old age, alarm'd, uncertain—a young woman's voice, appealing
    to me for comfort;
A young man's voice, *Shall I not escape?*

AS IF A PHANTOM CARESS'D ME

As if a phantom caress'd me,
I thought I was not alone walking here by the shore;
But the one I thought was with me as now I walk by the shore,
the one I loved that caress'd me,
As I lean and look through the glimmering light, that one has
utterly disappear'd,
And those appear that are hateful to me and mock me.

ASSURANCES[93]

I need no assurances, I am a man who is pre-occupied of his own
soul;
I do not doubt that from under the feet and beside the hands and
face I am cognizant of, are now looking faces I am not
cognizant of, calm and actual faces,
I do not doubt but the majesty and beauty of the world are latent
in any iota of the world,
I do not doubt I am limitless, and that the universes are limitless,
in vain I try to think how limitless,
I do not doubt that the orbs and the systems of orbs play their swift
sports through the air on purpose, and that I shall one day be
eligible to do as much as they, and more than they,
I do not doubt that temporary affairs keep on and on millions of
years,
I do not doubt interiors have their interiors, and exteriors have
their exteriors, and that the eyesight has another eyesight, and
the hearing another hearing, and the voice another voice,
I do not doubt that the passionately-wept deaths of young men are
provided for, and that the deaths of young women and the
deaths of little children are provided for,
(Did you think Life was so well provided for, and Death, the
purport of all Life, is not well provided for?)
I do not doubt that wrecks at sea, no matter what the horrors of
them, no matter whose wife, child, husband, father, lover, has
gone down, are provided for, to the minutest points,

I do not doubt that whatever can possibly happen anywhere at
    any time, is provided for in the inherences of things,
I do not think Life provides for all and for Time and Space, but I
    believe Heavenly Death provides for all.

QUICKSAND YEARS

Quicksand years that whirl me I know not whither,
Your schemes, politics, fail, lines give way, substances mock and
    elude me,
Only the theme I sing, the great and strong possess'd soul, eludes
    not,
One's-self must never give way—that is the final substance—that
    out of all is sure,
Out of politics, triumphs, battles, life, what at last finally
    remains?
When shows break up what but One's-Self is sure?

THAT MUSIC ALWAYS ROUND ME[94]

That music always round me, unceasing, unbeginning, yet long
    untaught I did not hear,
But now the chorus I hear and am elated,
A tenor, strong, ascending with power and health, with glad notes
    of daybreak I hear,
A soprano at intervals sailing buoyantly over the tops of immense
    waves,
A transparent base shuddering lusciously under and through the
    universe,
The triumphant tutti, the funeral wailings with sweet flutes and
    violins, all these I fill myself with,
I hear not the volumes of sound merely, I am moved by the
    exquisite meanings,
I listen to the different voices winding in and out, striving,
    contending with fiery vehemence to excel each other
    in emotion;

I do not think the performers know themselves—but now I think I
    begin to know them.

WHAT SHIP PUZZLED AT SEA

What ship puzzled at sea, cons for the true reckoning?
Or coming in, to avoid the bars and follow the channel a perfect
    pilot needs?
Here, sailor! here, ship! take aboard the most perfect pilot,
Whom, in a little boat, putting off and rowing, I hailing you offer.

A NOISELESS PATIENT SPIDER[95]

A noiseless patient spider,
I mark'd where on a little promontory it stood isolated,
Mark'd how to explore the vacant vast surrounding,
It launch'd forth filament, filament, filament, out of itself,
Ever unreeling them, ever tirelessly speeding them.

And you O my soul where you stand,
Surrounded, detached, in measureless oceans of space,
Ceaselessly musing, venturing, throwing, seeking the spheres to
    connect them,
Till the bridge you will need be form'd, till the ductile anchor
    hold,
Till the gossamer thread you fling catch somewhere, O my soul.

O LIVING ALWAYS, ALWAYS DYING

O living always, always dying!
O the burials of me past and present,
O me while I stride ahead, material, visible, imperious as ever;
O me, what I was for years, now dead, (I lament not, I am content;)
O to disengage myself from those corpses of me, which I turn and
    look at where I cast them,

To pass on, (O living! always living!) and leave the corpses
    behind.

TO ONE SHORTLY TO DIE

From all the rest I single out you, having a message for you,
You are to die—let others tell you what they please, I cannot
    prevaricate,
I am exact and merciless, but I love you—there is no escape for you.

Softly I lay my right hand upon you, you just feel it,
I do not argue, I bend my head close and half envelop it,
I sit quietly by, I remain faithful,
I am more than nurse, more than parent or neighbor,
I absolve you from all except yourself spiritual bodily, that is
    eternal, you yourself will surely escape,
The corpse you leave will be but excrementitious.

The sun bursts through in unlooked-for directions,
Strong thoughts fill you and confidence, you smile,
You forget you are sick, as I forget you are sick,
You do not see the medicines, you do not mind the weeping
    friends, I am with you,
I exclude others from you, there is nothing to be commiserated,
I do not commiserate, I congratulate you.

NIGHT ON THE PRAIRIES

Night on the prairies,
The supper is over, the fire on the ground burns low,
The wearied emigrants sleep, wrapt in their blankets;
I walk by myself—I stand and look at the stars, which I think now
    I never realized before.

Now I absorb immortality and peace,
I admire death and test propositions.

How plenteous! how spiritual! how resumé!
The same old man and soul—the same old aspirations, and the
    same content.

I was thinking the day most splendid till I saw what the not-day
    exhibited,
I was thinking this globe enough till there sprang out so noiseless
    around me myriads of other globes.

Now while the great thoughts of space and eternity fill me I will
    measure myself by them,
And now touch'd with the lives of other globes arrived as far along
    as those of the earth,
Or waiting to arrive, or pass'd on farther than those of the earth,
I henceforth no more ignore them than I ignore my own life,
Or the lives of the earth arrived as far as mine, or waiting to
    arrive.

O I see now that life cannot exhibit all to me, as the day cannot,
I see that I am to wait for what will be exhibited by death.

THOUGHT

As I sit with others at a great feast, suddenly while the music is
    playing,
To my mind, (whence it comes I know not,) spectral in mist of a
    wreck at sea,
Of certain ships, how they sail from port with flying streamers and
    wafted kisses, and that is the last of them,
Of the solemn and murky mystery about the fate of the
    President,
Of the flower of the marine science of fifty generations founder'd
    off the Northeast coast and going down—of the steamship
    Arctic going down,
Of the veil'd tableau—women gather'd together on deck, pale,
    heroic, waiting the moment that draws so close—O the
    moment!

A huge sob—a few bubbles—the white foam spirting up—and
    then the women gone,
Sinking there while the passionless wet flows on—and I now
    pondering, Are those women indeed gone?
Are souls drown'd and destroy'd so?
Is only matter triumphant?

THE LAST INVOCATION

At the last, tenderly,
From the walls of the powerful fortress'd house,
From the clasp of the knitted locks, from the keep of the well-
    closed doors,
Let me be wafted.

Let me glide noiselessly forth;
With the key of softness unlock the locks—with a whisper,
Set ope the doors O soul.

Tenderly—be not impatient,
(Strong is your hold O mortal flesh,
Strong is your hold O love.)

AS I WATCH'D THE PLOUGHMAN PLOUGHING

As I watch'd the ploughman ploughing,
Or the sower sowing in the fields, or the harvester harvesting,
I saw there too, O life and death, your analogies;
(Life, life is the tillage, and Death is the harvest according.)

PENSIVE AND FALTERING

Pensive and faltering,
The words *the Dead* I write,
For living are the Dead,

(Haply the only living, only real,
And I the apparition, I the spectre.)

THOU MOTHER WITH THY EQUAL BROOD

— 1 —

Thou Mother with thy equal brood,
Thou varied chain of different States, yet one identity only,
A special song before I go I'd sing o'er all the rest,
For thee, the future.

I'd sow a seed for thee of endless Nationality,
I'd fashion thy ensemble including body and soul,
I'd show away ahead thy real Union, and how it may be
    accomplish'd.

The paths to the house I seek to make,
But leave to those to come the house itself.

Belief I sing, and preparation;
As Life and Nature are not great with reference to the present only,
But greater still from what is yet to come,
Out of that formula for thee I sing.

— 2 —

As a strong bird on pinions free,
Joyous, the amplest spaces heavenward cleaving,
Such be the thought I'd think of thee America,
Such be the recitative I'd bring for thee.

The conceits of the poets of other lands I'd bring thee not,
Nor the compliments that have served their turn so long,
Nor rhyme, nor the classics, nor perfume of foreign court or
    indoor library;
But an odor I'd bring as from forests of pine in Maine, or breath
    of an Illinois prairie,

With open airs of Virginia or Georgia or Tennessee, or from Texas
  uplands, or Florida's glades,
Or the Saguenay's black stream, or the wide blue spread of
  Huron,
With presentment of Yellowstone's scenes, or Yosemite,
And murmuring under, pervading all, I'd bring the rustling sea-
  sound,
That endlessly sounds from the two Great Seas of the world.

And for thy subtler sense subtler refrains dread Mother,
Preludes of intellect tallying these and thee, mind-formulas fitted
  for thee, real and sane and large as these and thee,
Thou! mounting higher, diving deeper than we knew, thou
  transcendental Union!
By thee fact to be justified, blended with thought,
Thought of man justified, blended with God,
Through thy idea, lo, the immortal reality!
Through thy reality, lo, the immortal idea!

— 3 —

Brain of the New World, what a task is thine,
To formulate the Modern—out of the peerless grandeur of the
  modern,
Out of thyself, comprising science, to recast poems, churches, art,
(Recast, may-be discard them, end them—may-be their work is
  done, who knows?)
By vision, hand, conception, on the background of the mighty
  past, the dead,
To limn with absolute faith the mighty living present.

And yet thou living present brain, heir of the dead, the Old World
  brain,
Thou that lay folded like an unborn babe within its folds so
  long,
Thou carefully prepared by it so long—haply thou but unfoldest
  it, only maturest it,
It to eventuate in thee—the essence of the by-gone time contain'd
  in thee,

Its poems, churches, arts, unwitting to themselves, destined with
    reference to thee;
Thou but the apples, long, long, long a-growing,
The fruit of all the Old ripening to-day in thee.

– 4 –

Sail, sail thy best, ship of Democracy,
Of value is thy freight, 'tis not the Present only,
The Past is also stored in thee,
Thou holdest not the venture of thyself alone, not of the Western
    continent alone,
Earth's *résumé* entire floats on thy keel O ship, is steadied by thy
    spars,
With thee Time voyages in trust, the antecedent nations sink or
    swim with thee,
With all their ancient struggles, martyrs, heroes, epics, wars, thou
    bear'st the other continents,
Theirs, theirs as much as thine, the destination-port
    triumphant;
Steer then with good strong hand and wary eye O helmsman,
    thou carriest great companions,
Venerable priestly Asia sails this day with thee,
And royal feudal Europe sails with thee.

– 5 –

Beautiful world of new superber birth that rises to my eyes,
Like a limitless golden cloud filling the western sky,
Emblem of general maternity lifted above all,
Sacred shape of the bearer of daughters and sons,
Out of thy teeming womb thy giant babes in ceaseless procession
    issuing,
Acceding from such gestation, taking and giving continual
    strength and life,
World of the real—world of the twain in one,
World of the soul, born by the world of the real alone, led to
    identity, body, by it alone,

Yet in beginning only, incalculable masses of composite precious
     materials,
By history's cycles forwarded, by every nation, language, hither
     sent,
Ready, collected here, a freer, vast, electric world, to be
     constructed here,
(The true New World, the world of orbic science, morals,
     literatures to come,)
Thou wonder world yet undefined, unform'd, neither do I define
     thee,
How can I pierce the impenetrable blank of the future?
I feel thy ominous greatness evil as well as good,
I watch thee advancing, absorbing the present, transcending the
     past,
I see thy light lighting, and thy shadow shadowing, as if the entire
     globe,
But I do not undertake to define thee, hardly to comprehend
     thee,
I but thee name, thee prophesy, as now,
I merely thee ejaculate!

Thee in thy future,
Thee in thy only permanent life, career, thy own unloosen'd
     mind, thy soaring spirit,
Thee as another equally needed sun, radiant, ablaze, swift-
     moving, fructifying all,
Thee risen in potent cheerfulness and joy, in endless great
     hilarity,
Scattering for good the cloud that hung so long, that weigh'd so
     long upon the mind of man,
The doubt, suspicion, dread, of gradual, certain decadence of
     man;
Thee in thy larger, saner brood of female, male—thee in thy
     athletes, moral, spiritual, South, North, West, East,
(To thy immortal breasts, Mother of All, thy every daughter, son,
     endear'd alike, forever equal,)
Thee in thy own musicians, singers, artists, unborn yet, but
     certain,

Thee in thy moral wealth and civilization, (until which thy
    proudest material civilization must remain in vain,)
Thee in thy all-supplying, all-enclosing worship—thee in no
    single bible, saviour, merely,
Thy saviours countless, latent within thyself, thy bibles incessant
    within thyself, equal to any, divine as any,
(Thy soaring course thee formulating, not in thy two great wars,
    nor in thy century's visible growth,
But far more in these leaves and chants, thy chants, great Mother!)
Thee in an education grown of thee, in teachers, studies,
    students, born of thee,
Thee in thy democratic fêtes en-masse, thy high original festivals,
    operas, lecturers, preachers,
Thee in thy ultimata, (the preparations only now completed, the
    edifice on sure foundations tied,)
Thee in thy pinnacles, intellect, thought, thy topmost rational
    joys, thy love and godlike aspiration,
In thy resplendent coming literati, thy full-lung'd orators, thy
    sacerdotal bards, kosmic savans,
These! these in thee, (certain to come,) to-day I prophesy.

– 6 –

Land tolerating all, accepting all, not for the good alone, all good
    for thee,
Land in the realms of God to be a realm unto thyself,
Under the rule of God to be a rule unto thyself.

(Lo, where arise three peerless stars,
To be thy natal stars my country, Ensemble, Evolution, Freedom,
Set in the sky of Law.)

Land of unprecedented faith, God's faith,
Thy soil, thy very subsoil, all upheav'd,
The general inner earth so long so sedulously draped over, now
    hence for what it is boldly laid bare,
Open'd by thee to heaven's light for benefit or bale.

Not for success alone,
Not to fair-sail unintermitted always,
The storm shall dash thy face, the murk of war and worse than
    war shall cover thee all over,
(Wert capable of war, its tug and trials? be capable of peace, its
    trials,
For the tug and mortal strain of nations come at last in prosperous
    peace, not war;)
In many a smiling mask death shall approach beguiling thee,
    thou in disease shalt swelter,
The livid cancer spread its hideous claws, clinging upon thy
    breasts, seeking to strike thee deep within,
Consumption of the worst, moral consumption, shall rouge thy
    face with hectic,
But thou shalt face thy fortunes, thy diseases, and surmount
    them all,
Whatever they are to-day and whatever through time they may be,
They each and all shall lift and pass away and cease from thee,
While thou, Time's spirals rounding, out of thyself, thyself still
    extricating, fusing,
Equable, natural, mystical Union thou, (the mortal with
    immortal blent,)
Shalt soar toward the fulfilment of the future, the spirit of the
    body and the mind,
The soul, its destinies.

The soul, its destinies, the real real,
(Purport of all these apparitions of the real;)
In thee America, the soul, its destinies,
Thou globe of globes! thou wonder nebulous!
By many a throe of heat and cold convuls'd, (by these thyself
    solidifying,)
Thou mental, moral orb—thou New, indeed new, Spiritual
    World!
The Present holds thee not—for such vast growth as thine,
For such unparallel'd flight as thine, such brood as thine,
The FUTURE only holds thee and can hold thee.

A PAUMANOK PICTURE

Two boats with nets lying off the sea-beach, quite still,
Ten fishermen waiting—they discover a thick school of
    mossbonkers*—they drop the join'd seine-ends in the water,
The boats separate and row off, each on its rounding course to the
    beach, enclosing the mossbonkers,
The net is drawn in by a windlass by those who stop ashore,
Some of the fishermen lounge in their boats, others stand ankle-
    deep in the water, pois'd on strong legs,
The boats partly drawn up, the water slapping against them,
Strew'd on the sand in heaps and windrows, well out from the
    water, the green-back'd spotted mossbonkers.

---

*The mossbonker (also spelled mossbunker), or menhaden, is fish indigenous to
the Long Island waters Whitman describes.

FROM NOON TO STARRY NIGHT

━━━◆━━━

THOU ORB ALOFT FULL-DAZZLING

Thou orb aloft full-dazzling! thou hot October noon!
Flooding with sheeny light the gray beach sand,
The sibilant near sea with vistas far and foam,
And tawny streaks and shades and spreading blue;
O sun of noon refulgent! my special word to thee.

Hear me illustrious!
Thy lover me, for always I have loved thee,
Even as basking babe, then happy boy alone by some wood edge,
    thy touching-distant beams enough,
Or man matured, or young or old, as now to thee I launch my
    invocation.

(Thou canst not with thy dumbness me deceive,
I know before the fitting man all Nature yields,
Though answering not in words, the skies, trees, hear his voice —
    and thou O sun,
As for thy throes, thy perturbations, sudden breaks and shafts of
    flame gigantic,
I understand them, I know those flames, those perturbations
    well.)

Thou that with fructifying heat and light,
O'er myriad farms, o'er lands and waters North and South,
O'er Mississippi's endless course, o'er Texas' grassy plains,
    Kanada's woods,
O'er all the globe that turns its face to thee shining in space,

Thou that impartially infoldest all, not only continents, seas,
Thou that to grapes and weeds and little wild flowers givest so
    liberally,
Shed, shed thyself on mine and me, with but a fleeting ray out of
    thy million millions,
Strike through these chants.

Nor only launch thy subtle dazzle and thy strength for these,
Prepare the later afternoon of me myself—prepare my
    lengthening shadows,
Prepare my starry nights.

FACES[97]

– 1 –

Sauntering the pavement or riding the country by-road, lo,
    such faces!
Faces of friendship, precision, caution, suavity, ideality,
The spiritual-prescient face, the always welcome common
    benevolent face.
The face of the singing of music, the grand faces of natural
    lawyers and judges broad at the back-top,
The faces of hunters and fishers bulged at the brows, the shaved
    blanch'd faces of orthodox citizens,
The pure, extravagant, yearning, questioning artist's face,
The ugly face of some beautiful soul, the handsome detested or
    despised face,
The sacred faces of infants, the illuminated face of the mother of
    many children,
The face of an amour, the face of veneration,
The face as of a dream, the face of an immobile rock,
The face withdrawn of its good and bad, a castrated face,
A wild hawk, his wings clipp'd by the clipper,
A stallion that yielded at last to the thongs and knife of the
    gelder.

Sauntering the pavement thus, or crossing the ceaseless ferry,
       faces and faces and faces,
I see them and complain not, and am content with all.

— 2 —

Do you suppose I could be content with all if I thought them
       their own finalè?

This now is too lamentable a face for a man,
Some abject louse asking leave to be, cringing for it,
Some milk-nosed maggot blessing what lets it wrig to its hole.

This face is a dog's snout sniffing for garbage,
Snakes nest in that mouth, I hear the sibilant threat.

This face is a haze more chill than the arctic sea,
Its sleepy and wabbling icebergs crunch as they go.

This is a face of bitter herbs, this an emetic, they need no
       label,
And more of the drug-shelf, laudanum, caoutchouc, or hog's-lard.

This face is an epilepsy, its wordless tongue gives out the
       unearthly cry,
Its veins down the neck distend, its eyes roll till they show nothing
       but their whites,
Its teeth grit, the palms of the hands are cut by the turn'd-in
       nails,
The man falls struggling and foaming to the ground, while he
       speculates well.

This face is bitten by vermin and worms,
And this is some murderer's knife with a half-pull'd scabbard.

This face owes to the sexton his dismalest fee,
An unceasing death-bell tolls there.

– 3 –

Features of my equals would you trick me with your creas'd and
     cadaverous march?
Well you cannot trick me.

I see your rounded never-erased flow,
I see 'neath the rims of your haggard and mean disguises.

Splay and twist as you like, poke with the tangling fores of fishes
     or rats,
You'll be unmuzzled, you certainly will.

I saw the face of the most smear'd and slobbering idiot they had at
     the asylum,
And I knew for my consolation what they knew not,
I knew of the agents that emptied and broke my brother,
The same wait to clear the rubbish from the fallen tenement,
And I shall look again in a score or two of ages,
And I shall meet the real landlord perfect and unharm'd, every
     inch as good as myself.

– 4 –

The Lord advances, and yet advances,
Always the shadow in front, always the reach'd hand bringing up
     the laggards.

Out of this face emerge banners and horses—O superb! I see
     what is coming,
I see the high pioneer-caps, see staves of runners clearing the way,
I hear victorious drums.

This face is a life-boat,
This is the face commanding and bearded, it asks no odds of
     the rest,
This face is flavor'd fruit ready for eating,
This face of a healthy honest boy is the programme of all good.

These faces bear testimony slumbering or awake,
They show their descent from the Master himself.

Off the word I have spoken I except not one—red, white, black,
     are all deific,
In each house is the ovum, it comes forth after a thousand
     years.

Spots or cracks at the windows do not disturb me,
Tall and sufficient stand behind and make signs to me,
I read the promise and patiently wait.

This is a full-grown lily's face,
She speaks to the limber-hipp'd man near the garden
     pickets,
Come here she blushingly cries, *Come nigh to me limber-hipp'd
     man,
Stand at my side till I lean as high as I can upon you,
Fill me with albescent honey, bend down to me,
Rub to me with your chafing beard, rub to my breast and
     shoulders.*

– 5 –

The old face of the mother of many children,
Whist! I am fully content.

Lull'd and late is the smoke of the First-day morning,
It hangs low over the rows of trees by the fences,
It hangs thin by the sassafras and wild-cherry and catbrier under
     them.

I saw the rich ladies in full dress at the soiree,
I heard what the singers were singing so long,
Heard who sprang in crimson youth from the white froth and the
     water-blue.

Behold a woman!
She looks out from her quaker cap, her face is clearer and more
    beautiful than the sky.

She sits in an armchair under the shaded porch of the farmhouse,
The sun just shines on her old white head.

Her ample gown is of cream-hued linen,
Her grandsons raised the flax, and her grand-daughters spun it
    with the distaff and the wheel.

The melodious character of the earth,
The finish beyond which philosophy cannot go and does not wish
    to go,
The justified mother of men.

THE MYSTIC TRUMPETER[98]

— 1 —

Hark, some wild trumpeter, some strange musician,
Hovering unseen in air, vibrates capricious tunes to-night.

I hear thee trumpeter, listening alert I catch thy notes,
Now pouring, whirling like a tempest round me,
Now low, subdued, now in the distance lost.

— 2 —

Come nearer bodiless one, haply in thee resounds
Some dead composer, haply thy pensive life
Was fill'd with aspirations high, unform'd ideals,
Waves, oceans musical, chaotically surging,
That now ecstatic ghost, close to me bending, thy cornet echoing,
    pealing,
Gives out to no one's ears but mine, but freely gives to mine,
That I may thee translate.

− 3 −

Blow trumpeter free and clear, I follow thee,
While at thy liquid prelude, glad, serene,
The fretting world, the streets, the noisy hours of day withdraw,
A holy calm descends like dew upon me,
I walk in cool refreshing night the walks of Paradise,
I scent the grass, the moist air and the roses;
Thy song expands my numb'd imbonded spirit, thou freest,
    launchest me,
Floating and basking upon heaven's lake.

− 4 −

Blow again trumpeter! and for my sensuous eyes,
Bring the old pageants, show the feudal world.

What charm thy music works! thou makest pass before me,
Ladies and cavaliers long dead, barons are in their castle halls,
    the troubadours are singing,
Arm'd knights go forth to redress wrongs, some in quest of the
    holy Graal;
I see the tournament, I see the contestants incased in heavy
    armor seated on stately champing horses,
I hear the shouts, the sounds of blows and smiting steel;
I see the Crusaders' tumultuous armies—hark, how the cymbals
    clang,
Lo, where the monks walk in advance, bearing the cross on
    high.

− 5 −

Blow again trumpeter! and for thy theme,
Take now the enclosing theme of all, the solvent and the
    setting,
Love, that is pulse of all, the sustenance and the pang,
The heart of man and woman all for love,
No other theme but love—knitting, enclosing, all-diffusing love.

O how the immortal phantoms crowd around me!
I see the vast alembic ever working, I see and know the flames
     that heat the world,
The glow, the blush, the beating hearts of lovers,
So blissful happy some, and some so silent, dark, and nigh to death;
Love, that is all the earth to lovers—love, that mocks time and
     space,
Love, that is day and night—love, that is sun and moon and
     stars,
Love, that is crimson, sumptuous, sick with perfume,
No other words but words of love, no other thought but love.

                                   – 6 –

Blow again trumpeter—conjure war's alarums.

Swift to thy spell a shuddering hum like distant thunder rolls,
Lo, where the arm'd men hasten—lo, mid the clouds of dust the
     glint of bayonets,
I see the grime-faced cannoneers, I mark the rosy flash amid the
     smoke, I hear the cracking of the guns;
Not war alone—thy fearful music-song, wild player, brings every
     sight of fear,
The deeds of ruthless brigands, rapine, murder—I hear the cries
     for help!
I see ships foundering at sea, I behold on deck and below deck
     the terrible tableaus.

                                   – 7 –

O trumpeter, methinks I am myself the instrument thou playest,
Thou melt'st my heart, my brain—thou movest, drawest, changest
     them at will;
And now thy sullen notes send darkness through me,
Thou takest away all cheering light, all hope,
I see the enslaved, the overthrown, the hurt, the opprest of the
     whole earth,

I feel the measureless shame and humiliation of my race, it
    becomes all mine,
Mine too the revenges of humanity, the wrongs of ages, baffled
    feuds and hatreds,
Utter defeat upon me weighs—all lost—the foe victorious,
(Yet 'mid the ruins Pride colossal stands unshaken to the last,
Endurance, resolution to the last.)

– 8 –

Now trumpeter for thy close,
Vouchsafe a higher strain than any yet,
Sing to my soul, renew its languishing faith and hope,
Rouse up my slow belief, give me some vision of the future,
Give me for once its prophecy and joy.

O glad, exulting, culminating song!
A vigor more than earth's is in thy notes,
Marches of victory—man disenthral'd—the conqueror at last,
Hymns to the universal God from universal man—all joy!
A reborn race appears—a perfect world, all joy!
Women and men in wisdom innocence and health—all joy!
Riotous laughing bacchanals fill'd with joy!
War, sorrow, suffering gone—the rank earth purged—nothing but
    joy left!
The ocean fill'd with joy—the atmosphere all joy!
Joy! joy! in freedom, worship, love! joy in the ecstasy of life!
Enough to merely be! enough to breathe!
Joy! joy! all over joy!

TO A LOCOMOTIVE IN WINTER[99]

Thee for my recitative,
Thee in the driving storm even as now, the snow, the winter-day
    declining,
Thee in thy panoply, thy measur'd dual throbbing and thy beat
    convulsive,

Thy black cylindric body, golden brass and silvery steel,
Thy ponderous side-bars, parallel and connecting rods, gyrating,
      shuttling at thy sides,
Thy metrical, now swelling pant and roar, now tapering in the
      distance,
Thy great protruding head-light fix'd in front,
Thy long, pale, floating vapor-pennants, tinged with delicate
      purple,
The dense and murky clouds out-belching from thy smoke-stack,
Thy knitted frame, thy springs and valves, the tremulous twinkle
      of thy wheels,
Thy train of cars behind, obedient, merrily following,
Through gale or calm, now swift, now slack, yet steadily careering;
Type of the modern—emblem of motion and power—pulse of
      the continent,
For once come serve the Muse and merge in verse, even as here
      I see thee,
With storm and buffeting gusts of wind and falling snow,
By day thy warning ringing bell to sound its notes,
By night thy silent signal lamps to swing.

Fierce-throated beauty!
Roll through my chant with all thy lawless music, thy swinging
      lamps at night,
Thy madly-whistled laughter, echoing, rumbling like an
      earthquake, rousing all,
Law of thyself complete, thine own track firmly holding,
(No sweetness debonair of tearful harp or glib piano thine,)
Thy trills of shrieks by rocks and hills return'd,
Launch'd o'er the prairies wide, across the lakes,
To the free skies unpent and glad and strong.

O MAGNET-SOUTH

O magnet-South! O glistening perfumed South! my South!
O quick mettle, rich blood, impulse and love! good and evil!
      O all dear to me!

O dear to me my birth-things—all moving things and the trees
    where I was born—the grains, plants, rivers,
Dear to me my own slow sluggish rivers where they flow, distant,
    over flats of silvery sands or through swamps,
Dear to me the Roanoke, the Savannah, the Altamahaw, the
    Pedee, the Tombigbee, the Santee, the Coosa and the Sabine,
O pensive, far away wandering, I return with my soul to haunt
    their banks again,
Again in Florida I float on transparent lakes, I float on the
    Okeechobee, I cross the hummock-land or through pleasant
    openings or dense forests,
I see the parrots in the woods, I see the papaw-tree and the
    blossoming titi;
Again, sailing in my coaster on deck, I coast off Georgia, I coast
    up the Carolinas,
I see where the live-oak is growing, I see where the yellow-pine,
    the scented bay-tree, the lemon and orange, the cypress, the
    graceful palmetto,
I pass rude sea-headlands and enter Pamlico sound through an
    inlet, and dart my vision inland;
O the cotton plant! the growing fields of rice, sugar, hemp!
The cactus guarded with thorns, the laurel-tree with large white
    flowers,
The range afar, the richness and barrenness, the old woods
    charged with mistletoe and trailing moss,
The piney odor and the gloom, the awful natural stillness, (here
    in these dense swamps the freebooter carries his gun, and the
    fugitive has his conceal'd hut;)
O the strange fascination of these half-known half-impassable
    swamps, infested by reptiles, resounding with the bellow of
    the alligator, the sad noises of the night-owl and the wild-cat,
    and the whirr of the rattlesnake,
The mocking-bird, the American mimic, singing all the forenoon,
    singing through the moon-lit night,
The humming-bird, the wild turkey, the raccoon, the opossum;
A Kentucky corn-field, the tall, graceful, long-leav'd corn, slender,
    flapping, bright green, with tassels, with beautiful ears each
    well-sheath'd in its husk;

O my heart! O tender and fierce pangs, I can stand them not,
    I will depart;
O to be a Virginian where I grew up! O to be a Carolinian!
O longings irrepressible! O I will go back to old Tennessee and
    never wander more.

MANNAHATTA[100]

I was asking for something specific and perfect for my city,
Whereupon lo! upsprang the aboriginal name.

Now I see what there is in a name, a word, liquid, sane, unruly,
    musical, self-sufficient,
I see that the word of my city is that word from of old,
Because I see that word nested in nests of water-bays, superb,
Rich, hemm'd thick all around with sailships and steamships, an
    island sixteen miles long, solid-founded,
Numberless crowded streets, high growths of iron, slender, strong,
    light, splendidly uprising toward clear skies,
Tides swift and ample, well-loved by me, toward sundown,
The flowing sea-currents, the little islands, larger adjoining
    islands, the heights, the villas,
The countless masts, the white shore-steamers, the lighters, the
    ferry-boats, the black sea-steamers well-model'd,
The down-town streets, the jobbers' houses of business, the houses
    of business of the ship-merchants and money-brokers, the
    river-streets,
Immigrants arriving, fifteen or twenty thousand in a week,
The carts hauling goods, the manly race of drivers of horses, the
    brown-faced sailors,
The summer air, the bright sun shining, and the sailing clouds
    aloft,
The winter snows, the sleigh-bells, the broken ice in the
    river, passing along up or down with the flood-tide or ebb-tide,
The mechanics of the city, the masters, well-form'd, beautiful-
    faced, looking you straight in the eyes,

Trottoirs throng'd, vehicles, Broadway, the women, the shops and
      shows,
A million people—manners free and superb—open voices—
      hospitality—the most courageous and friendly young men,
City of hurried and sparkling waters! city of spires and masts!
City nested in bays! my city!

ALL IS TRUTH

O me, man of slack faith so long,
Standing aloof, denying portions so long,
Only aware to-day of compact all-diffused truth,
Discovering to-day there is no lie or form of lie, and can be none,
      but grows as inevitably upon itself as the truth does upon
      itself,
Or as any law of the earth or any natural production of the earth
      does.

(This is curious and may not be realized immediately, but it must
      be realized,
I feel in myself that I represent falsehoods equally with the rest,
And that the universe does.)

Where has fail'd a perfect return indifferent of lies or the truth?
Is it upon the ground, or in water or fire? or in the spirit of man?
      or in the meat and blood?
Meditating among liars and retreating sternly into myself, I see
      that there are really no liars or lies after all,
And that nothing fails its perfect return, and that what are called
      lies are perfect returns,
And that each thing exactly represents itself and what has
      preceded it,
And that the truth includes all, and is compact just as much as
      space is compact,
And that there is no flaw or vacuum in the amount of the truth—
      but that all is truth without exception;

And henceforth I will go celebrate any thing I see or am,
And sing and laugh and deny nothing.

A RIDDLE SONG[101]

That which eludes this verse and any verse,
Unheard by sharpest ear, unform'd in clearest eye or cunningest
    mind,
Nor lore nor fame, nor happiness nor wealth,
And yet the pulse of every heart and life throughout the world
    incessantly,
Which you and I and all pursuing ever ever miss,
Open but still a secret, the real of the real, an illusion,
Costless, vouchsafed to each, yet never man the owner,
Which poets vainly seek to put in rhyme, historians in prose,
Which sculptor never chisel'd yet, nor painter painted,
Which vocalist never sung, nor orator nor actor ever utter'd,
Invoking here and now I challenge for my song.

Indifferently, 'mid public, private haunts, in solitude,
Behind the mountain and the wood,
Companion of the city's busiest streets, through the assemblage,
It and its radiations constantly glide.

In looks of fair unconscious babes,
Or strangely in the coffin'd dead,
Or show of breaking dawn or stars by night,
As some dissolving delicate film of dreams,
Hiding yet lingering.

Two little breaths of words comprising it,
Two words, yet all from first to last comprised in it.

How ardently for it!
How many ships have sail'd and sunk for it!
How many travelers started from their homes and ne'er return'd!
How much of genius boldly staked and lost for it!
What countless stores of beauty, love, ventur'd for it!

How all superbest deeds since Time began are traceable to it—
    and shall be to the end!
How all heroic martyrdoms to it!
How, justified by it, the horrors, evils, battles of the earth!
How the bright fascinating lambent flames of it, in every age and
    land, have drawn men's eyes,
Rich as a sunset on the Norway coast, the sky, the islands, and the
    cliffs,
Or midnight's silent glowing northern lights unreachable.

Haply God's riddle it, so vague and yet so certain,
The soul for it, and all the visible universe for it,
And heaven at last for it.

EXCELSIOR

Who has gone farthest? for I would go farther,
And who has been just? for I would be the most just person of the
    earth,
And who most cautious? for I would be more cautious,
And who has been happiest? O I think it is I—I think no one was
    ever happier than I,
And who has lavish'd all? for I lavish constantly the best I have,
And who proudest? for I think I have reason to be the proudest
    son alive—for I am the son of the brawny and tall-topt city,
And who has been bold and true? for I would be the boldest and
    truest being of the universe,
And who benevolent? for I would show more benevolence than
    all the rest,
And who has receiv'd the love of the most friends? for I know
    what it is to receive the passionate love of many friends,
And who possesses a perfect and enamour'd body? for I do not
    believe any one possesses a more perfect or enamour'd body
    than mine,
And who thinks the amplest thoughts? for I would surround those
    thoughts,
And who has made hymns fit for the earth? for I am mad with
    devouring ecstasy to make joyous hymns for the whole earth.

AH POVERTIES, WINCINGS, AND SULKY RETREATS

Ah poverties, wincings, and sulky retreats,
Ah you foes that in conflict have overcome me,
(For what is my life or any man's life but a conflict with foes, the
    old, the incessant war?)
You degradations, you tussle with passions and appetites,
You smarts from dissatisfied friendships, (ah wounds the sharpest
    of all!)
You toil of painful and choked articulations, you meannesses,
You shallow tongue-talks at tables, (my tongue the shallowest of
    any;)
You broken resolutions, you racking angers, you smother'd
    ennuis!
Ah think not you finally triumph, my real self has yet to come
    forth,
It shall yet march forth o'ermastering, till all lies beneath me,
It shall yet stand up the soldier of ultimate victory.

THOUGHTS

Of public opinion,
Of a calm and cool fiat sooner or later, (how impassive! how
    certain and final!)
Of the President with pale face asking secretly to himself, *What
    will the people say at last?*
Of the frivolous Judge—of the corrupt Congressman,
    Governor, Mayor—of such as these standing helpless and
    exposed,
Of the mumbling and screaming priest, (soon, soon deserted,)
Of the lessening year by year of venerableness, and of the dicta of
    officers, statutes, pulpits, schools,
Of the rising forever taller and stronger and broader of the
    intuitions of men and women, and of Self-esteem and
    Personality;
Of the true New World—of the Democracies resplendent
    en-masse,

Of the conformity of politics, armies, navies, to them,
Of the shining sun by them — of the inherent light, greater than
    the rest,
Of the envelopment of all by them, and the effusion of all from
    them.

MEDIUMS[102]

They shall arise in the States,
They shall report Nature, laws, physiology, and happiness,
They shall illustrate Democracy and the kosmos,
They shall be alimentive, amative, perceptive,
They shall be complete women and men, their pose brawny and
    supple, their drink water, their blood clean and clear,
They shall fully enjoy materialism and the sight of products, they
    shall enjoy the sight of the beef, lumber, bread-stuffs,
    of Chicago the great city,
They shall train themselves to go in public to become orators and
    oratresses,
Strong and sweet shall their tongues be, poems and materials of
    poems shall come from their lives, they shall be makers and
    finders,
Of them and of their works shall emerge divine conveyers, to
    convey gospels,
Characters, events, retrospections, shall be convey'd in gospels,
    trees, animals, waters, shall be convey'd,
Death, the future, the invisible faith, shall all be convey'd.

WEAVE IN, MY HARDY LIFE

Weave in, weave in, my hardy life,
Weave yet a soldier strong and full for great campaigns to come,
Weave in red blood, weave sinews in like ropes, the senses, sight
    weave in,
Weave lasting sure, weave day and night the weft, the warp,
    incessant weave, tire not,

(We know not what the use O life, nor know the aim, the end,
    nor really aught we know,
But know the work, the need goes on and shall go on, the death-
    envelop'd march of peace as well as war goes on,)
For great campaigns of peace the same the wiry threads to weave,
We know not why or what, yet weave, forever weave.

SPAIN, 1873-74[103]

Out of the murk of heaviest clouds,
Out of the feudal wrecks and heap'd-up skeletons of kings,
Out of that old entire European debris, the shatter'd
    mummeries,
Ruin'd cathedrals, crumble of palaces, tombs of priests,
Lo, Freedom's features fresh undimm'd look forth—the same
    immortal face looks forth;
(A glimpse as of thy Mother's face Columbia,
A flash significant as of a sword,
Beaming towards thee.)

Nor think we forget thee maternal;
Lag'd'st thou so long? shall the clouds close again upon thee?
Ah, but thou hast thyself now appear'd to us—we know thee,
Thou hast given us a sure proof, the glimpse of thyself,
Thou waitest there as everywhere thy time.

BY BROAD POTOMAC'S SHORE

By broad Potomac's shore, again old tongue,
(Still uttering, still ejaculating, canst never cease this babble?)
Again old heart so gay, again to you, your sense, the full flush
    spring returning,
Again the freshness and the odors, again Virginia's summer sky,
    pellucid blue and silver,
Again the forenoon purple of the hills,

Again the deathless grass, so noiseless soft and green,
Again the blood-red roses blooming.

Perfume this book of mine O blood-red roses!
Lave subtly with your waters every line Potomac!
Give me of you O spring, before I close, to put between its
    pages!
O forenoon purple of the hills, before I close, of you!
O deathless grass, of you!

FROM FAR DAKOTA'S CAÑONS[104]

June 25, 1876

From far Dakota's cañons,
Lands of the wild ravine, the dusky Sioux, the lonesome stretch,
    the silence,
Haply to-day a mournful wail, haply a trumpet-note for heroes.

The battle-bulletin,
The Indian ambuscade, the craft, the fatal environment,
The cavalry companies fighting to the last in sternest heroism,
In the midst of their little circle, with their slaughter'd horses for
    breastworks,
The fall of Custer and all his officers and men.

Continues yet the old, old legend of our race,
The loftiest of life upheld by death,
The ancient banner perfectly maintain'd,
O lesson opportune, O how I welcome thee!

As sitting in dark days,
Lone, sulky, through the time's thick murk looking in vain for
    light, for hope,
From unsuspected parts a fierce and momentary proof,
(The sun there at the centre though conceal'd,

Electric life forever at the centre,)
Breaks forth a lightning flash.

Thou of the tawny flowing hair in battle,
I erewhile saw, with erect head, pressing ever in front, bearing a
     bright sword in thy hand,
Now ending well in death the splendid fever of thy deeds,
(I bring no dirge for it or thee, I bring a glad triumphal sonnet,)
Desperate and glorious, aye in defeat most desperate, most
     glorious,
After thy many battles in which never yielding up a gun or a
     color,
Leaving behind thee a memory sweet to soldiers,
Thou yieldest up thyself.

OLD WAR-DREAMS[105]

In midnight sleep of many a face of anguish,
Of the look at first of the mortally wounded, (of that indescribable
     look,)
Of the dead on their backs with arms extended wide,
          I dream, I dream, I dream.

Of scenes of Nature, fields and mountains,
Of skies so beauteous after a storm, and at night the moon so
     unearthly bright,
Shining sweetly, shining down, where we dig the trenches and
     gather the heaps,
          I dream, I dream, I dream.

Long have they pass'd, faces and trenches and fields,
Where through the carnage I moved with a callous composure, or
     away from the fallen,
Onward I sped at the time—but now of their forms at
     night,
          I dream, I dream, I dream.

THICK-SPRINKLED BUNTING

Thick sprinkled bunting! flag of stars!
Long yet your road, fateful flag—long yet your road, and lined
    with bloody death,
For the prize I see at issue at last is the world,
All its ships and shores I see interwoven with your threads greedy
    banner;
Dream'd again the flags of kings, highest borne, to flaunt
    unrival'd?
O hasten flag of man—O with sure and steady step, passing
    highest flags of kings,
Walk supreme to the heavens mighty symbol—run up above
    them all,
Flag of stars! thick sprinkled bunting!

WHAT BEST I SEE IN THEE[106]

To U. S. G. return'd from his World's Tour.

What best I see in thee,
Is not that where thou mov'st down history's great highways,
Ever undimm'd by time shoots warlike victory's dazzle,
Or that thou sat'st where Washington sat, ruling the land in
    peace,
Or thou the man whom feudal Europe feted, venerable Asia
    swarm'd upon,
Who walk'd with kings with even pace the round world's
    promenade;
But that in foreign lands, in all thy walks with kings,
Those prairie sovereigns of the West, Kansas, Missouri, Illinois,
Ohio's, Indiana's millions, comrades, farmers, soldiers, all to the
    front,
Invisibly with thee walking with kings with even pace the round
    world's promenade,
Were all so justified.

SPIRIT THAT FORM'D THIS SCENE[107]

Written in Platte Cañon, Colorado.

Spirit that form'd this scene,
These tumbled rock-piles grim and red,
These reckless heaven-ambitious peaks,
These gorges, turbulent-clear streams, this naked freshness,
These formless wild arrays, for reasons of their own,
I know thee, savage spirit—we have communed together,
Mine too such wild arrays, for reasons of their own;
Was't charged against my chants they had forgotten art?
To fuse within themselves its rules precise and delicatesse?
The lyrist's measur'd beat, the wrought-out temple's grace—
    column and polish'd arch forgot?
But thou that revelest here—spirit that form'd this scene,
    They have remembered thee.

AS I WALK THESE BROAD MAJESTIC DAYS

As I walk these broad majestic days of peace,
(For the war, the struggle of blood finish'd, wherein, O terrific
    Ideal,
Against vast odds erewhile having gloriously won,
Now thou stridest on, yet perhaps in time toward denser wars,
Perhaps to engage in time in still more dreadful contests, dangers,
Longer campaigns and crises, labors beyond all others,)
Around me I hear that eclat of the world, politics, produce,
The announcements of recognized things, science,
The approved growth of cities and the spread of inventions.

I see the ships, (they will last a few years,)
The vast factories with their foremen and workmen,
And hear the indorsement of all, and do not object to it.

But I too announce solid things,
Science, ships, politics, cities, factories, are not nothing,

Like a grand procession to music of distant bugles pouring,
  triumphantly moving, and grander heaving in sight,
They stand for realities—all is as it should be.

Then my realities;
What else is so real as mine?
Libertad and the divine average, freedom to every slave on the
  face of the earth,
The rapt promises and luminè of seers, the spiritual world, these
  centuries-lasting songs,
And our visions, the visions of poets, the most solid
  announcements of any.

A CLEAR MIDNIGHT

This is thy hour O Soul, thy free flight into the wordless,
Away from books, away from art, the day erased, the lesson done,
Thee fully forth emerging, silent, gazing, pondering the themes
  thou lovest best,
Night, sleep, death and the stars.

SONGS OF PARTING[108]

AS THE TIME DRAWS NIGH[109]

As the time draws nigh glooming a cloud,
A dread beyond of I know not what darkens me.

I shall go forth,
I shall traverse the States awhile, but I cannot tell whither or how
    long,
Perhaps soon some day or night while I am singing my voice will
    suddenly cease.

O book, O chants! must all then amount to but this?
Must we barely arrive at this beginning of us?—and yet it is
    enough, O soul;
O soul, we have positively appear'd—that is enough.

YEARS OF THE MODERN

Years of the modern! years of the unperform'd!
Your horizon rises, I see it parting away for more august dramas,
I see not America only, not only Liberty's nation but other nations
    preparing,
I see tremendous entrances and exits, new combinations, the
    solidarity of races,
I see that force advancing with irresistible power on the world's stage,
(Have the old forces, the old wars, played their parts? are the acts
    suitable to them closed?)
I see Freedom, completely arm'd and victorious and very haughty,
    with Law on one side and Peace on the other,

A stupendous trio all issuing forth against the idea of caste;
What historic denouements are these we so rapidly approach?
I see men marching and countermarching by swift millions,
I see the frontiers and boundaries of the old aristocracies broken,
I see the landmarks of European kings removed,
I see this day the People beginning their landmarks, (all others
    give way;)
Never were such sharp questions ask'd as this day,
Never was average man, his soul, more energetic, more like a
    God,
Lo, how he urges and urges, leaving the masses no rest!
His daring foot is on land and sea everywhere, he colonizes the
    Pacific, the archipelagoes,
With the steamship, the electric telegraph, the newspaper, the
    wholesale engines of war,
With these and the world-spreading factories he interlinks all
    geography, all lands;
What whispers are these O lands, running ahead of you, passing
    under the seas?
Are all nations communing? is there going to be but one heart to
    the globe?
Is humanity forming en-masse? for lo, tyrants tremble, crowns
    grow dim,
The earth, restive, confronts a new era, perhaps a general divine
    war,
No one knows what will happen next, such portents fill the days
    and nights;
Years prophetical! the space ahead as I walk, as I vainly try to
    pierce it, is full of phantoms,
Unborn deeds, things soon to be, project their shapes around me,
This incredible rush and heat, this strange ecstatic fever of dreams
    O years!
Your dreams O years, how they penetrate through me! (I know
    not whether I sleep or wake;)
The perform'd America and Europe grow dim, retiring in shadow
    behind me,
The unperform'd, more gigantic than ever, advance, advance,
    upon me.

ASHES OF SOLDIERS[110]

Ashes of soldiers South or North,
As I muse retrospective murmuring a chant in thought,
The war resumes, again to my sense your shapes,
And again the advance of the armies.

Noiseless as mists and vapors,
From their graves in the trenches ascending,
From cemeteries all through Virginia and Tennessee,
From every point of the compass out of the countless graves,
In wafted clouds, in myriads large, or squads of twos or threes or
 single ones they come,
And silently gather round me.

Now sound no note O trumpeters,
Not at the head of my cavalry parading on spirited horses,
With sabres drawn and glistening, and carbines by their thighs,
 (ah my brave horsemen!
My handsome tan-faced horsemen! what life, what joy and pride,
With all the perils were yours.)

Nor you drummers, neither at reveillé at dawn,
Nor the long roll alarming the camp, nor even the muffled beat
 for a burial,
Nothing from you this time O drummers bearing my warlike
 drums.

But aside from these and the marts of wealth and the crowded
 promenade,
Admitting around me comrades close unseen by the rest and
 voiceless,
The slain elate and alive again, the dust and debris alive,
I chant this chant of my silent soul in the name of all dead
 soldiers.

Faces so pale with wondrous eyes, very dear, gather closer yet,
Draw close, but speak not.

Phantoms of countless lost,
Invisible to the rest henceforth become my companions,
Follow me ever—desert me not while I live.

Sweet are the blooming cheeks of the living—sweet are the
     musical voices sounding,
But sweet, ah sweet, are the dead with their silent eyes.

Dearest comrades, all is over and long gone,
But love is not over—and what love, O comrades!
Perfume from battle-fields rising, up from the fœtor arising.

Perfume therefore my chant, O love, immortal love,
Give me to bathe the memories of all dead soldiers,
Shroud them, embalm them, cover them all over with tender
     pride.

Perfume all—make all wholesome,
Make these ashes to nourish and blossom,
O love, solve all, fructify all with the last chemistry.

Give me exhaustless, make me a fountain,
That I exhale love from me wherever I go like a moist perennial
     dew,
For the ashes of all dead soldiers South or North.

THOUGHTS

– 1 –

Of these years I sing,
How they pass and have pass'd through convuls'd pains, as
     through parturitions,
How America illustrates birth, muscular youth, the promise, the
     sure fulfilment the absolute success, despite of people—
     illustrates evil as well as good,
The vehement struggle so fierce for unity in one's-self;

How many hold despairingly yet to the models departed, caste,
　　myths, obedience, compulsion, and to infidelity,
How few see the arrived models, the athletes, the Western States,
　　or see freedom or spirituality, or hold any faith in results,
(But I see the athletes, and I see the results of the war glorious
　　and inevitable and they again leading to other results.)

How the great cities appear—how the Democratic masses,
　　turbulent, wilful, as I love them,
How the whirl, the contest, the wrestle of evil with good, the
　　sounding and resounding, keep on and on,
How society waits unform'd, and is for a while between things
　　ended and things begun,
How America is the continent of glories, and of the triumph of
　　freedom and of the Democracies, and of the fruits of society,
　　and of all that is begun,
And how the States are complete in themselves—and how all
　　triumphs and glories are complete in themselves, to lead
　　onward,
And how these of mine and of the States will in their turn be
　　convuls'd, and serve other parturitions and transitions,
And how all people, sights, combinations, the democratic masses
　　too, serve—and how every fact, and war itself, with all its
　　horrors, serves,
And how now or at any time each serves the exquisite transition of
　　death.

— 2 —

Of seeds dropping into the ground, of births,
Of the steady concentration of America, inland, upward, to
　　impregnable and swarming places,
Of what Indiana, Kentucky, Arkansas, and the rest, are to be,
Of what a few years will show there in Nebraska, Colorado,
　　Nevada, and the rest,
(Or afar, mounting the Northern Pacific to Sitka or Aliaska,)
Of what the feuillage of America is the preparation for—and of
　　what all sights, North, South, East and West, are,

Of this Union welded in blood, of the solemn price paid, of the
    unnamed lost ever present in my mind;
Of the temporary use of materials for identity's sake,
Of the present, passing, departing—of the growth of completer
    men than any yet,
Of all sloping down there where the fresh free giver the mother,
    the Mississippi flows,
Of mighty inland cities yet unsurvey'd and unsuspected,
Of the new and good names, of the modern developments, of
    inalienable homesteads,
Of a free and original life there, of simple diet and clean and
    sweet blood,
Of litheness, majestic faces, clear eyes, and perfect physique there,
Of immense spiritual results future years far West, each side of
    the Anahuacs,
Of these songs, well understood there, (being made for that area,)
Of the native scorn of grossness and gain there,
(O it lurks in me night and day—what is gain after all to
    savageness and freedom?)

SONG AT SUNSET[111]

Splendor of ended day floating and filling me,
Hour prophetic, hour resuming the past,
Inflating my throat, you divine average,
You earth and life till the last ray gleams I sing.

Open mouth of my soul uttering gladness,
Eyes of my soul seeing perfection,
Natural life of me faithfully praising things,
Corroborating forever the triumph of things.

Illustrious every one!
Illustrious what we name space, sphere of unnumber'd spirits,
Illustrious the mystery of motion in all beings, even the tiniest
    insect,
Illustrious the attribute of speech, the senses, the body,

Illustrious the passing light—illustrious the pale reflection on the
    new moon in the western sky,
Illustrious whatever I see or hear or touch, to the last.

Good in all,
In the satisfaction and aplomb of animals,
In the annual return of the seasons,
In the hilarity of youth,
In the strength and flush of manhood,
In the grandeur and exquisiteness of old age,
In the superb vistas of death.

Wonderful to depart!
Wonderful to be here!
The heart, to jet the all-alike and innocent blood!
To breathe the air, how delicious!
To speak—to walk—to seize something by the hand!
To prepare for sleep, for bed, to look on my rose-color'd flesh!
To be conscious of my body, so satisfied, so large!
To be this incredible God I am!
To have gone forth among other Gods, these men and women
    I love.

Wonderful how I celebrate you and myself!
How my thoughts play subtly at the spectacles around!
How the clouds pass silently overhead!
How the earth darts on and on! and how the sun, moon, stars,
    dart on and on!
How the water sports and sings! (surely it is alive!)
How the trees rise and stand up, with strong trunks, with branches
    and leaves!
(Surely there is something more in each of the trees, some living
    soul.)

O amazement of things—even the least particle!
O spirituality of things!
O strain musical flowing through ages and continents, now
    reaching me and America!

I take your strong chords, intersperse them, and cheerfully pass
    them forward.

I too carol the sun, usher'd or at noon, or as now, setting,
I too throb to the brain and beauty of the earth and of all the
    growths of the earth,
I too have felt the resistless call of myself.

As I steam'd down the Mississippi,
As I wander'd over the prairies,
As I have lived, as I have look'd through my windows my eyes,
As I went forth in the morning, as I beheld the light breaking in
    the east,
As I bathed on the beach of the Eastern Sea, and again on the
    beach of the Western Sea,
As I roam'd the streets of inland Chicago, whatever streets I have
    roam'd,
Or cities or silent woods, or even amid the sights of war,
Wherever I have been I have charged myself with contentment
    and triumph.

I sing to the last the equalities modern or old,
I sing the endless finalés of things,
I say Nature continues, glory continues,
I praise with electric voice,
For I do not see one imperfection in the universe,
And I do not see one cause or result lamentable at last in the
    universe.

O setting sun! though the time has come,
I still warble under you, if none else does, unmitigated adoration.

AS AT THY PORTALS ALSO DEATH[112]

As at thy portals also death,
Entering thy sovereign, dim, illimitable grounds,
To memories of my mother, to the divine blending, maternity,

To her, buried and gone, yet buried not, gone not from me,
(I see again the calm benignant face fresh and beautiful still,
I sit by the form in the coffin,
I kiss and kiss convulsively again the sweet old lips, the cheeks,
the closed eyes in the coffin;)
To her, the ideal woman, practical, spiritual, of all of earth, life,
love, to me the best,
I grave a monumental line, before I go, amid these songs,
And set a tombstone here.

MY LEGACY

The business man the acquirer vast,
After assiduous years surveying results, preparing for departure,
Devises houses and lands to his children, bequeaths stocks, goods,
funds for a school or hospital,
Leaves money to certain companions to buy tokens, souvenirs of
gems and gold.

But I, my life surveying, closing,
With nothing to show to devise from its idle years,
Nor houses nor lands, nor tokens of gems or gold for my friends,
Yet certain remembrances of the war for you, and after you,
And little souvenirs of camps and soldiers, with my love,
I bind together and bequeath in this bundle of songs.

PENSIVE ON HER DEAD GAZING

Pensive on her dead gazing I heard the Mother of All,
Desperate on the torn bodies, on the forms covering the
battlefields gazing,
(As the last gun ceased, but the scent of the powder-smoke
linger'd,)
As she call'd to her earth with mournful voice while she stalk'd,
Absorb them well O my earth, she cried, I charge you lose not my
sons, lose not an atom,

And you streams absorb them well, taking their dear blood,
And you local spots, and you airs that swim above lightly
    impalpable,
And all you essences of soil and growth, and you my rivers'
    depths,
And you mountain sides, and the woods where my dear children's
    blood trickling redden'd,
And you trees down in your roots to bequeath to all future trees,
My dead absorb or South or North—my young men's bodies
    absorb, and their precious precious blood,
Which holding in trust for me faithfully back again give me many
    a year hence,
In unseen essence and odor of surface and grass, centuries hence,
In blowing airs from the fields back again give me my darlings,
    give my immortal heroes,
Exhale me them centuries hence, breathe me their breath, let not
    an atom be lost,
O years and graves! O air and soil! O my dead, an aroma sweet!
Exhale them perennial sweet death, years, centuries hence.

CAMPS OF GREEN

Not alone those camps of white, old comrades of the wars,
When as order'd forward, after a long march,
Footsore and weary, soon as the light lessens we halt for the
    night,
Some of us so fatigued carrying the gun and knapsack, dropping
    asleep in our tracks,
Others pitching the little tents, and the fires lit up begin to
    sparkle,
Outposts of pickets posted surrounding alert through the dark,
And a word provided for countersign, careful for safety,
Till to the call of the drummers at daybreak loudly beating the
    drums,
We rise up refresh'd, the night and sleep pass'd over, and resume
    our journey,
Or proceed to battle.

Lo, the camps of the tents of green,
Which the days of peace keep filling, and the days of war keep
    filling,
With a mystic army, (is it too order'd forward? is it too only
    halting awhile,
Till night and sleep pass over?)

Now in those camps of green, in their tents dotting the world,
In the parents, children, husbands, wives, in them, in the old and
    young,
Sleeping under the sunlight, sleeping under the moonlight,
    content and silent there at last,
Behold the mighty bivouac-field and waiting-camp of all,
Of the corps and generals all, and the President over the corps
    and generals all,
And of each of us O soldiers, and of each and all in the ranks we
    fought,
(There without hatred we all, all meet.)

For presently O soldiers, we too camp in our place in the bivouac-
    camps of green,
But we need not provide for outposts, nor word for the countersign,
Nor drummer to beat the morning drum.

THE SOBBING OF THE BELLS[113]

(Midnight, Sept. 19–20, 1881)

The sobbing of the bells, the sudden death-news everywhere,
The slumberers rouse, the rapport of the People,
(Full well they know that message in the darkness,
Full well return, respond within their breasts, their brains, the sad
    reverberations,)
The passionate toll and clang—city to city, joining, sounding,
    passing,
Those heart-beats of a Nation in the night.

AS THEY DRAW TO A CLOSE

As they draw to a close,
Of what underlies the precedent songs—of my aims in
    them,
Of the seed I have sought to plant in them,
Of joy, sweet joy, through many a year, in them,
(For them, for them have I lived, in them my work is done,)
Of many an aspiration fond, of many a dream and plan;
Through Space and Time fused in a chant, and the flowing
    eternal identity,
To Nature encompassing these, encompassing God—to the
    joyous, electric all,
To the sense of Death, and accepting exulting in Death in its turn
    the same as life,
The entrance of man to sing;
To compact you, ye parted, diverse lives,
To put rapport the mountains and rocks and streams,
And the winds of the north, and the forests of oak and pine,
With you O soul.

JOY, SHIPMATE, JOY!

Joy, shipmate, joy!
(Pleas'd to my soul at death I cry,)
Our life is closed, our life begins,
The long, long anchorage we leave,
The ship is clear at last, she leaps!
She swiftly courses from the shore,
Joy, shipmate, joy.

THE UNTOLD WANT

The untold want by life and land ne'er granted,
Now voyager sail thou forth to seek and find.

PORTALS

What are those of the known but to ascend and enter the
    Unknown?
And what are those of life but for Death?

THESE CAROLS

These carols sung to cheer my passage through the world I see,
For completion I dedicate to the Invisible World.

NOW FINALÉ TO THE SHORE

Now finalé to the shore,
Now land and life finalé and farewell,
Now Voyager depart, (much, much for thee is yet in store,)
Often enough hast thou adventur'd o'er the seas,
Cautiously cruising, studying the charts,
Duly again to port and hawser's tie returning;
But now obey thy cherish'd secret wish,
Embrace thy friends, leave all in order,
To port and hawser's tie no more returning,
Depart upon thy endless cruise old Sailor.

SO LONG!*

To conclude, I announce what comes after me.

I remember I said before my leaves sprang at all,
I would raise my voice jocund and strong with reference to
    consummations.

---

*Slang expression used by the likes of sailors and prostitutes, "so long" signifies not
only "good-bye," but "'til we meet again."

When America does what was promis'd,
When through these States walk a hundred millions of superb
    persons,
When the rest part away for superb persons and contribute to
    them,
When breeds of the most perfect mothers denote America,
Then to me and mine our due fruition.

I have press'd through in my own right,
I have sung the body and the soul, war and peace have I sung,
    and the songs of life and death,
And the songs of birth, and shown that there are many births.

I have offer'd my style to every one, I have journey'd with
    confident step;
While my pleasure is yet at the full I whisper *So long!*
And take the young woman's hand and the young man's hand for
    the last time.

I announce natural persons to arise,
I announce justice triumphant,
I announce uncompromising liberty and equality,
I announce the justification of candor and the justification of
    pride.

I announce that the identity of these States is a single identity
    only,
I announce the Union more and more compact, indissoluble,
I announce splendors and majesties to make all the previous
    politics of the earth insignificant.

I announce adhesiveness, I say it shall be limitless, unloosen'd,
I say you shall yet find the friend you were looking for.

I announce a man or woman coming, perhaps you are the one,
    (*So long!*)
I announce the great individual, fluid as Nature, chaste,
    affectionate, compassionate, fully arm'd.

I announce a life that shall be copious, vehement, spiritual, bold,
I announce an end that shall lightly and joyfully meet its
    translation.

I announce myriads of youths, beautiful, gigantic, sweet-blooded,
I announce a race of splendid and savage old men.

O thicker and faster—(*So long!*)
O crowding too close upon me,
I foresee too much, it means more than I thought,
It appears to me I am dying.

Hasten throat and sound your last,
Salute me—salute the days once more. Peal the old cry once more.

Screaming electric, the atmosphere using,
At random glancing, each as I notice absorbing,
Swiftly on, but a little while alighting,
Curious envelop'd messages delivering,
Sparkles hot, seed ethereal down in the dirt dropping,
Myself unknowing, my commission obeying, to question it never
    daring,
To ages and ages yet the growth of the seed leaving,
To troops out of the war arising, they the tasks I have set
    promulging,
To women certain whispers of myself bequeathing, their affection
    me more clearly explaining,
To young men my problems offering—no dallier I—I the muscle
    of their brains trying,
So I pass, a little time vocal, visible, contrary,
Afterward a melodious echo, passionately bent for, (death making
    me really undying,)
The best of me then when no longer visible, for toward that I
    have been incessantly preparing.

What is there more, that I lag and pause and crouch extended
    with unshut mouth?
Is there a single final farewell?

My songs cease, I abandon them,
From behind the screen where I hid I advance personally solely
    to you.

Camerado, this is no book,
Who touches this touches a man,
(Is it night? are we here together alone?)
It is I you hold and who holds you,
I spring from the pages into your arms—decease calls me forth.

O how your fingers drowse me,
Your breath falls around me like dew, your pulse lulls the
    tympans of my ears,
I feel immerged from head to foot,
Delicious, enough.

Enough O deed impromptu and secret,
Enough O gliding present—enough O summ'd-up past.

Dear friend whoever you are take this kiss,
I give it especially to you, do not forget me,
I feel like one who has done work for the day to retire awhile,
I receive now again of my many translations, from my avataras
    ascending, while others doubtless await me,
An unknown sphere more real than I dream'd, more direct, darts
    awakening rays about me, *So long!*
Remember my words, I may again return,
I love you, I depart from materials,
I am as one disembodied, triumphant, dead.

Walt Whitman

Holding a butterfly—64 years old, 1883, photo taken at Ocean Grove,
New Jersey, by Phillips & Taylor. Courtesy of the Library of Congress,
Charles E. Feinberg Collection. Saunders #48.

SANDS AT SEVENTY[114]

MANNAHATTA

My city's fit and noble name resumed,
Choice aboriginal name, with marvellous beauty, meaning,
A *rocky founded island—shores where ever gayly dash the coming,
    going, hurrying sea waves.*

PAUMANOK

Sea beauty! stretch'd and basking!
One side thy inland ocean laving, broad, with copious commerce,
    steamers, sails,
And one the Atlantic's wind caressing, fierce or gentle—mighty
    hulls dark-gliding in the distance.
Isle of sweet brooks of drinking-water—healthy air and soil!
Isle of the salty shore and breeze and brine!

FROM MONTAUK POINT

I stand as on some mighty eagle's beak,
Eastward the sea absorbing, viewing, (nothing but sea and sky,)
The tossing waves, the foam, the ships in the distance,
The wild unrest, the snowy, curling caps—that inbound urge and
    urge of waves,
Seeking the shores forever.

TO THOSE WHO'VE FAIL'D

To those who've fail'd, in aspiration vast,
To unnam'd soldiers fallen in front on the lead,
To calm, devoted engineers—to over-ardent travelers—to pilots
    on their ships,
To many a lofty song and picture without recognition—I'd rear a
    laurel-cover'd monument,
High, high above the rest—To all cut off before their time,
Possess'd by some strange spirit of fire,
Quench'd by an early death.

A CAROL CLOSING SIXTY-NINE

A carol closing sixty-nine—a *résumé*—a repetition,
My lines in joy and hope continuing on the same,
Of ye, O God, Life, Nature, Freedom, Poetry;
Of you, my Land—your rivers, prairies, States—you, mottled Flag
    I love,
Your aggregate retain'd entire—Of north, south, east and west,
    your items all;
Of me myself—the jocund heart yet beating in my
    breast,
The body wreck'd, old, poor and paralyzed—the strange inertia
    falling pall-like round me,
The burning fires down in my sluggish blood not yet
    extinct,
The undiminish'd faith—the groups of loving friends.

THE BRAVEST SOLDIERS

Brave, brave were the soldiers (high named to-day) who lived
    through the fight;
But the bravest press'd to the front and fell unnamed,
    unknown.

A FONT OF TYPE[115]

This latent mine—these unlaunch'd voices—passionate
    powers,
Wrath, argument, or praise, or comic leer, or prayer devout,
(Not nonpareil, brevier, bourgeois, long primer merely,)
These ocean waves arousable to fury and to death,
Or sooth'd to ease and sheeny sun and sleep,
Within the pallid slivers slumbering.

AS I SIT WRITING HERE

As I sit writing here, sick and grown old,
Not my least burden is that dulness of the years, querilities,
Ungracious glooms, aches, lethargy, constipation, whimpering
    ennui,
May filter in my daily songs.

MY CANARY BIRD

Did we count great, O soul, to penetrate the themes of mighty
    books,
Absorbing deep and full from thoughts, plays, speculations?
But now from thee to me, caged bird, to feel thy joyous
    warble,
Filling the air, the lonesome room, the long forenoon,
Is it not just as great, O soul?

QUERIES TO MY SEVENTIETH YEAR

Approaching, nearing, curious,
Thou dim, uncertain spectre—bringest thou life or death?
Strength, weakness, blindness, more paralysis and heavier?
Or placid skies and sun? Wilt stir the waters yet?

Or haply cut me short for good? Or leave me here as now,
Dull, parrot-like and old, with crack'd voice harping,
    screeching?

THE WALLABOUT MARTYRS[116]

*[In Brooklyn, in an old vault, mark'd by no special recognition, lie
huddled at this moment the undoubtedly authentic remains of the
stanchest and earliest revolutionary patriots from the British prison
ships and prisons of the times of 1776–83, in and around New York,
and from all over Long Island; originally buried—many thousands of
them—in trenches in the Wallabout sands.]*

Greater than memory of Achilles or Ulysses,
More, more by far to thee than tomb of Alexander,
Those cart loads of old charnel ashes, scales and splints of mouldy
    bones,
Once living men—once resolute courage, aspiration,
    strength,
The stepping stones to thee to-day and here, America.

THE FIRST DANDELION

Simple and fresh and fair from winter's close emerging,
As if no artifice of fashion, business, politics, had ever been,
Forth from its sunny nook of shelter'd grass—innocent, golden,
    calm as the dawn,
The spring's first dandelion shows its trustful face.

AMERICA[117]

Centre of equal daughters, equal sons,
All, all alike endear'd, grown, ungrown, young or old,
Strong, ample, fair, enduring, capable, rich,

Perennial with the Earth, with Freedom, Law and Love,
A grand, sane, towering, seated Mother,
Chair'd in the adamant of Time.

MEMORIES

How sweet the silent backward tracings!
The wanderings as in dreams—the meditation of old times
    resumed—their loves, joys, persons, voyages.

TO-DAY AND THEE

The appointed winners in a long-stretch'd game;
The course of Time and nations—Egypt, India, Greece and
    Rome;
The past entire, with all its heroes, histories, arts, experiments,
Its store of songs, inventions, voyages, teachers, books,
Garner'd for now and thee—To think of it!
The heirdom all converged in thee!

AFTER THE DAZZLE OF DAY

After the dazzle of day is gone,
Only the dark, dark night shows to my eyes the stars;
After the clangor of organ majestic, or chorus, or perfect band,
Silent, athwart my soul, moves the symphony true.

ABRAHAM LINCOLN, BORN FEB. 12, 1809

To-day, from each and all, a breath of prayer—a pulse of
    thought,
To memory of Him—to birth of Him.
    (Publish'd Feb. 12, 1888.)

OUT OF MAY'S SHOWS SELECTED

Apple orchards, the trees all cover'd with blossoms;
Wheat fields carpeted far and near in vital emerald green;
The eternal, exhaustless freshness of each early morning;
The yellow, golden, transparent haze of the warm afternoon
     sun;
The aspiring lilac bushes with profuse purple or white flowers.

HALCYON DAYS

Not from successful love alone,
Nor wealth, nor honor'd middle age, nor victories of politics or war;
But as life wanes, and all the turbulent passions calm,
As gorgeous, vapory, silent hues cover the evening sky,
As softness, fulness, rest, suffuse the frame, like freshier, balmier air,
As the days take on a mellower light, and the apple at last hangs
     really finish'd and indolent-ripe on the tree,
Then for the teeming quietest, happiest days of all!
The brooding and blissful halcyon days!

FANCIES AT NAVESINK[118]

The Pilot in the Mist

Steaming the northern rapids—(an old St. Lawrence
     reminiscence,
A sudden memory-flash comes back, I know not why,
Here waiting for the sunrise, gazing from this hill;)*
Again 'tis just at morning—a heavy haze contends with
     daybreak,
Again the trembling, laboring vessel veers me—I press through
     foam-dash'd rocks that almost touch me,

---

*Navesink—a sea-side mountain, lower entrance of New York Bay [Whitman's note].

Again I mark where aft the small thin Indian helmsman
Looms in the mist, with brow elate and governing hand.

Had I the Choice

Had I the choice to tally greatest bards,
To limn their portraits, stately, beautiful, and emulate at will,
Homer with all his wars and warriors—Hector, Achilles, Ajax,
Or Shakspere's woe-entangled Hamlet, Lear, Othello—
        Tennyson's fair ladies,
Metre or wit the best, or choice conceit to wield in perfect rhyme,
        delight of singers;
These, these, O sea, all these I'd gladly barter,
Would you the undulation of one wave, its trick to me transfer,
Or breathe one breath of yours upon my verse,
And leave its odor there.

You Tides with Ceaseless Swell

You tides with ceaseless swell! you power that does this work!
You unseen force, centripetal, centrifugal, through space's spread,
Rapport of sun, moon, earth, and all the constellations,
What are the messages by you from distant stars to us? what
        Sirius'? what Capella's?
What central heart—and you the pulse—vivifies all? what
        boundless aggregate of all?
What subtle indirection and significance in you? what clue to all
        in you? what fluid, vast identity,
Holding the universe with all its parts as one—as sailing in a ship?

Last of Ebb, and Daylight Waning

Last of ebb, and daylight waning,
Scented sea-cool landward making, smells of sedge and salt
        incoming,
With many a half-caught voice sent up from the eddies,
Many a muffled confession—many a sob and whisper'd word,
As of speakers far or hid.

How they sweep down and out! how they mutter!
Poets unnamed—artists greatest of any, with cherish'd lost designs,
Love's unresponse—a chorus of age's complaints—hope's last words,
Some suicide's despairing cry, *Away to the boundless waste, and
      never again return.*

On to oblivion then!
On, on, and do your part, ye burying, ebbing tide!
On for your time, ye furious debouché!

And Yet Not You Alone

And yet not you alone, twilight and burying ebb,
Nor you, ye lost designs alone—nor failures, aspirations;
I know, divine deceitful ones, your glamour's seeming;
Duly by you, from you, the tide and light again—duly the hinges
      turning,
Duly the needed discord-parts offsetting, blending,
Weaving from you, from Sleep, Night, Death itself,
The rhythmus of Birth eternal.

Proudly the Flood Comes In

Proudly the flood comes in, shouting, foaming, advancing,
Long it holds at the high, with bosom broad outswelling,
All throbs, dilates—the farms, woods, streets of cities—workmen
      at work,
Mainsails, topsails, jibs, appear in the offing—steamers' pennants
      of smoke—and under the forenoon sun
Freighted with human lives, gaily the outward bound, gaily the
      inward bound,
Flaunting from many a spar the flag I love.

By That Long Scan of Waves

By that long scan of waves, myself call'd back, resumed upon
      myself,
In every crest some undulating light or shade—some retrospect,

Joys, travels, studies, silent panoramas—scenes ephemeral,
The long past war, the battles, hospital sights, the wounded and
 the dead,
Myself through every by-gone phase—my idle youth—old age at
 hand,
My three-score years of life summ'd up, and more, and past,
By any grand ideal tried, intentionless, the whole a nothing,
And haply yet some drop within God's scheme's ensemble—some
 wave, or part of wave,
Like one of yours, ye multitudinous ocean.

Then Last of All

Then last of all, caught from these shores, this hill,
Of you O tides, the mystic human meaning:
Only by law of you, your swell and ebb, enclosing me the same,
The brain that shapes, the voice that chants this song.

ELECTION DAY, NOVEMBER, 1884

If I should need to name, O Western World, your powerfulest
 scene and show,
'Twould not be you, Niagara—nor you, ye limitless prairies—nor
 your huge rifts of canyons, Colorado,
Nor you, Yosemite—nor Yellowstone, with all its spasmic geyser-
 loops ascending to the skies, appearing and disappearing,
Nor Oregon's white cones—nor Huron's belt of mighty lakes—
 nor Mississippi's stream:
—This seething hemisphere's humanity, as now, I'd name—*the
 still small voice* vibrating—America's choosing day,
(The heart of it not in the chosen—the act itself the main, the
 quadriennial choosing,)
The stretch of North and South arous'd—sea-board and inland—
 Texas to Maine—the Prairie States—Vermont, Virginia,
 California,
The final ballot-shower from East to West—the paradox and
 conflict,

The countless snow-flakes falling—(a swordless conflict,
Yet more than all Rome's wars of old, or modern Napoleon's:) the
  peaceful choice of all,
Or good or ill humanity—welcoming the darker odds, the dross:
—Foams and ferments the wine? it serves to purify—while the
  heart pants, life glows:
These stormy gusts and winds waft precious ships,
Swell'd Washington's, Jefferson's, Lincoln's sails.

WITH HUSKY-HAUGHTY LIPS, O SEA!

With husky-haughty lips, O sea!
Where day and night I wend thy surf-beat shore,
Imaging to my sense thy varied strange suggestions,
(I see and plainly list thy talk and conference here,)
Thy troops of white-maned racers racing to the goal,
Thy ample, smiling face, dash'd with the sparkling dimples of the
  sun,
Thy brooding scowl and murk—thy unloos'd hurricanes,
Thy unsubduedness, caprices, wilfulness;
Great as thou art above the rest, thy many tears—a lack from all
  eternity in thy content,
(Naught but the greatest struggles, wrongs, defeats, could make
  thee greatest—no less could make thee,)
Thy lonely state—something thou ever seek'st and seek'st, yet
  never gain'st,
Surely some right withheld—some voice, in huge monotonous
  rage, of freedom-lover pent,
Some vast heart, like a planet's, chain'd and chafing in those
  breakers,
By lengthen'd swell, and spasm, and panting breath,
And rhythmic rasping of thy sands and waves,
And serpent hiss, and savage peals of laughter,
And undertones of distant lion roar,
(Sounding, appealing to the sky's deaf ear—but now, rapport for
  once,
A phantom in the night thy confidant for once,)

The first and last confession of the globe,
Outsurging, muttering from thy soul's abysms,
The tale of cosmic elemental passion,
Thou tellest to a kindred soul.

DEATH OF GENERAL GRANT

As one by one withdraw the lofty actors,
From that great play on history's stage eterne,
That lurid, partial act of war and peace—of old and new
    contending,
Fought out through wrath, fears, dark dismays, and many a long
    suspense;
All past—and since, in countless graves receding, mellowing,
Victor's and vanquish'd—Lincoln's and Lee's—now thou with
    them,
Man of the mighty days—and equal to the days!
Thou from the prairies!—tangled and many-vein'd and hard has
    been thy part,
To admiration has it been enacted!

RED JACKET (FROM ALOFT)[119]

[*Impromptu on Buffalo City's monument to, and re-burial of the old Iroquois orator, October 9, 1884.*]

Upon this scene, this show,
Yielded to-day by fashion, learning, wealth,
(Nor in caprice alone—some grains of deepest meaning,)
Haply, aloft, (who knows?) from distant sky-clouds' blended shapes,
As some old tree, or rock or cliff, thrill'd with its soul,
Product of Nature's sun, stars, earth direct—a towering human
    form,
In hunting-shirt of film, arm'd with the rifle, a half-ironical smile
    curving its phantom lips,
Like one of Ossian's ghosts looks down.

WASHINGTON'S MONUMENT, FEBRUARY, 1885

Ah, not this marble, dead and cold:
Far from its base and shaft expanding—the round zones circling,
      comprehending,
Thou, Washington, art all the world's, the continents' entire—not
      yours alone, America,
Europe's as well, in every part, castle of lord or laborer's cot,
Or frozen North, or sultry South—the African's—the Arab's in his
      tent,
Old Asia's there with venerable smile, seated amid her ruins;
(Greets the antique the hero new? 'tis but the same—the heir
      legitimate, continued ever,
The indomitable heart and arm—proofs of the never-broken
      line,
Courage, alertness, patience, faith, the same—e'en in defeat
      defeated not, the same:)
Wherever sails a ship, or house is built on land, or day or night,
Through teeming cities' streets, indoors or out, factories or
      farms,
Now, or to come, or past—where patriot wills existed or exist,
Wherever Freedom, pois'd by Toleration, sway'd by Law,
Stands or is rising thy true monument.

OF THAT BLITHE THROAT OF THINE

[*More than eighty-three degrees north—about a good day's steaming
distance to the Pole by one of our fast oceaners in clear water—Greely
the explorer heard the song of a single snow-bird merrily sounding
over the desolation.*]

Of that blithe throat of thine from arctic bleak and blank,
I'll mind the lesson, solitary bird—let me too welcome chilling
      drifts,
E'en the profoundest chill, as now—a torpid pulse, a brain
      unnerv'd,

Old age land-lock'd within its winter bay—(cold, cold, O cold!)
These snowy hairs, my feeble arm, my frozen feet,
For them thy faith, thy rule I take, and grave it to the last;
Not summer's zones alone—not chants of youth, or south's warm
    tides alone,
But held by sluggish floes, pack'd in the northern ice, the
    cumulus of years,
These with gay heart I also sing.

BROADWAY

What hurrying human tides, or day or night!
What passions, winnings, losses, ardors, swim thy waters!
What whirls of evil, bliss and sorrow, stem thee!
What curious questioning glances—glints of love!
Leer, envy, scorn, contempt, hope, aspiration!
Thou portal—thou arena—thou of the myriad long-drawn lines
    and groups!
(Could but thy flagstones, curbs, façades, tell their inimitable
    tales;
Thy windows rich, and huge hotels—thy side-walks wide;)
Thou of the endless sliding, mincing, shuffling feet!
Thou, like the parti-colored world itself—like infinite, teeming,
    mocking life!
Thou visor'd, vast, unspeakable show and lesson!

TO GET THE FINAL LILT OF SONGS

To get the final lilt of songs,
To penetrate the inmost lore of poets—to know the mighty ones,
Job, Homer, Eschylus, Dante, Shakspere, Tennyson, Emerson;
To diagnose the shifting-delicate tints of love and pride and
    doubt—to truly understand,
To encompass these, the last keen faculty and entrance-price,
Old age, and what it brings from all its past experiences.

OLD SALT KOSSABONE[120]

Far back, related on my mother's side,
Old Salt Kossabone, I'll tell you how he died:
(Had been a sailor all his life—was nearly 90—lived with his
    married grandchild, Jenny;
House on a hill, with view of bay at hand, and distant cape, and
    stretch to open sea;)
The last of afternoons, the evening hours, for many a year his
    regular custom,
In his great arm chair by the window seated,
(Sometimes, indeed, through half the day,)
Watching the coming, going of the vessels, he mutters to
    himself—And now the close of all:
One struggling outbound brig, one day, baffled for long—cross-
    tides and much wrong going,
At last at nightfall strikes the breeze aright, her whole luck
    veering,
And swiftly bending round the cape, the darkness proudly
    entering, cleaving, as he watches,
"She's free—she's on her destination"—these the last words—
    when Jenny came, he sat there dead,
Dutch Kossabone, Old Salt, related on my mother's side, far back.

THE DEAD TENOR[121]

As down the stage again,
With Spanish hat and plumes, and gait inimitable,
Back from the fading lessons of the past, I'd call, I'd tell and
    own,
How much from thee! the revelation of the singing voice from
    thee!
(So firm—so liquid-soft—again that tremulous, manly timbre!
The perfect singing voice—deepest of all to me the lesson—trial
    and test of all:)
How through those strains distill'd—how the rapt ears, the soul of
    me, absorbing

Fernando's heart, *Manrico's* passionate call, *Ernani's*, sweet
    Gennaro's,
I fold thenceforth, or seek to fold, within my chants
    transmuting,
Freedom's and Love's and Faith's unloos'd cantabile,
(As perfume's, color's, sunlight's correlation:)
From these, for these, with these, a hurried line, dead tenor,
A wafted autumn leaf, dropt in the closing grave, the shovel'd
    earth,
To memory of thee.

CONTINUITIES

[From a talk I had lately with a German spiritualist.]

Nothing is ever really lost, or can be lost,
No birth, identity, form—no object of the world.
Nor life, nor force, nor any visible thing;
Appearance must not foil, nor shifted sphere confuse thy brain.
Ample are time and space—ample the fields of Nature.
The body, sluggish, aged, cold—the embers left from earlier
    fires,
The light in the eye grown dim, shall duly flame again;
The sun now low in the west rises for mornings and for noons
    continual;
To frozen clods ever the spring's invisible law returns,
With grass and flowers and summer fruits and corn.

YONNONDIO

[The sense of the word is *lament for the aborigines.* It is an Iroquois
term; and has been used for a personal name.]

A song, a poem of itself—the word itself a dirge,
Amid the wilds, the rocks, the storm and wintry night,
To me such misty, strange tableaux the syllables calling up;

Yonnondio—I see, far in the west or north, a limitless ravine, with
　　plains and mountains dark,
I see swarms of stalwart chieftains, medicine-men, and warriors,
As flitting by like clouds of ghosts, they pass and are gone in the
　　twilight,
(Race of the woods, the landscapes free, and the falls!
No picture, poem, statement, passing them to the future:)
Yonnondio! Yonnondio!—unlimn'd they disappear;
To-day gives place, and fades—the cities, farms, factories fade;
A muffled sonorous sound, a wailing word is borne through the
　　air for a moment,
Then blank and gone and still, and utterly lost.

LIFE

Ever the undiscouraged, resolute, struggling soul of man;
(Have former armies fail'd? then we send fresh armies—and fresh
　　again;)
Ever the grappled mystery of all earth's ages old or new;
Ever the eager eyes, hurrahs, the welcome-clapping hands, the
　　loud applause;
Ever the soul dissatisfied, curious, unconvinced at last;
Struggling to-day the same—battling the same.

"GOING SOMEWHERE"[122]

My science-friend, my noblest woman-friend,
(Now buried in an English grave—and this a memory-leaf for her
　　dear sake,)
Ended our talk—"The sum, concluding all we know of old or
　　modern learning, intuitions deep,
"Of all Geologies—Histories—of all Astronomy—of Evolution,
　　Metaphysics all,
"Is, that we all are onward, onward, speeding slowly, surely
　　bettering,

"Life, life an endless march, an endless army, (no halt, but it is
    duly over,)
"The world, the race, the soul—in space and time the universes,
"All bound as is befitting each—all surely going somewhere."

SMALL THE THEME OF MY CHANT

Small the theme of my Chant, yet the greatest—namely, One's-
    Self—a simple, separate person. That, for the use of the New
    World, I sing.
Man's physiology complete, from top to toe, I sing. Not
    physiognomy alone, nor brain alone, is worthy for the
    Muse;—I say the Form complete is worthier far. The Female
    equally with the Male, I sing.
Nor cease at the theme of One's-Self. I speak the word of the
    modern, the word En-Masse.
My Days I sing, and the Lands—with interstice I knew of hapless
    War.
(O friend, whoe'er you are, at last arriving hither to commence, I
    feel through every leaf the pressure of your hand, which I
    return.
And thus upon our journey, footing the road, and more than
    once, and link'd together let us go.)

TRUE CONQUERORS

Old farmers, travelers, workmen (no matter how crippled or
    bent,)
Old sailors, out of many a perilous voyage, storm and wreck,
Old soldiers from campaigns, with all their wounds, defeats and
    scars;
Enough that they've survived at all—long life's unflinching ones!
Forth from their struggles, trials, fights, to have emerged at all—in
    that alone,
True conquerors o'er all the rest.

THE UNITED STATES TO OLD WORLD CRITICS

Here first the duties of to-day, the lessons of the concrete,
Wealth, order, travel, shelter, products, plenty;
As of the building of some varied, vast, perpetual edifice,
Whence to arise inevitable in time, the towering roofs, the lamps,
The solid-planted spires tall shooting to the stars.

THE CALMING THOUGHT OF ALL

That coursing on, whate'er men's speculations,
Amid the changing schools, theologies, philosophies,
Amid the bawling presentations new and old,
The round earth's silent vital laws, facts, modes continue.

THANKS IN OLD AGE

Thanks in old age—thanks ere I go,
For health, the midday sun, the impalpable air—for life, mere
 life,
For precious ever-lingering memories, (of you my mother dear—
 you, father—you, brothers, sisters, friends,)
For all my days—not those of peace alone—the days of war the
 same,
For gentle words, caresses, gifts from foreign lands,
For shelter, wine and meat—for sweet appreciation,
(You distant, dim unknown—or young or old—countless,
 unspecified, readers belov'd,
We never met, and ne'er shall meet—and yet our souls embrace,
 long, close and long;)
For beings, groups, love, deeds, words, books—for colors, forms,
For all the brave strong men—devoted, hardy men—who've
 forward sprung in freedom's help, all years, all lands,
For braver, stronger, more devoted men—(a special laurel ere I
 go, to life's war's chosen ones.

The cannoneers of song and thought—the great artillerists—the
 foremost leaders, captains of the soul:)
As soldier from an ended war return'd—As traveler out of myriads,
 to the long procession retrospective,
Thanks—joyful thanks!—a soldier's, traveler's thanks.

LIFE AND DEATH

The two old, simple problems ever intertwined,
Close home, elusive, present, baffled, grappled.
By each successive age insoluble, pass'd on,
To ours to-day—and we pass on the same.

THE VOICE OF THE RAIN

And who art thou? said I to the soft-falling shower,
Which, strange to tell, gave me an answer, as here translated:
I am the Poem of Earth, said the voice of the rain,
Eternal I rise impalpable out of the land and the bottomless sea,
Upward to heaven, whence, vaguely form'd, altogether changed,
 and yet the same,
I descend to lave the drouths, atomies, dust-layers of the globe,
And all that in them without me were seeds only, latent, unborn;
And forever, by day and night, I give back life to my own origin,
 and make pure and beautify it;
(For song, issuing from its birth-place, after fulfilment, wandering,
Reck'd or unreck'd, duly with love returns.)

SOON SHALL THE WINTER'S FOIL BE HERE

Soon shall the winter's foil be here;
Soon shall these icy ligatures unbind and melt—A little while,
And air, soil, wave, suffused shall be in softness, bloom and
 growth—a thousand forms shall rise

From these dead clods and chills as from low burial graves.
Thine eyes, ears—all thy best attributes—all that takes
    cognizance of natural beauty,
Shall wake and fill. Thou shalt perceive the simple shows, the
    delicate miracles of earth,
Dandelions, clover, the emerald grass, the early scents and
    flowers,
The arbutus under foot, the willow's yellow-green, the blossoming
    plum and cherry;
With these the robin, lark and thrush, singing their songs—the
    flitting bluebird;
For such the scenes the annual play brings on.

WHILE NOT THE PAST FORGETTING

While not the past forgetting,
To-day, at least, contention sunk entire—peace, brotherhood
    uprisen;
For sign reciprocal our Northern, Southern hands,
Lay on the graves of all dead soldiers, North or South,
(Nor for the past alone—for meanings to the future,)
Wreaths of roses and branches of palm.
    (Publish'd May 30, 1888.)

THE DYING VETERAN

[A Long Island incident—early part of the present century.]

Amid these days of order, ease, prosperity,
Amid the current songs of beauty, peace, decorum,
I cast a reminiscence—(likely 'twill offend you,
I heard it in my boyhood;)—More than a generation since,
A queer old savage man, a fighter under Washington himself,
(Large, brave, cleanly, hot-blooded, no talker, rather
    spiritualistic,

Had fought in the ranks—fought well—had been all through the
  Revolutionary war,)
Lay dying—sons, daughters, church-deacons, lovingly tending
  him,
Sharping their sense, their ears, towards his murmuring, half-
  caught words:
"Let me return again to my war-days,
To the sights and scenes—to forming the line of battle,
To the scouts ahead reconnoitering,
To the cannons, the grim artillery,
To the galloping aids, carrying orders,
To the wounded, the fallen, the heat, the suspense,
The perfume strong, the smoke, the deafening noise;
Away with your life of peace!—your joys of peace!
Give me my old wild battle-life again!"

STRONGER LESSONS

Have you learn'd lessons only of those who admired you, and
  were tender with you, and stood aside for you?
Have you not learn'd great lessons from those who reject
  you, and brace themselves against you? or who
  treat you with contempt, or dispute the passage
  with you?

A PRAIRIE SUNSET

Shot gold, maroon and violet, dazzling silver, emerald, fawn,
The earth's whole amplitude and Nature's multiform power
  consign'd for once to colors;
The light, the general air possess'd by them—colors till now
  unknown,
No limit, confine—not the Western sky alone—the high
  meridian—North, South, all,
Pure luminous color fighting the silent shadows to the last.

TWENTY YEARS

Down on the ancient wharf, the sand, I sit, with a newcomer
　　chatting:
He shipp'd as green-hand boy, and sail'd away, (took some
　　sudden, vehement notion;)
Since, twenty years and more have circled round and round,
While he the globe was circling round and round,—and now
　　returns:
How changed the place—all the old land-marks gone—the
　　parents dead;
(Yes, he comes back *to lay in port for good—to settle*—has a well-
　　fill'd purse—no spot will do but this;)
The little boat that scull'd him from the sloop, now held in leash
　　I see,
I hear the slapping waves, the restless keel, the rocking in the
　　sand,
I see the sailor kit, the canvas bag, the great box bound with brass,
I scan the face all berry-brown and bearded—the stout-strong
　　frame,
Dress'd in its russet suit of good Scotch cloth:
(Then what the told-out story of those twenty years? What of the
　　future?)

ORANGE BUDS BY MAIL FROM FLORIDA

*[Voltaire closed a famous argument by claiming that a ship of war
and the grand opera were proofs enough of civilization's and France's
progress, in his day.]*

A lesser proof than old Voltaire's, yet greater,
Proof of this present time, and thee, thy broad expanse, America,
To my plain Northern hut, in outside clouds and snow,
Brought safely for a thousand miles o'er land and tide,
Some three days since on their own soil live-sprouting,
Now here their sweetness through my room unfolding,
A bunch of orange buds by mail from Florida.

TWILIGHT

The soft voluptuous opiate shades,
The sun just gone, the eager light dispell'd—(I too will soon be
     gone, dispell'd,)
A haze—nirwana—rest and night—oblivion.

YOU LINGERING SPARSE LEAVES OF ME

You lingering sparse leaves of me on winter-nearing boughs,
And I some well-shorn tree of field or orchard-row;
You tokens diminute and lorn—(not now the flush of May or July
     clover-bloom—no grain of August now;)
You pallid banner-staves—you pennants valueless—you over-
     stay'd of time,
Yet my soul-dearest leaves confirming all the rest,
The faithfulest—hardiest—last.

NOT MEAGRE, LATENT BOUGHS ALONE

Not meagre, latent boughs alone, O songs! (scaly and bare, like
     eagles' talons,)
But haply for some sunny day (who knows?) some future spring,
     some summer—bursting forth,
To verdant leaves, or sheltering shade—to nourishing fruit,
Apples and grapes—the stalwart limbs of trees emerging—the
     fresh, free, open air,
And love and faith, like scented roses blooming.

THE DEAD EMPEROR

To-day, with bending head and eyes, thou, too, Columbia,
Less for the mighty crown laid low in sorrow—less for the Emperor,
Thy true condolence breathest, sendest out o'er many a salt sea
     mile,

Mourning a good old man—a faithful shepherd, patriot.
(Publish'd March 10, 1888.)

AS THE GREEK'S SIGNAL FLAME[123]

[For Whittier's eightieth birthday, December 17, 1887.]

As the Greek's signal flame, by antique records told,
Rose from the hill-top, like applause and glory,
Welcoming in fame some special veteran, hero,
With rosy tinge reddening the land he'd served,
So I aloft from Mannahatta's ship-fringed shore,
Lift high a kindled brand for thee, Old Poet.

THE DISMANTLED SHIP

In some unused lagoon, some nameless bay,
On sluggish, lonesome waters, anchor'd near the shore,
An old, dismasted, gray and batter'd ship, disabled, done,
After free voyages to all the seas of earth, haul'd up at last and
    hawser'd tight,
Lies rusting, mouldering.

NOW PRECEDENT SONGS, FAREWELL

Now precedent songs, farewell—by every name farewell,
(Trains of a staggering line in many a strange procession,
    waggons,
From ups and downs—with intervals—from elder years, mid-age,
    or youth,)
"In Cabin'd Ships," or "Thee Old Cause" or "Poets to Come"
Or "Paumanok," "Song of Myself," "Calamus," or "Adam,"
Or "Beat! Beat! Drums!" or "To the Leaven'd Soil they Trod,"
Or "Captain! My Captain!" "Kosmos," "Quicksand Years," or
    "Thoughts,"

"Thou Mother with thy Equal Brood," and many, many more
    unspecified,
From fibre heart of mine—from throat and tongue—(My life's
    hot pulsing blood,
The personal urge and form for me—not merely paper, automatic
    type and ink,)
Each song of mine—each utterance in the past—having its long,
    long history,
Of life or death, or soldier's wound, of country's loss or safety,
(O heaven! what flash and started endless train of all! compared
    indeed to that!
What wretched shred e'en at the best of all!)

AN EVENING LULL

After a week of physical anguish,
Unrest and pain, and feverish heat,
Toward the ending day a calm and lull comes on,
Three hours of peace and soothing rest of brain.*

OLD AGE'S LAMBENT PEAKS

The touch of flame—the illuminating fire—the loftiest look at
    last,
O'er city, passion, sea—o'er prairie, mountain, wood—the earth
    itself;
The airy, different, changing hues of all, in falling twilight,
Objects and groups, bearings, faces, reminiscences;
The calmer sight—the golden setting, clear and broad:
So much i' the atmosphere, the points of view, the situations
    whence we scan,

---

*The two songs on this page are eked out during an afternoon, June, 1888, in my seventieth year, at a critical spell of illness. Of course no reader and probably no human being at any time will ever have such phases of emotional and solemn action as these involve to me. I feel in them an end and close of all [Whitman's note].

Bro't out by them alone—so much (perhaps the best) unreck'd
  before;
The lights indeed from them—old age's lambent peaks.

AFTER THE SUPPER AND TALK

After the supper and talk—after the day is done,
As a friend from friends his final withdrawal prolonging,
Good-bye and Good-bye with emotional lips repeating,
(So hard for his hand to release those hands—no more will they
  meet,
No more for communion of sorrow and joy, of old and young,
A far-stretching journey awaits him, to return no more,)
Shunning, postponing severance—seeking to ward off the last
  word ever so little,
E'en at the exit door turning—charges superfluous calling back—
  e'en as he descends the steps,
Something to eke out a minute additional—shadows of nightfall
  deepening,
Farewells, messages lessening—dimmer the forthgoer's visage and
  form,
Soon to be lost for aye in the darkness—loth, O so loth to depart!
Garrulous to the very last.

GOOD-BYE MY FANCY

PREFACE NOTE TO 2D ANNEX, CONCLUDING L. OF G. — 1891[124]

Had I not better withhold (in this old age and paralysis of me) such little tags and fringe-dots (maybe specks, stains,) as follow a long dusty journey, and witness it afterward? I have probably not been enough afraid of careless touches, from the first — and am not now — nor of parrot-like repetitions — nor platitudes and the commonplace. Perhaps I am too democratic for such avoidances. Besides, is not the verse-field, as originally plann'd by my theory, now sufficiently illustrated — and full time for me to silently retire? — (indeed amid no loud call or market for my sort of poetic utterance.)

In answer, or rather defiance, to that kind of well-put interrogation, here comes this little cluster, and conclusion of my preceding clusters. Though not at all clear that, as here collated, it is worth printing (certainly I have nothing fresh to write) — I while away the hours of my 72d year — hours of forced confinement in my den — by putting in shape this small old age collation:

> Last droplets of and after spontaneous rain,
> From many limpid distillations and past showers;
> (Will they germinate anything? mere exhalations as they
>   all are — the land's and sea's — America's;
> Will they filter to any deep emotion? any heart and
>   brain?)

However that may be, I feel like improving to-day's opportunity and wind up. During the last two years I have sent out, in the lulls of illness and exhaustion, certain chirps—lingering-dying ones probably (undoubtedly)—which now I may as well gather and put in fair type while able to see correctly—(for my eyes plainly warn me they are dimming, and my brain more and more palpably neglects or refuses, month after month, even slight tasks or revisions.)

In fact, here I am these current years 1890 and '91, (each successive fortnight getting stiffer and stuck deeper) much like some hard-cased dilapidated grim ancient shell-fish or time-bang'd conch (no legs, utterly non-locomotive) cast up high and dry on the shore-sands, helpless to move anywhere—nothing left but behave myself quiet, and while away the days yet assign'd, and discover if there is anything for the said grim and time-bang'd conch to be got at last out of inherited good spirits and primal buoyant centre-pulses down there deep somewhere within his gray-blurr'd old shell . . . . (Reader, you must allow a little fun here—for one reason there are too many of the following poemets about death, &c., and for another the passing hours (July 5, 1890) are so sunny-fine. And old as I am I feel to-day almost a part of some frolicsome wave, or for sporting yet like a kid or kitten—probably a streak of physical adjustment and perfection here and now. I believe I have it in me perennially anyhow.)

Then behind all, the deep-down consolation (it is a glum one, but I dare not be sorry for the fact of it in the past, nor refrain from dwelling, even vaunting here at the end) that this late-years palsied old shorn and shell-fish condition of me is the indubitable outcome and growth, now near for 20 years along, of too over-zealous, over-continued bodily and emotional excitement and action through the times of 1862, '3, '4 and '5, visiting and waiting on wounded and sick army volunteers, both sides, in campaigns or contests, or after them, or in hospitals or fields south of Washington City, or in that place and elsewhere—those hot, sad, wrenching times—the army volunteers, all States,—or North or South—the wounded, suffering, dying—the exhausting, sweating summers,

marches, battles, carnage—those trenches hurriedly heap'd by
the corpse-thousands, mainly unknown—Will the America of
the future—will this vast rich Union ever realize what itself
cost, back there after all?—those hecatombs of battle-deaths—
Those times of which, O far-off reader, this whole book is in-
deed finally but a reminiscent memorial from thence by me
to you?

SAIL OUT FOR GOOD, EIDÓLON YACHT!

Heave the anchor short!
Raise main-sail and jib—steer forth,
O little white-hull'd sloop, now speed on really deep
　　waters,
(I will not call it our concluding voyage,
But outset and sure entrance to the truest, best,
　　maturest;)
Depart, depart from solid earth—no more returning to these
　　shores,
Now on for aye our infinite free venture wending,
Spurning all yet tried ports, seas, hawsers, densities,
　　gravitation,
Sail out for good, eidólon yacht of me!

LINGERING LAST DROPS

And whence and why come you?

We know not whence, (was the answer,)
We only know that we drift here with the rest,
That we linger'd and lagg'd—but were wafted at last, and are now
　　here,
To make the passing shower's concluding drops.

GOOD-BYE MY FANCY

Good-bye* my fancy—(I had a word to say,
But 'tis not quite the time—The best of any man's word or say,
Is when its proper place arrives—and for its meaning,
I keep mine till the last.)

ON, ON THE SAME, YE JOCUND TWAIN!

On, on the same, ye jocund twain!
My life and recitative, containing birth, youth, mid-age
    years,
Fitful as motley-tongues of flame, inseparably twined and merged
    in one—combining all,
My single soul—aims, confirmations, failures, joys—Nor single
    soul alone,
I chant my nation's crucial stage, (America's, haply humanity's)—
    the trial great, the victory great,
A strange *eclaircissement* of all the masses past, the eastern world,
    the ancient, medieval,
Here, here from wanderings, strayings, lessons, wars, defeats—
    here at the west a voice triumphant—justifying all,
A gladsome pealing cry—a song for once of utmost pride and
    satisfaction;
I chant from it the common bulk, the general average horde,
    (the best no sooner than the worst)—And now I chant
    old age,
(My verses, written first for forenoon life, and for the summer's,
    autumn's spread,

---

*Behind a Good-bye there lurks much of the salutation of another beginning—to me,
Development, Continuity, Immortality, Transformation, are the chiefest life-
meanings of Nature and Humanity, and are the *sine qua non* of all facts, and each fact.

    Why do folks dwell so fondly on the last words, advice, appearance, of the de-
parting? Those last words are not samples of the best, which involve vitality at its
full, and balance, and perfect control and scope. But they are valuable beyond
measure to confirm and endorse the varied train, facts, theories and faith of the
whole preceding life [Whitman's note].

I pass to snow-white hairs the same, and give to pulses winter-
    cool'd the same;)
As here in careless trill, I and my recitatives, with faith and
    love,
Wafting to other work, to unknown songs, conditions,
On, on, ye jocund twain! continue on the same!

MY 71ST YEAR

After surmounting three score and ten,
With all their chances, changes, losses, sorrows,
My parents' deaths, the vagaries of my life, the many tearing
    passions of me, the war of '63 and '4,
As some old broken soldier, after a long, hot, wearying march, or
    haply after battle,
To-day at twilight, hobbling, answering company roll-call, *Here*,
    with vital voice,
Reporting yet, saluting yet the Officer over all.

APPARITIONS

A vague mist hanging 'round half the pages:
(Sometimes how strange and clear to the soul,
That all these solid things are indeed but apparitions, concepts,
    non-realities.)

THE PALLID WREATH

Somehow I cannot let it go yet, funeral though it is,
Let it remain back there on its nail suspended,
With pink, blue, yellow, all blanch'd, and the white now gray and
    ashy,
One wither'd rose put years ago for thee, dear friend;
But I do not forget thee. Hast thou then faded?

Is the odor exhaled? Are the colors, vitalities, dead?
No, while memories subtly play—the past vivid as ever;
For but last night I woke, and in that spectral ring saw
    thee,
Thy smile, eyes, face, calm, silent, loving as ever:
So let the wreath hang still awhile within my eye-reach,
It is not yet dead to me, nor even pallid.

AN ENDED DAY

The soothing sanity and blitheness of completion,
The pomp and hurried contest-glare and rush are done;
Now triumph! transformation! jubilate!*

---

*NOTE.—Summer country life.—Several years.—In my rambles and explorations I found a woody place near the creek, where for some reason the birds in happy mood seem'd to resort in unusual numbers. Especially at the beginning of the day, and again at the ending, I was sure to get there the most copious bird-concerts. I repair'd there frequently at sunrise—and also at sunset, or just before . . . Once the question arose in me: Which is the best singing, the first or the lattermost? The first always exhilarated, and perhaps seem'd more joyous and stronger; but I always felt the sunset or late afternoon sounds more penetrating and sweeter—seem'd to touch the soul—often the evening thrushes, two or three of them, responding and perhaps blending. Though I miss'd some of the mornings, I found myself getting to be quite strictly punctual at the evening utterances.

ANOTHER NOTE.—"He went out with the tide and the sunset," was a phrase I heard from a surgeon describing an old sailor's death under peculiarly gentle conditions.

    During the Secession War, 1863 and '4, visiting the Army Hospitals around Washington, I form'd the habit, and continued it to the end, whenever the ebb or flood tide began the latter part of day, of punctually visiting those at that time populous wards of suffering men. Somehow (or I thought so) the effect of the hour was palpable. The badly wounded would get some ease, and would like to talk a little, or be talk'd to. Intellectual and emotional natures would be at their best: Deaths were always easier; medicines seem'd to have better effect when given then, and a lulling atmosphere would pervade the wards.

    Similar influences, similar circumstances and hours, day-close, after great battles, even with all their horrors. I had more than once the same experience on the fields cover'd with fallen or dead [Whitman's notes].

OLD AGE'S SHIP & CRAFTY DEATH'S

From east and west across the horizon's edge,
Two mighty masterful vessels sailers steal upon us:
But we'll make race a-time upon the seas—a battle-contest yet!
    bear lively there!
(Our joys of strife and derring-do to the last!)
Put on the old ship all her power to-day!
Crowd top-sail, top-gallant and royal studding-sails,
Out challenge and defiance—flags and flaunting pennants
    added,
As we take to the open—take to the deepest, freest waters.

TO THE PENDING YEAR

Have I no weapon-word for thee—some message brief and fierce?
(Have I fought out and done indeed the battle?) Is there no shot
    left,
For all thy affectations, lisps, scorns, manifold silliness?
Nor for myself—my own rebellious self in thee?

Down, down, proud gorge!—though choking thee;
Thy bearded throat and high-borne forehead to the gutter;
Crouch low thy neck to eleemosynary gifts.

SHAKSPERE-BACON'S CIPHER[125]

I doubt it not—then more, far more;
In each old song bequeath'd—in every noble page or text,
(Different—something unreck'd before—some unsuspected
    author,)
In every object, mountain, tree, and star—in every birth and
    life,
As part of each—evolv'd from each—meaning, behind the ostent,
A mystic cipher waits infolded.

LONG, LONG HENCE

After a long, long course, hundreds of years, denials,
Accumulations, rous'd love and joy and thought,
Hopes, wishes, aspirations, ponderings, victories, myriads of readers,
Coating, compassing, covering—after ages' and ages'
    encrustations,
Then only may these songs reach fruition.

BRAVO, PARIS EXPOSITION![126]

Add to your show, before you close it, France,
With all the rest, visible, concrete, temples, towers, goods,
    machines and ores,
Our sentiment wafted from many million heart-throbs, ethereal
    but solid,
(We grand-sons and great-grand-sons do not forget your grand-sires,)
From fifty Nations and nebulous Nations, compacted, sent
    oversea to-day,
America's applause, love, memories and good-will.

INTERPOLATION SOUNDS

[General Philip Sheridan was buried at the Cathedral, Washington,
D.C., August, 1888, with all the pomp, music and ceremonies of the
Roman Catholic service.]

Over and through the burial chant,
Organ and solemn service, sermon, bending priests,
To me come interpolation sounds not in the show—plainly to
    me, crowding up the aisle and from the window,
Of sudden battle's hurry and harsh noises—war's grim game to
    sight and ear in earnest;
The scout call'd up and forward—the general mounted and his
    aides around him—the new-brought word—the
    instantaneous order issued;

The rifle crack—the cannon thud—the rushing forth of men
    from their tents;
The clank of cavalry—the strange celerity of forming ranks—the
    slender bugle note;
The sound of horses' hoofs departing—saddles, arms,
    accoutrements.*

TO THE SUN-SET BREEZE

Ah, whispering, something again, unseen,
Where late this heated day thou enterest at my window, door,
Thou, laving, tempering all, cool-freshing, gently vitalizing
Me, old, alone, sick, weak-down, melted-worn with sweat;
Thou, nestling, folding close and firm yet soft, companion better
    than talk, book, art,
(Thou hast, O Nature! elements! utterance to my heart beyond
    the rest—and this is of them,)
So sweet thy primitive taste to breathe within—thy soothing
    fingers on my face and hands,
Thou, messenger-magical strange bringer to body and spirit of
    me,
(Distances balk'd—occult medicines penetrating me from head to
    foot,)

---

*NOTE.—CAMDEN, N. J., August 7, 1888.—Walt Whitman asks the *New York Herald* "to add his tribute to Sheridan:"

"In the grand constellation of five or six names, under Lincoln's Presidency, that history will bear for ages in her firmament as marking the last life-throbs of secession, and beaming on its dying gasps, Sheridan's will be bright. One consideration rising out of the now dead soldier's example as it passes my mind, is worth taking notice of. If the war had continued any long time these States, in my opinion, would have shown and proved the most conclusive military talents ever evinced by any nation on earth. That they possess'd a rank and file ahead of all other known in points of quality and limitlessness of number are easily admitted. But we have, too, the eligibility of organizing, handling and officering equal to the other. These two, with modern arms, transportation, and inventive American genius, would make the United States, with earnestness, not only able to stand the whole world, but conquer that world united against us" [Whitman's note].

I feel the sky, the prairies vast—I feel the mighty northern lakes,
I feel the ocean and the forest—somehow I feel the globe itself
    swift-swimming in space;
Thou blown from lips so loved, now gone—haply from endless
    store, God-sent,
(For thou art spiritual, Godly, most of all known to my sense,)
Minister to speak to me, here and now, what word has never told,
    and cannot tell,
Art thou not universal concrete's distillation? Law's, all
    Astronomy's last refinement?
Hast thou no soul? Can I not know, identify thee?

OLD CHANTS

An ancient song, reciting, ending,
Once gazing toward thee, Mother of All,
Musing, seeking themes fitted for thee,
Accept for me, thou saidst, *the elder ballads*,
And name for me before thou goest each ancient poet.

(Of many debts incalculable,
Haply our New World's chiefest debt is to old poems.)

Ever so far back, preluding thee, America,
Old chants, Egyptian priests, and those of Ethiopia,
The Hindu epics, the Grecian, Chinese, Persian,
The Biblic books and prophets, and deep idyls of the Nazarene,
The Iliad, Odyssey, plots, doings, wanderings of Eneas,
Hesiod, Eschylus, Sophocles, Merlin, Arthur,
The Cid, Roland at Roncesvalles, the Nibelungen,
The troubadours, minstrels, minnesingers, skalds,
Chaucer, Dante, flocks of singing birds,
The Border Minstrelsy, the bye-gone ballads, feudal tales, essays,
    plays,
Shakspere, Schiller, Walter Scott, Tennyson,
As some vast wondrous weird dream-presences,
The great shadowy groups gathering around,

Darting their mighty masterful eyes forward at thee,
Thou! with as now thy bending neck and head, with courteous
    hand and word, ascending,
Thou! pausing a moment, drooping thine eyes upon them, blent
    with their music,
Well pleased, accepting all, curiously prepared for by them,
Thou enterest at thy entrance porch.

A CHRISTMAS GREETING

From a Northern Star-Group to a Southern, 1889–90.

Welcome, Brazilian brother—thy ample place is ready;
A loving hand—a smile from the north—a sunny instant hail!
(Let the future care for itself, where it reveals its troubles,
    impedimentas,
Ours, ours the present throe, the democratic aim, the acceptance
    and the faith;)
To thee to-day our reaching arm, our turning neck—to thee from
    us the expectant eye,
Thou cluster free! thou brilliant lustrous one! thou, learning well,
The true lesson of a nation's light in the sky,
(More shining than the Cross, more than the Crown,)
The height to be superb humanity.

SOUNDS OF THE WINTER

Sounds of the winter too,
Sunshine upon the mountains—many a distant strain
From cheery railroad train—from nearer field, barn, house,
The whispering air—even the mute crops, garner'd apples, corn,
Children's and women's tones—rhythm of many a farmer and of
    flail,
An old man's garrulous lips among the rest, *Think not we give out
    yet,*
Forth from these snowy hairs we keep up yet the lilt.

A TWILIGHT SONG

As I sit in twilight late alone by the flickering oak-flame,
Musing on long-pass'd war scenes—of the countless buried
    unknown soldiers,
Of the vacant names, as unindented air's and sea's—the
    unreturn'd,
The brief truce after battle, with grim burial-squads, and the
    deep-fill'd trenches
Of gather'd dead from all America, North, South, East, West,
    whence they came up,
From wooded Maine, New-England's farms, from fertile
    Pennsylvania, Illinois, Ohio,
From the measureless West, Virginia, the South, the Carolinas,
    Texas,
(Even here in my room-shadows and half-lights in the noiseless
    flickering flames,
Again I see the stalwart ranks on-filing, rising—I hear the
    rhythmic tramp of the armies;)
You million unwrit names all, all—you dark bequest from all the
    war,
A special verse for you—a flash of duty long neglected—your
    mystic roll strangely gather'd here,
Each name recall'd by me from out the darkness and death's
    ashes,
Henceforth to be, deep, deep within my heart recording, for
    many a future year,
Your mystic roll entire of unknown names, or North or
    South,
Embalm'd with love in this twilight song.

WHEN THE FULL-GROWN POET CAME

When the full-grown poet came,
Out spake pleased Nature (the round impassive globe, with all its
    shows of day and night,) saying, *He is mine*;

But out spake too the Soul of man, proud, jealous and
    unreconciled, *Nay, he is mine alone*;
—Then the full-grown poet stood between the two, and took each
    by the hand;
And to-day and ever so stands, as blender, uniter, tightly holding
    hands,
Which he will never release until he reconciles the two,
And wholly and joyously blends them.

OSCEOLA[127]

*[When I was nearly grown to manhood in Brooklyn, New York,
(middle of 1838,) I met one of the return'd U.S. Marines from Fort
Moultrie, S.C., and had long talks with him—learn'd the occur-
rence below described—death of Osceola. The latter was a young,
brave, leading Seminole in the Florida war of that time—was sur-
render'd to our troops, imprison'd and literally died of "a broken
heart," at Fort Moultrie. He sicken'd of his confinement—the doctor
and officers made every allowance and kindness possible for him;
then the close:]*

When his hour for death had come,
He slowly rais'd himself from the bed on the floor,
Drew on his war-dress, shirt, leggings, and girdled the belt around
    his waist,
Call'd for vermilion paint (his looking-glass was held before him,)
Painted half his face and neck, his wrists, and back-hands.
Put the scalp-knife carefully in his belt—then lying down, resting
    a moment,
Rose again, half sitting, smiled, gave in silence his extended hand
    to each and all,
Sank faintly low to the floor (tightly grasping the tomahawk
    handle,)
Fix'd his look on wife and little children—the last:

(And here a line in memory of his name and death.)

A VOICE FROM DEATH[128]

(The Johnstown, Penn., cataclysm, May 31, 1889.)

A voice from Death, solemn and strange, in all his sweep and
     power,
With sudden, indescribable blow—towns drown'd—humanity by
     thousands slain,
The vaunted work of thrift, goods, dwellings, forge, street, iron
     bridge,
Dash'd pell-mell by the blow—yet usher'd life continuing on,
(Amid the rest, amid the rushing, whirling, wild debris,
A suffering woman saved—a baby safely born!)

Although I come and unannounc'd, in horror and in pang,
In pouring flood and fire, and wholesale elemental crash, (this
     voice so solemn, strange,)
I too a minister of Deity.

Yea, Death, we bow our faces, veil our eyes to thee,
We mourn the old, the young untimely drawn to thee,
The fair, the strong, the good, the capable,
The household wreck'd, the husband and the wife the engulf'd
     forger in his forge,
The corpses in the whelming waters and the mud,
The gather'd thousands to their funeral mounds, and thousands
     never found or gather'd.

Then after burying, mourning the dead,
(Faithful to them found or unfound, forgetting not, bearing the
     past, here new musing,)
A day—a passing moment or an hour—America itself bends
     low,
Silent, resign'd, submissive.

War, death, cataclysm like this, America,
Take deep to thy proud prosperous heart.

E'en as I chant, lo! out of death, and out of ooze and slime,
The blossoms rapidly blooming, sympathy, help, love,
From West and East, from South and North and over sea,
Its hot-spurr'd hearts and hands humanity to human aid moves on;
And from within a thought and lesson yet.

Thou ever-darting Globe! through Space and Air!
Thou waters that encompass us!
Thou that in all the life and death of us, in action or in sleep!
Thou laws invisible that permeate them and all,
Thou that in all, and over all, and through and under all,
      incessant!
Thou! thou! the vital, universal, giant force resistless, sleepless,
      calm,
Holding Humanity as in thy open hand, as some ephemeral toy,
How ill to e'er forget thee!

For I too have forgotten,
(Wrapt in these little potencies of progress, politics, culture,
      wealth, inventions, civilization,)
Have lost my recognition of your silent ever-swaying power, ye
      mighty, elemental throes,
In which and upon which we float, and every one of us is buoy'd.

A PERSIAN LESSON

For his o'erarching and last lesson the graybeard sufi,
In the fresh scent of the morning in the open air,
On the slope of a teeming Persian rose-garden,
Under an ancient chestnut-tree wide spreading its branches,
Spoke to the young priests and students.

"Finally my children, to envelop each word, each part of the rest,
Allah is all, all, all—is immanent in every life and object,
May-be at many and many-a-more removes—yet Allah, Allah,
      Allah is there.

"Has the estray wander'd far? Is the reason-why strangely
  hidden?
Would you sound below the restless ocean of the entire world?
Would you know the dissatisfaction? the urge and spur of every
  life;
The something never still'd—never entirely gone? the invisible
  need of every seed?

"It is the central urge in every atom,
(Often unconscious, often evil, downfallen,)
To return to its divine source and origin, however distant,
Latent the same in subject and in object, without one exception."

THE COMMONPLACE

The commonplace I sing;
How cheap is health! how cheap nobility!
Abstinence, no falsehood, no gluttony, lust;
The open air I sing, freedom, toleration,
(Take here the mainest lesson—less from books—less from the
  schools,)
The common day and night—the common earth and waters,
Your farm—your work, trade, occupation,
The democratic wisdom underneath, like solid ground for all.

"THE ROUNDED CATALOGUE DIVINE COMPLETE"

*[Sunday,——.—— —Went this forenoon to church. A college profes-
sor, Rev. Dr.——, gave us a fine sermon, during which I caught the
above words; but the minister included in his "rounded catalogue" let-
ter and spirit, only the esthetic things, and entirely ignored what I
name in the following:]*

The devilish and the dark, the dying and diseas'd,
The countless (nineteen-twentieths) low and evil, crude and savage,

The crazed, prisoners in jail, the horrible, rank, malignant,
Venom and filth, serpents, the ravenous sharks, liars, the
　　dissolute;
(What is the part the wicked and the loathesome bear within
　　earth's orbic scheme?)
Newts, crawling things in slime and mud, poisons,
The barren soil, the evil men, the slag and hideous rot.

MIRAGES[129]

*(Noted verbatim after a supper-talk out doors in Nevada
with two old miners.)*

More experiences and sights, stranger, than you'd think for;
Times again, now mostly just after sunrise or before
　　sunset,
Sometimes in spring, oftener in autumn, perfectly clear weather,
　　in plain sight,
Camps far or near, the crowded streets of cities and the shop-
　　fronts,
(Account for it or not—credit or not—it is all true,
And my mate there could tell you the like—we have often
　　confab'd about it,)
People and scenes, animals, trees, colors and lines, plain as
　　could be,
Farms and dooryards of home, paths border'd with box, lilacs in
　　corners,
Weddings in churches, thanksgiving dinners, returns of long-
　　absent sons,
Glum funerals, the crape-veil'd mother and the daughters,
Trials in courts, jury and judge, the accused in the box,
Contestants, battles, crowds, bridges, wharves,
Now and then mark'd faces of sorrow or joy,
(I could pick them out this moment if I saw them again,)
Show'd to me just aloft to the right in the sky-edge,
Or plainly there to the left on the hill-tops.

L. OF G.'S PURPORT

Not to exclude or demarcate, or pick out evils from their
    formidable masses (even to expose them,)
But add, fuse, complete, extend—and celebrate the immortal and
    the good.

Haughty this song, its words and scope,
To span vast realms of space and time,
Evolution—the cumulative—growths and generations.

Begun in ripen'd youth and steadily pursued,
Wandering, peering, dallying with all—war, peace, day and night
    absorbing,
Never even for one brief hour abandoning my task,
I end it here in sickness, poverty, and old age.

I sing of life, yet mind me well of death:
To-day shadowy Death dogs my steps, my seated shape, and has
    for years—
Draws sometimes close to me, as face to face.

THE UNEXPRESS'D

How dare one say it?
After the cycles, poems, singers, plays,
Vaunted Ionia's, India's—Homer, Shakspere—the long, long
    times' thick dotted roads, areas,
The shining clusters and the Milky Ways of stars—Nature's pulses
    reap'd,
All retrospective passions, heroes, war, love, adoration,
All ages' plummets dropt to their utmost depths,
All human lives, throats, wishes, brains—all experiences' utterance;
After the countless songs, or long or short, all tongues, all lands,
Still something not yet told in poesy's voice or print—something
    lacking,
(Who knows? the best yet unexpress'd and lacking.)

GRAND IS THE SEEN

Grand is the seen, the light, to me—grand are the sky
    and stars,
Grand is the earth, and grand are lasting time and space,
And grand their laws, so multiform, puzzling, evolutionary;
But grander far the unseen soul of me, comprehending,
    endowing all those,
Lighting the light, the sky and stars, delving the earth, sailing
    the sea,
(What were all those, indeed, without thee, unseen soul? of what
    amount without thee?)
More evolutionary, vast, puzzling, O my soul!
More multiform far—more lasting thou than they.

UNSEEN BUDS

Unseen buds, infinite, hidden well,
Under the snow and ice, under the darkness, in every square or
    cubic inch,
Germinal, exquisite, in delicate lace, microscopic, unborn,
Like babes in wombs, latent, folded, compact, sleeping;
Billions of billions, and trillions of trillions of them
    waiting,
(On earth and in the sea—the universe—the stars there in the
    heavens,)
Urging slowly, surely forward, forming endless,
And waiting ever more, forever more behind.

GOOD-BYE MY FANCY![130]

Good-bye my Fancy!
Farewell dear mate, dear love!
I'm going away, I know not where,
Or to what fortune, or whether I may ever see you again,
So Good-bye my Fancy.

Now for my last—let me look back a moment;
The slower fainter ticking of the clock is in me,
Exit, nightfall, and soon the heart-thud stopping.

Long have we lived, joy'd, caress'd together;
Delightful!—now separation—Good-bye my Fancy.
Yet let me not be too hasty,
Long indeed have we lived, slept, filter'd, become really blended
    into one;
Then if we die we die together, (yes, we'll remain one,)
If we go anywhere we'll go together to meet what happens,
May-be we'll be better off and blither, and learn something,
May-be it is yourself now really ushering me to the true songs,
    (who knows?)
May-be it is you the mortal knob really undoing, turning—so now
    finally,
Good-bye—and hail! my Fancy.

A BACKWARD GLANCE O'ER TRAVEL'D
ROADS[131]

———◆———

Perhaps the best of songs heard, or of any and all true love, or life's fairest episodes, or sailors', soldiers' trying scenes on land or sea, is the *résumé* of them, or any of them, long afterwards, looking at the actualities away back past, with all their practical excitations gone. How the soul loves to float amid such reminiscences!

So here I sit gossiping in the early candle-light of old age—I and my book—casting backward glances over our travel'd road. After completing, as it were, the journey—(a varied jaunt of years, with many halts and gaps of intervals—or some lengthen'd ship-voyage, wherein more than once the last hour had apparently arrived, and we seem'd certainly going down—yet reaching port in a sufficient way through all discomfitures at last)—After completing my poems, I am curious to review them in the light of their own (at the time unconscious, or mostly unconscious) intentions, with certain unfoldings of the thirty years they seek to embody. These lines, therefore, will probably blend the weft of first purposes and speculations, with the warp of that experience afterwards, always bringing strange developments.

Result of seven or eight stages and struggles extending through nearly thirty years, (as I nigh my three-score-and-ten I live largely on memory,) I look upon "Leaves of Grass," now finish'd to the end of its opportunities and powers, as my definitive *carte visite* to the coming generations of the New World,* if I may assume to say

---

*When Champollion, on his death-bed, handed to the printer the revised proof of his "Egyptian Grammar," he said gayly, "Be careful of this—it is my *carte de visite* to posterity" [Whitman's note].

so. That I have not gain'd the acceptance of my own time, but have fallen back on fond dreams of the future—anticipations—("still lives the song, though Regnar dies")—That from a worldly and business point of view "Leaves of Grass" has been worse than a failure—that public criticism on the book and myself as author of it yet shows mark'd anger and contempt more than anything else—("I find a solid line of enemies to you everywhere,"—letter from W. S. K., Boston, May 28, 1884)—And that solely for publishing it I have been the object of two or three pretty serious special official buffetings—is all probably no more than I ought to have expected. I had my choice when I commenc'd. I bid neither for soft eulogies, big money returns, nor the approbation of existing schools and conventions. As fulfill'd, or partially fulfill'd, the best comfort of the whole business (after a small band of the dearest friends and upholders ever vouchsafed to man or cause—doubtless all the more faithful and uncompromising—this little phalanx!—for being so few) is that, unstopp'd and unwarp'd by any influence outside the soul within me, I have had my say entirely my own way, and put it unerringly on record—the value thereof to be decided by time.

In calculating that decision, William O'Connor and Dr. Bucke are far more peremptory than I am. Behind all else that can be said, I consider "Leaves of Grass" and its theory experimental—as, in the deepest sense, I consider our American republic itself to be, with its theory. (I think I have at least enough philosophy not to be too absolutely certain of any thing, or any results.) In the second place, the volume is a *sortie*—whether to prove triumphant, and conquer its field of aim and escape and construction, nothing less than a hundred years from now can fully answer. I consider the point that I have positively gain'd a hearing, to far more than make up for any and all other lacks and withholdings. Essentially, *that* was from the first, and has remain'd throughout, the main object. Now it seems to be achiev'd, I am certainly contented to waive any otherwise momentous drawbacks, as of little account. Candidly and dispassionately reviewing all my intentions, I feel that they were creditable—and I accept the result, whatever it may be.

After continued personal ambition and effort, as a young fellow, to enter with the rest into competition for the usual rewards, business, political, literary, &c.—to take part in the great *mêlée*, both for victory's prize itself and to do some good—After years of those aims and pursuits, I found myself remaining possess'd, at the age of thirty-one to thirty-three, with a special desire and conviction. Or rather, to be quite exact, a desire that had been flitting through my previous life, or hovering on the flanks, mostly indefinite hitherto, had steadily advanced to the front, defined itself, and finally dominated everything else. This was a feeling or ambition to articulate and faithfully express in literary or poetic form, and uncompromisingly, my own physical, emotional, moral, intellectual, and æsthetic Personality, in the midst of, and tallying, the momentous spirit and facts of its immediate days, and of current America—and to exploit that Personality, identified with place and date, in a far more candid and comprehensive sense than any hitherto poem or book.

Perhaps this is in brief, or suggests, all I have sought to do. Given the Nineteenth Century, with the United States, and what they furnish as area and points of view, "Leaves of Grass" is, or seeks to be, simply a faithful and doubtless self-will'd record. In the midst of all, it gives one man's—the author's—identity, ardors, observations, faiths, and thoughts, color'd hardly at all with any decided coloring from other faiths or other identities. Plenty of songs had been sung—beautiful, matchless songs—adjusted to other lands than these—another spirit and stage of evolution; but I would sing, and leave out or put in, quite solely with reference to America and to-day. Modern science and democracy seem'd to be throwing out their challenge to poetry to put them in its statements in contradistinction to the songs and myths of the past. As I see it now (perhaps too late,) I have unwittingly taken up that challenge and made an attempt at such statements—which I certainly would not assume to do now, knowing more clearly what it means.

For grounds for "Leaves of Grass," as a poem, I abandon'd the conventional themes, which do not appear in it: none of the stock ornamentation, or choice plots of love or war, or high, exceptional personages of Old-World song; nothing, as I may say, for beauty's sake—no legend, or myth, or romance; nor euphemism, nor rhyme. But the broadest average of humanity and its identities in the now ripening Nineteenth Century, and especially in each of their countless examples and practical occupations in the United States to-day.

One main contrast of the ideas behind every page of my verses, compared with establish'd poems, is their different relative attitude towards God, towards the objective universe, and still more (by reflection, confession, assumption, &c.) the quite changed attitude of the ego, the one chanting or talking, towards himself and towards his fellow-humanity. It is certainly time for America, above all, to begin this readjustment in the scope and basic point of view of verse; for everything else has changed. As I write, I see in an article on Wordsworth, in one of the current English magazines, the lines, "A few weeks ago an eminent French critic said that, owing to the special tendency to science and to its all-devouring force, poetry would cease to be read in fifty years." But I anticipate the very contrary. Only a firmer, vastly broader, new area begins to exist— nay, is already form'd—to which the poetic genius must emigrate. Whatever may have been the case in years gone by, the true use for the imaginative faculty of modern times is to give ultimate vivification to facts, to science, and to common lives, endowing them with the glows and glories and final illustriousness which belong to every real thing, and to real things only. Without that ultimate vivification— which the poet or other artist alone can give—reality would seem incomplete, and science, democracy, and life itself, finally in vain.

Few appreciate the moral revolutions, our age, which have been profounder far than the material or inventive or war-produced ones. The Nineteenth Century, now well towards its close (and ripening into fruit the seeds of the two preceding centuries*)—the

---

*The ferment and germination even of the United States to-day, dating back to, and in my opinion mainly founded on, the Elizabethan age in English history, the age of Francis Bacon and Shakspere. Indeed, when we pursue it, what growth or advent is there that does not date back, back, until lost—perhaps its most tantalizing clues lost—in the receded horizons of the past? [Whitman's note].

uprisings of national masses and shiftings of boundary-lines—the historical and other prominent facts of the United States—the war of attempted Secession—the stormy rush and haste of nebulous forces—never can future years witness more excitement and din of action—never completer change of army front along the whole line, the whole civilized world. For all these new and evolutionary facts, meanings, purposes, new poetic messages, new forms and expressions, are inevitable.

My Book and I—what a period we have presumed to span! those thirty years from 1850 to '80—and America in them! Proud, proud indeed may we be, if we have cull'd enough of that period in its own spirit to worthily waft a few live breaths of it to the future!

Let me not dare, here or anywhere, for my own purposes, or any purposes, to attempt the definition of Poetry, nor answer the question what it is. Like Religion, Love, Nature, while those terms are indispensable, and we all give a sufficiently accurate meaning to them, in my opinion no definition that has ever been made sufficiently encloses the name Poetry; nor can any rule of convention ever so absolutely obtain but some great exception may arise and disregard and overturn it.

Also it must be carefully remember'd that first-class literature does not shine by any luminosity of its own; nor do its poems. They grow of circumstances, and are evolutionary. The actual living light is always curiously from elsewhere—follows unaccountable sources, and is lunar and relative at the best. There are, I know, certain controling themes that seem endlessly appropriated to the poets—as war, in the past—in the Bible, religious rapture and adoration— always love, beauty, some fine plot, or pensive or other emotion. But, strange as it may sound at first, I will say there is something striking far deeper and towering far higher than those themes for the best elements of modern song.

Just as all the old imaginative works rest, after their kind, on long trains of presuppositions, often entirely unmention'd by themselves, yet supplying the most important bases of them, and without which they could have had no reason for being, so "Leaves of Grass," before a line was written, presupposed something different from any other, and, as it stands, is the result of such presupposition.

I should say, indeed, it were useless to attempt reading the book without first carefully tallying that preparatory background and quality in the mind. Think of the United States to-day—the facts of these thirty-eight or forty empires solder'd in one—sixty or seventy millions of equals, with their lives, their passions, their future—these incalculable, modern, American, seething multitudes around us, of which we are inseparable parts! Think, in comparison, of the petty environage and limited area of the poets of past or present Europe, no matter how great their genius. Think of the absence and ignorance, in all cases hitherto, of the multitudinousness, vitality, and the unprecedented stimulants of to-day and here. It almost seems as if a poetry with cosmic and dynamic features of magnitude and limitlessness suitable to the human soul, were never possible before. It is certain that a poetry of absolute faith and equality for the use of the democratic masses never was.

In estimating first-class song, a sufficient Nationality, or, on the other hand, what may be call'd the negative and lack of it, (as in Goethe's case, it sometimes seems to me,) is often, if not always, the first element. One needs only a little penetration to see, at more or less removes, the material facts of their country and radius, with the coloring of the moods of humanity at the time, and its gloomy or hopeful prospects, behind all poets and each poet, and forming their birth-marks. I know very well that my "Leaves" could not possibly have emerged or been fashion'd or completed, from any other era than the latter half of the Nineteenth Century, nor any other land than democratic America, and from the absolute triumph of the National Union arms.

And whether my friends claim it for me or not, I know well enough, too, that in respect to pictorial talent, dramatic situations, and especially in verbal melody and all the conventional technique of poetry, not only the divine works that to-day stand ahead in the world's reading, but dozens more, transcend (some of them immeasurably transcend) all I have done, or could do. But it seem'd to me, as the objects in Nature, the themes of æstheticism, and all special exploitations of the mind and soul, involve not only their own inherent quality, but the quality, just as inherent and important, of *their point of view,** the time had come to reflect all themes and things, old and new, in the lights thrown on them by the advent of America and democracy—to chant those themes through the utterance of one, not only the grateful and reverent legatee of the past, but the born child of the New World—to illustrate all through the genesis and ensemble of to-day; and that such illustration and ensemble are the chief demands of America's prospective imaginative literature. Not to carry out, in the approved style, some choice plot of fortune or misfortune, or fancy, or fine thoughts, or incidents, or courtesies—all of which has been done overwhelmingly and well, probably never to be excell'd—but that while in such æsthetic presentation of objects, passions, plots, thoughts, &c., our lands and days do not want, and probably will never have, anything better than they already possess from the bequests of the past, it still remains to be said that there is even towards all those a subjective and contemporary point of view appropriate to ourselves alone, and to our new genius and environments, different from anything hitherto; and that such conception of current or gone-by life and art is for us the only means of their assimilation consistent with the Western world.

Indeed, and anyhow, to put it specifically, has not the time arrived when, (if it must be plainly said, for democratic America's sake, if for no other) there must imperatively come a readjustment of the whole theory and nature of Poetry? The question is important, and I may turn the argument over and repeat it: Does not the best thought of our day and Republic conceive of a birth and spirit of song superior to anything past or present? To the effectual and moral consolidation of our lands (already, as materially establish'd, the greatest factors in known history, and far, far greater through what they prelude and necessitate, and are to be in future)—to conform with and build on the concrete realities and theories of the universe furnish'd by science, and henceforth the only irrefragable basis for anything, verse included—to root both influences

---

*According to Immanuel Kant, the last essential reality, giving shape and significance to all the rest [Whitman's note].

in the emotional and imaginative action of the modern time, and dominate all that precedes or opposes them—is not either a radical advance and step forward, or a new verteber of the best song indispensable?

The New World receives with joy the poems of the antique, with European feudalism's rich fund of epics, plays, ballads— seeks not in the least to deaden or displace those voices from our ear and area—holds them indeed as indispensable studies, influences, records, comparisons. But though the dawn-dazzle of the sun of literature is in those poems for us of to-day—though perhaps the best parts of current character in nations, social groups, or any man's or woman's individuality, Old World or New, are from them—and though if I were ask'd to name the most precious bequest to current American civilization from all the hitherto ages, I am not sure but I would name those old and less old songs ferried hither from east and west—some serious words and debits remain; some acrid considerations demand a hearing. Of the great poems receiv'd from abroad and from the ages, and to-day enveloping and penetrating America, is there one that is consistent with these United States, or essentially applicable to them as they are and are to be? Is there one whose underlying basis is not a denial and insult to democracy? What a comment it forms, anyhow, on this era of literary fulfilment, with the splendid day-rise of science and resuscitation of history, that our chief religious and poetical works are not our own, nor adapted to our light, but have been furnish'd by far-back ages out of their arriere and darkness, or, at most, twilight dimness! What is there in those works that so imperiously and scornfully dominates all our advanced civilization, and culture?

Even Shakspeare, who so suffuses current letters and art (which indeed have in most degrees grown out of him,) belongs essentially to the buried past. Only he holds the proud distinction for certain important phases of that past, of being the loftiest of the singers life has yet given voice to. All, however, relate to and rest upon conditions, standards, politics, sociologies, ranges of belief, that have been quite eliminated from the Eastern hemisphere, and never existed at all in the Western. As authoritative types of song they belong in America just about as much as the persons and institutes they depict.

True, it may be said, the emotional, moral, and aesthetic natures of humanity have not radically changed—that in these the old poems apply to our times and all times, irrespective of date; and that they are of incalculable value as pictures of the past. I willingly make those admissions, and to their fullest extent; then advance the points herewith as of serious, even paramount importance.

I have indeed put on record elsewhere my reverence and eulogy for those never-to-be excell'd poetic bequests, and their indescribable preciousness as heirlooms for America. Another and separate point must now be candidly stated. If I had not stood before those poems with uncover'd head, fully aware of their colossal grandeur and beauty of form and spirit, I could not have written "Leaves of Grass." My verdict and conclusions as illustrated in its pages are arrived at through the temper and inculcation of the old works as much as through anything else—perhaps more than through anything else. As America fully and fairly construed is the legitimate result and evolutionary outcome of the past, so I would dare to claim for my verse. Without stopping to qualify the averment, the Old World has had the poems of myths, fictions, feudalism, conquest, caste, dynastic wars, and splendid exceptional characters and affairs, which have been great; but the New World needs the poems of realities and science and of the democratic average and basic equality, which shall be greater. In the centre of all, and object of all, stands the Human Being, towards whose heroic and spiritual evolution poems and everything directly or indirectly tend, Old World or New.

Continuing the subject, my friends have more than once suggested—or may be the garrulity of advancing age is possessing me—some further embryonic facts of "Leaves of Grass," and especially how I enter'd upon them. Dr. Bucke has, in his volume, already fully and fairly described the preparation of my poetic field, with the particular and general plowing, planting, seeding, and occupation of the ground, till everything was fertilized, rooted, and ready to start its own way for good or bad. Not till after all this, did I attempt any serious acquaintance with poetic literature. Along in my sixteenth year I had become possessor of a stout, well-cramm'd one thousand page octavo volume (I have it yet,) containing Walter

Scott's poetry entire—an inexhaustible mine and treasury of poetic forage (especially the endless forests and jungles of notes)—has been so to me for fifty years, and remains so to this day.*

Later, at intervals, summers and falls, I used to go off, sometimes for a week at a stretch, down in the country, or to Long Island's seashores—there, in the presence of outdoor influences, I went over thoroughly the Old and New Testaments, and absorb'd (probably to better advantage for me than in any library or indoor room—it makes such difference *where* you read,) Shakspere, Ossian, the best translated versions I could get of Homer, Eschylus, Sophocles, the old German Nibelungen, the ancient Hindoo poems, and one or two other masterpieces, Dante's among them. As it happen'd, I read the latter mostly in an old wood. The Iliad (Buckley's prose version,) I read first thoroughly on the peninsula of Orient, northeast end of Long Island, in a shelter'd hollow of rocks and sand, with the sea on each side. (I have wonder'd since why I was not overwhelm'd by those mighty masters. Likely because I read them, as described, in the full presence of Nature, under the sun, with the far-spreading landscape and vistas, or the sea rolling in.)

Toward the last I had among much else look'd over Edgar Poe's poems—of which I was not an admirer, tho' I always saw that beyond their limited range of melody (like perpetual chimes of music bells, ringing from lower *b* flat up to *g*) they were melodious expressions, and perhaps never excell'd ones, of certain pronounc'd phases of human morbidity. (The Poetic area is very spacious—has room for all—has so many mansions!) But I was repaid in Poe's prose by the idea that (at any rate for our occasions, our day) there can be no such thing as a long poem. The same thought had been

---

*Sir Walter Scott's COMPLETE POEMS; especially including BORDER MINSTRELSY; then Sir Tristem; Lay of the Last Minstrel; Ballads from the German; Marmion; Lady of the Lake; Vision of Don Roderick; Lord of the Isles; Rokeby; Bridal of Triermain; Field of Waterloo; Harold the Dauntless; all the Dramas; various Introductions, endless interesting Notes, and Essays on Poetry, Romance, &c.

Lockhart's 1833 (or '34) edition with Scott's latest and copious revisions and annotations. (All the poems were thoroughly read by me, but the ballads of the Border Minstrelsy over and over again [Whitman's note].)

haunting my mind before, but Poe's argument, though short, work'd the sum out and proved it to me.

Another point had an early settlement, clearing the ground greatly. I saw, from the time my enterprise and questionings positively shaped themselves (how best can I express my own distinctive era and surroundings, America, Democracy?) that the trunk and centre whence the answer was to radiate, and to which all should return from straying however far a distance, must be an identical body and soul, a personality—which personality, after many considerations and ponderings I deliberately settled should be myself—indeed could not be any other. I also felt strongly (whether I have shown it or not) that to the true and full estimate of the Present both the Past and the Future are main considerations.

These, however, and much more might have gone on and come to naught (almost positively would have come to naught,) if a sudden, vast, terrible, direct and indirect stimulus for new and national declamatory expression had not been given to me. It is certain, I say, that, although I had made a start before, only from the occurrence of the Secession War, and what it show'd me as by flashes of lightning, with the emotional depths it sounded and arous'd (of course, I don't mean in my own heart only, I saw it just as plainly in others, in millions)—that only from the strong flare and provocation of that war's sights and scenes the final reasons-for-being of an autochthonic and passionate song definitely came forth.

I went down to the war fields in Virginia (end of 1862), lived thenceforward in camp—saw great battles and the days and nights afterward—partook of all the fluctuations, gloom, despair, hopes again arous'd, courage evoked—death readily risk'd—*the cause*, too—along and filling those agnostic and lurid following years, 1863-'64-'65—the real parturition years (more than 1776-'83) of this henceforth homogeneous Union. Without those three or four years and the experiences they gave, "Leaves of Grass" would not now be existing.

But I set out with the intention also of indicating or hinting some point-characteristics which I since see (though I did not then, at least not definitely) were bases and object-urgings toward those "Leaves" from the first. The word I myself put primarily for the description of them as they stand at last, is the word Suggestiveness. I round and finish little, if anything; and could not, consistently with my scheme. The reader will always have his or her part to do, just as much as I have had mine. I seek less to state or display any theme or thought, and more to bring you, reader, into the atmosphere of the theme or thought—there to pursue your own flight. Another impetus-word is Comradeship as for all lands, and in a more commanding and acknowledg'd sense than hitherto. Other word-signs would be Good Cheer, Content, and Hope.

The chief trait of any given poet is always the spirit he brings to the observation of Humanity and Nature—the mood out of which he contemplates his subjects. What kind of temper and what amount of faith report these things? Up to how recent a date is the song carried? What the equipment, and special raciness of the singer—what his tinge of coloring? The last value of artistic expressers, past and present—Greek æsthetes, Shakspere—or in our own day Tennyson, Victor Hugo, Carlyle, Emerson—is certainly involv'd in such questions. I say the profoundest service that poems or any other writings can do for their reader is not merely to satisfy the intellect, or supply something polish'd and interesting, nor even to depict great passions, or persons or events, but to fill him with vigorous and clean manliness, religiousness, and give him *good heart* as a radical possession and habit. The educated world seems to have been growing more and more ennuyed for ages, leaving to our time the inheritance of it all. Fortunately there is the original inexhaustible fund of buoyancy, normally resident in the race, forever eligible to be appeal'd to and relied on.

As for native American individuality, though certain to come, and on a large scale, the distinctive and ideal type of Western character (as consistent with the operative political and even money-making features of United States' humanity in the Nineteenth Century as chosen knights, gentlemen and warriors were the ideals of the centuries of European feudalism) it has not yet appear'd. I have allow'd the stress of my poems from beginning to end to bear upon American individuality and assist it—not only because that is a great lesson in Nature, amid all her generalizing laws, but as counterpoise to the leveling tendencies of

Democracy—and for other reasons. Defiant of ostensible literary and other conventions, I avowedly chant "the great pride of man in himself," and permit it to be more or less a *motif* of nearly all my verse. I think this pride indispensable to an American. I think it not inconsistent with obedience, humility, deference, and self-questioning.

Democracy has been so retarded and jeopardized by powerful personalities, that its first instincts are fain to clip, conform, bring in stragglers, and reduce everything to a dead level. While the ambitious thought of my song is to help the forming of a great aggregate Nation, it is, perhaps, altogether through the forming of myriads of fully develop'd and enclosing individuals. Welcome as are equality's and fraternity's doctrines and popular education, a certain liability accompanies them all, as we see. That primal and interior something in man, in his soul's abysms, coloring all, and, by exceptional fruitions, giving the last majesty to him—something continually touch'd upon and attain'd by the old poems and ballads of feudalism, and often the principal foundation of them—modern science and democracy appear to be endangering, perhaps eliminating. But that forms an appearance only; the reality is quite different. The new influences, upon the whole, are surely preparing the way for grander individualities than ever. To-day and here personal force is behind everything, just the same. The times and depictions from the Iliad to Shakspere inclusive can happily never again be realized—but the elements of courageous and lofty manhood are unchanged.

Without yielding an inch the working-man and working-woman were to be in my pages from first to last. The ranges of heroism and loftiness with which Greek and feudal poets endow'd their god-like or lordly born characters—indeed prouder and better based and with fuller ranges than those—I was to endow the democratic averages of America. I was to show that we, here and to-day, are eligible to the grandest and the best—more eligible now than any times of old were. I will also want my utterances (I said to myself before beginning) to be in spirit the poems of the morning. (They have been founded and mainly written in the sunny forenoon and early midday of my life.) I will want them to be the poems of women entirely as much as men. I have wish'd to put the complete Union of the States in my songs without any preference or partiality whatever. Henceforth, if they live and are read, it must be just as much South as North — just as much along the Pacific as Atlantic — in the valley of the Mississippi, in Canada, up in Maine, down in Texas, and on the shores of Puget Sound.

From another point of view "Leaves of Grass" is avowedly the song of Sex and Amativeness, and even Animality — though meanings that do not usually go along with those words are behind all, and will duly emerge; and all are sought to be lifted into a different light and atmosphere. Of this feature, intentionally palpable in a few lines, I shall only say the espousing principle of those lines so gives breath of life to my whole scheme that the bulk of the pieces might as well have been left unwritten were those lines omitted. Difficult as it will be, it has become, in my opinion, imperative to achieve a shifted attitude from superior men and women towards the thought and fact of sexuality, as an element in character, personality, the emotions, and a theme in literature. I am not going to argue the question by itself; it does not stand by itself. The vitality of it is altogether in its relations, bearings, significance — like the clef of a symphony. At last analogy the lines I allude to, and the spirit in which they are spoken, permeate all "Leaves of Grass," and the work must stand or fall with them, as the human body and soul must remain as an entirety.

Universal as are certain facts and symptoms of communities or individuals all times, there is nothing so rare in modern conventions and poetry as their normal recognizance. Literature is always calling in the doctor for consultation and confession, and always giving evasions and swathing suppressions in place of that "heroic nudity"* on which only a genuine diagnosis of serious cases can be built. And in respect to editions of "Leaves of Grass" in time to come (if there should be such) I take occasion now to confirm those lines with the settled convictions and deliberate renewals of thirty years, and to hereby prohibit, as far as word of mine can do so, any elision of them.

---

*Nineteenth Century," July, 1883 [Whitman's note].

Then still a purpose enclosing all, and over and beneath all. Ever since what might be call'd thought, or the budding of thought, fairly began in my youthful mind, I had had a desire to attempt some worthy record of that entire faith and acceptance ("to justify the ways of God to man" is Milton's well-known and ambitious phrase) which is the foundation of moral America. I felt it all as positively then in my young days as I do now in my old ones; to formulate a poem whose every thought or fact should directly or indirectly be or connive at an implicit belief in the wisdom, health, mystery, beauty of every process, every concrete object, every human or other existence, not only consider'd from the point of view of all, but of each.

While I can not understand it or argue it out, I fully believe in a clue and purpose in Nature, entire and several; and that invisible spiritual results, just as real and definite as the visible, eventuate all concrete life and all materialism, through Time. My book ought to emanate buoyancy and gladness legitimately enough, for it was grown out of those elements, and has been the comfort of my life since it was originally commenced.

One main genesis-motive of the "Leaves" was my conviction (just as strong to-day as ever) that the crowning growth of the United States is to be spiritual and heroic. To help start and favor that growth—or even to call attention to it, or the need of it—is the beginning, middle and final purpose of the poems. (In fact, when really cipher'd out and summ'd to the last, plowing up in earnest the interminable average fallows of humanity—not "good government" merely, in the common sense—is the justification and main purpose of these United States.)

Isolated advantages in any rank or grace or fortune—the direct or indirect threads of all the poetry of the past—are in my opinion distasteful to the republican genius, and offer no foundation for its fitting verse. Establish'd poems, I know, have the very great advantage of chanting the already perform'd, so full of glories, reminiscences dear to the minds of men. But my volume is a candidate for the future. "All original art," says Taine, anyhow, "is self-regulated, and no original art can be regulated from without; it carries its own counterpoise, and does not receive it from elsewhere—lives on its own blood"—a solace to my frequent bruises and sulky vanity.

As the present is perhaps mainly an attempt at personal statement or illustration, I will allow myself as further help to extract the following anecdote from a book, "Annals of Old Painters," conn'd by me in youth. Rubens, the Flemish painter, in one of his wanderings through the galleries of old convents, came across a singular work. After looking at it thoughtfully for a good while, and listening to the criticisms of his suite of students, he said to the latter, in answer to their questions (as to what school the work implied or belong'd,) "I do not believe the artist, unknown and perhaps no longer living, who has given the world this legacy, ever belong'd to any school, or ever painted anything but this one picture, which is a personal affair—a piece out of a man's life."

"Leaves of Grass" indeed (I cannot too often reiterate) has mainly been the outcropping of my own emotional and other personal nature—an attempt, from first to last, to put *a Person*, a human being (myself, in the latter half of the Nineteenth Century, in America,) freely, fully and truly on record. I could not find any similar personal record in current literature that satisfied me. But it is not on "Leaves of Grass" distinctively as *literature*, or a specimen thereof, that I feel to dwell, or advance claims. No one will get at my verses who insists upon viewing them as a literary performance, or attempt at such performance, or as aiming mainly toward art or æstheticism.

I say no land or people or circumstances ever existed so needing a race of singers and poems differing from all others, and rigidly their own, as the land and people and circumstances of our United States need such singers and poems to-day, and for the future. Still further, as long as the States continue to absorb and be dominated by the poetry of the Old World, and remain unsupplied with autochthonous song, to express, vitalize and give color to and define their material and political success, and minister to them distinctively, so long will they stop short of first-class Nationality and remain defective.

In the free evening of my day I give to you, reader, the foregoing garrulous talk, thoughts, reminiscences,

As idly drifting down the ebb,
Such ripples, half-caught voices, echo from the shore.

Concluding with two items for the imaginative genius of the West, when it worthily rises—First, what Herder taught to the young Goethe, that really great poetry is always (like the Homeric or Biblical canticles) the result of a national spirit, and not the privilege of a polish'd and select few; Second, that the strongest and sweetest songs yet remain to be sung.

As a dandy—29 years old, 1848, photo taken in New Orleans, Louisiana, by an unidentified photographer. Courtesy of the Walt Whitman House, Camden, New Jersey, and the Walt Whitman Birthplace Association, Huntington, New York. Not officially in Saunders, but sometimes referred to as Saunders #1.1.

ADDITIONAL POEMS

———◆———

Poems Written before 1855

Poems Excluded from the "Death-bed" Edition
(1891–1892)

Old Age Echoes
(1897)

CONTENTS

Additional Poems

POEMS WRITTEN BEFORE 1855 709

    Our Future Lot 709
    Fame's Vanity 710
    My Departure 711
    Young Grimes 713
    The Inca's Daughter 714
    The Love That Is Hereafter 716
    We All Shall Rest at Last 717
    The Spanish Lady 719
    The End of All 720
    The Columbian's Song 722
    The Punishment of Pride 723
    Ambition 726
    The Death and Burial of McDonald Clarke 728
    Time to Come 729
    A Sketch 730
    Death of the Nature-Lover 731
    The Play-Ground 732
    Ode 733
    The Mississippi at Midnight 735
    Song for Certain Congressmen 735
    Blood-Money 738
    The House of Friends 739
    Resurgemus 741

POEMS EXCLUDED FROM THE "DEATH-BED"
EDITION (1891–1892) 744

    Great Are the Myths 744
    Chants Democratic. 6 747
    Think of the Soul 748
    Respondez! 749

Enfans d'Adam. 11 754
Calamus. 16 754
Calamus. 8 755
Calamus. 9 756
Leaves of Grass. 20 756
Thoughts. 1 757
Thought 757
Says 758
Apostroph 759
O Sun of Real Peace 762
Primeval My Love for the Woman I Love 762
To You 763
Now Lift Me Close 763
To the Reader at Parting 763
Debris 764
Leaflets 768
Despairing Cries 768
Calamus. 5 769
Thoughts. 2 770
Thoughts. 4 771
Bathed in War's Perfume 771
Solid, Ironical, Rolling Orb 771
Not My Enemies Ever Invade Me 772
This Day, O Soul 772
Lessons 772
Ashes of Soldiers: Epigraph 772
The Beauty of the Ship 773
After an Interval 773
Two Rivulets 773
Or from That Sea of Time 774
From My Last Years 775
In Former Songs 775
As in a Swoon 775
[Last Droplets] 776
Ship Ahoy! 776
For Queen Victoria's Birthday 776
L of G 776
After the Argument 777
For Us Two, Reader Dear 777

OLD AGE ECHOES 779

    To Soar in Freedom and in Fullness of Power 779
    Then Shall Perceive 779
    The Few Drops Known 779
    One Thought Ever at the Fore 780
    While Behind All Firm and Erect 780
    A Kiss to the Bride 780
    Nay, Tell Me Not To-day the Publish'd Shame 781
    Supplement Hours 781
    Of Many a Smutch'd Deed Reminiscent 782
    To Be at All 782
    Death's Valley 783
    On the Same Picture 784
    A Thought of Columbus 784

INTRODUCTION TO
ADDITIONAL POEMS

Whitman published the poems in this section outside of the First Edition (1855) or culminating edition (1891–1892) of *Leaves of Grass.* "Poems Written before 1855" includes all the poems Whitman published during the so-called "seed-time of the *Leaves*"; these twenty-three poems date from 1838 to the early 1850s. "Poems Excluded from the 'Death-bed' Edition" gathers the works published in other editions of Whitman's poetry but dropped from the "Death-bed" Edition of *Leaves of Grass* (often cited as the "definitive" and "complete" edition, though it by no means includes all of Whitman's poetry). The *"Old Age Echoes"* section contains a collection of thirteen poems that first appeared in the 1897 edition of *Leaves of Grass.* Whitman's literary executor, Horace Traubel, claimed to have received Whitman's consent to publish this collection.

The reader is thus presented with all the poems that Whitman approved of publishing—*allegedly* approved of, in the case of *Old Age Echoes*—at some time during his life. Spanning almost sixty years and ranging widely in quality, the poems are interesting not only in their own right, but also for Whitman's reasons for excluding them from the definitive canon of the "Death-bed" Edition.

POEMS WRITTEN BEFORE 1855

Musing about "long foreground" of *Leaves of Grass* in his 1855 congratulatory letter to Whitman, Ralph Waldo Emerson was one of the first readers to express curiosity about Whitman's beginnings as a poet. What had Whitman written before 1855 that hinted of such great things to come? Determined to create a myth of his origins, Whitman did what he could to "cover his tracks": He destroyed significant amounts of manuscripts and letters upon at least two occasions and frequently reminded himself to "make no quotations, and no reference to any other writers. — Lumber the writing with nothing."

Sensitive to the public's curiosity concerning his development as a poet, but aware that much of his juvenilia was readily available in old newspapers, Whitman decided to publish some of his early pieces in an appendix to *Collect* (1882) entitled "Pieces in Early Youth, 1834–'42." "My serious wish were to have all those crude and boyish pieces quietly dropp'd in oblivion — but to avoid the annoyance of their surreptitious issue, (as lately announced, from outsiders), I have, with some qualms, tack'd them on here," he writes in *Collect*'s prefatory note. And yet the four poems, nine short stories, and a "Talk to an Art-Union" represented only a fraction of his early efforts; additionally, the works were often heavily revised to hide flaws of his early style.

Twenty-three poems written by Whitman were published before 1855. The awkwardness of Whitman's language and the conventional rhyme schemes and imagery will surprise anyone familiar with the energy and independence of his mature verse. Some of these pieces (like "The Death and Burial of McDonald Clarke" and "Young Grimes") are directly imitative of popular poems of the time; others ("The Mississippi at Midnight") are sensationalistic; still others ("Our Future Lot," "The Punishment of Pride") are didactic or overtly pious. One senses the insecurities of Whitman as man and artist: Trying so hard to please the average reader of New York's penny-daily newspapers, he has forgotten himself and his own voice.

Yet there are signs of the great poetry to be written in the next decade. "Resurgemus" and "The House of Friends" indicate that Whitman's political awareness was growing in the early 1850s; his interest in diverse peoples and cultures is exhibited in "The Spanish Lady" and "The Inca's Daughter." "Our Future Lot" and "The Love That Is Hereafter" are written on the themes of death and rebirth, key issues for his finest poems, including "The Sleepers" and "Out of the Cradle Endlessly Rocking."

For more examples of Whitman's pre-1855 writings, see Thomas L. Brasher's edition of *Early Poems and the Fiction* (see "For Further Reading"), Emory Holloway's edition of *Uncollected Poetry and Prose of Walt Whitman*, and the two-volume edition of *The*

Journalism. Whitman's temperance novel, *Franklin Evans* (1842), is also available (New York: Random House, 1929).

POEMS EXCLUDED FROM THE "DEATH-BED" EDITION (1891–1892)

Readying the final edition of *Leaves of Grass* to be published in his lifetime, Whitman wrote in the "Author's Note":

> As there are now several editions of L. of G., different texts and dates, I wish to say that I prefer and recommend this present one, complete, for future printing, if there should be any.

As a result of this announcement, the 1891–1892 edition has been considered the "definitive" or "complete" edition of his oeuvre.

There are several problems with the idea of considering the "Death-bed" Edition as "definitive." For one, though the 1891–1892 edition contains Whitman's greatest works, the style and sometimes the language of these poems reflects Whitman's more controlled and conservative "late style" rather than the original energy and rawness of his message in the 1850s and 1860s. A quick comparison between the 1855 and 1891–1892 versions of "Song of Myself" is a case in point. In time, Whitman substituted the ellipses and irregular line lengths with more conventional punctuation and more even-tempered flow of language; he also removed blatantly provocative lines—"I hear the trained soprano. . . . she convulses me like the climax of my love-grip" on p. 57—with more demure observations—"I hear the train'd soprano (what work with hers is this?)" on p. 218. The "good gray poet" idea of Whitman is a lifetime away from the young rebel of 1855, and readers should be aware that the poetry reflects those changes in Whitman the man and poet. Knowing where he began and ended is a good way to gain a knowledge of the poet, but a stronger understanding comes from looking into his "stops" along the way—including the sexually charged 1860 edition, the strong patriotism of *Drum-Taps* (1865), the melancholy dreaminess of so many of the 1871 poems.

The 1891–1892 Edition of *Leaves of Grass* is also not a "complete" edition, simply because Whitman dropped earlier poems and pieces of poems along the way. Why did he do so? The most obvious answer is that Whitman recognized the poorer quality of certain pieces; at other times, however, the older poet seems to have had second thoughts about an earlier opinion or feeling. In the interest of providing a more nuanced view of the poet's work, this selection includes the poems that appeared in one or more editions of Whitman's poems but were omitted by Whitman from the culminating edition of *Leaves of Grass*. In other words, these are poems that might "fall through the cracks" for readers acquainted only with Whitman's two best-known collections.

OLD AGE ECHOES (1897)

I said to W.W. today: "Though you have put the finishing touches on the Leaves, closed them with your good-by, you will go on living a year or two longer and writing more poems. The question is, what will you do with these poems when the time comes to fix their place in the volume?" "Do with them? I am not unprepared—I have even contemplated that emergency—I have a title in reserve: Old Age Echoes—applying not so much to things as to echoes of things, reverberant, an aftermath."

Whitman's friend and literary executor Horace Traubel records this 1891 conversation in the preface to *Old Age Echoes*, a collection of thirteen poems added to the 1897 Edition of *Leaves of Grass*. Whitman, who died in 1892, did not see or approve of this collection; in fact, Traubel seems to have changed some of the titles himself. But Traubel does claim that it was one of Whitman's final wishes to "collect a lot of prose and poetry pieces—small or smallish mostly, but a few larger—appealing to the good will, the heart—sorrowful ones not rejected—but no morbid ones given."

The thirteen works date from 1855 to Whitman's actual deathbed (Traubel noted that "A Thought of Columbus" was Whitman's "last deliberate composition") and range in quality from sketches for longer projects ("Then Shall Perceive") to carefully revised works ("Supplement Hours") and even a few previously published poems (such as "A Kiss to the Bride" and "Death's Valley").

—Karen Karbiener

POEMS WRITTEN BEFORE 1855

OUR FUTURE LOT

This breast which now alternate burns
  With flashing hope, and gloomy fear,
Where beats a heart that knows the hue
  Which aching bosoms wear;

This curious frame of human mould,
  Where craving wants unceasing play—
The troubled heart and wondrous form
  Must both alike decay,

Then cold wet earth will close around
  Dull, senseless limbs, and ashy face,
But where, O Nature! where will be
  My mind's abiding place?

Will it ev'n live? For though its light
  Must shine till from the body torn;
Then, when the oil of life is spent,
  Still shall the taper burn?

O, powerless is this struggling brain
  To pierce the mighty mystery;
In dark, uncertain awe it waits
  The common doom—to die!

*   *   *   *   *

Mortal! and can thy swelling soul
　　　Live with the thought that all its life
Is centred in this earthly cage
　　　Of care, and tears, and strife?

Not so; that sorrowing heart of thine
　　　Ere long will find a house of rest;
Thy form, re-purified, shall rise,
　　　In robes of beauty drest.

The flickering taper's glow shall change
　　　To bright and starlike majesty,
Radiant with pure and piercing light
　　　From the Eternal's eye!

FAME'S VANITY

O, many a panting, noble heart
　　　Cherishes in its deep recess
Th' hope to win renown o'er earth
　　　From Glory's priz'd caress.

And some will reach that envied goal,
　　　And have their fame known far and wide;
And some will sink unnoted down
　　　In dark Oblivion's tide.

But I, who many a pleasant scheme
　　　Do sometimes cull from Fancy's store,
With dreams, such as the youthful dream,
　　　Of grandeur, love, and power—

Shall I build up a lofty name,
　　　And seek to have the nations know
What conscious might dwells in the brain
　　　That throbs aneath this brow?

And have thick countless ranks of men
       Fix upon *me* their reverent gaze,
And listen to the deafening shouts,
       To *me* that thousands raise?

Thou foolish soul! the very place
       That pride has made for folly's rest;
What thoughts with vanity all rife,
       Fill up this heaving breast!

Fame, O what happiness is lost
       In hot pursuit of thy false glare!
Thou, whose drunk votaries die to gain
       A puff of viewless air.

So, never let me more repine,
       Though I live on obscure, unknown,
Though after death unsought may be
       My markless resting stone.

For mighty one and lowly wretch,
       Dull, idiot mind, or teeming sense
Must sleep on the same earthy couch,
       A hundred seasons hence.

MY DEPARTURE

Not in a gorgeous hall of pride,
       Mid tears of grief and friendship's sigh,
Would I, when the last hour has come,
       Shake off this crumbling flesh and die.

My bed I would not care to have
       With rich and costly stuffs hung round;
Nor watched with an officious zeal.
       To keep away each jarring sound.

Amidst the thunder crash of war,
 Where hovers Death's ensanguined cloud,
And bright swords flash, and banners fly,
 Above the sickening sight of blood.

Not there—not there, would I lay down
 To sleep with all the firm and brave;
For death in such a scene of strife,
 Is not the death that I do crave.

But when the time for my last look
 Upon this glorious earth should come,
I'd wish the season warm and mild,
 The sun to shine, and flowers bloom.

Just ere the closing of the day,
 My dying couch I then would have
Borne out in the refreshing air,
 Where sweet shrubs grow and proud trees wave

The still repose would calm my mind,
 And lofty branches overhead,
Would throw around this grassy bank,
 A cooling and a lovely shade.

At distance through the opening trees,
 A bay by misty vapours curled,
I'd gaze upon, and think the haven
 For which to leave this fleeting world.

To the wide winds I'd yield my soul,
 And die there in that pleasant place,
Looking on water, sun, and hill,
 As on their Maker's very face.

I'd want no human being near;
 But at the setting of the sun,

I'd bid adieu to earth, and step
        Down to the Unknown World—alone.

YOUNG GRIMES

When old Grimes died, he left a son—
        The graft of worthy stock;
In deed and word he shows himself
        A chip of the old block.

In youth, 'tis said, he liked not school—
        Of tasks he was no lover;
He wrote sums in a ciphering book,
        Which had a pasteboard cover.

Young Grimes ne'er went to see the girls
        Before he was fourteen;
Nor smoked, nor swore, for that he knew
        Gave Mrs. Grimes much pain.

He never was extravagant
        In pleasure, dress, or board;
His Sunday suit was of blue cloth,
        At six and eight a yard.

But still there is, to tell the truth,
        No stinginess in him;
And in July he wears an old
        Straw hat with a broad brim.

No devotee in fashion's train
        Is good old Grimes's son;
He sports no cane—no whiskers wears,
        Nor lounges o'er the town.

He does not spend more than he earns
        In dissipation's round;

But shuns with care those dangerous rooms
    Where sin and vice abound.

It now is eight and twenty years
    Since young Grimes saw the light;
And no house in the land can show
    A fairer, prouder sight.

For there his wife, prudent and chaste,
    His mother's age made sweet,
His children trained in virtue's path,
    The gazer's eye will meet.

Upon a hill, just off the road
    That winds the village side,
His farm house stands, within whose door
    Ne'er entered Hate or Pride.

But Plenty and Benevolence
    And Happiness are there—
And underneath that lowly roof
    Content smiles calm and fair.

Reader, go view the cheerful scene—
    By it how poor must prove
The pomp, and tinsel, and parade,
    Which pleasure's followers love.

Leave the wide city's noisy din—
    The busy haunts of men—
And here enjoy a tranquil life,
    Unvexed by guilt or pain.

THE INCA'S DAUGHTER

Before the dark-brow'd sons of Spain,
    A captive Indian maiden stood;

Imprison'd where the moon before
      Her race as princes trod.

The rack had riven her frame that day—
      But not a sigh or murmur broke
Forth from her breast; calmly she stood,
      And sternly thus she spoke:—

"The glory of Peru is gone;
      Her proudest warriors in the fight—
Her armies, and her Inca's power
      Bend to the Spaniard's might.

"And I—a Daughter of the Sun—
      Shall I ingloriously still live?
Shall a Peruvian monarch's child
      Become the white lord's slave?

"No: I'd not meet my father's frown
      In the free spirit's place of rest,
Nor seem a stranger midst the bands
      Whom Manitou has blest."

Her snake-like eye, her cheek of fire,
      Glowed with intenser, deeper hue;
She smiled in scorn, and from her robe
      A poisoned arrow drew.

"Now, paleface see! the Indian girl
      Can teach thee how to bravely die:
Hail! spirits of my kindred slain,
      A sister ghost is nigh!"

Her hand was clenched and lifted high—
      Each breath, and pulse, and limb was still'd;
An instant more the arrow fell:
      Thus died the Inca's child.

THE LOVE THAT IS HEREAFTER

O, beauteous is the earth! and fair
The splendors of Creation are:
Nature's green robe, the shining sky,
The winds that through the tree-tops sigh,
      All speak a bounteous God.

The noble trees, the sweet young flowers,
The birds that sing in forest bowers,
The rivers grand that murmuring roll,
And all which joys or calms the soul
      Are made by gracious might.

The flocks and droves happy and free,
The dwellers of the boundless sea,
Each living thing on air or land,
Created by our Master's hand,
      Is formed for joy and peace.

But man—weak, proud, and erring man,
Of truth ashamed, of folly vain—
Seems singled out to know no rest
And of all things that move, feels least
      The sweets of happiness.

Yet he it is whose little life
Is passed in useless, vexing strife,
And all the glorious earth to him
Is rendered dull, and poor, and dim,
      From hope unsatisfied.

He faints with grief—he toils through care—
And from the cradle to the bier
He wearily plods on—till Death
Cuts short his transient, panting breath,
      And sends him to his sleep.

O, mighty powers of Destiny!
When from this coil of flesh I'm free —
When through my second life I rove,
Let me but find *one* heart to love,
  As I would wish to love:

Let me but meet a single breast,
Where this tired soul its hope may rest,
In never-dying faith: ah, then,
That would be bliss all free from pain,
  And sickness of the heart.

For vainly through this world below
We seek affection. Nought but wo
Is with our earthly journey wove;
And so the heart must look above,
  Or die in dull despair.

WE ALL SHALL REST AT LAST

On earth are many sights of woe,
  And many sounds of agony,
And many a sorrow-wither'd check,
  . And many a pain-dulled eye.

The wretched weep, the poor complain,
  And luckless love pines on unknown;
And faintly from the midnight couch
  Sounds out the sick child's moan.

Each has his care — old age fears death;
  The young man's ills are pride, desire,
And heart-sickness; and in his breast
  The heat of passion's fire.

All, all know grief, and, at the close,
  All lie earth's spreading arms within —

The poor, the black-soul'd, proud, and low,
  Virtue, despair, and sin.

O, foolish, then, with pain to shrink
  From the sure doom we each must meet.
Is earth so fair—or heaven so dark—
  Or life so passing sweet?

No; dread ye not the fearful hour—
  The coffin, and the pall's dark gloom,
For there's a calm to throbbing hearts,
  And rest, down in the tomb.

Then our long journey will be o'er,
  And throwing off this load of woes,
The pallid brow, the feebled limbs,
  Will sink in soft repose.

Nor only this: for wise men say
  That when we leave our land of care,
We float to a mysterious shore,
  Peaceful, and pure, and fair.

So, welcome death! Whene'er the time
  That the dread summons must be met,
I'll yield without one pang of awe,
  Or sigh, or vain regret.

But like unto a wearied child,
  That over field and wood all day
Has ranged and struggled, and at last,
  Worn out with toil and play,

Goes up at evening to his home,
  And throws him, sleepy, tired, and sore,
Upon his bed, and rests him there,
  His pain and trouble o'er.

THE SPANISH LADY[1]

On a low couch reclining,
     When slowly waned the day,
Wrapt in gentle slumber,
     A Spanish maiden lay.

O beauteous was that lady;
     And the splendour of the place
Matched well her form so graceful,
     And her sweet, angelic face.

But what doth she lonely,
     Who ought in courts to reign?
For the form that there lies sleeping
     Owns the proudest name in Spain.

Tis the lovely Lady Inez.
     De Castro's daughter fair,
Who in the castle chamber,
     Slumbers so sweetly there.

O, better had she laid her
     Mid the couches of the dead;
O better had she slumbered
     Where the poisonous snake lay hid.

For worse than deadly serpent,
     Or mouldering skeleton,
Are the fierce bloody hands of men,
     By hate and fear urged on.

O Lady Inez, pleasant
     Be the thoughts that now have birth
In thy visions; they are last of all
     That thou shalt dream on earth.

Now noiseless on its hinges
    Opens the chamber door,
And one whose trade is blood and crime
    Steals slow across the floor.

High gleams the assassin's dagger;
    And by the road that it has riven,
The soul of that fair lady
    Has passed from earth to heaven.

THE END OF ALL

Behold around us pomp and pride;
    The rich, the lofty, and the gay,
Glitter before our dazzled eyes—
    Live out their brief but brilliant day;
Then when the hour for fame is o'er,
    Unheeded pass away.

The warrior builds a mighty name,
    The object of his hopes and fears,
That future times may see it where
    Her tower aspiring Glory rears.
Desist, O, fool! think what thou'lt be
    In a few fleeting years.

Beside his ponderous age worn book
    A student shades his weary brow;
He walks Philosophy's dark path—
    That journey difficult and slow:
But vain is all that teeming mind,
    He, too, to earth must go.

The statesman's sleepless, plodding brain
    Schemes out a nation's destiny;
His is the voice that awes the crowd,
    And his, the bold, commanding eye;

But transient is his high renown—
     He like the rest must die.

And beauty sweet, and all the fair,
     Who sail on fortune's sunniest wave;
The poor, with him of countless gold,
     Owner of all that mortals crave,
Alike are fated soon to lie
     Down in the silent grave.

Children of folly here behold
     How soon the fame of man is gone:
Time levels all. Trophies and names,
     Inscription that the proud have drawn
Surpassing strength—pillars and thrones
     Sink as the waves roll on.

Why, then, O, insects of an hour!
     Why, then, with struggling toil, contend
For honors you so soon must yield,
     When Death shall his stern summons send?
For honor, glory, fortune, wit,
     This is, to all, end.

Think not when you attain your wish,
     Content will banish grief and care;
High though your stand, though round you thrown
     The robes that rank and splendor wear,
A secret poison in the heart
     Will stick and rankle there.

In night to view the solemn stars,
     Ever in majesty the same—
Creation's world's; how poor must seem
     The mightiest honors earth can name—
And most of all this silly strife
     After the bubble, Fame!

THE COLUMBIAN'S SONG

What a fair and happy place
     Is the one where Freedom lives,
And the knowledge that our arm is strong,
     A haughty bearing gives!
For each sun that gilds the east,
When at dawn it first doth rise,
       Sets at night,
       Red and bright,
On a people where the prize
Which millions in the battle fight
Have sought with hope forlorn,
      Grows brighter every hour,
      In strength, and grace, and power,
      And the sun this land doth leave
      Mightier at filmy eve,
Than when it first arose, in the morn.

Beat the sounding note of joy!
     Let it echo o'er the hills,
Till shore and forest hear the pride,
     That a bondless bosom fills.
And on the plain where patriot sires
     Rest underneath the sod,
Where the stern resolve for liberty
     Was writ in gushing blood,
    Freeman go,
     With upright brow,
And render thanks to God.

O, my soul is drunk with joy,
     And my inmost heart is glad,
To think my country's star will not
     Through endless ages fade,
That on its upward glorious course
     Our red eyed eagle leaps,

While with the ever moving winds,
      Our dawn-striped banner sweeps:
That here at length is found
      A wide extending shore,
Where Freedom's starry gleam,
Shines with unvarying beam;
      Not as it did of yore,
With flickering flash, when CAESAR fell,
Or haughty GESLER heard his knell,
      Or STUART rolled in gore.

Nor let our foes presume
      That this heart-prized union band,
Will e'er be severed by the stroke
      Of a fraternal hand.
Though parties sometime rage,
      And Faction rears its form.
Its jealous eye, its scheming brain,
      To revel in the storm:
Yet should a danger threaten,
      Or enemy draw nigh,
Then scattered to the winds of heaven,
      All civil strife would fly;
And north and south, and east and west,
      Would rally at the cry—
'Brethren arise! to battle come,
For Truth, for Freedom, and for Home,
      And for our Fathers' Memory!'

THE PUNISHMENT OF PRIDE[2]

Once on his star-gemmed, dazzling throne,
Sat an all bright and lofty One,
      Unto whom God had given
To be the mightiest Angel-Lord
      Within the range of Heaven;

With power of knowing things to come,
To judge o'er man, and speak his doom.

O, he was pure! the fleecy snow,
Falling through air to earth below,
        Was not more undefiled:
Sinless he was as the wreathed smile
        On lip of sleeping child.
Haply, more like the snow was he,
Freezing—with all its purity.

Upon his forehead beamed a star,
Bright as the lamps of even are;
        And his pale robe was worn
About him with a look of pride,
        A high, majestic scorn,
Which showed he felt his glorious might,
His favor with the Lord of Light.

Years, thus he swayed the things of earth—
O'er human crime and human worth—
        Haughty, and high, and stern;
Nor ever, at sweet Mercy's call,
        His white neck would he turn;
But listening not to frailty's plea,
Launched forth each just yet stern decree.

At last, our Father who above
Sits throned with Might, and Truth, and Love,
        And knows our weakness blind,
Beheld him—proud, and pitying not
        The errors of mankind;
And doomed him, for a punishment,
To be forth from his birth-place sent.

So down this angel from on high
Came from his sphere, to live and die
        As mortal men have done;

That he might know the tempting snares
        Which lure each human son;
And dwell as all on earth have dwelt.
And feel the grief we all have felt.

Then he knew Guilt, while round him weaved
Their spells, pale Sickness, Love deceived,
        And Fear, and Hate, and Wrath;
And all the blighting ills of Fate
        Were cast athwart his path:
He stood upon the grave's dread brink,
And felt his soul with terror sink.

He learned why men to sin give way,
And how we live our passing day
        In indolence and crime;
But yet his eye with awe looked on,
        To see in all its prime
That godlike thing, the human mind,
A gem in black decay enshrined.

Long years in penance thus he spent,
Until the Mighty Parent sent
        His loveliest messenger—
Who came with step so noiselessly,
        And features passing fair;
Death was his name; the angel heard
The call, and swift to heaven he soared.

There in his former glory placed,
The star again his forehead graced;
        But never more that brow
Was lifted up in scorn of sin;
        His wings were folded now—
But not in pride: his port, though high,
No more spoke conscious majesty.

And O, what double light now shone
About that pure and heavenly one;
    For in the clouds which made
The veil around his seat of power,
    In silvery robes arrayed,
Hovered the seraph Charity,
And Pity with her melting eye.

AMBITION

    One day, an obscure youth, a wanderer,
Known but to few, lay musing with himself
About the chances of his future life.
In that youth's heart, there dwelt the coal Ambition,
Burning and glowing; and he asked himself,
"Shall I, in time to come, be great and famed?"
Now soon an answer wild and mystical
Seemed to sound forth from out the depths of air;
And to the gazer's eye appeared a shape
Like one as of a cloud — and thus it spoke:

    "O, many a panting, noble heart
        Cherishes in its deep recess
    The hope to win renown o'er earth
        From Glory's prized caress.

    "And some will win that envied goal,
        And have their deeds known far and wide;
    And some — by far the most — will sink
        Down in oblivion's tide.

    "But *thou*, who visions bright dost cull
        From the imagination's store,
    With dreams, such as the youthful dream
        Of grandeur, love, and power,

"Fanciest that thou shalt build a name
      And come to have the nations know
What conscious might dwells in the brain
      That throbs beneath that brow?

"And see thick countless ranks of men
      Fix upon *thee* their reverent gaze—
And listen to the plaudits loud
      To *thee* that thousands raise?

"Weak, childish soul! the very place
      That pride has made for folly's rest;
What thoughts, with vanity all rife,
      Fill up thy heaving breast!

"At night, go view the solemn stars
      Those wheeling worlds through time the same—
How puny seem the widest power,
      The proudest mortal name!

"Think too, that all, lowly and rich,
      Dull idiot mind and teeming sense,
Alike must sleep the endless sleep,
      A hundred seasons hence.

"So, frail one, never more repine,
      Though thou livest on obscure, unknown;
Though after death unsought may be
      Thy markless resting stone."

And as these accents dropped in the youth's ears,
He felt him sick at heart; for many a month
His fancy had amused and charmed itself
With lofty aspirations, visions fair
Of what he *might be*. And it pierced him sore
To have his airy castles thus dashed down.

THE DEATH AND BURIAL OF
McDONALD CLARKE[3]

A Parody

Not a sigh was heard, not a tear was shed,
  As away to the "tombs" he was hurried,
No mother or friend held his dying head,
  Or wept when the poet was buried.

They buried him lonely; no friend stood near,
  (The scoffs of the multitude spurning,)
To weep o'er the poet's sacred bier;
  No bosom with anguish was burning.

No polish'd coffin enclosed his breast,
  Nor in purple or linen they wound him,
As a stranger he died; he went to his rest
  With cold charity's shroud wrapt 'round him.

Few and cold were the prayers they said,
  Cold and dry was the cheek of sadness,
Not a tear of grief baptised his head,
  Nor of sympathy pardon'd his madness.

None thought, as they stood by his lowly bed,
  Of the griefs and pains that craz'd him;
None thought of the sorrow that turn'd his head,
  Of the vileness of those who prais'd him.

Lightly they speak of his anguish and woe,
  And o'er his cold ashes upbraid him,
By whatever he was that was evil below,
  Unkindness and *cruelty made* him.

Ye hypocrites! stain not his grave with a tear,
  Nor blast the fresh planted willow

That weeps o'er his grave; for while he was here,
     Ye refused him a crumb and a pillow.

Darkly and sadly his spirit has fled,
     But his name will long linger in story;
He needs not a stone to hallow his bed;
     He's in Heaven, encircled with glory.

TIME TO COME

O, Death! a black and pierceless pall
     Hangs round thee, and the future state;
No eye may see, no mind may grasp
     That mystery of Fate.

This brain, which now alternate throbs
     With swelling hope and gloomy fear;
This heart, with all the changing hues,
     That mortal passions bear—

This curious frame of human mould,
     Where unrequited cravings play,
This brain, and heart, and wondrous form
     Must all alike decay.

The leaping blood will stop its flow;
     The hoarse death-struggle pass; the cheek
Lay bloomless, and the liquid tongue
     Will then forget to speak.

The grave will tame me; earth will close
     O'er cold dull limbs and ashy face;
But where, O, Nature, where shall be
     The soul's abiding place?

Will it e'en live? for though its light
     Must shine till from the body torn;

Then, when the oil of life is spent,
      Still shall the taper burn?

O, powerless is this struggling brain
      To rend the mighty mystery;
In dark, uncertain awe it waits
      The common doom, to die.

A SKETCH

"The trail of the serpent is at times seen in every man's path."

Upon the ocean's wave-worn shore
   I marked a solitary form,
Whose brooding look, and features wore
   The darkness of the coming storm!
And, from his lips, the sigh that broke,
   So long within his bosom nursed,
In deep and mournful accents spoke,
   Like troubled waves, that shining burst!

And as he gazed on earth and sea,
   Girt with the gathering night; his soul,
Wearied and life-worn, longed to flee,
   And rest within its final goal!
He thought of her whose love had beamed,
   The sunlight of his ripened years;
But now her gentle memory seemed
   To brim his eye with bitter tears!

"Oh! thou bless'd Spirit!" thus he sighed—
   "Smile on me from thy realm of rest!
My dark and doubting spirit guide,
   By conflict torn, and grief oppressed!
Teach me, in every saddening care,
   To see the chastening hand of Heaven;

The Soul's high culture to prepare,
  Wisely and mercifully given!

"Could I this sacred solace share,
  'Twould still my struggling bosom's moan;
And the deep peacefulness of prayer,
  Might for thy heavy loss atone!
Earth, in its wreath of summer flowers,
  And all its varied scenes of joy,
Its festal halls and echoing bowers,
  No more my darkened thoughts employ.

"But here, the billow's heaving breast,
  And the low thunder's knelling tone,
Speak of the wearied soul's unrest,
  Its murmuring, and conflicts lone!
And yon sweet star, whose golden gleam,
  Pierces the tempest's gathering gloom,
In the rich radiance of its beam,
  Tells me of light beyond the tomb!"

DEATH OF THE NATURE-LOVER

Not in a gorgeous hall of pride
      Where tears fall thick, and loved ones sigh,
Wished he, when the dark hour approached
      To drop his veil of flesh, and die.

Amid the thundercrash of strife,
      Where hovers War's ensanguined cloud,
And bright swords flash and banners fly
      Above the wounds, and groans, and blood.

Not there—not there! Death's look he'd cast
      Around a furious tiger's den.

Rather than in the monstrous sight
  Of the red butcheries of men.

Days speed: the time for that last look
  Upon this glorious earth has come:
The Power he served so well vouchsafes
  The sun to shine, the flowers to bloom.

Just ere the closing of the day,
  His fainting limbs he needs will have
Borne out into the fresh free air,
  Where sweet shrubs grow, and proud trees wave.

At distance, o'er the pleasant fields,
  A bay by misty vapors curled,
He gazes on, and thinks the haven
  For which to leave a grosser world.

He sorrows not, but smiles content,
  Dying there in that fragrant place,
Gazing on blossom, field, and bay,
  As on their Maker's very face.

The cloud-arch bending overhead,
  There, at the setting of the sun
He bids adieu to earth, and steps
  Down to the World Unknown.

THE PLAY-GROUND

When painfully athwart my brain
  Dark thoughts come crowding on,
And, sick of worldly hollowness,
  My heart feels sad or lone—

Then out upon the green I walk,
  Just ere the close of day,

And swift I ween the sight I view
    Clears all my gloom away.

For there I see young children—
    The cheeriest things on earth—
I see them play—I hear their tones
    Of loud and reckless mirth.

And many a clear and flute-like laugh
    Comes ringing through the air;
And many a roguish, flashing eye,
    And rich red cheek, are there.

O, lovely, happy children!
    I am with you in my soul;
I shout—I strike the ball with you—
    With you I race and roll.—

Methinks white-winged angels,
    Floating unseen the while,
Hover around this village green,
    And pleasantly they smile.

O, angels! guard these children!
    Keep grief and guilt away:
From earthly harm—from evil thoughts
    O, shield them night and day!

ODE

To be sung on Fort Greene; 4th of July, 1846.
Tune "The Star Spangled Banner."

— 1 —

O, God of Columbia! O, Shield of the Free!
    More grateful to you than the fanes of old story,

Must the blood-bedewed soil, the red battle-ground, be
          Where our fore-fathers championed America's glory!

Then how priceless the worth of the sanctified earth,
We are standing on now. Lo! the slopes of its girth
Where the Martyrs were buried: Nor prayers, tears, or stones,
Mark their crumbled-in coffins, their white, holy bones!

— 2 —

Say! sons of Long-Island! in legend or song,
          Keep ye aught of its record, that day dark and cheerless—
That cruel of days—when, hope weak, the foe strong,
          Was seen the Serene One—still faithful, still fearless,
Defending the worth, of the sanctified earth
We are standing on now, &c.

— 3 —

Ah, yes! be the answer. In memory still
          We have placed in our hearts, and embalmed there forever!
The battle, the prison-ship, martyrs and hill,
—O, may *it* be preserved till those hearts death shall sever!
For how priceless the worth, etc.

— 4 —

And shall not the years, as they sweep o'er and o'er,
          Shall they not, even *here*, bring the children of ages—
To exult as their fathers exulted before,
          In the freedom achieved by our ancestral sages?
And the prayer rise to heaven, with pure gratitude given
And the sky by the thunder of cannon be riven?
Yea! yea! let the echo responsively roll
The echo that starts from the patriot's soul!

THE MISSISSIPPI AT MIDNIGHT

How solemn! sweeping this dense black tide!
  No friendly lights i' the heaven o'er us;
A murky darkness on either side,
  And kindred darkness all before us!

Now, drawn near the shelving rim,
  Weird-like shadows suddenly rise;
Shapes of mist and phantoms dim
  Baffle the gazer's straining eyes.

River fiends, with malignant faces!
  Wild and wide their arms are thrown,
As if to clutch in fatal embraces
  Him who sails their realms upon.

Then, by the trick of our own swift motion,
  Straight, tall giants, an army vast,
Rank by rank, like the waves of ocean,
  On the shore march stilly past.

How solemn! the river a trailing pall,
  Which takes, but never again gives back;
And moonless and starless the heavens' arch'd wall,
  Responding an equal black!

Oh, tireless waters! like Life's quick dream,
  Onward and onward ever hurrying—
Like Death in this midnight hour you seem,
  Life in your chill drops greedily burying!

SONG FOR CERTAIN CONGRESSMEN[4]

We are all docile dough-faces,
  They knead us with the fist,

They, the dashing southern lords,
    We labor as they list;
For them we speak—or hold our tongues,
    For them we turn and twist.

We join them in their howl against
    Free soil and "abolition,"
That firebrand—that assassin knife—
    Which risk our land's condition,
And leave no peace of life to any
    Dough-faced politician.

To put down "agitation," now,
    We think the most judicious;
To damn all "northern fanatics,"
    Those "traitors" black and vicious;
The "reg'lar party usages"
    For us, and no "new issues."

Things have come to a pretty pass,
    When a trifle small as this,
Moving and bartering nigger slaves,
    Can open an abyss,
With jaws a-gape for "the two great parties;"
    A pretty thought, I wis!

Principle—freedom!—fiddlesticks!
    We know not where they're found.
Rights of the masses—progress!—bah!
    Words that tickle and sound;
But claiming to rule o'er "practical men"
    Is very different ground.

Beyond all such we know a term
    Charming to ears and eyes,
With it we'll stab young Freedom,
    And do it in disguise;

Speak soft, ye wily dough-faces—
    That term is "compromise."

And what if children, growing up,
    In future seasons read
The thing we do? and heart and tongue
    Accurse us for the deed?
The future cannot touch us;
    The present gain we heed.

Then, all together, dough-faces!
    Let's stop the exciting clatter,
And pacify slave-breeding wrath
    By yielding all the matter;
For otherwise, as sure as guns,
    The Union it will shatter.

Besides, to tell the honest truth
    (For us an innovation,)
Keeping in with the slave power
    Is our personal salvation;
We've very little to expect
    From t' other part of the nation.

Besides it's plain at Washington
    Who likeliest wins the race,
What earthly chance has "free soil"
    For any good fat place?
While many a daw has feather'd his nest,
    By his creamy and meek dough-face.

Take heart, then, sweet companions,
    Be steady, Scripture Dick!
Webster, Cooper, Walker,
    To your allegiance stick!
With Brooks, and Briggs and Phoenix,
    Stand up through thin and thick!

We do not ask a bold brave front;
  We never try that game;
'Twould bring the storm upon our heads,
  A huge mad storm of shame;
Evade it, brothers—"compromise"
  Will answer just the same.   Paumanok

BLOOD-MONEY[5]

"Guilty of the body and the blood of Christ"

— 1 —

Of olden time, when it came to pass
That the beautiful god, Jesus, should finish his work on earth,
Then went Judas, and sold the divine youth,
And took pay for his body.

Curs'd was the deed, even before the sweat of the clutching hand
  grew dry;
And darkness frown'd upon the seller of the like of God,
Where, as though earth lifted her breast to throw him from her,
  and heaven refused him,
He hung in the air, self-slaughter'd.

The cycles, with their long shadows, have stalk'd silently
  forward,
Since those ancient days—many a pouch enwrapping
  meanwhile
Its fee, like that paid for the son of Mary.
And still goes one, saying,
"What will ye give me, and I will deliver this man unto you?"
And they make the covenant, and pay the pieces of silver.

— 2 —

Look forth, deliverer,
Look forth, first-born of the dead,
Over the tree-tops of Paradise;
See thyself in yet-continued bonds,
Toilsome and poor, thou bear'st man's form again,
Thou art reviled, scourged, put into prison,
Hunted from the arrogant equality of the rest;
With staves and swords throng the willing servants of
    authority,
Again they surround thee, mad with devilish spite;
Toward thee stretch the hands of a multitude, like vultures'
    talons,
The meanest spit in thy face, they smite thee with their
    palms;
Bruised, bloody, and pinion'd is thy body,
More sorrowful than death is thy soul.

Witness of anguish, brother of slaves,
Not with thy price closed the price of thine image:
And still Iscariot plies his trade.
      April, 1843   PAUMANOK

THE HOUSE OF FRIENDS[6]

"And one shall say unto him, What are those wounds in thy hands?
Then he shall answer, Those with which I was wounded in the
house of my friends."—Zachariah, xiii. 6.

    If thou art balked, O Freedom,
The victory is not to thy manlier foes;
    From the house of thy friends comes the death stab.

    Vaunters of the Free,
Why do you strain your lungs off southward?

Why be going to Alabama?
Sweep first before your own door;
Stop this squalling and this scorn
Over the mote there in the distance;
Look well to your own eye, Massachusetts—
Yours, New-York and Pennsylvania;
—I would say yours too, Michigan,
But all the salve, all the surgery
Of the great wide world were powerless there.

Virginia, mother of greatness,
Blush not for being also mother of slaves.
You might have borne deeper slaves—
Doughfaces, Crawlers, Lice of Humanity—
Terrific screamers of Freedom,
Who roar and bawl, and get hot i' the face,
But, were they not incapable of august crime,
Would quench the hopes of ages for a drink—
Muck-worms, creeping flat to the ground,
A dollar dearer to them than Christ's blessing;
All loves, all hopes, less than the thought of gain;
In life walking in that as in a shroud:
Men whom the throes of heroes,
Great deeds at which the gods might stand appalled
The shriek of a drowned world, the appeal of women,
The exulting laugh of untied empires,
Would touch them never in the heart,
But only in the pocket.

Hot-headed Carolina,
Well may you curl your lip;
With all your bondsmen, bless the destiny
Which brings you no such breed as this.

Arise, young North!
Our elder blood flows in the veins of cowards—
The gray-haired sneak, the blanched poltroon,

The feigned or real shiverer at tongues
That nursing babes need hardly cry the less for—
Are they to be our tokens always?
      Fight on, band braver than warriors,
Faithful and few as Spartans;
But fear not most the angriest, loudest malice—
Fear most the still and forked fang
That starts from the grass at your feet.

RESURGEMUS[7]

Suddenly, out of its stale and drowsy lair, the lair of
    slaves,
Like lightning Europe le'pt forth,
Sombre, superb and terrible,
As Ahimoth, brother of Death.

God, 'twas delicious!
That brief, tight, glorious grip
Upon the throats of kings.
You liars paid to defile the People,
Mark you now:
Not for numberless agonies, murders, lusts,
For court thieving in its manifold mean forms,
Worming from his simplicity the poor man's wages;
For many a promise sworn by royal lips
And broken, and laughed at in the breaking;
Then, in their power, not for all these,
Did a blow fall in personal revenge,
Or a hair draggle in blood:
The People scorned the ferocity of kings.

But the sweetness of mercy brewed bitter destruction,
And frightened rulers come back:
Each comes in state, with his train,
Hangman, priest, and tax-gatherer,

Soldier, lawyer, and sycophant;
An appalling procession of locusts,
And the king struts grandly again.

Yet behind all, lo, a Shape
Vague as the night, draped interminably,
Head, front and form, in scarlet folds;
Whose face and eyes none may see,
Out of its robes only this,
The red robes, lifted by the arm,
One finger pointed high over the top,
Like the head of a snake appears.

Meanwhile, corpses lie in new-made graves,
Bloody corpses of young men;
The rope of the gibbet hangs heavily,
The bullets of tyrants are flying,
The creatures of power laugh aloud:
And all these things bear fruits, and they are good.

Those corpses of young men,
Those martyrs that hang from the gibbets,
Those hearts pierced by the grey lead,
Cold and motionless as they seem,
Live elsewhere with undying vitality;
They live in other young men, O, kings,
They live in brothers, again ready to defy you;
They were purified by death,
They were taught and exalted.

Not a grave of those slaughtered ones,
But is growing its seed of freedom,
In its turn to bear seed,
Which the winds shall carry afar and resow,
And the rain nourish.

Not a disembodied spirit
Can the weapon of tyrants let loose,

But it shall stalk invisibly over the earth,
Whispering, counseling, cautioning.

Liberty, let others despair of thee,
But I will never despair of thee:
Is the house shut? Is the master away?
Nevertheless, be ready, be not weary of watching,
He will surely return; his messengers come anon.

POEMS EXCLUDED FROM THE
"DEATH-BED" EDITION (1891–1892)

GREAT ARE THE MYTHS

– 1 –

Great are the myths—I too delight in them;
Great are Adam and Eve—I too look back and accept them;
Great the risen and fallen nations, and their poets, women, sages,
    inventors, rulers, warriors, and priests.
Great is Liberty! great is Equality! I am their follower;
Helmsmen of nations, choose your craft! where you sail, I sail,
I weather it out with you, or sink with you.

Great is Youth—equally great is Old Age—great are the Day and
    Night;
Great is Wealth—great is Poverty—great is Expression—great is
    Silence.

Youth, large, lusty, loving—Youth, full of grace, force,
    fascination!
Do you know that Old Age may come after you, with equal grace,
    force, fascination?

Day, full-blown and splendid—Day of the immense sun, action,
    ambition, laughter,
The Night follows close, with millions of suns, and sleep, and
    restoring darkness.

Wealth, with the flush hand, fine clothes, hospitality;
But then the Soul's wealth, which is candor, knowledge, pride,
    enfolding love;
(Who goes for men and women showing Poverty richer than
    wealth?)

Expression of speech! in what is written or said, forget not that
    Silence is also expressive,
That anguish as hot as the hottest, and contempt as cold as the
    coldest, may be without words.

— 2 —

Great is the Earth, and the way it became what it is;
Do you imagine it has stopt at this? the increase
    abandon'd?
Understand then that it goes as far onward from this, as this is
    from the times when it lay in covering waters and gases,
    before man had appear'd.

Great is the quality of Truth in man;
The quality of truth in man supports itself through all
    changes,
It is inevitably in the man—he and it are in love, and never leave
    each other.

The truth in man is no dictum, it is vital as eyesight;
If there be any Soul, there is truth—if there be man or
    woman there is truth—if there be physical or moral,
    there is truth;
If there be equilibrium or volition, there is truth—if there be
    things at all upon the earth, there is truth.

O truth of the earth! I am determin'd to press my way toward
    you;
Sound your voice! I scale mountains, or dive in the sea after
    you.

— 3 —

Great is Language—it is the mightiest of the sciences,
It is the fulness, color, form, diversity of the earth, and of men
    and women, and of all qualities and processes;
It is greater than wealth—it is greater than buildings, ships,
    religions, paintings, music.

Great is the English speech—what speech is so great as the English?
Great is the English brood—what brood has so vast a destiny as
    the English?
It is the mother of the brood that must rule the earth with the
    new rule;
The new rule shall rule as the Soul rules, and as the love, justice,
    equality in the Soul rule.
Great is Law—great are the few old land-marks of the law,
They are the same in all times, and shall not be disturb'd.

— 4 —

Great is Justice!
Justice is not settled by legislators and laws—it is in the Soul;
It cannot be varied by statutes, any more than love, pride, the
    attraction of gravity, can;
It is immutable—it does not depend on majorities—majorities or
    what not, come at last before the same passionless and exact
    tribunal.

For justice are the grand natural lawyers, and perfect judges—is it
    in their Souls;
It is well assorted—they have not studied for nothing—the great
    includes the less;
They rule on the highest grounds—they oversee all eras, states,
    administrations.

The perfect judge fears nothing—he could go front to front
    before God;

Before the perfect judge all shall stand back—life and death shall
    stand back—heaven and hell shall stand back.

– 5 –

Great is Life, real and mystical, wherever and whoever;
Great is Death—sure as life holds all parts together, Death holds
    all parts together.

Has Life much purport?—Ah, Death has the greatest purport.

CHANTS DEMOCRATIC. 6

You just maturing youth! You male or female!
Remember the organic compact of These States,
Remember the pledge of the Old Thirteen thenceforward to the
    rights, life, liberty, equality of man,
Remember what was promulged by the founders, ratified by The
    States, signed in black and white by the Commissioners, and
    read by Washington at the head of the army,
Remember the purposes of the founders,—Remember
    Washington;
Remember the copious humanity streaming from every direction
    toward America;
Remember the hospitality that belongs to nations and
    men; (Cursed be nation, woman, man, without
    hospitality!)
Remember, government is to subserve individuals,
Not any, not the President, is to have one jot more than you or
    me,
Not any habitan of America is to have one jot less than you
    or me.

Anticipate when the thirty or fifty millions, are to become the
    hundred, or two hundred millions, of equal freemen and
    freewomen, amicably joined.

Recall ages—One age is but a part—ages are but a part;
Recall the angers, bickerings, delusions, superstitions, of the idea
    of caste,
Recall the bloody cruelties and crimes.

Anticipate the best women;
I say an unnumbered new race of hardy and well-defined women
    are to spread through all These States,
I say a girl fit for These States must be free, capable, dauntless,
    just the same as a boy.

Anticipate your own life—retract with merciless power,
Shirk nothing—retract in time—Do you see those errors, diseases,
    weaknesses, lies, thefts?
Do you see that lost character?—Do you see decay, consumption,
    rum-drinking, dropsy, fever, mortal cancer or inflammation?
Do you see death, and the approach of death?

THINK OF THE SOUL

Think of the Soul;
I swear to you that body of yours gives proportions to your Soul
    somehow to live in other spheres;
I do not know how, but I know it is so.

Think of loving and being loved;
I swear to you, whoever you are, you can interfuse yourself with
    such things that everybody that sees you shall look longingly
    upon you.

Think of the past;
I warn you that in a little while others will find their past in you
    and your times.

The race is never separated—nor man nor woman escapes;
All is inextricable—things, spirits, Nature, nations, you too—from
    precedents you come.

Recall the ever-welcome defiers, (The mothers precede them;)
Recall the sages, poets, saviors, inventors, lawgivers, of the earth;
Recall Christ, brother of rejected persons—brother of slaves,
    felons, idiots, and of insane and diseas'd persons.

Think of the time when you were not yet born;
Think of times you stood at the side of the dying;
Think of the time when your own body will be dying.

Think of spiritual results,
Sure as the earth swims through the heavens, does every one of its
    objects pass into spiritual results.

Think of manhood, and you to be a man;
Do you count manhood, and the sweet of manhood, nothing?

Think of womanhood, and you to be a woman;
The creation is womanhood;
Have I not said that womanhood involves all?
Have I not told how the universe has nothing better than the best
    womanhood?

RESPONDEZ!

Respondez! Respondez!
(The war is completed—the price is paid—the title is settled
    beyond recall;)
Let every one answer! let those who sleep be waked! let none
    evade!
Must we still go on with our affectations and sneaking?
Let me bring this to a close—I pronounce openly for a new
    distribution of roles;
Let that which stood in front go behind! and let that which was
    behind advance to the front and speak;
Let murderers, bigots, fools, unclean persons, offer new
    propositions!
Let the old propositions be postponed!

Let faces and theories be turn'd inside out! let meanings be freely
    criminal, as well as results!
Let there be no suggestion above the suggestion of drudgery!
Let none be pointed toward his destination! (Say! do you know
    your destination?)
Let men and women be mock'd with bodies and mock'd with
    Souls!
Let the love that waits in them, wait! let it die, or pass still-born to
    other spheres!
Let the sympathy that waits in every man, wait! or let it also pass,
    a dwarf, to other spheres!
Let contradictions prevail! let one thing contradict another! and
    let one line of my poems contradict another!
Let the people sprawl with yearning, aimless hands! let their
    tongues be broken! let their eyes be discouraged! let none
    descend into their hearts with the fresh lusciousness of love!
(Stifled, O days! O lands! in every public and private
    corruption!
Smother'd in thievery, impotence, shamelessness,
    mountain-high;
Brazen effrontery, scheming, rolling like ocean's waves around
    and upon you, O my days! my lands!
For not even those thunderstorms, nor fiercest lightnings of the
    war, have purified the atmosphere;)
—Let the theory of America still be management, caste,
    comparison! (Say! what other theory would you?)
Let them that distrust birth and death still lead the rest! (Say! why
    shall they not lead you?)
Let the crust of hell be neared and trod on! let the days be darker
    than the nights! let slumber bring less slumber than waking
    time brings!
Let the world never appear to him or her for whom it was all
    made!
Let the heart of the young man still exile itself from the heart of
    the old man! and let the heart of the old man be exiled from
    that of the young man!
Let the sun and moon go! let scenery take the applause of the
    audience! let there be apathy under the stars!

Let freedom prove no man's inalienable right! every one who can
    tyrannize, let him tyrannize to his satisfaction!

Let none but infidels be countenanced!

Let the eminence of meanness, treachery, sarcasm, hate, greed,
    indecency, impotence, lust, be taken for granted above all! let
    writers, judges, governments, households, religions,
    philosophies, take such for granted above all!

Let the worst men beget children out of the worst women!

Let the priest still play at immortality!

Let death be inaugurated!

Let nothing remain but the ashes of teachers, artists, moralists,
    lawyers, and learn'd and polite persons!

Let him who is without my poems be assassinated!

Let the cow, the horse, the camel, the garden-bee—let the
    mud-fish, the lobster, the mussel, eel, the sting-ray, and the
    grunting pig-fish—let these, and the like of these, be put on a
    perfect equality with man and woman!

Let churches accommodate serpents, vermin, and the corpses of
    those who have died of the most filthy of diseases!

Let marriage slip down among fools, and be for none but fools!

Let men among themselves talk and think forever obscenely of
    women! and let women among themselves talk and think
    obscenely of men!

Let us all, without missing one, be exposed in public, naked,
    monthly, at the peril of our lives! let our bodies be freely
    handled and examined by whoever chooses!

Let nothing but copies at second hand be permitted to exist upon
    the earth!

Let the earth desert God, nor let there ever henceforth be
    mention'd the name of God!

Let there be no God!

Let there be money, business, imports, exports, custom,
    authority, precedents, pallor, dyspepsia, smut, ignorance,
    unbelief!

Let judges and criminals be transposed! let the prison-keepers be
    put in prison! let those that were prisoners take the keys! Say!
    why might they not just as well be transposed?)

Let the slaves be masters! let the masters become slaves!

Let the reformers descend from the stands where they are forever
  bawling! let an idiot or insane person appear on each of the
  stands!
Let the Asiatic, the African, the European, the American, and the
  Australian, go armed against the murderous stealthiness of
  each other! let them sleep armed! let none believe in good
  will!
Let there be no unfashionable wisdom! let such be scorn'd and
  derided off from the earth!
Let a floating cloud in the sky—let a wave of the sea—let growing
  mint, spinach, onions, tomatoes—let these be exhibited as
  shows, at a great price for admission!
Let all the men of These States stand aside for a few smouchers!
  let the few seize on what they choose! let the rest gawk,
  giggle, starve, obey!
Let shadows be furnish'd with genitals! let substances be deprived
  of their genitals!
Let there be wealthy and immense cities—but still through any of
  them, not a single poet, savior, knower, lover!
Let the infidels of These States laugh all faith away!
If one man be found who has faith, let the rest set upon him!
Let them affright faith! let them destroy the power of breeding
  faith!
Let the she-harlots and the he-harlots be prudent! let them dance
  on, while seeming lasts! (O seeming! seeming! seeming!)
Let the preachers recite creeds! let them still teach only what they
  have been taught!
Let insanity still have charge of sanity!
Let books take the place of trees, animals, rivers, clouds!
Let the daub'd portraits of heroes supersede heroes!
Let the manhood of man never take steps after itself!
Let it take steps after eunuchs, and after consumptive and genteel
  persons!
Let the white person again tread the black person under his heel!
  (Say! which is trodden under heel, after all?)
Let the reflections of the things of the world be studied in mirrors!
  let the things themselves still continue unstudied!
Let a man seek pleasure everywhere except in himself!

With Nigel and Catherine Jeanette Chomeley-Jones—68 years old, 1887, photo taken by George C. Cox in New York, New York. Courtesy of the Library of Congress, Charles E. Feinberg Collection. Saunders #97.3.

Let a woman seek happiness everywhere except in herself!
(What real happiness have you had one single hour through your
　　whole life?)
Let the limited years of life do nothing for the limitless years of
　　death! (What do you suppose death will do, then?)

ENFANS D'ADAM. 11

In the new garden, in all the parts,
In cities now, modern, I wander,
Though the second or third result, or still further, primitive yet,
Days, places, indifferent—though various, the same,
Time, Paradise, the Mannahatta, the prairies, finding me
　　unchanged,
Death indifferent—Is it that I lived long since? Was I buried very
　　long ago?
For all that, I may now be watching you here, this moment;
For the future, with determined will, I seek—the woman of the
　　future,
You, born years, centuries after me, I seek.

CALAMUS. 16

Who is now reading this?

May-be one is now reading this who knows some wrong-doing of
　　my past life,
Or may-be a stranger is reading this who has secretly loved me,
Or may-be one who meets all my grand assumptions and egotisms
　　with derision,
Or may-be one who is puzzled at me.

As if I were not puzzled at myself!
Or as if I never deride myself! (O conscience-struck! O self-
　　convicted!)

Or as if I do not secretly love strangers! (O tenderly, a long time, and never avow it;)
Or as if I did not see, perfectly well, interior in myself, the stuff of wrong-doing,
Or as if it could cease transpiring from me until it must cease.

CALAMUS. 8

Long I thought that knowledge alone would suffice me—O if I could but obtain knowledge!
Then my lands engrossed me—Lands of the prairies, Ohio's land, the southern savannas, engrossed me—For them I would live—I would be their orator;
Then I met the examples of old and new heroes—I heard of warriors, sailors, and all dauntless persons—And it seemed to me that I too had it in me to be as dauntless as any—and would be so;
And then, to enclose all, it came to me to strike up the songs of the New World—And then I believed my life must be spent in singing;
But now take notice, land of the prairies, land of the south savannas, Ohio's land,
Take notice, you Kanuck woods—and you Lake Huron—and all that with you roll toward Niagara—and you Niagara also,
And you, Californian mountains—That you each and all find somebody else to be your singer of songs,
For I can be your singer of songs no longer—One who loves me is jealous of me, and withdraws me from all but love,
With the rest I dispense—I sever from what I thought would suffice me, for it does not—it is now empty and tasteless to me,
I heed knowledge, and the grandeur of The States, and the example of heroes, no more,
I am indifferent to my own songs—I will go with him I love,
It is to be enough for us that we are together—We never separate again.

CALAMUS. 9

Hours continuing long, sore and heavy-hearted,
Hours of the dusk, when I withdraw to a lonesome and
    unfrequented spot, seating myself, leaning my face in my
    hands;
Hours sleepless, deep in the night, when I go forth, speeding
    swiftly the country roads, or through the city streets, or pacing
    miles and miles, stifling plaintive cries;
Hours discouraged, distracted—for the one I cannot content
    myself without, soon I saw him content himself without me;
Hours when I am forgotten, (O weeks and months are passing,
    but I believe I am never to forget!)
Sullen and suffering hours! (I am ashamed—but it is useless—I
    am what I am;)
Hours of my torment—I wonder if other men ever have the like,
    out of the like feelings?
Is there even one other like me—distracted—his friend, his lover,
    lost to him?
Is he too as I am now? Does he still rise in the morning, dejected,
    thinking who is lost to him? and at night, awaking, think who
    is lost?
Does he too harbor his friendship silent and endless? harbor his
    anguish and passion?
Does some stray reminder, or the casual mention of a name,
    bring the fit back upon him, taciturn and deprest?
Does he see himself reflected in me? In these hours, does he see
    the face of his hours reflected?

LEAVES OF GRASS. 20

So far, and so far, and on toward the end,
Singing what is sung in this book, from the irresistible impulses
    of me;
But whether I continue beyond this book, to maturity,
Whether I shall dart forth the true rays, the ones that wait unfired,

(Did you think the sun was shining its brightest?
No—it has not yet fully risen;)
Whether I shall complete what is here started,
Whether I shall attain my own height, to justify these, yet
    unfinished,
Whether I shall make THE POEM OF THE NEW WORLD,
    transcending all others—depends, rich persons, upon you,
Depends, whoever you are now filling the current Presidentiad,
    upon you,
Upon you, Governor, Mayor, Congressman,
And you, contemporary America.

THOUGHTS. 1

Of the visages of things—And of piercing through to the accepted
    hells beneath;
Of ugliness—To me there is just as much in it as there is in
    beauty—And now the ugliness of human beings is acceptable
    to me;
Of detected persons—To me, detected persons are not, in any
    respect, worse than undetected persons—and are not in any
    respect worse than I am myself;
Of criminals—To me, any judge, or any juror, is equally
    criminal—and any reputable person is also—and the
    President is also.

THOUGHT

Of what I write from myself—As if that were not the resume;
Of Histories—As if such, however complete, were not less
    complete than the preceding poems;
As if those shreds, the records of nations, could possibly be as
    lasting as the preceding poems;
As if here were not the amount of all nations, and of all the lives
    of heroes.

SAYS

− 1 −

I say whatever tastes sweet to the most perfect person, that is
finally right.

− 2 −

I say nourish a great intellect, a great brain;
If I have said anything to the contrary, I hereby retract it.

− 3 −

I say man shall not hold property in man;
I say the least developed person on earth is just as important and
sacred to himself or herself, as the most developed person is
to himself or herself.

− 4 −

I say where liberty draws not the blood out of slavery, there slavery
draws the blood out of liberty,
I say the word of the good old cause in These States, and resound
it hence over the world.

− 5 −

I say the human shape or face is so great, it must never be made
ridiculous;
I say for ornaments nothing outre can be allowed,
And that anything is most beautiful without ornament,
And that exaggerations will be sternly revenged in your own
physiology, and in other persons' physiology also;
And I say that clean-shaped children can be jetted and conceived
only where natural forms prevail in public, and the human
face and form are never caricatured;

And I say that genius need never more be turned to romances,
(For facts properly told, how mean appear all romances.)

– 6 –

I say the word of lands fearing nothing—I will have no other land;
I say discuss all and expose all—I am for every topic openly;
I say there can be no salvation for These States without
    innovators—without free tongues, and ears willing to hear the
    tongues;
And I announce as a glory of These States, that they respectfully
    listen to propositions, reforms, fresh views and doctrines, from
    successions of men and women,
Each age with its own growth.

– 7 –

I have said many times that materials and the Soul are great, and
    that all depends on physique;
Now I reverse what I said, and affirm that all depends on the
    æsthetic or intellectual,
And that criticism is great—and that refinement is greatest of all;
And I affirm now that the mind governs—and that all depends on
    the mind.

– 8 –

With one man or woman—(no matter which one—I even pick
    out the lowest,)
With him or her I now illustrate the whole law;
I say that every right, in politics or what-not, shall be eligible to
    that one man or woman, on the same terms as any.

APOSTROPH

O mater! O fils!
O brood continental!

O flowers of the prairies!
O space boundless! O hum of mighty products!
O you teeming cities! O so invincible, turbulent, proud!
O race of the future! O women!
O fathers! O you men of passion and the storm!
O native power only! O beauty!
O yourself! O God! O divine average!
O you bearded roughs! O bards! O all those slumberers!
O arouse! the dawn-bird's throat sounds shrill! Do you not hear
    the cock crowing?
O, as I walk'd the beach, I heard the mournful notes foreboding a
    tempest—the low, oft-repeated shriek of the diver, the long-
    lived loon;
O I heard, and yet hear, angry thunder;—O you sailors! O ships!
    make quick preparation!
O from his masterful sweep, the warning cry of the eagle!
(Give way there, all! It is useless! Give up your spoils;)
O sarcasms! Propositions! (O if the whole world should prove
    indeed a sham, a sell!)
O I believe there is nothing real but America and freedom!
O to sternly reject all except Democracy!
O imperator! O who dare confront you and me?
O to promulgate our own! O to build for that which builds for
    mankind!
O feuillage! O North! O the slope drained by the
    Mexican sea!
O all, all inseparable—ages, ages, ages!
O a curse on him that would dissever this Union for any reason
    whatever!
O climates, labors! O good and evil! O death!
O you strong with iron and wood! O Personality!
O the village or place which has the greatest man or woman!
    even if it be only a few ragged huts;
O the city where women walk in public processions in the streets,
    the same as the men;
O a wan and terrible emblem, by me adopted!
O shapes arising! shapes of the future centuries!
O muscle and pluck forever for me!

O workmen and workwomen forever for me!
O farmers and sailors! O drivers of horses forever for me!
O I will make the new bardic list of trades and tools!
O you coarse and wilful! I love you!
O South! O longings for my dear home! O soft and sunny airs!
O pensive! O I must return where the palm grows and the
    mocking-bird sings, or else I die!
O equality! O organic compacts! I am come to be your born
    poet!
O whirl, contest, sounding and resounding! I am your poet,
    because I am part of you;
O days by-gone! Enthusiasts! Antecedents!
O vast preparations for These States! O years!
O what is now being sent forward thousands of years to
    come!
O mediums! O to teach! to convey the invisible faith!
To promulge real things! to journey through all The States!
O creation! O to-day! O laws! O unmitigated adoration!
O for mightier broods of orators, artists, and singers!
O for native songs! carpenter's, boatman's, ploughman's songs!
    shoemaker's songs!
O haughtiest growth of time! O free and extatic!
O what I, here, preparing, warble for!
O you hastening light! O the sun of the world will ascend,
    dazzling, and take his height—and you too will ascend;
O so amazing and so broad! up there resplendent, darting and
    burning;
O prophetic! O vision staggered with weight of light! with
    pouring glories!
O copious! O hitherto unequalled!
O Libertad! O compact! O union impossible to dissever!
O my Soul! O lips becoming tremulous, powerless!
O centuries, centuries yet ahead!
O voices of greater orators! I pause—I listen for you
O you States! Cities! defiant of all outside authority! I spring at
    once into your arms! you I most love!
O you grand Presidentiads! I wait for you!
New history! New heroes! I project you!

Visions of poets! only you really last! O sweep on! sweep on!
O Death! O you striding there! O I cannot yet!
O heights! O infinitely too swift and dizzy yet!
O purged lumine! you threaten me more than I can stand!
O present! I return while yet I may to you!
O poets to come, I depend upon you!

O SUN OF REAL PEACE

O sun of real peace! O hastening light!
O free and extatic! O what I here, preparing, warble for!
O the sun of the world will ascend, dazzling, and take his
    height—and you too, O my Ideal, will surely ascend!
O so amazing and broad—up there resplendent, darting and
    burning!
O vision prophetic, stagger'd with weight of light! with pouring
    glories!
O lips of my soul, already becoming powerless!
O ample and grand Presidentiads! Now the war, the war
    is over!
New history! new heroes! I project you!
Visions of poets! only you really last! sweep on! sweep on!
O heights too swift and dizzy yet!
O purged and luminous! you threaten me more than I can
    stand!
(I must not venture—the ground under my feet menaces me—it
    will not support me:
O future too immense,)—O present, I return, while yet I may,
    to you.

PRIMEVAL MY LOVE FOR THE WOMAN I LOVE

Primeval my love for the woman I love,
O bride! O wife! more resistless, more enduring than I can tell,
    the thought of you!
Then separate, as disembodied, the purest born,

The ethereal, the last athletic reality, my consolation,
I ascend—I float in the regions of your love, O man,
O sharer of my roving life.

TO YOU

Let us twain walk aside from the rest;
Now we are together privately, do you discard ceremony,
Come! vouchsafe to me what has yet been vouchsafed to none—
    Tell me the whole story,
Tell me what you would not tell your brother, wife, husband, or
    physician.

NOW LIFT ME CLOSE

Now lift me close to your face till I whisper,
What you are holding is in reality no book, nor part of a
    book;
It is man, flush'd and full-blooded—it is I—*So long!*
—We must separate awhile—Here! Take from my lips this
    kiss;
Whoever you are, I give it especially to you;
So long!—And I hope we shall meet again.

TO THE READER AT PARTING

Now, dearest comrade, lift me to your face,
We must separate awhile—Here! take from my lips this kiss.
Whoever you are, I give it especially to you;
So long!—And I hope we shall meet again.

DEBRIS

*

He is wisest who has the most caution,
He only wins who goes far enough.

*

Any thing is as good as established, when that is established that
    will produce it and continue it.

*

What General has a good army in himself, has a good army;
He happy in himself, or she happy in herself, is happy,
But I tell you you cannot be happy by others, any more than you
    can beget or conceive a child by others.

*

Have you learned lessons only of those who admired you, and
    were tender with you, and stood aside for you?
Have you not learned the great lessons of those who rejected you,
    and braced themselves against you? or who treated you with
    contempt, or disputed the passage with you?
Have you had no practice to receive opponents when they come?

*

Despairing cries float ceaselessly toward me, day and night,
The sad voice of Death—the call of my nearest lover, putting
    forth, alarmed, uncertain,

This sea I am quickly to sail, come tell me,
Come tell me where I am speeding—tell me my destination.

*

I understand your anguish, but I cannot help you,
I approach, hear, behold—the sad mouth, the look out of the
    eyes, your mute inquiry,
Whither I go from the bed I now recline on, come tell me;
Old age, alarmed, uncertain—A young woman's voice appealing
    to me, for comfort,
A young man's voice, *Shall I not escape?*

*

A thousand perfect men and women appear,
Around each gathers a cluster of friends, and gay children and
    youths, with offerings.

*

A mask—a perpetual natural disguiser of herself,
Concealing her face, concealing her form,
Changes and transformations every hour, every moment,
Falling upon her even when she sleeps.

*

One sweeps by, attended by an immense train,
All emblematic of peace—not a soldier or menial among
    them.

One sweeps by, old, with black eyes, and profuse white hair,
He has the simple magnificence of health and strength,

His face strikes as with flashes of lightning whoever it turns
　　toward.

*

Three old men slowly pass, followed by three others, and they by
　　three others,
They are beautiful—the one in the middle of each group holds
　　his companions by the hand,
As they walk, they give out perfume wherever they walk.

*

Women sit, or move to and fro—some old, some young,
The young are beautiful—but the old are more beautiful than the
　　young.

*

What weeping face is that looking from the window?
Why does it stream those sorrowful tears?
Is it for some burial place, vast and dry?
Is it to wet the soil of graves?

*

I will take an egg out of the robin's nest in the orchard,
I will take a branch of gooseberries from the old bush in the
　　garden, and go and preach to the world;
You shall see I will not meet a single heretic or scorner,
You shall see how I stump clergymen, and confound
　　them,

You shall see me showing a scarlet tomato, and a white pebble
from the beach.

＊

Behavior—fresh, native, copious, each one for himself or
herself,
Nature and the Soul expressed—America and freedom
expressed—In it the finest art,
In it pride, cleanliness, sympathy, to have their chance,
In it physique, intellect, faith—in it just as much as to
manage an army or a city, or to write a book—perhaps
more,
The youth, the laboring person, the poor person, rivalling all the
rest—perhaps outdoing the rest,
The effects of the universe no greater than its;
For there is nothing in the whole universe that can be
more effective than a man's or woman's daily behavior
can be,
In any position, in any one of These States.

＊

Not the pilot has charged himself to bring his ship
into port, though beaten back, and many times
baffled,
Not the path-finder, penetrating inland, weary and long,
By deserts parched, snows chilled, rivers wet, perseveres till he
reaches his destination,
More than I have charged myself, heeded or unheeded, to
compose a free march for These States,
To be exhilarating music to them, years, centuries hence.

＊

I thought I was not alone, walking here by the shore,
But the one I thought was with me, as now I walk by the
    shore,
As I lean and look through the glimmering light—that one has
    utterly disappeared,
And those appear that perplex me.

LEAFLETS

What General has a good army in himself, has a good army:
He happy in himself, or she happy in herself, is happy.

DESPAIRING CRIES

— 1 —

Despairing cries float ceaselessly toward me, day and night,
The sad voice of Death—the call of my nearest lover, putting
    forth, alarmed, uncertain,
This sea I am quickly to sail, come tell me,
Come tell me where I am speeding—tell me my destination.

— 2 —

I understand your anguish, but I cannot help you,
I approach, hear, behold—the sad mouth, the look out of the
    eyes, your mute inquiry,
Whither I go from the bed I now recline on, come tell me;
Old age, alarmed, uncertain—A young woman's voice appealing
    to me, for comfort,
A young man's voice, *Shall I not escape?*

CALAMUS. 5

States!
Were you looking to be held together by the lawyers?
By an agreement on a paper? Or by arms?

Away!
I arrive, bringing these, beyond all the forces of courts and
    arms,
These! to hold you together as firmly as the earth itself is held
    together.

The old breath of life, ever new,
Here! I pass it by contact to you, America.

O mother! have you done much for me?
Behold, there shall from me be much done for you.

There shall from me be a new friendship—It shall be called after
    my name,
It shall circulate through The States, indifferent of place,
It shall twist and intertwist them through and around each
    other—Compact shall they be, showing new signs,
Affection shall solve every one of the problems of freedom,
Those who love each other shall be invincible,
They shall finally make America completely victorious, in my
    name.

One from Massachusetts shall be comrade to a Missourian,
One from Maine or Vermont, and a Carolinian and an
    Oregonese, shall be friends triune, more precious to each
    other than all the riches of the earth.

To Michigan shall be wafted perfume from Florida,
To the Mannahatta from Cuba or Mexico,
Not the perfume of flowers, but sweeter, and wafted beyond
    death.

No danger shall balk Columbia's lovers,
If need be, a thousand shall sternly immolate themselves for
    one,
The Kanuck shall be willing to lay down his life for the Kansian,
    and the Kansian for the Kanuck, on due need.

It shall be customary in all directions, in the houses and streets, to
    see manly affection,
The departing brother or friend shall salute the remaining brother
    or friend with a kiss.

There shall be innovations,
There shall be countless linked hands—namely, the
        Northeasterner's, and the Northwesterner's, and the
        Southwesterner's, and those of the interior, and all their
        brood,
These shall be masters of the world under a new power,
They shall laugh to scorn the attacks of all the remainder of the
    world.

The most dauntless and rude shall touch face to face lightly,
The dependence of Liberty shall be lovers,
The continuance of Equality shall be comrades.

These shall tie and band stronger than hoops of iron,
I, extatic, O partners! O lands! henceforth with the love of lovers
    tie you.

THOUGHTS. 2

Of waters, forests, hills,
Of the earth at large, whispering through medium of me;
Of vista—Suppose some sight in arriere, through the formative
        chaos, presuming the growth, fulness, life, now attained on
        the journey;
(But I see the road continued, and the journey ever continued;)

Of what was once lacking on the earth, and in due time has
    become supplied—And of what will yet be supplied,
Because all I see and know, I believe to have purport in what will
    yet be supplied.

THOUGHTS. 4

Of ownership—As if one fit to own things could not at pleasure
    enter upon all, and incorporate them into himself or
    herself;
Of Equality—As if it harmed me, giving others the same chances
    and rights as myself—As if it were not indispensable to my
    own rights that others possess the same;
Of Justice—As if Justice could be any thing but the same ample
    law, expounded by natural judges and saviours,
As if it might be this thing or that thing, according to decisions.

BATHED IN WAR'S PERFUME

Bathed in war's perfume—delicate flag!
(Should the days needing armies, needing fleets, come
    again,)
O to hear you call the sailors and the soldiers! flag like a beautiful
    woman!
O to hear the tramp, tramp, of a million answering men! O the
    ships they arm with joy!
O to see you leap and beckon from the tall masts of ships!
O to see you peering down on the sailors on the decks!
Flag like the eyes of women.

SOLID, IRONICAL, ROLLING ORB

Solid, ironical, rolling orb!
Master of all, and matter of fact!—at last I accept your
    terms;

Bringing to practical, vulgar tests, of all my ideal dreams,
And of me, as lover and hero.

NOT MY ENEMIES EVER INVADE ME

Not my enemies ever invade me—no harm to my pride from
    them I fear;
But the lovers I recklessly love—lo! how they master me!
Lo! me, ever open and helpless, bereft of my strength!
Utterly abject, grovelling on the ground before them.

THIS DAY, O SOUL

This day, O Soul, I give you a wondrous mirror;
Long in the dark, in tarnish and cloud it lay—But the cloud has
    pass'd, and the tarnish gone;
. . . Behold, O Soul! it is now a clean and bright mirror,
Faithfully showing you all the things of the world.

LESSONS

There are who teach only the sweet lessons of peace and
    safety;
But I teach lessons of war and death to those I love,
That they readily meet invasions, when they come.

ASHES OF SOLDIERS: EPIGRAPH

Again a verse for sake of you,
You soldiers in the ranks—you Volunteers,
Who bravely fighting, silent fell,
To fill unmention'd graves.

THE BEAUTY OF THE SHIP

When, staunchly entering port,
After long ventures, hauling up, worn and old,
Batter'd by sea and wind, torn by many a fight,
With the original sails all gone, replaced, or mended,
I only saw, at last, the beauty of the Ship.

AFTER AN INTERVAL

(Nov. 22, 1875, midnight—Saturn and Mars in conjunction.)

After an interval, reading, here in the midnight,
With the great stars looking on—all the stars of Orion looking,
And the silent Pleiades—and the duo looking of Saturn and
    ruddy Mars;
Pondering, reading my own songs, after a long interval, (sorrow
    and death familiar now,)
Ere closing the book, what pride! what joy! to find them,
Standing so well the test of death and night!
And the duo of Saturn and Mars!

TWO RIVULETS

Two Rivulets side by side,
Two blended, parallel, strolling tides,
Companions, travelers, gossiping as they journey.

For the Eternal Ocean bound,
These ripples, passing surges, streams of Death and Life,
Object and Subject hurrying, whirling by,
The Real and Ideal,

Alternate ebb and flow the Days and Nights,
(Strands of a Trio twining, Present, Future, Past.)

In You, whoe'er you are, my book perusing,
In I myself—in all the World—these ripples flow,
All, all, toward the mystic Ocean tending.

(O yearnful waves! the kisses of your lips!
Your breast so broad, with open arms, O firm, expanded shore!)

OR FROM THAT SEA OF TIME

− 1 −

Or, from that Sea of Time,
Spray, blown by the wind—a double winrow-drift of weeds and
    shells;
(O little shells, so curious-convolute! so limpid-cold and voiceless!
Yet will you not, to the tympans of temples held,
Murmurs and echoes still bring up—Eternity's music, faint and far,
Wafted inland, sent from Atlantica's rim—strains for the Soul of
    the Prairies,
Whisper'd reverberations—chords for the ear of the West, joyously
    sounding
Your tidings old, yet ever new and untranslatable;)
Infinitessimals out of my life, and many a life,
(For not my life and years alone I give—all, all I give;)
These thoughts and Songs—waifs from the deep—here, cast high
    and dry,
Wash'd on America's shores.

− 2 −

Currents of starting a Continent new,
Overtures sent to the solid out of the liquid,
Fusion of ocean and land—tender and pensive waves,
(Not safe and peaceful only—waves rous'd and ominous too.
Out of the depths, the storm's abysms—Who knows whence?
    Death's waves,
Raging over the vast, with many a broken spar and tatter'd sail.)

FROM MY LAST YEARS

From my last years, last thoughts I here bequeath,
Scatter'd and dropt, in seeds, and wafted to the West,
Through moisture of Ohio, prairie soil of Illinois—through
    Colorado, California air,
For Time to germinate fully.

IN FORMER SONGS

In former songs Pride have I sung, and Love, and passionate,
    joyful Life,
But here I twine the strands of Patriotism and Death.

And now, Life, Pride, Love, Patriotism and Death,
To you, O FREEDOM, purport of all!
(You that elude me most—refusing to be caught in songs of mine,)
I offer all to you.

— 2 —

'Tis not for nothing, Death,
I sound out you, and words of you, with daring tone—embodying
    you,
In my new Democratic chants—keeping you for a close,
For last impregnable retreat—a citadel and tower,
For my last stand—my pealing, final cry.

AS IN A SWOON

As in a swoon, one instant,
Another sun, ineffable, full-dazzles me,
And all the orbs I knew—and brighter, unknown orbs;
One instant of the future land, Heaven's land.

[LAST DROPLETS]

Last droplets of and after spontaneous rain,
From many limpid distillations and past showers;
(Will they germinate anything? mere exhalations as they all are—
    the land's and sea's—America's;
Will they filter to any deep emotion? any heart and brain?)

SHIP AHOY!

In dreams I was a ship, and sail'd the boundless seas,
Sailing and ever sailing—all seas and into every port, or out upon
    the offing,
Saluting, cheerily hailing each mate, met or pass'd, little or big,
"Ship ahoy!" thro' trumpet or by voice—if nothing more, some
    friendly merry word at least,
For companionship and good will for ever to all and each.

FOR QUEEN VICTORIA'S BIRTHDAY

*An American arbutus bunch to be put in a little vase on the royal
breakfast table, May 24th, 1890*

Lady, accept a birth-day thought—haply an idle gift and token,
Right from the scented soil's May-utterance here,
(Smelling of countless blessings, prayers, and old-time thanks,)
A bunch of white and pink arbutus, silent, spicy, shy,
From Hudson's, Delaware's, or Potomac's woody banks.

L OF G

Thoughts, suggestions, aspirations, pictures,
Cities and farms—by day and night—book of peace and war,
Of platitudes and the commonplace.

For out-door health, the land and sea—for good will,
For America—for all the earth, all nations, the common people,
(Not of one nation only—not America only.)

In it each claim, ideal, line, by all lines, claims, ideals temper'd;
Each right and wish by other wishes, rights.

AFTER THE ARGUMENT

A group of little children with their ways and chatter flow in,
Like welcome, rippling water o'er my heated nerves and flesh.

FOR US TWO, READER DEAR

Simple, spontaneous, curious, two souls interchanging,
With the original testimony for us continued to the last.

OLD AGE ECHOES

TO SOAR IN FREEDOM AND IN FULLNESS OF POWER

I have not so much emulated the birds that musically sing,
I have abandon'd myself to flights, broad circles.
The hawk, the seagull, have far more possess'd me than the
    canary or mocking-bird.
I have not felt to warble and trill, however sweetly,
I have felt to soar in freedom and in the fullness of power, joy,
    volition.

THEN SHALL PERCEIVE

In softness, languor, bloom, and growth,
Thine eyes, ears, all thy sense—thy loftiest attribute—all that
    takes cognizance of beauty,
Shall rouse and fill—then shall perceive!

THE FEW DROPS KNOWN

Of heroes, history, grand events, premises, myths, poems,
The few drops known must stand for oceans of the
    unknown,
On this beautiful and thick peopl'd earth, here and there a little
    specimen put on record,
A little of Greeks and Romans, a few Hebrew canticles, a few
    death odors as from graves, from Egypt—

What are they to the long and copious retrospect of
    antiquity?

ONE THOUGHT EVER AT THE FORE

One thought ever at the fore—
That in the Divine Ship, the World, breasting Time and Space,
All Peoples of the globe together sail, sail the same voyage, are
    bound to the same destination.

WHILE BEHIND ALL FIRM AND ERECT

While behind all, firm and erect as ever,
Undismay'd amid the rapids—amid the irresistible and deadly
    urge,
Stands a helmsman, with brow elate and strong hand.

A KISS TO THE BRIDE[9]

Marriage of Nelly Grant, May 21, 1874.

Sacred, blithesome, undenied,
With benisons from East and West,
And salutations North and South,
Through me indeed to-day a million hearts and hands,
Wafting a million loves, a million soul felt prayers;
—Tender and true remain the arm that shields thee!
Fair winds always fill the ship's sails that sail thee!
Clear sun by day, and light stars at night, beam on thee!
Dear girl—through me the ancient privilege too,
For the New World, through me, the old, old wedding
    greeting:
O youth and health! O sweet Missouri rose! O bonny bride!
Yield thy red cheeks, thy lips, to-day,
Unto a Nation's loving kiss.

NAY, TELL ME NOT TO-DAY THE PUBLISH'D SHAME[10]

Winter of 1873, Congress in Session.

Nay, tell me not to-day the publish'd shame,
Read not to-day the journal's crowded page,
The merciless reports still branding forehead after forehead,
The guilty column following guilty column.
To-day to me the tale refusing,
Turning from it—from the white capitol turning,
Far from these swelling domes, topt with statues,
More endless, jubilant, vital visions rise
Unpublish'd, unreported.

Through all your quiet ways, or North or South, you Equal States,
    you honest farms,
Your million untold manly healthy lives, or East or West, city or
    country,
Your noiseless mothers, sisters, wives, unconscious of their
    good,
Your mass of homes nor poor nor rich, in visions rise—(even your
    excellent poverties,)
Your self-distilling, never-ceasing virtues, self-denials, graces,
Your endless base of deep integrities within, timid but certain,
Your blessings steadily bestow'd, sure as the light, and still,
(Plunging to these as a determin'd diver down the deep hidden
    waters),
These, these to-day I brood upon—all else refusing, these will I
    con,
To-day to these give audience.

SUPPLEMENT HOURS

Sane, random, negligent hours,
Sane, easy, culminating hours,
After the flush, the Indian summer, of my life,

Away from Books—away from Art—the lesson learn'd, pass'd
    o'er,
Soothing, bathing, merging all—the sane, magnetic,
Now for the day and night themselves—the open air,
Now for the fields, the seasons, insects, trees—the rain and
    snow,
Where wild bees flitting hum,
Or August mulleins grow, or winter's snowflakes fall,
Or stars in the skies roll round—
The silent sun and stars.

OF MANY A SMUTCH'D DEED REMINISCENT

Full of wickedness, I—of many a smutch'd deed reminiscent—of
    worse deeds capable,
Yet I look composedly upon nature, drink day and night the joys
    of life, and await death with perfect equanimity,
Because of my tender and boundless love for him I love and
    because of his boundless love for me.

TO BE AT ALL

(Cf. Stanza 27, Song of Myself)

To be at all—what is better than that?
I think if there were nothing more developed, the clam in its
    callous shell in the sand were august enough.
I am not in any callous shell;
I am cased with supple conductors, all over
They take every object by the hand, and lead it within me;
They are thousands, each one with his entry to himself;
They are always watching with their little eyes, from my head to
    my feet;
One no more than a point lets in and out of me such bliss and
    magnitude,

I think I could lift the girder of the house away if it lay between
    me and whatever I wanted.

DEATH'S VALLEY[11]

To accompany a picture; by request. "The Valley of the Shadow of Death,"
from the painting by George Inness.

Nay, do not dream, designer dark,
Thou hast portray'd or hit thy theme entire;
I, hoverer of late by this dark valley, by its confines, having
    glimpses of it,
Here enter lists with thee, claiming my right to make a symbol
    too.
For I have seen many wounded soldiers die,
After dread suffering—have seen their lives pass off with
    smiles;
And I have watch'd the death-hours of the old; and seen the
    infant die;
The rich, with all his nurses and his doctors;
And then the poor, in meagreness and poverty;
And I myself for long, O Death, have breath'd my every breath
Amid the nearness and the silent thought of thee.

And out of these and thee,
I make a scene, a song (not fear of thee,
Nor gloom's ravines, nor bleak, nor dark—for I do not fear thee,
Nor celebrate the struggle, or contortion, or hard-tied knot),
Of the broad blessed light and perfect air, with meadows, rippling
    tides, and trees and flowers and grass,
And the low hum of living breeze—and in the midst God's
    beautiful eternal right hand,
Thee, holiest minister of Heaven—thee, envoy, usherer, guide at
    last of all,
Rich, florid, loosener of the stricture-knot call'd life,
Sweet, peaceful, welcome Death.

ON THE SAME PICTURE[12]

Intended for first stanza of "Death's Valley."

Aye, well I know 'tis ghastly to descend that valley:
Preachers, musicians, poets, painters, always render it,
Philosophs exploit—the battlefield, the ship at sea, the myriad
    beds, all lands,
All, all the past have enter'd, the ancientest humanity we know,
Syria's, India's, Egypt's, Greece's, Rome's;
Till now for us under our very eyes spreading the same to-day,
Grim, ready, the same to-day, for entrance, yours and mine,
Here, here 'tis limn'd.

A THOUGHT OF COLUMBUS[13]

The mystery of mysteries, the crude and hurried ceaseless flame,
    spontaneous, bearing on itself.
The bubble and the huge, round, concrete orb!
A breath of Deity, as thence the bulging universe unfolding!
The many issuing cycles from their precedent minute!
The eras of the soul incepting in an hour,
Haply the widest, farthest evolutions of the world and man.

Thousands and thousands of miles hence, and now four centuries
    back,
A mortal impulse thrilling its brain cell,
Reck'd or unreck'd, the birth can no longer be postpon'd:
A phantom of the moment, mystic, stalking, sudden,
Only a silent thought, yet toppling down of more than walls of
    brass or stone.
(A flutter at the darkness' edge as if old Time's and Space's secret
    near revealing.)
A thought! a definite thought works out in shape.
Four hundred years roll on.
The rapid cumulus—trade, navigation, war, peace, democracy,
    roll on;

The restless armies and the fleets of time following their leader—
    the old camps of ages pitch'd in newer, larger areas,
The tangl'd, long-deferr'd eclaircissement of human life and,
    hopes boldly begins untying,
As here to-day up-grows the Western World.

(An added word yet to my song, far Discoverer, as ne'er before
    sent back to son of earth—
If still thou hearest, hear me,
Voicing as now—lands, races, arts, bravas to thee,
O'er the long backward path to thee—one vast consensus, north,
    south, east, west,
Soul plaudits! acclamation! reverent echoes!
One manifold, huge memory to thee! oceans and lands!
The modern world to thee and thought of thee!)

Outdoors, sitting, with cane—71 years old, 1890, photo taken by Dr. John Johnston on a wharf in Camden, New Jersey. Courtesy of the Bayley-Whitman Collection of Ohio Wesleyan University, Delaware, Ohio, and the Walt Whitman Birthplace Association, Huntington, New York. Saunders #109.

ENDNOTES

FIRST EDITION (1855)

1. (p. 7) [Preface]: The bracketed titles of this section and the following twelve poems were provided by Whitman in later editions of *Leaves of Grass*. In the 1855 edition, Whitman did not provide a title for the preface and wrote "Leaves of Grass" as a header for the first six poems, leaving the last six without any title (see "Publication Information").

Whitman claimed that he had written the preface and included it in his book at the last minute. As he was assisting the Rome brothers with the printing of *Leaves of Grass* in their Brooklyn Heights shop, Whitman felt that his literary experiment needed an introduction. It is part of Whitman lore that the poet composed what turned out to be ten double-columned, tightly printed pages in one sitting. Whether or not the preface was a spontaneous creation, its fluid, conversational language—as well as its strong call to consciousness to American poets and their readers—make it a revolutionary statement in American culture.

The idea for a ground-breaking prefatory statement was not original to Whitman. Though Whitman's preface is thoroughly American in voice, imagery, and intention, it also can be read as a response to or expansion of William Wordsworth's epoch-making "Preface to *Lyrical Ballads*" (1798). Wordsworth's popularity after his death in 1850 resulted in a flood of new American editions of his poetry; Whitman's notebooks indicate that he was familiar with Wordsworth's writings, and parts of Whitman's preface seem to borrow from the poet laureate's manifesto.

2. (p. 9) *His spirit responds to his country's spirit . . . he incarnates its geography and natural life and rivers and lakes:* Whitman here shows how the poet's patriotism and spirit take actual shape. It is the first instance of one of Whitman's favorite themes: the connection between physicality and spirituality. His interest in this subject is evinced by his inclusion of his phrenological chart in advertisements for *Leaves of Grass*. (Phrenology, a popular pseudoscience of Whitman's day, was based on the assumption that intellectual and emotional qualities could be manifested on the body as bumps on the head.) On page 17

787

of the "[Preface]," Whitman names phrenologists (along with lexi-cographers) as among the "lawgivers of poets."

3. (p. 10) *Of all nations the United States with veins full of poetical stuff most need poets and will doubtless have the greatest and use them the greatest:* For Whitman, the "need" here is particularly urgent. The 1850s were a time of unprecedented political corruption. A series of weak presidencies (Millard Fillmore, president 1850–1853; Franklin Pierce, 1853–1857; and James Buchanan, 1857–1861) eroded Ameri-cans' confidence in leadership. Just a few months before the printing of the First Edition, Pierce's failed leadership helped set the stage in "Bleeding Kansas" for what amounted to a local civil war between pro-slavery and abolitionist settlers.

4. (p. 13) *This is what you shall do:* The following passage is inspired by Paul's dictates in Romans 12:1–21. The rolling lines and stately rhythms of many of Whitman's writings were inspired by passages from the Bible, particularly Psalms and the Gospels.

5. (p. 27) *The soul of the largest and wealthiest and proudest nation . . . his country absorbs him as affectionately as he has absorbed it:* These pow-erful lines are the foundation of Whitman's philosophy of literature: The poet must reflect his people, and the people embrace their poet. As he brought forth subsequent editions of *Leaves of Grass* without re-ceiving the general support of the American public, Whitman realized he would not experience this symbiotic relationship with his readers during his lifetime (see note 130, to "A Backward Glance o'er Travel'd Roads," his end-of-career response to the demands of the "[Preface]").

6. (p. 29) *loveroot, silkthread, crotch and vine:* This is the reader's intro-duction to Whitman's use of "sexualized" plant life. All four words are names of plants, though they bring to mind parts of the human body as well. Whitman's suggestiveness here has led critics to hypothesize about the tie between "grass" and pubic hair, especially in the next few pages of "Song of Myself."

7. (p. 31) *plumb in the uprights, . . . braced in the beams:* These are car-penter's terms. Whitman's father was a skilled carpenter, and Whit-man himself worked in the trade while getting *Leaves of Grass* ready for publication. In addition to using carpentry terms throughout his poems, Whitman often includes the terminology of printing, his first real profession and a trade that remained dear to him throughout his life.

8. (p. 32) *But they are not the Me myself:* In the following section, Whit-man differentiates between soul and self ("the other I am"), spiritual and physical Walt. He sees a symbiotic relationship between the two, which is typical of the connections between physical and spiritual realms throughout *Leaves of Grass*.

9. (p. 33) *and elder and mullen and pokeweed:* The preceding section has been subject to a myriad of interpretations, many of them concerned with the sexuality of the passage; for the infamous "oral sex" interpretation, as well as others, see Edwin Haviland Miller's *Walt Whitman's "Song of Myself": A Mosaic of Interpretations*, Iowa City: University of Iowa Press, 1989, pp. 59–67. The intimacy and moment of revelation shared by the "me" and "you" of the passage need not be purely sexual, however; it might well be a dialogue between the "self" and the "soul" that is referenced in the section immediately preceding this one in "Song of Myself."

10. (p. 36) *there the pistol had fallen:* When the grandson of American statesman Henry Clay shot himself in New Orleans, Whitman was there to report it. The "still photo" feeling of many of the images in "Song of Myself" was inspired by Whitman's years as a journalist.

11. (p. 39) *Twenty-eight young men bathe by the shore . . . They do not think whom they souse with spray:* The "swimmers" passage has intrigued many of Whitman's readers, including Thomas Eakins (who painted "The Swimming Hole" in 1885). Especially intriguing is the number twenty-eight (or twenty-nine). In *Walt Whitman's America* (see "For Further Reading"), David Reynolds provides a telling example of Whitman's "encoded" language in his reference to Pete Doyle, with whom he began a friendship in 1865, as "16.4" (the letter numbers of his initials); there is reason to believe, then, that the number twenty-eight holds significance (whether it has something to do with the lunar or female reproductive cycle or with Whitman's age when he experienced a particularly important event).

12. (p. 39) *shuffle and breakdown:* An example of how Whitman used his journalism to inspire his poetry. In an editorial for the New York *Aurora*, Whitman describes butchers in the marketplace: "With sleeves rolled up, and one corner of their white apron tucked under the waist string—to whoever casts an enquiring glance at their stand, they gesticulate . . . and when they have nothing else to do, they amuse themselves with a jig, or a break-down. The capacities of the 'market roarers' in all the mystery of a double shuffle, it needs not our word to endorse" (1842).

13. (p. 43) *must sit for her daguerreotype:* In the middle of this collage of everyday life, Whitman introduces one of his fascinations: the new and popular art of photography. Starting in the 1840s, daguerreotype studios lined Broadway. Matthew Brady and Gabriel Harrison were among the best, and Whitman's favorites. Whitman was allegedly the most photographed nineteenth-century American poet; more then 100 images of him are available at the Walt Whitman Archive (see "For Further Reading").

14. (p. 43) *The opium eater reclines with rigid head and just-opened lips*:
Opium use was at an all-time high in Whitman's New York, particularly in slum areas such as Five Points. Though there is no evidence that Whitman ever experimented with opium, he certainly saw it in use. Whitman had a fear of addictions that may be rooted in his father's alleged alcoholism; the poet was active in the popular Temperance Movement through the early 1840s.

15. (p. 47) *I cock my hat as I please indoors or out*: From his own cocky image on the frontispiece of *Leaves of Grass*, to his order in the "[Preface]" to "take off your hat to nothing known or unknown or to any man or number of men," Whitman defied the polite conventions of hat wear of his day. Clothes did indeed make the man, according to Whitman: For him, the reflection of the inner self in outer wear was analogous to the connection between the spiritual and the physical.

16. (p. 52) *Walt Whitman, an American, one of the roughs, a kosmos*: This line, approximately halfway into the first poem in the 1855 First Edition of *Leaves of Grass*, is the poet's first use of his name. Thus one can identify the "anonymous" author only if one has read into the heart of the poem—a point that calls into question whether some reviewers had actually read "Song of Myself" in its entirety (in the *New York Tribune* of July 23, 1855, Charles A. Dana writes of "our nameless bard").

17. (p. 52) *Unscrew the doors themselves from their jambs!*: These lines appear on the title page of the City Lights edition of Allen Ginsberg's 1955 poem "Howl," a poem meant to respond to and extend Whitman's message 100 years after the First Edition of *Leaves of Grass*.

18. (p. 56) *I hear the bravuras of birds*: Throughout this passage, Whitman "hears" traditional musical instruments and sounds in nature. Thus he also listens to the fish-pedlars' "recitative" (a term normally reserved for opera singers), the anchor-lifters' "refrain" (or repeated chorus), and the drum-like "solid roll of the train."

19. (p. 58) *I have instant conductors all over me . . . lead it harmlessly through me*: Whitman's idea here is inspired by his knowledge of such popular pseudosciences as the study of animal magnetism, a phenomenon in which electrical impulses flow through the body.

20. (p. 63) *Where triphammers crash . . . . where the press is whirling its cylinders*: In this line, Whitman includes references to the art of printing. These are wonderfully appropriate to the 1855 edition of *Leaves of Grass*, which he helped typeset.

21. (p. 63) *or a good game of base-ball*: Whitman was a fan of the new sport, the rules and features of which were standardized in the 1840s by members of the New York Knickerbocker Club. Though the birthplace of baseball is still in question, many argue that it was Whitman's beloved Brooklyn.

22. (p. 67) *the crowded and rudderless wreck of the steamship, and death chasing it up and down the storm:* On December 22, 1853, the ship *San Francisco* set sail for South America; from December 23 to January 5 it was rudderless. Many lost their lives. Whitman probably read about this event in the *New York Tribune* of January 21, 1854.

23. (p. 68) *I am the mashed fireman with breastbone broken:* As a journalist in the 1840s, Whitman was well aware of the terrible fires that ravaged Manhattan throughout that decade. In the *Brooklyn Daily Eagle* of February 24, 1847, he described a scene to which he had been an eyewitness: "When my eyes caught a full view of it, I beheld a space of several lots, all covered with smoldering ruins, mortar, red hot embers, piles of smoking, half-burnt walls—a sight to turn a man's heart sick. . . . the most pitiful thing in the whole affair was the sight of shivering women, their eyes red with tears, and many of them dashing wildly through the crowd, in search, no doubt, of some member of their family, who, for what they knew, might be burned in smoking ruins near by."

   After September 11, 2001, this "Song of Myself" passage appeared on numerous firehouse doors in New York City, as a tribute to firefighters killed in the line of duty.

24. (p. 69) *I tell not the fall of Alamo:* Whitman's years as a newspaper reporter continue to flavor this section, which tells a lesser-known tale of a bloodier battle than the battle of the Alamo, which ended on March 6, 1836. In late March of that year some 400 Americans were murdered after they surrendered to the Mexicans near Goliad, Texas.

25. (p. 70) *Did you read in the seabooks of the oldfashioned frigate-fight?:* Whitman here describes a Revolutionary War sea battle that took place on September 23, 1779, between the American ship the *Bonhomme Richard* and the British *Serapis.* He was interested in preserving important moments in American history in his poem.

26. (p. 76) *Magnifying and applying come I:* In this bold passage, the poet claims that gods and priests have made too little of the divinity of man. Whitman's self-education in world religions is evinced by this passage, which runs through the names of gods from Jehovah to Manito (an Algonquin god), Odin (the chief Norse deity), and Mexitli (an Aztec war god).

27. (p. 78) *Here and there with dimes on the eyes walking:* For an earlier version of this passage, see "The House of Friends" (p. 739). The early version was first published in the *New York Tribune* of June 14, 1850.

28. (p. 83) *And slept while God carried me through the lethargic mist, / And took my time . . . . and took no hurt from the foetid carbon:* Whitman had read enthusiastically about pre-Darwinian evolutionary theory in the years leading up to *Leaves of Grass.* "Lethargic mist" and "foetid

carbon" are references to pre-human ages, earlier even than the period of "monstrous sauroids" (Whitman probably means dinosaurs) he refers to in the next few lines.

29. (p. 90) *I sound my barbaric yawp over the roofs of the world:* The title of Allen Ginsberg's poem "Howl" (1955), written 100 years after the publication of *Leaves of Grass*, was inspired by this line.

30. (p. 91) *I stop some where waiting for you:* The lack of end punctuation here is intentional, as the poem and its message were not supposed to have an end. The last word "you" circles back to the first word ("I"), as Whitman's personal epic continues as the reader's own.

31. (p. 91) *I pass so poorly with paper and types:* Whitman begins "[A Song of Occupations]" with allusions to his own first occupation in the printing industry. When he first wrote the poem, he was engaged in newspaper publishing and would continue to be—hence the "unfinished business" of "cold types" and "wet paper."

32. (p. 101) *Woman in your mother or lover or wife:* This is one of many examples in which Whitman ties femaleness with motherhood first but leaves out references to a father figure as far as masculinity is concerned. See also the body-skimming passage at the end of "I Sing the Body Electric" (p. 254), in which Whitman looks at the male form in detail but fixates upon the maternal elements of women. In "[There Was a Child Went Forth]" (p. 138), Whitman speaks lovingly of his mother, but his father is described as "mean" and even "unjust."

33. (p. 111) *I am the actor and the actress:* The dream sequence that starts here demonstrates extraordinary fluidity of identity. The poet is neither male nor female—or perhaps he is both. While the imagery remains heterosexual, the speaker now has the opportunity to identify his lover as a "he." Whitman, who was gay but not completely "out," is thus able to write about same-sex love under the guise of heterosexual passion.

34. (p. 112) *and the best liquor afterward:* It is difficult to determine the precise nature of this passage, a convolution of natural and sexual imagery. But it is a moment of bliss and resolution after a particularly difficult "exposure" passage in which the poet seemed to find himself "naked" and confronting deep-set anxieties.

35. (p. 112) *through the eddies of the sea:* This is the first of four "dream sequence" passages. The description of the swimmer sounds like the poet himself, who also identified himself as the "twenty-ninth swimmer" in "[Song of Myself]." This particular scene, with its shipwreck and washed-up bodies, was inspired by Whitman's witnessing of the wreck of the *Mexico* off Hempstead Beach in 1840.

36. (p. 114) *Now of the old war-days:* The second dream sequence evokes scenes from Revolutionary War days. In the first stanza, Washington

becomes emotional over the battle of Brooklyn Heights on August 27, 1776; next, Washington is once again teary-eyed, this time over bidding his troops farewell after America's victory.

37. (p. 114) *as we sat at dinner together:* The third dream sequence, like the previous two, concerns the longing for missed human connections, and the grief over loss. Here, the mother figure mourns the disappearance of the aborigine—perhaps regretting the lost bond with indigenous American culture.

38. (p. 115) *Now Lucifer was not dead . . . . or if he was I am his sorrowful terrible heir:* The powerful "Black Lucifer" passage was deleted after 1855. Whitman evokes the Bible's Lucifer, who, by fearlessly confronting God and fighting for his freedom from the ultimate master, became a revolutionary hero for the Romantic poets. Whitman thus vilifies the slave ("Black Lucifer") who chooses to defy his master (the "sportsman" or hunter of the passage). Written during a time when slave revolts were on the increase, the passage is deliberately incendiary. "The vast dusk bulk that is the whale's bulk" may well be the latent power of the enslaved masses waiting to arise—though the phrase is also sexually provocative, and may have been inspired by Melville's 1851 novel *Moby Dick*.

39. (p. 119) *and duly return to you:* A rephrasing of the Bible, Job 1:21: "Naked came I out of my mother's womb, and naked shall I return thither" (King James Version). Here, as in "Out of the Cradle Endlessly Rocking" (p. 400), the darkness and quiet of the maternal womb is evoked as a desirable place to which to return.

40. (p. 119) *whether those who defiled the living were as bad as they who defiled the dead?:* The poem begins and ends with indictments against those who "corrupt" their bodies and "defile" the living and the dead. Here masturbation ("corruption") seems to be viewed negatively, which contrasts with the opinion dominating "Bunch Poem" of 1856 (retitled "Spontanous Me" in 1867).

41. (p. 127) *This is a face of bitter herbs . . . . caoutchouc, or hog's lard:* In these lines, the poet compares human faces with items that speak of inner troubles—a face that evokes the putridity of a vomit-inducer (emetic), the addictive pull of laudanum (a mixture of opium and alcohol), the hardness of caoutchouc (crude rubber), and the soft greasiness of hog's lard.

42. (p. 128) *that emptied and broke my brother:* Mental-health problems plagued the Whitman family, so it is possible that there is biographical truth to these lines. Walt's older brother, Jesse, was eventually confined to and died in an insane asylum in 1870; his youngest brother, Edward, was mentally retarded at birth (and possibly afflicted with Down's syndrome or epilepsy).

43. (p. 133) *[Europe: The 72d and 73d Years of These States]*: Whitman is reacting with favor to the revolutions going on in Austria, Hungary, Germany, and Italy; they were set off by the dethroning of Louis-Philippe of France in 1848, when the second French Republic was declared.

44. (p. 135) *[A Boston Ballad]*: This poem is Whitman's vigorous and sarcastic protest against the way state and federal authorities handled the case of Anthony Burns in 1854. Burns was an African and a slave belonging to Charles Suttle of Alexandria, Virginia. He escaped on a Boston-bound ship in early 1854; in May he was arrested, and after a weeklong trial, Judge Edward Loring ruled that Burns had to return to his master. Antislavery agitators like Wendell Phillips championed Burns as a martyr and led rallies. Because most of Boston protested the ruling, federal troops were called in to escort Burns back to the ship. Crowds jeered, and the American flag was hung upside down. On July 4 activists held a huge rally in Framingham, Massachusetts. It was there that Henry David Thoreau delivered a powerful address, "Slavery in Massachusetts," and William Lloyd Garrison burned copies of the Fugitive Slave Law and the Constitution.

45. (p. 138) *And clap the skull on top of the ribs, and clap a crown on top of the skull:* The poet sarcastically bids the silent, passive onlookers to glue the corrupt King George III together again and set him up for the United States Congress to "worship."

46. (p. 139) *The father, strong, selfsufficient, manly, mean, angered . . . the tight bargain, the crafty lure:* These lines have been cited in support of the theory that Whitman had a troubled relationship with his father. Alternately, maternal imagery in this poem is comforting and attractive, from the image of the Quaker mother to the "mother" schooner with the "baby" boat "slacktowed astern."

47. (p. 142) *thirty-six years old in 1855:* The birth date, height, and age correspond to factual data on Whitman.

DEATH-BED EDITION (1891–1892)

1. (p. 147) *Come, said my Soul:* Whitman "framed" the experience of reading the "Death-bed" Edition with this introductory poem (which also appeared on the title pages of the two variants of the 1876 Centennial Edition—*Leaves of Grass: Author's Edition, with Portraits and Intercalations* and *Leaves of Grass: Author's Edition, with Portraits from Life*—as well as *Complete Poetry and Prose* of 1888) and "So Long!", the farewell poem for every edition since 1860.

2. (p. 165) *the word En-Masse:* The first lines of the first poem in the "Death-bed" Edition recall the message of the first poem in the 1855 *Leaves of Grass* ("[Song of Myself]"): The poem celebrates Whitman himself and through him all others. Here Whitman seems to be simplifying and modifying his earlier, more blatantly egotistical statement.

3. (p. 173) *temperate, chaste, magnetic:* Throughout the 1850s, Whitman was intrigued by several developing pseudosciences. Animal magnetism was the study of the flow of "electricity" within the human body, including how this energy might be exchanged with the help of mediums or machines.

4. (p. 173) *To a Certain Cantatrice:* The poem was dedicated to Marietta Alboni (1823–1894), an Italian contralto who visited America in 1852 and 1853. Whitman often referred to his love for opera; as he wrote for the *Atlantic Monthly*, "but for the opera, I could never have composed Leaves of Grass."

"To a Certain Cantatrice," "The Dead Tenor" (p. 648), and "The Singer in the Prison" (p. 520) are all dedicated to opera singers; many other poems and passages—including "That Music Always Round Me" (p. 583) and the "trained soprano" passage of "[Song of Myself]" (p. 29)—relate how moved and inspired he was by this musical genre. See Robert Faner's *Walt Whitman and Opera*, Carbondale: Southern Illinois University Press, 1951.

5. (p. 175) *I Hear America Singing:* Whitman's vision of himself as a "singer" and "chanter of songs" was in part inspired by the popularity of family singing groups in mid-nineteenth-century America. In the *Brooklyn Daily Eagle* of April 3, 1846, Whitman wrote: "We have now several American vocal bands that in *true* music really surpass almost any of the *artificial* performers from abroad: there are the Hutchinsons, the Cheneys, the Harmoneons, the Barton family, and the Ethiopian serenaders—all of them well trained, and full of both natural and artistic capacity."

6. (p. 183) *camerado:* One of Whitman's variants for "comrade," this word carries a suggestion of intimacy and tenderness. Whitman often associated the word "camerado" with "adhesiveness," a term from phrenology that designates a love and closeness between friends (and one of Whitman's code words for homosexual love).

7. (p. 190) *and us two only:* In 1860 four lines were included between this and the next line; they were omitted from all succeeding editions. The original lines are typical of the strong "adhesive" sentiments of the 1860 *Leaves of Grass*—feelings that Whitman chose to tone down or leave out of later editions.

O power, liberty, eternity at last!
O to be relieved of distinction! To make as much of
  vices as virtues!
O to level occupations and the sexes! O to bring all to
  common ground! O adhesiveness!
O the pensive aching to be together—you know not why,
  and I know not why.

8. (p. 190) *Song of Myself*: See the "Publication Information" section of this edition. Major changes over the years include the addition of stanza numbers in 1860 and the addition of section numbers in 1867. After 1855 (see p. 29) Whitman also began substituting dashes and more regular punctuation for his original ellipses, the length of which he sometimes modified to signify the length and depth of pauses. Additionally, he modified and toned down many of the more provocative passages. Many believe that the 1855 version of "Song of Myself" has a spontaneous, vital quality that is missing from the more ordered later editions. The later "Song of Myself" is, however, easier to read, and the poetry often has a more graceful, even feel.

9. (p. 214) *Walt Whitman, a kosmos, of Manhattan the son:* This important identifying line went through several transitions before achieving its current smoothness and combination of universality and specificity. In 1855 it was the energetic but clumsy "Walt Whitman, an American, one of the roughs, a kosmos" (p. 52); in 1867 it became the stronger statement "Walt Whitman am I, of mighty Manhattan the son"; in 1871 the line became overcrowded again: "Walt Whitman am I, a Kosmos, of mighty Manhattan the son." The line achieved its final version in 1881.

10. (p. 218) *I hear the traind'd soprano (what work with hers is this?)*: This line was toned down significantly in 1867. In 1855 it read: "I hear the trained soprano . . . . she convulses me like the climax of my love-grip" (p. 57). In 1867 the line became "I hear the trained soprano—(what work, with hers, is this?)."

11. (p. 233) *And feel the dull intermitted pain:* The alterations made to this passage illustrate that over time Whitman's style became more condensed and focused but also lost some of its specificity and energy. Consider the nonspecific imagery of the first stanza of section 37 and compare it to this section's appearance in 1855:

O Christ! My fit is mastering me!
What the rebel said gaily adjusting his throat to the rope-noose,

> What the savage at the stump, his eye-sockets empty,
>> his mouth spirting whoops and defiance,
> What stills the traveler come to the vault at Mount Vernon,
> What sobers the Brooklyn boy as he looks down the shores
>> of the Wallabout and remembers the prison ships,
> What burnt the gums of the redcoat at Saratoga when he
>> surrendered his brigades,
> These become mine and me every one, and they are but little,
> I become as much more as I like.

> I become any presence or truth of humanity here,
> And see myself in prison shaped like another man,
> And feel the dull intermitted pain (p. 72).

Most of the lines of the first stanza were removed for the 1856 edition; the second stanza began changing significantly after 1860.

12. (p. 234) *Enough! enough! enough!*: In 1855 the following lines appeared instead of this one:

> I rise extatic through all, and sweep with the true gravitation,
> The whirling and whirling is elemental within me (p. 73).

After 1860 all signs of this culminating moment were removed, which was typical of the regularized pacing and modified dramatic moments of the later editions.

13. (p. 244) *The great Camerado, the lover true for whom I pine will be there:* In 1855 this section read: "Our rendezvous is fitly appointed . . . . God will be there and wait till we come" (p. 84). The alterations that culminate in the present shaping of these lines (which appeared first in 1876) demonstrate Whitman's turn from more intimate, informal relationships to universal prototypes for love: The rendezvous morphs from one between Whitman and us, the readers, to Whitman and God, who becomes his "great Camerado, the lover true."

14. (p. 251) *I stop somewhere waiting for you:* Perhaps the most significant change in editions of "Song of Myself" after 1855 was the addition of end punctuation to this line. The new period at the end of the sentence seems unfortunate: The open-endedness of the line in 1855 was a perfect affirmation of the poet's message.

15. (p. 252) *Children of Adam:* This group of poems (then "Enfans d'Adam") and "Calamus" both appeared first in the 1860 edition, and Whitman himself hinted at the relationship between these collections.

While the "Calamus" cluster has as a focus manly friendship and affection, the poems in "Children of Adam" involved heterosexual love and the products of connections between men and women (as the title suggests). Readers have long noted the coherence of the poems in the "Calamus" cluster, which seem to tell a personal tale of the poet's own love and losses, while the "Children of Adam" poems are varied and seem less intimate. Whitman may have purposefully juxtaposed what was important for the individual (the deep emotions of "Calamus") and the human race as a whole (the emphasis on procreation and continuity in "Children of Adam"); perhaps unconsciously, he demonstrates his sympathies for homosexual expression in the finessed quality of the "Calamus" cluster.

16. (p. 254) *From sex, from the warp and from the woof*: Following this line, these two lines were omitted after 1860:

> (To talk to the perfect girl who understands me—the girl
>   of The States,
> To waft to her these from my own lips—to effuse them from
>   my own body).

17. (p. 254) *I Sing the Body Electric*: This poem, along with "The Dalliance of the Eagles" (p. 425), "A Woman Waits for Me" (p. 263), and several others, came under attack in 1882. Publisher James R. Osgood of Boston asked Whitman to alter several lines and passages on the grounds that the poems violated the public statutes concerning obscene literature. Whitman consented to a few changes, but when Osgood claimed they weren't drastic enough, Whitman wrote back: "The whole list and entire is rejected by me, and will not be thought of under any circumstances." He immediately wrote the essay "A Memorandum at a Venture," a condemnation of the two prevailing attitudes toward sex in America: suppression and exploitation. It was published in June 1882 in the *North American Review*.

18. (p. 261) *For they do not conceal themselves, and cannot conceal themselves*: With these two lines and the following section, Whitman made a major addition to this poem in 1856. In section 9, Whitman seems to trace his hand over the human body; when one reads the passage, one gets the sensation that the poet is lovingly "touching" the reader from head to toe. Though he claims equal interest in all human bodies in the fourth line of section 9, the anatomical "tour" certainly favors the male form. When he does finally get to "womanhood," his description is more maternal than sensual—and notably shorter.

D. H. Lawrence was one admirer of Whitman who nevertheless found reasons to question Whitman's take on women, citing the poet's "'Athletic mothers of these States—' Muscles and wombs. They needn't have had faces at all" (*Studies in Classic American Literature*, 1923).

19. (p. 263) *They know how to swim, row, ride, wrestle, shoot, run, strike, retreat, advance, resist, defend themselves:* These lines depicting women as confident, active, and aggressive seem wonderfully progressive even today, though critics have pointed out that Whitman "masculinized" these female objects of his affection. A friend of many early suffragettes, including Fanny Wright and Lucretia Mott, Whitman was probably familiar with many of the writings on the "new womanhood." *The Illustrated Family Gymnasium* (published in 1857 by Fowler and Wells, who sold Whitman's First Edition in their bookstore) even contained images of uncorseted women lifting barbells.

20. (p. 264) *I dare not withdraw till I deposit what has so long accumulated within me:* These surprisingly aggressive lines have offended many readers. In an 1883 diary entry, feminist Elizabeth Cady Stanton wrote of this poem: "He speaks as if the female must be forced to the creative act, apparently ignorant of the natural fact that a healthy woman has as much passion as a man, that she needs nothing stronger than the law of attraction to draw her to the male." Some have looked more critically at this rape-like scene, while others see it as further evidence that Whitman simply did not know how to describe a heterosexual love scene.

21. (p. 267) *I toss it carelessly to fall where it may:* The condemnation of masturbation—the "solitary vice"—was a major goal of American social reformers in the 1840s and '50s. Through the last twenty lines, the poet wrestles with guilt even as he equates the act and the elements with beautiful, organic imagery. The last six lines reference a story from Genesis 38 that is traditionally used to explain the condemnation of masturbatory practices: Onan was put to death by God for "spilling his seed" and thus defying God's order to mankind to "be fruitful, and multiply" (Genesis 1:28). The speaker of "Spontaneous Me" may be as self-absorbed and greedy about his seed as Onan; notably, however, Whitman's protagonist escapes Onan's punishment.

22. (p. 270) *Once I Pass'd Through a Populous City:* In *Whitman's Manuscripts: Leaves of Grass (1860)* (Chicago: University of Chicago Press, 1955, p. 64), Fredson Bowers includes an early manuscript draft of this poem, originally titled "Enfans d'Adam. 9," that alters the sexuality of the love interest:

Once I passed through a populous celebrated city, imprinting
    on my brain for future use, its shows, with its shows, architecture,
    customs and traditions
But now of all that city I remember only the man who
    wandered with me, there, for love of me,
Day by day, and night by night, we were together,

All else has long been forgotten by me—I remember, I say, only
    one rude and ignorant man who, when I departed, long and
    long held me by the hand, with silent lips, sad and tremulous.

23. (p. 274) *Calamus:* (See note 15, above, to *Children of Adam.*) Fitting for a collection of poems within *Leaves of Grass*, "Calamus" takes its name from an herb with pointy, narrow leaves. Whitman explained his choice to his English editor, William Michael Rossetti: "Calamus is a common word here. It is the very large & aromatic grass, or rush, growing about water-ponds in the valleys—spears about three feet high—often called 'sweet flag'—grows all over the Northern and Middle States" (*The Correspondence*, vol. 1, p. 347). Whitman's stress here is clearly on the universality of the plant, but there is another reason it may have caught his attention: The shape of its floral spike is suggestive of an erect phallus. Indeed, he had already sexualized "sweet-flag" in "Song of Myself" (section 24). Considering that the poems in the "Calamus" cluster are held together by the sentiment of "male bonding" (Whitman used the phrenological term "adhesiveness" to refer to this attachment between men), the choice of plant seems especially fitting.

    The "Calamus" cluster has been cited as the "homoerotic" cluster compared with the predominantly heterosexual passion of the "Children of Adam" poems. The more unified and intimate feel of the "Calamus" poems suggests that Whitman was more in his element with the theme of same-sex love. Scholar Fredson Bowers—in *Whitman's Manuscripts: Leaves of Grass (1860)*—discovered that Whitman had written twelve of the "Calamus" poems as a separate series entitled "Live Oak with Moss"; these poems can be read as the story of an unhappy love affair, and many Whitman scholars have suggested an autobiographical component to these works. The series can be approximated by reading the poems in this sequence (numbers of poems are given in the annotations in the "Publication Information" section): Calamus 14, 20, 11, 23, 8, 32, 10, 9, 34, 43, 36, and 42. For a full discussion of the "Live Oak with Moss" series, see Bowers, pp. lxiii–lxxiv.

24. (p. 276) *Whoever You Are Holding Me Now in Hand*: The teachings of Jesus in the Gospels (particularly the Book of John) inform Whitman's message and language throughout this poem. This high, majestic tone permeates several of the poems new to the 1860 edition of *Leaves of Grass*: Consider also "To One Shortly to Die" (p. 585, originally part of the "Messenger Leaves" cluster) and "Ages and Ages Returning at Intervals" (p. 268; "Enfans d'Adam. 12" in 1860).

25. (p. 279) *Here, out of my pocket, some moss which I pull'd off a live-oak in Florida as it hung trailing down*: This is the first mention of the live oak in the Calamus series. The action of "pulling off" a twig is significant, particularly because it is the central act of "I Saw in Louisiana a Live-Oak Growing" (p. 286).

26. (p. 280) *Not in any or all of them O adhesiveness!*: Adhesiveness was a phrenological term for same-sex friendship. On the phrenological maps of the human mind published in Fowler and Wells's *Illustrated Family Gymnasium*, "adhesiveness" occupied a large site and thus had tremendous potential for affecting a person's behavior. Whitman claimed he scored a 6 (the highest number) in "adhesiveness" on the phrenological chart he included in early editions of *Leaves of Grass*.

27. (p. 281) *The Base of All Metaphysics*: This poem shows Whitman in the role of professor—an unusual one for him, since, as he wrote in "Whoever You Are Holding Me Now in Hand," "in any roof'd room of a house I emerge not, nor in company, / And in libraries I lie as one dumb" (p. 276). For an interesting juxtaposition, see "When I Heard the Learn'd Astronomer" (p. 423).

28. (p. 286) *I Saw in Louisiana a Live-Oak Growing*: This is possibly the first poem written for the "Calamus" series; it is also credited with being the second in the "Live Oak with Moss" series (see note 23, above). The poet is clearly comparing himself with the strong, solitary tree—though he has doubts about his ability to remain so. The doubt of the last line introduces the theme of yearning that runs throughout the "Live Oak with Moss" grouping.

29. (p. 290) *A Glimpse*: The "Calamus" cluster was written and first published during what might be called Whitman's bohemian years. On September 8, 1858, he wrote an article entitled "Bohemianism in Literary Circles" for the *Brooklyn Times*; after he was fired from the newspaper the next year, he began frequenting New York's first bohemian meeting place, Pfaff's Cellar. The restaurant/bar/café, at the corner of Broadway and Bleecker, was a second home to actors like Ada Clare and radical journalists such as Henry Clapp (whose *Saturday Press* published several of Whitman's poems). "A Glimpse" is thought to be a description of the poet meeting a lover—perhaps Fred Vaughan—at Pfaff's.

30. (p. 291) *I Dream'd in a Dream:* In *Whitman's Manuscripts: Leaves of Grass (1860)* (p. 114), Fredson Bowers includes this earlier, more focused version of the poem's first lines:

I dreamed in a dream of a city where all the men were like brothers,
O I saw them tenderly love each other—I often saw them,
   in numbers walking hand in hand,
I dreamed that was the city of robust friends—Nothing was
   greater there than manly love—it led the rest,
It was seen every hour in the actions of the men of that city,
   and in all their looks and words—

31. (p. 298) *I see the tracks of the railroads:* Whitman fully embraced progress in the name of democracy. In the following five lines, he celebrates two new wonders: the American rail system, which had grown quickly after 1830, and the electric telegraph. When Whitman first published this poem in 1856, Americans were still experimenting with various methods of telegraphing; by 1866 the first permanently successful transatlantic cable had been laid. Whitman's poem "Passage to India," published in 1871, applauds this technological advancement.

32. (p. 305) *Song of the Open Road:* The title and subject of this poem were particularly influential on the Beat poets of the 1950s. Jack Kerouac embraced Whitman's ideas of the romance and freedom of travel and the joys of the journey (rather than the destination) in his 1957 novel *On the Road.*

33. (p. 309) *Something there is in the float of the sight of things:* Whitman also uses the word "float" in "Crossing Brooklyn Ferry"—in the passage "I too had been struck from the float forever held in solution" (p. 319). The connotation is of a disembodied vision or knowledge, though the poet seems to be purposefully elusive here.

34. (p. 316) *Crossing Brooklyn Ferry:* From the mid-1840s to 1862 (when he left New York to help with the Civil War effort), Whitman rode the Brooklyn ferry almost daily. For Whitman and many of his fellow New Yorkers, the ferry was a necessary "frame" to the working day: The eight-minute trip from Brooklyn's Fulton Street to Manhattan's Fulton Street, and then back again, was the commute between Brooklyn's bedroom communities and Manhattan's workplaces. From the early 1600s until it closed some years after the completion of the Brooklyn Bridge in 1883, the Brooklyn Ferry represented an important "passage" that was, for Whitman and others, also a destination in itself: Even while riders moved toward a destination, they were part of a common, shared experience.

35. (p. 319) *the dark patches fall:* This self-revelatory passage underwent significant revision from 1856 through later editions. Also notable are early drafts of this poem, which indicate that Whitman was struggling with identity issues and second thoughts about his literary calling. Consider this passage, found in Whitman's *Notebooks and Unpublished Prose Manuscripts*, edited by Edward F. Grier, New York: New York University Press, 1984, vol. 1, p. 230. The verbal stutter—an oral "coming to terms"—is especially moving:

> I too have—
> Have—have—
> I too have—felt the curious questioning come upon me.
> In the day they came
> In the silence of the night came upon me

36. (p. 322) *you dumb, beautiful ministers:* Originally this line ended with the additional phrase "you novices," which strengthens the religious associations of the word "minister." The people and scenes looking on the ferry as it rides from shore to shore are divine agents of a greater force— yet the ferry riders have achieved the greater spiritual awakening.

37. (p. 339) *Weapon shapely, naked, wan:* The first six lines of the poem are a rare instance of rhyme in Whitman's poetic oeuvre; for another example that was much despised by Whitman himself, see "O Captain! My Captain!" p. 484). This passage appeared in much the same form in its original version in the 1856 edition (with the addition of exclamation marks).

38. (p. 353) *Blazon'd with Shakspere's purple page, / And dirged by Tennyson's sweet sad rhyme:* William Shakespeare (1564–1616) and Alfred Tennyson (1809–1892) were among a handful of British writers whom Whitman admitted to reading and admiring. His anger at the ongoing popularity of British writers in America and his interest in creating a new American literary culture did not often allow him room to admire British "representative men."

39. (p. 356) *Away with old romance!:* In the following stanza, the poet takes aim at two of his favorite targets: the patriarchal literary traditions of Europe, and the decadence associated with Old World attitudes. "Take no illustrations whatever from the ancients or classics, nor from the mythology, nor Egypt, Greece, or Rome—nor from the royal and aristocratic institutions and forms of Europe. Make no mention or allusion to them whatever," wrote Whitman in manuscripts dating from the early 1850s (*Notebooks and Unpublished Prose Manuscripts*, vol. 1, p. 101).

40. (p. 357) *the Brooklyn bridge:* One of Whitman's few references to a bridge often closely associated with his poetry. Construction of the bridge began in 1870 and was completed in 1883, long after Whitman had left New York and settled in Camden, New Jersey. In 1876, the year that "Song of the Exposition" appeared in *Two Rivulets*, the completion of the Brooklyn and New York bridge towers inspired a Festival of Connection.

41. (p. 361) *Song of the Redwood-Tree:* This poem is exceptional in that it earned Whitman a tidy sum: He received $100 when it appeared in *Harper's Magazine* of February 1874. He later included it in *Two Rivulets* (1876) and in the 1881 edition of *Leaves of Grass*.

42. (p. 375) *Of the interminable sisters:* The poet seems to be speaking of celestial bodies, including the "beautiful sister we know" (earth). His use of numbers (such as the twenty-four who appear daily, and the three hundred and sixty-five moving around the sun) recalls his use of the number twenty-eight in the "swimmers" passage of "Song of Myself": Each number relates to cyclical movements of the planets charted by calendars.

43. (p. 389) *France, The 18th Year of These States:* Whitman is alluding to 1794, the year of the culmination of the Reign of Terror. After the execution of Robespierre on July 28, 1794, a reconstituted Committee of Public Safety was established, and many former terrorists were executed.

44. (p. 392) *Year of Meteors (1859–60):* Whitman probably had witnessed at least two meteor showers before writing this poem (one in 1833, another in 1858), but the "meteors" here refer to stellar individuals rather than heavenly bodies.

45. (p. 395) *A Broadway Pageant:* The poem was originally written to commemorate the arrival of the envoys of the new Japanese Embassy in New York, where treaties between Japan and America were negotiated that year.

46. (p. 400) *Sea-Drift:* This group of eleven poems first appeared in the 1881 edition of *Leaves of Grass*. As the title suggests, each of the poems is set in or on the sea, or at the seashore—a favorite childhood haunt of the poet's, and a place for reflection and inspiration throughout his life.

47. (p. 400) *Out of the Cradle Endlessly Rocking:* One of Whitman's major statements, this was the last poem written during his most important decade as an artist (1850–1860). The references to childhood on Long Island (the Native American name is Paumanok) have led many to read this poem as Whitman's personal statement regarding his development as a poet; it also anticipates the themes of love and loss in the "Calamus" poems that Whitman probably was also composing at this time. Remembering too the strong antebellum tensions of 1859 (a frequent point of discussion at Pfaff's), one might also read the poem as an elegy for the United States on the eve of the Civil War: The happy pair of Alabama birds is eventually separated, and the remaining bird is trapped in an alien and violent landscape.

Despite all the possibilities of meaning now seen in "Out of the Cradle Endlessly Rocking," the first critical reaction to the poem was that it was "meaningless." This attack on the poem, which appeared in the *Cincinnati Daily Commercial* on December 28, 1859, was quickly refuted by Whitman in an article entitled "All About a Mocking Bird" (*Saturday Press*, January 7, 1860).

"Out of the Cradle Endlessly Rocking" has been set to music more than any of Whitman's other poems, and it demonstrates his interest in opera. In *Walt Whitman and Opera* (pp. 86–89), Robert Faner suggests that the alternation of italicized and non-italicized passages reflects the relationship in opera of arias (sung parts) and recitatives (story lines). In New York City the 1840s and 1850s were great times for the performance of Italian opera, of which Whitman was particularly fond. The Astor Place Opera House opened in 1847 and was America's largest theater until the Academy of Music started hosting performances in 1854; throughout these years, such artists as Marietta Alboni, Pasquale Brignoli, and Jenny Lind sang at New York venues. Whitman frequently attended operatic performances.

48. (p. 400) *From the word:* The poet refers to "Death," the word repeated by the sea near the end of the poem. Death, in other words, is present in the beginnings of life too—and is one of the poet's points of departure.

49. (p. 401) *Shine! shine! shine!:* The first of the arias alluded to by the poet on page 404. Here, one of the two mockingbirds "sings" words that the gifted boy-listener can understand.

50. (p. 406) *Death, death, death, death, death:* This onomatopoeic sound uttered by the crashing and retreating waves echoes the five-time repetition of "loved" (p. 404). Facing loss and life's dreaded mysteries, the boy becomes an artist.

51. (p. 406) *As I Ebb'd with the Ocean of Life:* Like other poems written at this particular moment of Whitman's career, "As I Ebb'd with the Ocean of Life" has a confessional feel: Whitman apparently was disappointed with the mild reception of the first two editions of *Leaves of Grass* and was also channeling the unrest and discontent of antebellum America.

52. (p. 410) *To the Man-of-War-Bird:* The poem was twice published in periodicals—the *London Athenaeum* of April 1, 1876, and the *Philadelphia Progress* of November 16, 1878. In the latter publication,

Whitman acknowledged that his poem nearly paraphrased an English translation of Jules Michelet's French poem "The Bird." Such acknowledgments were absent from further publications, which speaks to Whitman's lifelong "anxiety of influence" and reticence regarding his sources and readings. It is strange, however, that the poet did not seek to alter the rather un-Whitmanesque use of "thou."

53. (p. 413) *and of the future:* Some nineteen lines that followed this stanza in 1856 were removed for subsequent editions. It was typical of the mature poet to omit many of his most personal sentiments in revisions. Consider, for example, three of the lines left out of all but the poem's first edition:

> I am not uneasy but I am to be beloved by young and old men,
> and to love them the same,
> I suppose the pink nipples of the breasts of women with whom
> I shall sleep will taste the same to my lips,
> But this is the nipple of a breast of my mother, always near
> and always divine to me, her true child and son.

54. (p. 417) *A Boston Ballad:* See note 44 to the First Edition. A comparison of the 1855 version of this poem with this final one indicates some of the changes in Whitman's style throughout his career: He replaced ellipses with dashes, controlled and regularized line length, and toned down the heightened drama of exclamations.

55. (p. 419) *Europe, The 72d and 73d Years of These States:* See the note 43 to the First Edition (p. 133). Revisions made on this poem between 1855 and 1860 indicate Whitman's growing appreciation for more even-toned meter and clarified (if less dramatic) statements. Compare, for example, the second stanza of 1860 (set in a more traditional four-line format that evokes blues rhythms) with the breathless two-line stanza of the 1855 edition.

56. (p. 421) *A Hand-Mirror:* If the first two poems of "By the Roadside" represent Whitman's awakening as a political poet, "A Hand-Mirror" indicates his increasing interest and involvement in the bohemian subcultures of New York throughout the late 1850s. Although there is no evidence that Whitman himself overindulged in alcohol or drugs, he socialized with heavy drinkers at Pfaff's Cellar and regularly walked through the Five Points area, where many an "unwholesome [opium] eater's face" was seen on the streets.

57. (p. 421) *Gods:* This poem's regular refrain, almost hymn-like, places it in a small group of more traditionally patterned poems, along with "O Captain! My Captain!" (p. 484) and "Song of the Broad-Axe" (p. 339).

58. (p. 425) *The Dalliance of the Eagles*: When Whitman was courting Boston publisher James R. Osgood for the publication of *Leaves of Grass* in 1882, Osgood asked Whitman to remove several poems and passages on the grounds that they violated the "Public Statutes concerning obscene literature." Surprisingly, "The Dalliance of the Eagles" was one of the "banned" poems—along with the much racier "A Woman Waits for Me" and "Spontaneous Me."

59. (p. 426) *Roaming in Thought*: Late in his career, Whitman became an avid reader of the German philosopher Georg Wilhelm Friedrich Hegel (1770–1831).

60. (p. 430) *Drum-Taps*: Published in a thin, black-covered book, this collection of poems was designed to be a separate effort from *Leaves of Grass*: Whitman saw *Drum-Taps* as reflecting his time and place more specifically than his other collections. He had left New York for Virginia in December 1862, to search for his wounded brother; from that time until the end of the Civil War, Whitman spent most of his time in Washington as a hospital nurse and governmental office worker. What he saw and experienced went into *Drum-Taps*, the most patriotic and accessible poetry he had yet written.

61. (p. 435) *Song of the Banner at Daybreak*: The "call and response" format is not typical of Whitman's style. English poet William Wordsworth (1770–1850) used it in such popular poems such as "Expostulation and Reply" and "We Are Seven."

62. (p. 444) *City of Ships*: Lines 8 and 9 of this poem form part of the balustrade at the World Financial Center in New York City.

63. (p. 445) *The Centenarian's Story*: A man old enough to remember the battle of Long Island (August 1776) recalls his story to a Civil War soldier. Whitman thus places two fights for freedom in a comparison.

64. (p. 457) *The Wound-Dresser*: This poem catalogues Whitman's experiences as a Civil War hospital nurse. For the classic commentary on Whitman's engagement in the war, see *Walt Whitman and the Civil War*, edited by Charles Glicksberg, Philadelphia: University of Pennsylvania Press, 1933.

65. (p. 462) *Dirge for Two Veterans*: Note the unusual regular stanzaic form of this poem; as in "O Captain! My Captain!" (p. 484), the closed form seems to bring solemnity to the poem's subject.

66. (p. 465) *The Artilleryman's Vision*: This poem is an interesting nineteenth-century explanation of "shell shock."

67. (p. 470) *Delicate Cluster*: In this poem Whitman uses language ("cluster," "orbs") he had earlier employed in the "Calamus" and "Children of Adam" poems to connote male sexuality; he now applies those words to a feminized American flag.

68. (p. 471) *Lo, Victress on the Peaks:* It was typical of Whitman's "late style" (after 1871) to remove more dramatic lines and phrasing. This poem exhibits another of the poet's later tendencies: to feminize neutral imagery, in this case Libertad ("Freedom"). See also note 67, above.

69. (p. 473) *To the Leaven'd Soil They Trod:* Whitman often carefully selected the opening and closing poems of his collections (see, for example, the Publication Information note for "So Long!"), and "To the Leaven'd Soil They Trod" is no exception: It gives the sense of America as a "clean slate" and "equal ground" after the Civil War.

70. (p. 475) *When Lilacs Last in the Dooryard Bloom'd:* In 1865–1866, lines 9–13 of what is now section 16 read as follows:

> Must I leave thee, lilac with heart-shaped leaves?
> Must I leave thee there in the door-yard, blooming, returning
>   with spring?
> Must I pass from my song for thee;
> From my gaze on thee in the west, fronting the west,
>   communing with thee,
> O comrade lustrous, with silver face in the night?

These dramatic questions reflect Whitman's immediate and utter despondency over the loss of his "redeemer president." Whitman had first seen Lincoln on February 19, 1861—Lincoln's second visit to New York City. From the top of an omnibus gridlocked in traffic, Whitman had a "capital view" of Lincoln despite the crowd of about 40,000 gathered to see him. And so began Whitman's fascination with Lincoln, a representation of the poet's supreme values for humanity, both political and personal (some critics have suggested that the poet may have even had a "crush" on the president). When he was working in Washington, Whitman allegedly waited by the White House gates just to catch a glimpse of Lincoln when he stepped out. In a lecture entitled "Death of Abraham Lincoln" delivered several times between 1879 and 1881 (and recorded in *Collect,* the literary miscellany included in *Specimen Days and Collect* of 1882), Whitman concluded: "Dear to the Muse—thrice dear to Nationality—to the whole human race—precious to the Union—precious to Democracy—unspeakably and forever precious—their first great Martyr Chief."

As for the strong symbols of the lilac sprig (Whitman's love for the president) and the star (Lincoln himself) used throughout, Whitman was struck by two particular visions in the month before the assassination: the lilacs that bloomed early due to an unusually warm spring, and the beauty of Venus sinking into the west. The thrush resembles

the "solitary singer" of "Out of the Cradle Endlessly Rocking," a fig-
uration of Whitman as "chanter of songs."

71. (p. 476) *Night and day journeys a coffin:* In sections 5 and 6, the poet
describes the procession of Lincoln's funeral train from Washington
to Springfield, Illinois. Nine railroad cars draped in black traveled the
1,662 miles to Lincoln's hometown, and 7 million Americans gath-
ered alongside the tracks to watch it pass.

72. (p. 481) Come lovely and soothing death: As in "Out of the Cradle
Endlessly Rocking" (p. 400), the bird's voice is set in italics. Whitman
did not use italics in the first publication of "When Lilacs Last in the
Dooryard Bloom'd."

73. (p. 484) *O Captain! My Captain!:* The most popular of Whitman's
poems is also uncharacteristic of his style. Whitman grew to dislike
the poem and its clumsy attempt at regularity. "The thing that tanta-
lizes me most is not its rhythmic imperfection or its imperfection as a
ballad or rhymed poem (it is damned bad in all that, I do believe) but
the fact that my enemies and some of my friends who half doubt me,
look upon it as a concession made to the philistines—that makes me
mad," he told his friend Horace Traubel (see *With Walt Whitman in
Camden,* vol. 2, p. 333).

74. (p. 485) *By Blue Ontario's Shore:* From its first appearance in 1856,
this poem has functioned as Whitman's definitive social statement. In
1856 it constituted a broad directive for how the country might be uni-
fied; the poem echoed many of the commands of the "[Preface]"
(p. 7) and actually used or modified many of its most powerful state-
ments. Section 14 of "By Blue Ontario's Shore," for example, places
Whitman's well-known passage from the "[Preface]" (the lines begin-
ning with "This is what you shall do," p. 13) in a poetic format.

Whitman continued to revise this poem through subsequent edi-
tions, adding historical detail and topical references, and the changes
between editions are interesting to note. Consider section 7, for ex-
ample; this angry indictment of Southern slave-owners was added
only for the 1867 *Leaves of Grass.*

75. (p. 501) *Reversals:* "Reversals" is a fitting name for this poem, since
the commands are either "reversals" or seem to oppose Whitman's
typical commands; however, "Respondez," the title it carried in the
1867, 1871, and 1876 editions, also fits the deliberately provocative na-
ture of Whitman's indictments.

76. (p. 502) *Autumn Rivulets:* Like the three clusters that followed it in 1881
("Whispers of Heavenly Death," "From Noon to Starry Night," and
"Songs of Parting"), "Autumn Rivulets" has a title that reflects the poet's
sense of impending death. His personal history provides a clear indica-
tion of why mortality was so much on his mind at this time. Beginning

in his fifties, Whitman was plagued with health problems and emotional trials: He suffered a paralytic stroke in January 1873 and his mother died in May of that year; he became involved in an ill-fated relationship with Harry Stafford in 1876; and he was taken ill again in 1879 while traveling west.

Despite the aches of his deteriorating body and a heavy heart, Whitman rarely brought a sense of hopelessness or sadness to these late collections. Many of the poems he selected to include in them focus on the themes of immortality and the cycles of life. The selections exhibit a thoughtful "backward glance" at a life that spanned the nineteenth century, and a sense that Whitman saw a progression and continuance in his own career as poet.

77. (p. 502) *As Consequent*, Etc.: Notable are Whitman's use of the "rivulets" metaphor, an old-age echo of his image of the American poet in the 1855 "[Preface]:" "His spirit responds to his country's spirit . . . he incarnates its geography and natural life and rivers and lakes" (p. 9). The "windrow-drift of weeds and shells" are the scenes of American life "washed up" by the poet's "currents."

78. (p. 511) *Old Ireland*: This is Whitman's single poem on the Irish, which is surprising in that they were the largest group of working-class immigrants during Whitman's New York years. In *Whitman and the Irish* (Iowa City: University of Iowa Press, 2000, p. xii), Joann Krieg notes that a full 30 percent of New York's population in 1855 were Irish by birth. Though "Old Ireland" is a sympathetic portrait of the Irish and the revolutionary organization the Fenian Brotherhood, Krieg and others have wondered at Whitman's silence regarding this important population in his city.

79. (p. 517) *Song of Prudence*: Like "By Blue Ontario's Shore" (p. 485), "Song of Prudence" is greatly influenced by the language of the 1855 "[Preface]." See the passage on prudence—undoubtedly inspired by Emerson's essay "Prudence"—which begins on page 21; the section beginning "Only the soul is of itself" (p. 22) corresponds with Whitman's third stanza here. The fine line between Whitman's prose and poetry is particularly interesting to note in this case.

80. (p. 520) *The Singer in the Prison*: This is one of the three poems in this cluster—along with "Vocalism" (p. 526), "Italian Music in Dakota" (p. 541), and "Proud Music of the Storm" (p. 543)—to be inspired specifically by the power of music, and one of the very few poems in Whitman's entire oeuvre to be inspired by a particular event ("When Lilacs Last in the Dooryard Bloom'd," on page 475, is probably the best-known example). Whitman is said to have attended a concert given by the Italian tenor Carl Parepa-Rosa at a New York prison in 1869.

81. (p. 533) *Unfolded Out of the Folds:* The 1881 publication of the poem garnered this celebration of womanhood more attention than had its previous revisions: It was one of the poems (along with "The Sleepers," also included in the "Autumn Rivulets" cluster) that was considered indecent by Boston district attorney Oliver Stevens. Before the D.A. would allow publication of this edition, he asked publisher James R. Osgood to alter and omit particular lines of "Unfolded Out of the Folds."

82. (p. 537) *O Star of France:* As the subtitle suggests, Whitman wrote this poem in 1871 as a reaction to the defeat of France in the Franco-Prussian War (1870–1871).

83. (p. 541) *Italian Music in Dakota:* An enthusiastic fan of Italian opera since the 1840s, Whitman mentions three of his favorites; the military band of the subtitle probably played the overtures. His taste for European opera, which always seemed in conflict with his support for an independent American culture, here finds resolution: The music of Vincenzo Bellini (1801–1835; composer of *Norma* and *La Sonnambula*) and Gaetano Donizetti (1797–1848; *Poliuto*) sound as "native" as the natural sounds of the Dakota plains.

84. (p. 543) *Proud Music of the Storm:* In *Walt Whitman and Opera* (pp. 103–105), Robert Faner describes section 3 of the poem as Whitman's "musical autobiography": The poet recounts that his love of music developed from his mother's lullabies through the folk songs of his youth to his love of Italian opera. Critics have also commented on the poem's "symphonic structure" and musical rhythms, though Whitman himself admitted he was a musical illiterate who could not carry a tune.

85. (p. 549) *Passage to India:* A celebration of progress and modern life, "Passage to India" reflects Whitman's admiration of Columbus in its title (see "Prayer of Columbus," below). He praises the accomplishments of explorers, engineers, architects, and inventors throughout, with special emphasis on the three grand achievements in lines 5, 6, and 7: the Suez canal (opened in 1869), the transcontinental railroad (Union Pacific and Central Pacific lines were joined in 1869), and the transatlantic cable (laid in 1866). Machines and the workings of man "connect" humanity here—a very different message from the more spiritual, poet-centered proclamations of the 1855 poems.

86. (p. 558) *Prayer of Columbus:* The poet here assumes the voice of Columbus, who was imprisoned after his third voyage and plagued by ill health before his death. Whitman's admiration for the explorer leads to strong identification with him. Like Columbus, the aging poet had not gained the widespread appeal he had hoped for, and in 1873 Whitman suffered a paralytic stroke that brought on dizzy spells for the better part of a year.

87. (p. 560) *The Sleepers*: See notes 33–39 to the First Edition. This final version of "The Sleepers," prepared for the 1881 edition of *Leaves of Grass*, excludes two notable paragraphs from the original work: the "discovery and mortification" passage ("O hotcheeked and blushing!", p. 111), and the "black Lucifer" passage ("Now Lucifer was not dead", p. 115). The omission of these highly charged, sexual (and politically radical, in the case of the plotting slave Lucifer) passages is a typical "late style" revision, as is the refigured punctuation (dashes and periods substitute for the original ellipses). The numbering of the passages is a later addition as well.

88. (p. 570) *To Think of Time*: A comparison of this poem with its first incarnation (p. 102) reveals much about Whitman's changing editorial practices.

89. (p. 577) *Whispers of Heavenly Death*: The poems of "Whispers of Heavenly Death" are taken from several editions, though not so many as were used for "Autumn Rivulets"; nine of the eighteen are from the 1860 edition. Like the other clusters new to the 1881 edition, this one shows Whitman in a philosophical, almost mystical mode. The word "soul" predominates among the eighteen works.

90. (p. 577) *Whispers of Heavenly Death*: This poem is interesting for its use of female-based imagery for night ("labial gossip," "sibilant chorals"), which connects with the final "birthing" metaphor.

91. (p. 578) *Chanting the Square Deific*: The first of the allusions to the "square deific," this poem is divided into four parts: The first describes four supreme authority figures (the god of the Hebrews, Jehovah; the Hindu supreme spirit, Brahma; the Roman god Saturnius, or Saturn; and the Greek god Kronos); the second part details divinities of sacrifice and love; the third, Satan; and the fourth, the Christian idea of the Holy Spirit.

92. (p. 580) *Of Him I Love Day and Night*: The poem's themes make it a good fit for the provocative "Calamus" series, but a better match for this soul-searching group of poems. It's interesting to compare "Of Him I Love Day and Night" with Wordsworth's "Lucy" poems.

93. (p. 582) *Assurances*: The poem defies its title by including a negative statement in each of its twelve lines.

94. (p. 583) *That Music Always Round Me*: This poem is one of several in which Whitman celebrates the power of music (specifically opera or vocal music). See also "The Dead Tenor" (p. 648), "The Mystic Trumpeter" (p. 600), "To a Certain Cantatrice" (p. 173), "Proud Music of the Storm" (p. 543), and "Italian Music in Dakota" (p. 541).

95. (p. 584) *A Noiseless Patient Spider*: See the "Publication Information" note for "Darest Thou Now O Soul" (p. 577). Whitman's use of an unusually easy to understand metaphor (the spider's creation of a web

for the soul's exploration of space and time) has made this poem a popular favorite.

96. (p. 595) *From Noon to Starry Night:* The idea of the title begins with the high noon described in the first poem ("Thou Orb Aloft Full-Dazzling") and ends with the vision of "A Clear Midnight" (p. 617). The poems also follow Whitman's career from his "noon" on through the evening of his life, with poems selected from the First Edition as well as new works for 1881. In addition to a feeling of time that has passed, these poems convey a sense of great distances crossed: from south to north, Spain to Colorado, and back to Whitman's beloved Mannahatta.

97. (p. 596) *Faces:* Among the faces described are several possible family members, including Whitman's brother Eddie, who was possibly retarded or epileptic (the "idiot" of section 3), and his grandmother (the woman wearing a Quaker cap in section 5).

98. (p. 600) *The Mystic Trumpeter:* This is yet another poem celebrating the powers of music—in this case, its ability to evoke the past and herald the future.

99. (p. 603) *To a Locomotive in Winter:* Along with such poems as "Passage to India," this is an example of Whitman's celebration of progress and invention.

100. (p. 606) *Mannahatta:* This poem appeared in 1881 with the three final lines substituting for seven original lines:

The parades, processions, bugles playing, flags flying, drums beating,
A million people—manners free and superb—open voices—
    hospitality—the most courageous and friendly young men,
The free city! No slaves! No owners of slaves!
The beautiful city, the city of hurried and sparkling waters!
    The city of spires and masts!
The city nested in bays! My city!
The city of such women, I am mad to be with them!
    I will return after death to be with them!
The city of such young men, I swear I cannot live happy without
    I often go talk, walk, eat, drink, sleep with them!

It is interesting to compare the force and effectiveness of "Mannahatta" with the poem immediately preceding it, "O Magnet-South." Though Whitman was clearly trying to portray his love for all corners of the United States, his attachment to New York City clearly shines through the superior lines of this poem.

101. (p. 608) A *Riddle Song:* This poem contains a question without an answer—and follows Whitman's 1855 directive to the reader, to "listen to all sides, and filter them from yourself" ("[Song of Myself]").

102. (p. 611) *Mediums:* The "mediums" of the title are Americans who will represent and convey ideas of democracy through their physical selves and actions. The poem clearly draws on the 1855 "[Preface]" (p. 7) for its thesis.

103. (p. 612) *Spain, 1873–74:* Whitman here supports Spain's attempt to establish a constitutional republic and asks Americans to consider their past and offer support for the Spanish revolutionaries.

104. (p. 613) *From Far Dakota's Cañons:* In the last stanza, Whitman romanticizes Custer's last stand at Little Big Horn.

105. (p. 614) *Old War-Dreams:* The poem is interesting for its suggestion of just how much the poet was emotionally affected by his Civil War experiences; it reads as an insider's understanding of "shell shock."

106. (p. 615) *What Best I See in Thee:* This poem celebrates General Ulysses S. Grant's 1877–1879 world tour.

107. (p. 616) *Spirit That Form'd This Scene:* In 1879 Whitman took a trip to the western states; he commemorates its memory in these lines.

108. (p. 618) *Songs of Parting:* As the title suggests, the themes of this cluster are death and departure: The poet glances backward, but also ponders his legacy and the future of America. Just as this title is a more forthright statement of Whitman's feelings of mortality than are "Autumn Rivulets," "Whispers of Heavenly Death," and "From Noon to Starry Night" (the other three newly organized clusters in the 1881 *Leaves of Grass*), the poems in this cluster focus more directly and intensely on the themes of death and swiftly passing time.

109. (p. 618) *As the Time Draws Nigh:* Among the lines that were dropped or changed in revisions are these, which appeared after line 6 in 1860:

> The glances of my eyes, that swept the daylight,
> The unspeakable love I interchanged with women,
> My joys in the open air—my walks through the Mannahatta,
> The continual good will I have met—the curious attachment
>   of young men to me,
> My reflections alone—the absorption into me from the
>   landscape, stars, animals, thunder, rain, and snow, in my
>   wanderings alone . . .

110. (p. 620) *Ashes of Soldiers:* Whitman's inclusion of this poem, along with "Pensive on Her Dead Gazing" (p. 626) and "Camps of Green" (p. 627) in 1881 confirms the enduring impact of his Civil War experiences.

111. (p. 623) *Song at Sunset:* This poem's ecstatic, celebratory mode has made it a favorite with readers.

112. (p. 625) *As at Thy Portals Also Death:* New for 1881, this poem was inspired by the death in 1873 of Whitman's beloved mother, Louisa Van Velsor Whitman.

113. (p. 628) *The Sobbing of the Bells:* Whitman penned this poem after hearing of President James A. Garfield's death on September 19.

114. (p. 635) *First Annex: Sands at Seventy:* Each poem in this cluster is brief, at least for Whitman; one after another, they read as a series of spontaneous "thought-bubbles" floating through the poet's mind. In "You Lingering Sparse Leaves of Me" (p. 657), the poet writes of his special affection for these "soul-dearest leaves confirming all the rest, / The faithfulest—hardiest—last."

115. (p. 637) *A Font of Type:* This poem celebrates the art of printing; the names for different type styles listed in line 3 show off Whitman's insider knowledge of the "language" of printing.

116. (p. 638) *The Wallabout Martyrs:* This poem celebrates the Revolutionary soldiers buried in a mass grave in Brooklyn. Wallabout Bay is a bend in the East River just north of the Brooklyn Bridge.

117. (p. 638) *America:* A recording of Whitman reading the first four lines of this poem was allegedly made by Thomas Edison in 1891.

118. (p. 640) Fancies at Navesink: Whitman may have visited Navesink, on the New Jersey coast, in the summer of 1883 or 1884. "With Husky-Haughty Lips, O Sea!" (p. 644), another "Sands at Seventy" poem, was also inspired by the poet's visits to the Jersey shore.

119. (p. 645) *Red Jacket (From Aloft):* This poem—like "Yonnondio" (p. 649), also in "Sands at Seventy"—demonstrates Whitman's interest in Native American culture. Red Jacket was an Iroquois leader who is said to have made the Iroquois sympathetic to the American cause in the War of 1812.

120. (p. 648) *Old Salt Kossabone:* This poem celebrates Whitman's maternal heritage. Dutch Kossabone was the grandfather of Louisa Van Velsor Whitman, the poet's mother.

121. (p. 648) *The Dead Tenor:* This poem is a memorial to the great Italian tenor Pasquale Brignoli (1824–1884). Whitman had enjoyed the singer's performance of some of his favorite roles; those he mentions in the poem include Fernando in Donizetti's *La Favorita*, Manrico in Verdi's *Il Trovatore*, the title role in Verdi's *Ernani*, and Gennaro in Donizetti's *Lucrezia Borgia*.

122. (p. 650) *"Going Somewhere":* This poem alludes to Anne Gilchrist, an Englishwoman (and wife of William Blake's biographer) who greatly admired Whitman and developed a friendship with him. Gilchrist died in 1885.

123.(p. 658) *As the Greek's Signal Flame:* First published in the *New York Herald* of December 15, 1887, the poem celebrates the birthday of the American poet John Greenleaf Whittier (1807–1892), who had corresponded with Whitman.

124.(p. 661) *Preface Note to 2d Annex, Concluding L. of G.—1891:* Spontaneous-sounding remarks like these introduce or expand the themes of other poems in the collection, giving this cluster a "conversational" tone.

125.(p. 667) *Shakspere-Bacon's Cipher:* This poem engages in the questions regarding Shakespeare's identity and the authorship of the plays.

126.(p. 668) *Bravo, Paris Exposition!:* This poem celebrates the 1889 Paris Exposition and indicates Whitman's interest in progress and invention in his final years.

127.(p. 673) *Osceola:* This poem memorializes the bravery of the Seminole leader Osceola, who died, as Whitman indicates, in 1838.

128.(p. 674) *A Voice from Death:* This poem memorializes the thousands who died when a dam collapsed in Johnstown, Pennsylvania.

129.(p. 677) *Mirages:* This poem's introductory note is fictional: Whitman never visited Nevada. The veracity of other unverifiable introductory statements—such as the one for "The Rounded Catalogue Divine Complete"—is thus called into question.

130.(p. 679) *Good-Bye My Fancy!:* Though "fancy" more commonly designates the imagination, the poet may be bidding his own body or physical presence farewell in this poem (consider the line "Exit, nightfall, and soon the heart-thud stopping"). "Fancy" might also be something (or someone) the poet has treasured and fantasized about for an extended time.

131.(p. 681) *A Backward Glance o'er Travel'd Roads:* In a note to his "Prefatory Letter to the Reader, *Leaves of Grass* 1889," Whitman told his public that he favored this edition of his writings: "As there are now several editions of L. of G., different texts and dates, I wish to say that I prefer and recommend the present one, complete, for future printing." The essay "A Backward Glance o'er Travel'd Roads" has thus remained in volumes of his collected poetry, while also collected in *Complete Prose Works* (1892). Along with the "[Preface]" to the 1855 edition of *Leaves of Grass*, "A Backward Glance" frames Whitman's career and the body of his work. Although he had grown more pessimistic about his reception since his poetic beginnings, he remained determined when explaining the motivations of his project and when calling American artists to consciousness.

ADDITIONAL POEMS

Poems Written before 1855

1. (p. 719) *The Spanish Lady:* This poem retells the tragic tale of Inez de Castro (1320–1355).

2. (p. 723) *The Punishment of Pride:* In 1894 Whitman's friend and companion Horace Traubel interviewed Charles A. Roe, one of Whitman's former students from Little Bay Side, Queens. Roe claimed that Whitman made his students memorize a poem entitled "The Fallen Angel"; to prove it, Roe recited the poem, which turned out to be a variant of "The Punishment of Pride." See Traubel's article "Walt Whitman, Schoolmaster: Notes of a Conversation with Charles A. Roe, 1894," in the *Walt Whitman Fellowship Papers* 14 (April 1895), pp. 81–87.

3. (p. 728) *The Death and Burial of McDonald Clarke:* This poem was signed "W." and designated "For the Aurora" (the *Aurora* was a New York newspaper of the day). Clarke (1798–1842), the so-called "Mad Poet of Broadway," wrote several volumes of unconventional poetry and was himself a symbol of the "outsider artist."

4. (p. 735) *Song for Certain Congressmen:* This poem mocks supporters of the Compromise of 1850, which granted California admittance to the Union but did not enforce legal restrictions on slavery in Utah and New Mexico. "Song for Certain Congressmen" is Whitman's first truly political poem, and his growing political awareness is evident in the following three poems (all published over a period of less than four months).

5. (p. 738) *Blood-Money:* In this poem, supporters of the Compromise of 1850 are compared with Judas Iscariot, the disciple who betrayed Jesus in the New Testament.

6. (p. 739) *The House of Friends:* The third poem inspired by the hypocrisies of the Compromise of 1850, the poem demonstrates Whitman's increasing awareness of the division between South and North.

7. (p. 741) *Resurgemus:* Whitman's inspiration here is the spirit of the European revolutions of the late 1840s; despite loss and death, the ideas of liberty and democracy live on.

Poems Excluded from the "Death-bed" Edition of Leaves of Grass (1891–1892)

8. (p. 755) *Calamus. 8:* Like "Calamus. 9," the poem openly addresses the narrator's passion for a male companion.

Poems Published after the *1891–1892* "Death-bed" Edition: Old Age Echoes

9. (p. 780) A *Kiss to the Bride*: This poem commemorates the wedding of the daughter of Ulysses S. Grant.

10. (p. 781) *Nay, Tell Me Not To-day the Publish'd Shame*: This poem critiques the passing of an act to increase the salaries of the U.S. president and other government officials.

11. (p. 783) *Death's Valley*: "Death's Valley" was inspired by the artwork of American landscape painter George Inness (1825–1894).

12. (p. 784) *On the Same Picture*: The title is Horace Traubel's. The title of the manuscript ("Death's Valley") indicates that the stanza was meant to be included in the poem "Death's Valley," above.

13. (p. 784) A *Thought of Columbus*: In the July 16, 1892, edition of the newspaper *Once a Week*, Traubel explains how Whitman finished the poem and handed it to him a few days before his death.

PUBLICATION INFORMATION

———◆•◆———

LEAVES OF GRASS: FIRST EDITION (1855)

[*Preface*], p. 7: Whitman told an admirer in 1870 that the preface had been "written hastily" before publication, and that "I do not consider it of permanent value." He never included it in another edition of *Leaves of Grass* after 1855, though he revised and edited it for inclusion in *Specimen Days and Collect* (1882), *Complete Poems and Prose* (1888), and *Complete Prose Works* (1892). Passages from the preface have found their way into several poems, including "By Blue Ontario's Shore" and "Song of the Answerer."

[*Song of Myself*], p. 29: In the 1855 edition each of the first six poems shared the title of the book: "Leaves of Grass." In 1856 this poem was titled "Poem of Walt Whitman, an American"; in editions from 1860 to 1871 it was simply "Walt Whitman." "Song of Myself" was first used as a title in 1881. Through the years, Whitman's major poetic statement was steadily revised and edited, with stanza numbers added in 1860 and section numbers in the 1867 edition of *Leaves of Grass*.

[*A Song for Occupations*], p. 91: This poem was headed "Leaves of Grass" in 1855. In 1856 the title became "Poem of the Daily Work of the Workmen and Workwomen of These States"; in 1860, "Chants Democratic. 3"; in 1867, "To Workingmen"; in 1871 and 1876, "Carol of Occupations." It received the current title in 1881. Whitman added stanza numbers in 1860 and section numbers in 1867.

[*To Think of Time*], p. 102: Given the header "Leaves of Grass" in the First Edition, this poem became "Burial Poem" in 1856 and

"Burial" in 1860. "To Think of Time" was adopted as the title in 1871.

[*The Sleepers*], p. 109: This poem, titled "Leaves of Grass" in 1855, became "26—Night Poem" in 1856, "Sleep-Chasings" in 1860, and "The Sleepers" in 1871. Stanza numbers were added in 1860; section numbers were included in 1867. The poem is often read as the "dark twin" of "[Song of Myself]," since its action takes place at night (versus the first poem's brilliantly illuminated daytime scenes), and its subject is an exploration of the deep levels of common psychic territory rather than the American landscape of "[Song of Myself]."

[*I Sing the Body Electric*], p. 119: This poem was titled "Leaves of Grass" in 1855, "7—Poem of the Body" in 1856, "Enfans d'Adam. 3" in 1860, and "I Sing the Body Electric" in 1867. Stanza numbers were added in 1860, and section numbers in 1867. See p. 254 for Whitman's final "Death-bed" Edition version of this poem, which includes a remarkable, sweeping listing of human body parts (added in 1856).

[*Faces*], p. 126: Titled "Leaves of Grass" in 1855, this poem became "27—Poem of Faces" in 1856, "Leaf of Faces" in 1860, "A Leaf of Faces" in 1867, and "Faces" in 1867. Stanza numbers were added in 1860; section numbers were added in 1867.

[*Song of the Answerer*], p. 130: Untitled in the 1855 edition, in 1856 lines 3–52 became "14—Poem of the Poet," and lines 54–66 and 69–83 became "19—Poem of the Singers and of the Words of Poems." In 1860 lines 3–52 became "Leaves of Grass," and lines 54–66 and 69–83 became "Leaves of Grass. 6." In 1867 lines 1–52 were titled "Now List to My Morning's Romanza," and lines 53–66 and 69–85 were titled "The Indications." In 1871 lines 1–52 became "Now List to My Morning's Romanza," and lines 53–83 became "The Indications." In 1881 lines 1–83 became "Song of the Answerer."

[*Europe, The 72d and 73d Years of These States*], p. 133: This is the only poem published before 1855 that appeared in an edition of

Leaves of Grass. It appeared as "Resurgemus" in the *New York Tribune* of June 21, 1850; significant modifications of the poem's rhythms and symbolism were made between the more conventional early poem and this one. In 1855 it became the untitled eighth of the twelve First Edition poems; in 1856 it was known as "16—Poem of the Dead Young Men of Europe, The 72d and 73d Years of These States"; in 1860, "Europe, The 72d and 73d Years of These States."

[*A Boston Ballad*], p. 135: Untitled in 1855, this poem became "22—Poem of Apparitions in Boston, the 78th Year of These States" in 1856; "A Boston Ballad / The 78th Year of These States" in 1860; "To Get Betimes in Boston Town" in 1867; and "A Boston Ballad (1854)" in 1871. A protest against the authorities' handling of the 1854 Anthony Burns case (see endnote 44 to the First Edition), the poem is one of two (along with "[Europe]"; see just above) *Leaves of Grass* poems that are known to have been completed before 1855.

[*There Was a Child Went Forth*], p. 138: Untitled in 1855, this poem became "25—Poem of the Child That Went Forth, and Always Goes Forth, Forever and Forever" in 1856. In 1860 it was "Leaves of Grass. 9;" in 1867, "Leaves of Grass. 1." It gained its current title in 1871. Several significant revisions were made to the poem over time, such as the exclusion of the last line after 1856; see "There Was a Child Went Forth" in the "Death-bed" Edition (p. 509).

[*Who Learns My Lesson Complete*], p. 140: Untitled in 1855, the poem became "29—Lesson Poem" in 1856, "Leaves of Grass. 11" in 1860, "Leaves of Grass. 3" in 1867, and "Who Learns My Lesson Complete?" in 1871. This poem was heavily revised over time, with all of Whitman's personal details (birth date, height, age) eventually dropped; see "Who Learns My Lesson Complete?" in the "Death-bed" Edition (p. 535).

[*Great Are the Myths*], p. 142: In 1855 this poem was untitled. In 1856 it became "6—Poem of a Few Greatnesses"; in 1860, "Leaves of Grass. 2"; from 1867 to 1871, "Great Are the Myths." Whitman chose to exclude this poem from *Leaves of Grass* after 1881, except for lines 9–12, which became "Youth, Day, Old Age, and Night." Stanzas were added in 1860, section numbers in 1871. For revisions, compare with "Great Are the Myths" on p. 744 of the "Additional Poems" section of this edition.

LEAVES OF GRASS: "DEATH-BED" EDITION (1891–1892)

Come, said my Soul, p. 147: This poem, signed in the poet's hand, was the epigraph for *Leaves of Grass* (1876), *Leaves of Grass* (1882), *Complete Poems and Prose* (1888), and the "Death-bed" Edition of *Leaves of Grass* (1891–1892). It first appeared in the *New York Daily Graphic* of December 1874.

Inscriptions, p. 165: Whitman first used this cluster title in the 1871 *Leaves of Grass* for a group of nine poems. The present twenty-four poems were first assembled under this title in 1881.

One's-Self I Sing, p. 165: A shortened and simplified version of the poem on the frontispiece of the 1867 edition (included here as "Small the Theme of My Chant"; see p. 651), "One's-Self I Sing" gained its title and current form in 1871.

As I Ponder'd in Silence, p. 165: First included, and in its final form, in the 1871 *Leaves of Grass*. Note Whitman's use of italics to indicate a speaking voice, which he had already experimented with in 1860's "A Word Out of the Sea" (now known as "Out of the Cradle Endlessly Rocking"; see p. 400).

In Cabin'd Ships at Sea, p. 166: First included, and in its final form, in the "Inscriptions" cluster, in the 1871 edition of *Leaves of Grass*.

To Foreign Lands, p. 167: First appeared in the "Messenger Leaves" cluster of the 1860 edition; in its final form in 1871.

To a Historian, p. 167: In its first form as "Chants Democratic. 10" in the 1860 edition, the poem gained its current title and form in the "Songs before Parting" annex of 1867.

To Thee Old Cause, p. 168: First appeared in 1871; in its final form in 1881.

Eidólons, p. 168: First published in the *New York Tribune* of February 19, 1876, the poem was included in *Two Rivulets* (1876) and moved to the "Inscriptions" cluster in the 1881 edition of *Leaves of Grass*.

For Him I Sing, p. 171: First included, and in its final form, as part of the "Inscriptions" cluster, which was new to the 1871 edition of *Leaves of Grass*.

When I Read the Book, p. 172: First included in a shorter version in 1867; in its final form in 1871.

Beginning My Studies, p. 172: First included in *Drum-Taps* (1865); in its final form in 1871.

Beginners, p. 172: First included in 1860, the poem gained minor revisions in the 1867 and 1871 editions of *Leaves of Grass*.

To the States, p. 173: First included in 1860 as "Walt Whitman's Caution," "To the States" took its current title in 1881.

On Journeys Through the States, p. 173: Known as "Chants Democratic. 17" in 1860, the poem was left out of the 1867 edition but restored as "On Journeys Through the States" in 1871.

To a Certain Cantatrice, p. 173: "To a Cantatrice" in the 1860 edition, the poem gained its current title in 1867, and finally was included in the "Inscriptions" cluster in 1881.

Me Imperturbe, p. 174: First included as "Chants Democratic. 18" in the 1860 edition of *Leaves of Grass*, the poem gained its final title and form in 1881.

Savantism, p. 174: First included, and in its final form, in the 1860 edition of *Leaves of Grass*.

The Ship Starting, p. 175: First appearing in *Drum-Taps* (1865), "The Ship Starting" was included in the "Inscriptions" cluster of 1881.

I Hear America Singing, p. 175: "Chants Democratic. 20" in 1860, "I Hear America Singing" gained its title in 1867.

What Place Is Besieged?, p. 176: First included as part of "Calamus. 31" in 1860, the poem gained its current title and form in 1867.

Still Though the One I Sing, p. 176: First included, and in its final form, in the "Songs of Insurrection" cluster of *Leaves of Grass* (1871).

Shut Not Your Doors, p. 176: First written for *Drum-Taps* in 1865, this poem was in its final form in 1871.

Poets to Come, p. 176: The original, longer version of this poem was known as "Chants Democratic. 14" in the 1860 edition. The poem gained its current title and form in 1867.

To You, p. 177: First included, and in its final form, as the last poem in the "Messenger Leaves" cluster of 1860.

Thou Reader, p. 177: The concluding poem of the "Inscriptions" section was included, and in its final form, in 1881.

Starting from Paumanok, p. 177: First included in 1860 as "Proto-Leaf," this poem became "Starting from Paumonok" in 1871 and achieved its final form in 1881. The poem has always had an important placement in *Leaves of Grass*: It was first in 1860 (as its title suggests) and the first poem following the "Inscriptions" cluster beginning in 1871.

Song of Myself, p. 190: See notes to the 1855 version of "[Song of Myself]," above. "Song of Myself" appeared in its final form in 1881.

Children of Adam, p. 252: This cluster of poems first appeared in the 1860 edition as "Enfans d'Adam." All but one of the original fifteen poems ("In the New Garden, in all the Parts") appeared in the collection in the 1867 edition of *Leaves of Grass*, and the title was then changed to "Children of Adam." In 1871 Whitman added "Out of the Rolling Ocean the Crowd" and "I Heard You Solemn-Sweet Pipes of the Organ," making up the sixteen poems that have since comprised the group.

To the Garden the World, p. 252: Known as "Enfans d'Adam. 1" in 1860, this poem gained its current title in 1867 and remained unrevised through successive editions. It has also maintained its position as first poem in the "Children of Adam" grouping, probably because of its image of the poet "ascending" as Adam.

From Pent-up Aching Rivers, p. 252: "Enfans d'Adam. 2" in 1860, this celebration of heterosexual passion gained its current title in 1867, and minor revisions through the 1871 edition.

I Sing the Body Electric, p. 254: This was the fifth poem in the 1855 edition of *Leaves of Grass*. In 1856 it became "Poem of the Body"; in 1860, "Enfans d'Adam. 3"; and in 1867 it received its current title and section numbers. Minor revisions were made to the poem in the 1871 and 1881 editions of *Leaves of Grass*.

A Woman Waits for Me, p. 263: "Poem of Procreation" in the 1856 edition, this became "Enfans d'Adam. 6" in 1860 and received its current title in 1867. Minor changes were made through the 1871 edition.

Spontaneous Me, p. 264: Originally titled "Bunch Poem" in 1856, this poem became "Enfans d'Adam. 5" in 1860 and received its present title and form in 1867. Both the first and final titles allude to the poem's subject: masturbation.

One Hour to Madness and Joy, p. 267: Originally "Enfans d'Adam. 6" in 1860, this poem received its present title in the 1867 edition of *Leaves of Grass*. The current form of the text was achieved in 1881.

Out of the Rolling Ocean the Crowd, p. 268: This poem originally appeared in *Drum-Taps* (1865) and was moved to the "Children of Adam" cluster in *Leaves of Grass* (1871).

Ages and Ages Returning at Intervals, p. 268: "Enfans d'Adam. 12" in 1860, this poem gained its present title (and capitalized "Sex" for the first time) in 1867.

We Two, How Long We Were Fool'd, p. 269: Known as "Enfans d'Adam. 7" in 1860, this poem received its current title in 1867. Minor revisions (mostly punctuation changes) were made through the 1881 edition.

O Hymen! O Hymenee!, p. 269: "Enfans d'Adam. 13" in 1860, this poem received its current title in 1867.

I Am He That Aches with Love, p. 270: Originally "Enfans d'Adam. 14" in 1860, the poem's title was permanently changed in 1867.

Native Moments, p. 270: "Enfans d'Adam. 8" in 1860, this poem received its current title in 1867.

Once I Pass'd Through a Populous City, p. 270: Originally "Enfans d'Adam. 9" in 1860, this poem gained its present title in 1867.

I Heard You Solemn-Sweet Pipes of the Organ, p. 271: First published in the *New York Leader* of October 12, 1861, as "Little Bells Last Night," the poem was included in *Sequel to Drum-Taps* (1865–1866) and moved to the "Children of Adam" cluster in *Leaves of Grass* (1871).

Facing West from California's Shores, p. 271: "Enfans d'Adam. 10" in 1860, this poem gained its current title in 1867. Minor revisions (mostly changes in punctuation) were made between these editions.

As Adam Early in the Morning, p. 272: "Enfans d'Adam. 15" in 1860, this poem was permanently renamed in 1867. It has always been the final poem of the "Children of Adam" cluster; along with the first poem ("To the Garden the World"), it frames the collection with Edenic scenes.

Calamus, p. 274: The manuscript source for this cluster is a series of twelve poems now known as the "Live Oak with Moss" cluster, narrating an unhappy love affair that may have had special significance for Whitman. Assembled as a cluster of forty-five poems in the 1860 edition of *Leaves of Grass*, "Calamus" was reduced to forty-two poems in 1867 (excluded were "Calamus" 8, 9, and 16 — "Long I Thought That Knowledge Would Suffice," "Hours Continuing Long," and "Who Is Now Reading This?"). In 1871 Whitman added "The Base of All Metaphysics" to the cluster and removed four others to *Passage to India*, making a final total of thirty-nine "Calamus" poems.

In Paths Untrodden, p. 274: "Calamus. 1" in 1860, this poem took its current title in 1867.

Scented Herbage of My Breast, p. 274: "Calamus. 2" in 1860, this poem gained its present title in 1867.

Whoever You Are Holding Me Now in Hand, p. 276: "Calamus. 3" in 1860, this poem took its current title in 1867.

For You O Democracy, p. 278: The lines of this poem are taken from "Calamus. 5" of the 1860 edition. "Calamus. 5" (titled "States!" when it was reprinted in 1901) did not appear in another edition of *Leaves of Grass* during Whitman's lifetime (see "Poems Excluded from the 'Death-bed' Edition," below). Whitman used the poetic text to form two poems: "Over the Carnage Rose Prophetic a Voice," which appeared in *Drum-Taps*, and "A Song" of 1867, which became "For You O Democracy" in 1881.

These I Singing in Spring, p. 278: "Calamus. 4" in 1860, this poem gained its present title and form in 1867.

Not Heaving from My Ribb'd Breast Only, p. 280: "Calamus. 6" in 1860, the poem was given its current title in 1867.

Of the Terrible Doubt of Appearances, p. 280: "Calamus. 7" in 1860, this poem gained its current title in 1867.

The Base of All Metaphysics, p. 281: Not part of the original 1860 "Calamus" cluster, this new poem was added to the collection in 1871.

Recorders Ages Hence, p. 282: Originally "Calamus. 10" in 1860, the poem gained its present title in 1867.

When I Heard at the Close of the Day, p. 283: "Calamus. 11" in 1860, this poem gained its current title in 1867.

Are You the New Person Drawn toward Me?, p. 283: "Calamus. 12" in 1860, this poem was given its present title in 1867.

Roots and Leaves Themselves Alone, p. 284: "Calamus. 13" in 1860, this poem was given its final title in 1867.

Not Heat Flames Up and Consumes, p. 284: "Calamus. 14" in 1860, this poem gained its present title and form in 1867.

Trickle Drops, p. 285: "Calamus. 15" in 1860, this poem was given its final title and form in 1867.

City of Orgies, p. 285: "Calamus. 18" in 1860, this poem gained its present title in 1867.

Behold This Swarthy Face, p. 286: "Calamus. 19" in 1860, this poem gained its present title in 1867, when it also lost its first two lines ("Mind you the timid models of the rest, the majority? / Long I minded them, but hence I will not—for I have adopted models for myself, and now offer them to you").

I Saw in Louisiana a Live-Oak Growing, p. 286: "Calamus. 20" in 1860, this poem gained its current title and form in 1867.

To a Stranger, p. 287: "Calamus. 22" in 1860, this poem received its final title in 1867.

This Moment Yearning and Thoughtful, p. 287: "Calamus. 23" in 1860, the poem gained its final title and form in 1867.

I Hear It Was Charged Against Me, p. 288: "Calamus. 24" in 1860, the poem received its final title in 1867.

The Prairie-Grass Dividing, p. 288: "Calamus. 25" in 1860, this poem received its current title in 1867.

When I Peruse the Conquer'd Fame, p. 289: "Calamus. 28" in 1860, this poem received its final title in 1867.

We Two Boys Together Clinging, p. 289: "Calamus. 26" in 1860, this poem gained its current title in 1867, when it also lost one descriptive line (between current lines 7 and 8).

A Promise to California, p. 289: "Calamus. 30" in 1860, the poem gained its present title in 1867.

Here the Frailest Leaves of Me, p. 290: "Calamus. 44" in 1860, the poem gained its present title in 1867.

No Labor-saving Machine, p. 290: "Calamus. 33" in 1860, the poem gained its current title in 1867. It received minor revisions through 1881.

A Glimpse, p. 290: "Calamus. 29" in 1860, the poem received its final title in 1867.

A Leaf for Hand in Hand, p. 291: "Calamus. 37" in 1860, the poem was permanently retitled in 1867.

Earth, My Likeness, p. 291: "Calamus. 36" in 1860, the poem was titled "Earth! My Likeness!" in 1867, and its punctuation was finalized in 1871.

I Dream'd in a Dream, p. 291: "Calamus. 34" in 1860, this poem became "I Dreamed in a Dream" in 1867, with the current wording taking shape in 1871.

What Think You I Take My Pen in Hand?, p. 292: "Calamus. 32" in 1860, the poem gained its present title in 1867.

To the East and to the West, p. 292: "Calamus. 35" in 1860, this poem gained its current title in 1867.

Sometimes with One I Love, p. 292: "Calamus. 39" in 1860, this poem gained its current title in 1867.

To a Western Boy, p. 293: "Calamus. 42" in 1860, the poem gained its current title in 1867.

Fast-anchor'd Eternal O Love!, p. 293: "Calamus. 38" in 1860, this poem gained its current title in 1867. The first line of the 1860 version read: "Primeval my love for the woman I love."

Among the Multitude, p. 293: "Calamus. 41" in 1860, this poem gained its current title in 1867.

O You Whom I Often and Silently Come, p. 293: "Calamus. 43" in 1860, this poem gained its present title in 1867.

That Shadow My Likeness, p. 294: "Calamus. 40" in 1860, the poem gained its current title in 1867, and received minor revisions until 1881.

Full of Life Now, p. 294: "Calamus. 45" in 1860, the poem gained its final title in 1867 and its last revisions for the 1871 edition.

Salut au Monde!, p. 294: Originally titled "Poem of Salutation," this poem was first published in *Leaves of Grass* (1856). It gained its current title, as well as its stanza numbers, in 1860, with section numbers following in 1867. Minor revisions were made until the text achieved its current form in 1881.

Song of the Open Road, p. 305: "Poem of the Road" in 1856 and 1860, the poem received its current title in the 1867 edition of *Leaves of Grass*. The poem was given very minor revision, with only one new line added to the final text in 1881 (line 6).

Crossing Brooklyn Ferry, p. 316: Originally "Sun-down Poem" in 1856, the poem received its current title in 1860. Stanza numbers were added in 1860, section numbers in 1871. Several lines were changed or dropped, including (originally after line 21): "I project myself, also I return—I am with you, and know how it is." The poem achieved its final form in 1881.

Song of the Answerer, p. 322: This poem underwent many revisions from its beginnings as the seventh poem ("A Young Man Came to Me . . .") in the 1855 edition of *Leaves of Grass*. In 1856 the poem was split into two parts, as "14—Poem of the Poet" and "19—Poem of the Singers, and of the Words of Poems": In 1860 these poems became "Leaves of Grass. 3" and "Leaves of Grass. 6," respectively. These poems were retitled "Now List to My Morning's Romanza" and "The Indications" in the 1867 edition, and included as the first and second poems in the new cluster "The Answerer" in 1871. In 1881 the poem was assembled out of the two sections and titled "The Answerer." It received a new section and its present title in 1881.

Our Old Feuillage, p. 327: "Chants Democratic. 4" in 1860, this poem became "American Feuillage" in 1867. It took its present title and form in 1881.

A Song of Joys, p. 332: First appearing in 1860 as "Poem of Joys," the poem became "Poems of Joy" in 1867. Two more title switches and many revisions later, "A Song of Joys" appeared in its present form in 1881.

Song of the Broad-Axe, p. 339: First appearing as "Broad-Axe Poem" in 1856 and "Chants Democratic. 2" in 1860, the poem took its final title in 1867, though its text was much revised through 1881. Stanza numbers were added in 1856, section numbers in 1867.

Song of the Exposition, p. 351: This poem was written as a tribute to the Annual Exhibition of the American Institute in 1871. It first appeared in several newspapers, and then as a booklet entitled "After All Not to Create Only: Recited by Walt Whitman on Invitation of Managers American Institute, on Opening Their 40th Annual Exhibition, New York, Noon, September 7, 1871." "After All, Not to Create Only" was annexed to the 1872 impression of *Leaves of Grass*; in 1876 it was published as "Song of the Exposition" in "Centennial Songs," a separately published cluster annexed to *Two Rivulets*. An explanatory preface explaining the "impulses" that led to the poem's initial "oral delivery" was dropped in 1881.

Song of the Redwood-Tree, p. 361: First published in *Harper's Magazine* in February 1874, the poem was one of four in "Centennial Songs," a separately published cluster annexed to *Two Rivulets* (1876). It appeared in its final form in the 1881 edition of *Leaves of Grass*.

A Song for Occupations, p. 365: Originally the second poem in the 1855 edition of *Leaves of Grass*, "A Song for Occupations" underwent many revisions and changes in title until it appeared in its final state in 1881. In the 1856 edition of *Leaves of Grass* it was titled "Poem of the Daily Work of the Workmen and Workwomen of These States"; in 1860, "Chants Democratic. 3"; in 1867, "To Workingmen"; and "Carol of Occupations" in 1871 and 1876. Comparisons of this last revision with the first reveal some of the major changes in Whitman's verse over the course of his career, including diminished intimacy and specific references, as well as regularized line lengths and punctuation. Stanza numbers were added in 1860, and section numbers in 1867.

A Song of the Rolling Earth, p. 373: Originally "Poem of the Sayers of the Words of the Earth" in 1856, this poem became "To the Sayers of Words" in 1860 and 1867, and "Carol of Words" in 1871 and 1876. It gained its present title and form in 1881, with stanza numbers added in 1860 and section numbers in 1867.

Youth, Day, Old Age and Night, p. 379: This poem is lines 19–22 of "[Great Are the Myths]," the last of the twelve poems of the 1855 edition. When Whitman excluded "Great Are the Myths" from the 1881 edition, he retained these four lines as a separate work.

Birds of Passage, p. 380: This cluster of seven poems first appeared in 1881, though the individual poems had all appeared in earlier editions of *Leaves of Grass*.

Song of the Universal, p. 380: On June 17, 1874, this poem was included as part of commencement exercises at Tufts College. In 1876 it became one of the four "Centennial Songs," a separately published cluster annexed to *Two Rivulets*.

Pioneers! O Pioneers!, p. 382: First appearing in *Drum-Taps* (1865), the poem also appeared in the "Drum-Taps" annex of *Leaves of Grass* (1867). It was included in a cluster entitled "Marches Now the War Is Over" in 1871 and 1876, and took its final form in 1881.

To You, p. 387: First appearing in the 1856 edition as "Poem of You, Whoever You Are," this poem became "To You Whoever You Are" in 1860, and "Leaves of Grass. 4" in 1867. In 1871 it achieved its present title.

France, The 18th Year of These States, p. 389: The poem first appeared in the 1860 edition of *Leaves of Grass*, under its current title.

Myself and Mine, p. 390: "Leaves of Grass. 10" in 1860 and "Leaves of Grass. 2" in 1867, the poem gained its present title in 1871.

Year of Meteors (1859–60), p. 392: First appearing in *Drum-Taps* (1865), this poem was moved to a "Leaves of Grass" cluster in 1871 and finally included in the "Birds of Passage" cluster in 1881.

With Antecedents, p. 393: First published in the *New York Saturday Press* of January 14, 1860, as "You and Me and To-Day," this poem was included in the 1860 edition as "Chants Democratic. 7." It gained its present title in 1867.

A Broadway Pageant, p. 395: First published in the *New York Times* of June 27, 1860, as "The Errand-Bearers," the poem was included in *Drum-Taps* (1865) as "A Broadway Pageant (Reception Japanese Embassy, June 16, 1860)"; in 1870 it was retitled "Broadway Pageant. Reception Japanese Embassy, June, 1860." It gained its current title in 1871. Stanza numbers were included in 1865, section numbers in 1871.

Sea-Drift, p. 400: This cluster of eleven poems was new to the 1881 edition. It absorbed the "Sea-Shore Memories" cluster of *Passage to India* (1871), plus two new poems and two transferred poems.

Out of the Cradle Endlessly Rocking, p. 400: The poem was first published as "A Child's Reminiscence" in the New York *Saturday Press* on Christmas Eve 1859. For the 1860 edition of *Leaves of Grass*, Whitman heavily revised the poem and retitled it "A Word Out the Sea." The present title was first seen in *Passage to India* (1871), and the poem took its final form by 1881.

As I Ebb'd with the Ocean of Life, p. 406: In April 1860 this poem was published in the *Atlantic Monthly* under the title "Bardic Symbols." It became "Leaves of Grass. 1" in 1860 and "Elemental Drifts" for the 1867 edition, and gained its current title in 1881.

Tears, p. 409: Originally appearing as "Leaves of Grass. 2" in 1867, the poem gained its current title in *Passage to India* (1871).

To the Man-of-War-Bird, p. 410: The poem was first published in the *London Athenaeum* on April 1, 1876. One of six poems that were intercalations in copies of the 1876 *Leaves of Grass* "Author's Edition, with Portraits and Intercalations" (along with "As in a Swoon," "The Beauty of the Ship," "When the Full-grown Poet Came," "After an Interval," and "From Far Dakota's Canons"). It appeared in its final form in the 1881 edition.

Aboard at a Ship's Helm, p. 411: "Leaves of Grass. 3" in 1867, the poem received its current title in *Passage to India* (1871). It was first included in *Leaves of Grass* in 1881.

On the Beach at Night, p. 411: First included under the current title in *Passage to India* (1871), the poem became part of the "Sea-Drift" cluster in *Leaves of Grass* of 1881.

The World below the Brine, p. 412: "Leaves of Grass. 16" in 1860 and "Leaves of Grass. 4" in 1867, the poem first appeared under its present title in *Passage to India* (1871). Whitman moved it to *Leaves of Grass* in 1881.

On the Beach at Night Alone, p. 413: In 1856 this poem appeared as a much longer version entitled "15 — Clef Poem." More than twenty lines were omitted when it was shaped into "Leaves of Grass. 12" in 1860, and it was further truncated when it appeared as "Leaves of Grass. 1" in 1867. It assumed its present title in *Passage to India* (1871) and was included again in *Leaves of Grass* of 1881.

Song for All Seas, All Ships, p. 414: The poem was first published in the *New York Daily Graphic* on April 4, 1873. Along with "Song of the Redwood-Tree," "Song of the Universal," and "Song of the Exposition," it was published in "Centennial Songs," a separately published cluster annexed to *Two Rivulets* (1876). It appeared in the "Sea-Drift" section of *Leaves of Grass* in 1881.

Patroling Barnegat, p. 415: This poem was first included in *Leaves of Grass* of 1881, though it appeared previously in *The American* of June 1880.

After the Sea-Ship, p. 415: First published in the *New York Daily Graphic* of December 1874 as "In the Wake Following," this poem gained its present title in *Two Rivulets* (1876). In 1881 it became part of the "Sea-Drift" series in *Leaves of Grass.*

By the Roadside, p. 417: Whitman devised this title for a cluster of old and new poems in 1881. He wrote the twenty-nine poems at various stages of his journey "down life's road" (hence, perhaps, the title); "A Boston Ballad" was among the first poems Whitman published, while three others were written for the 1881 edition of *Leaves of Grass.*

A Boston Ballad (1854), p. 417: See note to "[A Boston Ballad]," p. 417.

Europe, The 72d and 73d Years of These States, p. 419: See note to "[Europe, The 72d and 73d Years of These States]," p. 419.

A Hand-Mirror, p. 421: This poem's title and format remained unchanged from its first appearance in the 1860 edition of *Leaves of Grass*.

Gods, p. 421: First published in *Passage to India* (1871), "Gods" also appeared in *Leaves of Grass* (1876).

Germs, p. 422: Titled "Leaves of Grass. 19" in 1860 and "Leaves of Grass. 2" in 1867, the poem was titled "Germs" in 1871.

Thoughts, p. 422: In the 1860 edition of *Leaves of Grass*, Whitman published a series of seven poems called "Thoughts." This 1881 poem starts with the first line from "Thoughts. 4" and the last four lines of "Thoughts. 2." Other poems with this title (including three more in "By the Roadside") were similarly pulled together—as fluidly and spontaneously, one might say, as thoughts themselves.

When I Heard the Learn'd Astronomer, p. 423: First included in *Drum-Taps* (1865), this poem was part of the "Songs of Parting" cluster in *Leaves of Grass* of 1871 and 1876. It became part of "By the Roadside" in 1881.

Perfections, p. 423: First appearing in *Leaves of Grass* (1860), this poem was reprinted in all subsequent editions without revisions.

O Me! O Life!, p. 423: This question-answer poem was first included in *Sequel to Drum-Taps* (1865–1866). It was included in *Leaves of Grass* (1881) with very minor revisions.

To a President, p. 424: First printed in the 1860 edition of *Leaves of Grass*, the poem was originally addressed to James Buchanan, Lincoln's predecessor. The poem was not included in *Drum-Taps* or

Sequel to Drum-Taps (collections inspired by Lincoln and the Civil War) but reappeared in the 1867 and 1871 editions of *Leaves of Grass*.

I Sit and Look Out, p. 424: "Leaves of Grass. 17" in 1860, "Leaves of Grass. 5" in 1867, the poem gained its present title in the 1871 edition of *Leaves of Grass*.

To Rich Givers, p. 425: Appearing under this title in 1860, the poem was included with minor revisions in 1867, 1871, and 1876, and achieved its final form in 1881.

The Dalliance of the Eagles, p. 425: New to *Leaves of Grass* in 1881, this poem was published a year earlier in the magazine *Cope's Tobacco Plant*.

Roaming in Thought, p. 426: A new poem in the 1881 edition of *Leaves of Grass*, the poem remained unrevised through Whitman's lifetime.

A Farm Picture, p. 426: The poem first appeared under the present title, but without the third line, in *Drum-Taps* (1865). The final line was added for the 1871 edition of *Leaves of Grass*.

A Child's Amaze, p. 426: The poem first appeared with its present title in *Drum-Taps* (1865).

The Runner, p. 426: The poem first appeared in *Leaves of Grass* in 1867 and was included in all subsequent editions.

Beautiful Women, p. 427: Originally part of the "Debris" cluster, a series of seventeen untitled poems published in the 1860 edition of *Leaves of Grass*, the poem was entitled "Picture" in 1867 and gained its current title in 1871.

Mother and Babe, p. 427: First published under its current title in *Drum-Taps* (1865), the poem remained ungrouped until it was included in "By the Roadside" in 1881.

Thought, p. 427: The seventh of the "Thoughts" poem series of 1860, this poem gained its current "singular" title in 1871.

Visor'd, p. 427: Part of the "Debris" cluster in 1860, these lines gained their present title in 1867.

Thought, p. 427: Originally part of "Thoughts. 4" in the 1860 edition of *Leaves of Grass*, these lines gained their current title in 1871.

Gliding o'er All, p. 428: This poem originally appeared untitled and italicized, on the title page of *Passage to India* (1871). It gained its current title in the 1872 edition.

Hast Never Come to Thee an Hour, p. 428: This poem first appeared in the 1881 edition of *Leaves of Grass*.

Thought, p. 428: A single line of "Thoughts. 4" in 1860, the poem received its current title in the 1871 edition of *Leaves of Grass*.

To Old Age, p. 428: First appearing under this title in 1860, the poem was also published in 1867, 1871, 1872, and 1876 before being moved to the "By the Roadside" cluster in 1881.

Locations and Times, p. 428: Originally part of "Sun-down Poem" (the 1856 version of "Crossing Brooklyn Ferry"), this poem became "Leaves of Grass. 23" in 1860 and "Leaves of Grass. 5" in 1867. It gained its current title in 1871.

Offerings, p. 429: Originally part of the "Debris" cluster of the 1860 edition of *Leaves of Grass*, this poem was titled "Picture" in 1867 and received its present title in 1871.

To the States, To Identify the 16th, 17th, or 18th Presidentiad, p. 429: This poem was first published under its current title in 1860 and was placed in all subsequent editions.

Drum-Taps, p. 430: This 1881 collection of forty-three poems gathers thirty-eight of its works from either *Drum-Taps* (1865) or *Sequel to Drum-Taps* (1865–1866). Only five of the poems were from other collections: "Virginia—The West," "Not the Pilot," "Ethiopia Saluting the Colors," "Delicate Cluster," and "Adieu to a Soldier."

First O Songs for a Prelude, p. 430: This poem was originally entitled "Drum Taps" in 1865, taking its first line for its title in 1881. Four lines beginning "Aroused and angry" were placed at the beginning of the poem in 1871 and 1876; these lines were eventually moved to "The Wound-Dresser," another *Drum-Taps* poem.

Eighteen Sixty-One, p. 432: In *Drum-Taps*, the poem was titled "1861." It gained its present title in the 1881 edition of *Leaves of Grass*.

Beat! Beat! Drums!, p. 433: Under this title, the poem was originally published in two periodicals (*Harper's Weekly* and the *New York Leader*) on September 28, 1861. It was included in *Drum-Taps* (1865).

From Paumanok Starting I Fly like a Bird, p. 434: The poem has maintained this title since its first appearance in *Drum-Taps* (1865).

Song of the Banner at Daybreak, p. 435: The poem was published under this title in *Drum-Taps* (1865).

Rise O Days from Your Fathomless Deeps, p. 441: The poem's title remains the same as in 1865. It became part of the "Drum-Taps" annex in the 1867 edition of *Leaves of Grass*, and the "Drum-Taps" clusters of 1871 and 1881.

Virginia—The West, p. 444: First published in the *Kansas Magazine* of March 1872, the poem was part of *As a Strong Bird on Pinions Free*, an 1872 collection that was integrated into the 1881 edition of *Leaves of Grass* as "Thy Mother with Thy Equal Brood." Whitman moved "Virginia—The West" to "Drum-Taps" in this edition.

City of Ships, p. 444: First appearing in *Drum-Taps* (1865), the poem was part of the "Drum-Taps" annex in the 1867 edition of *Leaves of Grass*, and the "Drum-Taps" clusters of 1871 and 1881.

The Centenarian's Story, p. 445: The poem's title and original form were preserved from 1865 through all subsequent editions.

Cavalry Crossing a Ford, p. 449: The 1865 title remained unchanged in following editions.

Bivouac on a Mountain Side, p. 450: The 1865 title remained unchanged, and the poem was subject to minor revisions through following editions.

An Army Corps on the March, p. 450: Originally entitled "An Army on the March," the poem was included in *Sequel to Drum-Taps* (1865–1866). It received its present title in the 1871 edition of *Leaves of Grass*.

By the Bivouac's Fitful Flame, p. 451: The title and poem are unchanged from their first appearance in *Drum-Taps* (1865).

Come Up from the Fields Father, p. 451: Title remained unchanged from its first appearance in 1865. The poem remains one of the most anthologized in the *Drum-Taps* series.

Vigil Strange I Kept on the Field One Night, p. 453: The title remained unchanged from its first appearance in 1865; the poem received minor revisions in following editions.

A March in the Ranks Hard-prest, and the Road Unknown, p. 454: The poem's title remained unchanged from its first version in 1865.

A Sight in Camp in the Daybreak Gray and Dim, p. 455: Entitled "A Sight in Camp in the Day-Break Grey and Dim" when it first appeared in 1865, the poem had numbered stanzas through the 1871 edition of *Leaves of Grass*.

As Toilsome I Wander'd Virginia's Woods, p. 456: The title and poem itself remain unchanged since their first appearance in *Drum-Taps* (1865).

Not the Pilot, p. 457: Originally part of the "Debris" cluster in the 1860 edition of *Leaves of Grass*, it was given its current title in 1867 and put into the "Drum-Taps" cluster in *Leaves of Grass* (1871).

Year That Trembled and Reel'd Beneath Me, p. 457: The poem and title remain unchanged since their first appearance in *Drum-Taps* (1865).

The Wound-Dresser, p. 457: Entitled "The Dresser" in 1865, the poem received its current title in the 1876 "Centennial" Edition of *Leaves of Grass*.

Long, Too Long America, p. 460: Originally entitled "Long, Too Long, O Land" in 1865, the poem gained its current title in 1881.

Give Me the Splendid Silent Sun, p. 461: The poem retains its 1865 title and form.

Dirge for Two Veterans, p. 462: First appearing in *Sequel to Drum-Taps* (1865–1866), the poem was subject to only minor revisions in punctuation through subsequent editions.

Over the Carnage Rose Prophetic a Voice, p. 464: This poem (along with "For You O Democracy," a Calamus poem from 1867 to 1881) has its roots in "Calamus. 5" from the 1860 edition of *Leaves of Grass*. It gained its current title when it was revised and included in *Drum-Taps* (1865).

I Saw Old General at Bay, p. 465: The poem preserves its original 1865 title; Whitman made only minor revisions to punctuation through subsequent editions.

The Artilleryman's Vision, p. 465: Originally entitled "The Veteran's Vision" in 1865, the poem gained its current title in 1871. For the most part, Whitman made only minor alterations to the poem's punctuation through subsequent editions.

Ethiopia Saluting the Colors, p. 466: Originally subtitled "A Reminiscence of 1864," this poem was first published in the 1871 edition of *Leaves of Grass*. It was placed in the "Drum-Taps" cluster in 1881.

Not Youth Pertains to Me, p. 467: The poem retains its 1865 title, though in 1871 the last two lines were revised from: "[Intervals] I have strung together a few songs, / Fit for war, and the life of the camp."

Race of Veterans, p. 467: First included in *Sequel to Drum-Taps* (1865–1866), the poem has kept its original title and form, with minor revisions in punctuation.

World Take Good Notice, p. 468: Originally "World, Take Good Notice," this poem retains its 1865 title and content; only the number of line 3 was altered from "thirty-six," reflecting the addition of two states to the union.

O Tan-faced Prairie-Boy, p. 468: The poem retains its 1865 title and most of its original form, with minor revisions to punctuation.

Look Down Fair Moon, p. 468: The poem carries its 1865 title. Only minor revisions in punctuation were made through subsequent editions.

Reconciliation, p. 468: Originally included in *Sequel to Drum-Taps* (1865–1866), the poem retains its original title and most of its original wording.

How Solemn as One by One, p. 469: Originally included in *Sequel to Drum-Taps* (1865–1866), the poem gained its subtitle in 1871.

As I Lay with My Head In Your Lap Camerado, p. 469: First included in *Sequel to Drum-Taps* (1865–1866), the poem gained one major revision in 1871: two lines originally included after line 4 were omitted: "Indeed I am myself the real soldier; / It is not he, there, with his bayonet, and not the red-striped artilleryman."

Delicate Cluster, p. 470: The poem as titled first appeared in the 1871 edition of *Leaves of Grass* and was placed in the "Drum-Taps" cluster of *Leaves of Grass* (1881).

To a Certain Civilian, p. 470: Entitled "Did You Ask Dulcet Rhymes from Me?" in 1865, the poem gained its current title (and four additional lines to its original six) in *Passage to India* (1871). In 1881 it was included in the "Drum-Taps" cluster of *Leaves of Grass*.

Lo, Victress on the Peaks, p. 471: Originally included in *Sequel to Drum-Taps* (1865–1866) as "Lo! Victress on the Peaks!", the poem gained its present, calmer title in 1876.

Spirit Whose Work Is Done, p. 471: Originally included in *Sequel to Drum-Taps* (1865–1866), the poem gained its subtitle in 1871.

Adieu to a Soldier, p. 472: First published in 1871, the poem was included in the "Drum-Taps" cluster of *Leaves of Grass* (1881).

Turn O Libertad, p. 473: Originally included under its present title in *Drum-Taps* (1865), the poem was subject to minor revisions through subsequent editions.

To the Leaven'd Soil They Trod, p. 473: The final poem in the "Drum-Taps" cluster since its first appearance in *Sequel to Drum-Taps* (1865–1866).

Memories of President Lincoln, p. 475: While the previous cluster, "Drum-Taps," focuses on the theme of the Civil War, the four poems comprising the cluster "Memories of President Lincoln" all make explicit mention of Whitman's hero, Abraham Lincoln. These poems here were first grouped as "President Lincoln's Burial Hymn" in *Passage to India* (1871) and became known as "Memories of President Lincoln" in 1881.

When Lilacs Last in the Dooryard Bloom'd, p. 475: This great elegy to Lincoln was first included in *Sequel to Drum-Taps* (1865–1866). Minor changes in punctuation and word choice were made in subsequent editions, with the exception of one particular revision near the end of the poem (see endnote 70 to the "Death-bed" Edition). Some minor revisions were made to the poem for the 1871 and 1881 publications.

O Captain! My Captain!, p. 484: Published in the New York *Saturday Press* on November 4, 1865, the poem appeared in *Sequel to Drum-Taps* (1865–1866) and *Passage to India* (1871) and the annex of the same title in 1876.

Hush'd Be the Camps To-Day, p. 485: When the poem was first published in *Drum-Taps* (1865), the subtitle read: "A. L. Buried April 19, 1865." He corrected the erroneous date in the 1871 edition of *Passage to India*.

This Dust Was Once the Man, p. 485: First published in *Passage to India* (1871), this poem was not revised in its 1871, 1876, and 1881 publications.

By Blue Ontario's Shore, p. 485: In *Leaves of Grass* (1856) this poem was "8—Poem of Many in One." For the 1860 edition Whitman changed the title to "Chants Democratic. 1"; it appeared in the 1867 annex "Songs before Parting" as "As I Sat Alone by Blue Ontario's Shore" and gained its present title in 1881. Stanza numbers were added in 1860, section numbers in 1867. The form of the poem was much revised through these editions, and a good portion of its original 280 lines was taken from (or inspired by) the 1855 "[Preface]."

Reversals, p. 501: These six lines have their origin in a fifty-seven-line poem entitled "Poem of the Proposition of Nakedness" first published in 1856. In 1860 the poem became "Chants Democratic. 5"; in 1867, 1871, and 1876 it was retitled "Respondez." The poem took its final form and title in 1881.

Autumn Rivulets, p. 502: This cluster was new to the 1881 edition of *Leaves of Grass*, though most of the poems were previously published in earlier editions or periodicals.

As Consequent, Etc., p. 502: This introductory poem is one of the few in "Autumn Rivulets" that is new to the 1881 edition of *Leaves of Grass* (though some lines were taken from the 1876 poems "Two Rivulets" and "Or from That Sea of Time").

The Return of the Heroes, p. 503: First published in *The Galaxy* in September 1867 as "A Carol of Harvest for 1867," the poem found its way into *Passage to India* (1871) and *Two Rivulets* (1876). Stanza and section numbers were added in 1871, and the present title was first used in 1881.

There Was a Child Went Forth, p. 509: See note to "There Was a Child Went Forth," p. 138.

Old Ireland, p. 511: The poem was first published in the *New York Leader* of November 2, 1861; in its final forum, it was placed in *Drum-Taps* in 1865.

The City Dead-House, p. 511: Published under this title in the 1867 edition of *Leaves of Grass*, the poem was subject to very minor revisions through 1881.

This Compost, p. 512: In 1856 this poem was known as "9 — Poem of Wonder at The Resurrection of The Wheat." The title was changed to "Leaves of Grass—4" in 1860, "This Compost!" in 1867, and its present title in 1871. Minor revisions (mostly changes in punctuation) were made to it until its 1881 publication.

To a Foil'd European Revolutionaire, p. 514: First published in *Leaves of Grass* (1856) as "Liberty Poem for Asia, Africa, Europe, America, Australia, Cuba, and the Archipelagoes of the Sea," the poem became "To a Foiled Revolter or Revoltress" in 1860 and 1867, and received its current title in 1871. Stanza numbers were added in 1860, section numbers in 1871. The poem was subject to revision, and several lines were removed between 1856 and 1860.

Unnamed Lands, p. 516: The poem was published in the 1860 edition under its present title and was subject to minor revisions after 1871. It achieved its final form in 1881.

Song of Prudence, p. 517: Entitled "Poem of the Last Explanation of Prudence" in 1856, the poem became "Leaves of Grass. 5" in 1860 and "Manhattan's Streets I Saunter'd Pondering" in 1865. It gained its present title in 1881. Many of its lines were taken from Whitman's 1855 "[Preface]."

The Singer in the Prison, p. 520: First published in the *Saturday Evening Visitor* on December 25, 1869, the poem was included in the 1871 edition of *Passage to India* and gained its final revisions for the 1881 edition of *Leaves of Grass*.

Warble for Lilac-Time, p. 522: First published in *The Galaxy* in May 1870, the poem appeared in *Passage to India* (1871) as "Warble for Lilac Time" and lost several lines before achieving its final form in 1881.

Outlines for a Tomb, p. 523: First published in *The Galaxy* in January 1870 under the title "Brother of All, with Generous Hand," this poem was written for millionaire philanthropist George Peabody (1795–1869). Whitman included it in *Passage to India* (1871); he gave it the title "Outlines for a Tomb" and shortened it by several lines for the 1881 edition.

Out from Behind This Mask, p. 525: After first appearing in the *New York Tribune* in 1876, the poem was published in the "Centennial" Edition of *Leaves of Grass* (1876) as well as *Two Rivulets*, a companion volume to *Leaves of Grass* also published that year. Included in *Leaves of Grass* (1876) was a portrait engraving of Whitman by W. J. Linton (based on an 1871 photo of the poet taken by G. C. Potter). This portrait was not included in the 1881 edition of *Leaves of Grass*.

Vocalism, p. 526: The 1881 poem is a conflation of two earlier works. "Chants Democratic. 12" of 1860 contributed the first stanza;

"Leaves of Grass. 21" of 1860 is the source of the second. Both stanzas lost lines in the fusion of 1881.

To Him That Was Crucified, p. 528: First published in the "Messenger Leaves" cluster of the 1860 edition, the poem retained its original title and most of its form through republications.

You Felons on Trial in Courts, p. 528: "Leaves of Grass. 13" in 1860, the poem was reduced by several lines and received its present title in 1867.

Laws for Creations, p. 529: "Chants Democratic. 13" in 1860 and "Leaves of Grass. 3" in 1867, the poem gained its present title in 1871. After 1860 the poem was shortened by several lines.

To a Common Prostitute, p. 530: The poem appeared under this title as one of the "Messenger Leaves" in the 1860 edition of *Leaves of Grass*. It was not revised for future publications.

I Was Looking a Long While, p. 530: "Chants Democratic. 19" in 1860, the poem received its current title in 1867 and underwent only minor revisions.

Thought, p. 531: "Thoughts. 3" in the 1860 edition, the poem became "Thought" in 1871.

Miracles, p. 531: "Poem of Perfect Miracles" in 1856 and "Leaves of Grass. 8" in 1860, the poem took its present title in 1867. Revisions included shortening the poem by eleven lines for the 1881 edition.

Sparkles from the Wheel, p. 532: The poem possessed this title and text when it was first published in *Passage to India* (1871).

To a Pupil, p. 533: The poem had this title and text upon its first appearance in the "Messenger Leaves" cluster of *Leaves of Grass* (1860).

Unfolded Out of the Folds, p. 533: First published in *Leaves of Grass* (1856) as "Poem of Women," the poem received its present title and final revisions for *Leaves of Grass* (1871).

What Am I After All, p. 534: "Leaves of Grass. 22" in 1860 and "Leaves of Grass. 4" in the 1867 annex "Songs before Parting," the poem gained its present title in *Passage to India* (1871).

Kosmos, p. 534: Published in *Leaves of Grass* (1860) under its current title, the poem was subject to minor revisions for its 1867 republication.

Others May Praise What They Like, p. 535: Published under this title in *Drum-Taps* (1865), the poem underwent minor revisions before achieving its final form in 1881.

Who Learns My Lesson Complete?, p. 535: The eleventh of the twelve original poems in the 1855 edition, the poem became "29—Lesson Poem" in 1856, "Leaves of Grass. 11" in 1860, and "Leaves of Grass. 3" in 1867, and it achieved its current title in *Passage to India* (1871). It was heavily revised, especially between the 1855 and 1860 editions.

Tests, p. 537: Published in this form and with this title in *Leaves of Grass* (1860).

The Torch, p. 537: First published under this title in *Drum-Taps* (1865), the poem was subject to very minor revision before achieving its final form in 1871.

O Star of France (1870–71), p. 537: First published in *The Galaxy* in June 1871, the poem was included in *As a Strong Bird on Pinions Free and Other Poems* (1872), reprinted in *Two Rivulets* (1876), and revised in *Leaves of Grass* (1881).

The Ox-tamer, p. 539: Published in the *New York Daily Graphic* in December 1874, the poem appeared under its current title in *Two Rivulets* (1876) and achieved its final form for *Leaves of Grass* (1881).

An Old Man's Thought of School. For the Inauguration of a Public School, Camden, New Jersey, 1874, p. 540: Published in the *New York Daily Graphic* of November 1874, the poem was included in *Two Rivulets* (1876) and revised for inclusion in *Leaves of Grass* (1881).

Wandering at Morn, p. 540: Published in the *New York Daily Graphic* in March 1873 as "The Singing Thrush," the poem was published in *Two Rivulets* (1876) and under its present title in *Leaves of Grass* (1881).

Italian Music in Dakota, p. 541: This poem was new to the 1881 edition of *Leaves of Grass.*

With All Thy Gifts, p. 542: Published in the *New York Daily Graphic* of March 1873 under this title, and reprinted in *Two Rivulets* (1876) and *Leaves of Grass* (1881).

My Picture-Gallery, p. 542: This poem has its beginnings in a pre-1855 notebook entitled "Pictures." First published in *The American* on October 30, 1880, the poem was published in *Leaves of Grass* (1881).

The Prairie States, p. 542: The poem was first published in *Leaves of Grass* (1881), though the manuscript of the poem was printed in the *Art Autograph* of May 1880.

Proud Music of the Storm, p. 543: First published in the *Atlantic Monthly* of February 1869, the poem was included in *Passage to India* (1871) and *Two Rivulets* (1876) before becoming part of the "Autumn Rivulets" cluster of *Leaves of Grass* (1881).

Passage to India, p. 549: First published as the title piece to *Passage to India* (1871), the poem appeared in *Leaves of Grass* 1871 and 1872 and in *Two Rivulets* (1876) before its inclusion in "Autumn Rivulets" in 1881. The poem was lightly revised after 1871.

Prayer of Columbus, p. 558: First published in *Harper's* of March 1874, the poem was included in *Two Rivulets* (1876) and underwent final revisions for its publication in *Leaves of Grass* (1881).

The Sleepers, p. 560: See note to "The Sleepers" (p. 109), above.

Transpositions, p. 570: This poem is constructed of three lines taken from "Poem of the Propositions of Nakedness" in the 1856 edition (lines 46, 44, and 22).

To Think of Time, p. 570: Originally the third of the twelve untitled poems in the 1855 edition, this poem was heavily revised before appearing in this version in 1881. Entitled "Burial Poem" in 1856 and "Burial" in 1860 and 1867, it achieved its current title in *Passage to India* (1871). Stanza numbers were added in 1860, section numbers in 1867.

Whispers of Heavenly Death, p. 577: Whitman first used this title for a cluster of fifteen poems in *Passage to India* (1871); for the 1881 edition of *Leaves of Grass*, he included five more poems to make up the current eighteen.

Darest Thou Now O Soul, p. 577: Whitman published a series of five poems in the *Broadway Magazine* of October 1868, together entitled "Whispers of Heavenly Death." In order, the current titles of the poems as they appear in this cluster are: "Whispers of Heavenly Death"; "Darest Thou Now O Soul"; "A Noiseless Patient Spider"; "The Last Invocation"; and "Pensive and Faltering." "Whispers of Heavenly Death" was included in *Passage to India* (1871) and achieved its final form in the 1881 edition of *Leaves of Grass*.

Whispers of Heavenly Death, p. 577: See note to "Darest Thou Now O Soul," above. The poem remained unchanged from its inclusion in *Passage to India* (1871) to its 1881 incarnation here.

Chanting the Square Deific, p. 578: Originally written for *Sequel to Drum-Taps* (1865–1866), this poem was lightly revised before appearing in its final version in 1881.

Of Him I Love Day and Night, p. 580: Originally "Calamus. 17," the poem was retitled "Of Him I Love Day and Night" for the 1867 edition, with minor revisions made to its text between its 1860 and 1871 publications.

Yet, Yet, Ye Downcast Hours, p. 581: The poem of three stanzas and with the current title first appeared in the original "Whispers of Heavenly Death" cluster of *Passage to India* (1871). The second and third stanzas have their root in sections five and six of the 1860 poem "Debris."

As if a Phantom Caress'd Me, p. 582: Like "Yet, Yet, Ye Downcast Hours," this poem has roots in the 1860 poem "Debris" (the final section). "As if a Phantom Caress'd Me" took its final title and form in 1867.

Assurances, p. 582: First appearing as the sixteen-line "Faith Poem" in 1856, the poem was revised for the 1860 and 1867 editions before appearing in its final form in the "Whispers of Heavenly Death" cluster in *Passage to India* (1871).

Quicksand Years, p. 583: First published in *Drum-Taps* (1865), the poem took its final title and form in the "Whispers of Heavenly Death" cluster of *Passage to India* (1871).

That Music Always Round Me, p. 583: "Calamus. 21" in 1860, the poem took on its present form and title in 1867, and appeared in the cluster "Whispers of Heavenly Death" in *Passage to India* (1871).

What Ship Puzzled at Sea, p. 584: The first four lines of "Calamus. 31" in 1860, the poem was published in 1867, 1871, and 1876, but assumed its present title only for the 1881 edition of *Leaves of Grass*.

A Noiseless Patient Spider, p. 584: One of the five poems published in the *Broadway Magazine* of October 1868 (see above note to "Darest Thou Now O Soul," p. 577), the poem was included in *Passage to India* (1871) and underwent its final revisions for the 1881 edition of *Leaves of Grass*.

O Living Always, Always Dying, p. 584: "Calamus. 27" in 1860, the poem took its present title and form in 1867.

To One Shortly to Die, p. 585: Published with the current title in *Leaves of Grass* (1860), the poem achieved its final form in *Passage to India* (1871).

Night on the Prairies, p. 585: "Leaves of Grass. 15" in 1860 and "Leaves of Grass. 3" in 1867, the poem achieved its current title and form in *Passage to India* (1871).

Thought, p. 586: This poem was the fifth in a series of poems entitled "Thoughts" in 1860 and 1867. It was first included in the cluster "Whispers of Heavenly Death" in 1881.

The Last Invocation, p. 587: One of the five poems published in the *Broadway Magazine* of October 1868 (see above note to "Darest Thou Now O Soul," p. 577), the poem was included in *Passage to India* (1871), *Leaves of Grass* (1872), *Two Rivulets* (1876), and *Leaves of Grass* (1881) without revisions.

As I Watch'd the Ploughman Ploughing, p. 587: Published with this title and in its final form in *Passage to India* (1871).

Pensive and Faltering, p. 587: One of the five poems published in the *Broadway Magazine* of October 1868 (see above note to "Darest Thou Now O Soul," p. 577), the poem was included in *Passage to India* (1871), *Leaves of Grass* (1872), *Two Rivulets* (1876), and *Leaves of Grass* (1881).

Thou Mother with Thy Equal Brood, p. 588: This work has its beginnings as "As a Strong Bird on Pinions Free," a commencement poem Whitman delivered at Dartmouth College on June 26, 1872. He published this poem and six others the same year, in a small volume of the same title; in 1876 the cluster "As a Strong Bird on Pinions Free" was published as part of *Two Rivulets*. The poem was revised, expanded, and given the title "Thou Mother with Thy Equal Brood" in *Leaves of Grass* (1881).

A Paumanok Picture, p. 594: These seven lines first became a poem for the 1881 edition of *Leaves of Grass*. From *Leaves of Grass* (1856) to *Leaves of Grass* (1876), they served as the eighth canto of "Salut au Monde."

From Noon to Starry Night, p. 595: This cluster of twenty-two poems was new to the 1881 edition of *Leaves of Grass*, as was the "Autumn Rivulets" cluster. Five of the poems are new to *Leaves of Grass*, and the others are taken from seven different editions, though a majority of them were written in the 1870s.

Thou Orb Aloft Full-Dazzling, p. 595: First published in *The American* on June 4, 1881, as "A Summer Invocation," the poem was published with its current title in *Leaves of Grass* (1881).

Faces, p. 596: This poem was originally the sixth of the twelve poems in *Leaves of Grass* (1855). "Poem of Faces" in 1856, "A Leaf of Faces" in 1867, and finally "Faces" in 1881, it achieved its final form for the 1881 edition.

The Mystic Trumpeter, p. 600: First published in *Kansas Magazine* in February 1872, the poem was one of seven poems in the 1872 annex "As a Strong Bird on Pinions Free" (1872). It appeared in its final form in the 1881 edition of *Leaves of Grass*.

To a Locomotive in Winter, p. 603: This popular favorite was first published in the *New York Daily Tribune* of February 19, 1876, then in *Two Rivulets* (1876) and *Leaves of Grass* (1881) without revision.

O Magnet-South, p. 604: Published as "Longings from Home" in *Leaves of Grass* (1860), the poem received its final form and present title in *Leaves of Grass* 1881.

Mannahatta, p. 606: Included in the 1860, 1867, and 1871 editions of *Leaves of Grass*, this poem appeared in 1881 with three final lines substituting for seven original lines (see endnote 100 to the "Deathbed" Edition).

All Is Truth, p. 607: "Leaves of Grass. 18" in 1860 and "Leaves of Grass. 1" in the "Songs before Parting" annex to *Leaves of Grass* (1867), the poem achieved its current title in 1871.

A Riddle Song, p. 608: A new poem for the 1881 edition, "A Riddle Song" was first published in *Forney's Progress* on April 17, 1880.

Excelsior, p. 609: "Poem of the Heart of the Son of Manhattan Island" in 1856 and "Chants Democratic. 15" in 1860, the poem gained its present title in 1867. It was revised until its publication in the 1881 edition of *Leaves of Grass*.

Ah Poverties, Wincings, and Sulky Retreats, p. 610: First appearing in *Sequel to Drum-Taps* (1865–1866), the poem was republished with only one minor revision through all later editions up to 1881.

Thoughts, p. 610: First titled "Thought" in 1860 and 1867, the poem gained its current title in 1871.

Mediums, p. 611: "Chants Democratic. 16" in 1860, this poem gained its present title in the 1867 edition and also appeared in *Passage to India* in 1871 before inclusion in the 1881 *Leaves of Grass*.

Weave in, My Hardy Life, p. 611: First published in *Drum-Taps* (1865), the poem was only slightly revised before achieving its final form in 1881.

Spain, 1873–74, p. 612: First appearing in the *New York Daily Graphic* of March 24, 1873, the poem was reprinted in *Two Rivulets* (1876) before inclusion in the 1881 edition of *Leaves of Grass*.

By Broad Potomac's Shore, p. 612: Published under this title in *As a Strong Bird on Pinions Free* (1872), the poem was also included in *Two Rivulets* (1876) before appearing in *Leaves of Grass* (1881).

From Far Dakota's Cañons, p. 613: First appearing in the *New York Tribune* of June 18, 1876, as "A Death Sonnet for Custer," the poem was included in the 1876 edition of *Leaves of Grass* before gaining its final position in the "From Noon to Starry Night" cluster in 1881.

Old War-Dreams, p. 614: First appearing in *Sequel to Drum-Taps* (1865–1866), the poem was revised and published in 1867 and 1871 before its inclusion in the 1881 edition.

Thick-sprinkled Bunting, p. 615: First published as "Flag of Stars, Thick-sprinkled Bunting" in *Drum-Taps* (1865), the poem received its present title in 1871.

What Best I See in Thee, p. 615: The dedication to Ulysses S. Grant first appeared in the 1881 edition of *Leaves of Grass*.

Spirit That Form'd This Scene, p. 616: This poem was a new inclusion in *Leaves of Grass* (1881).

As I Walk These Broad Majestic Days, p. 616: "Chants Democratic. 21" in 1860 and "As I Walk Solitary, Unattended" in the "Songs before Parting" annex to *Leaves of Grass* (1867), the poem was given its current title in 1871. It was revised until it achieved its final form in 1881.

A Clear Midnight, p. 617: This was a new inclusion to the 1881 edition of *Leaves of Grass*.

Songs of Parting, p. 618: This cluster is new to the 1881 edition, though all but two of the seventeen poems ("As at Thy Portals Also Death" and "The Sobbing of the Bells") appeared in earlier editions.

As the Time Draws Nigh, p. 618: Originally titled "To My Soul" in the 1860 edition of *Leaves of Grass*, this poem was originally much longer and more personal; it was revised for inclusion in the "Songs before Parting" annex of 1867 and was retitled "As the Time Draws Nigh" in 1871.

Years of the Modern, p. 618: Published as "Years of the Unperformed" in *Drum-Taps* (1865), the poem took on its present title when it appeared in "Songs of Parting" in *Leaves of Grass* (1872).

Ashes of Soldiers, p. 620: First published in *Drum-Taps* of 1865 as "Hymn of Dead Soldiers," this poem was also included in *Passage to India* of 1871, the 1872 edition of *Leaves of Grass*, and the 1876 companion volume *Two Rivulets*.

Thoughts, p. 621: The first part of this poem was "Chants Democratic. 9" and the second part "Chants Democratic. 11" in *Leaves of Grass* (1860). In 1867 the poems were combined and formed the first two sections of "Thoughts," which was republished in 1871 and 1881.

Song at Sunset, p. 623: Originally entitled "Chants Democratic. 8" in the 1860 edition, this poem gained its present title in 1867 was republished in 1871 and 1881.

As at Thy Portals Also Death, p. 625: This elegy to Whitman's mother was new to the 1881 edition of *Leaves of Grass*.

My Legacy, p. 626: First published as "Souvenirs of Democracy" in *As a Strong Bird on Pinions Free* (1872), the poem was reprinted in *Two Rivulets* (1876) and appeared in *Leaves of Grass* (1881) under its present title.

Pensive on Her Dead Gazing, p. 626: Appearing first in *Drum-Taps* (1865), the poem underwent minor revisions through its republication in 1867, 1871, and 1881.

Camps of Green, p. 627: This poem shares the publication history of "Pensive on Her Dead Gazing," appearing first in *Drum-Taps* (1865) and in final form in *Leaves of Grass* (1881).

The Sobbing of the Bells, p. 628: First published in the *Boston Daily Globe* of September 27, 1881, it was included in *Leaves of Grass* (1881).

As They Draw to a Close, p. 629: First published in *Passage to India* (1871) as "Thought," the poem achieved its final form in 1881.

Joy, Shipmate, Joy!, p. 629: Published with the current title and text in *Passage to India* (1871).

The Untold Want, p. 629: Published with the current title and text in *Passage to India* (1871).

Portals, p. 630: Published with the current title and text in *Passage to India* (1871).

These Carols, p. 630: Published with the current title and text in *Passage to India* (1871).

Now Finalé to the Shore, p. 630: Published in *Passage to India* (1871) and included with minor revisions in *Leaves of Grass* (1881).

So Long!, p. 630: First published in *Leaves of Grass* (1860), "So Long!" maintained its place as the farewell poem in all subsequent editions of *Leaves of Grass*. After 1860, the poem was shortened by more than twenty lines.

First Annex: Sands at Seventy, p. 635: This cluster of sixty-five poems was first published in the miscellany *November Boughs* in 1888 (a year before Whitman's seventieth birthday). "Sands at Seventy" was first included in *Leaves of Grass* in 1889. Like the poems of "Second Annex: Good-Bye My Fancy," most of these poems were written after 1884.

Mannahatta, p. 635: First published in the *New York Herald* on February 27, 1888, the poem was included in the "Sands at Seventy" annex of *November Boughs* (1888) with minor revision.

Paumanok, p. 635: First published in the *New York Herald* on February 29, 1888, the poem was included in the "Sands at Seventy" annex of *November Boughs* (1888).

From Montauk Point, p. 635: First published in the *New York Herald* on March 1, 1888, the poem was included in the "Sands at Seventy" annex of *November Boughs* (1888).

To Those Who've Fail'd, p. 636: First published in the *New York Herald* on January 27, 1888, the poem was included in the "Sands at Seventy" annex of *November Boughs* (1888) with minor revision.

A Carol Closing Sixty-nine, p. 636: First published in the *New York Herald* on May 21, 1888, the poem was included in the "Sands at Seventy" annex of *November Boughs* (1888).

The Bravest Soldiers, p. 636: First published in the *New York Herald* on March 18, 1888, the poem was included in the "Sands at Seventy" annex of *November Boughs* (1888).

A Font of Type, p. 637: First published in the "Sands at Seventy" annex of *November Boughs* (1888).

As I Sit Writing Here, p. 637: First published in the *New York Herald* on May 14, 1888, the poem was included in the "Sands at Seventy" annex of *November Boughs* (1888).

My Canary Bird, p. 637: First published in the *New York Herald* on March 2, 1888, the poem was included in the "Sands at Seventy" annex of *November Boughs* (1888).

Queries to My Seventieth Year, p. 637: First published in the *New York Herald* on May 2, 1888, the poem was included in the "Sands at Seventy" annex of *November Boughs* (1888).

The Wallabout Martyrs, p. 638: First published in the *New York Herald* on March 16, 1888, the poem was included in the "Sands at Seventy" annex of *November Boughs* (1888).

The First Dandelion, p. 638: First published in the *New York Herald* on March 12, 1888, the poem was included in the "Sands at Seventy" annex of *November Boughs* (1888).

America, p. 638: This poem was published in the *New York Herald* of April 23, 1888, and then included in the "Sands at Seventy" annex of *November Boughs* (1888).

Memories, p. 639: First published in the "Sands at Seventy" annex of *November Boughs* (1888).

To-Day and Thee, p. 639: First published in the *New York Herald* on April 23, 1888, the poem was included in the "Sands at Seventy" annex of *November Boughs* (1888).

After the Dazzle of Day, p. 639: First published in the *New York Herald* on February 3, 1888, the poem was included in the "Sands at Seventy" annex of *November Boughs* (1888).

Abraham Lincoln, Born Feb. 12, 1809, p. 639: First published in the *New York Herald* on February 12, 1888, the poem was included in the "Sands at Seventy" annex of *November Boughs* (1888).

Out of May's Shows Selected, p. 640: First published in the *New York Herald* of May 10, 1888, the poem was included in the "Sands at Seventy" annex of *November Boughs* (1888).

Halcyon Days, p. 640: First published in the *New York Herald* of January 29, 1888, the poem was included in the "Sands at Seventy" annex of *November Boughs* (1888).

Fancies at Navesink, p. 640: This group of eight poems was first published in the London publication *Nineteenth Century* in August 1885; all were included with the same text and title in the "Sands at Seventy" annex of *November Boughs* (1888).

Election Day, November, 1884, p. 643: First published in the *Philadelphia Press* of October 26, 1884, the poem was included in the "Sands at Seventy" annex of *November Boughs* (1888).

With Husky-Haughty Lips, O Sea!, p. 644: First published in *Harper's Monthly* in March 1884, the poem was included in the "Sands at Seventy" annex of *November Boughs* (1888).

Death of General Grant, p. 645: First published in *Harper's Weekly* on May 16, 1885, the poem was included in the "Sands at Seventy" annex of *November Boughs* (1888).

Red Jacket (From Aloft), p. 645: First published in the *Philadelphia Press* of October 10, 1884, the poem was included in the "Sands at Seventy" annex of *November Boughs* (1888).

Washington's Monument, February, 1885, p. 646: First published in the *Philadelphia Press* of February 22, 1885, the poem was included in the "Sands at Seventy" annex of *November Boughs* (1888).

Of That Blithe Throat of Thine, p. 646: First published in *Harper's Monthly* of January 1885, the poem was included in the "Sands at Seventy" annex of *November Boughs* (1888).

Broadway, p. 647: First published in the *New York Herald* on April 10, 1888, the poem was included in the "Sands at Seventy" annex of *November Boughs* (1888).

To Get the Final Lilt of Songs, p. 647: First published in the *New York Herald* of April 16, 1888, the poem was included in the "Sands at Seventy" annex of *November Boughs* (1888).

Old Salt Kossabone, p. 648: First published in the *New York Herald* of February 25, 1888, the poem was included in the "Sands at Seventy" annex of *November Boughs* (1888).

The Dead Tenor, p. 648: First published in the *Critic* of November 8, 1884, the poem was included in the "Sands at Seventy" annex of *November Boughs* (1888).

Continuities, p. 649: First published in the *New York Herald* of March 20, 1888, the poem was included in the "Sands at Seventy" annex of *November Boughs* (1888).

Yonnondio, p. 649: First published in the *Critic* of November 26, 1887, the poem was included in the "Sands at Seventy" annex of *November Boughs* (1888).

Life, p. 650: First published in the *New York Herald* of April 15, 1888, the poem was included in the "Sands at Seventy" annex of *November Boughs* (1888).

"Going Somewhere," p. 650: First published in *Lippincott's Magazine* in November 1887, the poem was included in the "Sands at Seventy" annex of *November Boughs* (1888).

Small the Theme of My Chant, p. 651: This was the introductory poem to *Leaves of Grass* (1867); revised and condensed, it headed the "Inscriptions" cluster in 1871.

True Conquerors, p. 651: First published in the *New York Herald* of February 15, 1888, the poem was included in the "Sands at Seventy" annex of *November Boughs* (1888).

The United States to Old World Critics, p. 652: First published in the *New York Herald* of May 8, 1888, the poem was included in the "Sands at Seventy" annex of *November Boughs* (1888).

The Calming Thought of All, p. 652: First published in the *New York Herald* of May 27, 1888, the poem was included in the "Sands at Seventy" annex of *November Boughs* (1888).

Thanks in Old Age, p. 652: First published in the *Philadelphia Press* of November 24, 1887, the poem was included in the "Sands at Seventy" annex of *November Boughs* (1888).

Life and Death, p. 653: First published in the *New York Herald* of May 23, 1888, the poem was included in the "Sands at Seventy" annex of *November Boughs* (1888).

The Voice of the Rain, p. 653: First published in *Outing* in August 1885, the poem was included in the "Sands at Seventy" annex of *November Boughs* (1888).

Soon Shall the Winter's Foil Be Here, p. 653: First published in the *New York Herald* of February 21, 1888, the poem was included in the "Sands at Seventy" annex of *November Boughs* (1888).

While Not the Past Forgetting, p. 654: The poem's first appearance was in the "Sands at Seventy" annex of *November Boughs* (1888).

The Dying Veteran, p. 654: First published in *McClair's Magazine* in June 1887, the poem was included in the "Sands at Seventy" annex of *November Boughs* (1888).

Stronger Lessons, p. 655: These two lines were originally part of the 1860 poem "Debris." In 1867 the lines were given the present title.

A *Prairie Sunset*, p. 655: First published in the *New York Herald* of March 9, 1888, the poem was included in the "Sands at Seventy" annex of *November Boughs* (1888).

Twenty Years, p. 656: First published in the *Magazine of Art* in July 1888, the poem was included in the "Sands at Seventy" annex of *November Boughs* (1888).

Orange Buds by Mail from Florida, p. 656: First published in the *New York Herald* of March 19, 1888, the poem was included in the "Sands at Seventy" annex of *November Boughs* (1888).

Twilight, p. 657: First published in *Century* magazine in December 1887, the poem was included in the "Sands at Seventy" annex of *November Boughs* (1888).

You Lingering Sparse Leaves of Me, p. 657: First published in *Lippincott's* in November 1887, the poem was included in the "Sands at Seventy" annex of *November Boughs* (1888).

Not Meagre, Latent Boughs Alone, p. 657: First published in *Lippincott's* in November 1887, the poem was included in the "Sands at Seventy" annex of *November Boughs* (1888).

The Dead Emperor, p. 657: The poem was first published in the *New York Herald* of March 10, 1888, the day after the death of Wilhelm I of Germany. The poem was included in the "Sands at Seventy" annex of *November Boughs* (1888).

As the Greek's Signal Flame, p. 658: First published in the *New York Herald* of December 15, 1887, the poem was included in the "Sands at Seventy" annex of *November Boughs* (1888).

The Dismantled Ship, p. 658: First published in the *New York Herald* of February 23, 1888, the poem was included in the "Sands at Seventy" annex of *November Boughs* (1888).

Now Precedent Songs, Farewell, p. 658: This poem was first published in the "Sands at Seventy" annex of *November Boughs* (1888).

An Evening Lull, p. 659: This poem was first published in the "Sands at Seventy" annex of *November Boughs* (1888).

Old Age's Lambent Peaks, p. 659: First printed in *Century* magazine in September 1888, this poem was not collected in *November Boughs* but in the "Sands at Seventy" annex of *Leaves of Grass* (1888).

After the Supper and Talk, p. 660: First published in *Lippincott's* in November 1887, the poem was included in the "Sands at Seventy" annex of *November Boughs* (1888).

Second Annex: Good-Bye My Fancy, p. 661: This cluster of thirty-one poems was first assembled as a sixty-six-page volume of prose and poetry, published by David McKay in May 1891; the grouping was included in the 1892 edition of *Leaves of Grass*. Most of these works were written in the poet's final decade and first published in periodicals after 1888.

Preface Note to 2d Annex, Concluding L. of G. — 1891, p. 661: Whitman included these spontaneous-sounding notes in the 1891 volume entitled *Good-Bye My Fancy*; they also prefaced the "Second Annex" of the 1891–1892 edition of *Leaves of Grass*.

Sail Out for Good, Eidólon Yacht!, p. 663: Published as "Old Age Echoes" along with three other poems ("Sound of the Winter," "The Unexpress'd," and "After the Argument") in *Lippincott's* of March 1891, the poem was collected in *Good-Bye My Fancy* (1891).

Lingering Last Drops, p. 663: The poem was first published in *Good-Bye My Fancy* (1891).

Good-Bye My Fancy, p. 664: The poem was first published in *Good-Bye My Fancy* (1891).

On, On the Same, Ye Jocund Twain!, p. 664: The poem was first published in *Good-Bye My Fancy* (1891).

My 71st Year, p. 665: First published in *Century* magazine in November 1889, the poem was collected in *Good-Bye My Fancy* (1891).

Apparitions, p. 665: The poem was first published in *Good-Bye My Fancy* (1891).

The Pallid Wreath, p. 665: First published in the *Critic* of January 10, 1891, the poem was collected in *Good-Bye My Fancy* (1891).

An Ended Day, p. 666: The poem was first published in *Good-Bye My Fancy* (1891).

Old Age's Ship & Crafty Death's, p. 667: First published in *Century* magazine in February 1890, the poem was collected in *Good-Bye My Fancy* (1891).

To the Pending Year, p. 667: First published in the *Critic* of January 5, 1889 as "To the Year 1889," the poem received its current title in *Good-Bye My Fancy* (1891).

Shakspere-Bacon's Cipher, p. 667: First published in the *Cosmopolitan* magazine of October 1887, the poem was collected in *Good-Bye My Fancy* (1891).

Long, Long Hence, p. 668: The poem was first published in *Good-Bye My Fancy* (1891).

Bravo, Paris Exposition!, p. 668: First published in *Harper's Weekly* on September 28, 1889, the poem was collected in *Good-Bye My Fancy* (1891).

Interpolation Sounds, p. 668: First published in the *New York Herald* of August 12, 1888, under the title "Over and Through the Burial Chant," the poem received its current title in *Good-Bye My Fancy* (1891).

To the Sun-set Breeze, p. 669: First published in *Lippincott's* for December 1890, the poem was collected in *Good-Bye My Fancy* (1891).

Old Chants, p. 670: First published in *New York Truth* of March 19, 1881, the poem was collected in *Good-Bye My Fancy* (1891).

A Christmas Greeting, p. 671: The poem was first published in *Good-Bye My Fancy* (1891).

Sounds of the Winter, p. 671: Published as "Old Age Echoes" along with three other poems ("Sail Out for Good, Eidólon Yacht!," "The Unexpress'd," "After the Argument") in *Lippincott's* for March 1891, the poem was collected in *Good-Bye My Fancy* (1891).

A Twilight Song, p. 672: First published in the *Century* of May 1890, the poem was collected in *Good-Bye My Fancy* (1891).

When the Full-Grown Poet Came, p. 672: An intercalation in *Leaves of Grass: Author's Edition, with Portraits and Intercalations* (1876), the poem was printed in the same position in *Leaves of Grass: Author's Edition, with Portraits from Life* (1876). Left out of subsequent editions, it reappeared in *Good-Bye My Fancy* (1891).

Osceola, p. 673: First published in *Munson's Illustrated World* of April 1890, the poem was collected in *Good-Bye My Fancy* (1891).

A Voice from Death, p. 674: First published in the *New York World* of June 7, 1889, the poem was collected in *Good-Bye My Fancy* (1891).

A Persian Lesson, p. 675: The poem was first published in *Good-Bye My Fancy* (1891).

The Commonplace, p. 676: *Munson's Magazine* published a facsimile of the manuscript of this poem in March 1891. It was first collected in *Good-Bye My Fancy* (1891).

"The Rounded Catalogue Divine Complete," p. 676: The poem was first published in *Good-Bye My Fancy* (1891).

Mirages, p. 677: The poem was first published in *Good-Bye My Fancy* (1891).

L. of G.'s Purport, p. 678: The poem was first published in *Good-Bye My Fancy* (1891).

The Unexpress'd, p. 678: Published as "Old Age Echoes" along with three other poems ("Sail Out for Good, Eidólon Yacht!," "Sounds of the Winter," and "After the Argument") in the *Lippincott's* of March 1891, the poem was collected in *Good-Bye My Fancy* (1891).

Grand Is the Seen, p. 679: The poem was first published in *Good-Bye My Fancy* (1891).

Unseen Buds, p. 679: The poem was first published in *Good-Bye My Fancy* (1891).

Good-Bye My Fancy!, p. 679: The poem first concluded the volume of the same title (1891) and maintained its place in the "Second Annex" of *Leaves of Grass* (1891–1892).

A Backward Glance o'er Travel'd Roads, p. 681: This essay was completed in 1888 and first appeared in *November Boughs* (1888), a volume of prose that also included the cluster "Sands at Seventy." It also appeared with "Sands at Seventy" in *Complete Poems and Prose*, published that same year; in the 1889 edition of *Leaves of*

Grass printed for the poet's seventieth birthday; and the "Death-bed" Edition of *Leaves of Grass* published by David McKay in 1891–1892.

ADDITIONAL POEMS

Poems Written before 1855

Our Future Lot, p. 709: Published in the *Long Island Democrat* of October 31, 1838, and labeled "from the *Long Islander*," "Our Future Lot" is Whitman's earliest extant published poem. The poem was heavily revised and published as "Time to Come" in the New York *Aurora* of April 9, 1842.

Fame's Vanity, p. 710: Published in the *Long Island Democrat* of October 23, 1839, the poem was the basis for "Ambition" (see note below), published in *Brother Jonathan* on January 29, 1842.

My Departure, p. 711: The poem first appeared in the *Long Island Democrat* of November 27, 1839; the poem was shortened, revised, and published as "Death of the Nature Lover" (see note below), in *Brother Jonathan* on March 11, 1843.

Young Grimes, p. 713: Published in the *Long Island Democrat* of January 1, 1840, the poem is Whitman's response to Albert Gordon Greene's "Old Grimes," first published in 1822 and frequently re-published thereafter.

The Inca's Daughter, p. 714: The poem was first published in the *Long Island Democrat* of May 5, 1840.

The Love That Is Hereafter, p. 716: The poem first appeared in the *Long Island Democrat* of May 19, 1840.

We Shall All Rest at Last, p. 717: First published in the *Long Island Democrat* of July 14, 1840, the poem was lightly revised and published as "Each Has His Grief" in the New York *New World* of November 20, 1841.

The Spanish Lady, p. 719: First appeared in the *Long Island Demo-crat* of August 4, 1840.

The End of All, p. 720: First published in the *Long Island Democrat* of September 22, 1840, "The End of All" was lightly revised and published as "The Winding Up" in the same newspaper on June 22, 1841.

The Columbian's Song, p. 722: The poem first appeared in the *Long Island Democrat* of October 27, 1840.

The Punishment of Pride, p. 723: First published in the New York *New World* of December 18, 1841, the poem was allegedly written by Whitman two years earlier.

Ambition, p. 726: Appearing in *Brother Jonathan* on January 29, 1842, this poem is the heavily revised version of an earlier work entitled "Fame's Vanity" (see note above).

The Death and Burial of McDonald Clarke, p. 728: Published in the New York *Aurora* of March 18, 1842.

Time to Come, p. 729: Published in the New York *Aurora* of April 9, 1842, this poem is the heavily revised version of an earlier poem entitled "Our Future Lot" (see note above).

A Sketch, p. 730: Published in the *New World* on December 10, 1842, this poem was first attributed to Whitman in 1994.

Death of the Nature-Lover, p. 731: Published in *Brother Jonathan* on March 11, 1843, this poem is the heavily revised version of "My Departure" (see note above).

The Play-Ground, p. 732: The poem was published in the *Brooklyn Daily Eagle* of June 1, 1846, which was three months after Whitman assumed the editorship of the newspaper.

Ode, p. 733: The poem appeared in the *Brooklyn Daily Eagle* of July 2, 1846, while Whitman was editor.

The Mississippi at Midnight, p. 735: Originally published in the *New Orleans Crescent* of March 6, 1848, the poem was revised and re-named "Sailing the Mississippi at Midnight" for inclusion in *Collect* (the literary miscellany included in *Specimen Days and Collect*) in 1882.

Song for Certain Congressmen, p. 735: Originally published in the *New York Evening Post* of March 2, 1850, the poem was republished as "Dough-Face Song" in *Collect* in 1882, where Whitman also added the epigraph: "Like dough; soft; yielding to pressure; pale.— *Webster's Dictionary*.

Blood-Money, p. 738: First published in the *New York Tribune Supplement* of March 22, 1850, the poem was reprinted in the *Evening Post* of April 30, 1851. With very minor changes to punctuation, the poem was republished in *Collect* in 1882.

The House of Friends, p. 739: Published in the *New York Tribune* of June 14, 1850, the poem was revised and published as "Wounded in the House of Friends" in *Collect* in 1882.

Resurgemus, p. 741: Appearing in the *New York Tribune* on June 21, 1850, "Resurgemus" was revised and included as the eighth of the twelve untitled poems in the 1855 edition of *Leaves of Grass*. To date, it is the only poem published before 1855 to have been included in the First Edition. In 1856, with further revisions, it was known as "16—Poem of the Dead Young Men of Europe, The 72d and 73d Years of These States"; in 1860, "Europe, The 72d and 73d Years of These States."

Poems Excluded from the "Death-bed" Edition (1891–1892)
Great Are the Myths, p. 744: The poem appears as it did in its final publication during Whitman's lifetime, the 1876 "Centennial" Edition of *Leaves of Grass*. The idea of the poem has its basis in the last of the twelve untitled poems of the 1855 edition; in various states of revision, it was published in 1856 ("Poem of a Few Greatnesses"), 1860 ("Leaves of Grass. 2"), 1867 (under its present title), and 1871. "Great Are the Myths" was dropped from all subsequent editions;

only lines 9–12 were separated and printed as "Youth, Day, Old Age, and Night" in the 1881 edition.

Chants Democratic. 6, p. 747: The poem appears in its final published version from the 1860 edition. Without the first line and with twenty-three additional lines attached to the end, the poem was included in the 1856 edition under the title "Poem of Remembrance for a Girl or a Boy of These States." The last twenty-three lines of the "Poem of Remembrance" eventually became "Think of the Soul" in 1867 (see note below).

Think of the Soul, p. 748: See note for "Chants Democratic. 6," above. These twenty-three lines were originally part of "Poem of Remembrance for a Girl or a Boy of These States" in 1856. In 1867 they became "Leaves of Grass. 1"; in 1871, the lines gained their present title, "Think of the Soul." The poem was dropped from the 1881 edition.

Respondez!, p. 749: The poem appears as it did in the 1876 "Centennial" Edition of *Leaves of Grass*; it was dropped from all subsequent editions. It appeared first in 1856 as "Poem of the Proposition of Nakedness"; with minor revisions, it became "Chants Democratic. 5" in 1860 and "Respondez!" in 1867.

Enfans d'Adam. 11, p. 754: The poem appeared only in the 1860 edition. All other "Enfans d'Adam" poems were retained in various forms in subsequent editions.

Calamus. 16, p. 754: The poem appeared only in the 1860 edition. Of the forty-five poems in the "Calamus" series, only four (numbers 5, 8, 9, and 16) were not retained in future editions.

Calamus. 8, p. 755: The poem appeared only in the 1860 edition.

Calamus. 9, p. 756: The poem appeared only in the 1860 edition.

Leaves of Grass. 20, p. 756: The poem was published in the 1860 edition only.

Thoughts. 1, p. 757: The poem appeared in the 1860 and 1867 edition of *Leaves of Grass* and was dropped from subsequent editions.

Thought, p. 757: The poem appears as it did in its final publication, in the 1876 "Centennial" Edition, as well as in the 1871 edition of *Leaves of Grass*. Earlier versions of the poem in the 1860 and 1867 editions include minor changes in wording and a different title, "Thoughts. 6."

Says, p. 758: The poem was first published in 1860. Though the title was retained in 1867, Whitman removed stanzas 2, 3, 4, and 6. For the 1871, 1872, and 1876 editions, stanzas 1, 5, 7, and 8 were renumbered 1 through 4, revised and published as "Suggestions." All variants of the poem were dropped from subsequent editions.

Apostroph, p. 759: In this form, in 1860 the poem made its first and last appearance during Whitman's lifetime. For the 1867 edition lines 49–64 were revised as "Leaves of Grass. 1." Whitman worked on the lines yet again for the 1871 edition and retitled the poem "O Sun of Real Peace" (see note below).

O Sun of Real Peace, p. 762: See the note to "Apostroph" (above) for the history of this poem, which was excluded from *Leaves of Grass* editions after 1871.

Primeval My Love for the Woman I Love, p. 762: The poem was published but once, in the 1860 edition of *Leaves of Grass*. See the note for "Fast-anchor'd Eternal O Love!" (p. 293), above.

To You, p. 763: The poem appeared in this title and form in the 1860 and 1867 editions of *Leaves of Grass*. For inclusion in the annex to *Leaves of Grass* (1872) entitled "Passage to India" and for *Two Rivulets* (1876), Whitman added a new line 4: "Come let us talk of death—unbosom all freely." The poem was dropped from subsequent editions.

Now Lift Me Close, p. 763: The poem first appeared as the last ("24") of the "Leaves of Grass" cluster in 1860. In 1867 it gained its present title and retained its placement at the end of the "Leaves of Grass" grouping. "Now Lift Me Close" was dropped from subsequent editions (probably because Whitman decided that "So Long!" was a sufficient farewell poem), though a derivative entitled "To the Reader at Parting" appeared in 1871 (see note below).

To the Reader at Parting, p. 763: For an explanation of the poem's history, see the note to "Now Lift Me Close." "To the Reader at Parting" appeared in this form for the first and final time during Whitman's lifetime in *Passage to India* (1871).

Debris, p. 764: The poem appeared in its entirety only in the 1860 edition. Whitman later mined "Debris" for other poems, including "Stronger Lessons," "Yet, Yet, Ye Downcast Hours," "Offerings," "Visor'd," "Beautiful Women," "Not the Pilot," and "As if a Phantom Caress'd Me."

Leaflets, p. 768: Originally part of "Debris" in 1860, this separate poem appeared in the 1867 edition of *Leaves of Grass* and was removed thereafter.

Despairing Cries, p. 768: Originally part of "Debris" in 1860, "Despairing Cries" was published as its own poem in 1867. It was dropped from subsequent editions, though some lines were used in "Yet, Yet, Ye Downcast Hours" (see note to "Debris," above).

Calamus. 5, p. 769: The poem appeared only in the 1860 edition of *Leaves of Grass*, with a final seven lines that provided the basis for the poem "For You O Democracy." Lines 15–35 were used as the basis for the poem "Over the Carnage Rose Prophetic a Voice."

Thoughts. 2, p. 770: The poem appeared in the 1860 and 1867 editions of *Leaves of Grass* and did not appear in this form in subsequent editions.

Thoughts. 4, p. 771: The poem appeared as the fourth part of the "Thoughts" grouping in the 1860 and 1867 editions of *Leaves of Grass*, and did not appear in this form thereafter.

Bathed in War's Perfume, p. 771: This is the 1871 text of the poem, which was also included in the 1876 "Centennial" Edition but excluded from *Leaves of Grass* thereafter. The poem first appeared in *Drum-Taps* of 1865 and the 1867 edition of *Leaves of Grass*, without the current second line, which was included in 1871, six years after the end of the Civil War.

Solid, Ironical, Rolling Orb, p. 771: First published in *Drum-Taps* (1865), the poem appeared in 1867, 1871, and 1876 but was left out of the 1881 edition of *Leaves of Grass*.

Not My Enemies Ever Invade Me, p. 772: First published in *Sequel to Drum-Taps* (1865–1866), the poem was reprinted in 1867 and excluded from all subsequent editions.

This Day, O Soul, p. 772: First published in *Sequel to Drum-Taps* (1865–1866,) the poem appeared in the 1867 edition, the 1872 "Passage to India" annex and *Two Rivulets* (1876). It was excluded from *Leaves of Grass* thereafter.

Lessons, p. 772: This poem appeared for the first and last time during Whitman's lifetime in *Passage to India* (1871).

Ashes of Soldiers: Epigraph, p. 772: This epigraph first preceded the poem "Ashes of Soldiers" in *Passage to India* (1871). It supplemented "Ashes of Soldiers" in the "Passage to India" annexes of 1872 and 1876 but was excluded from all subsequent editions.

The Beauty of the Ship, p. 773: The text of this poem was published only in 1876. Along with "After an Interval" (see note below), "The Beauty of the Ship" was an intercalation in the 1876 *Leaves of Grass: Author's Edition, with Portraits and Intercalations* (an "intercalation" was Whitman's word for a clipping that was pasted in place in one edition and printed on the same page in later pressings). The poem was printed in the 1876 *Leaves of Grass: Author's Edition, with Portraits from Life*.

After an Interval, p. 773: See note to "The Beauty of the Ship," above. "After an Interval" was also an intercalation in the 1876

Leaves of Grass: Author's Edition, with Portraits and Intercalations; it was published in the later pressing of this edition, the 1876 *Leaves of Grass: Author's Edition, with Portraits from Life*.

Two Rivulets, p. 773: Published in this form only once, in *Two Rivulets*, the companion volume to the 1876 edition of *Leaves of Grass*. Lines 10–12 were used in "As Consequent, Etc.," a poem new to the 1881 edition. All in all, four poems in *Two Rivulets* appeared only in that volume: "Two Rivulets," "Or from That Sea of Time," "From My Last Years," and "In Former Songs" (see notes, below).

Or from That Sea of Time, p. 774: The text to this poem appeared in this form only in the 1876 companion volume *Two Rivulets*. The first twelve lines were revised and became lines 22–33 of "As Consequent, Etc"; lines 13–18 were altered slightly to form lines 16–21 of that poem.

From My Last Years, p. 775: This poem appeared once only in *Two Rivulets* (1876).

In Former Songs, p. 775: This poem appears but once, in the companion volume *Two Rivulets* (1876).

As in a Swoon, p. 775: The poem first appeared as an intercalation in the 1876 *Leaves of Grass: Author's Edition, with Portraits and Intercalations*; it was published in the 1876 edition *Leaves of Grass: Author's Edition, with Portraits from Life* (see the note, above, on "The Beauty of the Ship" for information about Whitman's intercalations). Though it was included in *Good-Bye My Fancy* (1891) and *Complete Prose Works* (1892), it was not included in *Leaves of Grass* (1891–1892).

[Last Droplets], p. 776: Whitman never titled these lines, which appear only once: in the prefatory note to the literary miscellany *Good-Bye My Fancy* (1891).

Ship Ahoy!, p. 776: The poem first appeared in the literary miscellany *Good-Bye My Fancy* (1891) and was also published in *Complete*

Prose Works (1892), though it was never included in the culminating 1891–1892 edition of *Leaves of Grass*.

For Queen Victoria's Birthday, p. 776: This tribute poem appeared first in the *Philadelphia Public Ledger* (May 22, 1890) and was included in *Complete Prose Works* (1892), though Whitman decided not to include it in the 1891–1892 edition of *Leaves of Grass*.

L of G, p. 776: The poem appeared first in the literary miscellany *Good-Bye My Fancy* (1891) and finally in *Complete Prose Works* (1892). The poet chose not to include it in his culminating edition of 1891–1892.

After the Argument, p. 777: Published in *Good-Bye My Fancy* (1891) and *Complete Prose Works* (1892), the poem was not included in Whitman's culminating edition of *Leaves of Grass*.

For Us Two, Reader Dear, p. 777: Published in the literary miscellany *Good-Bye My Fancy* (1891) as well as *Complete Prose Works* (1892), the poem was excluded from the 1891–1892 edition of *Leaves of Grass*.

Old Age Echoes (1897)

To Soar in Freedom and in Fullness of Power, p. 779: First published in *Old Age Echoes* (1897).

Then Shall Perceive, p. 779: First published in *Old Age Echoes* (1897).

The Few Drops Known, p. 779: First published in *Old Age Echoes* (1897).

One Thought Ever at the Fore, p. 780: First published in *Old Age Echoes* (1897).

While Behind All Firm and Erect, p. 780: First published in *Old Age Echoes* (1897).

A Kiss to the Bride, p. 780: Published in the *New York Daily Graphic* of May 21, 1874, this poem was first collected in *Old Age Echoes* (1897).

Nay, Tell Me Not To-day the Publish'd Shame, p. 781: Published in the *New York Daily Graphic* of March 5, 1873, this poem was first collected in *Old Age Echoes* (1897).

Supplement Hours, p. 781: First published in *Old Age Echoes* (1897).

Of Many a Smutch'd Deed Reminiscent, p. 782: First published in *Old Age Echoes* (1897).

To Be at All, Cf. Stanza 27, *"Song of Myself,"* p. 782: Though this poem was first published in *Old Age Echoes* (1897), it appears to be a draft or revision of stanza 27 of "Song of Myself."

Death's Valley, p. 783: First published—ironically—the month after Whitman's death in *Harper's New Monthly Magazine* (April 1982), the poem was collected in *Old Age Echoes* (1897).

On the Same Picture, p. 784: First published in *Old Age Echoes* (1897).

A Thought of Columbus, p. 784: First published in *Once a Week* on July 9, 1892, a few months after Whitman's death, the poem was collected in *Old Age Echoes* (1897).

INSPIRED BY *LEAVES OF GRASS*

Whitman poems on every subject—war, love, travel, compassion—continue to inspire artists in many genres.

POETRY

In "Poets to Come" Walt Whitman addresses future generations of poets, commanding, "Arouse! for you must justify me." They have done so. Among them is Ezra Pound, whose poem "A Pact" (1913) begins, "I make a pact with you, Walt Whitman—/ I have detested you long enough." Other notable poems invoking Whitman include "Retort to Whitman" (late 1920s), by D. H. Lawrence, and "Old Walt" (1954), by Langston Hughes (who also edited a collection of Whitman's verse in 1946). T. S. Eliot and Carl Sandburg both published essays in the 1920s addressing the importance of Whitman in American poetry. Though Eliot found the poet's style to be primitive and even distasteful, Sandburg's *Chicago Poems* (1916) and *The People, Yes!* (1936) reflect Whitman's style.

In his "Cape Hatteras" (1920) Hart Crane asks: "Walt, tell me, Walt Whitman, if infinity / Be still the same as when you walked the beach / Near Paumanok." The last lines of the poem envision Crane and Whitman together on the beach, walking hand in hand. Crane summons his venerated predecessor into the future, attempting to carry his legacy onward.

Two important post-World War II American poets, William Carlos Williams and John Berryman, also took Whitman as an artistic guide. Williams's essay "The American Idiom" (1967) addresses Whitman's impact on language. Likewise, Beat-generation poets Jack Kerouac and Allen Ginsberg often cited Whitman as the major influence in their work. In "Supermarket in California" (1955), Ginsberg imagines his predecessor roving among modern store aisles, examining meats and vegetables, darting desirous glances at the grocery boys. Kerouac, too, invokes Whitman, in his poem "168th Chorus" (1959). Louis Simpson named his collection *At the End of the Open Road* (1963) in reference to Whitman's "Song of the Open Road," and in some of his closing verse he carries on a lengthy dialogue with the older poet regarding new problems in a modernized America. Across the Atlantic, Whitman has been the subject of poems by Spanish writers Pedro Mir, Pablo Neruda, Federico García Lorca, and Jorge Luis Borges.

Walt Whitman: The Measure of His Song (edited by Dan Campion, Ed Folsom, and Jim Perlman; see "For Further Reading") anthologizes works of the many poets Whitman has influenced and includes Whitman-related letters and essays by such writers as Gerard Manley Hopkins, Matthew Arnold, Henry David Thoreau, Sherwood Anderson, Henry Miller, and Robert Bly. In *Whitman's Wild Children*, Neeli Cherkovski provides in-depth discussions of twelve poets who represent the Whitmanic tradition, and *The Outlaw Bible of American Poetry* begins and ends with Whitman's verse.

FICTION

Willa Cather took the title of her novel *O Pioneers!* (1913) from the Whitman poem "Pioneers! O Pioneers!" Set on the Nebraska prairie, the novel chronicles the struggles of Swedish immigrant Alexandra Bergson, whose father's death leaves her with a plot of sickly farmland that she transforms into a thriving enterprise. The novel includes this Whitmanesque line: "The history of every country begins in the heart of a man or a woman." British novelist E. M. Forster took the title of Whitman's poem as that of his masterpiece *A Passage to India* (1924).

Jack Kerouac refers directly to Whitman as his muse in the freewheeling *On the Road* (1957), the title of which echoes Whitman's "Song of the Open Road." Perhaps the seminal text of the Beat generation, the novel details the adventures of writer Sal Paradise and recent jailbird Dean Moriarty as they hitchhike and travel by bus across America, smoking marijuana, drinking heavily, and visiting jazz clubs and brothels.

Another incarnation of Whitman hit the road in 1989, in Maxine Hong Kingston's novel *Tripmaster Monkey*. The protagonist, a young Chinese-American poet named Wittman Ah Sing, recites poetry to fellow passengers on the buses of San Francisco.

PAINTING

Whitman's rich imagery translates well into painting. The poet has been a favorite among artists since the time of Vincent van Gogh, who praised Whitman vigorously in letters to his family while he painted *Starry Night* (1889). Indeed, van Gogh may even have taken his title from Whitman's poem cluster "From Noon to Starry Night," which was published in France just before the artist began work on the famous painting.

Realist painter Thomas Eakins enjoyed a close friendship with Whitman. While the poet was frequently photographed and painted, he most admired his portrait by Eakins, saying it represented him truly, without glossing over his physical imperfections. Eakins's best-known work, *The Swimming Hole* (1889), is widely thought to be a response to "Song of Myself" in which "twenty-eight young men bathe by the shore."

Inspired by the poem "I Hear America Singing," Whitman's ode to the noble and tireless workers of the country, in 1939 Ben Shahn and Bernarda Bryson Shahn painted the epic series *Resources of America* for the walls of the Bronx County Post Office in New York City. The eighteen-foot-high frescoes depict ordinary Americans performing the everyday tasks that keep the country running. Several panels focus on people engaged in such jobs as harvesting wheat and reading construction blueprints. Other panels depict technology, including hydroelectric dams and electrical blast furnaces, and one panel shows Whitman himself reciting poetry to citizens gathered below.

MUSIC

Weda Cook, a popular singer, friend of Whitman, and model for painter Thomas Eakins, was the first musician to set "O Captain! My Captain!" and other Whitman poems to music. Classical music has also strongly favored Whitman. Composer Charles Ives, deemed the "Walt Whitman of American Music," provided a setting of one of the outspoken passages of "Song of Myself": "Who goes there? Hankering, gross, mystical, nude . . ." (from "Walt Whitman"). In the early twentieth century, the good gray poet sparked the interest of three important British composers: Frederick Delius, Ralph Vaughn Williams, and Gustav Holst. Delius set Whitman's poems to music in "Seadrift" (1904), "Songs of Farewell" (1930), and "Idyll" (1932). Williams's "Toward the Unknown Reason" (1906) sets the poem "Darest Thou Now O Soul" to music; his "Sea Symphony" (1910) uses words from "A Passage to India" and several Whitman poems about ships; and his "Dona Nobis Pacem" ("Grant Us Peace," 1936) is an antiwar piece incorporating Whitman's Civil War poems. Holst set Whitman's "When Lilacs Last in the Dooryard Bloom'd" to music in "Ode to Death" (1919), which memorialized friends killed during World War I. In the years leading up to World War II, a number of anti-Nazi composers set Whitman to music. Among them were Kurt Weill, Paul Hindemith, Hans Werner Henze, Friedrich Wildgans, Franz Schreker, and Karl Amadeus Hartmann.

Whitman's immense influence on folk and progressive music by the likes of Woody Guthrie and Bob Dylan is discussed by Bryan Garman in *A Race of Singers: Whitman's Working-class Hero from Guthrie to Springsteen.*

COMMENTS & QUESTIONS

In this section, we aim to provide the reader with an array of perspectives on the text, as well as questions that challenge those perspectives. The commentary has been culled from sources as diverse as reviews contemporaneous with the work, letters written by the author, literary criticism of later generations, and appreciations written throughout the work's history. Following the commentary, a series of questions seeks to filter Walt Whitman's Leaves of Grass *through a variety of points of view and bring about a richer understanding of this enduring work.*

COMMENTS

RALPH WALDO EMERSON

I am not blind to the worth of the wonderful gift of "Leaves of Grass." I find it the most extraordinary piece of wit and wisdom that America has yet contributed. I am very happy in reading it, as great power makes us happy. It meets the demand I am always making of what seemed the sterile and stingy Nature, as if too much handiwork, or too much lymph in the temperament, were making our western wits fat and mean.

I give you joy of your free and brave thought. I have great joy in it. I find incomparable things said incomparably well, as they must be. I find the courage of treatment which so delights us, and which large perception only can inspire.

I greet you at the beginning of a great career, which yet must have had a long foreground somewhere, for such a start. I rubbed my eyes a little, to see if this sunbeam were no illusion; but the solid sense of the book is a sober certainty. It has the best merits, namely, of fortifying and encouraging.

I did not know until I, last night, saw the book advertised in a newspaper, that I could trust the name as real and available for a post-office. I wish to see my benefactor, and have felt much like striking my tasks, and visiting New York to pay you my respects.

—from a letter to Walt Whitman (July 21, 1855)

CHARLES A. DANA

[Whitman's] *Leaves of Grass* are doubtless intended as an illustration of the natural poet. They are certainly original in their external form, have been shaped on no pre-existent model out of the author's own brain. Indeed, his independence often becomes coarse and defiant. His language is too frequently reckless and indecent though this appears to arise from a naive unconsciousness rather than from an impure mind. His words might have passed between Adam and Eve in Paradise, before the want of fig-leaves brought no shame; but they are quite out of place amid the decorum of modern society, and will justly prevent his volume from free circulation in scrupulous circles. With these glaring faults, the *Leaves of Grass* are not destitute of peculiar poetic merits, which will awaken an interest in the lovers of literary curiosities. They are full of bold, stirring thoughts—with occasional passages of effective description, betraying a genuine intimacy with Nature and a keen appreciation of beauty—often presenting a rare felicity of diction, but so disfigured with eccentric fancies as to prevent a consecutive perusal without offense, though no impartial reader can fail to be impressed with the vigor and quaint beauty of isolated portions.

—from an unsigned article in the
New York Daily Tribune (July 23, 1855)

WALT WHITMAN

An American bard at last! One of the roughs, large, proud, affectionate, eating, drinking, and breeding, his costume manly and free, his face sunburnt and bearded, his posture strong and erect, his voice bringing hope and prophecy to the generous races of young and old. We shall cease shamming and be what we really are. We shall start an athletic and defiant literature. We realize now how it is, and what was most lacking. The interior American republic shall also be declared free and independent. . . .

Self-reliant, with haughty eyes, assuming to himself all the attributes of his country, steps Walt Whitman into literature, talking like a man unaware that there was hitherto such a production as a book, or such a being as a writer. Every move of him has the free play of the muscle of one who never knew what it was to feel that he stood in the presence of a superior. Every word that falls from his mouth shows silent disdain and defiance of the old theories and forms. Every phrase announces new laws; not once do his lips unclose except in conformity with them. With light and rapid touch he first indicates in prose the principles of the foundation of a race of poets so deeply to spring from the American people, and become ingrained through them, that their Presidents shall not be the common referees so much as that great race of poets shall.

—from an unsigned review of
Leaves of Grass in *United States Review* (September 1855)

FANNY FERN

Well baptized: fresh, hardy, and grown for the masses. Not more welcome is their natural type to the winter-bound, bed-ridden, and spring-emancipated invalid. *Leaves of Grass* thou art unspeakably delicious, after the forced, stiff, Parnassian exotics for which our admiration has been vainly challenged.

Walt Whitman, the effeminate world needed thee. The timidest soul whose wings ever drooped with discouragement, could not choose but rise on thy strong pinions.

—from the *New York Ledger* (May 10, 1856)

WILLIAM DEAN HOWELLS

We are to suppose that Mr. Whitman first adopted his method as something that came to him of its own motion. This is the best possible reason, and only possible excuse, for it. In its way, it is quite as artificial as that of any other poet, while it is unspeakably inartistic. On this account it is a failure. The method of talking to one's self in rhythmic and ecstatic prose is one that surprises at first, but, in the end, the talker can only have the devil for a listener, as happens in other cases when people address their own individualities; not, however, the devil of the proverb, but the devil of reasonless, hopeless, all-defying egotism. An ingenious French critic said very acutely of Mr. Whitman that he made you partner of the poetical enterprise, which is perfectly true; but no one wants to share the enterprise. We want its effect, its success; we do not want to plant corn, to hoe it, to drive the crows away, to gather it, husk it, grind it, sift it, bake it, and butter it, before eating it, and then take the risk of its being at last moldy in our mouths. And this is what you have to do in reading Mr. Whitman's rhythm.

—from Round Table (November 11, 1865)

HENRY JAMES

The most that can be said of Mr. Whitman's vaticinations is, that, cast in a fluent and familiar manner, the average substance of them might escape unchallenged. But we have seen that Mr. Whitman prides himself especially on the substance—the life—of his poetry. It may be rough, it may be grim, it may be clumsy—such we take to be the author's argument—but it is sincere, it is sublime, it appeals to the soul of man, it is the voice of a people. He tells us, in the lines quoted, that the words of his book are nothing. To our perception they are everything, and very little at that. A great deal of verse that is nothing but words has, during the war, been sympathetically sighed over and cut out of newspaper corners, because it has possessed a certain simple melody. But Mr. Whitman's verse, we are confident, would have failed even of this triumph, for the simple reason that no triumph, however small, is won but through the exercise of art, and that this volume is an offense against art. It is not enough to be grim and rough and careless; common sense is also necessary, for it is by common sense that we are judged. There exists in even the commonest minds, in literary matters, a certain precise instinct of conservatism, which is very shrewd in detecting wanton eccentricities. To this instinct Mr. Whitman's attitude seems monstrous. It is monstrous because it pretends to persuade the soul while it slights the intellect; because it pretends to gratify the feelings while it outrages the taste. The point is that it does this *on theory*, wilfully, consciously, arrogantly. It is the little nursery game of "open your mouth and shut your eyes." Our hearts are often touched through a compromise with the artistic sense, but never in direct violation of it. Mr. Whitman sits down at the outset and counts out the intelligence.

—from an unsigned review of
Drum-Taps in The Nation (November 16, 1865)

WILLIAM DOUGLAS O'CONNOR

Walt Whitman's [*Leaves of Grass*] is a poem which Schiller might have hailed as the noblest specimen of naïve literature, worthy of a place beside Homer. It is, in the first place, a work purely and entirely American, autochthonic, sprung from our own soil; no savor of Europe nor of the past, nor of any other literature in it; a vast carol of our own land, and of its Present and Future; the strong and haughty psalm of the Republic. There is not one other book, I care not whose, of which this can be said.

—from *The Good Gray Poet: A Vindication* (1866)

JOHN BURROUGHS

When *Leaves of Grass* was written and published, the author was engaged in putting up small frame houses in the suburbs of Brooklyn, partly with his own hands and partly with hired help. The book was still-born. To a small job printing office in that city belongs the honor, if such, of bringing it to light. Some three score copies were deposited in a neighboring book store, and as many more in another book store in New York. Weeks elapsed and not one was sold. Presently there issued requests from both the stores that the thin quarto, for such it was, should be forthwith removed. The copies found refuge in a well-known phrenological publishing house in Broadway, whose proprietors advertised it and sent specimen copies to the journals and to some distinguished persons. The journals remained silent, and several of the volumes sent to the distinguished persons were returned with ironical and insulting notes. The only attention the book received was, for instance, the use of it by the collected *attaches* of a leading daily paper of New York, when at leisure, as a butt and burlesque—its perusal aloud by one of the party being equivalent to peals of ironical laughter from the rest.

A small but important occurrence seems to have turned the tide. This was the appearance of a letter from the most illustrious literary man in America, brief, but containing a magnificent eulogium of the book. A demand arose, and before many months all the copies of the thin quarto were sold. At the present date, a curious person, poring over the shelves of second-hand book stalls in side places of the city, may light upon a copy of this quarto, for which the stall-keeper will ask him treble its first price. *Leaves of Grass,* considerably added to, and printed in the new shape of a handy 16mo. of about 350 pages, again appeared in 1857. This edition also sold. The newspaper notices of it both here and in Great Britain were numerous, and nearly all of them scoffing, bitter and condemnatory. The most general charge made was that it had passages of serious indelicacy. . . .

The full history of the book, if it could ever be written, would be a very curious one. No American work has ever before excited at once such diametrically opposite judgments, some seeing in it only matter for ridicule and contempt; others, eminent in the walks of literature, regarding it as a great American poem. Its most enthusiastic champions are young men, and students and lovers of nature; though the most pertinent and suggestive criticism of it we have ever seen, and one that accepted it as a whole, was by a lady—one whose name stands high on the list of our poets. Some of the poet's warmest personal friends, also, are women of this mould. On the other hand, the most bitter and vindictive critic of him of whom we have heard was a Catholic priest, who evoked no very mild degree of damnation upon his soul; if, indeed, we except the priestly official at the seat of government who, in administering the affairs of his department, on what he had the complacency to call Christian principles, took occasion, for reason of the poet's literary heresies alone, to expel him from a position in his office. Of much more weight than the opinion of either of these Christian gentlemen is the admiration of that Union soldier we chanced to hear of, who by accident came into possession of the book, and without any previous knowledge of it or its author, and by the aid of his mother wit alone, came to regard it with feelings akin to those which personal friendship and intercourse alone awaken; carrying it in his knapsack through three years of campaigning on the Potomac, and guarding it with a sort of jealous affection from the hands of his comrades.

—from *Galaxy* (December 1, 1866)

ROBERT LOUIS STEVENSON

[Whitman's] book, he tells us, should be read "among the cooling influences of external nature"; and this recommendation, like that other famous one which Hawthorne prefixed to his collected tales, is in itself a character of the work. Every one who has been upon a walking or a boating tour, living in the open air, with the body in constant exercise and the mind in fallow, knows true ease and quiet. The irritating action of the brain is set at rest; we think in a plain, unfeverish temper; little things seem big enough, and great things no longer portentous; and the world is smilingly accepted as it is. This is the spirit that Whitman inculcates and parades. He thinks very ill of the atmosphere of parlours or libraries. Wisdom keeps school outdoors. And he has the art to recommend this attitude of mind by simply pluming himself upon it as a virtue; so that the reader, to keep the advantage over his author which most readers enjoy, is tricked into professing the same view. And this spirit, as it is his chief lesson, is the greatest charm of his work. Thence, in spite of an uneven and emphatic key of expression, something trenchant and straightforward, something simple and surprising, distinguishes his poems. He has sayings that come home to one like the Bible. We fall upon Whitman, after the works of so many men who write better, with a sense of relief from strain, with a sense of touching nature, as when one passes out of the flaring, noisy thoroughfares of a great city into what he himself has called, with unexcelled imaginative justice of language, "the huge and thoughtful night." And his book in consequence, whatever may be the final judgment of its merit, whatever may be its influence on the future, should be in the hands of all parents and guardians as a specific for the distressing malady of being seventeen years old. Green-sickness yields to his treatment as to a charm of magic; and the youth, after a short course of reading, ceases to carry the universe upon his shoulders.

—from *Familiar Studies of Men and Books* (1882)

WILLIAM JAMES

Walt Whitman owes his importance in literature to the systematic expulsion from his writings of all contractile elements. The only sentiments he allowed himself to express were of the expansive order; and he expressed these in the first person, not as your mere monstrously conceited individual might so express them, but vicariously for all men, so that a passionate and mystic ontological emotion suffuses his words, and ends by persuading the reader that men and women, life and death, and all things are divinely good.

Thus it has come about that many persons to-day regard Walt Whitman as the restorer of the eternal natural religion. He has infected them with his own love of comrades, with his own gladness that he and they exist. Societies are actually formed for his cult; a periodical organ exists for its propagation, in which the lines of orthodoxy and heterodoxy are already beginning to be drawn; hymns are written by others in his peculiar prosody; and he is even explicitly compared with the founder of the Christian religion, not altogether to the advantage of the latter.

—from *The Varieties of Religious Experience* (1902)

EZRA POUND

His crudity is an exceeding great stench, but it *is* America. He is the hollow place in the rock that echoes with his time. He *does* 'chant the crucial stage' and he is the 'voice triumphant.' He is disgusting. He is an exceedingly nauseating pill, but he accomplishes his mission.

—from "What I Feel About Walt Whitman" (1909), in
Selected Prose: 1909–1965 (1973)

D. H. LAWRENCE

Whitman was the first to break the mental allegiance. He was the first to smash the old moral conception, that the soul of man is something "superior" and "above" the flesh. Even Emerson still maintained this tiresome "superiority" of the soul. Even Melville could not get over it. Whitman was the first heroic seer to seize the soul by the scruff of her neck and plant her down among the potsherds.

—from *Studies in Classic American Literature* (1923)

LANGSTON HUGHES

Walt Whitman wrote without the frills, furbelows, and decorations of conventional poetry, usually without rhyme or measured prettiness. Perhaps because of his simplicity, timid poetry lovers over the years have been frightened away from his Leaves of Grass, poems as firmly rooted and as brightly growing as the grass itself. Perhaps, too, because his all-embracing words lock arms with workers and farmers, Negroes and whites, Asiatics and Europeans, serfs and freemen, beaming democracy to all, many academic-minded intellectual isolationists in America have little use for Whitman, and so

have impeded his handclasp with today by keeping him impris-
oned in silence on library shelves. Still his words leap from their
pages and their spirit grows steadily stronger everywhere.
— "The Ceaseless Rings of Walt Whitman," in
I Hear the People Singing: Selected Poems of Walt Whitman (1946)

ALLEN GINSBERG
   Where are we going, Walt Whitman? The doors close in a hour.
      Which way does your beard point tonight?
   (I touch your book and dream of our odyssey in the
      supermarket and feel absurd.)
   Will we walk all night through solitary streets? The trees add shade
      to shade, lights out in the houses, we'll both be lonely.
   Will we stroll dreaming of the lost America of love past
      blue automobiles in driveways, home to our silent cottage?
   Ah, dear father, graybeard, lonely old courage-teacher,
      what America did you have when Charon quit poling his ferry
      and you got out on a smoking bank and stood watching
      the boat disappear on the black waters of Lethe?
                                    — from "A Supermarket in California" (1955)

PABLO NERUDA
There are many kinds of greatness, but let me say (though I be a
poet of the Spanish tongue) that Walt Whitman has taught me
more than Spain's Cervantes: in Walt Whitman's work one never
finds the ignorant being humbled, nor is the human condition ever
found offended.

We continue to live in a Whitmanesque age, seeing how new
men and new societies rise and grow, despite their birth-pangs.
Walt Whitman was the protagonist of a truly geographical person-
ality: the first man in history to speak with a truly continental Amer-
ican voice, to bear a truly American name.
                                    — from "We Live in a Whitmanesque Age" in
                                    the *New York Times* (April 14, 1972)

ALICIA OSTRIKER
But what moves me, and I suspect other American women poets, is
less the agreeable programmatic utterances than the gestures

whereby Whitman enacts the crossing of gender categories in his own person. It is not his claim to be "of the woman" that speeds us on our way but his capacity to be shamelessly receptive as well as active, to be expansive on an epic scale without a shred of nostalgia for narratives of conquest, to invent a rhetoric of power without authority, without hierarchy, and without violence. The omnivorous empathy of his imagination wants to incorporate All and therefore refuses to represent anything as unavailably Other. So long as femaleness in our culture signifies Otherness, Whitman's greed is our gain.

—from "Loving Walt Whitman and the Problem of America," in
The Continuing Presence of Walt Whitman (1992)

QUESTIONS

1. Why do you think Whitman is so often thought of as prototypically American? Is it because of his inclusiveness? His "barbaric yawp," as he called it? His refusal to adhere to traditional forms? His optimism?

2. In 1882 the district attorney of Boston, Oliver Stevens, sent publisher James R. Osgood an order to stop publication of *Leaves of Grass* on the grounds that it violated "the Public Statutes concerning obscene literature." Do you see any lines in *Leaves* as obscene or, in any case, as an outrage to public decency? You may want to examine closely the poems Osgood wanted Whitman to remove or change, such as "A Woman Waits for Me," "Spontaneous Me," and "The Dalliance of the Eagles."

3. How would you formulate Whitman's spirituality? Is it Christian? Just a loose religiosity? A body mystique? A version of an Asian religion, such as Buddhism?

4. Whitman maintained strong sympathies for women's rights activists, such as Abby Price and Frances Wright. But D. H. Lawrence criticized Whitman's descriptions of women—"athletic mothers of the states . . . depressing. Muscle and wombs—functional creatures—no more." What is your own take on Whitman's treatment of women?

FOR FURTHER READING

———◆———

WHITMAN: WRITINGS AND CONVERSATIONS

The Complete Writings of Walt Whitman. Edited by Richard Maurice
Bucke, Thomas B. Harned, and Horace L. Traubel. New York: G. P.
Putnam's Sons, 1902.

The Correspondence. 5 vols. Edited by Edwin Haviland Miller. New York:
New York University Press, 1961–1969.

Daybooks and Notebooks. 3 vols. Edited by William White. New York:
New York University Press, 1978.

The Early Poems and the Fiction. Edited by Thomas L. Brasher. New York:
New York University Press, 1963.

Faint Clews and Indirections: Manuscripts of Walt Whitman and His Family. Edited by Clarence Gohdes and Rollo G. Silver. New York: AMS
Press, 1965.

The Gathering of the Forces. 2 vols. Edited by Cleveland Rodgers and John
Black. New York: G. P. Putnam's Sons, 1920.

I Sit and Look Out: Editorials from the Brooklyn Daily Times. Edited by
Emory Holloway and Vernolian Schwarz. New York: Columbia University Press, 1932.

The Journalism. Edited by Herbert Bergman, Douglas A. Noverr, and Edward J. Recchia. 2 vols. New York: Peter Lang, 1998, 2003.

Leaves of Grass: A Textual Variorum of the Printed Poems. 3 vols. Edited by
Sculley Bradley, Harold W. Blodgett, Arthur Golden, and William
White. New York: New York University Press, 1980.

*New York Dissected: A Sheaf of Recently Discovered Newspaper Articles by
the Author of Leaves of Grass.* Edited by Emory Holloway and Ralph
Adimari. New York: R. R. Wilson, 1936.

Notebooks and Unpublished Prose Manuscripts. 6 vols. Edited by Edward
F. Grier. New York: New York University Press, 1984. New York: New
York University Press, 1961.

Notes and Fragments. Edited by Richard Maurice Bucke. Ontario, Canada: A. Talbot, 1899.

Specimen Days and Collect. 1882. New York: Dover, 1995.

Uncollected Poetry and Prose of Walt Whitman. 2 vols. Edited by Emory Holloway. Gloucester, MA: Peter Smith, 1972.

Walt Whitman and the Civil War: A Collection of Original Articles and Manuscripts. Edited by Charles I. Glicksberg. Philadelphia: University of Pennsylvania Press, 1933.

The Walt Whitman Archive: A Facsimile of the Poet's Manuscripts. 6 vols. Edited by Joel Myerson. New York: Garland, 1993.

Walt Whitman of the New York Aurora. Edited by Joseph Jay Rubin and Charles H. Brown. State College, PA: Bald Eagle Press, 1950.

Walt Whitman: Selected Poems 1855–1892. Edited by Gary Schmidgall. New York: St. Martin's Press, 1999.

Walt Whitman's Journalism: A Bibliography. Edited by William White. Detroit, MI: Wayne State University Press, 1969.

Walt Whitman's New York: From Manhattan to Montauk. Edited by Henry Christman. New York: New Amsterdam, 1989.

Whitman and Rolleston: A Correspondence. Edited by Horst Frenz. Dublin: Browne and Nolan, 1952.

With Walt Whitman in Camden. 9 vols. Edited by Horace Traubel. Various publishers, 1906–1961.

WHITMAN: REVIEWS AND CRITICISM

Allen, Gay Wilson. *The Solitary Singer: A Critical Biography of Walt Whitman.* New York: New York University Press, 1967.

—— and Folsom, Ed. *Walt Whitman and the World.* Iowa City: University of Iowa Press, 1995.

Aspiz, Harold. "Walt Whitman, Feminist." In *Walt Whitman Here and Now,* edited by Joann P. Krieg. Westport, CT: Greenwood Press, 1985, pp. 9–88.

Asselineau, Roger. *The Evolution of Walt Whitman.* Cambridge, MA: Harvard University Press, 1962.

Beach, Christopher. "'A Strong and Sweet Female Race': Cultural Discourse and Gender in Whitman's *Leaves of Grass.*" *American Transcendental Quarterly* 9:4 (December 1995), pp. 283–298.

Binns, Henry Bryan. *A Life of Walt Whitman.* London: Methuen, 1905.

Bradley, Sculley. "The Fundamental Metrical Principle in Whitman's Poetry." *American Literature* 10:4 (January 1939), pp. 437–459.

Brasher, Thomas L. *Whitman as Editor of the Brooklyn Daily Eagle*. Detroit: Wayne State University Press, 1970.

Bucke, Richard Maurice. *Walt Whitman*. Philadelphia: David McKay, 1883.

Burroughs, John. *Notes on Walt Whitman as Poet and Person*. New York: American News Company, 1867.

Callow, Philip. *From Noon to Starry Night: A Life of Walt Whitman*. Chicago: Ivan R. Dee, 1992.

Ceniza, Sherry. " 'Being a Woman . . . I Wish to Give My Own View': Some Nineteenth Century Women's Responses to the 1860 *Leaves of Grass*." In *The Cambridge Companion to Walt Whitman*, edited by Ezra Greenspan. Cambridge: Cambridge University Press, 1995.

——. *Walt Whitman and Nineteenth-century Women Reformers*. Tuscaloosa: University of Alabama Press, 1998.

Cherkovski, Neeli. *Whitman's Wild Children: Portraits of Twelve Poets*. South Royalton, VT: Steerforth Press, 1999.

Epstein, Daniel Mark. *Lincoln and Whitman: Parallel Lives in Civil War Washington*. New York: Ballantine Books, 2004.

Erkkila, Betsy. *Whitman the Political Poet*. New York: Oxford University Press, 1989.

Erkkila, Betsy, and Jay Grossman, eds. *Breaking Bounds: Whitman and American Cultural Studies*. New York: Oxford University Press, 1996.

Folsom, Ed. "The Whitman Recording." *Walt Whitman Quarterly Review* 9 (Spring 1992), pp. 214–216.

——, ed. *Whitman East and West: New Contexts for Reading Walt Whitman*. Iowa City: University of Iowa Press, 2002.

Garman, Bryan K. *A Race of Singers: Whitman's Working-class Hero from Guthrie to Springsteen*. Chapel Hill: University of North Carolina Press, 2000.

Garrett, Florence Rome. *The Rome Printing Shop*. Privately circulated, 1955.

Goodale, David. "Some of Walt Whitman's Borrowings." *American Literature* 10 (1938), pp. 202–213.

Greenspan, Ezra. *Walt Whitman and the American Reader*. New York: Cambridge University Press, 1990.

Hindus, Milton. *Walt Whitman: The Critical Heritage*. New York: Routledge, 1997.

Holloway, Emory. "Whitman as Journalist." *Yale Review* 11:2 (January 1922), pp. 212–215.

Kaplan, Justin. *Walt Whitman: A Life*. New York: Simon and Schuster, 1980.

Kaufman, Alan. *The Outlaw Bible of American Poetry*. New York and Emeryville, CA: Thunder's Mouth Press, 1999.

Killingsworth, M. Jimmie. *Whitman's Poetry of the Body: Sexuality, Politics, and the Text*. Chapel Hill: University of North Carolina Press, 1989.

Krieg, Joann P. *A Whitman Chronology*. Iowa City: University of Iowa Press, 1998.

Loving, Jerome. *Emerson, Whitman, and the American Muse*. Chapel Hill: University of North Carolina Press, 1982.

——. *Walt Whitman: The Song of Himself*. Berkeley: University of California Press, 1999.

——. "Whitman's Idea of Women." In *Walt Whitman of Mickle Street: A Centennial Collection*, edited by Geoffrey M. Sill. Knoxville: University of Tennessee Press, 1994, pp. 151–167.

Martin, Robert K., ed. *The Continuing Presence of Walt Whitman: The Life after the Life*. Iowa City: University of Iowa Press, 1992.

Miller, James E., Jr. *The American Quest for a Supreme Fiction: Whitman's Legacy in the Personal Epic*. Chicago: University of Chicago Press, 1979.

Mullins, Maire. "Leaves of Grass as a Woman's Book." *Walt Whitman Quarterly Review* 10:4 (Spring 1993), pp. 195–208.

Myerson, Joel. *Walt Whitman: A Descriptive Bibliography*. Pittsburgh, PA: University of Pittsburgh Press, 1993.

——. *Whitman in His Own Time: A Biographical Chronicle of His Life, Drawn from Recollections, Memoirs, and Interviews by Friends and Associates*. Expanded edition. Iowa City: University of Iowa Press, 2000.

Perlman, Jim, Ed Folsom, and Dan Campion, eds. *Walt Whitman: The Measure of His Song*. Duluth, MN: Holy Cow! Press, 1998.

Perry, Bliss. *Walt Whitman, His Life and Work*. Boston and New York: Houghton Mifflin, 1906.

Pollack, Vivian. *The Erotic Whitman*. Berkeley: University of California Press, 2000.

Price, Kenneth M., ed. *Walt Whitman: The Contemporary Reviews.* New York: Cambridge University Press, 1996.

Reynolds, David S. *A Historical Guide to Walt Whitman.* New York: Oxford University Press, 2000.

——. *Walt Whitman's America: A Cultural Biography.* New York: Vintage, 1996.

Rubin, Joseph Jay. *The Historic Whitman.* University Park: Pennsylvania State University Press, 1973.

Schmidgall, Gary. *Walt Whitman: A Gay Life.* New York: Dutton, 1997.

Schyberg, Frederik. *Walt Whitman.* New York: Columbia University Press, 1951.

Shephard, Esther. *Walt Whitman's Pose.* New York: Harcourt, Brace, 1938.

Sill, Geoffrey, ed. *Walt Whitman of Mickle Street.* Knoxville: University of Tennessee Press, 1994.

Stovall, Floyd. *The Foreground of Leaves of Grass.* Charlottesville: University of Virginia Press, 1974.

Traubel, Horace, Richard M. Bucke, and Thomas Harned, eds. *In re Walt Whitman.* Philadelphia: David McKay, 1893.

Woodress, James, ed. *Critical Essays on Walt Whitman.* Boston: G. K. Hall, 1983.

WHITMAN AND NEW YORK: CONTEXTS

Anbinder, Taylor. *Five Points.* New York: Free Press, 2001.

Asbury, Herbert. *The Gangs of New York.* New York: Alfred A. Knopf, 1928.

Black, Mary, ed. *Old New York in Early Photographs.* New York: Dover Publications, 1976.

Burrows, Edwin G., and Mike Wallace, eds. *Gotham: A History of New York City to 1898.* New York: Oxford University Press, 1999.

Gray, Christopher. *New York Streetscapes: Tales of Manhattan's Significant Buildings and Landmarks.* New York: Harry N. Abrams, 2003.

Homberger, Eric. *The Historical Atlas of New York City.* New York: Holt, 1994.

Jackson, Kenneth T., ed. *Encyclopedia of New York City.* New Haven, CT: Yale University Press, 1995.

Jackson, Kenneth T., and David S. Dunbar, eds. *Empire City: New York Through the Centuries.* New York: Columbia University Press, 2002.

LeMaster, J. R., and Donald D. Kummings, eds. *Walt Whitman: An Encyclopedia.* New York: Garland, 1998.

Lopate, Phillip, ed. *Writing New York: A Literary Anthology.* New York: Library of America, 1998.

O'Connell, Shaun. *Remarkable, Unspeakable New York: A Literary History.* Boston: Beacon Press, 1995.

Sante, Luc. *Low Life: Lures and Snares of Old New York.* New York: Vintage, 1992.

Voorsanger, Catherine Hoover, and John K. Howat, eds. *Art and the Empire City: New York, 1825–1861.* New York: Metropolitan Museum of Art, 2000.

USEFUL WEB SITES

Library of Congress site for the Thomas Biggs Harned Walt Whitman Collection: *http://memory.loc.gov/ammem/wwhtml/wwhome.html*

The Mickle Street Review: An Electronic Journal of Whitman and American Studies: *http://www.micklestreet.rutgers.edu/*

The Walt Whitman Archive: *http://www.whitmanarchive.org/*

Whitman and the Development of Leaves of Grass: *http://www.sc.edu/library/spcoll/amlit/whitman.html*

INDEX OF TITLES
AND FIRST LINES

Poem titles (in italics) and first lines of poems are listed together alphabetically, with reference to page numbers. In cases where first lines and titles are identical, only the title is listed. As in the text, titles from the First Edition are listed in brackets as their own entry.

A

A batter'd, wreck'd old man 558

A carol closing sixty-nine—a résumé—a repetition 636

A glimpse through an interstice caught 290

A great year and place 389

A group of little children with their ways and chatter flow in 778

A lesser proof than old Voltaire's, yet greater 656

A line in long array where they wind betwixt green islands 449

A mask, a perpetual natural disguiser of herself 427

A newer garden of creation, no primal solitude 542

A song, a poem of itself-the word itself a dirge 649

A song of the rolling earth, and of words according 373

A thousand perfect men and women appear 429

A vague mist hanging 'round half the pages: 665

A voice from Death, solemn and strange, in all his sweep and power 674

A woman waits for me, she contains all, nothing is lacking 263

A young man came to me with a message from his brother 130

Aboard at a Ship's Helm 411

Abraham Lincoln, Born Feb. 12, 1809 639

Add to your show, before you close it, France 668

Adieu O soldier 472

Adieu to a Soldier 472

Afoot and light-hearted I take to the open road 305

After a long, long course, hundreds of years, denials 668

After a week of physical anguish 659

After an Interval 774

After an interval, reading, here in the midnight 774

After surmounting three score and ten 665

After the Argument 778

After the dazzle of day is gone 639

After the Dazzle of Day 639

After the Sea-Ship 415

After the sea-ship, after the whistling winds 415

After the Supper and Talk 660

After the supper and talk-after the day is done 660

Again a verse for sake of you 772

Ages and Ages Returning at Intervals 268

(Ah little recks the laborer 351

Ah, not this marble, dead and cold 646

Ah Poverties, Wincings, and Sulky Retreats 610

Ah, whispering, something again, unseen 669

All Is Truth 607

All submit to them where they sit, inner, secure, unapproachable to analysis in the soul 537

All you are doing and saying is to America dangled mirages 424

Always our old feuillage! 327

Ambition 726

America 638

Amid these days of order, ease, prosperity 654

Among the men and women the multitude 293

Among the Multitude 293

An ancient song, reciting, ending 670

An old man bending I come among new faces 457

And now gentlemen, 281

And whence and why come you? 663

And who art thou? said I to the soft-falling shower 653

And Yet Not You Alone 642

And yet not you alone, twilight and burying ebb 642

Apostroph 759

Apparitions 665

Apple orchards, the trees all cover'd with blossoms 640

Approaching, nearing, curious 637

Are You the New Person Drawn toward Me? 283

Arm'd year-year of the struggle 432

Army Corps on the March, An 450

Artilleryman's Vision, The 465

As Adam Early in the Morning 272

As at Thy Portals Also Death 625

As consequent from store of summer rains 502

As Consequent, Etc. 502

As down the stage again 648

As I Ebb'd with the Ocean of Life 406

As I Lay with My Head in Your Lap Camerado 469

As I Ponder'd in Silence 165

As I sit in twilight late alone by the flickering oak-flame 672

As I sit with others at a great feast, suddenly while the music is playing 586

As I Sit Writing Here 637

As I sit writing here, sick and grown old 637

As I walk these broad majestic days of peace 616

As I Walk These Broad Majestic Days 616

As I Watch'd the Ploughman Ploughing 587

As if a Phantom Caress'd Me 582

As in a Swoon 776

As in a swoon, one instant 776

As one by one withdraw the lofty actors 645

As the Greek's Signal Flame 658

As the Greek's signal flame, by antique records told 658

As the time draws nigh glooming a cloud 618

As the Time Draws Nigh 618

As They Draw to a Close 629

As Toilsome I Wander'd Virginia's Woods 456

Ashes of soldiers South or North 620
Ashes of Soldiers 620
Ashes of Soldiers: Epigraph 772
Assurances 582
At the last, tenderly 587
AUTUMN RIVULETS 502
Aye, well I know 'tis ghastly to descend that valley: 784

B

Backward Glance o'er Travel'd Roads 681
Base of All Metaphysics, The 281
Bathed in War's Perfume 771
Bathed in war's perfume-delicate flag! 771
Be composed—be at ease with me—I am Walt Whitman, liberal and lusty as Nature 530
Beat! Beat! Drums! 433
Beat! beat! drums!—blow! bugles! blow! 433
Beautiful Women 427
Beauty of the Ship, The 773
Before the dark-brow'd sons of Spain 714
Beginners 172
Beginning my studies the first step pleas'd me so much 172
Beginning My Studies 172
Behold around us pomp and pride; 720
Behold This Swarthy Face 286
BIRDS OF PASSAGE 380
Bivouac on a Mountain Side 450
Blood-Money 738
[Boston Ballad, A] 135
Boston Ballad (1854), A 417
Brave, brave were the soldiers (high named to-day) who lived through the fight 636
Bravest Soldiers, The 636
Bravo, Paris Exposition! 668
Broadway 647

Broadway Pageant, A 395
By Blue Ontario's Shore 485
By Broad Potomac's Shore 612
By broad Potomac's shore, again old tongue 612
By That Long Scan of Waves 642
By that long scan of waves, myself call'd back, resumed upon myself 642
By the Bivouac's Fitful Flame 450
By the city dead-house by the gate 511
BY THE ROADSIDE 417

C

CALAMUS 274
Calamus. 16 754
Calamus. 5 769
Calamus. 8 755
Calamus. 9 756
California song, A 361
Calming Thought of All, The 652
Camps of Green 627
Carol Closing Sixty-nine, A 636
Cavalry Crossing a Ford 449
Centenarian's Story, The 445
Centre of equal daughters, equal sons 638
Chanting the Square Deific 578
Chanting the square deific, out of the One advancing, out of the sides 578
Chants Democratic. 6 747
CHILDREN OF ADAM 252
Child's Amaze, A 426
Christmas Greeting, A 671
City Dead-House, The 511
City of Orgies 285
City of orgies, walks and joys 285
City of Ships 444
Clear Midnight, A 617
Clear the way there Jonathan! 135
Columbian's Song, The 722
Come closer to me, 91

Come, I will make the continent indissoluble 278

Come my tan-faced children, 382

Come said the Muse, 380

Come Up from the Fields Father 451

Come up from the fields father, here's a letter from our Pete 451

Commonplace, The 676

Continuities 649

Courage yet, my brother or my sister! 514

Crossing Brooklyn Ferry 316

D

Dalliance of the Eagles, The 425

Darest Thou Now O Soul 577

Dead Emperor, The 657

Dead Tenor, The 648

Death and Burial of McDonald Clarke, The 728

Death of General Grant 645

Death of the Nature-Lover 731

Death's Valley 783

Debris 764

Delicate Cluster 470

Delicate cluster! flag of teeming life! 470

Despairing Cries 768

Despairing cries float ceaselessly toward me, day and night 768

Did we count great, O soul, to penetrate the themes of mighty books 637

Did you ask dulcet rhymes from me? 470

Dirge for Two Veterans 462

Dismantled Ship, The 658

Down on the ancient wharf, the sand, I sit, with a newcomer chatting: 656

DRUM-TAPS 430

Dying Veteran, The 654

E

Earth, My Likeness 291

Eidólons 168

Eighteen Sixty-One 432

Election Day, November 1884 643

End of All, The 720

Ended Day, An 666

Enfans d'Adam. 11 754

Ethiopia Saluting the Colors 466

[Europe: The 72d and 73d Years of These States] 133

Europe, The 72d and 73d Years of These States 419

Evening Lull, An 659

Ever the undiscouraged, resolute, struggling soul of man; 650

Excelsior 609

F

[Faces] 126

Faces 596

Facing West from California's Shores 271

Fame's Vanity 710

Fancies at Navesink 640

Far back, related on my mother's side 648

Far hence amid an isle of wondrous beauty 511

Farm Picture, A 426

Fast-anchor'd Eternal O Love! 293

Fast-anchor'd eternal O love! O woman I love! 293

Few Drops Known, The 779

FIRST ANNEX: SANDS AT SEVENTY 635

First Dandelion, The 638

First O Songs for a Prelude 430

Flood-tide below me! I see you face to face! 316

Font of Type, A 637

For Him I Sing 171

For his o'erarching and last lesson the graybeard sufi 675

For Queen Victoria's Birthday 777

For the lands and for these
    passionate days and for myself 503
For Us Two, Reader Dear 778
For You O Democracy 278
Forms, qualities, lives, humanity,
    language, thoughts 422
France, The 18th Year of these States
    389
From all the rest I single out you,
    having a message for you 585
From east to west across the
    horizon's edge 667
From Far Dakota's Cañons 613
From Montauk Point 635
From My Last Years 773
From my last years, last thoughts I
    here bequeath 773
FROM NOON TO STARRY
    NIGHT 595
*From Paumanok Starting I Fly like a
    Bird* 434
From Pent-up Aching Rivers 252
Full of Life Now 294
Full of life now, compact, visible
    294
Full of wickedness, I—of many a
    smutch'd deed reminiscent—of
    worse deeds capable 782

G

Germs 422
Give Me the Splendid Silent Sun 461
Give me the splendid silent sun with
    all his beams full-dazzling 461
Give me your hand old
    Revolutionary 445
Gliding o'er All 428
Gliding o'er all, through all, 428
Glimpse, A 290
Gods 421
Good-Bye My Fancy 664
Good-Bye my Fancy! 679
Good-bye my fancy—(I had a word
    to say 664

Grand Is the Seen 679
Grand is the seen, the light, to me-
    grand are the sky and stars 679
[Great Are the Myths] 142
Great are the myths . . . . I too
    delight in them 142
Great Are the Myths 744
Great are the myths-I too delight in
    them; 744
Greater than memory of Achilles or
    Ulysses 638

H

Had I the choice to tally greatest
    bards 641
Had I the Choice 641
Halcyon Days 640
Hand-Mirror, A 421
Hark, some wild trumpeter, some
    strange musician 600
Hast Never Come to Thee an Hour
    428
Have I no weapon-word for
    thee—some message brief and
    fierce? 667
Have you learn'd lessons only of
    those who admired you, and were
    tender with you, and stood aside
    for you? 655
He is wisest who has the most
    caution 764
Heave the anchor short! 663
Here first the duties of to-day, the
    lessons of the concrete 652
Here the frailest leaves of me and yet
    my strongest lasting 290
Here the Frailest Leaves of Me 290
Here, take this gift, 173
Hold it up sternly—see this it sends
    back, (who is it? is it you?) 421
Hours continuing long, sore, and
    heavy-hearted 756
House of Friends, The 739
How dare one say it? 678

How Solemn as One by One 469

How solemn! sweeping this dense black tide! 735

How sweet the silent backward tracings 639

How they are provided for upon the earth, (appearing at intervals,) 172

Hush'd Be the Camps To-day 485

I

I am he that aches with amorous love; 270

I Am He That Aches with Love 270

I celebrate myself 29

I celebrate myself, and sing myself 190

I doubt it not—then more, far more; 667

I Dream'd in a Dream 291

I dream'd in a dream I saw a city invincible to the attacks of the whole of the rest of the earth 291

I have not so much emulated the birds that musically sing 779

I Hear America Singing 175

I hear America singing, the varied carols I hear 175

I hear it was charged against me that I sought to destroy institutions 288

I Hear It Was Charged Against Me 288

I heard that you ask'd for something to prove this puzzle the New World 167

I Heard You Solemn-Sweet Pipes of the Organ 271

I heard you solemn-sweet pipes of the organ as last Sunday morn I pass'd the church 271

I met a seer, 168

I need no assurances, I am a man who is pre-occupied of his own soul 582

I Saw in Louisiana a Live-Oak Growing 286

I Saw Old General at Bay 465

I say whatever tastes sweet to the most perfect person, that is finally right. 758

I see before me now a traveling army halting 450

I see in you the estuary that enlarges and spreads itself grandly as it pours in the great sea. 428

I see the sleeping babe nestling the breast of its mother 427

[I Sing the Body Electric] 119

I Sing the Body Electric 254

I Sit and Look Out 424

I sit and look out upon all the sorrows of the world, and upon all oppression and shame 424

I stand as on some mighty eagle's beak 635

I wander all night in my vision, 109

I wander'd all night in my vision 560

I was asking for something specific and perfect for my city 606

I Was Looking a Long While 530

I was looking a long while for Intentions 530

If I should need to name, O Western World, your powerfulest scene and show 643

If thou art balked, O Freedom 739

In a far-away northern county in the placid pastoral region 539

In a little house keep I pictures suspended, it is not a fix'd house 542

In Cabin'd Ships at Sea 166

In dreams I was a ship, and sail'd the boundless seas 777

In Former Songs 776

In former songs Pride have I sung, and Love, and passionate, joyful Life 776

In midnight sleep of many a face of anguish 614

In Paths Untrodden 274

In softness, languor, bloom, and growth 779

In some unused lagoon, some nameless bay 658

In the new garden, in all the parts 754

Inca's Daughter, The 714

INSCRIPTIONS 165

Interpolation Sounds 668

Is reform needed? is it through you? 533

Italian Music in Dakota 541

J

Joy, Shipmate, Joy! 629

K

Kiss to the Bride 780

Kosmos 534

L

L of G 777

L. of G.'s Purport 678

Lady, accept a birth-day thought— haply and idle gift and token 777

[Last Droplets] 776

Last droplets of and after spontaneous rain 776

Last Invocation, The 587

Last of Ebb, and Daylight Waning 641

Laws for Creations 529

Leaf for Hand in Hand, A 291

Leaflets 768

Leaves of Grass. 20 756

Lessons 772

Let that which stood in front go behind 501

Let the reformers descend from the stands where they are forever

bawling—let an idiot or insane person appear on each of the stands 570

Let us twain walk aside from the rest; 763

Life and Death 653

Life 650

Lingering Last Drops 663

Lo, the unbounded sea, 175

Lo, Victress on the Peaks 471

Locations and Times 428

Locations and times—what is it in me that meets them all, whenever and wherever, and makes me at home? 428

Long I thought that knowledge alone would suffice me—O if I could but obtain knowledge! 755

Long, Long Hence 668

Long, Too Long America 460

Look down fair moon and bathe this scene 468

Look Down Fair Moon 468

Love That Is Hereafter, The 716

Lover divine and perfect Comrade 421

M

Manhattan's streets I saunter'd pondering 517

Mannahatta 606

Mannahatta 635

Many things to absorb I teach to help you become eleve of mine 293

March in the Ranks Hard-Prest, and the Road Unknown, A 454

Me Imperturbe 174

Me imperturbe, standing at ease in Nature, 174

Mediums 611

Memories 638

MEMORIES OF PRESIDENT LINCOLN 475

Miracles 531

Mirages 677

Mississippi at Midnight, The 735

More experiences and sights, stranger, than you'd think for; 677

Mother and Babe 427

My 71st Year 665

My Canary Bird 637

My city's fit and noble name resumed 635

My Departure 711

My Legacy 626

My Picture-Gallery 542

My science-friend, my noblest woman-friend 650

My spirit to yours dear brother 528

Myself and Mine 390

Myself and mine gymnastic ever 390

Mystic Trumpeter, The 600

N

Nations ten thousand years before these States, and many times ten thousand years before these States 516

Native Moments 270

Native moments—when you come upon me—ah you are here now 270

Nay, do not dream, designer dark 783

Nay, Tell Me Not To-day the Publish'd Shame 781

Night on the Prairies 585

No Labor-saving Machine 290

Noiseless Patient Spider, A 584

Not a sigh was heard, not a tear was shed 728

Not alone those camps of white, old comrades of the wars 627

Not from successful love alone 640

Not Heat Flames up and Consumes 284

Not Heaving from My Ribb'd Breast Only 280

Not in a gorgeous hall of pride 711

Not in a gorgeous hall of pride 731

Not Meagre, Latent Boughs Alone 657

Not meagre, latent boughs alone, O songs! (scaly and bare, like eagles' talons) 657

Not My Enemies Ever Invade Me 772

Not my enemies ever invade me—no harm to my pride from them I fear; 772

Not the Pilot 457

Not the pilot has charged himself to bring his ship into port, though beaten back and many times baffled 457

Not to exclude or demarcate, or pick out evils from their formidable masses (even to expose them,) 678

Not Youth Pertains to Me 467

Nothing is ever really lost, or can be lost 649

Now Finalé to the Shore 630

Now Lift Me Close 763

Now lift me close to your face till I whisper 763

Now list to my morning's romanza, I tell the signs of the Answerer 322

Now Precedent Songs, Farewell 658

Now, dearest comrade, lift me to your face 763

Now precedent songs, farewell—by every name farewell 658

O

O a new song, a free song 435

O, beauteous is the earth! and fair 716

O Captain! My Captain! 484

O Captain! my Captain! our fearful trip is done 484

O, Death! a black and pierceless pall 729

O, God of Coumbia! O, Shield of the Free! 733

O Hymen! O Hymenee! 269

O hymen! O hymenee! Why do you tantalize me thus? 269

O Living Always, Always Dying 584

O Magnet-South 604

O magnet-South! O glistening perfumed South! my South! 604

O, many a panting, noble heart 710

O mater! O fils! 759

O Me! O Life! 423

O me! O life! of the questions of these recurring 423

O me, man of slack faith so long 607

O sight of pity, shame and dole! 520

O Star of France (1870-71) 537

O Sun of Real Peace 762

O sun of real peace! O hastening light! 762

O take my hand Walt Whitman! 294

O Tan-faced Prairie-Boy 468

O to make the most jubilant song! 332

O You Whom I Often and Silently Come 293

O you whom I often and silently come where you are that I may be with you 293

Ode 733

Of Equality—as if it harm'd me, giving others the same chances and rights as myself—as if it were not indispensable to my own rights that others possess the same. 428

Of heroes, history, grand events, premises, myths, poems 779

Of Him I Love Day and Night 580

Of him I love day and night I dream'd I heard he was dead 580

Of Justice—as if Justice could be any thing but the same ample

law, expounded by natural judges and saviors 427

Of Many a Smutch'd Deed Reminiscent 782

Of obedience, faith, adhesiveness; 427

Of olden time, when it came to pass 738

Of ownership—as if one fit to own things could not at pleasure enter upon all, and incorporate them into himself or herself; 422

Of ownership—As if one fit to own things could not at pleasure enter upon all, and incorporate them into himself or herself; 771

Of persons arrived at high positions, ceremonies, wealth, scholarships, and the like; 531

Of public opinion 610

Of That Blithe Throat of Thine 646

Of that blithe throat of thing from arctic bleak and blank 646

Of the Terrible Doubt of Appearances 280

Of these years I sing 621

Of the visages of things—And of piercing through to the accepted hells beneath; 757

Of waters, forests, hills 770

Of what I write from myself—As if that were not the resume; 757

Offerings 429

OLD AGE ECHOES 779

Old Age's Lambent Peaks 659

Old Age's Ship & Crafty Death's 667

Old Chants 670

Old farmers, travelers, workmen (no matter how crippled or bent,) 651

Old Ireland 511

Old Man's Thought of School, An 540

Old Salt Kossabone 648

Old War-Dreams 614

On a flat road runs the well-train'd runner 426

On a low couch reclining 719

On earth are many sights of woe 717

On journeys through the States we start 173

On Journeys Through the States 173

On my Northwest coast in the midst of the night a fishermen's group stands watching 537

On the Beach at Night 411

On the Beach at Night Alone 413

On the Same Picture 784

On, On the Same, Ye Jocund Twain! 664

Once I Pass'd Through a Populous City 270

Once I pass'd through a populous city imprinting my brain for future use with its shows, architecture, customs, traditions 270

Once on his star-gemmed, dazzling throne 723

One day, an obscure youth, a wanderer 726

One Hour to Madness and Joy 267

One hour to madness and joy! O furious! O confine me not! 267

One Thought Ever at the Fore 780

One's-Self I Sing 165

One's-self I sing, a simple separate person 165

Only themselves understand themselves and the like of themselves 423

Or from That Sea of Time 775

Orange Buds by Mail from Florida 656

Osceola 673

Others May Praise What They Like 535

Our Future Lot 709

Our Old Feuillage 327

Out from behind this bending rough-cut mask 525

Out from Behind This Mask 525

Out of May's Shows Selected 640

Out of the Cradle Endlessly Rocking 400

Out of the murk of heaviest clouds 612

Out of the Rolling Ocean the Crowd 268

Out of the rolling ocean the crowd came a drop gently to me 268

Outlines for a Tomb 523

Over and through the burial chant 668

Over the Carnage Rose Prophetic a Voice 464

Over the Western sea hither from Niphon come 395

Ox-tamer, The 539

P

Pallid Wreath, The 665

Passage to India 549

Passing stranger! you do not know how longingly I look upon you 287

Patroling Barnegat 415

Paumanok 635

Paumanok Picture, A 594

Pensive and Faltering 587

Pensive on her dead gazing I heard the Mother of All 626

Pensive on Her Dead Gazing 626

Perfections 423

Persian Lesson, A 675

Pilot in the Mist, The 640

Pioneers! O Pioneers! 382

Play-Ground, The 732

Poets to Come 176

Poets to come! orators, singers, musicians to come! 176

Portals 630

Prairie States, The 542

Prairie Sunset, A 655
Prairie-Grass Dividing, The 288
Prayer of Columbus 558
[Preface] 7
Preface Note to 2d Annex 661
Primeval My Love for the Woman I Love 762
Promise to California, A 289
Proud Music of the Storm 543
Proudly the Flood Comes In 642
Proudly the flood comes in, shouting, foaming, advancing 642
Punishment of Pride, The 723

Q

Queries to My Seventieth Year 637
Quicksand Years 583
Quicksand years that whirl me I know not whither 583

R

Race of Veterans 467
Race of veterans—race of victors! 467
Reconciliation 468
Recorders Ages Hence 282
Red Jacket (From Aloft) 645
Respondez! 749
Respondez! Respondez! 749
Resurgemus 741
Return of the Heroes, The 503
Reversals 501
Riddle Song, A 608
Rise O Days from Your Fathomless Deeps 441
Rise O Days from your fathomless deeps, till you loftier, fiercer sweep 441
Roaming in Thought 426
Roaming in thought over the Universe, I saw the little that is Good steadily hastening towards immortality 426
Roots and Leaves Themselves Alone 284

Roots and leaves themselves alone are these 284
"Rounded Catalogue Divine Complete, The" 676
Runner, The 426

S

Sacred, blithesome, undenied 780
Sail Out for Good, Eidólon Yacht! 663
Salut au Monde! 294
Sane, random, negligent hours 781
Sauntering the pavement or riding the country byroads here then are faces 126
Sauntering the pavement or riding the country by-road, lo such faces! 596
Savantism 174
Says 758
Scented Herbage of My Breast 274
Sea beauty! stretched and basking! 635
SEA-DRIFT 400
SECOND ANNEX: GOOD-BYE MY FANCY 661
Shakspere-Bacon's Cipher 667
Ship Ahoy! 777
Ship Starting, The 175
Shot gold, maroon and violet, dazzling silver, emerald, fawn 655
Shut Not Your Doors 176
Shut not your doors to me proud libraries 176
Sight in Camp in the Daybreak Gray and Dim, A 455
Silent and amazed even when a little boy 426
Simple and fresh and fair from winter's close emerging 638
Simple, spontaneous, curious, two souls interchanging 778
Singer in the Prison, The 520
Singing my days 549

Sketch, A 730

Skirting the river road, (my forenoon walk, my rest,) 425

[Sleepers , The] 109

Sleepers, The 560

Small the Theme of My Chant 651

Small the theme of my Chant, yet the greatest—namely, One's-Self—a simple, separate person. 651

So far, and so far, and on toward the end 756

So Long! 630

Sobbing of the Bells, The 628

Solid, Ironical, Rolling Orb 771

Somehow I cannot let it go yet, funeral though it is 665

Something startles me where I thought I was safest 512

Sometimes with One I Love 292

Sometimes with one I love I fill myself with rage for fear I effuse unreturn'd love 292

Song at Sunset 623

Song for All Seas, All Ships 414

Song for Certain Congressmen 735

[Song for Occupations, A] 91

Song for Occupations, A 365

Song of Exposition 351

Song of Joys, A 332

[Song of Myself] 29

Song of Myself 190

Song of Prudence 517

[Song of the Answerer] 130

Song of the Answerer 322

Song of the Banner at Daybreak 435

Song of the Broad-Axe 339

Song of the Open Road 305

Song of the Redwood-Tree 361

Song of the Rolling Earth, A 373

Song of the Universal 380

SONGS OF PARTING 618

Soon Shall the Winter's Foil Be Here 653

Soon shall the winter's foil be here; 653

Sounds of the Winter 671

Sounds of the winter too 671

Spain, 1873-74 612

Spanish Lady, The 719

Sparkles from the Wheel 532

Spirit That Form'd This Scene 616

Spirit Whose Work Is Done 471

Spirit whose work is done—spirit of dreadful hours! 471

Splendor of ended day floating and filling me 623

Spontaneous Me 264

Spontaneous me, Nature 264

Starting from fish-shape Paumanok where I was born 177

Starting from Paumanok 177

States! 769

Steaming the northern rapids—(an old St. Lawrence reminiscence) 640

Still Though the One I Sing 176

Stranger, if you passing meet me and desire to speak to me, why should you not speak to me? 177

Stronger Lessons 655

Suddenly out of its stale and drowsy lair, the lair of slaves 133

Suddenly out of its stale and drowsy lair, the lair of slaves 419

Suddenly, out of its stale and drowsy lair, the lair of slaves 741

Supplement Hours 781

T

Tears 409

Tears! tears! tears! 409

Tests 537

Thanks in Old Age 652

Thanks in old age—thanks ere I go 652

That coursing on, whate'er men's speculations 652

That Music Always Round Me 583

That music always round me, unceasing, unbeginning, yet long untaught I did not hear 583

That Shadow My Likeness 294

That shadow my likeness that goes to and fro seeking a livelihood, chattering, chaffering, 294

That which eludes this verse and any verse 608

The appointed winners in a long-stretch'd game; 639

The bodies of men and women engirth me, and I engirth them 119

The business man the acquirer vast 626

The commonplace I sing; 676

The devilish and the dark, the dying and diseas'd 676

The last sunbeam 462

The mystery of mysteries, the crude and hurried ceaseless flame, spontaneous, bearing on itself 784

The noble sire fallen on evil days 444

The prairie-grass dividing, its special odor breathing 288

The sobbing of the bells, the sudden death-news everywhere 628

The soft voluptuous opiate shades 657

The soothing sanity and blitheness of completion 666

The touch of flame—the illuminating fire—the loftiest look at last 659

The two old, simple problems ever intertwined 653

The untold want by life and land ne'er granted 629

Thee for my recitative 603

Then Last of All 643

Then Last of All, caught from these shores, this hill 643

Then Shall Perceive 779

There are who teach only the sweet lessons of peace and safety; 772

[There Was a Child Went Forth] 138

There Was a Child Went Forth 509

There was a child went forth every day 138

There was a child went forth every day 509

These Carols 630

These carols sung to cheer my passage through the world I see 630

These I Singing in Spring 278

These I singing in spring collect for lovers 278

They shall arise in the States 611

Thick-sprinkled Bunting 615

Thick sprinkled bunting! flag of stars! 615

Think of the Soul 748

This breast which now alternate burns 709

This Compost 512

This Day, O Soul 772

This day, O Soul, I give you a wondrous mirror; 772

This Dust Was Once the Man 485

This is thy hour O Soul, thy free flight into the wordless 617

This latent mine—these unlaunch'd voices—passionate powers 637

This moment yearning and thoughtful sitting alone 287

This Moment Yearning and Thoughtful 287

Thither as I look I see each result and glory retracing itself and nestling
close, always obligated 174

Thou hast slept all night upon the storm 410

Thou Mother with Thy Equal Brood 588

Thou Orb Aloft Full-Dazzling 595

Thou orb aloft full-dazzling! thou hot October noon! 595

Thou reader throbbest life and pride and love the same as I 177

Thou Reader 177

Thought 427

Thought 427

Thought 428

Thought 531

Thought 586

Thought 757

Thought of Columbus, A 784

Thoughts 422

Thoughts 610

Thoughts 621

Thoughts. 1 757

Thoughts. 2 770

Thoughts. 4 771

Thoughts, suggestions, aspirations, pictures 777

Through the ample open door of the peaceful country barn 426

Through the soft evening air enwinding all 541

Time to Come 729

To a Certain Cantatrice 173

To a Certain Civilian 470

To a Common Prostitute 530

To a Foil'd European Revolutionaire 514

To a Historian 167

To a Locomotive in Winter 603

To a President 424

To a Pupil 533

To a Stranger 287

To a Western Boy 293

To Be at All 782

To be at all—what is better than that? 782

To conclude, I announce what comes after me. 630

To Foreign Lands 167

To get betimes in Boston town I rose this morning early 417

To Get the Final Lilt of Songs 647

To Him That Was Crucified 528

To Old Age 428

To One Shortly to Die 585

To Rich Givers 425

To Soar in Freedom and in Fullness of Power 779

To the East and to the West 292

To the Garden the World 252

To the garden the world anew ascending 252

To the Leaven'd Soil They Trod 473

To the leaven'd soil they trod calling I sing for the last 473

To the Man-of-War-Bird 410

To the Pending Year 667

To the Reader at Parting 763

To the States 173

To the States or any one of them, or any city of the States, *Resist much, obey little* 173

To the States, To Identify the 16th, 17th, or 18th Presidentiad 429

To the Sun-set Breeze 669

To Thee Old Cause 168

[To Think of Time] 102

To Think of Time 570

To think of time—of all that retrospection 570

To think of Time . . . .to think through the retrospection 102

To Those Who've Fail'd 636

To those who've fail'd, in aspiration vast 636

To You 177

To You 387

To You 763

To-day a rude brief recitative 414

To-day and Thee 639

To-day, from each and all, a breath of prayer—a pulse of thought 639

To-day, with bending head and eyes, thou, too, Columbia 657

Torch, The 537

Transpositions 570

Trickle Drops 285

Trickle drops! My blue veins leaving! 285

True Conquerors 651

Turn O Libertad 473

Turn O libertad, for the war is over 473

Twenty Years 656

Twilight 657

Twilight Song, A 672

Two Rivulets 774

Two Rivulets side by side 774

U

Unexpress'd, The 678

Unfolded Out of the Folds 533

Unfolded out of the folds of the woman man comes unfolded, and is always to come unfolded 533

Unnamed Lands 516

United States to Old World Critics, The 652

Unseen Buds 679

Unseen buds, infinite, hidden well 679

Untold Want, The 629

Upon the ocean's wave-worn shore 730

Upon this scene, this show 645

V

Vigil Strange I Kept on the Field One Night 453

Virginia-The West 444

Visor'd 427

Vocalism 526

Vocalism, measure, concentration, determination, and the divine power to speak words 526

Voice from Death, A 674

Voice of the Rain, The 653

W

Wallabout Martyrs, The 638

Wandering at Morn 540

Warble for Lilac-Time 522

Warble me now for joy of lilac-time, (returning in reminiscence,) 522

Washington's Monument, February, 1885 646

We All Shall Rest at Last 717

We are all docile dough-faces 735

We Two Boys Together Clinging 289

We Two, How Long We Were Fool'd 269

Weapon shapely, naked, wan 339

Weave In, My Hardy Life 611

Weave in, weave in, my hardy life 611

Welcome, Brazilian brother—thy ample place is ready; 671

What a fair and happy place 722

What Am I After All 534

What am I after all but a child, pleas'd with the sound of my own name? repeating it over and over 534

What are those of the known but to ascend and enter the Unknown? 630

What Best I See in Thee 615

What General has a good army in himself, has a good army: 768

What hurrying human tides, or day or night! 647

What may we chant, O thou within this tomb? 523

What Place Is Besieged? 176

What place is besieged, and vainly tries to raise the siege? 176

What Ship Puzzled at Sea 584

What ship puzzled at sea, cons for
the true reckoning? 584

*What Think You I Take My Pen in
Hand?* 292

What you give me I cheerfully
accept 425

When his hour for death had come
673

*When I Heard at the Close of the
Day* 283

When I heard at the close of the day
how my name had been receiv'd
with plaudits in the capitol, still it
was not a happy night for
me that follow'd 283

*When I Heard the Learn'd
Astronomer* 423

When I Peruse the Conquer'd Fame
289

When I peruse the conquer'd fame
of heroes and the victories of
mighty generals, I do not envy the
generals 289

When I Read the Book 172

When I read the book, the biography
famous 172

*When Lilacs Last in the Dooryard
Bloom'd* 475

When old Grimes died, he left a
son—713

When painfully athwart my brain
732

When the Full-Grown Poet Came 672

When, staunchly entering port 773

Where the city's ceaseless crowd
moves on the livelong day 532

While Behind All Firm and Erect 780

While behind all, firm and erect as
ever 780

While my wife at my side lies
slumbering, and the wars are over
long 465

While Not the Past Forgetting 654

Whispers of heavenly death
murmur'd I hear 577

*WHISPERS OF HEAVENLY
DEATH* 577

Whispers of Heavenly Death 577

Who are you dusky woman, so
ancient hardly human 466

Who has gone farthest? for I would
go farther 609

Who includes diversity and is Nature
534

Who is reading this? 754

[Who Learns My Lesson Complete]
140

Who Learns My Lesson Complete?
535

*Whoever You Are Holding Me Now in
Hand* 276

Whoever you are, I fear you are
walking the walks of dreams
387

Why reclining, interrogating? why
myself and all drowsing? 429

Why, who makes much of a miracle?
531

Wild, wild the storm, and the sea
high running 415

With All Thy Gifts 542

With all thy gifts America 542

With Antecedents 393

With Husky-Haughty Lips, O Sea!
644

With its cloud of skirmishers in
advance 450

Woman Waits for Me, A 263

Women sit or move to and fro, some
old, some young 427

Word over all, beautiful as the sky
468

World Below the Brine, The 412

World Take Good Notice 468

World take good notice, silver stars
    fading 468
Wound-Dresser, The 457

Y

Year of Meteors (1859-60) 392
Year of meteors! brooding year! 392
*Year That Trembled and Reel'd
    Beneath Me* 457
Years of the Modern 618
Years of the modern! years of the
    unperform'd! 618
Yet, Yet, Ye Downcast Hours 581
Yet, yet, ye downcast hours, I know
    ye also 581
Yonnondio 649
You Felons on Trial in Courts 528

You just maturing youth! You male
    or female! 747
You lingering sparse leaves of me on
    winter-nearing boughs 657
You Lingering Sparse Leaves of Me
    657
You Tides with Ceaseless Swell 641
You tides with ceaseless swell! you
    power that does this work! 641
You who celebrate bygones 167
Young Grimes 713
Youth, Day, Old Age and Night 379
Youth, large, lusty, loving—youth full
    of grace, force, fascination 379